EUPHEMIA

broadview editions
series editor: L.W. Conolly

EUPHEMIA

Charlotte Lennox

edited by Susan Kubica Howard

broadview editions

Library and Archives Canada Cataloguing in Publication

Lennox, Charlotte, ca. 1729-1804
  Euphemia / Charlotte Lennox ; edited by Susan Kubica Howard.

(Broadview editions)
Originally publ.: London : Printed for T. Cadell, 1790.
Includes bibliographical references.
ISBN 978-1-55111-618-1

  I. Howard, Susan Kubica, 1958-.   II. Title.   III. Series.

PR3541.L27E97 2008   823'.6   C2008-902798-1

Broadview Editions
The Broadview Editions series represents the ever-changing canon of literature in English by bringing together texts long regarded as classics with valuable lesser-known works.

Advisory editor for this volume: Colleen Franklin

Broadview Press is an independent, international publishing house, incorporated in 1985. Broadview believes in shared ownership, both with its employees and with the general public; since the year 2000 Broadview shares have traded publicly on the Toronto Venture Exchange under the symbol BDP.

We welcome comments and suggestions regarding any aspect of our publications—please feel free to contact us at the addresses below or at broadview@broadview-press.com.

North America
Post Office Box 1243, Peterborough, Ontario, Canada K9J 7H5
2215 Kenmore Avenue, Buffalo, NY, USA 14207
Tel: (705) 743-8990; Fax: (705) 743-8353;
email: customerservice@broadviewpress.com

UK, Ireland, and continental Europe
NBN International, Estover Road, Plymouth, UK PL6 7PY
Tel: 44 (0) 1752 202300   Fax: 44 (0) 1752 202330
email: enquiries@nbninternational.com

Australia and New Zealand
UNIREPS, University of New South Wales
Sydney, NSW, Australia 2052
Tel: 61 2 9664 0999; Fax: 61 2 9664 5420
email: info.press@unsw.edu.au

www.broadviewpress.com

This book is printed on paper containing 100% post-consumer fibre.

Typesetting and assembly: True to Type Inc., Claremont, Canada.

PRINTED IN CANADA

Mixed Sources

Product group from well-managed forests, controlled sources and recycled wood or fiber
www.fsc.org Cert no. SW-COC-000952
© 1996 Forest Stewardship Council

For my Family

Contents

Acknowledgements

I am grateful to many people who have helped me as I have worked on this edition. My family and friends have supported me through my work in numerous ways. My son, Ben, has provided hours of babysitting, as well as conversation on Colonial America, while my daughters, Amy and Lena, have given me ample opportunities for play breaks along the way. My parents, Helen and Walter Kubica, my brother, John Kubica, and friends Becky Spurlock and Kathy Pivak gave my children their attention so that I could give mine to this project. Jessica Jost-Costanzo and Tim Ruppert served as committed research assistants, entering text and researching annotations. I am grateful to the reference staff (especially Leslie Lewis), circulation personnel, and interlibrary loan staff at Duquesne University's Gumberg Library for their help in locating primary texts. I benefitted from two internal NEH grants that funded research assistants; a Wimmer grant, which paid for some childcare; and a sabbatical, part of which I used to work on this project. I gratefully acknowledge permission to use, in an abridged form, material first published in my essay, "Seeing Colonial America and Writing Home About It: Charlotte Lennox's *Euphemia*, Epistolarity, and the Feminine Picturesque," in *Studies in the Novel*, Vol. 37, Number 3 (Fall 2005), 273-91. I have also appreciated the helpful comments on the proposal for this edition by the generous scholars who serve as readers for Broadview Press, as well as the professional and friendly aid given me and my project by the Broadview production personnel, editors Julia Gaunce and Leonard Conolly, and copy editor Colleen Franklin.

Introduction

Harriot Stuart and Euphemia

Over the course of a long literary career, Charlotte Ramsay Lennox published a volume of poetry, many translations, several adaptations of plays—and a number of novels. Her first novel, *The Life of Harriot Stuart, Written by Herself*, published in 1750, was partially set in America and told the story of a young girl's trials and tribulations as she negotiated her family's efforts to find her a suitable husband and her own sense of the kind of man she would marry. It is a novel about courtship, with an exotic setting and adventures among pirates and the aboriginal peoples of North America. Its heroine is young, and somewhat naive, but she knows herself, and she actively defends her virtue; she is rewarded, finally, with marriage to the right man, and a safe harbor in England, away from the high seas and the American wilderness.

Lennox suggested at the time of publication that her first novel was at least somewhat autobiographical, and while it is difficult to know what intrinsic similarities existed between Harriot Stuart and the young Charlotte Ramsay, it is probable that, like Harriot Stuart, Lennox spent her middle teenage years in Colonial New York, c. 1738-43, where her father served in an official capacity with the British army; that when her father died, she travelled to London seeking the protection of an aunt, only to find her ill; and that at that point, she was taken under the wing of two wealthy aristocratic sisters, who acted as her guardians for a time. One could say, then, that there is something of Charlotte Ramsay in Lennox's depiction of Harriot Stuart, and this is true as well of the heroine of her final novel, *Euphemia*, published at the end of her career in 1790. Like Lennox's first novel, this final work also has a Colonial American setting, an epistolary framework, and a heroine caught in the throes of courtship woes. However, in the case of *Euphemia*, while one of the correspondents, Maria Harley, is very much in the mold of Harriot Stuart, and as such may resemble the youthful Charlotte Ramsay in her struggles to find the right partner in life, the titular character, Euphemia Neville, leads the life of a married woman that in its unhappiness and frustration mirrors what we know of Lennox's own married life. Lennox's decision to focus on Euphemia's married life, to a greater extent even than on Maria's courtship with her cousin Harley, is an unusual move for a late-eighteenth-century novelist since for most novels of the period marriage was foreign territory.[1]

Maria's story is much more the norm for novels of the time, as the *Critical Review* notes when remarking that the "history of Maria Harley approaches more nearly to the general style of novels" (396)[2] and the reviewer for the *General Magazine and Impartial Review* states that, like many of her fictional peers, "Maria Harley is an amiable young lad[y] ... rather awkwardly situated":

> Maria Harley ... is dependent on Sir John Harley, a rich uncle, who, although a worthy man, is apparently duped by a young, designing wife, to whom the niece is a kind of eye-sore, and whom she endeavours to supplant and ruin in her uncle's estimation. (399)

Over the course of her twelve-year correspondence with Euphemia, Maria chronicles how she wins back her uncle's trust and affection, and in the process, manages a reconciliation between her uncle and his estranged nephew, Edward Harley, whom she eventually marries. Maria's trials match those of many eighteenth-century novelistic heroines, including Harriot Stuart, whose delicate sensibilities and ignorance of the ways of the world are combined with a firm sense of what is right in human relationships and the forthrightness to act when the occasion demands it. Maria's difficulties are domestic, they are confined to England and France, and they are happily resolved in the usual

---

1 One of the few novels written during the eighteenth century that deals significantly with the life of a married woman is Frances Sheridan's *Memoirs of Miss Sidney Bidulph* (1761) which portrays a woman who, like Euphemia, married her mother's choice of husband and endured an unhappy marriage as a result. Janet Todd suggests that women novelists avoided focusing on married life in their works because they were writing from within unhappy marriages themselves and therefore could not countenance romanticizing such a state (145). Those women, including Lennox, Sheridan, and Charlotte Smith, who did write about the frustration and bitterness below the surface in the lives of many wives, did not go far enough because they preserved the surface (261), in Dale Spender's judgement.

2 This and other contemporary reviews of *Euphemia* appear in Appendix A. Citations to works within the appendices, as well as to *Euphemia*, are to the present edition.

way over time and after many misunderstandings and near crises by the mediating efforts of Mr. Greville, a family friend; the affectionate and worthy natures of the hero and heroine; and the ability of Maria's uncle to admit he has been wrong. Maria's story, while certainly never dull, would probably have struck contemporary readers as somewhat familiar and predictable. This cannot be said of Euphemia's story, which is why it is hers that holds us as it did contemporary readers.

Marriage in *Euphemia*

Euphemia's Marriage

As the *Critical Review* notes, *Euphemia* begins "where novels usually end, by [Euphemia's] marriage, a marriage dictated by duty and convenience, rather than affection" (395). Mrs. Lumley, a recent widow in poor health who has discovered that her husband, through extravagance and imprudence had left his family in financial straits, desires to see her only child settled before she dies. Euphemia, wishing to ease her mother's mind, agrees to marry a man she does not know or love; she writes, "I never had any other will but her's and her choice regulated mine" (108). Though the reader is not privy to Mr. Neville's motivations, certainly Euphemia is a gentlewoman, well educated and attractive, and, he may believe, still an heiress. While he has deceived others into believing that he is a prudent, responsible young man who is financially secure, Mr. Neville's pursuit of Euphemia seems to be motivated at least in part by a need for money.

While economics play a role in all eighteenth-century marriages according to Bridget Hill (174), it was felt by people of all classes that the ideal union was one that "'combined *both* practical viability *and* strong affection'" (Reay, qtd. in Hill 193). In such a union, affection, rather than an "instilled obedience" would provide the "main cohesive force within the ... family" (Houlbrooke 1), and this kind of "companionable marriage," according to Stone (1977, 136), was becoming the norm by the middle of the century. Unfortunately, the portrait that emerges from the letters written by Euphemia and her companion, Mrs. Benson, of Euphemia's married life with Mr. Neville is of an emotionally barren, unequal relationship. While Mr. Neville is not physically abusive or adulterous, his character is weak; he is irresponsible, self-centered, arrogant and authoritarian, as well as quick to anger. Euphemia, whose "indisposition to the married state" (58), as a young woman was well known, suffers under his domestic tyranny over important issues, such as the education of her son, as well as seemingly trivial points, such as a winter afternoon's excursion. She remains true to her marriage vows, but her letters to Maria (who actually does marry a man she knows, loves, and respects) register her sense of frustration at his inadequacy and his power over her. While she sees marriage as a sacred vow, and a wife's submission as necessary, she looks to the afterlife for happiness, aware she will not find it in her life as a wife.

An impediment to Euphemia's happiness is the lack of equality in her marriage, and the fact that the power in their relationship lies in the wrong hands. Time and again, Mr. Neville's insistence on his patriarchal authority, an authority that was supported by the Common Law of England developed in the Middle Ages, and by the Protestant Church (Houlbrooke 22, 31), compromises the happiness and well-being of his family. Because his gambling debts have depleted his inheritance, and he cannot trust himself to remain in London and not gamble or live extravagantly, he buys a commission in an Independent Company bound for America, forcing his wife to leave her home and parent. Euphemia's outrage at such an inhumane and selfish act—her mother is unwell and unable to accompany them—causes the reader to wonder whether she will disobey her husband in order to remain with her mother, but the conflict is resolved by her mother's death, and Euphemia obeys, without pleasure, her husband's demands. That such discord occurs early in their marriage, but after the reader has come to know and respect Euphemia's character, allows Lennox to align the reader's sympathy wholly with Euphemia and begin a critique of the patriarchal authority within this marriage supported by the reader's righteous indignation at Euphemia's emotional suffering.

Once in New York, Mr. Neville continues his program of ill-considered, self-centered decision-making which leads to near tragic consequences. On one occasion, as winter is coming on, he and his family and friends have rather incautiously embarked on an excursion to a newly purchased property of a friend when it begins to snow. Even after Euphemia begs him to "let us return," Mr. Neville insists that they continue to the farm. He was "immoveable in his opinion, that this severity of weather, being premature, would not hold long"(307); and to this, Euphemia and her friends were "obliged to submit" (307), only to become snowbound in a house without food or fuel as a winter storm closes in on them. In her letter to Maria, Euphemia calls this an example of her husband's "obstinacy" and to his face, out of concern for the dangerous situation they are in, she declares "Oh! what imprudence to venture on, when the first fall of snow warned us of what we had to expect" (309). In an unsuccessful effort to rescue them from what Euphemia refers to as their "captivity," Mr. Neville enlists the aid of a snowshoeing Mohawk to carry a message to the nearest fort, but he gives him rum for the journey, with the result that the man becomes drunk and dies of exposure before going too far. The party is rescued finally after Mr. Neville, using the dead man's snowshoes, makes it back to the fort for help.

On yet another occasion, during Euphemia's lying-in with her first child, Mr. Neville is angered by what he calls the "savage" Dutch custom of washing the floor of the bedchamber of a newly delivered woman—a practice at odds with English customs related to childbirth;[1] he kicks over the bucket of dirty water, soaking the entire bedchamber floor. This action, born of ignorance coupled with a sense of cultural superiority, has the potential, Mrs. Benson and Euphemia both realize, to be more harmful to the mother and child than the initial floor washing, and it is Mrs. Benson's quick thinking that salvages this situation after Mr. Neville storms out of the room.[2]

And finally, in an act that leads to the greatest catastrophe of Euphemia's married life, Mr. Neville requests a transfer to a post in Schenectady, an outlying fort, more remote and less comfort-

---

1 Adrian Wilson calls childbirth during the eighteenth century a "social occasion, specifically an occasion for women" (70). While the husband and his male friends waited in the parlor, his wife, surrounded by her midwife and her female friends, labored in her bedroom. After the child's birth and swaddling, the mother's lying-in began, and extended for about a month. During the first few weeks of this period, the woman stayed in bed, receiving few visitors; her room remained darkened, and her linen was not changed. Certainly, it was not customary in Britain to clean the lying-in woman's room. Mr. Neville's anger may be a result of his fear that his wife's and child's lives are endangered by the Dutch nurse's actions, or he may be frustrated by not being allowed to participate in the birth or its aftermath, which were solely female activities, within a female domain.

2 Mr. Neville's bias against the Dutch is in contrast with most eighteenth-century views which found the Dutch inhabitants of New York pragmatic and hospitable. See selections from Sarah Knight, the Abbé Raynal, and Priscilla Wakefield in Appendix C.

able than the fort at Albany where he is presently stationed, because, as his wife writes, he would rather be a large fish in a small pool. It is while the family is in Schenectady that Mr. Neville, in an effort to impress a visitor with the grandeur of Britain's North American possessions, takes his family to the Falls of Cohas[1]—this despite Euphemia's forebodings and her request to stay behind with her children. While Mr. Neville and his friend are sightseeing, his young son, Edward, wanders away from the servant who is caring for him, and supposedly drowns. While both parents feel the tragedy, Euphemia's distress is compounded by her sense of powerlessness. This event also suggests that while Mr. Neville is a poor husband, he is an even less effective parent, since it is his irresponsible behavior which leads to the loss of his son.

Throughout their marriage, Euphemia does question her husband's poor decisions; however, she has little recourse but to obey him because as a gentlewoman, decorum demands this of her. Yet in her correspondence with Maria, she reveals "a just picture" of her situation which forces her to "touch upon the faults of one who, from the near relation in which he stands to me, has claims upon my tenderness and respect, which even those faults cannot dispense with me from allowing him" (95). Yet, while she strives to respect Mr. Neville, she is not cowed by him, unlike Mrs. Mansell, who entrusts her son to Euphemia during the transatlantic crossing. Mr. Mansell, like Mr. Neville, is both "domineering and insensitive," but while his public displays of anger, condescension, and disrespect toward his wife meet with meekness from her, Euphemia expresses in her letters a more critical view of her husband and thereby retains a sense of herself as Mrs. Mansell does not.

Euphemia's refusal to accept unconditionally her husband's decrees, her questioning of his decisions, and her voicing of her own views prepare us for the final example of the couple's lack of shared values and goals, and its resolution. After Edward's return to the bosom of his family, Euphemia and Mr. Neville disagree on the best mode of educating him. While Euphemia patiently instructs her studious son in appropriate subjects, her husband takes the boy away from his studies to accompany him on his

---

1　See Appendix C for descriptions of Cahoes Falls by Timothy Dwight and Priscilla Wakefield, and contemporary descriptions of Albany, Schenectady and New York City by Dwight, Wakefield, Edmund Burke, and Sarah Knight.

forays into fashionable society. Before Euphemia is forced to open a breach with her husband that might prove irreparable, Mr. Neville's uncle dies and leaves £15,000 to Euphemia, who had nursed him through his last illness when his nephew ignored him. This money is "for her sole use and benefit, not subject to the controul of her husband, and entirely at her own disposal" (392). Mrs. Benson notes in a letter to Maria that "the precautions taken to secure this legacy in its full extent and design to Mrs. Neville, is an indirect reflexion upon Mr. Neville" (392). That old Mr. Neville changes his will on his deathbed to provide for Euphemia allows her to pursue her educational aims for her children without Mr. Neville's interference. Mrs. Benson also notes that Euphemia's decision to finance Edward's education completely "will throw power enough in her hands, to enable her to follow the light of her own excellent understanding, in an affair of too much consequence to be left to the guidance of a man, who is always counselled by his passions, appetites, and caprice" (392). Euphemia's good fortune is deserved because throughout her marriage she has conformed to society's view of the good wife, an "able companion who maintains harmony by maintaining order" (Ezell 42) and recognizes her place in the hierarchy. She has been submissive and obedient, as William Fleetwood in his *The Relative Duties of Parents and Children, Husbands and Wives, Masters and Servants* (1705), advises her to be. She has tried to be the wife Priscilla Wakefield, writing in *Reflections on the Present Condition of the Female Sex* at the latter end of the century, suggests she should be:

> the participator of her husband's cares, the consoler of his sorrow, his stimulator, to every praise-worthy undertaking, his partner in the labours and vicissitudes of life, the faithful and oeconomical manager of his affairs, the judicious superintendant of his family, the wise and affectionate mother of his children, the preserver of his honour, his chief counsellor, and, to sum up all, the chosen friend of his bosom. (416)[1]

She has tried to be all these to Mr. Neville, but she has failed as his "chief counsellor," as he is unwilling throughout their marriage to be guided by her, and she seems not to have been the

---

1   See Appendix B for selections from the works of William Fleetwood, Sarah Pennington, the pseudonymous Philogamus, George Booth, Earl of Warrington, Priscilla Wakefield, and Mary Astell.

"chosen friend of his bosom," since it was not she whom he wished to impress, but those in power. As Sarah Pennington enjoins her daughter to do in *An Unfortunate Mother's Advice to Her Absent Daughters* (1761), so Euphemia has attempted to "learn to be satisfied with the Consiousness of acting Right, according to your best Ability, and look with an unconcerned Indifference on the Reception every successless Attempt to please may meet with" (415). Both Euphemia and Pennington recognize that this is

> a hard Lesson of Philosophy; it requires no less than an absolute Command over the Passions; but let it be remembered, that such a Command, will itself most amply recompence every Difficulty, every Pain the obtaining it may cost; besides, 'tis, I believe, the only Way to preserve any Tranquillity of Mind under so disagreeable a Connection. (415)

Mr. Neville does not seem to honor his side of the marital agreement as it was understood during the eighteenth century. While Fleetwood suggests that a married woman acquiesce to being governed by her husband, "in return for this Submission and Obedience" her husband should love her "above all the World" (405); he should make it easy for his wife to love him by being prudent and good-natured. Along with Fleetwood, the pseudonymous Philogamus, in *The Present State of Matrimony* (1739), also admonishes men not to play the tyrant toward their wives:

> The first Cause of Dislike given to the Woman from the Man ... is his putting on the Husband too soon; and exerting his Authority.... [Wives] are made to be governed, not to govern; but you will never bring them to a just Sense of this Duty, by a rough, rude, and shocking Behaviour. (412)

The more enlightened eighteenth-century essayists dealing with marriage suggest that there could be equality between a wife and a husband, that both should be trusted as autonomous adults, and that, according to Warrington and Fleetwood, all relations in the world have reciprocal duties (Warrington 406), including the duties of husbands and wives toward one another. Mary Astell, writing in 1706, reminds her readers, of which Mr. Neville is obviously not one, that "Subjection ... is not over easie, none of us whether Men or Women but have so good an Opinion of our own Conduct as to believe we are fit, if not to direct others, at least to govern our selves" (402).

Women's Status within Marriage

This is exactly the problem Euphemia faces in her marriage with Mr. Neville, as did all married women in eighteenth-century Britain (as well as those in Europe and Colonial America)—their inability to legally govern themselves. As Sir William Blackstone in his *Commentaries on the Laws of England* (1765-69) writes:

> By marriage, the husband and wife are one person in law: that is, the very being or legal existence of the woman is suspended during the marriage, or at least incorporated and consolidated into that of the husband: under whose wing, protection, and *cover* she performs everything; and is therefore called in our law French a *femme covert*....; [she] is said to be covert-baron, or under the protection and influence of her husband. (qtd. in Greenberg 173)

What this meant in practice for a woman was that she could not make contracts under the law; any unprotected property she brought with her into the marriage became her husband's; and, as Greenberg notes, a husband's "title further extended to personal property given to his wife after marriage, unless the gift was to her separate use" (174). This last provision is an important one—and proves so for Euphemia—because it allowed a married woman to achieve or maintain control over property despite common law; however, it occurred only when

> a relative ... bequeath[ed] a personal estate to a woman, stipulating in the will that the heir was to hold the estate to her particular and separate use. [The Court of] Chancery would likely enforce the conditions of the will by prohibiting the husband from interfering with his wife's legacy, even to the extent of barring his curtesy. (Greenberg 176)[1]

While such a means towards a married woman's autonomy did exist, David Narrett is quick to point out that, at least in New

---

1 In eighteenth-century America, this was called a trust estate (Narrett 106).

York, not many women "achieved this degree of autonomy in wedlock" (101). And, while relationships between husbands and wives of Dutch descent in Colonial New York, despite the English conquest of 1674 and the subsequent adoption of English Common Law by the Dutch inhabitants, appeared to be more equal, with married Dutch women "exercis[ing] a considerable degree of authority within the family" (Hoffman 102), such a phenomenon did not greatly influence English immigrants to the New World. Englishmen like Mr. Neville, who, as we have seen, looked at Dutch customs as primitive, continued instead to perpetuate this typical scenario as described by Philogamus in 1739:

> We pay the greatest Deference to the Ladies of any Place in the World before Marriage, and the least after, of any People, who allow Women to be born free, as well as Men. Yesterday she was assured by her Lover, that his Life depended on her's; what she said or did, was a Law; one kind Look filled him with Raptures; an unkind one threw him into Despair: But as soon as the Parson has pronounced the fatal Words, he puts on the Lord and Master, and in a short Time lets her see, that she must obey. The Bird is lured into the Cage, where it may beat itself against the Sides, till it is forced to live in Thrall, or knock its Brains out. (411)

Such commentary suggests that most women who were wives in the eighteenth century experienced at best what Beatrice Gottlieb calls a state of "loving despotism" (92).

Women's Options When Unhappy in Marriage[1]

What options did a woman unhappy in her marriage have in mid-eighteenth-century Colonial America and Britain? Stone points out the irony of the fact that while marriage laws before 1753, when Lord Hardwicke's Marriage Act was passed, were "extraordinarily lax," divorce laws by contrast were "extraordinarily

---

1   This section deals specifically with options open to women, since men had a greater number of options when seeking to free themselves from unhappy marriages, including divorce, abandonment, and wife sale, a practice whereby a husband could sell his wife at market to the highest bidder (see Stone, *Divorce*, 141).

strict" until 1857.[1] Even in Massachusetts where divorce was legal and affordable, "the tendency, especially before the middle of the eighteenth century, was to avoid actual divorce and revert to the more traditional legal separation (without permission to remarry), especially if the wife brought the suit" (Gottlieb 106).[2] And, given the fact that women who sued for divorce, even in the ecclesiastical courts, would rarely win, and could lose their children,[3] their property, and their right to future legacies in the process, few women tried; most well-to-do women in the eighteenth century who were unhappy in their marriages, like Euphemia, suffered through them. Their only solace was that because, in general, people did not live much beyond their forties, most marriages only lasted ten to twenty years anyway, and usually it was the husband who died first, despite the high incidence of women's death in childbirth (Hay and Rogers 43).

This rather hopeless situation began to change as revolution brewed. Gottlieb notes that in Massachusetts, for example, there was a

clear shift [around 1760] to more divorce petitions by women. They often had to settle for legal separations, but they apparently felt freer to initiate such actions than they had earlier. The idea that someone was entitled to a degree of personal satisfaction in marriage came to be more openly expressed in court records in this pivotal period. (108)

Cott also suggests that the rise in the divorce rate in the 1760s might be due to a change in "'outlook ... [to one] that implied self-assertion and regard for the future [which] ... may have led a person to seek divorce and also to support independence'" (qtd. in Fliegelman 124). In addition to the slow changes within the marriage practices among colonists of European ancestry during

---

1 Stone, *Divorce*, 12. MacFarlane maintains that "between 1603 and 1857, English marriage was almost indissoluable" (225) and Gottlieb notes that before 1800, only "about 100 such bills of divorcement were ... granted" in England (106).

2 Such a separation would be private, and was really only viable if "family pressure" convinced both partners to honor it (Hay and Rogers 42; Staves 163f.)

3 Stone notes that it was not until the Custody of Infants Act in 1839 that mothers were given some rights over their children (*Divorce* 4-5).

the second half of the century that indicated a movement toward greater equality for married women in the colony than in Britain,[1] Lennox would most likely have been aware that among aboriginal tribal societies, if a marriage did not prove satisfactory to either party, the dissolution of the marriage contract was straightforward and painless. As the Abbé Raynal reports in his *Philosophical and Political History of the British Settlements and Trade in North America* (1770),

> The very idea of an indissoluble tie never once entered the thoughts of these people who are free till death. When those who are married disagree, they part by consent, and divide their children between them. Nothing appears to them more repugnant to nature and reason than the contrary system which prevails among Christians. *The great spirit*, say they, *hath created us all to be happy: and we should offend him, were we to live in a perpetual state of constraint and uneasiness.* (441)[2]

Sarah Knight offers a much less positive view of tribal divorce customs when, writing in early eighteenth-century Boston, she notes that "they marry many wives and at pleasure put them away, and on the ye least dislike or fickle humor, on either side, saying *stand away* to one another is a sufficient Divorce" (419); she suggests that this Native American practice has affected the European community in Massachusetts:

> And indeed those uncomely *Stand aways* are too much in Vougue [sic] among the English in this (Indulgent Colony) as their Records plentifully prove, and that on very trivial

---

1 This despite the fact that as a result of a British ruling, Colonial divorce bills were effectively rescinded in the decade preceding the Revolution. Pennsylvania and New York, for instance, granted no divorces before the Revolution.

2 See Appendix C for selections from the Abbé Raynal, and for Sarah Knight. Raynal's contemporary, Thomas Paine, in his 1775 *Reflections on Unhappy Marriages*, writes in an aboriginal persona about marriage customs within tribal society. There, marriages have "'no other ceremony than mutual affection and last no longer than they bestow mutual pleasures;'" people in such a society "'being at liberty to separate, seldom or never feel the inclination. But if any should be found so wretched among us as to hate where the only commerce ought to be to love, we instantly dissolve the bond: ... no creature was ever intended to be miserable'" (qtd. in Fliegelman 124).

matters, of which some have been told me, but are not proper to be Related by a Female pen, tho some of that foolish sex have had too large share in the story. (419)

Clearly, the dissolution of the union between husband and wife was a controversial issue throughout the eighteenth century in Britain and Colonial America, with men and women arguing on both sides of the issue, with one's stance often depending on one's personal experience of marriage, as well as one's view of its place as an institution within society and as a metaphor for more expansive unions.

Charlotte Lennox's Marriage

In mid-eighteenth-century New York or London, then, divorce was not a viable option for Euphemia. Fortunately, via her uncle-in-law's will, she was granted what amounted to a separation of sorts: control over her own money and therefore her children, and protection from her husband's controlling nature. Lennox herself was not so fortunate. That she experienced some frustration in her marriage to Alexander Lennox is evident from her correspondence. In a 1781 letter, Samuel Johnson, her mentor and friend, wrote that Lennox had been "'very harshly treated by her husband'" ("Lennox Collection" 426, n. 213). Certainly, they disagreed about such things as their children's education, as is evident in a draft of a letter c. 1775-80. Lennox writes to her husband, from whom she must have been separated either by choice or necessity, about his view that their daughter, Harriot Holles, should be sent to Boulogne for her education. Lennox attests that her friends all say that a boarding school in England would be "equally advantageous, equally cheap, and is liable to fewer inconveniences than a convent" ("Lennox Collection" 426). In some frustration, she goes on to proclaim that her friends' "reasons have convinced me, and that is the cause that they will never convince you—therefore I submit to your despotick will, with this condition only, that I go with her, and see her settled—this point I never will give up" (426). This letter makes clear the similarities between Euphemia's situation and Lennox's, down to the very subject under dispute.[1] But unlike her novel, which ends with the sense that Euphemia will be able

---

1   Philippe Séjourné also suggests that "*Euphemia* tells us the story of Charlotte's own relations with her husband" (150).

to assert her beneficial guidance in her children's lives, Lennox's efforts were not as successful: her daughter died while still in her teens, and her son was forced to emigrate to America, for which Lennox blamed the bad influence of his father. In a 1793 letter to Dr. Richard Johnson, of the Royal Literary Fund, Lennox pleads for money to send her son to America. Apologizing for such an indecorous appeal, she writes:

> but I am a Mother, and see an only child upon the brink of utter ruin. Driven as he was first, to desperation by a most unnatural father, and then deserted.... I have in vain used my utmost endeavors to mortgage the poor income I hold from a husband whose fortune I have made by the sacrifice of my own. (qtd. in Small 59)

The same year, Lennox wrote to James Dodsley, calling her husband "'the most ungrateful of Men'" ("Lennox Collection" 426, n. 213). Clearly, hers was overall an unhappy marriage, and like Euphemia, her frustration at her subordinate position to an incompetent master is also registered in her letters and those of her friends.

Revolution and Divorce

In *Euphemia*, marriage is seen from the woman's perspective: Euphemia's, her mother's, Mrs. Benson's, Maria's, that of the women Maria's letters chronicle; but the novel also examines marriage as a social institution. In this regard, it joins the conversation occurring in the eighteenth century[1] on both sides of the Atlantic about family structures in general, and about the relationship between wife and husband in particular by such writers as Mary Astell, William Fleetwood, George Booth, Earl of Warrington, Priscilla Wakefield, Thomas Paine and Sarah Pennington. This conversation was often broadened to include national interests in the middle of the century: as tensions between America and Britain mounted, marriage and divorce became metaphors for the union that existed between the two

---

1   Of course this conversation was taking place during the seventeenth century as well, with John Milton and others arguing for freer divorce laws, and more conservative writers on the family—Robert Abbott, Jeremy Taylor, and William Hill—championing the traditional patriarchal family.

countries and the way that union might be broken.[1] Though *Euphemia* is set in Colonial America, its post-Revolution publication in 1790 would have meant that many readers would have been aware of the use of the marriage and divorce metaphors in this national conversation and probably also of the many tracts published in both Britain and America during this period on this topic. Indeed, Lennox's depiction of Euphemia's unhappy marriage, along with the stories Maria tells of other women unhappy in love, and their tragic ends, would certainly have called to mind for contemporary readers the long history of critiques on domestic partnerships as well as national unions. Mary Astell, in *Reflections on Marriage* (1700), had early collapsed the one into the other:

> If absolute sovereignty be not necessary in a state, how comes it to be so in a family? Or if in a family, why not in a state? ... Is it not then partial in men to the last degree to contend for and practise that arbitrary dominion in their families which they abhor and exclaim against in the state? ... If all men are born free, how is it that all women are born slaves? (qtd. in Stone, *Family* 240)

While Astell is writing with the Revolution of 1688 in mind, the kind of despotism both Euphemia and Lennox experienced as the wives of greedy, inflexible, imprudent, and selfish men, and the rhetoric used to justify such marriages, would have seemed all too familiar to many Americans. To the eighteenth century, the family (or household) and the state were mirror-images of one another; and to many conservative thinkers of the time, within the family/state, the father/king must be in complete control. This view had been challenged by Locke when he suggested that "*Conjugal* Society is made by a voluntary Compact between Man and Woman ... and in this power the Mother too has her share with the Father" (qtd. in Gottlieb 235). Revolutionary rhetoric applied Locke's emphasis on equality within the family dynamic

---

1 One would perhaps expect that because more contemporary tracts in the seventeenth and eighteenth centuries deal with the parent/child relationship than with the relationship between husband and wife, the relationship between Britain and America would be viewed as a paternalistic one, but this was not so, and Lennox conceives of the post-Revolutionary situation in America as she does marriage, as a potential union of equals.

to the state. As Jay Fliegelman points out, "central to the rationalist ideology of the American Revolution was the belief that in an ideal world all relationships would be contractual" and entered into with "all obligations and expectations" clarified at the outset (123). If either party in the relationship failed to do his or her part, the contract would be considered null and void. As support for the close connection between national relationships and domestic partnerships, Fliegelman quotes from Thomas Paine's "Reflections on Unhappy Marriages," published in June 1775, in the *Pennsylvania Magazine* (which Paine edited), just six months before he was to write his call to revolution, *Common Sense*. Having suffered in an unhappy marriage himself, Paine contends that in a civilized world, only marriages based on affection would exist. Fleigelman suggests that this essay and others like it published immediately before the American Revolution and dealing ostensibly with unhappiness within marriage but metaphorically with the relationship between Britain and America[1] show "the extent to which the theme of domestic tyranny of all sorts preoccupied the American mind on the eve of Revolution" (125).

There had been much in Britain's dealings with mid-century Colonial America that called forth this rhetoric. As J.A. Alden notes, "'during the years 1763-65, the ministry headed by George Grenville [had] ... goaded the colonists into open revolt by a series of ill-advised measures'" (qtd. in Plumb 113-14). These had included restricting the settlement of land beyond the Alleghenies; keeping a British army in America, 6000 men strong, that the colonists must feed and shelter; setting up British oversight of aboriginal affairs; enforcing the Acts of Trade and overhauling the Customs Office; restricting trade between America and the West Indies; and promoting greater revenue from America in the case of the Stamp Act and other taxes imposed on the colonies for the benefit of Britain (Plumb 114). These efforts to bring America under greater control were associated in the colonial mind with George III, rather than with his

---

1 See also for instance "One Cause of Uneasiness in the Married State," by an anonymous writer, published in Dec. 1775 in the *Pennsylvania Magazine*. Fliegelman points out that while there were a good many essays published in the years before the Revolution that criticized marriage and argued in favor of divorce, there were just as many that celebrated marriage, and that the revolutionaries remained supportive of healthy unions while denouncing dysfunctional ones.

ministers, so that charges of tyrannical behavior fell on his head. And he, taking his responsibilities as head of the British Empire seriously, had embraced the role of inflexible head of state. J.H. Plumb suggests that George III's "stupidity and obstinacy" didn't help matters, and he became "the symbol of tyranny" (121, 125).

The first readers of *Euphemia* could not help but recall how the political arguments for and against dissolution of America's union with Britain fifteen years before the novel's publication had been couched in terms similar to those used in the tracts on marriage and divorce. The idea that relationships should be contractual, and thus dissolvable when a contract was no longer honored or viable, was the foundation of arguments for both revolution and divorce. George Booth, Earl of Warrington had suggested in his *Considerations on the Institution of Marriage* (1739) that marriage is a promise to man only, not a vow to God; as such, it is dissoluble, either by separation or divorce. However, this perspective threatened patriarchal authority, which viewed women's subservience as sanctioned by God. It therefore also threatened the ultimate authority of the state over its citizens and the Empire over its colonies. As Susan Staves suggests,

> a wife who could ... renegotiate her marriage contract into a separate maintenance contract would appear to be in some respects in a position analogous to that of the king's subjects after the Revolution of 1688. Like the king's, the husband's authority appeared less absolute. (164)

Any apprehension of such weakness could become a weapon in Revolutionary hands. Thus, Britain had a vested interest in denying divorce within domestic partnerships, despite the fact that divorce was "written into the laws of Protestant countries," including England after King Henry VIII's breach with the Pope in 1534 (Gottlieb 105).

Indeed, as one might expect, one consequence of the American Revolution was a more "generous" attitude toward divorce (Bolt 15), with Pennsylvania in 1785 and New York in 1787 allowing divorce. However, Cathy Davidson notes that the results of the American Revolution for women in America were not in general revolutionary. She suggests that "for the most part, the new Republic modestly revised British principles and procedures and did so essentially to maintain the existing power structures of class, race, and gender in America" (117). Quoting Marylynn Salmon, Davidson writes that "most of the legal changes that occurred in America between 1775 and 1800, especially those bearing on women's rights, were 'gradual, conservative, and frequently based upon English developments'" (117). Blackstone's *Commentaries* still informed American law as it did English law, especially as regarded a married woman's status as *femme covert*. Thus, the American Revolution "freed America from a repressive colonial status, but it had not freed American women from their subservient status" (Davidson 118), despite Abigail Adams's injunction to her husband as he met to write the new Constitution that he "'Remember the Ladies: ... Do not put such unlimited power into the hands of the Husbands ... [because] all men would be tyrants if they could'" (qtd. in Davidson 119).

While Davidson allows that "a spirit of 'woman's rights' was felt throughout post-revolutionary America," she also points out the paradox of the married woman's situation in America after the Revolution: her

> restricted status within marriage (and the corresponding restrictions on divorce) presumed a patriarchal domestic order often breached during the Revolutionary War years when many American women were suddenly forced to survive without the economic assistance or legal protection of a husband. (120)

While the American Revolution is literally absent from *Euphemia*, it is present in Lennox's awareness of the above irony. Like these women, Euphemia suffers the restrictions of marriage without the compensation of a strong man to provide for her and protect her; indeed, Mr. Neville is often a liability, responsible for most of his family's troubles. But *Euphemia* challenges patriarchal marriage as the status quo because, against her husband's incompetence, Euphemia's ability to manage her home and family capably and with compassion is evident, and she is finally rewarded with legal, financial, and parental autonomy.

The Community of Women and Epistolarity

While Lennox lived in London during the period of the American Revolution, several of her family members had remained in America after her father's death, and her son eventually emigrated to the country in which she had spent her youth. Hers may have been a divided loyalty; if nothing else, she would have brought a more informed perspective than many of her fellow

Britons to the debate over whether America should remain Britain's colony. She had an intimate knowledge of the country and its people that many of them lacked. And she had the experience of living for forty years in a less than satisfactory marriage to draw from as she wrote what could be viewed as the continuation of Harriot Stuart's story. Always an independent woman— an assertive, even aggressive force—one can see how these two experiences might come together for her in what she must have realized was her final novel. As such, and all the time recognizing that she needed to write what her audience wished to read so that this work might sell and thereby relieve her poverty, it was her last chance to say what she needed to say about the situation of the marginalized in society: women, aboriginal peoples, slaves, the poor—people who had been oppressed by the dominant powers and who deserved a voice. While *Euphemia* is not a rant, it does quietly voice alternatives to the dominant perspective.

W. Austen Flanders suggests that in many eighteenth-century novels, "supportive relationships outside the conjugal family compensate somewhat for the ineffectiveness of family structures" (159).[1] Certainly, Lennox is concerned to show that the expanded household is more vigorous than the nuclear family, since the relationship between Euphemia and Neville is fraught with difficulty and inequity, and stronger bonds of affection exist between mother and child, and between women. Lennox uses the "motif of adoption" (Flanders 160) to suggest the flexibility of the concept of family. For instance, before she has children of her own, Euphemia fosters Master Mansell, a twelve-year-old whose parents are not on board the man-of-war that takes them to America, and whose mother is not in favor of his trip, but whose father believes it will make a man of him. Euphemia devotedly nurses the boy through the smallpox, and when the adult Master Mansell is introduced to Edward at the end of the Nevilles' stay in America, it is as "another son," who tells Edward that "the son of that dear lady, will always be considered as a brother by me" (386).

In the same way that she fosters Master Mansell, Euphemia is herself nurtured by Mrs. Benson and Maria. Mrs. Benson was

---

1 Julia Ellison also notes this focus in *Euphemia* "on how communities of feminine sensibility can be a rational way to survive the absence of sentimental gratifications in marriage" (315). Where our arguments differ is in my sense that *Euphemia* suggests a much broader means of survival, a larger embrace of the American experience.

Euphemia's governess, but stays on with Mrs. Lumley and Euphemia, without pay, after Mr. Lumley's death. Mrs. Benson acts as a friend and nurse to Mrs. Lumley in her final illness, a companion to Euphemia as she journeys to America, and a nanny to the Neville children when they arrive. It is Mrs. Benson who writes for Euphemia when Euphemia is overcome by the travails of childbirth or the loss of her son. Her comments about Mr. Neville in her own letters to Maria, or as reported in Euphemia's, voice Euphemia's sense of frustration and unhappiness over the marriage into which she was forced and through which she has suffered, while they allow Euphemia to maintain her wifely decorum, since she does not herself openly criticize a man whom the *Critical Review* felt should have been "sent to sleep with his fathers" (395). Additionally, despite or perhaps because of her status as a servant, Mrs. Benson serves as the voice of reason and recognition of the value of diversity in America: when others are unable to appreciate the Dutch customs—whether it is that of washing the lying-in chamber floor or serving a large meal at tea time to guests, Mrs. Benson intervenes to mediate between cultures, classes, races, religions, and genders. Lennox uses Mrs. Benson's actions and words as the indicator of the correct perspective, one that shows the limitations of the British colonial view as well as the costs associated with the silence imposed on married women by society. And, in return for her loyalty, Euphemia puts off her long-anticipated return to England to stay in America to nurse Mrs. Benson when she falls ill, "with more than the tenderness of a daughter, with the solicitude of a grateful friend, whom her goodness has laid under the highest obligations" (365).

In Euphemia's words, a friend is "a witness of conscience, a physician of secret griefs, a moderator in prosperity, and a guide in adversity" (150).[1] Maria and Euphemia meet these needs for one another and as a result the correspondence between them is intimate, heartfelt, and sustaining.[2] Through their correspondence, Lennox explores the ironic truth that physical distance is easily overcome by two friends with much to communicate, while

1 Sarah Pennington echoes these sentiments in her description of friendship (see Appendix B).

2 While *Harriot Stuart* is technically an epistolary novel, since Harriot is writing to her friend Amanda, it is much less sophisticated in technique than *Euphemia* because Amanda never writes back; the novel is, therefore, more of a memoir than an epistolary correspondence.

emotional distance between husband and wife, despite close physical proximity, sometimes cannot be bridged. As Maria asserts to Euphemia, "you cannot complain, nor be unhappy, by yourself alone; I partake of all your good or evil fortune" (251). Lennox's use of the epistolary technique, applauded by contemporary reviewers as ingenious and pleasing, endows her heroine with the ability to interpret and communicate what she sees to another woman. Both Euphemia and Maria, under the English social system in which they had been brought up, had limited power for self-expression; while their epistolary correspondence is private and confined for the most part to the domestic, Lennox's use of it has political implications: in this novel, epistolarity challenges the accepted cultural and political practices that have silenced women.[1] The epistolarity of Lennox's novel, which tapped into what had by the end of the eighteenth century become a very popular novelistic technique, emphasizes and facilitates Euphemia's relationships with other women in the novel who are all affected by England's colonial program.

If Euphemia's letters to Maria allow her to share her experiences in America and to emphasize the way in which travel within various cultures has gifted her with a sense of interconnectedness with those she might once have seen as "other," then the epistolary novel form, with its emphasis on communication between the self and another, allows Lennox to share such an experience with her reader. She uses the epistolary form as a counter to the static, framed, closed presentation of experience typical of the masculine travel narrative. As Elizabeth MacArthur notes, the epistolary narrative resists closure, emphasizes "the process of creating meanings" rather than of assigning them, and acts to "question the moral and political status quo" (18). While Euphemia's letters initially fall into the static and crafted tour-guide descriptions of places and people typical of male travellers seeing America, they soon register the uncontrolled, unforeseen nature of lived experience in an unknown place among strange and surprising people. Her letters, like her experiences in America, are marked by a need to make connections that expand rather than limit her frame of reference, as well as that of her correspondent. Her letters also reflect what Jay Fliegelman refers to as "the issue of personal autonomy within a structure of family obligation" and they "affirm ... the importance of the individual

---

1 See Beebee 105, 119.

voice" (29); they are then a fitting form for the post-revolutionary era in which *Euphemia* was written.

Travel Narratives and the Picturesque

The expansion of one's community as well as one's perspective is both necessitated by and a consequence of travel through new landscapes, among new peoples. Miriam Rossiter Small suggests that

> [it] is in the American scenes of *Harriot Stuart* and *Euphemia* that we find something original with Mrs. Lennox and interesting historically and biographically. The accurate simple accounts of a passage up the Hudson and of life in the fort at Albany with occasional excursions into the surrounding country are the most valuable and unusual portions of these novels. (152)

But where in *Harriot Stuart* description of the North American countryside and its inhabitants is minimal, in *Euphemia* Lennox paints a vivid and detailed picture of Colonial New York and the people living there. Perhaps this is a result of the growing interest among eighteenth-century English readers in "descriptions of the primitive Indians and of adventures in the wilderness" (Séjourné 45), as well as interest in the picturesque landscape as popularized by William Gilpin and Uvedale Price. Given her financial distress in the last quarter of the eighteenth century, Lennox would have been sensitive to the demands of the London literary marketplace, and indeed, critics responded well to Lennox's handling of the American scenes in *Euphemia*. The *Critical Review* found the novel "interesting from some of its descriptions; accounts of a country which, though long in our possession, has scarcely ever been described in a picturesque narrative" (395); and the *London Review* judged that "the picturesque beauties of the province of New York, the manners and customs of its inhabitants, together with the vagrant life of the savages, are described, in the course of this correspondence, with great beauty and effect" (397). The *General Magazine and Impartial Review* also affirms that "[m]ost of the interesting scenes lie in America, and that romantic country is always prolific of adventure. The writer knows it well; and her information has this advantage, that it is authentic" (400).

Lennox's valuation of the American landscape in *Euphemia* is complex and, while overtly conservative, it manages to question the underlying political, cultural, and aesthetic assumptions of her readers. She gives the aesthetic eye to a married Englishwoman who is a traveller in America against her will and whose position vis-à-vis the colonized landscape and peoples of North America is therefore far closer to them than to that of her husband, a member of the military, sent to safeguard Britain's colonial interests in mid-eighteenth-century New York against the French and their aboriginal allies. It is Mr. Neville's job to ensure that British tourists, settlers, and military personnel are protected not only from the European forces opposing British colonization in North America, but from those other British subjects, the "large numbers of alien peoples [who had been] incorporated into the empire by conquest, not consent" (K. Wilson 153). While colonialism succeeded through accretion, Neville's efforts within the fort are essentially toward maintaining separation of the British from all others. As a representative of British imperialist interests, Neville sees New York only as a colony, remarking to his wife that "it is one of the finest of our American provinces" (107). He becomes a tourist,[1] a man who visits sites in the North American wilderness out of "that restlessness of temper, which makes every change, even for the worse, desirable" (265), or because they are known attractions and therefore marked as noteworthy colonial possessions. Indeed, the tragedy at Cahoes Falls, as noted above, occurs as a direct result of Neville's touristic impulse: arrogant and ignorant, Mr. Neville is unable to properly assess the potential danger of his surroundings because he does not respect them and therefore views them as safe and exploitable. This episode clearly shows Lennox to be critical of the phenomena of tourism, of the aesthetic valuation of a site/sight for public consumption. Not only do such sites/sights further the colonial cause, but the nature of tourism emphasizes a transient, artificial, and ultimately unappreciative relationship between the tourist and the land.[2] And despite the loss of his son, or perhaps because of it, Neville continues to go on "excursions to Philadelphia, Boston, and other places whither curiosity or a desire of changing the scene has led him" (303). His curiosity is "align[ed] ... with purposeless movement onwards," with what

---

1   John Sears contends that tourism was not established in America until the 1820s and 1830s (3).

2   See Blunt 20, and Brewer 635.

Chloe Chard suggests is "a form of travel which, where it is mentioned in eighteenth-century writings, is rejected as evidence of complete inadequacy in managing the experience of the foreign" (28). His is the perspective condemned by the Abbé Raynal, who asserts that "barbarous soldiers and rapacious merchants were not proper persons to give us just and clear notions of this half of the universe" (*Philosophical History* VI, 11). In his *Philosophical and Political History of the British Settlements and Trade in North America* (1772), Raynal examines the "natural state" of North America "before the arrival of the English, and what it is become under their dominion"(Raynal 24).[1] He conjectures that prior to European colonization, North America was "sublime," a land of "unbounded space," of "dark, thick, and deep forests," a place where "the imagination of a painter or a poet would have been raised, animated, and filled with those ideas which leave a lasting impression on the mind" (Raynal 56). While he praises the early Dutch settlers in America for their "spirit of order and oeconomy," (438) and their lack of pretense, along with the exemplary moderation and justness of William Penn's settling of Pennsylvania, in general the European settlement of America inspires him with "disgust, horror, or melancholy.... Hitherto we have only seen these barbarians spreading depopulation before they took possession, and laying every thing waste before they cultivated" (Raynal 97). In particular, the European introduction of alcohol has caused the aboriginal people to have been "made barbarous" and thus, conveniently, "othered." This process is at the root of what Raynal sees wanting in British America—"its not forming precisely one people" (443).

Despite shared commercial interests, Raynal asserts that true communication between the aboriginal peoples and the colonists is absent: prejudice limits perspective. British settlers do not appreciate the singing or dancing of aboriginal cultures, he states, possibly because their ears are not "properly adapted to their music" (441), their imaginations not properly receptive to the dance. Benjamin Franklin begins his *Remarks Concerning the Savages of North America* (1784) by noting the relative nature of the American perspective when he writes: "Savages we

---

1 Quotations marked with Raynal's name are taken from Justamond's 1779 translation of Raynal's *A Philosophical and Political History of the British Settlements and Trade in North America* while those followed by pagination only are found in Appendix C, as are those passages by Benjamin Franklin which follow.

call them, because their manners differ from ours, which we think the perfection of civility; they think the same of theirs (444)." He goes on to suggest, as does Raynal, that a broadening of perspective is necessary: "Perhaps if we could examine the manners of different nations with impartiality, we should find no people so rude as to be without any rules of politeness; nor any so polite as not to have some remains of rudeness" (444). Both Franklin and Raynal attempt to redress this European perspective on the aboriginal peoples of North America as "other" by placing the responsibility for bridging the gap on the European entering America, rather than on the aboriginal, whose attitude toward the interlopers Raynal suggests elsewhere in his treatise was initially welcoming and, even when under attack, often conciliatory. Greater sensitivity, open-mindedness, and imagination must inform the perspective of the European visitor to America if she/he is to fully appreciate the American scene. And indeed, as Mary Geiter and W.A. Speck suggest, it would seem that the formation of an American identity begins as early as the 1740s, the period in which *Euphemia* is set, as "the development of the colonies, for example the interaction of Europeans with native North Americans and Africans imported as slaves, created a society very different from that of the mother country" (28).

While Neville clearly embodies Raynal's "barbarous soldier" and his actions throughout the novel attest to his unimaginative and unappreciative view of everyone in North America who is not English-born, Lennox gives voice to many of Raynal's sympathetic sentiments toward aboriginal peoples through the words of Mr. Euston, a British gentleman who, like many other European tourists, came to America originally "merely to gratify a curiosity," but remains out of fascination with and compassion for the aboriginal peoples with whom he has lived.[1] On the occasion when Euphemia and others are accosted by two drunken, bellicose aboriginals, it is Mr. Euston's calm and respectful conversation with them that allows them to be civil men, and the potentially volatile situation is disarmed.

Euphemia's position with regard to Britain's mid-eighteenth-century colonial agenda is not as clear cut as her husband's, nor, initially, Mr. Euston's: while she begins the novel allied to her husband and his role in the imperial project of England, she is

---

1 Séjourné points out that many of Mr. Euston's speeches are direct quotations from Raynal's work (52).

not emotionally supportive of either. Yet while she is critical of European influence in America, especially concerning the corruption of the aboriginal peoples with alcohol, and she notes, in true Raynalian fashion, that the aboriginals' "virtues are their own; their vices often copied from their enlightened allies" (226), she condemns the violence sometimes practiced by the aboriginal men on their wives and on European settlers, aligning herself with the critical European perspective. Euphemia progresses through the course of the novel to a position more in line with the Abbé Raynal's: colonizers must be responsible and respectful toward those whom they colonize. This progress is meant to be instructive to the English reader in particular: although England had lost its American colonies by 1790, its imperial program was still voracious. Euphemia's ambivalence about her position as colonizer—and therefore Britain's colonial endeavor in general—mirrors the concerns of many in pre- and post-Revolutionary Britain who regarded their country's colonial enterprise from a more enlightened philosophical position, and it benefits from hindsight, from the arguments made for and against colonialism during the fifty years that separate the novel's setting from its publication.

Euphemia's progress toward this more enlightened position is both impeded and impelled by her position as a woman traveller because, however much she may be identified with the colonial endeavor as wife of a British soldier, her gender marginalizes her, pushing her to an awareness of the similarity between her dependent and subordinate position and that of the people around her who have been marginalized by colonialism. Coming to this recognition of similarity is complicated by the nature of the picturesque conventions by which Euphemia is meant to see America and its people. Male travellers to the New World, suggests Annette Kolodny, saw its landscape not as it was, necessarily, but as they wished it to be. They looked to America with the "European pastoral" in mind, and therefore saw the land as edenic, feminized for ease of conquest (*Lay* 6-7). They viewed in order to appreciate, but also to assess with an eye to eventual domination and possession. This assessing eye became part of the picturesque aesthetic realized by gentlemen, and in colonial America, the picturesque was appropriated to the colonial endeavor by British men.

In his *An Essay upon Prints: Containing Remarks Upon the Principles of Picturesque Beauty* (1768), William Gilpin defined the picturesque as "a term expressive of that peculiar kind of beauty, which is agreeable in a picture."[1] The picturesque perspective as theorized by Gilpin, Sir Uvedale Price, and Richard Payne Knight during the last quarter of the eighteenth century was to be achieved by "the subjective and individual ... recognition of beauty" in the landscape, as opposed to the apprehension of beauty by means of a set of classical, "absolute," rules (Andrews 41), to the point that the natural world being perceived sometimes paled in comparison to the artistic composition achieved. Gilpin suggests that while "Nature is wonderfully fertile. The invention of the painter may form a *composition* more agreeable to the rules of his art, than nature commonly produces" (448). As David Marshall, in "The Problem of the Picturesque," observes,

> [t]he picturesque represents a point of view that frames the world and turns nature into a series of *living tableaux*. It begins as an appreciation of natural beauty, but it ends by turning people into figures in a landscape or figures in a painting. Coinciding with a discovery of the natural world, anticipating an imaginative projection of self into the landscape through an act of transport or identification, it assumes an attitude that seems to depend on distance and separation. (414)

This separation of self from scene allows the "picturesque eye" (449) to appreciate what Gilpin views as the "wild and rough parts of nature" and those "objects we often meet with in the wild scenes of the forest, ... cattle sheds, cottages, winding pales ... which have often as beautiful an effect, when seen at a *distance* ... [because] distance ... hides many defects; and many an object may appear well in a remove, which brought nearer, would disgust the eye" (449). The picturesque eye aims for an idealized version of the countryside, romanticized, sanitized, both sublime

---

1   Qtd. in Ross 12. The term "picturesque" had been used as early as 1705 in England, but it was not until Gilpin published (anonymously) his *Dialogue upon the Gardens of the Right Honourable The Lord Viscount Cobham at Stow [sic] in Buckinghamshire* in 1748 that the term was more fully explained and more widely disseminated. His *Three Essays: On Picturesque Beauty; On Picturesque Travel; and on Sketching Landscape*, published in 1792, but written and discussed at least a decade and a half earlier, brought the term into general use. By 1790, the term, originally yoked to the paintings of the continental artists Claude Lorraine, Salvator Rosa, and Nicolas Poussin, had transcended particular national boundaries and was associated with landscapes that shared certain characteristics, regardless of the country in which they were found.

and beautiful, but never the brutish, poverty-filled, close-up reality of rural life.[1] As Elizabeth Helsinger notes, this framing perspective invites the viewer of the landscape to reshape the land—if only visually—which implies a right to possess the land. The viewer was usually a man of leisure, the traditional landowner—not "women, children, the laboring classes, or the native inhabitants of the lands to which Britain was extending her empire" (18). Such a view emphasizes the general rather than the particular, which allows one to distance himself from the moral prospect inherent in the landscape; it also allows for the maintaining of the status quo, and the separation of people according to class, gender, and racial hierarchies.

The picturesque as practiced by women retains the appreciation of variety, but it is more often a domestic vision, that of the marginalized and so compassionate toward the marginalized it views. It is appreciative of the details of the scene, and apprehends the figures in the landscape as individual people whose circumstances must be responded to personally rather than solely aesthetically. Women writing of what they saw on their travels emphasized the relationships that developed between themselves and their travelling companions, as well as with the people they met as they travelled (Labbe 117). An example of the way in which Euphemia's gaze shifts from the traditional picturesque tourist's view to a more humanized and individual view consistent with the feminine picturesque[2] and with Raynal's instructions on how to see America is evident in the episode of the Dutch cottagers.[3] As she voyages up the Hudson River from New York City to Albany, where her husband is initially stationed, Euphemia describes the river as "the most delightful river imaginable, the shores on each side exhibiting a prospect, sometimes all beautifully wild and

---

1 See Copley 151, 153; Ross 19, 34; Bermingham 11; Labbe xxi; Andrews 59; Buzard 16.

2 Elizabeth Bohls uses the term "female picturesque" to suggest a similar, though more narrow concept, and Sara Suleri uses the term "feminine picturesque" to describe the process as experienced by women in India.

3 Berg (394) and Garside (x) also mention this scene, and the *Critical Review* quoted this scene—and this one alone—in its entirety as an example of Lennox's descriptive abilities.

romantic, sometimes rich with flourishing plantations, and elegant mansions" (219). That she admires both wild nature as well as a nature shaped by art and exhibiting commercial success marks her perspective as significantly different from that of many male travellers in the New World whose aesthetics were more wholly "imperial" (Seelye 51) because they emphasized the land's usefulness to those colonizing it and valued the transformation of nature.

As Euphemia travels further into the American wilderness, however, her perspective changes. While on their way up the Hudson, Euphemia notes "the trees of many species unknown to us" (219); while the landscape, with its unrecognizable vegetation, seems foreign, it is still identifiably picturesque: groves of trees and beautiful verdure conjure visions of the English pastoral countryside through which the English took tours, armed with their Claude glasses and bent on seeing as many framed prospects as possible. Such a landscape "inspired a soft and pleasing melancholy, which we enjoyed in silence" (220). But this perspective changes as Euphemia and her party, enticed by their Dutch skipper's stories of the "sequestered inhabitants" of the forested areas beyond the river's banks, become "impatient to see these persons, whose manners, we supposed, must be as savage as their way of life" (220). Leaving the boat and entering the forest, they come to a "delightful spot" whose beauty seems to "have been a little assisted by art" (220). They discover a cottage such as Gilpin's picturesque traveler would view as "a dwelling, where happiness may reside, unsupported by wealth— ... a resource, where we may still continue to enjoy peace, tho we should be deprived of all the favours of fortune" (448). They confidently enter the empty cottage, help themselves to refreshment, and are about to depart when the owner of the cottage, a Dutch woman, and her child appear. The fear the tourists feel is far overshadowed by the terror of the cottager who was "in so much astonishment and terror at our appearance, that she seemed ready to fall to the ground," and her child "almost stunned us with its screams" (221). Their terror is lightened only after the Dutch skipper calms them; as they are very poor, the travellers give them money, aprons, and handkerchiefs. Euphemia concludes that "the condition of these poor people seems to be bad; and I do not find that they receive much relief from the wealthy owners of the rich plantations, which are in the neighbourhood of these high lands. The many that need, and the many that deny pity, make up the bulk of mankind" (222).[1]

This scene illustrates the way in which Euphemia's initial aesthetic response to the landscape—distant, romantic, self-indulgent—is transformed upon closer contact. Just as in her correspondence with Maria she reveals the darker side of married life, so her criticism of social and economic hierarchies, rising out of the landscape that had appeared so picturesque from a distance, reveals to the reader the tensions often hidden from the view of the cursory tourist—the bleak, unidealized side of rural life; Euphemia and her party discover the poor Dutch family living in the wilderness only by infiltrating the apparently prosperous colonial landscape via the picturesque "rugged path." Venturing into the interior, Euphemia comes to a realization of the detail-laden perspective that reveals the reality of rural poverty. In so doing, Euphemia practices the picturesque from a feminized perspective, thereby revealing the limitations of the masculine picturesque which severed aesthetics from morality. The feminine picturesque embraces an emotive response to what is seen, allowing a morally informed version of the picturesque. Ultimately, Euphemia does not see the Dutch cottagers with the western "journalistic eye, ... [an] instrument of colonial authority [that pursues] ... penetration of the interiors of human habitations [and] ... the bodies and faces of people with the same freedom that it brings to the survey of a landscape" (Spurr 19). Instead, in this "confrontation of cultures," compassion is a mediating force. While I would agree with Séjourné that to Euphemia the Dutch initially appear as foreign as the aboriginal peoples and that at the outset she is prone to "consider them as only one more sight in the general picture of the country" (93), her experience with the Dutch cottager that moves her out of the garrison mentality of "we vs. them" meliorates this tendency. Finally, it is Euphemia's female experience of the New World, a female perspective on the land and its people—informed by the experiences of an upper-middle-class woman's domestic life, sunk in the reality of the quotidian—that is validated, rather

---

1 Sarah Knight, in her travels in early eighteenth-century New England, also comes upon a "hutt" in which very poor folk are living; it is, she writes, "one of the wretchedest I ever saw a habitation for human creatures" (see Appendix C, 417). Her response is very similar to Euphemia's: a recognition of the deplorable conditions some people are forced to endure, and a sense of perspective regarding her own hardships in comparison with those of the hut dwellers.

than the more prevalent masculine perspective. It is her perspective, finally, that Raynal invites.

The Captivity Narrative

The aboriginal peoples of New York, especially the Iroquois, struck the Abbé Raynal, Thomas Paine, J. Hector St. John de Crèvecoeur and many other eighteenth-century writers as "exemplars of liberty" (Grinde and Johansen), a people among whom democracy had evolved to such a level that American revolutionaries took note. This may explain their evolution in Lennox's works.[1] Certainly, by including quotations from Raynal's work, passages which Lois Whitney suggests "contrast, to the disparagement of civilization, the simplicity of savage life with the enervating complexities and the injustices of life in cultivated society" (55-56), Lennox's aim is to critique eighteenth-century European society. In this attempt she was not alone; other British novelists of the period had used the figure of the aboriginal North American similarly, though few had the first-hand experience with aboriginal people that Lennox seems to have had.[2]

Lennox's first novel, *Harriot Stuart*, uses the more traditional form of the captivity narrative,[3] which depicts a white woman

---

1 H.N. Fairchild notes that Lennox presents the aboriginal peoples in her first novel much more negatively than she does in her last novel, where they receive what Lois Whitney terms "guarded praise" (55). Fairchild assumes this is because the publication of *Euphemia* coincided with "the fashionableness of sentimental primitivism" (159).

2 Benjamin Bissell suggests that "the sentimentalized or idealized Indian" does not play a significant role in English fiction before 1800, but "during the latter half of the century, novels having their scene in America became much more common and in many of these the Indian plays a conspicuous role" (116, 87). In addition to *Euphemia*, aboriginal peoples of North America appear in Charlotte Smith's *Old Manor House* (1793); Gilbert Imlay's *The Emigrants* (1793); Robert Bage's *Hermsprong* (1796); Charles Brockden Brown's *Edgar Huntly* (1799); Eliza Winkfield's *The Female American* (1767); John Shebbeare's *Lydia* (1755); Frances Brooke's *History of Emily Montague* (1769); Tobias Smollett's *Humphry Clinker* (1773).

3 O'Donnell notes that in "a more sophisticated variation [of the captivity narrative], the white victim is a child ... captured by Indians and brought up in their ways, which he ... adopts as his own" (246-47). This variation was especially popular in New York fiction after the 1824 publication of Mary Jemison's captivity narrative, a section of which is included in Appendix D, along with the abduction scene from *Harriot Stuart*.

who is captured, tortured, and made to journey into the wilderness: Harriot is herself captured by what she takes to be a group of aboriginal people and rowed up river away from the fort at Albany, into the wilderness. However, Lennox inverts the captivity narrative in *Harriot Stuart* when she places at the head of the group of aboriginal people an Englishman in disguise: Harriot's spurned lover, Belmein. Harriot's initial fear at being captured by Mohawks is quickly replaced by anger when she realizes that it is Belmein who is her captor. Dressed in Mohawk garb, Belmein had been convincing in his disguise and Harriot had at first taken him for a Mohawk. The interchangeableness of Belmein and the Mohawks who accompany him suggests that in this pseudo-captivity narrative Lennox is concerned to show that the reputation the natives had for savagery and the fear they evoked in the British in North America, while in some instances warranted, is in this case only a shadow play when viewed against the actual savagery of the "civilized" gentleman who has violently taken Harriot from the fort garden and into the wilderness with little actual concern for her physical safety or the security of her reputation. Harriot Stuart sees herself as a victim, but not of the Mohawk tribe; her victimization occurs at the hands of libertine men and a father who insists that she marry a man whom she does not love.

In *Euphemia*, Lennox uses the more sophisticated form of the captivity narrative; in this case, it is Euphemia's son, Edward, who is taken. Euphemia is left to suffer the loss of her son, though his is only a captivity narrative for her after the fact, since she does not find out what happened to him until he returns to her after nine years spent with a Huron tribe and the Jesuits in Canada.

Edward is three years old when he and William, his father's servant, become lost in the forest near the falls of Cohas and are found by a group of Hurons from Canada, who have come to New York to sell furs to the English settlements. The Hurons, having lost a member of their group through an accident while on this expedition, carry William back "to the mother of the deceased, in order, that by adopting him, she might replace her dead son" (374). Edward is adopted by a woman in the expedition whose son had died just before she set out: in William's words, she "showed an affection for him equal to that she had felt for her own son" (374). Indeed, her dying request is that Edward be given back to his birth family, but because his family is unknown, he is sent by the local Jesuit missionary to the Father

Rector at the Jesuit College in Montreal, who is so taken with Edward that he does not try very hard to find Edward's parents and instead, Euphemia later surmises, educates Edward with the idea of making a Jesuit of him. William, who had been adopted happily into a Huron family, was subsequently taken prisoner by the Algonquins and adopted into another family; he manages to escape from this harsher environment and tracks Edward down. The Father Rector, when confronted, agrees to release Edward, who feels great "gratitude, tenderness, and grief" upon parting with him (379).

Euphemia regains her son through the good-hearted actions of both Europeans and aboriginal peoples. When she had feared that her son had been captured, Euphemia's view of aboriginal North Americans had reverted to the dehumanizing: they were beasts, savages, and she imagined that their reputed cannibalistic tendencies would impel them to eat her son.[1] But once Edward has been recovered, she is forced to deal with the human face of the aboriginal in the person of her son, who initially appears to Mrs. Benson as "a young Indian" (369) and who is called "the young Huron" even after his return to England. In addition to his adoption of traditional Huron clothing and hairstyle, Edward bears a birthmark in the image of a bow and arrow, the arms born by one of the aboriginal men who frightened Euphemia in the forest while she was pregnant with Edward. Mrs. Benson suggests that the mark attests to "the power of imagination" (263). In *Euphemia*, then, Lennox is willing to go further than she had in *Harriot Stuart* in suggesting sympathy between British colonials and aboriginal peoples. *Harriot Stuart*'s Belmein simply dresses as an aboriginal, whereas Edward carries the mark of America back to England as a part of his identity and a result of his mother's imaginative response to her vivid experience in America. Indeed, his birthmark is what convinces Mrs. Benson of his identity as Edward Neville upon his return from captivity. And while his rough, incongruous appearance and mannerisms suggest picturesque spectacle, closer inspection reveals how these diverse elements coexist in a beloved son. Edward's captivity

---

1   In addition to passages from Raynal's work, which is generally appreciative of the cultures of the tribal societies of North America, Lennox also uses material from Edmund Burke's *An Account of the European Settlements in North America* (see Appendix C), which offers a negative picture of the aboriginal peoples, describing them in bestial terms. Euphemia's fears are articulated in this more Burkean manner in the novel.

results in his transculturation—from English to Huron to French to Mohawk, moving further away from a pure and simple English identity with each successive culture he enters.[1] Her son's multi-layered identity requires that Euphemia acknowledge the Mohawks and Hurons, along with the French and the English, who helped her son to freedom. It takes members of three cultures and several social classes to achieve her son's return: the members of the tribes that adopted Edward and William; the French priests who received Edward from the Hurons and educated him; Mr. Parker, the British officer who kept boy and man safe from the wicked Lt. Blood; and the two Mohawks who changed clothes with Edward and William, allowing them a disguise, and who escorted them back through the wilderness to their home.

In both *Harriot Stuart* and *Euphemia*, then, Lennox evokes the idea of the captivity narrative only to complicate the reader's initial response, making the reader step back to question her assumptions. The initial culprit in both captivities is the North American aboriginal; but, in both novels, that initial assumption is only partially correct: in *Harriot Stuart*, yes, Belmein is actually accompanied by two Mohawks, but it turns out they have been converted to Christianity, and speak in the Dutch language; while they may lend an air of credibility to Belmein's scheme, they do no more in Harriot's capture than row the boat—this despite the reputation of the Mohawks among both settlers and other tribes for being "a most ambitious, haughty, and bloodthirsty people" (VanDerBeets 106). Belmein, on the other hand, has behaved with violence toward the woman for whom he purports to care; he has shown himself to be a "savage." In *Euphemia*, Edward is indeed taken by the Hurons, but treated well, and the culpability for the event rests partially with his father, who had persisted in taking him on a journey into dangerous country and then did not attend to him. Additionally, the violence of Euphemia's grief over the loss of her son is muted for the reader because it is mediated through Mrs. Benson's reporting of it; it is she who writes to Maria in the aftermath of the loss, not Euphemia. Thus it seems clear that, while Lennox was more concerned in *Harriot Stuart* to show the depravity of Englishmen than to vindicate the North American aboriginal peoples, in *Euphemia* she follows Raynal's

---

1 Michelle Burnham discusses the process of transculturation many captives experienced (52).

lead in appreciating the value of the indigenous North American cultures as she indicates ways in which many of their customs and manners are essentially superior to those of the English.

The inclusion of a captivity narrative in a novel would usually signal a standard emotional response of outrage from the late eighteenth-century reader, who was primed by more than a century of captivity narratives. Some of these, such as Mary Rowlandson's well-known account of her capture, written in 1682, dwell on the violence of the aboriginal people toward their white captives, their insensibility to their captives' suffering, the physical hardships of the journey, and especially the emotional suffering of the captives over the violent, often horrific deaths of loved ones. While Rowlandson's captivity narrative is clearly meant to evidence God's power and grace, it can also be seen as a vehicle for expressing hatred of the tribes and their French allies (VanDerBeets xvii). Others, like Robert Eastburn's narrative, suggest the physical discomfort of the march with the aboriginal people, but reveal that it is discomfort shared equally by captor and captive alike, which suggests to the reader the harsh conditions aboriginal people routinely endured and may mitigate the charge of cruelty toward prisoners somewhat. Gilbert Imlay's *The Emigrants* (1794) chronicles the capture of Caroline T—n, but this novelistic treatment, like Eastburn's non-fiction account, de-emphasizes aboriginal violence: Caroline relates that she had no fear as a prisoner, and was treated with kindness by her captors; further, the novel suggests, through its description of her rescue by Captain Arl—ton as a "re-taking," that the lack of a woman's agency in America amounted to a captive life.[1] This view is articulated as well in Frances Brooke's novel, *The History of Emily Montague* (1769), set partly in Canada, when Edward Rivers, writing to his sister, observes that

> In the true sense of the word, we are the savages, who so impolitely deprive you of the common rights of citizenship, and leave you no power but that of which we cannot deprive you, the resistless power of your charms. (40)

Like Imlay and Brooke, Lennox has done all she can in *Euphemia* to denude the captivity experience of much of its impact, assigning little of the onus associated with the act of capture to the abo-

---

1   See Appendix D for selections by Imlay and Eastburn.

riginal people themselves, and mitigating even that little by making the two Mohawks integral to Edward's safe passage home. The captivity narrative in *Euphemia* initially places Lennox's heroine in a passive position, as the one who waits, the one who is betrayed by the wilderness and its inhabitants, a position similar to her role as wife. However, the captivity narrative also suggests an active role for her in its happy resolution as it forces her to recognize the true nature of life in America: the wilderness is not a pastoral garden, but neither are the aboriginal peoples savages.

Conclusion

There are some among Lennox's critics who see *Euphemia* as a rehashing of her first novel, *Harriot Stuart*. Yes, they are set in the same place and time, but the forty years that lie between the two novels both cause and allow Lennox to suggest in *Euphemia* a clear reformist agenda, one which is every bit as revolutionary as Mary Wollstonecraft's or Thomas Paine's, and which marks this last novel as the realistic, balanced successor of a first novel written in its author's more hopeful youth.

Euphemia offers, through the give and take of the epistolary form, the provision of two strong, but very differently situated heroines; the embrace of the feminine picturesque perspective; its recommendation of alternative family configurations; and its reworking of the captivity narrative, a recognition that both men and women have a right to express dissatisfaction and to find a satisfactory solution to a problem, whether it be a complete breaking of the bond, as was the consequence of the American Revolution, or a reconfiguring of family that would redress imbalances therein, as occurs in Euphemia's relationship with her husband. Was Lennox advocating divorce be made as accessible in Britain, where she lived most of her life, as it was in post-revolutionary America, where she had spent her girlhood? As a sufferer in her own unhappy marriage, it would make sense that Lennox would see such a need, and it is suggestive that while her first novel was written soon after her marriage to Alexander Lennox, deals with courtship in an American setting, and ends hopefully with the marriage of the heroine, her final novel, the only other work set in America, situates the reader squarely in the reality of the life of a woman married to an imprudent, selfish, tyrannical man. Even Maria's happy marriage cannot dislodge this reality from the reader's attention. Euphemia does not divorce her husband—that would be impossible within the mid-eighteenth-century British legal system—but fortune allows her, and she grasps, the opportunity to take greater control in her marriage, especially over the education of her children. Such a solution, Lennox might say, was her only option in 1750; it should not be in 1790.[1]

In *Euphemia* there is an acknowledgment of America as a potential nation of many diverse peoples, and a greater examination of the components of the nation in the depictions of aboriginal peoples, slaves of African origin, European groups other than the British—the French and Dutch, for instance—various religious and class viewpoints, and gender and generational differences, than there was in *Harriot Stuart*. As Kathleen Wilson points out, the American Revolution "undermined long-held beliefs in the morality and virtue of the imperial project" (152); it is the morality of this project, considered through its aesthetic and gendered underpinnings, that Lennox questions in *Euphemia*; her silence on the American Revolution accentuates Lennox's recognition that the problematic nature of Britain's colonial practices was apparent long before the Revolution, to those who could see it. In its emphasis on travel and the epistolary frame as means to closing distances between people, *Euphemia* offers to a post-Revolutionary world some hope for a new idea of union between two equal and independent nations, rather than a dwelling on the mistakes of the past. Just as the marriage between Euphemia and Neville at the end of the novel must adjust to Euphemia's changed financial circumstances, so America and England must find a new way to see one another, one which recognizes the equal value of the disparate individuals who make up the two nations. Who better to recognize such a solution than a woman who was born in and lived most of her life in England, but whose imagination was fired by the American landscape and people she knew as a girl?

---

1 *Euphemia* is written as a cautionary tale for a British audience of young unmarried women. It could just as easily have been written for an American audience of the same (though it was never published in America) because, as Cathy Davidson notes, like many of the sentimental novels to be written in America from 1800 onward, *Euphemia* portrays the consequences of a poor marriage decision. These novels also "acknowledge that marriage can be bitterly unhappy"; they "encourage women to circumvent disaster by weighing any prospective suitors in the balance of good sense—society's and ... [their] own" (113).

Charlotte Ramsay Lennox:
A Brief Chronology

1727-29? Charlotte Ramsay born (possibly in Gibraltar where her father, James Ramsay, was stationed as Captain-Lieutenant of Clayton's Regiment (14th Foot)

1739-42 James Ramsay appointed Captain of an Independent Company in New York; family moves to Albany, New York

1742-46 James Ramsay dies in New York in 1742; Charlotte returns to London, lives under the patronage of Lady Cecilia Isabella Finch and the Countess of Rockingham

1747 *Poems on Several Occasions* published in November by S. Paterson, London; marries Alexander Lennox, Assistant to W. Strahan, printer, in London, Oct. 6, at St. George's, Mayfair

1748-50 Actress in London productions

1750 *The Life of Harriot Stuart, Written by Herself* (novel) published in December by J. Payne and J. Bouquet (trans. into French 1795)

1752 *The Female Quixote* (novel) published in March; *The Age of Louis XIV* (trans.) published

1753-4 *Shakespeare Illustrated* (trans. of Italian sources of Shakespeare's plays, and criticism), 3 vols., published

1755 *The Memoirs of Maximilian de Bethune, Duke of Sully* (trans.) published

1756 *The Memoirs of the Countess of Berci* (trans.) published

1757 *Memoirs for the History of Madame de Maintenon and of the Last Age* (trans.); *Philander* (play; rejected by Garrick)

1758 *Henrietta* (novel) published; second edition 1761

1760 *The Greek Theatre of Father Brumoy* (trans.) published

1760-61 *The Lady's Museum* (magazine) published (11 numbers)

1762 *Sophia* (novel) published (first serialized March 1760-February 1761 as *The History of Harriot and Sophia* in the *Lady's Museum*)

1765	Daughter, Harriot Holles, christened April 28; Catherine Ramsay, CL's mother, dies in New York
1769	*The Sister* (comedy) produced at Covent Garden
1771	Son, George Louis, born
1774	*Meditations and Penitential Prayers Written by the Celebrated Duchess De La Valliere* (trans.); adaptation and trans. of Racine's *Bajazet*, rejected by Garrick
1775-76	*Old City Manners* (adaptation of *Eastward Hoe* by Ben Jonson, John Marston, and George Chapman) produced at Drury Lane; published 1775
1783-4	Death of daughter, Harriot Holles
1790	*Euphemia* published by T. Cadell and J. Evans
1792	Receives financial assistance from Royal Literary Fund (continued until her death)
1793	George Louis emigrates under duress to America, possibly to relatives in Baltimore
1804	Charlotte Ramsay Lennox dies January 4 in Dean's Yard, Westminster; buried in an unmarked grave

A Note on the Text

Euphemia was published in June, 1790 by T. Cadell and J. Evans in London; the four-volume novel sold for twelve shillings, sewn. There were no editions other than the first, which serves as the copy text for this edition. No manuscript of the novel is extant.

While spelling has not been regularized, except in the case of obvious printer's errors, punctuation and capitalization have been modernized to the extent that dialogue is now marked by one set of double quotation marks; sentences receive end punctuation when followed by a capitalized letter denoting the beginning of a new sentence; the display capitals used for the first word of a new paragraph have not been reproduced; and the word at the beginning of a sentence is capitalized when preceded by end punctuation (except occasionally when an exclamation mark is followed by a number of short phrases in the exclamatory mode, none of which begins with a capitalized letter). In addition, the long S has been replaced by the modern S, and the length of dashes has been normalized. I have retained the hyphens in compound words hyphenated at the margin in the copy text unless the *Oxford English Dictionary* suggests this was not the common practice for a given word in the eighteenth century. I have followed the above practices in editing the appendices as well as the text of *Euphemia*. I have not altered the practice of capitalizing substantives, which occurs in some works in the appendices. For the appendices, I chose as my copy text the first edition of a work when possible.

Lennox's two footnotes are indicated by asterisks in the text. My annotations appear as footnotes and aim to contextualize the works historically, culturally, geographically, and literarily. They also clarify issues raised by the text, such as when a character is misnamed. While Lennox and her contemporaries referred to the aboriginal peoples of North American as "Indians," I have used the terms "aboriginal" and "aboriginal peoples," as well as the First Nations' names for their peoples, such as "Huron" and "Mohawk" when these affiliations are clear, throughout my introduction, annotations, and headnotes for the appendices. I consulted a number of reference works as I worked on the annotations, and have abbreviated their titles as the list that follows indicates.

Abbreviations of Sources Used for Annotations

AFP   *A Factious People*. Patricia Bonami. New York: Columbia UP, 1971.

CBD   *Chambers' Biographical Dictionary*. Rev. ed. Ed. J.O. Thorne and T.C. Collocott. Edinburgh: Chambers, 1986.

CCB   *The Customs and Ceremonies of Britain*. Charles Kightly. London: Thames and Hudson, 1986.

CCE   *Concise Columbia Encyclopedia*. Ed. Judith S. Levey and Agnes Greenhall. New York: Avon, 1983.

CDQS   *The Columbia Dictionary of Quotations from Shakespeare*. Mary and Reginald Foakes. New York: Columbia UP, 1998.

CGEL   *The Cambridge Guide to English Literature*. Michael Stapleton. Cambridge: Cambridge UP, 1983.

DAIH   *The Dictionary of American Immigration History*. Ed. Francesco Cordasco. Metuchen, NJ: The Scarecrow Press, 1990.

DCM   *Dictionary of Classical Mythology*. J.E. Zimmerman. New York: Harper and Row, 1978.

ECEL   *Eighteenth-Century English Literature*. Ed. Geoffrey Tillotson et al. New York: Harcourt Brace Jovanovich, 1969.

HNY   *History of New York*. David Ellis, et al. New York: Cornell UP, 1967.

HPNY   *A History of the Province of New York*. William Smith. 1757. 2 vols. Ed. Michael Kammen. Cambridge, MA: Harvard UP, 1972.

LE   *The London Encyclopedia*. Ed. Ben Weinreb and Christopher Hibbert. London: Macmillan, 1983.

LPP   *London Past and Present*. Henry Wheatley. 3 vols. London: J. Murray, 1891.

NOCLF   *The New Oxford Companion to Literature in French*. Ed. Peter France. Oxford: Clarendon, 1995.

OCCL   *The Oxford Companion to Classical Literature*. Ed. M.C. Howatson. New York: Oxford UP, 1989.

OCEL   *The Oxford Companion to English Literature*. Ed. Margaret Drabble. 5th ed. New York: Oxford UP, 1985.

OED   *The Oxford English Dictionary*. J.A. Simpson and

E.S.C. Weiner. 2nd ed. Oxford: Clarendon, 1989.

PDEH   *The Penguin Dictionary of Eighteenth-Century English History.* Ed. Jeremy Black and Roy Porter. London: Penguin, 1994.

Séjourné   *The Mystery of Charlotte Lennox, First Novelist of Colonial America.* Philippe Séjourné. Aix-en-Provence: Publications des Annales de la Faculté des Lettres, 1967.

EUPHEMIA.

BY

Mrs. CHARLOTTE LENNOX.

IN FOUR VOLUMES.

LONDON:
PRINTED FOR T. CADELL, IN THE STRAND,
AND J. EVANS, PATERNOSTER-ROW.
MDCCXC.

EUPHEMIA.
VOL. I

Letter I.
MISS HARLEY TO MRS. NEVILLE.

ONE of the greatest pleasures I proposed to myself, on my return to England, was to meet my dear Euphemia; to bind, if possible, in faster bands, that tender friendship which has united us from our earliest years; to live in sweet society together: to suffer only short absences; rendered tolerable by frequent letters, and the dear hope of meeting soon again. But how are these expectations destroyed! You are going to leave me; and, too probably, for ever. Long tracts of land, and an immeasurable ocean, will soon divide us. I shall hear from you once or twice in a year, perhaps: my dear Euphemia will be lost to me; and all that now remains of that friendship, which was the pride and happiness of my life, will be the sad remembrance of a good I once enjoyed, but which is fled for ever!

How shall I teach my heart to forget you! How shall I hear the conversation of other young women of our age and condition, after being used to yours! It was some merit to be capable of tasting it with so high a relish, as to render that of my other companions insipid. There are friendships that serve only to pass away the time, and soften the tediousness of solitude; but yours, besides being delightful, was profitable. I never read your letters, but I brought away pleasures that remained, and advantages that did you no hurt. I grew rich by what I took from you, without impoverishing you by my gain. In a word, I was happy, and I am so no more. I must lose you! there is no remedy! My tears efface my letters as I write! I cannot, I would not, restrain them! The wise may call these tender feelings infirmities of the mind, if they will; I do not wish to be without them, and I had rather have my malady than their health.

But tell me, my Euphemia, by what strange fatality have all these things happened? When I went to France, I left you rich and happy; the reputed heiress of a large fortune, both your beloved parents alive, and every prospect brightening before you. What a reverse, in the space of a few months! An orphan! your inheritance lost! married; and, in consequence of that marriage, becoming an exile from your country, doomed to waste your days in America! I cannot bear to think of it! But you go with a husband you love. I never thought my Euphemia very susceptible of that passion. Mr. Neville undoubtedly must possess an uncommon share of merit, to have so soon conquered your indifference, your reserve, and if I may now venture to say so, your indisposition to the married state. Oh! had it been otherwise, with what pleasure should I have communicated to you the happy change in my fortune; a fortune which, by sharing with you, I should have doubly enjoyed! I cannot enter into particulars now; my mind is too much agitated. Write to me soon: yet what can you say to comfort me? If you cannot say that you are not to quit England, it will be the first of your letters that I shall not receive with transport. Adieu, my ever dear Euphemia!

MARIA HARLEY.

Letter II.
MISS HARLEY TO MRS. NEVILLE.
IN CONTINUATION.

MY DEAR EUPHEMIA,

I CANNOT let the post go away without giving you the particulars of that happy change in my fortune, which, while my heart was so full of your loss that I could utter nothing but complaints, I only hinted at: but you would have reason to be offended with me if I was silent on this subject, knowing so well as I do the tender interest you take in whatever concerns me.

You never could be persuaded to think that my uncle's marriage with Miss Fenwick would make any alteration in his conduct towards me, having brought me up with a tenderness and care that supplied the loss of my parents; a loss which I could only know by reflection, being but an infant when they died, and which the kindness of my uncle made it impossible for me to feel. But in this you was mistaken, my dear friend: Lady Harley was a true step-mother, and contrived to alienate my uncle's affection from me by artifices which imposed upon us both. I will give you two or three instances of her plan of operations, as they have been since explained to me.

My uncle, who really loved me, and viewed all my actions in a favourable light, was particularly pleased with a certain attention which prevented his wishes, and made him perceive that I was delighted when I could be useful to him. There is nothing so necessary as to know how to bear tedious moments. My uncle did not possess this art: he is, as you know, a man of sense, and some learning; but having passed the greatest part of his life in the common track of men of fortune and fashion, his amusements must come all from without: he knew not how to strike out any for himself, from resources which a mind more cultivated might have afforded him.

Some time after his marriage, the gout[1] began to visit him with periodical fits: he bore the pain and the confinement with much impatience. Lady Harley, whose fondness for him always appeared excessive, rather tired than relieved him by her importunate caresses: which, however, he received without any apparent peevishness; for, to be sure, he knew how to value a love so tender and passionate, with which he had inspired a woman twenty years younger than himself!

My company was now more acceptable than my aunt's. I sung, I played to him: I gave the rein to my natural vivacity, and endeavoured to divert him by a thousand lively sallies of imagination. I read to him sometimes; and perceived, with great satisfaction, that he began to acquire a taste for this amusement. My voice and manner pleased him. He had a well-stored library; and he approved my choice of the books which were to furnish out his entertainment. You will easily imagine how much this taste for reading increased upon him, when I tell you that I read all Plutarch's Lives[2] to him in less than a fortnight.[3] Thus this long fit of the gout passed away; during which, my aunt had time to make observations on her own insufficiency on such occasions, and my apparent superiority over her. A second attack of the gout gave her an opportunity to practice some of those artifices which she had imagined, in order to lessen my uncle's regard for me. She redoubled her cares and assiduity; she scarce ever left him a moment; she watched his looks, and every turn of his distemper, with such an anxious solicitude, as if her life depended upon his. She would rise several times in the night and run into his chamber to know if he slept, and if the nurse was attentive. A thousand things of this kind she did, which left me, fond as I was of my uncle, far behind her in these outward testimonies of affection.

---

1 A hereditary disease experienced mostly by men in which uric acid deposits in the joints cause inflammation and acute pain (*OED*).
2 Plutarch (c. AD 50–c. 125), Greek biographer, author of *Parallel Lives*, a collection of moral anecdotes.
3 Two weeks.

It is common for people to judge of friendship by the shew it makes, without considering that superstition is fuller of ceremonies than true devotion. My attentions appeared cold and constrained, compared with those of my aunt; and were received with indifference. My uncle now seldom desired me to read; and when I offered to take a book, he would ask me, if I did not think reading so much had hurt me. I sometimes smiled at this: and he would add, with a significant look—"Reading aloud is not good for one who has weak lungs."—"That is not my case, Sir," replied I. "I am glad of it," said he, coldly: "but, however, you shall not read to me." I was quite confounded at his peremptory refusal, and knew not what to say to him; but though vexed and mortified to the last degree, I suffered no complaints to escape me, because I was not willing to discompose my uncle or gratify the malice of Lady Harley, who, I judged, was at the bottom of this peevishness in him: and I judged right; for this was the manner in which she effected her purpose, as my uncle afterwards informed me.

One day, when he desired her to bid me come and read to him, she regretted her not having equal talents with me for that employment—"Which, if I had," said she, "I should not be afraid of falling into a consumption by using them."—"Why, has Maria that notion?" said Sir John. "She certainly has," said my aunt: "but you must not mention to her what I tell you. She complains of a pain in her breast; of shortness of breath; and declares, that when she has read to you an hour or two, she feels as if she was ready to expire with a strange oppression and faintness. She has carried her apprehension so far, as to send her case to an eminent physician; whose answer is, that if she continues to read aloud, she will fall into a decline."

My uncle was amazed and confounded at hearing this, for I never looked better in my life; and he took notice of that circumstance. Lady Harley assured him I was perfectly well, and in very good spirits; "And therefore," added she, "it is the more surprising that she should give way to such strange fancies."

My aunt followed this first blow with many others of the same kind, which would be tedious to enumerate: so that at length my uncle viewing all my actions in an unfavourable light, set me down in his mind as a perfect hypocrite; a character which he ever despised and hated. But although, in consequence of this opinion, he withdrew his affection from me; yet, as it produced no other alteration in his behavior than a certain coldness and reserve, which rather increased than lessened that politeness which was so natural to him, I knew not on what ground to build a complaint. My expences were as liberally supplied as before; my requests as readily granted. My uncle, as he has since told me, could never be brought to hate his brother's daughter, though he ceased to love me as his own.

Being in this unfavourable disposition towards me, he was easily persuaded to press me to a marriage, in which my inclinations were much less consulted than my interest. You know the man I refused, my dear Euphemia; and you did not chide me for my disobedience. My uncle, however, was offended; and as I was absolutely incapable of repairing my fault, or even repenting of it, his continued displeasure gave me so deep a concern, that my situation became very miserable.

Mrs. Irwin was about this time preparing to go to the south of France, for the recovery of her health: as she was a near relation of my mother's, and a very worthy woman, I asked and obtained leave to attend her. I left England without any regret, but parting with you my sweet friend; for my uncle appeared so happy in the passionate tenderness of his young wife, and so compleatly estranged from me, that I could not suppose my absence would give him any uneasiness. He provided for my expences, however, with his usual generosity. When I took leave of him, my tears, and the ardour with which I kissed his hand, seemed to awaken some tender emotions; for he turned aside, and wiped his eyes: but immediately afterwards, as if hardened by some unfavourable recollection, he relapsed into his former coldness, and took a much more ceremonious than kind leave of me. My aunt acted her part extremely well; regretted the loss of my company, and comforted herself with the hope of a happy meeting in a few months. Mrs. Irwin was amazed at the ascendant Lady Harley had gained over a man of my uncle's good sense: "This woman," said she, "will as the poet says—

'Mould his passions till she makes his will.'

But it is my opinion, that your excursion to the Continent will prove less favorable to her machinations than your stay here. With friends and lovers, absence is a kind of death, which sheds oblivion over faults, and heightens every virtue and amiable quality. Lady Harley will now miss a thousand opportunities of hurting you with your uncle, which artifice on her side, and innocent security on yours, would have furnished her with, if you had staid here." It is certain, that the fine fabrick she had raised with such an expence of falshood, was destroyed on a sudden, by means which she could neither foresee nor prevent.

With what pleasure do I turn from this dark side of my fortune, to one in which my dear Euphemia will share in my satisfaction! But what do I say? My Euphemia is going to leave me! This thought, like the stings of a guilty conscience, saddens all my enjoyments; and, when I should be happy, gives me up to tears and complainings. But you will chide me if I continue this strain. Adieu, my dear friend.

In my next you shall have a full account of all that remains for you to know concerning my present situation. Meantime, pity my impatience, my anxiety; and explain to me the causes of this sad reverse of fortune, and all that has happened to you in a separation of a few months; and which, alas! is so soon to be followed by one of many years. But I will fly this thought. Adieu!

MARIA HARLEY.

Letter III.
MRS. NEVILLE TO MISS HARLEY.

WHY does my dear Maria imagine I would chide her for a sensibility so amiable in her, so flattering to me who am the object of it? Am I qualified to recommend apathy to you, who share so deeply with you in an affliction that is common to us both; and while my heart is still smarting with a wound which never, never can be healed? You knew my mother, Maria; you knew her excellence; judge what my grief must be for her loss. But she is happy! her patient suffering virtue has its just reward.

So little do events depend upon the most prudent measures, that had she lived to see the unprosperous event of a marriage which, was her own work; and from which in her last moments, she owed all her consolation with regard to me; she would have been miserable. Heaven spared her this affliction: and, did not self mingle too frequently in our most justifiable passions, I should not now grieve so much for her death, as rejoice in her exemption from an evil which she might not perhaps have borne with her usual fortitude. But you shall have my history from the time of our separation; and an eventful one it is, for the time. I have leisure enough; and to rehearse the past, when the present is unhappy, and the future presents only a gloomy prospect, is not so irksome a task as to make me decline obeying you.

Scarce were my tears dried up for your sudden and unexpected departure, when a surprising alteration in the temper and behaviour of my father filled my mother and myself with the most uneasy apprehensions. He became peevish, melancholy, silent, and reserved: he shunned company, staid much at home, and passed the greatest part of his time shut up in his closet;[1] and was inaccessible even to my mother, who certainly was not even then wholly ignorant of the cause of this great change in him. A stroke of the palsy followed these first symptoms, and completed our distress. It was but slight, however; and by the great skill and care of his physicians he was restored to some degree of health, and able to take a journey to Bath,[2] which they judged necessary to his perfect recovery. I never doubted but I should be permitted to attend him thither, as well as my mother, but my father had resolved otherwise. I durst not dispute his will: tender and affectionate as he always seemed to me, he exacted, and never failed to receive, an implicit obedience to it. Spare me the description of this sad parting! My father, as he turned from me, shed tears, which he endeavoured to hide. I had thrown myself into the arms of my governess; but, raising my head to snatch a parting glance as he stepped into the coach, at that moment he appeared to me more like a corpse than my living father: I shrieked, and fainted away. My dear mother, who had taken every precaution to make this absence more supportable to me, directed my governess to carry me immediately to Richmond, where I was impatiently expected by Mrs. Highmore and her family, with whom I was to reside till my parents returned from Bath. You know this lady, my dear Maria; you know how greatly she was esteemed by my mother, whose confidence she had acquired by the appearance of an uncommon attachment to her. She had daughters of an age fit to be my companions; and their birth and accomplishments made them very proper ones.

During our little journey, Mrs. Burton[3] employed every soothing art to alleviate my grief: but that image, that death-like image of my father, filled my imagination, and swam continually before my sight. I was for a long time insensible to all the caresses of Mrs. Highmore and the young ladies; which were, indeed, carried to excess, particularly on the part of Mrs. Highmore and the

---

1 A small, private room used for study.
2 In Somerset County, southwestern England, a resort in the eighteenth century because of the Roman baths built there in the first and second centuries CE which were thought to have restorative powers.
3 This should read "Mrs. Benson," the name of Euphemia's governess.

eldest daughter: but I was more touched with the behaviour of Lucy, the youngest of these ladies, whose professions of friendship for me had an air of candour and sweetness which won my confidence and engaged my gratitude.

The first letter I received from my mother, gave me so favourable an account of my father's health, that my melancholy apprehensions began to abate; and I was once more able to mix in society, and to share in those amusements which the family were eager to procure for me. This attention, apparently so obliging, would certainly have made an impression upon me, if I had not been disgusted with the adulation which Mrs. Highmore and her eldest daughter were perpetually pouring in my ears. I have heard it said, that it is a mark of grandeur to be hated by those who do not know us, and flattered by those who do: a young woman of fortune has this, in common with royalty, that she seldom hears truth. My governess would have it, that Mrs. Highmore had some design upon me; and her suspicions were strengthened by a visit made by her son, a youth of nineteen, from college, though it was not vacation-time.

The young gentleman had probably received orders to be violently in love with me; for he seemed to court opportunities of speaking to me alone, which I believe were often contrived for him: but he was too bashful to profit by them as was expected; for, after some general conversation about the weather, he used to withdraw to a window, and whistle a tune. His behaviour might have afforded me some diversion, had my mind been more at ease: but now every letter from Bath brought me still less favourable accounts of my father's health. At length, the fatal news of his death arrived; which, notwithstanding the caution that was used, the melancholy looks of my governess, and the rest of the family, announced to me, before the tender Lucy, whose sad task it was to prepare me for this stroke, could utter a word. "My father is dead!" cried I, trembling: "is it not so?" Lucy answered me only by her tears. "Then I have seen him," said I, "for the last time; and the last time I saw him, he looked as he is now."

I continued several days in a most melancholy situation; during which time the family took part in my affliction with an appearance of the most tender sympathy: they shut themselves up with me, and neither paid nor received any visits;[1] each solicitous

---

1   Formal visits were an important social obligation in the eighteenth century. If one received a visit, one was expected to return the visit within a short time.

to outdo the other in endeavouring to calm my grief. On a sudden, this attention ceased; they saw company as usual; and their engagements, both at home and abroad, took up their time so much that they had scarce a few moments to bestow on me; and I have sometimes passed a whole day without seeing them in my apartment. The young man was sent back to college, without leaving even a compliment for me. A strange alteration now took place in their manner of conversing with me: respect and adulation were no more; their kindness was disgustingly familiar, their pity humiliating, and their civility constrained.

All this passed unnoticed for some time: but when the violence of my grief was in some degree abated, my attention was awakened first to little neglects and failures in their usual politeness, that led to a fuller observation of their behaviour towards me; which I found so changed, that they did not seem to be the same persons with whom I had conversed so long. Perplexed and astonished at what I now for the first time discovered, I asked my governess the meaning of this strange alteration. "My dear," said she, "you now see the world as it is: and you will probably," added she, sighing, "have but too many opportunities of assenting to the truth of that maxim, which seems to bear hard upon human nature; but which is nevertheless too true, That the generality are bad."—"But, Lucy," said I, without taking in the full meaning of her words, "Lucy is still the same; she is not changed." At that moment the dear girl entered the room. I flew into her arms; and my heart being greatly oppressed, I burst into tears. She looked at Mrs. Benson significantly, as I afterwards recollected; and then applied herself, with her usual tender solicitude, to console me. My governess retired upon Mrs. Highmore's coming in: "Why my good girl," said she to me, "will you never have done grieving?" Struck with the unusual coarseness of her phrase, I stared at her without making any answer. "Come," pursued she, "you must not stay moping in the house: take an airing in your chariot; you may not always have one." Here Lucy, in great agitation, stopped her; crying eagerly—"Mamma!" Mrs. Highmore, as if recollecting herself, replied—"You are right.—But, Miss Lumley," said she to me, "have you had a letter from your mamma? How is she? does she talk of returning?"—"Would to heaven I were with her!" said I, passionately. "Ah, poor woman!" said Mrs. Highmore, "she is in trouble enough; she is greatly to be pitied." My tears now flowed afresh: "Pray, Madam," said Lucy, receiving my declining head on her bosom, "leave me to comfort Miss Lumley: she will be more calm when we are alone."—"Well, I am going," said Mrs. Highmore. "Pray, my good girl, moderate your affliction.—And Lucy, do you hear? I cannot possibly dispense with your dining at table to-day: I have company, you know. You will hardly have time to dress." She went out of the room at these words; and I, with some peevishness, pressed Miss Lucy to go and dress: but she declared she would not quit me that day, Mrs. Benson being obliged to go to town to transact some business my mother had charged her with.

I have related this little scene circumstantially to you, my dear Maria, that you may have some notion of the astonishment I must be in at the alteration of this woman's stile and behaviour, who a few weeks before had carried her respects and attentions to me even to servility. But the mystery was soon to be unravelled.

Two days after this, Mrs. Benson told me I should soon see my mother. "When?" cried I impatiently. "Tomorrow, perhaps," said she, smiling; "and, perhaps, to-night." I rose from my chair in a transport. "Ah! She is here," said I; "let me fly to her!"—"No, my dear," said Mrs. Benson, "she is not here; she would not come here: but she is in London. I have a note from her, ordering me to bring you to her. The chariot is getting ready, and we will set out in a few minutes." Lucy came running to me all in tears: I took an affectionate leave of her; and received the parting civilities of Mrs. Highmore and her eldest daughter with great coolness. Mrs. Highmore charged me to assure her good friend, so she stiled my mother, that it should not be long before she called upon her. As supercilious as this speech was, the air that accompanied it was still more so. I answered only by a slight bow; and we drove away.

My thoughts, wholly employed on the expected meeting with my dear mother, a meeting at once so wished and dreaded, prevented my taking notice of the extreme dejection of Mrs. Benson, who scarce spoke to me all the way. Nor was I rouzed from my reverie, till I found myself in St. James's Square;[1] when the carriage, instead of crossing into Pall Mall,[2] where our house was,

---

1 St. James's Square designed by the Earl of St. Albans in 1663, was originally known as the Piazza and became a much sought after residence. George III was born there and other members of the nobility lived there during the eighteenth century, including the Duke of Ormond and the Earl of Derby, as well as Sir Robert Walpole, and William Pitt.

2 Pall Mall was a wide street which extended from St. James's Street to the Haymarket. In the eighteenth century, it was the home to Lord Bolingbroke, and place of business of Robert Dodsley, the bookseller.

drove directly to Charles Street,[1] and stopped at a small house, upon the window of which I observed a bill for lodgings. "Have you any business here?" said I to my governess. "My dear," replied she, sighing, "we shall find your mamma here."—"My mamma here!" cried I eagerly; and, springing out of the chariot, I flew up stairs, upon the top of which I saw her coming to meet me.

Her deep mourning,[2] her pale and emaciated countenance, the transient gleam of joy which the first sight of me occasioned, effaced by a flood of tears, affected me with such poignant anguish, that I sunk down at her feet; and, clasping her knees, remained there speechless and drowned in tears. Mrs. Benson raised me, and led us both into the room. My dear mother continued gazing on me for some time in silent sorrow; while I wept, and kissed the hand with which she affectionately pressed mine. "My dear child," said she, recovering herself, "you have, no doubt, paid your just tribute of tears to the memory of your father. The time calls upon us for fortitude. You have, alas! many evils to struggle against. Poverty is a more dreadful monster than any Hercules[3] overcame: and, to bear it with patience, to preserve our integrity, our independence of mind; in a word, to fall with dignity; is to be a greater hero than he was."

At the word Poverty I started, and gazed on my mother eagerly. "Yes, my dear," pursued she, "we are no longer rich; you are no longer an heiress to a great fortune. From the small provision your father made for me on our marriage, before he succeeded to his uncle's great riches, and which will cease at my

---

1 Charles Street, St. James's Square. The western part of the street built in 1673, was named after Charles II and remained a fashionable address. The portion east of Regent Square however, was much narrower and called "Six Bell Alley." It is probably this latter portion of the street, which was no longer in existence after the mid-eighteenth century, that Euphemia's mother must live in due to her impoverished circumstances.

2 As a new widow, Mrs. Lumley would be wearing a dress the color of which was deep black and which was unornamented; as the period of her widowhood lengthened—usually after a year—she might begin to wear dresses trimmed with gray or purple, though some widows continued to wear unrelieved black.

3 Roman god, son of Zeus and Alcmena, who performed the Twelve Labors, feats of great strength that included cleaning the Augean stables, killing the Nemean lion, and capturing the girdle of the Amazonian queen, Hippolyta.

death, we must for the future draw our subsistence. Mr. Lumley died insolvent. Houses, plate, jewels, furniture, all are seized by the creditors! This small apartment in which you now see me, is my habitation; and even this I must soon exchange for one less expensive, and more suitable to my circumstances: for it must be my part now to live in such a manner that my dear child may not be wholly destitute at my death. Something, I hope, I shall be able, by the strictest parsimony, to leave behind me, to put off the bad day of beggary!" My mother could not restrain her tears at this word. She rose up, and said she would retire to her bed-chamber for a few moments, and endeavour to compose herself.

When she was gone, I gave free vent to those emotions which respect and tenderness for her had hitherto restrained. Mrs. Benson endeavoured to comfort me. "Tell me," said I, "if you know; tell me by what means this ruin was brought about?"— "Your father," replied she, "would have been a happy man, if he had continued in that easy mediocrity which once bounded his wishes: but no sooner was he become possessed of the great riches your uncle had acquired in the Indies,[1] than he plunged deep into all the fashionable excesses of the age." The word All she pronounced with a deep emphasis, and a meaning look that went to my heart. "His seat in parliament," continued she, "cost him an immense sum. He played high, and always with ill success. In a word, he was ruined, my dear, before the continued dissipation in which he lived gave him leisure to look into his affairs. Reflection, which came too late to prevent the wreck of his fortune, now produced a remorse that preyed upon his mind, and brought on those disorders which put a period[2] to his life."

My mother's entrance obliged me to restrain those emotions which Mrs. Benson's discourse had excited: I dried my tears; I endeavoured to console my mother by every soothing power I possessed. Her piety and good sense had already brought her to a state of perfect resignation in every thing that respected herself; it was for me only that she felt: and it was to relieve her from that tender anxiety which preyed upon her spirits, and destroyed her health, that I made a sacrifice which I cannot repent of; though,

---

1 In the eighteenth century this term referred to lands in the western Hemisphere discovered in the fifteenth and sixteenth centuries by European explorers who thought them part of India. These lands yielded great wealth to Europeans who traveled there as traders or who owned plantations there.

2 Put an end to his life.

alas! it proved fruitless. But here let me break off for the present: I will continue my narrative some other time. This free communication of my misfortunes to a dear and sympathizing friend, seems to lessen their force.

> "The grief that must not speak,
> Whispers the o'ercharg'd heart, and bids it break,"

says my favourite poet.[1] I will go on, then, and speak to you.— But, my Maria, remember, you must give me the remainder of your little history as soon as possible; you will easily imagine how much I am interested in it. Adieu, my dear friend.

EUPHEMIA NEVILLE.

Letter IV.
MISS HARLEY TO MRS. NEVILLE.

MY DEAR EUPHEMIA,

I HAVE almost effaced every word of your tender and affecting narrative with my tears. Alas! my sweet friend, what have you not suffered! Why was I not with you during these hard trials? Why did you conceal your situation from me? I never received but two letters from you while I was in France. In the last there were some obscure hints, which greatly perplexed me, and which you have now but too well explained. My uncle expresses great tenderness and concern for you; and speaks of your mother in terms of the highest admiration. He says, he was intimate enough with Mr. Lumley, to use the liberty of remonstrating against some of those errors in his conduct which have been the source of his misfortunes: "But," added he very sententiously, "there is a wide distance between being simply persuaded that a thing is wrong, to the being sufficiently so as to make us fall to action, when we must act contrary to our inclinations. Mr. Lumley acknowledged there was reason in what I said; but did not alter his conduct."— "How much easier," thought I, "it is to be wiser for others than ourselves!" Had your father represented to Sir John the imprudence of marrying, at his years, a gay young girl, he might have

---

1 Euphemia's "favourite poet" is Shakespeare. This couplet is from *Macbeth* 4.3 and should read "The grief that does not speak,/ Whispers the o'erfraught heart, and bids it break."

made the same observations: but this truth he was soon convinced of by his own experience.

I had been near a year in France, when I received a letter from my uncle, very different from any of his former ones; for it was extremely affectionate. He expressed great uneasiness at my long absence, and much impatience for my return. This letter was accompanied with a large order upon his banker at Paris,[1] whither we were now going, and permission to stay there a month: after which, he said, he would expect me; and, if his health permitted, Lady Harley and he would meet me at ——. He said not a word of those causes of uneasiness which he had given me, (for when do men own they are in the wrong?) but concluded with professions of the tenderest attachment to me. You will easily conceive that, after the receipt of this letter, I passed my time very pleasantly at Paris; when, a few days before our intended departure, I received another letter from my uncle: it contained but a few lines; and those surprised me with an account of the death of Lady Harley. As I have not naturally a hard heart, nor an unforgiving temper, the death of this lady gave me a real concern, particularly on my uncle's account, who, I supposed, would be greatly afflicted. Mrs. Irwin agreed, that this news ought to hasten our journey, and accordingly we set out immediately upon our return.

My uncle was surprised when he heard of my arrival so much sooner than he expected; and, I could perceive, was pleased at my readiness to oblige him. He received my very kindly; and, as I did not observe any signs of immoderate grief in his countenance, my compliments of condolence were but short. He mentioned my aunt only once, and employed but a few words on the subject. "Her illness," said he, "was sudden, and reached its height before she was thought to be in any danger. The faculty complained of her obstinacy in refusing to be bled,[2] and attributed her death to the want of that remedy." When my uncle took leave of me for the night, he said—"I will send Martin to you as soon as I am in bed; he will inform you of some circumstances that have happened during your absence." I believe you have seen this man: an old confidential servant, who had lived with him many years; and who, by his zeal and attachment, merited the great regard he expressed for him.

1 Cheque for a large amount of money, which his banker in Paris will cash.
2 Surgically bled for medical purposes.

My curiosity was strongly excited, as well by my uncle's behaviour as by these words, which seemed to indicate that something extraordinary had really happened. As soon as the good old man appeared, he congratulated me on my return with tears; and assured me the tenants and servants had constantly prayed for it: "And they did not scruple," pursued he, "to tell my lady herself how much they longed to see you: and this seemed to displease her, for my lady was cunning by halves only; and although she persuaded my master that she was grieved for your absence, she did not take the same pains to deceive us."

"She has certainly," said I, "been less guarded on some occasion or other than usual, for my uncle is greatly altered with respect to her; he appears not to regret her death, and speaks of her with little affection."

"Ah, Madam!" said Mr. Martin, "there is good reason for that. I have a curious history to relate to you, if you can have the patience to hear it: my master ordered me to tell you every circumstance."—"Pray sit down," said I, "and let me have it all." He did so: and here is what he told me, and in his own words.

"You may remember, Madam," said he, "how childishly fond my lady affected to be of her husband; it was much worse after you was gone. She was continually taking his hand, stroking his cheek, and would often kiss him before the servants. I was sorry to see my good master so played upon; and, if I durst, I would have told him that all was not gold that glisters. Mr. Greville, who, you know, Madam, is a very facetious old gentleman, and has a power of wit, used to joke with my master about his young wife's prodigious fondness for him; and would often say very *home* things,[1] which my master would sometimes take very well, and sometimes answer peevishly to; but they had been great friends from their youth, so that it was not a little matter would part them. Now it happened that my master was taken with another fit of the gout, and grievous bad he was, so that the doctors were afraid that it was getting up into his stomach; and then, you know, Madam, all would have been over with him. My lady sat by his bed-side almost continually, sighing most piteously, and shedding rivers of tears while she was with him: but her maid used to say that, when she was in her own apartment, she had no need of an handkerchief to dry her eyes. Well, Madam, my poor master grew worse and worse; and my lady, to

---

1 Pointed, effective, searching things (*OED*).

be sure, more and more sorrowful. And now my master resolved to alter his will: you may guess, Madam, who put that into his head. I was ordered to ride to town, and fetch Lawyer Grasp, and some more gentlemen of that *persuasion*.[1] I perceived what was going forward: and, to be sure, Madam, I thought a new will, under my lady's direction, would not be favourable to you, and that it was fit some friend of yours should be present; and no one was more proper than Mr. Greville, who loves you so dearly, and was, besides, my master's most dear friend. So I ventured to say to my master—'Does not your honour please that I should send or go for Mr. Greville upon this occasion?' My lady looked as if she could have eat me; and my master said weakly—'Mr. Greville is at his seat in ——, that is more than seventy miles distant: it will be too much trouble for him to come on such short notice.'— 'Sir,' said I, 'I am sure he will not think so.' My master seemed to pause upon it; when my lady, losing her temper quite, called me an officious fool; and bursting into tears, said—'Do you want to persuade your master that he is dying.—My dear Sir John, the physicians assure me you are better. Mr. Greville will be here in a week or two. Do not let this blockhead put such sad thoughts into your head!' She sobbed violently while she was speaking, holding my master's hand to her lips all the time. My master then said—'Let him go for the lawyers, however.' Upon which my lady, looking very spitefully at me said—'Do as you are ordered!' and I left the room immediately, with my heart full, as well for my dear master's danger, as for the injustice you were likely to suffer, my dear young lady."

I interrupted the honest man here, to thank him for the affection he had shewn for me at a time when selfish policy would have pointed out a different conduct; and I do assure you, I thanked him with an effusion of heart equal to his own. But I must break off here; I am summoned to dinner. My uncle has been riding this morning, which has given me leisure to scribble so much: he has brought Mr. Greville home to dinner. You cannot imagine how greatly I am obliged to this gentleman; but you shall know all in my next. My dear Euphemia, adieu!

MARIA HARLEY.

The post not being yet gone out, I have time to add a few lines. Something that fell from Mr. Greville, relating to you, has

---

1 I.e., of that profession.

alarmed me greatly. I fear, I fear, my sweet friend, you are not likely to be as happy in the married state as you deserve to be. Your husband, forgive my freedom, is thought to be ill-tempered; you are all sweetness, patience, and condescension: I foresee from this contrast, continual encroachments on one side; continual recedings on the other. You are one of those few persons who never contest what they think they cannot obtain. What a dangerous power will such a disposition throw into the hands of one who is disposed to use it tyrannically! Mr. Greville knows your husband; and this is what he said upon my telling my uncle, in answer to his enquiry how I had been amusing myself all the morning, that I had been writing to you. "Poor Miss Lumley!" said he; "she is married to Mr. Neville, then! There is nothing—a friend of mind said of himself, and may be applied to her—that could persuade a believer in modern miracles to confess that any thing is impossible to be done, but her ill fortune, which is unchangeable."—"I hope not," said my uncle. "There is no more room for hope," replied Mr. Greville: "she is married to the worst-tempered man in the world; and that has crowned all her misfortunes."

You may judge, my dear Euphemia, how I was affected by this discourse: I asked a thousand questions about Mr. Neville; and every answer I received served to convince me that his temper will make you very miserable. Good Heaven! and is it with this man that you are to cross the Atlantic! This the protector, the friend, the companion, with whom you are to traverse an immense ocean, and live in unknown regions, far from your country and all you love! Surely you can never consent to it; he cannot be so unreasonable as to desire it. If his duty calls him hence, his tenderness for you ought to make him dispense with your accompanying him. You must stay with me, my dear Euphemia; my fortune is yours: my uncle will be a father to us both; he offers you his house for a retreat, and me for your companion till your husband returns.

I have not time to add more. Pray think on what I have proposed, and the necessity there is for complying with it. Once more adieu, my dear friend!

Letter V.
MISS HARLEY TO MRS. NEVILLE.
IN CONTINUATION.

MY uncle is gone to spend a day or two with Mr. Greville; so I shall have full leisure for my pen, which is never so pleasingly employed as when I am writing to my dear Euphemia. Well, Martin went on with his story, which I shall continue to give you in his own words. "Finding I was not permitted to send for Mr. Greville in my master's name, I resolved, however, to write to him, and let him know what was going on; and this I did before I set out for the lawyer's, and put my letter myself into the post. I was sorry to find Mr. Grasp at home; so there could be no delay on that side. He told me he would call upon Counsellor Worden in his way, and bring him with him. With this answer I returned. My lady seemed not at all satisfied with the haste I had made, and her woman told me she shewed great impatience, and was very restless and uneasy all the time I was gone.

"Well, Madam, the lawyers came at last; they were shut up with my master several hours, and my lady went backwards and forwards continually. At last the chaplain and I were called to witness this fine will: the chaplain set his name, but, as Fortune would have it, I had cut my right thumb so desperately about an hour before, that I could not hold my pen, so I was excused, and Counsellor Worden's clerk signed instead of me; and right glad was I that I had escaped this odious office.

"My lady looked marvelously pleased when this affair was over; that is, when she was not in my master's chamber, for there her countenance was like December, all cold and surly, but all sunshine every-where else.

"As I waited on the lawyers to their carriage, I heard Counsellor Worden say to the attorney, 'Sir John's next heir will not thank him for burthening his estate with such an enormous jointure for so young a life as Lady Harley's.' 'And Miss Harley,' said the attorney, 'has no reason to be pleased with the small provision that is made for her.' They shook their heads at each other, and smiled, as much as to say, 'Somebody has played her cards well.'—Heaven forgive me, but I could not help hating them a little for the part they had in making his will: though, to be sure, they were no ways to blame, you know, Madam."

"No, certainly," said I, "but I long to hear of my uncle's recovery: methinks you leave him too long on this sick bed, Mr. Martin."

"Why, Madam," replied the honest man, "he grew better and better every day after this, and was soon able to leave his bed, and when Mr. Greville came he found him walking about his chamber. I had just time to tell Mr. Greville all I knew of the matter, and he was sorely grieved at it, and lamented his not getting my letter sooner. My lady complained much of what she had suffered during my master's illness. 'And yet you never looked better in your life, Madam,' said he, dryly; 'if grief is such a friend to your complexion, what will joy be? Why, your ladyship looks like May; but I am sorry,' said he, turning to my master, 'to see my good friend here look so much like January.'

"There was some joke in this, I found; for Mr. Greville looked archly at my master, who blushed, and my lady seemed half pleased and half angry. My lady's woman went tittering out of the room, and I followed, curious to know what she laughed at. 'Oh Mr. Martin,' said she, 'if you had read as many books as I have, you would know what that comical gentleman *luded* to.[1] Why, there is a tale in rhyme about January,[2] an old knight, who married a young lady called May, and she made a fool of him; and Mr. Greville as good as called my master and lady January and May—there was the jest, Mr. Martin.'"

I was afraid the old man might have sported with this idea too far, so I thought fit to look very grave; upon which he recollected himself and went on.

"Mr. Greville staid several days at the Hall, and during that time I believe he talked in a pretty home manner to my master; for I observed, that, whenever they had had some private conversation, my master would be in a musing mood a long time afterwards. My lady on these occasions always redoubled her fondness; and Mr. Greville used to cut his jokes without mercy. At length he went away; and now my lady, having my master all to herself, played all her old tricks over, but not with the same success as formerly; for my master, though he recovered his health, did not appear half so well pleased as usual; and used to be often talking of you, Madam, and wishing for your return: and at last he said he would write to you, and insist upon your coming home immediately. My lady was confounded, and brought a great many bad reasons, as my master told her, to put him off this design: and finding she could not prevail that way, she fairly told

---

1 I.e., alluded to.
2 Lady Harley's lady's maid refers to Chaucer's "The Merchant's Tale" in *The Canterbury Tales*.

him, that your temper was so bad, it was impossible to live with you; and hereupon she cried bitterly.

"My master was not moved, as she expected, but seemed a little angry, and defended you, Madam, very cordially, and in conclusion wrote to you, and gave me the letter before her face to get it properly conveyed to you, and glad was I of the office, you may be sure. After this his Honour was continually speaking of you, and always in your praise, so that my lady was sufficiently mortified."

I have often observed, my dear Euphemia, let a calumniator be ever so artful, all that which does not directly hurt the persons abused, turns to their advantage. This charge of bad tempers appeared to my uncle so ill-founded, that it led him to weigh thoroughly many other faults she had accused me of, and to compare my behaviour with the picture she used to draw of my disposition; and the result of this candid investigation was so favourable for me, that upon my return I had reason to believe I stood higher in his opinion than ever, as the sequel of my little history will shew you.

But here I will conclude for the present. A letter from you is this moment brought me; does it or does it not bring an answer favourable to my wishes?—I break the seal with eagerness.—Ah, my dear Euphemia, your first words destroy all my hopes. Adieu.

MARIA HARLEY.

Letter VI.
MRS. NEVILLE TO MISS HARLEY.

MY DEAR MARIA,

DESTINED to live under the control of another, I find obedience to be a very necessary virtue, and in my case it is an indispensable duty. I am a wife; I know to what that sacred tie obliges me: I am determined, by Heaven's assistance, to fulfil the duties of my station. My lot is cast perhaps for misery here; the future will be like the past: so my foreboding heart suggests. I have drawn a blank in the great lottery of life, but there is a state beyond this, in which my hopes aspire to a prize: to that all my wishes, all my endeavours tend. Philosophy may teach us to bear the past and future evils; but it is the Christian only that can endure the present with fortitude. Oh, my dear Maria, what could have supported me under my affliction for the death of my mother, but that active faith which made resignation to the will of Heaven at once my duty and my reward?—I perceive all the hardships of my situation, but I cannot avoid them without a crime; it is my duty to follow my husband; and what in other circumstances I should certainly have done from inclination, I do now from better motives—from a sense of those sacred obligations which the state I have entered into lays upon me; and which, whatever mortifications I may meet with in the discharge of them, are still indispensable.

But how shall I thank you, my dear friend, for your kind and generous offers? How shall I make you sensible of the gratitude that fills, that more than fills, that oppresses my heart, for this proof of your friendship? Words here are weak, and deeds, alas! are not in my power, for I am poor in every thing but in will. Do not, however, imagine my leaving this country such a misfortune; except you, I have nothing to regret, for the unfortunate have few friends: here every object reminds me of my former state, and makes the present more sensibly felt. Every place where I have seen my mother, renews my grief for her loss. Change of scene, new objects, and different cares, may perhaps weaken this sad idea, and restore me some degree of tranquility. Let this consideration reconcile you to my departure; and though separated, we will not be wholly absent—our minds shall meet in converse—a constant intercourse of letters shall bring us within view of each other—shall communicate our joys and sorrows, our hopes and fears, and all the little, as well as considerable events of our lives.

I will make it a rule to retire every day to my closet, for an hour at least, to talk to you; and every ship that sails for England shall bring a packet[1] from your Euphemia, which shall leave you ignorant of nothing that concerns her. Tell me, Maria, how you like this scheme, and whether you can resolve to be as punctual in the performance of your part of it, as I propose to be of mine: meantime I will continue to give you a relation of such of my affairs as you are yet ignorant of, but not in this letter, which I dispatch immediately, to bear my warmest acknowledgments for your most generous offers, to acquaint you with my reasons for declining them, and to share with you that comfort I derive from the plan I communicate. Present my best respects, and grateful thanks, to your good uncle, for his kind proposals; and do not let

---

1 Short for packet-boat, a boat that travelled between two ports at regular intervals, originally to carry mail, but later passengers (*OED*).

me wait long for the rest of your history. My curiosity is wound up to a very high pitch by what you have already related; and I am charmed with the honest zeal and affecting simplicity of your humble friend. I wait impatiently for the remainder of his narration:—My griefs are all suspended while I read your letters; and is not this a sufficient motive to make you hasten them to me? Farewel, my dear and most valuable friend!

EUPHEMIA NEVILLE.

Letter VII.
MISS HARLEY TO MRS. NEVILLE.

MY DEAR EUPHEMIA,

NOTHING can be offered in opposition to the arguments you use in support of your resolution to leave England with your husband. My heart murmurs, it is true; but my reason approves—Approves, did I say?—I admire, I love, I almost adore you, my excellent friend; —Blame not the warmth of my expressions. Must we not revere virtue, unless it be consecrated by antiquity? What were the merits of an Arrias, or a Portia,[1] to your's?—Love produced in them those great actions, for which they are so famous. Religion and duty are the nobler motives which influence your's. To die for the man one loves, is not an act of such heroism, as to chuse misery with the man one has no reason to love, because we consider it to be our duty to do so.

It is the fate of the best things to be either wholly neglected, or at most but little known. Such is this noble conduct of your's; for few will know it, and fewer still admire it. I, who am the greatest loser by it, am yet capable of admiring it; and this is a merit you must permit me to be vain of, since it costs me so dear.

But it is time to introduce Mr. Martin again. You tell me your griefs are suspended while you read my letters; and this is sufficient to make me devote the greatest part of my time to writing, were I at liberty to follow my inclinations. But I have no will of my own, my dear Euphemia; I am a slave to that of another. Reconcile this, if you can, with what I told you of the happy change in my fortune; or, if you cannot, wait patiently for my explana-

---

1 Roman women considered political heroines for their honorable contributions to the Republic.

tion, which will come in due time. But now hear Mr. Martin, who went on in this manner:

"The doctors, Madam, finding my master in so fine a way of recovery, told him that change of air would set him quite up again; and so he accepted Mr. Greville's invitation to pass a week or two at his seat.[1] Mr. Greville being a single man, my lady thought she should be troublesome to him; so she stayed behind at the Hall: but she wept over my master when he took leave of her, as if they were never to meet again. However, she quickly recovered her spirits, and passed her time very merrily with Lady Flareit, and some other gay ladies in the neighbourhood. There was nothing but airings and visiting, and dining and supping; and Colonel Flareit, Lady Flareit's kinsman, always made one; and he was so very obsequious to my lady, that her woman said, If my master should happen to die, it would certainly be a match; but my lady was wiser, I believe, than that comes to; for Colonel Flareit, you know, Madam, has no estate.

"Well, Madam, in the midst of all this jollity news came, that my master being out a hunting, had fallen from his horse and was taken up dead. The whole family was in tears and lamentation; but my lady was more composed, because she did not believe the report; 'for if it was true,' she said, 'she should have notice of it by a messenger sent express by Mr. Greville.' This seemed likely: but, for all that, I was impatient to set out for Greville Park, to know the truth: but it being very late in the evening when the news came, my lady ordered me not to stir till the next morning, when I might set out as soon as I pleased. And now she thought fit to make a show of sorrow, and shed a few tears before her woman and I. But for all that, we thought we could perceive that she would not be sorry to be a rich young widow.

"Well, Madam, I passed an anxious night, Heaven knows! and the moment it was light I mounted and rode away.

"Being still weak with my distemper, I could not make as much haste as my impatience required; and at the very second stage I saw Mr. Greville's post-chaise,[2] and himself in it, drive into the inn yard. I was now seized with such a fit of trembling, that I could neither sit my horse nor alight; so one of the hostlers helped me, and I followed Mr. Greville to a room where he was sitting.—'Oh, Sir! my master!' was all I could

---

1 I.e., estate.

2 I.e., in Britain, a closed, four-wheeled horse-drawn carriage which carried passengers and mail.

bring out. His very looks, however, relieved me instantly, as well as his words.

"'What does the simpleton mean,' said he, 'by trembling and looking so pale? What, you have heard of the accident then?—Well, your master has got off for only a few slight bruises.'—'Heaven be praised,' said I, 'for this good news! but we heard that he had broke his neck, and all us at the Hall are in the deepest affliction.' 'How!' said Mr. Greville, 'Does your lady believe Sir John is dead?' 'Not absolutely, Sir,' replied I; 'she said, if it was true, a messenger would be sent express to inform her, and no one had come yet.'—'A wise woman,' said Mr. Greville; 'she was in the right not to be lavish with tears upon an uncertainty: but, Martin,' pursued he, after thinking a little, 'I have a mind to know how she will take his death, when she believes it to be certain. Sir John, poor man, believing his confinement is likely to be long, though that is by no means the case, was desirous of his lady's company; so I could do no less than offer my service to conduct her to him, and that was the sole motive of my journey: but now I am resolved to have a little diversion from it. Can you keep a secret, Martin?'—'Ah, I do not doubt it,' said Mr. Greville, shaking his head: 'Well, then, my design is, to tell your lady that the report of Sir John's death was but too true.'—'Oh, Sir,' cried I, 'you know how fond my lady is of her husband; this trial will be very hard upon her.'—'You are a rogue,' said he smiling, 'I see that; but you will be secret.'—'But Sir,' said I, 'your servants will betray the matter.'—'Never fear that,' said he; 'I will give them their instructions; so send them up to me.' I did so; and after Mr. Greville had tutored them properly, we all set out for the Hall.

"Mr. Greville, in consideration of my late illness, had the goodness to take me into the chaise with him; and all the way he diverted himself with the scheme he had formed, and with telling me what to say and how to behave.

"Well, Madam, we had scarce entered the avenue, when, Mr. Greville's carriage and servants being perceived by one of our men, the whole family was in motion, and came crowding round us. 'Is the sad news true?' cried several voices at once. Mr. Greville's servants shook their heads in a melancholy way. 'Alas! then it is too true,' they all repeated, and ran back in great disorder into the house, which they filled with their lamentations. Mr. Greville, alighting, said in a solemn tone, 'If Lady Harley is at leisure, let her be informed I am come.' He followed the butler, who with eyes full of tears, shewed him into my master's library, and withdrew to acquaint my lady.

"It was with difficulty I could break from the servants, who hung upon me, lamenting and enquiring—but I was curious to see how my lady would receive Mr. Greville; so I hastened after him.

"He was seated, and had taken a book; 'for,' said he to me, 'I cannot expect to have an audience so soon: the lady will take time to settle the face she is to wear upon this trying occasion:' and to be sure, Madam, my lady was a full hour before she sent to desire Mr. Greville would be pleased to come to her dressing-room.

"Mr. Greville obeyed immediately, but with a slow step, and solemn air. I attended him; but I believe I did not act my part so well as his Honour; for my fellow-servants have since told me, that they thought my grief was not very violent. We found my lady half-lying on a settee, with a handkerchief at her eyes, so that she did not perceive our entrance. Her woman was standing close by her with a smelling bottle[1] which she offered to her, and at the same time told her, Mr. Greville was there. My lady then, drawing aside her handkerchief, just looked up, and crying, 'Ah, Mr. Greville!' clapped it close to her eyes again, and continued silent.

"'I cannot blame you, Madam; I cannot blame you,' said Mr. Greville; 'your grief is great, and so is your cause for grief:—you have lost a good husband, but that is not all;—you have lost—' At that word my lady started, let fall her handkerchief, and fixed her eyes upon Mr. Greville, impatiently expecting him to proceed; for here the poor gentleman was seized with a violent cough, which held him for two or three minutes.

"All that time I observed my lady heedfully: her colour went and came—she seemed hardly able to draw her breath, still keeping her looks fixed upon Mr. Greville, who, recovering, went on:— 'Yes Madam, as I was saying, you have lost, beside a good husband'—My lady seemed now ready to die with impatience, for Mr. Greville paused, as if fearful of his cough returning; then slowly added, 'You have lost a friend, a protector, an amiable companion;—Sir John was all this to you, Madam; and how dear you were to him, you will (if you do not know it already) soon know.'

"My lady was again at leisure for her tears: she resumed her handkerchief, and Mr. Greville his fine speeches, which lasted till

---

1 Bottle of "smelling salts"—ammonium-carbonate mixed with perfume— used to restore someone to consciousness after a bout of faintness. Also known as "hartshorn," as it was made from deer antlers.

I was desired to let my lady know that dinner was served. Mr. Greville then offered his hand to lead her down stairs, but she declined it, saying, she must intreat him to dispense with her attending him at table, since her melancholy situation would plead her excuse. Mr. Greville allowed it; and only beseeching her to moderate her sorrow, if possible, bowed, and quitted the room.

"I then advanced, and asked if her Ladyship had any commands for me? She answered haughtily, 'No!' and I followed Mr. Greville, who, seeing me enter the dining parlour, said to the other servants, 'You need not wait, my lads, my old friend here will be sufficient to attend me:' accordingly they left the room.

"Mr. Greville made a sign to me to fasten the door, which I did: 'And now,' said he, 'let me have my laugh out, for I am almost strangled.'

"What diverted Mr. Greville most, Madam, was, that he had thrown my lady quite off her guard when he made her apprehend a greater loss than that of her husband; for to be sure, Madam, my lady was quite in earnest then, and looked frighted out of her wits; for she supposed, as Mr. Greville intended she should, that my master had made some alteration in his will before the accident happened."

But here I must drop Mr. Martin and his narration for the present, for I have only time to make up my letter, which you must acknowledge is of a tolerable length; therefore adieu, my dear Euphemia. Alas, the moment is approaching when I must bid you adieu for a long, an indefinite time. This is a sad thought; but since I have well considered your admirable reasons for a resolution so contrary to my hopes and wishes, I perceive a sort of calm acquiescence steal upon my mind, which gathers strength every moment. Yet you must not on this account imagine I love you less; I endeavour to imitate your fortitude, and to make myself worthy of your esteem.

MARIA HARLEY.

Why have I not a letter from you? Must I charge you with breach of promise in not sending me the remainder of your affecting story?

Letter VIII.
MRS. NEVILLE TO MISS HARLEY.

NO, my dear Maria, I do not think you love me less than you did, but that you love me more wisely. But were it possible for me to suspect the sincerity of your affection, it would be from the extravagant eulogium you bestow on me, for what in my opinion is but an ordinary effect of duty and obedience.

Surely then you mean to excite me to virtue by a new subtilty, and the praises you give me are but disguised exhortations. Take notice, this is the construction I shall put down upon all such language from you; and if you would not be thought rather to dictate than to commend, avoid it for the future.

But to shew you that I am as little disposed to submit to unjust censure as to undeserved praise, I will not receive patiently your charge of being a promise breaker. Every thing that is promised and not done, is not a violation of faith or breaking of promise, since accident has so much to do in the ordering of small events. The large packet that will soon follow this letter, will convince you that I have been employed in obeying your commands; and I have given you my History, as you call it, down to the present moment, without interruption, that you may no longer be ignorant of the causes and motives of the most important transaction of my life, and from which that life must hereafter take all its colour.

I have been very much entertained with your friend Martin's relation, and like his manner extremely well, which your memory has faithfully preserved; but I am not quite pleased with the method Mr. Greville hit upon to release his doubts of Lady Harley's sincerity. He laid himself under the necessity of telling a direct falsehood, and of supporting that falsehood by many little artifices, not easily practiced by an ingenuous mind. But your men of wit and ridicule have a very relaxed moral on certain occasions. A man of plain good sense starts at these humorous violations of truth, and thinks his reputation would be ruined for ever by such bold flights.

But I ought to remember that it is my dear Maria's friend whose conduct I am censuring, and that it was for her service chiefly he devised this stratagem: therefore, though I cannot absolve, yet I am willing to pardon; for I confess my integrity is scarcely proof against so high a bribe. My dear friend, adieu!

EUPHEMIA NEVILLE.

Letter IX.
MISS HARLEY TO MRS. NEVILLE.

MY DEAR EUPHEMIA,

AND do you really resolve to put such a strange construction upon the just tribute paid by a friend to your merit? Must my praises be considered as disguised exhortations? Let me tell you, you avoid presumption by a contrary extreme, since envy itself would give you that which your own modesty takes away.

But, not to offend you further by dwelling on this theme, you shall now have the remainder of Mr. Martin's relation: his simplicity pleases you; and I have been careful to make no alteration in his style and manner: thus when he went on:—

"Mr. Greville, as soon as he had dined, sent to beg my lady would favour him with a short interview before his departure, which he said the occasion required should be immediately. Accordingly he was admitted to see her. He told her that he intended to get as far on his way home that night as he possibly could, and would call upon Mr. Mainwaring, and the executor, to settle all matters relating to the funeral. He desired to know if her Ladyship had any particular commands to favour him with: to which she answered, 'Pray, Mr. Greville, do not consult me upon these sad affairs; I leave all to your discretion.'

"'But, Madam,' said Mr. Greville, 'I earnestly recommend it to you to arm yourself with fortitude; the body must be brought here to-morrow or next day at farthest.'

"'As you please,' said my lady, 'but I entreat you spare me any further discourse upon this melancholy subject.'

"All this, Madam, Mr. Greville told me was said with the utmost composure of look and accent; so, to be short, Madam, he took his leave; and, as my ague[1] now returned with great violence, this served for a good reason for my not going with him, so I went up to my chamber; but, as I afterwards found, my lady did not know I was in the house, for she concluded I was gone with Mr. Greville.

"That very evening Lady Flareit came to condole my lady, and supper was served up in her dressing-room; and nobody was allowed to wait but her woman, in whom my lady had great confidence, which she did not deserve, for she was very deceitful.

---

1 Fever (*OED*).

Now it happened that my name was mentioned upon some occasion or other, upon which Mrs. Wilson said I was very ill.

"My lady was much surprised to hear I was in the house, and declared I should not stay another moment in it. 'He is a busy meddling fellow,' said she; 'he gained his master's good-will by his fawning and his lies. Poor Sir John had no very strong head, and even this paltry fellow could make a dupe of him. Go, Wilson, and tell him to leave the Hall immediately.' Mrs. Wilson told her that I was ill and gone to bed.

"'No matter,' said my lady; 'he may go to the next inn; he is rich enough to procure accommodation any where—I am determined he shall not stay in the house—I am mistress here, and will be obeyed.'

"'Lord Madam!' said Mrs. Wilson, as she told me afterwards, 'does your ladyship consider what a clamour this will make: every one knows my late good master had a great regard for Mr. Martin; he has served him faithfully many years, you know Madam, and faithful servants ought not to be used so.'

"'Your late *good* master,' said my lady, 'has well rewarded him for his services, such as they were. But methinks you are very bold to stand arguing with me thus; go and deliver my orders—tell him to be gone: and here,' said she, kicking a little French dog that my master was very fond of—'bid him take his animal with him. This was a favorite too, and was allowed to snarl, and bark, and spoil the carpets, and no one, not even myself, durst find fault with him.'

"Mrs. Wilson took up the dog, and came to my room, and told me all that had passed. I was thunderstruck in a manner; and making no answer, she asked me what she should say to my lady?

"'Give my duty to her ladyship,' said I, 'and tell her that I will obey her commands to-morrow morning as soon as it is day, but for this night I hope she will excuse me; and as for the dog, I will take care of it for my dear master's sake; and so good night, Mrs. Wilson.' She smiled, and said I acted quite right; so she went away, and I bolted the door after her, and went to bed.

"I know not how my lady took this answer, for early the next morning I got up, and finding myself much better, I went to the stable, made the groom saddle my horse, and I set out for Mr. Greville's seat.

"I arrived there the next day about noon, and had the satisfaction to hear that my master was quite well; for indeed his hurt had been very inconsiderable. I desired Mr. Greville's valet to tell his master that I was come, and begged to speak to him in private before I waited on my master.

"Mr. Greville ordered me to come to him in his study, and expressed much surprise at seeing me. I told him all that had passed, and how my lady had turned me out of doors, and the little dog with me.

"Mr. Greville rubbed his hands, and cried out joyfully, 'So, this goes well; she has shewn the cloven foot:[1] what will my old friend say to this?'

"'Does my master know, Sir,' said I, 'of the trick you have put upon my lady?'

"'Oh, yes,' said he, 'and laughs at the jest: but I fancy the story you have to tell will put some serious thoughts into his head. Come, I will bring you to him.'

"I followed Mr. Greville into my master's chamber, who was walking about, and looked so well that my joy quite overpowered me, and I burst into tears.

"'Well, Martin,' said my master, 'I believe you are glad to find me alive: but what brings you here? I heard you was not well: and why have you brought my poor Fidelle with you?' added he, caressing the dog, who had got out of my arms, and was jumping about him.

"I cast down my eyes and was silent, not knowing how to tell the matter. My master then perceived that something extraordinary had happened, and said hastily, 'Why don't you answer me, Martin?'

"'I believe I must answer for him,' said Mr. Greville, 'for the poor man is half ashamed of the matter; but the truth is, my lady, firmly believing that she is now whole and sole sovereign, has, in the plenitude of her power, taken upon her to turn your faithful servant, and your favourite dog, out of doors.'

"'How is this?' said my master, eagerly: then suddenly stopping, he mused a little, and added, with a smile, 'she has played you trick for trick; but considering that Martin was ill, this was carrying the jest too far. But, pray what cause did she assign for this treatment?'

"'My lady accuses me of being a spy, a busy body, and a mischief-maker, Sir,' said I, 'and as for the dog, her ladyship makes heavy complaints of him, for such faults as dogs are often guilty of, to be sure; but I never thought Fidelle was one of those.'

"My master now laughed heartily, at which I thought Mr.

---

1   Associated with the devil, a cloven foot is a divided hoof, an external marking of satanic presence.

Greville looked a little silly. 'I see you take this matter right,' said he to my master, in a peevish tone.

"'Why yes,' said my master, 'I believe I do: but come, I am resolved to act a part in this farce: I find myself strong enough to undertake a longer journey than that to my own house; so, if you please, we will set out to-morrow; and I will surprise Lady Harley with the ghost of her husband.'

"'With all my heart,' said Mr. Greville, 'but if your sudden appearance should frighten her into fits, I am guiltless of the consequences; for I do assure you, she thinks you are actually dead.'

"'Indeed, I am persuaded she has been laughing at you all this time,' said my master.

"'Well,' replied Mr. Greville, 'I have no more to say; but I hope you will have your jest too.'

"'That is what I intend,' said my master. He then ordered me to go and take care of myself; and I withdrew, a little apprehensive of his displeasure, because he did not take this matter as Mr. Greville expected.

"However, I had an opportunity of speaking to Mr. Greville that evening, and he assured me, my master was not angry with any of us; that was his phrase. 'Though some of us,' says he, 'certainly deserve that he should be so. He talks of what has past very pleasantly; but I think I can perceive he has some serious thoughts about it, for he is often pensive and silent.'

"Well, Madam, my master set out next day at noon, with Mr. Greville, for the Hall. He would have had me stay behind a day or two to recover myself; but I told him, I found myself well enough to attend him: and truly I would not upon any account have missed the scene I expected to see.

"We lay that night at a friend of Mr. Greville's, who had heard the report of my master's death, and was rejoiced to find it without foundation. We left this gentleman's house so late in the day, that it was night before we reached the Hall. No one took any notice of my master, who was wrapt up in his great coat and his hat slouched; he followed Mr. Greville up stairs, who had asked for my lady, and was told she was in her own apartment.

"A servant announced Mr. Greville to my lady's woman who was in waiting; and Mr. Greville, without ceremony, followed her into my lady's dressing room, my master being close at his heels; and to be sure, Madam, there was my lady, not mourning like a sorrowful widow, but sitting at supper with Lady Flareit and the Colonel, and they all seemed very cheerful.

"'Your servant, your servant, good people,' said my master,

gaily taking off his hat, 'will you permit a couple of hungry travellers to partake with you?'

"My lady, who had seemed lost in astonishment and terror at the sound of his voice, no sooner saw his face, than she screamed aloud and fell into a fainting fit. Lady Flareit cried out, 'A ghost!,' hid her eyes with her apron, and trembled like an aspen leaf; and the Colonel starting up, clapped his hand 'instinctively,' aye, that was Mr. Greville's word, upon his sword; and opening his eyes as wide as he could, stood staring at my master from a corner of the room, who was very busy in endeavouring to recover my lady, which at last, with the assistance of her woman, who sprinkled her face plentifully with water, he effected.

"But as soon as she opened her eyes, and saw my master, she seemed ready to relapse; upon which Lady Flareit, who was now by the assistance of Mr. Greville, quite recovered from her fright, approached, and taking her hand, said, 'Come, Lady Harley, let me lead you to your chamber; Sir John, this was a cruel jest.'—'It was all Greville's doings,' said my master; 'therefore, pray, my dear,' said he to my lady, who went tottering out of the room, leaning upon Lady Flareit's arms, 'do not be too much discomposed, but return again soon, if you would not spoil my supper.'

"Colonel Flareit then came forward, looking a little foolish, I thought, as if he did not know how to take my master's gaiety. 'Come, Colonel,' said my master, 'come and finish your supper, otherwise I shall think you are still afraid.'

"'Afraid, Sir!' said the Colonel. 'Aye, afraid,' said my master; 'why Colonel, a soldier may be afraid of a ghost, without any disparagement to his courage: but after all,' continued my master, laughing, 'you have all acted your parts very well; and my friend Greville need not boast much of the success of his trick; for I am confident there is not one of you that was imposed upon for a single moment, by the story he invented of my death; therefore the laugh, I think, is fairly turned upon him.'

"The Colonel said not a word; and Mr. Greville seemed utterly at a loss how to understand my master, so he continued to eat in silence.

"At length Lady Flareit came in, looking very grave; and was going to speak, but my master prevented her; crying out, 'So, Lady Harley is not with you, I see; she would fain carry on the jest a little further, and persuade me that she really thought I was dead; but I know better; she is not so good an actress as she thinks; and yet after all, she imposed upon Greville, I believe.'

"Lady Flareit now cleared up all on a sudden. 'Ah,' said she to my master, 'you have found us out; we intended to mortify you by our pretended indifference; but, however, your sudden appearance surprised Lady Harly; you know she has very weak nerves; she is really not well, and is gone to bed.'—'I am sorry for that,' said my master, 'I hoped she would have joined the laugh against this plotter here,' clapping Mr. Greville on the back.

"Lady Flareit now returned to my lady; telling the Colonel, that she would go home in a quarter of an hour. Mrs. Wilson informed me that this time was spent in close conversation between the two ladies, which she could not hear distinctly; but Lady Flareit seemed endeavouring to persuade my lady to something. She was sent to acquaint the Colonel, that her ladyship was ready; so he took leave of my master and Mr. Greville, and they went away together.

"Early the next morning, I saw my master and Mr. Greville walking together upon the lawn, seemingly in deep discourse. When they came in to breakfast, my lady sent her woman with an apology for her not being able to attend them, having had a very indifferent night. My master expressed great concern for her illness; and desired her woman to let her know when she was up, that he might go and see her: then hastily turning to me, he said, 'Get ready immediately to go for Worden and Grasp; I have some business for them to do, which I think ought not to be delayed, lest I should die in good earnest.' Mrs. Wilson heard these words, and hurried away to tell her lady; and I was eager to execute my commission.

"I brought them both with me to the Hall. My master was in my lady's chamber when they arrived; and as soon as he had notice of it, he joined them in his study. Mr. Greville was there; and they continued a long time together.

"My master detained the two lawyers to dinner; at which my lady, being still indisposed, did not appear. The next morning, Mr. Greville set out for his own seat: he shook my hand, as I attended him to his carriage, saying, in a low voice, 'All goes right, honest Martin.' I understood his Honour, and was heartily glad of it.

"When Mr. Greville was gone, my lady appeared at table as usual; but so sullen, so silent, that my master could hardly get a word out of her, though he was very complaisant and civil to her. Mrs. Wilson told me, that she could hear Lady Flareit, who seldom missed a day coming to see her, often chide her for her behaviour: telling her, she was wrong, quite wrong: but my lady could not be persuaded to alter it; continuing cold, reserved, and even peevish. But my master seemed to take no notice of this strange alteration in her manner towards him: he was often talking of you, Madam, and pleasing himself with the expectation of seeing you soon. He ordered your apartment to be prepared for you, and a set of wrought dressing-plate for your toilet[1] came from London, which my lady fearcely condescended to look at; saying coldly, when my master asked her opinion, that it was mighty pretty.

"A great alteration now appeared in my lady's looks; and it was apparent that her secret discontents had hurt her health. My master proposed to her change of air, and a journey to Paris; she said she would rather go to some of the watering places.[2] But she grew visibly worse, and at length was seized with a violent fever. The physicians had very little hopes from the first; and all their arguments and intreaties could not prevail upon her to be bled: so she died, as one may say, by her own fault.

"My master was very kind to her during her illness; but she was seldom sensible, and scarce ever spoke. The day she died, he continued shut up in his closet for several hours; and the next morning set out for Mr. Greville's seat. She was buried in the family vault with great solemnity; but, I am sorry to say, not much lamented; for her ladyship was not very charitable to the poor; and she always behaved to the tenants and small gentry in the neighbourhood with great haughtiness."

Here Mr. Martin ended his narration, which took up two or three of my evenings in listening to; and I have given it to you almost in his very words. What more I have to tell you on this subject must be deferred till my next. But now adieu! my ever dear Euphemia.

MARIA HARLEY.

Letter X.
MRS. NEVILLE TO MISS HARLEY.

MY DEAR MARIA,

I SHALL never for the future rank your uncle with men of common understanding; his whole conduct with regard to Lady

---

1 Dressing-plate for your toilet: Articles for the dressing table.
2 Watering places: Resorts.

Harley, on the most trying occasion imaginable, displays a fund of good sense and philosophy, rarely to be met with in persons, who, like him, have spent so great a part of their lives in the pursuit of pleasure.

How nicely has he steered between two extremes, equally fatal to his reputation. Had he appeared insensible of her levities, and indifferent to the ungrateful returns she made to his affection, he would have passed for a dupe: had he avowed his resentment, he would have authorized suspicions that would have ruined her character, and fixed ridicule upon his own; he escaped both these rocks by the most masterly management imaginable, and neither malice nor ridicule can find a shaft to hit him.

I am not surprised at the despair which Lady Harley seems to have fallen into. The most common view persons have, when they commit imprudent actions, is the probability of always finding out some resource or other: but Lady Harley, in this case, could have no such hope; she had fixed her husband's opinion of her irrevocably, and the very methods he used to render her less contemptible in the eyes of the world, served only to lessen her more in her own. But peace be to her ashes, and oblivion to her memory!

I am particularly impatient for your next letter, in hopes that it will clear up an ambiguous expression in one of your former ones, that has puzzled me greatly; you say, you have no will of your own, and that you are a slave to that of another; pray make me understand this. Adieu! my dear Maria.

Letter XI.
MISS HARLEY TO MRS. NEVILLE.

MY DEAR EUPHEMIA,

I WISH I could with any propriety have shewn my uncle some part of your last letter; even the wise might be pardoned for indulging a little vanity at receiving praises from judgment and sincerity like yours; but you will easily conceive this would not have been proper, at least at this time, after what I am going to tell you.

Martin having informed him that he had obeyed his commands, and given me a very particular (and you must own, my friend; that it *was* a very particular) account of all that had happened during my absence, my uncle spoke to me in this manner:

"You have heard from Martin some very interesting circumstances relating to your aunt and me; you have candour and good sense; I doubt not but you will judge rightly of my conduct. I only intreat you never to mention Lady Harley to me in private, and in public be as reserved on that subject as I am. Mr. Greville," he added, "is certainly your friend; you owe him some acknowledgments;" and these, my dear, I did not fail to pay him the very first opportunity, with an effusion of heart which convinced him of my gratitude.

I was obliged to listen to some humorous sallies on my aunt's account, and even to smile at them, for indeed it would have been very difficult to refrain; however, he always spared my uncle, which, considering his fondness for raillery, was an instance of self-denial that had some merit in it.

My aunt's woman was still in the house; she expected to have made her court to me by throwing out some reflections upon her late lady, and by making an ample discovery of all she knew; but I silenced her by a severe look, and an absolute command never to speak to me on the subject.

My uncle left it to me to do as I pleased with regard to her; I had reason to think her very deceitful, and incapable of being true to anyone; I resolved to discharge her immediately; so I gave her all her late lady's clothes and linen, with what money she had in her pockets when she died, and dismissed her, to the great joy of the servants, who had all of them, at one time or other, experienced her treachery.

You will call Mr. Greville a bold man, when I tell you he would read your last letter, notwithstanding all I could do to hinder him; he came in when I was writing, and saw it lying on my table, and actually read it through; and this is what he said when he returned it to me: "No modesty is able to resist the praises that come from your amiable friend; and although I have hitherto thought vanity a ridiculous quality, yet I protest I should take a pleasure in being corrupted by her."

He prest me much to shew my uncle what you said of him; but I pleaded his absolute command not to mention Lady Harley to him; and he agreed that he ought to be obeyed.

This unlooked for intrusion of Mr. Greville's will teach me caution; I will always fasten my door for the future when I sit down to write to you. But I will now explain to you what I meant when I told you my uncle was kinder to me than ever, and yet I had no will of my own, but was a slave to that of another.

It is that kindness of his that has enslaved my will, my dear

Euphemia, that has loaded me with a debt of gratitude which I can never be able to pay, and has fixed shackles upon my mind which it is impossible for me ever to unloose. Mark the method he took to produce this voluntary subjection.

Some little time after my return from France, Mr. Greville being upon a visit at the Hall, my uncle sent for me into his study, where he was sitting with his friend; they had papers lying upon the table before them, one of which, upon my entrance, my uncle took, and, presenting it to Mr. Greville, "Here, Sir," said he, "is a deed of gift to my niece of the greatest part of my personal estate, amounting to about twenty thousand pounds, which, as her guardian and trustee, I lodge in your hands. It is all placed on government securities, for the interest of which you are to be accountable to her only from the present moment, and to pay into her hands for her sole use and benefit.

"Be not surprised," pursued he, "child," taking my hand, and leading me, all amazed and speechless, to a chair next his own, "I believe you have a sincere affection for me, and I am willing to enjoy the pleasure this thought gives me, pure and unmixed with the least shadow of a doubt. What I intended to bequeath you at my death I give you now, irrevocably, that you may be free and absolute mistress of yourself, and that having nothing more to hope, or any thing to fear, from me, your actions may be as unconstrained as your thoughts, and your real affection for me liable to no misconstructions."

It was easy to perceive, my dear Euphemia, what an impression Lady Harley's duplicity and artifice had made upon his mind, and how much he apprehended being thought the dupe of female subtilty a second time. His favourable opinion of me was also evident; and this was the point to which, as I conceived, delicacy obliged me only to answer.

My heart was full, but I endeavoured to suppress my emotions; and taking his hand, which I respectfully kissed, while an involuntary tear at the same time dropped upon it, "I am obliged to you, Sir," said I, "not so much for making me rich, or for making me rich before my time, but for putting it in my power to shew you"—"I understand you, my dear niece," said he, hastily interrupting me,—"we understand one another, I believe, and we shall both be the happier for it. Would to heaven," added he, with some emotion, "that the estate of my family, which falls to a collateral branch which I have no reason to love, could have been your's likewise."—"Come, no more of this," said Mr. Greville, "my fair ward here will have enough of that pelf,[1] which, as Pope says,

> 'Buys the sex a tyrant in itself.'"[2]

Mr. Greville very judiciously endeavoured to give the conversation a gayer turn, to relieve my uncle and me from the very awkward situation we found ourselves in, while he was afraid of hearing acknowledgments, which my full heart left me not the power of expressing. And thus, my friend, has the independence my uncle bestowed on me been the beginning of my slavery, for I cannot, I ought not, to have any will but that of a benefactor who has acted with such uncommon generosity.

The power to follow my inclinations is secured to me, but my will is fettered by the obligations I lie under. Thus, for instance, my heart impels me to fly to you, to sooth, to comfort, to assist you in your situation; and I should most certainly have asked his permission for a short absence, if he had not, by making me my own mistress, deprived himself, as he thinks, of the power of refusing; and my company being now more necessary to him than ever, I cannot give the least hint that I have a wish that way, for fear of laying him under the necessity of doing what may be disagreeable to him. But perhaps his own good sense may suggest to him to offer what I cannot ask, and then you may depend upon seeing me in London.

I have this moment received the long-expected packet; but I must rein in my impatience, and not open it till I retire for the night; for this whole day I shall be employed in reading to my uncle, who is a little indisposed, and cannot take his usual ride. My dear Euphemia, adieu.

Letter XII.
MRS. NEVILLE TO MISS HARLEY.

BEFORE I continue my little narrative, I must entreat you, my dear Maria, not to suffer these papers to be seen by any person

---

1 Pelf: Money.
2 Alexander Pope (1688-1744), *Moral Essays*, Epistle II, "To a Lady": "the pelf/ That buys your sex a tyrant o'er itself," i.e., the fortune that attracts a husband.

but yourself; they will contain a faithful account of my affairs, and give you a just picture of my situation: and consequently I shall be obliged to touch upon the faults of one who, from the near relation in which he stands to me, has claims upon my tenderness and respect, which even those faults cannot dispense with me from allowing him. Mine, I know, your friendship would spare and conceal; and he, being a part of myself, for him I expect the same indulgence.

I have already repeated what Mrs. Benson told me concerning my father's imprudent management of his affairs, the consequence of which has involved his family in ruin. My mother, always gentle and kind, endeavoured to palliate those errors by which she was so great a sufferer.

There is nothing, said she, more commendable than generosity, but nothing ought less to be stretched too far. Mr. Lumley served his friends with too little attention to his own ability, which, together with other imprudences, produced that bitter remorse which shortened his days.

Her tears flowed fast at these words; I suppressed my own emotions that I might comfort her, and endeavoured to detach her thoughts from the melancholy idea, by giving her a detail of the inequality of Mrs. Highmore's behaviour to me during the first and the last days of my residence with her, which the wreck of our fortunes now enabled me to account for.

My mother smiled at my story; and taking two letters out of her pocketbook, put them into my hand. "Here are two letters from Mrs. Highmore," said she, "of different dates: the first is to Mrs. Lumley in affluence; the second to the same Mrs. Lumley in distress; read them." I did so, and here is what they contained.

TO MRS. LUMLEY.

"DEAR MADAM,

"My whole family have been transported with joy ever since I communicated to them your resolution to give us the inestimable blessing of Miss Lumley's company during your stay at Bath. My daughters will think themselves honoured by her accepting their services, and I shall be proud to stand in the place of a mother to such excellence, during the absence of you, her incomparable mother! Most devoutly do I pray for the perfect recovery of good

Mr. Lumley, and for all imaginable blessings to your worthy self, being, with great respect,

Dear Madam,
Your obliged, most humble,
And most obedient servant,
A. HIGHMORE.

P.S. The dear young lady is in perfect health."

TO MRS. LUMLEY.

"I am sincerely sorry, my very good friend, for your late loss, which is attended with such dreadful consequences to your affairs. Your daughter takes on greatly for her father's death, but we keep her in ignorance of the rest of her misfortunes—against my judgment, indeed; for it moves my pity to see the poor thing so unsuspicious of the sad reverse of her fortune.

"I wish I could offer you any consolation in this great calamity; but, as you are a good Christian, and a woman of sense, you will doubtless reflect that all are not born to be rich, and that it behoves us to be resigned and humble under difficult situations. Pray let me know when you design to leave Bath, and whether I can be of any use to you here on this occasion, for I shall always be glad to shew myself your very sincere friend,

And humble servant,
A. HIGHMORE.

"The poor child is well as can be expected, considering her affliction."

My mother answered this extraordinary epistle no otherwise than by cancelling a note for sixty pounds, which Mrs. Highmore had borrowed of her about a year before, and enclosing it in a cover, which contained only these words: "Mrs. Lumley's compliments, and desires Mrs. Highmore will accept the enclosed as payment for her daughter's and her governess's board for five weeks."

This billet was sent by a porter to Mrs. Highmore's house in town, whither we had heard she was come, with orders not to stay for an answer. She came herself a few days afterwards to visit my mother, who pleaded indisposition, and refused to see her.

Mrs. Highmore's behaviour was imitated by many other persons of our acquaintance, whose cool kindness, and constrained civility, marked too well the change of our fortunes.

Some of our relations were of high rank; and these kept us at a distance by their very ceremonious behaviour. Some were only rich, and to them poverty appeared rather a crime than a misfortune; so that in strict morality they were obliged to treat us with great coldness and reserve.

My mother appeared calm and unruffled by this general depravity. "Persons of quicker sensibility than myself," said she, "would, on this occasion, complain of the world; but I shall content myself with forgetting it."

Having settled all her affairs in London, we retired to a small house, which my mother had taken in a neighbouring town, and furnished with a simplicity suitable to her fortune, and a neatness that gave elegance to that simplicity.

Mrs. Benson refused the part of governess to a young lady of high distinction, in order to accompany us in this retreat. "I have income," said she, "which, though small, is sufficient to prevent my being an incumbrance to you. I acquired part of it in your service; and I will never quit you while my attendance can be either useful or agreeable to you."

You will easily imagine, my dear Maria, how acceptable such an instance of faithful attachment must be to my mother, at a time when she seemed forsaken by all the world. She embraced, and thanked her with tears of tenderness and joy; yet represented to her, that her interest required she should accept the advantageous proposal that was made to her.

"Honour, gratitude, and friendship," replied she, "impel me to attach myself to you, and my beloved pupil; in doing so I find my interest."

We were soon settled in our new habitation: one maid-servant composed our whole equipage. We worked, we read, we dressed our little garden—all was peace, friendship, and mutual complacency.

"I see," said I one day to my mother, "that one may cease to be rich without being unhappy."—"A life led in tranquility, and with judgment," replied my mother, "which is the work of reason, is preferable to one half of those sudden and great successes which the world admires, and which are scarce ever the rewards of merit, but the mere vagaries of fortune."

The privacy my mother so earnestly desired was not like to be interrupted in a neighbourhood chiefly composed of families grown wealthy by the successful arts of trade, and had chosen this retreat for their summer residence, who had no idea of any merit but riches, and allowed no claims to respect, but what were derived from the ostentatious display of them. The Lumley name sounded less respectable in their ears than that of Jackson or Wilson, because Jackson or Wilson kept coaches, and could afford to fare sumptuously every day.

"Nothing," says the immortal Bacon, "can make that great which nature meant to be little."[1] Our situation afforded us many opportunities of observing how fortune and nature were at strife, when the lavish gifts bestowed by the one, could not efface the despicable stamp impressed by the other. The Indian plunderer, raised from the condition of a link-boy[2] to princely affluence, in the midst of this blaze of grandeur, looked like a robber going in mock state to execution; and the forestalling trader enjoyed his clumsy magnificence with the same aspect as when he had over-reached a less cunning dealer in a bargain.

Such were the observations of Mrs. Benson, when these sons and daughters of sudden opulence rolled in unwieldy state by our humble habitation.

My mother used sometimes to chide her for the severity of her sarcasms; but her spleen was often roused by the inconveniences which our contiguity to these great personages exposed us to: for money, which, as she said, cost them nothing to acquire, but what they valued as nothing, consequently, was expended so lavishly, as raised the prices of necessaries; and this grievance was severely felt by their less opulent neighbours.

My mother, who chiefly subsisted upon milk, could hardly procure any that was genuine, although the cows were milked under her window, because the brokers, the soap-boilers, and the rope-makers ladies'[3] numerous servants could not drink their tea without cream; and therefore vast quantities of milk were

---

1   Bacon qt.: "Of Nature in Men" in *Essays* by Francis Bacon, Baron Verulam and Viscount St. Alban (1561-1625), English essayist.
2   Link-boy: A boy paid to carry a lantern for people in the street (*OED*). East-India Co.: Incorporated in 1600, this company was a group of London merchants who carried on lucrative trade in the East Indies (*OED*).
3   The wives of the newly rich pawnbrokers, soap-markers, and rope-makers, having moved financially if not in manners and polish into the middle class, can afford to pay for cream in their servants' tea.

bespoke every day, to furnish this indispensable article to their afternoon regale.

Such inconveniences as these my mother bore without murmuring; but she was not so easy under the difficulty she found of procuring a seat in the church, "which," said Mrs. Benson, "are almost all taken up with the worshippers of Mammon,[1] to whom, as they have erected an altar in their own houses, they might as well perform their devotions at home, and let Christians have access to the house of God."

My mother, however, sometimes, by the force of a bribe, got admission into a pew;[2] and one Sunday, making use of the same powerful oratory, she was let into a pew where there was only one lady, of a diminutive figure indeed, but a soul so vast, as seemed to oe'r-inform her small tenement of clay, and made her fancy herself large enough to occupy the whole pew; so that upon my mother's entrance, she spread her flounces and hoop over the whole bench, and wedging my mother close in a corner, looked askance upon her, without making the least return to the courtesy she made her after she had risen from her knees.

When the service was over, the little great lady, being in a hurry to get out, flounced by my mother, and said, loud enough to be heard by my mother, to the woman who attended to open the door, "I wonder at your assurance, to put people that nobody knows into my pew—I shall complain to the church-warden, I assure you."

"Madam," said the woman, "you have a right to but one seat in the pew, and the gentlewoman looks as much like a lady as any body."

This speech called forth a contemptuous smile, and a repetition of the word "lady!" for although my mother was, as you know, my Maria, a most elegant figure, and had an air of dignity, which was rendered more interesting by the gentle sorrow which shaded her features, yet as she had no footman with her, that barrier, in this polite country town, between the high and the low, it was impossible to imagine she could have any claim to civility.

---

1 Originally, the name of the devil of greed; later, the personification of wealth as idol.
2 Pew: Church pews, enclosed seats, were often reserved for the use of particular, important, wealthy individuals, or entire families. Worshippers were escorted to a pew by a pew-opener, whom one tipped for his or her services.

Shocked, but not mortified, at the ridiculous pride of this daughter of trade, my mother was preparing to go out of the pew, when she was accosted by a lady, who, by her air and manner, seemed to be indeed a gentlewoman; she had heard what had been said to the pew-opener, and appeared much affected at it.

"I perceive, Madam," said she to my mother, "that you are not provided with a seat in this church, which indeed is very difficult to procure in the summer season, but you will be extremely welcome to one in my pew; there is room enough, and I shall be happy to accommodate you; you need only desire to be shewn to Mrs. Howard's pew, and it will always be open to you."

The lady curtseyed, and passed on, giving my mother time to pay her acknowledgments for this favour, only by a deep curtsey and an expressive look.

She related this incident to Mrs. Benson and me when she came home, telling us, at the same time, the name of the benevolent lady. "I should have been surprised," said Mrs. Benson, "if any of the plebian gentry of this lofty place had been capable of such an instance of civility to a stranger; from the noble name of Howard one might expect it."[1]

"It is true," replied my mother, "that pride and meanness are generally found together; but there are persons, even of high birth, who can submit to be proud, and whose whole greatness lie in their titles; so that if they would have us respect them, they must send a herald before to announce their claims."

I believe you and I, my dear Maria, know several of these undignified great ones; and, to my sorrow, some may be found among my own relations.

My mother did not fail to go to church next Sunday, and the pew-opener, who had heard what Mrs. Howard said, immediately conducted her to that lady's pew: Mrs. Howard was already there, and received her with smiles, that shewed the satisfaction she felt at seeing her offer so readily accepted. My mother had now an opportunity of paying her acknowledgments, which she did with her usual politeness, and a heart glowing with gratitude.

Mrs. Howard, judging by the paleness of her looks that she was in a weak state of health, desired, as soon as the service was over, that she would permit her to set her down at her own door;

---

1 Howard family: A famous family in England, founded in the thirteenth century and headed by the Duke of Norfolk, the most prestigious duke in the nation.

which my mother, after a short apology for the trouble it would give her, consented to.

My mother being desired to tell the servant where the coach was to stop, directed him to the place, and said he would see the name of Lumley upon the door.

"Is your name Lumley, Madam?" said Mrs. Howard hastily: my mother bowing.

"Then you are the widow of the late Mr. Lumley, who died at Bath, I presume?" said she.

"I am, Madam," replied my mother, sighing.

"How happy am I to meet with you thus unexpectedly," said Mrs. Howard; "I have often wished for the pleasure of your acquaintance; but I know not how it was, I never met you at any of my parties; but you must promise that we shall be good neighbours now; I generally pass three or four months every year at a little pleasant house I have about a short mile from hence, before I go to our seat in Hertfordshire. I will not part with you till you have promised to spend a day with me."

My mother assured her, she would with great pleasure. Mrs. Howard insisted upon alighting when the coach stopped, that she might be introduced to me, for I had hastened to the door to receive my mother. She saluted me tenderly; said some very civil things, and took leave of us; having first made us promise to dine with her the next day, and to name the hour when we chose the coach should come for us. But little did I imagine the influence this visit was to have over my future fortunes.

The coach came for us at the appointed time, and carried us to a small, but elegant building. The grounds about it were laid out with a beautiful simplicity, and the apartments all furnished in the same taste.

Mrs. Howard received us both with an easy politeness, which soon banished the idea of being but the acquaintance of a day. When we were summoned to the dining parlour, we found there no other company but one gentleman, who by his dress we knew to be an officer, whom Mr. Howard introduced to us as his kinsman.

This was Mr. Neville, my dear Maria, now the husband of your Euphemia. His age seemed to be about thirty; he was well bred, talked sensibly, and had something very gracious and insinuating in his manner, which, I know not how it was, had not the same effect upon me that it had upon most other persons, on whom it generally produced a favourable prepossession.

Although I could perceive I had attracted his notice, his eyes being almost instantly fixed on me, and following all my motions, yet his attentions were chiefly directed to my mother; he sat with her at table, and served her with everything in the most polite and obliging manner imaginable. We walked in the gardens after dinner; he kept close to my mother, whom he prevailed upon to lean on his arm, and entertained her with all the gallantry of an admirer, yet with all the respect and reverence of a son. My mother was quite pleased with him; he seemed solicitous to gain her good opinion, and frequently threw out sentiments which did prodigious honour to his heart.

My mother was greatly struck with one thing he said, which she declared was worthy of Socrates[1] himself. Having, upon some instance of his obliging assiduity, complimented him upon his politeness, Mrs. Howard said, with a smile, "I do assure you, Madam, Mr. Neville is a general favourite."

"I protest to you, Madam," replied Mr. Neville, "I do not think I have any reason to be vain of such a commendation; the favour of the multitude is seldom procured by honest and lawful means. I aspire indeed to the approbation of the few, for I do not number voices, but weigh them."

"Pray," said Mrs. Benson, when my mother repeated this speech to her, "how old is this sententious gentleman?" My mother replied, "that she believed he was under thirty," "Ah!" replied she, "a philosopher of that age will always be suspected by me; these fine sayings come more from the head than the heart."

"Your satire is too keen, my dear Benson," said my mother, "it is easy to perceive you are out of humour with the world; but having no reason to be so on your own account, I must place it to your friendship for me, who am so uneasily situated in it; however, Fortune may justify herself for having favoured me so little, for I am sure I never courted her."

"But I would fain know," said Mrs. Benson, "what my young pupil here thinks of this grave young gentleman?"

"My mama thinks well of him," said I, "her judgment ought to be a guide to mine; but if I may be permitted to speak my sentiments, I think the air of his countenance and the graciousness of his manner, are not of a piece; his smiles are rather forbidding than conciliating, and do not seem calculated to invite confidence in the goodness of his temper."

---

1 Socrates (469-399 BCE) was a Greek philosopher whose teachings are chronicled in Plato's *Dialogues* and in Xenophon's *Memorabilia*. His primary teachings centered on ethics.

"Upon my word," said my mother, half smiling, "Mrs. Benson seems to have infused part of her spirit in you; but my dear," pursued she in a grave tone, "I wish he were your husband; I am persuaded he would make you happy; and to see you settled, is all the wish I have on this side of Heaven."

"Dear Madam," said I, a little disconcerted, "the gentleman has no thought of me." "I do not know that," replied my mother, "I am sure he took a very particular notice of you; and as he seems to be a man of much worth and honour, it would make me happy to leave you under such a protection."

This last thought affected me with a tender concern; and made Mrs. Benson look grave. We changed the discourse; but my mother often mentioned Mr. Neville, still finding something in his manners and behaviour to ground a good opinion of his morals on.

He called the next day to enquire after our health, but only left his name, without staying to be asked in, which afforded my mother new matter for praise, as his modesty seemed in this instance to be equal to his politeness.

It soon became a custom to dine every Sunday with Mrs. Howard, who carried us home with her from church, and we were always sure to find Mr. Neville there. His behaviour to me was now particular enough to be observed by every body. Mrs. Howard, railing me on my conquest, was pleased to say, "there are few men worthy of you, but, in point of birth or fortune, Mr. Neville is no improper match. On the death of his uncle, who is now seventy, he will succeed to an estate of eight hundred a year; he is likely to rise in the army, and his own fortune, which is about five thousand pounds, is, I believe, still entire, as I never heard he was addicted to any extravagance."

My mother was very well pleased with this account of his circumstances. "Such an establishment for my daughter," said she to Mrs. Benson, "is in her situation not to be rejected, especially when the man is so worthy."

Mrs. Benson, who knew how little I was disposed to become a wife, and did not perhaps think so highly of Mr. Neville's good qualities as my mother did, shewed no great satisfaction at Mr. Neville's addresses, and wished the affair not to be hurried on too fast.

"It is dangerous," said she, "to enter the state of marriage rashly, and by the conduct of fortune; all the eyes that prudence hath, are not too many to serve as a guide in this business; for errors are mortal, where repentance is unprofitable."

She sometimes expressed her surprise to me at my mother's earnestness to conclude this affair. Alas! the motive soon became too obvious; her health was declining fast, her anxiety for me preyed upon her spirits; I could often observe her look at me earnestly for a minute till her eyes filled with tears, and then she would hastily turn away to conceal her emotion.

Mr. Neville's behaviour, all this time, was so tender, so obliging, so eager to do us little services, so attentive to my mother, so passionate, yet so respectful to me, that he even brought over Mrs. Benson, in some degree, to his party. She would sometimes tell me, that since I was absolutely certain his addresses to me were not actuated by any motives of interest, I owed him some gratitude for the sincerity of his affection.

My mother's illness now increased so fast upon her, as to fill us with the most dreadful apprehensions; the physicians acknowledged they thought her case dangerous. I passed my days, and the greatest part of my nights, by her bedside, indulging my tears in her intervals of rest—for I carefully concealed from her the agonizing fears that filled my mind.

Mr. Neville, on this occasion, shewed all the tenderness of a son, and all the sympathy of the most cordial friendship.

"Oh! that you could love this man," said my mother to me one day, "what satisfaction would it give me to leave you under his protection; for indeed, my dear child," pursued she, "I have reason to think my anxiety for you is one of the chief sources of my illness."

I started from the chair where I was sitting, I threw myself on my knees at her bedside, and bathing the dear hand she held out to me with my tears, "My dear mama," said I, "why, oh! why did you not explain yourself before? Could you doubt my ready obedience to your will?"

"In this case, my Euphemia," said she, "I would exact nothing from your obedience; my wish went no farther than that you could love Mr. Neville. Your good opinion of him I am sure he has."

"He has, Madam," said I, "and I will teach my heart to love him, since he is your choice, and since the peace of your mind depends upon my being settled; should my compliance restore you to your health, I shall be the happiest of human beings."

"And to see you happy," said my mother, "is all my wish upon earth; I am persuaded Mr. Neville will make you so, provided you have no dislike to him."

"How is that possible, Madam," said I, "that I can have any

dislike to a person for whom you have so great a regard? Doubt not but I shall love Mr. Neville, when it is my duty so to do; and I will make it my duty whenever you please to command me."

"My dear child," said my mother, "Heaven will, I doubt not, reward you for this, as well as every other instance of your filial piety. From a young woman of your reserved and delicate turn of mind, I expected no sudden attachment, no romantic flights of passion; but I am well assured, that the man whom your judgment approves, will, when entitled to your affection, possess it entirely."

From that day my mother began to be not only composed, but cheerful; the easy state of her mind had such a powerful effect upon her health, that in a few days she left her bed, and her recovery seemed no longer doubtful.

Mr. Neville received my consent with transports that seemed to border, I thought, upon madness, and rather frighted than pleased me. He asked his uncle's consent for form's sake, which was neither granted nor refused; for the old gentleman, who was not satisfied with his conduct in general, had long ceased to trouble himself about his affairs; and it was thought that his disgust had risen to such a height, that if he could have disinherited him, he would certainly have done it.

Mr. Neville's security on this point was perhaps one cause of the little care he took to conciliate him.

My mother made no reflections to the disadvantage of Mr. Neville on account of this coolness between him and his relation; for there are times when some persons are always in the right. We were married; and my husband, in about a fortnight afterwards, carried me to a genteel house in Hill-street,[1] which he had taken ready furnished for my reception.

The parting with my mother, whose state of health did not permit her to live in London, would have been very grievous to me, if I had not been enabled to visit her constantly every day; for, among other articles of expence which I did not expect, from the very moderate income my husband possessed at present, I had a chariot and servants in elegant liveries. My mother gently hinted her fears, that his great fondness for me would, in the œconomy of his house and appearance, make him consider rather the affluence in which I had been bred, than the humble condition to which fortune had reduced me.

---

1   This street wound through both the Berkeley and Grosvenor Estates, and was home to such respected residents as Henry Brougham, later Lord Chancellor, and Elizabeth Montagu.

I have heard it observed, that it is common for persons who are conscious that they have done things deserving of blame, to answer their own thoughts, rather than what is said to them. Mr. Neville, therefore, hastily replied, "I have no intention to mislead my Euphemia into an opinion that I am richer than I really am. I never deceived her with regard to my present circumstances, nor my future prospects; what you object to was not done to cast a mist before her eyes."

"My dear son," said my mother, hastily interrupting him, "how vastly do you mistake my meaning. You are incapable of deceit; but you are also incapable of reflecting, that your wife having brought you no fortune, has no claim to any increase of expence beyond conveniences."

My husband's countenance now cleared up, and this short debate ended with a kind compliment to me, which I was pleased with, because it gave her satisfaction.

Mr. Neville, however, had deceived several of his friends, and Mrs. Howard in particular, with regard to his circumstances, and consequently my mother; for of his own fortune, which was five thousand pounds, the greatest part was spent. He had commanded a company of foot[1] in a regiment which was lately reduced, and his half-pay[2] was almost all he had to subsist on. Without reflecting upon the causes of disgust he had given his uncle, he hoped that upon his marriage, an event which he had often wished for, he would have made him a decent allowance out of an estate which must one day be his, and of which he did not spend the half upon himself; but in this he was disappointed; after many fruitless endeavours to soften his uncle, he took a sudden resolution (for his resolutions are always sudden) to extricate himself from his difficulties by going abroad; and fortune, on this occasion, favoured his designs.

A young gentleman, who was appointed first Lieutenant to one of the independent companies in New York,[3] having no incli-

---

1 I.e., foot soldiers; infantry.
2 Half-pay: Reduced pay given to an army or navy officer when not in active service or upon retirement.
3 According to Séjourné, there were four Independent Companies stationed in New York in the mid-eighteenth century, two at the fort in New York City, and two at the frontier forts. The four companies consisted of three hundred and sixty "private men"; of the two Independent Companies protecting the frontiers, there was a garrison at Schenectady of twenty men, one in the "Mohawks' country" of twenty men, one at

nation to leave England, entered eagerly into a proposal Mr. Neville made him, to exchange this commission for his Captain's half-pay; and having very considerable interest, the affair was soon accomplished. Mr. Neville, who has very high notions of the prerogatives of a husband, and doubtless foreseeing the opposition I should make to this scheme, never deigned to consult me upon it. Little did I expect the storm that was ready to burst upon my head; when one evening, having staid later than usual with my mother, on my return I found him at home, very busy at his escrutore[1] looking over papers, and settling accounts.

After some enquiries concerning my mother's health, he asked me abruptly, "if I should like to travel?" I said, "I should like it extremely in certain circumstances." "And pray what are these certain circumstances, my dear?" said he. "Why," replied I, "a full purse, and my mother's company." "I cannot promise for either," said he; "and yet I believe we must travel." He said this with so grave a look and accent, that although I could hardly think him in earnest, yet I was strangely alarmed; and I asked him, with some emotion, "what he meant?"

"I mean what I say," replied he, "that we must go abroad, me dear; it is absolutely necessary."

"Absolutely necessary to go abroad!" I repeated, trembling, and scarce able to speak.

"It is really as I tell you," said he, without taking notice of the disorder I was in. "My uncle is incorrigible, he will make no addition to my income, which is too small to support you properly. I am besides incumbered with some debts, which, without his assistance, I am not able to pay; and he has had the cruelty to refuse me a few hundreds, which would have set me at ease. Fortunately an opportunity offers, which will enable me to extricate myself from these difficulties without his help. I have made an advantageous exchange with an officer who was going to New-York. It is one of the finest of our American provinces; the climate is delightful, the air healthy, the people polished; all the luxuries

---

Oswego of twenty men, and the rest at Albany (94). There were three lieutenants and one captain assigned to each Independent Company. These Independent Companies "made up the permanent element of the King's forces in the colony, whereas ... the militia, mostly composed of Dutch officers and soldiers, ... only had a local role" (94). The soldiers of the Independent Companies "were poorly equipped, badly commanded and ... on several occasions, they simply deserted" (95).

1 I.e., escritoire; writing desk.

of life are there more easily purchased than common necessaries here. There will be no great hardship in passing three or four years there. My uncle's death will be the period of our banishment, if you will have me call it so: his age and infirmities scarce make it possible that he can last long; we will then return to England."

All the time he was speaking, I sat with my hands folded, and my eyes fixed on the ground, in an agony of thought. He paused, as if expecting me to answer him.

"You say nothing to me, Euphemia," said he at length. "You think it a hardship, no doubt, to follow a husband who has given you such uncommon proofs of his affection."

"Oh! my dear mother," cried I, "am I to be torn from you, at a time when my attendance on you is so necessary?"

"Your mother will go with us, perhaps," said he. "The voyage is not so long a one as you imagine; they often run it in less than three weeks."[1]

"I charge you," interrupted I, rising hastily, and holding him as if he was going that instant to my mother, "I charge you, do not carry this dreadful news to my mother; you will kill her; she will not survive this parting with me. Alas! was it for this"—I paused.

"Go on," said Mr. Neville, "was it for this you married? I know to whom I was obliged for your reluctant consent."

This was a sad thought.—Agitated as I was with other griefs, I perceived instantly all the inconveniencies this notion, if it took too deep root, would bring upon me: but it was not possible for me to eradicate it, without descending to the meanness of falsehood; my soul was unacquainted with those emotions, which, on this occasion, would have suggested professions of fondness and attachment, such as he perhaps expected. I answered, therefore, with great simplicity, "It is true, Sir, you were my mother's choice; I never had any other will but her's, and her choice regulated mine; but I would not have married an emperor, if by that marriage I should have been obliged to leave her."

"Well," answered he, carelessly, "I believe your mother will be the only rival I shall ever have in your affections: we must endeav-

---

1 Such crossings were not unusual, but many crossings were longer due to variable winds and bad weather. Indeed, most sea travellers making the crossing to America at this time dealt with weeks of cold, cramped conditions below deck, dependent upon the rations they brought on board, which often fell short.

our to prevail upon her to go with us. But pray," pursued he, in a kinder accent, "compose yourself; this separation is yet too distant to occasion all this uneasiness."

"But still it is certain," said I; "is it not so?"

"I am afraid it is," he replied. "My affairs are in such perplexity, that it must be so."

At this decisive word my tears flowed afresh. His patience (for, alas! he has but a small share of that useful quality) seemed now exhausted; he rose up, and taking his hat, told me, he was obliged to go out, and hoped when he returned to find me in a better humour.

I was not sorry to be left alone, that I might give free vent to my tears. But scarce had I passed a few minutes in this sad employment, when my servant informed me a gentleman from Lord S. desired to speak with me. This nobleman, my dear Maria, was a relation of my mother's, and was my god-father, as I believe you have heard me say. He was but very lately returned from the Continent, where he had spent two years in search of health, which, however, he had not found; as his letter, which his gentleman now delivered to me, informed me. He expressed great concern for my father's death, and the situation in which he had left my mother and me; wished me happy in my marriage, and desired my acceptance of five hundred pounds as a nuptial present, lamenting his inability to do more for me; which indeed I knew to be true, as he had but a small estate, and several children to provide for.

My surprise at this unexpected piece of good fortune, at a time when I was overwhelmed with despair, was so great, that the letter fell out of my hands, and the bank-notes enclosed in it were scattered about the room. My soul was filled with joy and gratitude; in this providential relief I felt, I acknowledged the gracious hand of Heaven! It was with difficulty I could compose myself to write a few lines to my kind benefactor; and, when I sent for his messenger to deliver my billet to him myself, the transport I was in might easily be read in my countenance. Delivered from my fears of being separated from my mother, by being thus enabled to supply the necessities of my husband, I felt as if a mountain was removed from my breast. I expected his return with inconceivable impatience; and as soon as he entered the room I flew eagerly to him.

"My dear Mr. Neville," said I, delivering him the letter with the notes, "see how Providence has interposed to prevent a separation, that would have given death to my mother, and made me miserable. These sums will, I hope, be sufficient to set you at ease, and make it unnecessary for you to go abroad."

He read the letter, and examined the notes.—"It must be confessed," said he coldly, "this is a fortunate circumstance, considering your great unwillingness to leave England.—Well, Euphemia, I hope you will now be easy, since you have your wish." I saw he expected I should thank him for his ready acquiescence to my will; and by this piece of policy he escaped what to him would have been a very great mortification—the appearance of being under any obligation to me or my friends. My answer was calculated to please him, and I left him the next day in very good humour, in order to visit my mother.

My heart was light, and the inward satisfaction I felt gave such an air of cheerfulness to my countenance, that upon entering my mother's apartment she took notice of it. Holding out her hand to me, which I kissed, "May I always see you," said she, "with this contented air; and may you never have reason to be otherwise!"

Alas! how soon was my cheerfulness to be overcast; I felt her hand intensely hot. I fixed my eager looks upon her face; the alteration I perceived there froze me with terror. "I have had but an indifferent night, but I am better now," said she, forcing a smile to dissipate my apprehensions.

Mrs. Benson that moment entered the room: in the fixed concern that was visible in her face I read my impending misfortune. She was followed by the physician; but from him I could collect no comfort: he even acknowledged to me that my mother was in great danger. Shall I attempt to describe my feelings to you on this occasion? Oh! no, it is impossible to give you an idea of my distress. I had sent back the carriage to town, which returned again immediately with Mr. Neville, who had been informed, by a billet from Mrs. Benson, of my mother's situation.

The most dutiful, the most affectionate of sons, could not have behaved otherwise than he did: and I have the comfort to reflect, that my mother, to the last moment of her life, was fully persuaded that I was perfectly happy in the choice she had made for me.

I left her no more after this day, nor ever parted from her bedside a moment while she lived. I had command enough over myself to suppress my sighs and tears, that I might not interrupt that saint-like composure with which she waited for her dissolution. All the moments that were not spent in her devotions, she employed in consoling, fortifying, and instructing me. With the most pathetic sweetness she recommended me to my husband's care. She intreated Mrs. Benson to continue her friendship for me; and heard, with great satisfaction, her promise never to forsake me. She talked sensibly, she reasoned justly, to the last moment of her life. It was not more than a quarter of an hour before she died, when, faintly pressing my hand, which she held in her's, and looking earnestly on me,—"It has been said," said she, "with more wit than truth, that virtue was the most beautiful and the most profitable thing in the world. Can that be called unprofitable which, when supported by faith, can, in the hour of death, give a calm like this?" My heart, sunk as it was with sorrow, caught the enthusiasm of her words.

"Oh!" cried I, lifting up my swimming eyes to Heaven, "may I die the death of the righteous, and may my latter end be like their's!"—A smile of joy beamed over her countenance, now beginning to be overspread with the dark shades of death—once more I felt the faint pressure of her hand, now cold and clammy, and withdrawing from mine.—To the last moment she kept her eyes fixed upon me—then, gently closing them, her head sunk upon my bosom, and with one soft sigh she breathed out her pure and innocent soul.

Here let me draw a veil over the sad scene that ensued.—My husband carried me in his arms, and put me into the chariot, where I continued without sense or motion till we arrived at our own house. I had no reason to complain of his behaviour to me on this occasion; it was tender, affectionate, and assiduous, and filled my heart with the warmest sentiments of gratitude.

Mrs. Benson came in the evening, and spent two hours with me; and then returned to watch by the dear remains of her friend and benefactor. Lord S. desired to be at the expence of the funeral, which was performed in a manner suitable to her birth and happier fortunes.—She lies in the family vault at ——. Oh, my Maria, I must pause here for a while; when I can detach my thoughts from this affecting subject, I will continue my narration.

★ ★ ★ ★ ★

As soon as I was recovered from a dangerous fever, with which I was seized immediately after the death of my mother, Lord S. insisted upon my passing a few weeks at his country-seat with his lady and daughters. Mr. Neville was also invited; but he pleaded business in town that required his attendance, and contented himself with sometimes coming to pass a day or two with us.

When I returned to town, I found Mrs. Benson had, with the concurrence of my husband, settled all my mother's affairs. She had taken lodgings in the same street where I lived, that she might be near me: and, now my mind being a little more composed, I thought it necessary to represent to Mr. Neville, that in the present state of our circumstances, prudence required we should adopt some plan of living less expensive, and more suitable to our income. I took care to avoid giving this discourse the air of advice; I even complimented his tenderness, by ascribing to that motive the figure we had hitherto made, which I said I was by no means intitled to.

Mr. Neville, as usual, answered his own thoughts—"I suppose," says he, "you think it strange that I have not yet acquainted you with the manner in which I have disposed of your five hundred pounds; but the time has not been favourable for such discussions."

"Alas! no," said I, bursting into tears at the sad remembrance he excited by these last words.—"And perhaps," pursued he, "I have now introduced this subject unseasonably; if you please we will talk no more of it at present."

It was not long, however, before he renewed it himself.—"I cannot submit to alter my mode of living," said he; "and I cannot continue it without involving myself in difficulties—there is no help for it—we must go abroad.—If your mother had lived, I should have found it very difficult to have mentioned this to you again; but as it is, I think you can have no objection to changing the scene for a few years."

My surprise and confusion were so great at this unexpected declaration, that I continued silent for some moments; during which his countenance was marked with so much impatience, that I thought proper to tell him, I would endeavour to overcome the reluctance I had to quit my native country, and those few friends which the wreck of my fortunes had left me; but he must permit me to say, "that I wish this hard task had not been imposed upon me."—"He said, that it was impossible for him to break through his engagement, without bringing such a stain upon his honour, as could never be wiped off."—"Since that is the case," I replied, "I have nothing more to say;" and from that moment I have never suffered him to perceive that I had any reluctance to this voyage.

My dear Mrs. Benson goes with me. She has nothing dearer, she says, than me in the world; and no claims upon her that would hinder her from keeping the promise she made to my mother never to forsake me.

Mr. Neville seems to approve of her design; I say *seems*, because he never heartily approves of any thing that he is not the first mover of himself.

You are now, my dear Maria, informed of all those circumstances of my life which led to my present situation. Some particulars I wish, indeed, may be known to none but yourself; for, when I discover secrets to you, I think I hide them. Adieu.

EUPHEMIA NEVILLE.

Letter XIII.
MISS HARLEY TO MRS. NEVILLE.

MY DEAR EUPHEMIA,

WHAT an affecting narrative is your's? If Nature herself could speak, she could not make use of more significant terms. You are above all praise; therefore, without incurring the guilt of making you vain, I may venture to tell you how we talk of you here in our set. "She is a woman," said Mr. Greville, "either lifted up by her own strength above the passions of her sex, or Nature hath exempted her from them by a peculiar privilege."—"Miss Lumley," said my uncle, "is indeed a wonderful young woman; she had an excellent monitress in her mother; and she has profited well both by her lessons and example. Young as she is, she is strict in the performance of all her duties, yet she affects no peculiar gravity in her aspect and manners, but tempers her reserve with so much sweetness, that, without endeavouring to please any, she pleases all the world."

Had any persons been present at this discourse, who were ignorant of my sentiments for you, they might have judged, from my silence and discontented air, that I was envious of your praises. This is the friend, thought I, I must lose; and she, of whom hardly any man can be worthy, must follow one, who assuredly cannot be ranked among the best, to the wilds of America.

I am afraid you will be angry with me, my Euphemia, for these impatient repinings, and for profiting so little by the example you set me; but you well know, that there are some of us of such spirits, that neither time nor philosophy can work upon us; while there are others again, who prevent the work of time and philosophy by their own natural disposition.

We are going to spend a week at Mr. Greville's: he sets out to-day, to prepare for our reception, and two days afterwards we are to follow him. My chief pleasure there, as well as here, will be writing to you. I hope to have a letter from you before we leave the Hall. Adieu, my dear friend.

MARIA HARLEY.

Letter XIV.
MRS. NEVILLE TO MISS HARLEY.

YESTERDAY Mr. Neville told me he had been to pay his respects to Colonel Bellenden, whose first Lieutenant he now is, and who is appointed commander of the forces stationed at New York, under the governor, who, it seems, is captain-general.[1] The colonel introduced him to his lady and daughters: he was greatly pleased with his reception; and, having desired leave to present me to Mrs. Bellenden, and the young ladies, we received a polite invitation to dine there to-day, which we accepted.

Mr. Neville is much out of humour that, being still in mourning for my dear mother, I cannot appear with eclat;[2] that is his expression in this my first visit. He takes upon him to judge what ornaments I may wear with propriety, and has actually laid out my jewels, which, he says, will receive additional lustre from my sable habit.

It has been observed, that obstinate persons are ever most obstinate in error. Unhappily I experience the truth of this observation every day, on some occasion or other. When Mr. Neville has once given his opinion, however erroneous it may be, it is impossible by argument to set him right, for reason itself would seem to be wrong if it is not of his side. I was sadly perplexed; for I saw nothing but determined opposition would save me from an absurdity, and upon this I could not resolve; when, fortunately for me, he took it into his head to make an appeal to Mrs. Benson, who sat smiling all the time, without meddling in the dispute. But first, he endeavoured, by a long speech, to convince her, that what he proposed was the fittest thing in the world to be done.

"I know not who it is," said Mrs. Benson, very gravely, "who says that eloquence is that powerful, efficacious, and dangerous

---

1 The governor of New York State was very much a military governor in the eyes of the imperial British crown.
2 Brilliant display (*SOED*). Her dress would necessarily be muted, both in color and in ornamentation.

gift, alike capable of persuading both to what is right and what is wrong. There is no answering your arguments, that is certain; but you are too gallant not to yield up this point to Mrs. Neville, since the article of dress is entirely her own affair."—"Oh, to be sure," said Mr. Neville, "she is at liberty to dress as she pleases; I only wanted to convince her I was right in what I proposed;—but I am satisfied if you think me so."

He was indeed satisfied with the compliment Mrs. Benson paid to his eloquence, yet he could not help, now and then, returning to the charge, with—"How plainly you are dressed, my dear; if you would but add a few ornaments you would look much better."—I constantly replied with a smile, "Have you not said I should dress as I please?"—"Oh, to be sure, to be sure," he cried, "I shall never contradict you;"—and the next moment, "Certainly, my dear, you might wear diamond ear-rings, at least."—But I see the chariot at the door—my husband is coming to fetch me. I protest he surveys me with a look of disapprobation; I must remind him of the compliment Mrs. Benson paid him to put him in a good humour again. Farewel, my dear Maria, I will give you an account of our new acquaintance when we return, if we are not kept too late.

TEN O'CLOCK.

We are just come home.—Mr. Neville is engaged with a gentleman in the parlour, who having business with him, waited his return; so I have an hour before supper, which I shall devote to you, my dear Maria, to acquit myself of my promise.

We were set down at a handsome house in St. James's Square,[1] and shewn into a genteel drawing-room; into which, immediately afterwards, came Mrs. Bellenden, followed by three young ladies, her daughters. Mrs. Bellenden is about-five-and-forty years of age, or something more. She has, in her youth, been handsome, though her complexion is brown,[2] for her features are regular and

---

1 A fashionable residential area, to the north-east of St. James's Palace in London.

2 Brown complexion: A mark of a woman's delicacy, wealth, and social standing was the whiteness of her skin. Women during the eighteenth and nineteenth centuries took great pains to cover themselves from the sun even during the hot summer months, wearing long sleeves, gloves, and large-brimmed bonnets. Freckles were caused by exposure to sun, and as such were to be avoided, or, if one were born with them, powdered over.

pleasing, and her eyes remarkably fine. She is well made; her motions perfectly genteel; and, in her behaviour, she has all that easy politeness which distinguishes persons in a certain rank of life. After saluting me with a mixture of ceremony and cordiality, both as a stranger, and one with whom an intimate connection was likely soon to take place, she presented her three daughters to me by name.

Miss Bellenden, the eldest,[1] is about two-and-twenty, tall, and well-shaped, and may doubtless be called a good figure: yet her proportions are not fine, and her motions want grace. She is reckoned extremely handsome, Mr. Neville says; and it is certain that she has a fine complexion, and very regular features; but they are merely regular, cold and insipid. Her eyes are not animated with any thing but motion, and so totally devoid of expression, that they may more properly be said to see than to look. She made me a short compliment, which gave me an opportunity of observing, that the tones of her voice are unpleasing, and her expression confused.

Louisa, the second daughter, resembles her eldest sister in the delicacy of her complexion, and the air of her features; but has greatly the advantage of her in the elegance of her form, which has besides more dignity in it than I ever remember to have seen in one so young. This young lady is about fifteen; she seems grave and reserved; and returned my salute with a deep curtsey, without scarce raising her eyes.

Clara, the youngest daughter, is about fourteen, all life, soul and sensibility. She appeared, in her impatience to salute[2] me, almost ready to prevent her mother, who introduced her in her turn. The same powerful sympathy drew me towards her; I could scarcely help embracing her tenderly; but I checked this involuntary emotion, and confined myself to form. How shall I give you an idea of this amiable girl, whose loveliness is rather felt than seen, how paint the ever-varying charms of a countenance which is never the same for three minutes together, yet pleasing in every change. She is not thought so handsome as either of her sisters, her complexion being less fair, and her features not so delicate. Her eyes, however, are the finest in the world; large, dark, full of fire, full of softness: languishing, yet bright; lively yet tender: so

---

1 The eldest daughter would be given the title "Miss" while her younger sisters would be addressed by their first names.
2 Salute: In this case, to greet with a kiss or hug.

full of expression, that it is scarce necessary for her to speak, the intelligence of her looks conveying her thoughts as distinctly as her words. The make of her face is genteel, and her smile bewitching. She does not promise to be quite so tall as her eldest sister, nor to equal her second in the dignity of her person; but she excels them both in the elegance and symmetry of her form. Her voice, in speaking, is so sweet, so modulated, that it is a kind of oratory in itself, and persuades as much as her words. She continued to sit near me the whole day, which gave me great pleasure.

In about half an hour after our arrival, Colonel Bellenden entered the room. With an air of dignity he apologized to us for not being able to join us sooner, having been detained at the coffee house by some persons of business. It is impossible, my dear Maria, to look upon this gentleman without feeling for him, even at first sight, love, esteem, and reverence. He has a fine figure, a noble air, a most engaging countenance, in which every virtue that adorns the human heart is apparent. He is not a man of letters, having, as he told us, been a soldier from the age of fourteen; but nature has given him an excellent understanding. He talks little, but that little is always to the purpose; and he possesses so much natural grace, that all he says and does is pleasing.

Such, my Maria, is the family with whom I am to make a voyage to the New World; and, I believe, you will not think I shall find it a difficult matter to pass my time agreeably with them.

When tea was announced, we returned to the drawing-room, leaving the two gentlemen to their wine. Miss Bellenden then drawing her chair near me, said in a low voice, and a half sigh—

"Do you know, Madam, when this terrible voyage is to take place?"—"Not exactly, Madam," I replied, "but I am sorry to find you are so much afraid of the sea."

"Oh dear, no," said she, "I am not afraid of the sea, I never thought about it; but I am very sorry to leave England."

"Oh," said Clara, "we shall find London in every place where there are balls, and concerts, and assemblies, and plays."—"And who tells you," said Miss Bellenden, "that there are any such things in the strange part of the world to which we are going?"

"Your sister may have heard so from me," said Mrs. Bellenden, who seemed anxious to quiet her daughter's mind about these matters. "I have been told, by persons who have resided some years in the province of New York, that it is a very gay place, that the people are fond of polite amusements, and are in general very well bred." That last article, I found, had great weight with Mrs. Bellenden, for she spoke it with emphasis.

"I am informed too," proceeded Mrs. Bellenden, "that the air is pure, the climate agreeable, and the face of the country romantic and beautiful."

"Then Clara will be delighted with it," said Miss Bellenden, "for she would rather wander in woods and groves, she says, than mix in the most fashionable assemblies; nay, I have known her to prefer a walk in the most solitary part of Hyde-Park,[1] where she could see nothing but trees and grass, than accompany me to the Mall,[2] when it has been so crowded with persons of fashion, that we could hardly move." Here I observed Clara cast down her eyes, and Miss Louisa smiling significantly.

"Is solitude your taste too, Miss?" said I. "No, indeed, Madam," said she, "I like to be among persons of fashion; but not in such a crowd as my sister speaks of; for then every body looks alike, and there is no distinction of persons."

From these lights, thus artlessly held out, it was no difficult matter to discover the different dispositions of these young ladies; which were made still plainer, by the manner in which their portraits are taken by the inimitable pencil of Sir Joshua Reynolds,[3] whose pieces are so full of mind, that you have the character, as well as form, of those who sit to him. But I am interrupted with a summons to supper; and as I shall not have an opportunity of filling up the remainder of my paper till to-morrow, I will here bid you good night.

MRS. NEVILLE, IN CONTINUATION.

The Colonel and Mr. Neville having joined us, Mrs. Bellenden carried us into her dressing-room, to look at her daughters' pictures. "I was resolved," said she, "to have them drawn before we left England, and by our great artist; because they are designed for presents to some of their nearest relations."

She then directed my eyes to the portrait of Miss Bellenden, which was placed in the most conspicuous part of the room. It is a whole-length, and finely executed. She is dressed for a mas-

---

1 One of the largest and oldest parks in London, Hyde Park consists of over 340 acres.
2 In St. James's Park, the Mall was a fashionable place in which to walk.
3 Sir Joshua Reynolds (1723-92) was the most successful portrait painter of the period.

querade;[1] her habit that of a Circassian Lady;[2] she holds her masque in one hand, and, with the other, adjusts a curl of her bright auburn hair, which seems falling on her ivory neck; her countenance expresses all the self-complacency of conscious beauty, and communicates to the spectator part of that pleasure which she herself feels in the contemplation of it.

While I was gazing attentively upon this finished piece, Miss Bellenden, who seemed impatient for my opinion, glided up to me, and said in a loud whisper, "the painter has flattered me excessively; yet, I think there is some resemblance."

Mr. Neville took the word, and, in a high strain of compliment, expatiated upon the beauties of the picture, and the skill of the artist.

Miss Bellenden smiled, and interrupting him at last, said, "but I would have Mrs. Neville's opinion."

"The painter has done you justice, Madam," said I, "and only justice."

"Ah," replied she, "I perceive you can compliment as well as your lord here."

I left it to Mr. Neville to satisfy the lady's scruples about our veracity, and turned my eyes upon Miss Louisa's picture; her dress is a robe of pale blue sattin, ornamented with festoons of flowers; her hair hangs in loose ringlets upon her fine turned neck, and its luxurious growth about the forehead and temples is confined by a tiara of pearls; she is represented standing in a garden; her left arm leaning on a marble column; her right extended towards a beautiful little boy, as if to receive a small basket of flowers, which he offers her. Her attitude is extremely graceful, and calculated to mark the dignity of her form; she smiles upon the child who presents her with the flowers, who seems to have gathered them from a parterre[3] at a distance, to which he points. There is a beautiful distinction between the flowers on her robe, and those in the basket: we see that the former are artificial, only because they are contrasted with the others, which look like nature itself.

---

1 A ball at which the guests wear masks and often other fantastic or opulent disguises.
2 A woman from Circassia, a region in the north Caucasus mountain range, between the Black Sea and the Caspian Sea (*OED*).
3 An ornamental arrangement of flower-beds in a level garden (*OED*).

"You have gazed long enough," said the colonel, "upon these two fine ladies; now let me have your opinion of my little pastoral nymph here." Miss Louisa, while we were looking at her picture, stood by with an air quite easy and unconcerned; and replied to our compliments no otherwise than by a respectful curtsey.

My attention was now fixed upon the picture of my young favourite; which, both for design and execution, is one of the most pleasing pieces I ever saw. She is represented in a wood, and as just risen from the foot of a spreading oak; her book, a large folio volume,[1] lying near it; a young fawn, at a distance, seems hastening to hide itself in a thicket; a length of ribband, which it trails along, shews that it has been her captive, and has made its escape; she seems springing forwards to recover it; a sweet anxiety is expressed in her animated countenance; her hair is tied behind with a ribband, and floats in the wind. The admirable symmetry of her form is shewn to advantage by a thin white robe, which she gathers up with one hand, that it may not impede her flight; the other she holds out invitingly towards the little animal. I perceived the book was lettered on the back, it was Sidney's Arcadia;[2] I smiled. "That is a romance,[3] is it not, Madam?" said Mrs. Belleden; "Clara is very fond of those sort of books, too fond I think." Clara blush'd, and seemed apprehensive of more rebukes on this subject. "It is a romance, Madam," said I, "but it is a very ingenious work, and contains excellent lessons of morality: it was wrote by one of the bravest soldiers, and most accomplished gentlemen of the age he lived in; an age too, that was fruitful in great men."

"I see you are an advocate for romances, Mrs. Neville," said Mrs. Bellenden, half grave, and half smiling, "and indeed, you are still of an age to relish them." I smiled assentingly; and the colonel leading me again to the drawing room, the discourse turned upon matters relating to our intended voyage, and the country we were going to, till it was time to take leave.

---

1 A book or manuscript made up of sheets of paper folded once; a volume of the largest size (*OED*).

2 Sir Philip Sidney's (1554-86) *Arcadia*, probably written by 1581, was published posthumously in 1590 and in a revised version in 1593.

3 Popular stories in verse which dealt with three subjects: Arthur; Charlemagne and his knights; and classical heroes, especially Alexander. Unlike the initially more realistic genre of the novel that followed the romances, they are full of fantastic incidents and their characters are of noble birth and exhibit heroic actions.

I am apprehensive this voyage will take place sooner than I expected; but I could easily reconcile myself to all the difficulties of it, except parting with you, my dear Maria.—Alas! this is a subject I dare not trust myself to write on.

This moment your short letter (which to make amends for its shortness, it must be owned is very sweet) is brought me. By lavishing such praises on me, you do me a favour no doubt, but I cannot say you do me justice; and you seem to have a design to please me at the hazard of offending truth. But you will tell me, these high commendations come from your uncle and Mr. Greville.—'Tis well, I will rate them at their just value; for do we not all know, my dear Maria, what politeness obliges men of wit and gallantry to, when ladies are the subjects of their panegyric?—But enough of this. Write to me soon; let me know all that passes in this little excursion; every thing interests me that relates to you. Adieu.

EUPHEMIA NEVILLE.

Letter XV.
MISS HARLEY TO MRS. NEVILLE.

MY DEAR EUPHEMIA,

IT is some comfort to me to reflect, that if you must take this hated voyage, the Bellenden family will afford agreeable companions in it. Mr. Greville is well acquainted with the Colonel: he speaks of him with a kind of enthusiasm. In the language of Pope, he cried out,

> "'A wit's a feather, a chief's a rod,
> An honest man's the noblest work of God.'"[1]

"Colonel Bellenden," said he, "is that noblest work; and to this truth the candid bear testimony by their words, and detractors by their silence." I asked him his opinion of the ladies.

"Mrs. Bellenden," said he, "by her politeness and attention to please, supplies, in some degree, the defect of her education; which being confined to mere accomplishments, as they are

---

1 Alexander Pope's *An Essay on Man*, Epistle IV, ll. 247-48: "A Wit's a feather, and a Chief a rod;/ An honest Man's the noblest work of God."

called, has left the nobler powers of her mind uncultivated. She sings well; she dances finely; she performs on the harpsichord with great skill; she can carry on the small talk of a tea-table in French; draws prettily; and is allowed to shade her flowers in embroidery extremely well; but her reading has been wholly confined to her Psalter[1] and Bible, a few devotional tracts and some sermons; and, among profane authors, the Seven Champions of Christendom,[2] pamphlets, poems, and some other works of the same kind. She has a great contempt for what she calls book-learning in women; and thinks chastity and good breeding, for so she pairs them, the highest of female virtues. She is an obedient wife, a tender mother, and an easy companion; is gentle in her censures of her acquaintance, except when they offend against the laws of modesty, or the rules of ceremony, and then, it must be owned, she is very severe."

"Your characters," said I, "seem to be drawn with so much skill, that I wish to have Miss Bellenden's by the same hand. She will be the companion of my dear friend in a long voyage, and I shall be happy to know that she will be an agreeable one."

"I do not," said Mr. Greville, "think Miss Bellenden qualified to be an agreeable companion to one of your friend's solid understanding: but she is good-tempered, and will not give offence; she is very handsome, and has no idea of any higher excellence in women than beauty; she is greedy of admiration, and would be a coquet,[3] if she had wit enough to secure her conquests; but although nature directs her to throw the bait, and the gaudy fry often catch at it, yet she has not skill enough to bring her prey to land; and they always escape her. These disappointments affect her but little; for a constant succession of new conquests keeps her in good humour with her own charms, and leaves her no leisure to regret, that their effect is not lasting."

"Her two sisters are too young to have any character yet; but they are both fine girls in their persons; and Clara, the youngest, seems, I think, to give the promise of being superior to the others, in the endowments of her mind." "My friend has found that out already," said I. "Then," replied Mr. Greville, "I shall have some opinion of my own penetration."

My uncle this moment sends to let me know that he is ready,

---

1 I.e., book of psalms.
2 *The Famous History of the Seven Champions of Christendom* (c. 1597), a popular romance written by Richard Johnson (1573-1659?).
3 A flirt.

and the carriage is at the gate. We are to spend a week at least at Mr. Greville's, and from thence my next letter will be dated, unless I should find leisure to write to you at the inn where my uncle puts up the first night. Ever, ever your's,

MARIA HARLEY.

Letter XVI.
MISS HARLEY TO MRS. NEVILLE.

Bell Inn.

HERE we are, my dear Euphemia, somewhat fatigued with our journey, for the roads were very heavy, and the day unpleasant; and, to complete our dissatisfaction, we met with some disagreeable occurrences on our arrival at this place, which have had a surprising effect on my uncle's temper, and for which, at present, I can by no means account.

When our carriage drove into the inn-yard, a young gentleman, who was talking to Mrs. Deering, the landlady, hastily advanced, and with great politeness offered his hand to help me out: he bowed low to my uncle, and observing that he descended with some difficulty, he assisted him with equal attention; my uncle thanked him very cordially, which the young gentleman answered only by a most respectful bow, and withdrew. Both my uncle and I thought him extremely handsome; and indeed, my dear Euphemia, he has a most engaging countenance, and is one of the finest figures I ever saw.

Mrs. Deering having conducted us to a parlour, appeared to be in some confusion. "Your honour," said she, "used always to give me notice when you intended to come here, and then I prepared every thing for your reception."

"And have you not had notice," said my uncle; "I sent Robert before me, early in the morning." "Indeed, Sir," said she, "not a soul has been here from you: and I am in the greatest quandary in the world; for I have not a bed for your honour, my house is so full: I can make a shift to accommodate the young lady, if she will put up with a little bed in a dark closet, and her maid can sleep with one of mine; but the room your honour used always to have, is engaged by that young gentleman you saw in the yard, and I have not another room in the house, but what is taken up."

My uncle fretted very much at this disappointment, and at the negligence of the groom. "What is to be done, Maria?" said he to me; "do you think you can bear the fatigue of travelling to the next stage this cold dark night?"

"I can bear it very well, Sir," said I, "but I am sure you cannot; therefore, I must entreat that you will accept of the dark room and the little bed Mrs. Deering talks of; and Fanny shall sit up with me in this room: here are two easy chairs; and if I can get a book, I shall pass my time well enough." "I cannot consent to that," said my uncle; then turning to Mrs. Deering, who had uttered a thousand good lacks[1] all the time, he ordered her to get a boiled chicken for supper; and in the mean time he would resolve upon something.

I continued to press my uncle to agree to my proposal; which he could not prevail upon himself to approve.

All this time we heard nothing of the groom. The night became wet and stormy. I trembled for my uncle's health; for he was immoveable in his resolution not to let me sit up all night; but rather to go forward to the next stage; when Mrs. Deering entered the room smiling, and told us, that the young gentleman, who had engaged the room, hearing of the inconveniences we were likely to suffer for want of an apartment, had politely resigned it to my uncle; and was actually set out on horseback, in the midst of the storm, in order to reach the house of a friend, who lived about ten miles distant.

"Blessings on his heart for it!" said Mrs. Deering, "it was as good a deed as ever was done; and it was all his own offer."

My uncle appeared very much affected with this young man's civility. "Who is he?" said he to Mrs. Deering: "I hope I shall have an opportunity, some time or other, of thanking him." "He is your namesake," said Mrs. Deering.

"Harley!" interrupted my uncle, impatiently, "Whose son is he?"

"He is son to the Reverend Doctor Harley," answered Mrs. Deering; "and is just returned from Germany. He was sent to get his learning at a *Versity* there; because his father, it seems, is not rich, and could not maintain him at one of our own *Versities*."

My uncle had been used to this good woman's language, and was able to listen to her gravely; but it was with some difficulty that I could not help smiling. However, my mirth was immediately clouded, when casting my eyes upon my uncle, I per-

---

1 I.e., Mrs. Deering repeatedly utters the term "Good lack!," an expression of dissatisfaction, regret, surprise, etc. (*OED*).

ceived all the marks of astonishment, anger and confusion in his countenance.

"Pray hasten supper," said he to Mrs. Deering, at the same time making a motion to her with his hand to be gone. She left the room; and he continued to walk about in it silently, with a hasty unequal step.

My astonishment at this evident discomposure, kept me silent also for some moments. At length I asked him, if any thing extraordinary had happened, to make him uneasy.

"Yes," replied he, throwing himself into a chair, "I have reason to be uneasy, when, contrary to my intentions, I am laid under obligations to persons I hate. This young fellow has insulted me by his mock-civility. Cannot you guess who he is?" "Is he not, Sir," said I, "related to us?"

"He is so, to your and my misfortune," said he. "His father is my enemy, my mortal enemy: and upon him, since I have no male heir, my estates are entailed. Oh! that my brother had left me a son instead of a daughter!"

"Well, Sir," said I, endeavouring to laugh him out of his ill humour, "it is always a misfortune enough to be a woman, without any aggravation. But I am not avaricious; and you have made me as rich as I desire to be. I wish, indeed, your heir was more worthy of your regard. But has this young man affronted you, as well as his father?"

"His father is a villain!" cried my uncle, starting from his chair, and pacing again furiously about the room; then suddenly stopping, and grasping my hand eagerly,

"Oh! Maria," said he, "I have cause for hatred; that base man betrayed me! betrayed me in the tenderest point! betrayed me, who was his kinsman, his friend, his benefactor!"

His voice failed; his eyes filled with tears; he turned from me, and throwing himself again into his chair, fixed his looks, altered as they were from rage to melancholy, stedfastly upon the fire.

While he continued in this affecting silence, I could not refrain from tears; which I endeavoured to conceal, upon Mrs. Deering's entrance with supper. Sir John was so absorbed in thought, that he did not perceive she was in the room; I drew near to tell him softly, that supper was on the table.

"I hope his Honour is not ill!" said Mrs. Deering, coming up officiously towards him. "Sir John is fatigued," said I, "with his journey." "Ah! no doubt of it," said she. "What a mercy it was, that his honour did not go further to-night. Blessings on good young Mr. Harley, for leaving us his bed!"

At that name my uncle started up in some emotion; and then, for the first time, perceiving our loquacious landlady, he recollected himself, and drew his chair near the table.

"It is a bitter night," pursued she; "poor heart! I warrant he is drenched through with the rain by this time: but as long as his Honour is safe and warm, I am contented."

Sensible how much my uncle must suffer in the present state of his mind, by this woman's idle talk, I desired her to get his apartment ready for him as soon as possible; "for I suppose, Sir," said I, "you will choose to retire when you have supped?" "Certainly," he said: upon which Mrs. Deering withdrew.

My uncle, still pensive and silent, carved the chicken, helped me and himself, but scarce ate any thing; and my supper being finished as soon as his, he drank one glass of wine; and ordering his valet, who attended, to light him to his room, he wished me a good night and left me.

I was glad to be alone, that I might give free vent to my tears; for the gentle melancholy my uncle fell into, after the first sallies of his anger were over, affected me greatly. I could have wished he had opened his heart to me, and acquainted me with the cause of his enmity against his kinsman. That there was no cordiality nor correspondence between them, I knew; but I never imagined their differences were of a nature to excite such a strong and lasting enmity. But what has this poor young man done, to deserve so great a share of my uncle's dislike? For it seems he never saw him before, and was disposed to like him, till he heard his name: and indeed, it must be acknowledged, that he has something extremely interesting in his countenance, and his person and address are engaging to a great degree. Poor youth! his complaisance may probably cost him dear; the night is dark and stormy, his road lies across the country, and he has ten miles to travel, with no attendant but an old countryman, whom, at a large expence, he hired to serve him as a guide.

Here is Mrs. Deering with her alasses![1] again; she puts a thousand frightful thoughts into one's head. I have always observed, that low people take a pleasure in creating fears, when there is no cause for them, and in aggravating them when there is. But I will go to bed: I am tired, but not sleepy. I have been writing ever since my uncle left me.—Good night, my dear Euphemia.

---

1 I.e., many repetitions of the interjection "alas."

I cannot sleep, the tempest without is so violent; and, to say the truth, the agitations of my mind have raised a kind of tempest within me. I am risen, and I am got again to my pen. I dread seeing my uncle; his uneasiness affects me greatly. Methinks, I can now account for his ill-suited marriage with Miss Fenwick.— Doubtless, he hoped for an heir, to disappoint the expectations of his hated kinsman, and his race. But, why should his race be hated too? Whatever the father's guilt may be, ought it to involve the innocent son? Bless me! there is a loud knocking at the gate. This stormy night has driven some bewildered travellers hither. Poor Mr. Harley! perhaps, he too, may be in difficulties. Good Heaven! how they thunder at the gate! This impatience speaks some emergency. So, the house is roused, I perceive: my window looks into the inn-yard; cold and dreary as it is, I must open it, and see what is the matter.

A post-chaise drives into the yard; they help a man out of it, who seems to be hurt: some dreadful accident has happened. I must ring for somebody to come to me; I am terrified, and cannot bear to be alone.

Alas! my dear Euphemia, the wounded man I saw brought in is Mr. Harley! My maid, whom the noise had wakened, came to my chamber; I sent her to make some enquiries; she returned with my uncle's groom, who told me, that the young gentleman was dangerously hurt. I was excessively angry with this fellow, by whose neglect all this mischief has been brought about. I could hardly bear him in my sight; yet I was impatient to know, how he happened to be in Mr. Harley's company, for he was in the chaise with him, it seems: he told me, after some awkward excuses for his transgression, which I impatiently interrupted, that having met with a brother, who was just returned from sea, and whom he'd not seen for many years, he was by him persuaded to go into a public house; where drink and discourse beguiled the time, he said, in such a manner, that it was late in the evening before they parted; but the storm was so violent, that he could not have proceeded, if he had not met with a returned post-chaise, the driver of which was his acquaintance, who invited him to take a seat in it; he set out with his friend, who promised to leave him at this inn. In their way, they were alarmed with the cries of a man, who begged them to alight and assist a gentleman, whose horse had thrown him, and who, he believed, was dangerously hurt: this was poor Mr. Harley, my dear. They found him lying under a tree, which afforded him but indifferent shelter against the rain; and in this condition, it seems, he had remained near an hour, being unable to rise, much less to sit his horse; and in all this time, no carriage of any sort had passed by till their arrival; his guide, poor fellow! had taken off his own great coat[1] to cover the poor youth as he lay, supporting his head upon his knees, hollowing in vain for help, where there was none to hear; and uncertain whether he ought to leave him, in that condition, to seek for assistance, or stay near him, in expectation that Providence would send them relief.

With some difficulty they raised him, and put him into the chaise; Robert supporting him in it. The humanity he had shewn upon this occasion prevented any further reproaches from me for his negligence, and I promised to prevail with my uncle to pardon him; who, upon the report of what had happened, had risen, and having sent to know if I was up, desired I would come to him in the parlour. He took notice that my eyes were red. "I do not blame you for your sensibility," said he; "I am concerned, as well as you, for the accident that has happened to this young man. That I should be undesignedly made, in part, the occasion of it, is one of those good turns which I am used to meet with from that family."

I perceived he was in an ill humour; so I made him no answer to this speech, which, I thought, was a very strange one at this time. He walked hastily backwards and forwards in the room, as his manner is, when he is vexed.

"I have sent to tell Mrs. Deering," said he, "that she may accommodate her guest with my bed, which I have left for that purpose; so there, I think, we are even." There was no answering to this, you know; so I was still silent.

"I am impatient to be gone," pursued he, "therefore ring, and order some breakfast to be prepared immediately; we will set out as soon as it is light."

I rung, and my maid appearing, I ordered her to get breakfast ready: "for I suppose," said I, "they have business enough below to employ them." My uncle looked wishfully at Fanny, then at me, as if desirous to know what was passing. I asked no questions, though I was really in a great deal of anxiety myself, being resolved to see how far good nature would work. He seemed disappointed when Fanny went out of the room; and going to the door, called her back.

---

1   Great coat: Heavy overcoat (*OED*).

"Why do you not tell us," said he, "how the gentleman is?" "He is very bad, Sir," said Fanny; "he is very much bruised, and has got a large cut on the side of his head, for it seems he fell against a huge stone that lay in the road: Mrs. Deering says, he bleeds like a pig, and he has fainted away twice. There is no surgeon to be had nearer than the next town, and that is seven miles off."

My uncle now walked about faster than before. "Cursed accident!" muttered he: then, suddenly stopping, "Is any one gone for this surgeon?" asked he, hastily. Fanny told him, a man and horse were gone full speed. "Well, make haste with breakfast," said he, "it grows light; and tell the men to get the carriage ready; I will be gone immediately."

Mrs. Deering brought in the chocolate herself, and told us, that as good luck would have it, one of her guests, being a physical gentleman,[1] had visited Mr. Harley, who was now in bed; that he said, he ought to be bled immediately, and undertook to do it himself, though he did not practice that profession; that he had *subscribed* [2] something to anoint his bruises, and to compose him to sleep; and that he was actually in a fine breathing sweat, and was very quiet.

Sir John, I could observe, listened to her strange jargon very attentively, which, at any other time, would have made me smile. But I was really concerned for the young gentleman, extremely concerned; it was natural I should be so, for he is our kinsman, you know, and whatever may be his father's demerits, he is blameless.

My uncle heard all she said without making any reply; and having drank his chocolate, seated himself in an easy chair, complaining that he was very sleepy. I retired to my own room, and wrote thus far, expecting to be soon summoned to depart, for I see the coach is drawn out. Methinks I could wish the surgeon was come, that we might have his opinion of the poor young man's case: common humanity, you know, my dear, would suggest this. Sure, Sir John will not go till he knows what degree of danger Mr. Harley is in. I was mistaken; he sends this moment to know if I am ready.—Well, I will attend him.

---

1 A physician.
2 Subscribed: I.e., prescribed.

I am retired for the night to my own chamber; the fatigue and agitation of the day affording me a reasonable excuse for desiring to rest; but I shall devote an hour or two to you before I go to-bed.

I told you, my uncle sent to let me know he was ready to set out from the inn, and I hastened down to him. I found him reading a news-paper, and so leisurely, that he even read all the advertisements; at length, he laid down the paper, walked to the window, and looked at his watch. My maid coming in with my cloak, he asked her, "If the surgeon was come?" She answered, "No; but that the coach was ready." I rose up, my uncle gave me his hand; I thought we were going away immediately, when he stopped short at the parlour door: "I fancy, Maria," said he, "you would be glad of a dish of tea before you go; you have had very little rest, it will refresh you, and you are not used to breakfast upon chocolate."

It appeared to me, that my uncle was desirous of staying till the surgeon came, though he would not own it. I accepted his proposal, and tea was ordered. In about half an hour afterwards, Fanny told us the surgeon was come: "Well," said my uncle, with an assumed carelessness, "we shall now hear his opinion of this case." And accordingly Mrs. Deering came, in a great hurry, to tell us.

"Well, Heaven be praised," said she, "matters are not so bad as we imagined; Surgeon Parker has examined the wound, and shook his head; but says, he hopes it will not be attended with very great danger. He is a fine man; he will cure him, if any body can. He says, the young gentleman is very much bruised, but he hopes not dangerously; and his fever is pretty high, but he hopes not dangerous. He says, he must be kept quiet; for it will be a work of time to set him upon his legs again. Oh, he is a fine man; the young gentleman will be very safe in his hands. But I must go, and get ready the things he has *subscribed* for him." And accordingly she left us, in as great a hurry as she came in.

"I fancy this fine man," said my uncle, half smiling, "will make a fine job of this." Then pausing a little; "the wounded gentleman," said he, "is probably not provided with money enough to answer such extraordinary expences as he may be brought into; and the wretch, his father, lives at a great distance: can you think of any method, Maria, of conveying this to him," taking a bank-note of fifty pounds out of his pocket-book; "it will hurt his deli-

cacy, I suppose, to put it into Mrs. Deering's hands for his use."
I could have wished my uncle had completed this act of benevo-
lence, by making Mr. Harley a visit, and giving it to himself; but
I durst not mention this to him.

"There is no other way, Sir," said I, "than to inclose it, and
send it to him by Mrs. Deering." He said, that would do; and
taking his hat, walked into the garden, to give me an opportunity.
Accordingly, I inclosed the note in a blank sheet of paper, and
sealed it with my own cypher.[1] I then sent for Mrs. Deering, and
desired her to deliver it to Mr. Harley herself. She told me he was
asleep, which I was glad to hear; and, smiling significantly,
assured me, he should have it as soon as he waked. She was going
to oppress me with her usual loquacity; but my uncle coming in,
she stopped short. He gave me his hand to lead me to the coach,
and we drove away immediately; my uncle not once speaking to
me, till we came within five miles of Greville-park; when he perceived Mr. Greville, on horse back, coming to meet us; and he
pointed him out to me.

Mr. Greville, full of the pleasure this visit gave him, said a
great many civil things to me; and thanked Sir John for the favour
he did him, in prevailing upon me to accompany him. But my
uncle continued to be grave and pensive; so that when we arrived
at the Park, Mr. Greville, as he handed me out of the coach,
expressed some surprise at the humour his friend seemed to be
in; and asked me in a whisper, "What was the matter?" I replied,
"That we had met with disagreeable accidents at the inn, which,
I supposed, Sir John would acquaint him with; and that I should
then expect an explanation from him; for I knew he was too much
in his confidence, to be ignorant of any thing that materially concerned him."

This is a delightful seat, my dear Euphemia; sweetly romantic
in its situation and prospects. The house is not very large, but
elegant, and furnished with great taste. I complimented the
house-keeper, who is a grave matronly woman, upon the exquisite neatness that reigned in all the apartments. That which is
allotted for me, during my stay, is one of the best.

I have had a long conversation with Mr. Greville this morning.
My uncle, being a little fatigued with his journey, did not accompany us in our walk in the park, which is a very extensive one. I
was impatient to know what had passed between them, after I left

---

1 Maria seals her letter with wax, which she impresses with her monogram.

them last night, concerning our adventures on the road; and Mr. Greville, to my wish, entered of himself into the subject.

"So, Sir John has seen this young kinsman," said he, "I find. It must have been a trying interview for him; and, no doubt, opened all those wounds, which neither time nor reason have been able entirely to heal."

"What are those wounds," said I, "which, in a mind so generous as my uncle's naturally is, could produce such fatal effects, as to make him confound innocence with guilt, and reject the blameless son for the faults of the offending father? Yet, it must be owned, that, angry as he was, he forgot not the duties of humanity."

"That is exactly my friend," replied Mr. Greville; "his passions may sometimes mislead him, but his inclinations are always good, and never fail to bring him again into the right path. But you will not be surprised at the continuance of his resentment against the father, when you know the injuries he has received from him; and I have his leave to make you acquainted with them. 'For I am not willing,' said he, 'that my niece should think meanly of me, as she probably will, till she is convinced, that resentment is but proportioned to the offence that has been given me.'"

"You must know then, that Sir John and Dr. Harley had contracted a great friendship for each other in their early youth. They received the first rudiments of their education at the same academy, and were sent together to the same university. Dr. Harley's father was but in indifferent circumstances, and would have found it very difficult to have supported his son at college, had not his expences been liberally supplied by your uncle, whose father, Sir Henry Harley, gave him a very large allowance. The two friends were inseparable; and their mutual attachment was so steady and so ardent, that they were called Pilades and Orestes.[1] Mr. Harley, your uncle, during one of the vacations, became acquainted in a gentleman's family, the daughter of which was exquisitely handsome, and highly accomplished; for her father, having no fortune to give her, was at an expence for her education, which but little suited his circumstances, not doubting but her beauty, aided by such advantages, would procure her a very honourable establishment. Your uncle conceived a violent passion for her; he made her a declaration of it, which was not ill received; but the prudent young lady referred him to her father, which put

---

1 In Greek myth, Pilades remained a faithful friend to his cousin Orestes even when Orestes committed matricide.

matters in such a train, that your uncle was soon engaged in a formal matrimonial address, which, for the present, however, was to be carried on secretly, as it was not expected that Sir Henry would be easily prevailed upon to give his consent, and the young gentleman was still master enough of himself, to reject all thoughts of a complete disobedience.

"His young kinsman, you may be sure, became his confident; and he undertook to manage a correspondence between the lovers; which, for some time, was carried on undiscovered; at length, some hints of the affair had been given to Sir Henry, who, when his son came next to visit him, caused him to be watched so closely, that he soon became master of the whole secret. He came to an explanation with his son, who had too much candour to deny his attachment to Miss Denby; but assured him, that he never entertained a thought of engaging himself further without his consent.

"Sir Henry seemed satisfied with this assurance, and gave him to understand, that he relied entirely upon his honour, and expected that he would break off this connexion; and, to make all sure, proposed, that he should set out immediately upon his travels.[1] This was a sad stroke: Mr. Harley endeavoured to ward it off by many bad arguments, which he brought to prove, that it would be better to defer this expedition for a year at least.

"Sir Henry, who never had recourse to authority when the case in question could be decided by reason, was sensible, that to combat passion with remonstrances was engaging with unequal arms; therefore he put an end to the debate with a positive *I will have it so*; and preparations were immediately made for his departure.

"The lovers, at parting, exchanged a thousand vows of constancy, and their faithful confident[2] promised to manage their correspondence as usual, which went on unsuspected for near a year when Mr. Harley's governor[3] discovered it by chance, and gave immediate notice to Sir Henry.

"The Baronet[4] began now to apprehend very serious consequences from a passion which had stood the test of time and

---

1 Harley is to leave on the Grand Tour of Europe, a rite of passage for wealthy young men of the period that enabled them to study the cultural riches of Europe over a period of several years, usually accompanied by a tutor, as they themselves matured.
2 Confident: I.e., confidante.
3 Tutor.
4 A member of the lowest hereditary titled British order (*OED*).

absence; and the active part young Harley had taken in the affair giving him just offence, he sent for him in order to reprove him severely for it. Mr. Harley, finding it in vain to deny the truth to one who was so well informed, pleaded in his own excuse the force of friendship, and in your uncle's, the fascinating power of Miss Denby's charms; and on this last point he spoke so feelingly, as put a scheme into Sir Henry's head, which, if it succeeded would effectually prevent the misfortune he feared from his son's imprudent attachment.

"Dropping therefore the first severity of his tone and aspect, he began to expostulate mildly with him.

"'If my son,' said he, 'continues his addresses to this girl, he will offend me greatly; but, if he should be mad enough to marry her, never let him hope for my pardon; I will banish him from my heart, and from my sight for ever; tell him this, and use all your influence with him to prevent such an insult to parental authority; in doing so you will shew your friendship to him, and will secure mine to yourself.'

"Mr. Harley's father was lately dead, and had left him a very small fortune; he had taken orders, but had little hopes of obtaining any preferment in the church[1] but by the interest of Sir Henry. He perceived all the advantages of this opening towards gaining his confidence and friendship; and Sir Henry was convinced by the suppleness of his answers, that it would not be a very difficult matter to lead him as far as he pleased. He resolved, therefore, to explain his whole design at once, founding his hopes of success in it, on the observations he had made on the warmth with which the young man expatiated upon the beauty and merit of Miss Denby. He knew that the shortest way to persuade was to please; therefore, he instantly proposed to him to marry the young lady himself, whom he would portion with a thousand pounds, and give him the reversion of the living of ———, which was worth three hundred pounds a year, and was likely to be soon vacant, the present incumbent being then above four-score.[2]

"The once faithful Pilades could not resist these strong temptations; he sacrificed his Orestes without scruple, persuading himself that the friendship he had vowed for him required that he

1 Mr. Harley has been ordained a minister in the Anglican Church, but he does not expect to receive a "living," an appointment by the Church of England to a parish, except through Sir Henry's influence with the owner of the estate in which the church is located.

2 Eighty years old.

should use every means in his power to prevent his incurring the guilt of disobedience to his father; and knowing that in great affairs there are no small steps, he went boldly to work, represented to Mr. Denby the danger of offending a man so powerful by his fortune and interest as Sir Henry Harley; by encouraging his son's clandestine address to Miss Denby; that the young gentleman himself did not entertain a thought of marrying her without his father's consent, which would never be obtained; that the Baronet's death alone could open a prospect of success in this affair; and this prospect, considering the vigour of his years and constitution, was very remote. He advised him, therefore, to listen to another proposal for his daughter, which, though not so splendid yet was certain, and might be productive of more happiness.

"Mr. Denby was a reasonable man; he considered that nothing is less certain than the future—nothing apter to deceive than hope. He was anxious to settle his daughter, and resolved not to reject a present good for the bare possibility of a greater in future; and, after some reflection, desired Mr. Harley to explain himself, which he accordingly did, relating very candidly Sir Henry's proposal; for even knaves can be honest when their interest points that way.

"The two gentlemen were soon agreed; the greatest difficulty seemed to be the persuading Miss Denby to this new regulation:— but even this was got over in a little time, either because the young lady's passion for her absent lover was not very violent, or she had given way to a growing inclination for the present; or, what indeed was most likely, the precarious condition of her fortune, her sole dependence being upon the life of her father, whose health was declining, and whose income, arising from a place in the revenue,[1] did not enable him to lay up any thing for her future support.

"Sir Henry had soon the satisfaction to hear that this marriage was completed; he performed the first part of his promise immediately, and caused the thousand pounds he gave Miss Denby to be settled on herself; and in a very few weeks he was enabled to perform the second part of it; the living became vacant, and Mr. Harley was put in possession of it.

"Your uncle was at Brussels, on his way to England, when he heard of this marriage, which, upon report, he did not believe:

---

1   The governmental department responsible for collecting taxes.

but a letter from his father put it past a doubt. He received one at the same time from Dr. Harley, which he returned unopened. He made no reproaches, he expressed no resentment; satisfied with the resolution he had taken, never for the future to hold any converse with a man who had so basely betrayed him, he confined his grief and rage within his own breast; and, in his letter to his father, took not the least notice of what had happened, but desired he would approve of his intention to continue abroad some time longer.

"Dr. Harley was deeply wounded by the contemptuous silence of his injured friend, which carried with it more keen reproach than the severest invectives. His remorse, it was said, cost him a fit of sickness; and he had the mortification to find that Sir Henry, though he profited by his treachery, yet despised him for it, confining his acknowledgments to the bare performance of his promise, without keeping up any correspondence with him, or pushing his interest any further.

"Your uncle continued on the continent three years longer, visiting most of the European courts; and being furnished with remittances to make a large expence, he amused himself so effectually, that he returned to England perfectly cured of his passion; but retaining all his resentment against the perfidious pair who had so basely betrayed him.

"Sir Henry pressed him to marry, to which he seemed greatly averse; and when his father, to prevail upon him, mentioned the entail of his estates upon Mr. Harley in default of issue in his line,[1] your uncle said, his brother's marriage might as effectually prevent that misfortune as his. Accordingly Mr. Edward Harley was, with the consent of all parties, married to your amiable mother; and Sir Henry, before he died, had the satisfaction to be grandfather to three fine boys and yourself. It pleased Heaven, however, to take your brothers to himself; and your parents, too much affected with their loss, followed them in a few months. Then it was that your uncle resolved upon marriage, but was not

---

1   The settlement of the succession of land or other property. Sir Henry Harley tries to convince his eldest son, Sir John Harley, that he should marry because if he does not, and thereby produces no legitimate children, Sir Henry's line will die out and his estate will go to Dr. Harley, Sir John's cousin, and his childhood friend who had lately betrayed him by marrying the woman Sir John had loved. The matter is resolved, and the inheritance kept within Sir Henry's family line, by Sir Henry's younger son, Edward, marrying instead and producing Maria.

able to fix till he saw Miss Fenwick. A most injudicious choice, as it has proved; and he has now the mortification to know, that the person whom he hates most, and has most reason to hate, plumes himself with the hope of succeeding to his fortune."

This was what Mr. Greville told me, my dear Euphemia; and it must be confessed, that my uncle's fixed resentment against the elder Mr. Harley is very justifiable. It was natural, you know, my dear, to be a little inquisitive about the character of the son. Mr. Greville, it seems, knows him very well, having met him several times in company since his return from Leyden.[1] He speaks of his merit in very high terms: he says he is a most amiable youth, is possessed of a fine understanding, and besides being an excellent scholar, is highly accomplished. He resembles his father, he says, in nothing but the graces of his person; and even in these he has the advantage of him.

"He would be no bad representative," added Mr. Greville, "of the honours of your family; but, if it be true what some have observed, that the qualities of the mind are hereditary, though the order of succession is not always observed, young Harley may have a son that will resemble his grandfather, and disgrace those honours."

I smiled at this conceit, and I must confess I was glad to hear so good an account of the young man, for I was willing to be justified in the favourable prepossession—I mean the good opinion I had conceived of him from his very polite and engaging behaviour. "Mr. Greville told me that he would dispatch a man and horse to-day to the Bell Inn, to know how the young gentleman is, and, by some means or other," said he, "I will contrive to let Sir John know the state of his health, about which I am sure he has good nature enough to be anxious, though he will not own it."

Our walk ended with this little history. My uncle himself mentioned Mr. Harley, and said he should be glad to know if the young man's hurt was really as bad as the surgeon represented it.

"We shall know, presently," said Mr. Greville, "for I ordered Will, as he passed by the Bell Inn, to enquire; he must be come back I suppose by this time."—He rang the bell, and Will himself appeared.—"Well, how is the wounded gentleman?" said Sir John, carelessly.—"Sir," replied the man, "he is much better; so well, indeed, that he talks of setting out tomorrow in a post-chaise for his father's house; but the surgeon and Mrs. Deering say he is mad to think of any such thing, and would fain have him stay a

---

1 Also "Leiden." A city in the Netherlands.

week longer, at least; but the young gentleman seems to be a very positive young gentleman, and will do as he pleases."

When William left the room, my uncle said he was glad the young man was not likely to be a great sufferer by his civility, which, whether it proceeded, said he, from an interested policy, or real benevolence, I profited by, and therefore owed him my thanks for it: and now, that the matter is all over, I must insist upon never having his name mentioned to me again.

He spoke this with so severe a look, and so firm an accent, that Mr. Greville did not think fit to make any reply; much less did I, you may be sure. But is this just, my dear Euphemia, to shew so much rancour?—Rancour did I say! no, that is too harsh a word. My uncle is incapable of harbouring any rancour in his breast; but so much dislike to one who never offended him—one whose amiable qualities—yes, I think that praise may be allowed to him from what we observed of his behaviour, even though Mr. Greville may have drawn his character with some exaggeration. But why should one suppose that Mr. Greville, whose penetration and sincerity nobody ever called in question, could either be mistaken in the character of his youth, or draw it in false colours? If then he is what he represents him to be, and what his behaviour to us gives us reason to think he is, I must say it is unreasonable, nay, it is unjust in my uncle to confound him with his unworthy parents, and make him answerable for their faults.

I expected to have had a letter from you by yesterday's post. How does it happen that I am disappointed? Does the Bellenden family engross you wholly? Have you not a few moments to spare to your friend? Let me not accuse you of neglect, my Euphemia; at this time it would affect me greatly.—I am low-spirited—I know not why, but I am really so; and yet have I not too much cause for low spirits—are we not to be separated, perhaps for ever? Mr. Greville quarrels with me for spending so many hours in the Park; its romantic scenes charm me—"solitude is the nurse of tender thought," the poet says;[1] and in the silence and gloom

---

1 A reference to a song in Hannah More's popular play, *The Search After Happiness: A Pastoral Drama for Young Ladies* (pub. 1773) known as "Sweet Solitude":

Sweet Solitude! Thou placid queen
Of Modest air, and brow serene!
This thou inspirest the sage's theme,
The poet's visionary dreams.

of these shades I undergo the melancholy reveries of divided friendship—divided, but never to be lessened.—Yes, my dear Euphemia, I think of you with more tenderness than ever; my fortitude has quite forsaken me, and my tears flow at the bare idea of our separation. How then shall I suppress the trial when it comes? But I must lay down my pen; Mr. Greville makes an entertainment tomorrow for some of the neighbouring families, who come to welcome us to this part of the country; and my maid tells me it is time to dress. The post carries you a large packet this time. Adieu.

MARIA HARLEY.

END OF THE FIRST VOLUME.

Parent of virtue, nurse of thought!
By thee were saints and patriarchs taught,
Wisdom from thee her treasures drew,
And in thy lap fair science grew.

Whate'er exalts, refines, and charms,
Invites to thought, to virtue warms;
Whate'er is perfect, fair, and food,
We owe to thee, sweet Solitude!

In these bless'd shades dost thou maintain
Thy peaceful, unmolested reign;
Let no disordered thoughts intrude
On thy repose, sweet Solitude!

With the charm of life shall last,
E'en when its rosy bloom is past,
And when slow pacing Time shall spread
Its silver blossoms o'er my head;

No more with this vain world perplex'd,
Thou shall prepare me for the next;
The springs of life shall gently cease,
And angels point the way to peace.

EUPHEMIA.
VOL. II

Letter XVII.
MISS HARLEY TO MRS. NEVILLE.

HERE am I escaped again to my beloved solitude, sitting under the shade of a spreading oak, well furnished with pens, ink, and paper, and a thick folio on my knee, which serves me for a table to write on. I have given orders to my maid not to find me till within half an hour of dinner, which will be sufficient time for me to dress; and all the hours, till then, I will devote to you, my dear Euphemia.

I have, for some days past, been taken up with returning visits to the neighbouring ladies; but these afford me no matter for observation, either of praise or censure, and consequently nothing for your entertainment. They are neither handsome nor ugly, witty nor foolish, awkward nor well-bred; they are in that class of mediocrity which leaves one nothing to say, but that they are good sort of people. However, there was another lady expected, who, I supposed, had some claim to distinction; for upon the mention of Lady Jackson, every one had something to say of her. "She was at church last Sunday," said one lady, "quite new dressed in her fourth mourning, that is, for the last quarter, you know, and looked mighty well."[1] "To be sure, she is a very *personable* woman," said another, "and has a fine presence: but any one would look well, dressed to such advantage as she is; I dare say, she had not less than twenty pounds value of gauzes, and blonds, and feathers about her." "Aye, she had plenty of white plumes on her head," said a third lady. "I suppose it is the

---

1 Lady Jackson has moved through "deep mourning," immediately after her husband's death, when she was required by social convention as a widow to wear unornamented black, usually for the period of a "year and a day," to "second," "third," and then "half mourning" when grey or purple ornamentation was permissible, and finally to what Lennox here calls "fourth mourning," which is the last step before she will be able to wear clothing of any color without restriction. Clearly, Lady Jackson is chomping at the bit to be free of a social convention whose meaning she seems not to feel very strongly, since she is wearing a dress of gauze (i.e., silk or linen), trimmed with blond lace (also made of silk), and plumes of feathers.

fashion in London to wear so many; for Lady Jackson would rather be dead than out of the fashion: and they say, indeed, she spends two-thirds of her income in clothes, though she is not young, and never was handsome; and to my thinking, that prodigious quantity of feathers she wears is frightful; for when she came into church, being a very tall woman, and walking through the crowd, she overtopped every body, and her white plumes, nodding as she moved, appeared like those carried before the hearse of some bachelor or maid in a funeral."[1]

Everyone laughed at this conceit; and Mr. Greville happening to sit near me, I asked him, in a low voice, "who is this Lady Jackson?" "She is the widow of a rich citizen,"[2] said he, "who was knighted in the last promotion of bob-wigs and laced waistcoats. The lady so little understands this honour, so envied by every alderman's wife in London that she thinks it equals her with a countess; and if she knew how, she would assume the dignified manners of quality, as well as their dress; but her breeding is coarse, and her opportunities for improvement few. One leading card in her character I cannot pass over; it is her insuperable vanity, which makes her imagine that every man who looks upon her is in love with her. No maiden can be secure of the constancy of her lover, no wife of the fidelity of her husband, if Lady Jackson comes in the way. This folly of hers is so apparent, that it draws a great deal of ridicule upon her from the men, who feed it with the grossest flattery, which she swallows as greedily as if—as Shakspeare says,

'Her appetite grew with what it fed on.'[3]

---

1 The white feathers attached to the heads of the horses that pulled the hearse of an unmarried man or woman signified the dead person's chastity. The company laugh at the irony of this analogy given that Lady Jackson is not a virgin, having been married, and given her amorous propensities.

2 Lady Jackson's husband was given a knighthood by the king, which entitled him to be called "Sir"; usually such honors were given for merit or for service, but Lennox implies here that this knighthood was parceled out with many others to men whose wealth alone—evident in their fashionable and costly waistcoats and wigs—garnered them the honor. As a widow, Lady Jackson had rights under the law that no married women did: she could make contracts, control her money, and sue.

3 From Shakespeare's *Hamlet* (1.2): She would hang on him/ As if her appetite *grew* by what it *fed on.*

But it is not only to the praise of beauty she aspires; she unites, if you believe her professions, every amiable quality in her mind, as well as every grace in her person. She is far gone in the refinements of friendship; she tastes, with the highest relish, the luxury of benevolence; while her insincerity incapacitates her for the one, and her selfishness for the other."

"It must be confessed," said I, "that you are going to introduce me to a very valuable acquaintance." "I could not avoid inviting her," replied he, "as she is upon a visit to a lady in the neighbourhood, who is my intimate friend; besides, I am fond of extraordinary characters. I have given you but the bare outlines of Lady Jackson's; the lady will finish the picture herself."

I was obliged, however, to wait some time longer for this satisfaction; and dinner was ready to be served, before Lady Jackson came; doubtless, this delay was an effect of the same policy, which makes our celebrated beauties enter the church and the play-house, when the service is half over in the former, and the second act of the comedy begun in the latter.

At length Lady Jackson was announced; she entered the room with a masculine step, and such an air of confidence in the superiority of her charms and dress, as at the first moment inspired me with disgust.

Mr. Greville, who knew that dinner only waited for her, led her immediately into the dining-hall, expressing his concern, by the way, that Mrs. Derwent did not accompany her. Lady Jackson told him, that Mrs. Derwent was so much indisposed, that she could not venture abroad, and that she had sat by her bed-side, in great uneasiness, all the morning. This was the first time I had heard her voice, which is loud and harsh; and so little did her countenance express the sensibility she would be thought to possess, that her mouth was screwed up into an affected simper, while her eyes were fixed upon the large glass that fronted the door by which she entered, and shewed her figure at full length. This sight had the force of magic, and seemed to have riveted her feet to the spot where she stood; when Mr. Greville, by a gentle violence, led her to her seat at the table, which was on my right hand. She soon entered into a particular conversation with me; admired the elegance of my undress;[1] asked who was my milliner,[2] and how much my lace

---

1 Referred in the eighteenth century to dress of a kind not ordinarily worn in public; informal.
2 Hat maker/seller.

cost a yard; and, in a decisive tone, assured me every thing I had on was perfectly fashionable.

After dinner, when we were got back to the drawing-room, being still seated near me, she renewed the discourse; and making a sudden transition from the trimming of gowns, to which she condescended to ask my opinion of, she talked of books; ran over the names of Milton, Shakespeare, Dryden, Pope:[1]—But her observations and criticisms were confined to exclamations of—excellent! divine! inimitable! which she uttered with great vehemence; while she entered more deeply into the merits of Mariveaux and Marmontel;[2] the characters of the former were so natural—the tales of the latter so charming—so interesting!—This flow of erudition was stopped by the attention the company seemed willing to give, to a lady who was relating to the person that sat next her, a melancholy accident which had happened to an acquaintance of her's—a gentleman who was killed by a fall from his horse, and brought home dead to his wife a few hours after he had left her in high health and spirits. The wretched wife was seised with convulsions at the sight, and died the next day.

Lady Jackson, being a widow herself, it was her part to be more affected than any one else with this sad story: she sighed aloud. My uncle observed, that such instances of conjugal affection were very rare.

"Very rare indeed," said Mr. Greville; "for one such afflicted widow, we shall see a hundred, who, as Pope, one of your admired authors, Madam," said he addressing himself to Lady Jackson, "has it,

---

1 John Milton (1608-74), poet and essayist, author of the epic, *Paradise Lost*; William Shakespeare (1564-1616), actor, dramatist, poet; John Dryden (1631-1700), critic, political and occasional poet, dramatist, poet laureate; and Alexander Pope (1688-1744), poet, translator, and satirist were English authors whose works were well respected during the eighteenth century.

2 Pierre Carlet de Chamberlain de Marivaux (1688-1763) and Jean François Marmontel (1723-99) were both French novelists, dramatists, and prose writers. Lady Jackson's interest in these authors, and relative disinterest in and ignorance of the English authors listed above—all of whom were dead and whose literary reputations were solid by the mid-eighteenth century—may be a result of Marivaux's sympathetic treatment of women in society in his works, or the more fashionable nature of French literature and fashions among English society men and women; but it is also a mark against her since, especially in the latter half of the century, England was distrustful of all things foreign, and especially French.

'Bear about the mockery of woe
To midnight dances, and the public shew.'[1]

"Oh, dear Sir," said Lady Jackson, "you are very severe."

"Not at all, Madam," said he, "for although my censures are general, I admit of some exceptions. But, to speak the truth, there is no virtue now so common as fortitude, nor any thing so superfluous as the custom of comforting. All the poisons of Thessaly[2] might safely be trusted in the hands of the mourners of our time."

"I hope, Sir," said Lady Jackson, "you include the male mourners in this observation."

"Certainly, Madam," said Mr. Greville, "there are men, I believe, who would be glad to outlive, not only their friends and relations, but even the age they live in, and their very country; and rather than die, would willingly stay in the world alone."

"I am sure there is no woman of that mind," said Lady Jackson.

"For a very good reason, Madam," said Mr. Greville; "there would be nobody to admire her."

"You are a perfect cynic," replied the Lady, gravely; and rising, walked up to a window, from which there was a prospect of a very fine flowering garden, which she commended greatly. Mr. Greville assured her, it was part of his business every morning to dress that garden. "For," added he, "I am a great admirer of beauty, wherever I meet it: but because it is a dangerous thing in women's faces, I had rather contemplate it in these flowers."

Lady Jackson, who has, it seems, a very happy facility in appropriating these sort of speeches to herself, immediately changed her manner; she became lively, witty, good-humoured; but her vivacity shewed itself in boisterous laughs at a jest of her own finding out; her wit, in scraps of poetry quoted at random; and her good humour, in familiar nods, smiles, indelicate praise, and taps on the shoulder, rather heavy indeed, for the hand that gave them was robust, and the manner truly masculine.

Mr. Greville kept up the scene so long, that the lady departed in full persuasion that she had made a conquest; and this notion of her's afforded my uncle some diversion; but I was concerned that her folly had been soothed so agreeably; for if happiness be

---

1   From Pope's "Elegy to the Memory of an Unfortunate Lady," lines 58-59.
2   In ancient times, Thessaly, in northeastern Greece, was thought to be the richest source of poisonous plants in the classical world.

but opinion, Mr. Greville had made her happy; and what was this but to reward and continue folly?

I was malicious enough to wish she had been a secret witness of the ridicule cast upon her by the very man whom she imagined was beginning to feel the influence of her charms. But enough, and indeed too much of this lady; if it were not that she has earnestly requested me to make her the bearer of a letter to you, whose character she professes to be an idolater of. She says she has some relations in New York, who by their station and connections may be of use to Mr. Neville; and this being confirmed to me by Mr. Greville, she will have the happiness to present this letter to you. Oh! envied happiness! Could she taste it—but that is impossible, for minds like your's and her's can never mix. Adieu! my dear Euphemia!

Letter XVIII.
MISS HARLEY TO MRS. NEVILLE.

MY DEAR EUPHEMIA,

BY this time you have received my last letter, which Lady Jackson, transported with the opportunity it gave her of being acquainted with you, promised to deliver to you herself. I am impatient till you give me an account of your interview; I am sure you will be diverted with her peculiarities; for you only smile at follies which make me peevish.

I have been surprised with a letter from Mr. Harley; a country fellow gave it to my maid. She asked if it required an answer; he said he had no orders about that, but he would wait.

It should seem that he had chosen his time well; for Mr. Greville and my uncle had rode out to take the air, about a quarter of an hour before he came.

TO MISS HARLEY.

"MADAM,

"LOW as my fortunes are, I never till now laboured under the weight of my pecuniary obligations. But can any thing be humiliating that comes from you? Oh! why was this soft attention to my situation shewn me at a time when my reason was still free enough to combat those sentiments which the first sight of you inspired. Sentiments, which the implacability of your uncle, and a just sense of my own unworthiness, convinced me I ought to suppress—I ought, it is true, but I never can suppress them: and all I dare to hope for from your goodness is, that you will pardon the boldness of this confession, and pity the misfortune of him that makes it. I am, and ever will be, Madam,

Your devoted servant,
EDWARD HARLEY."

Well, my dear Euphemia, what do you think of this letter? Is there not something extremely affecting in the manner in which this young man speaks of his situation? He is humble without meanness, and dignifies poverty by the nobleness of his sentiments. Dearly as I love my uncle, grateful as my heart is for his generosity to me, I must blame him a little for the implacability of his temper (as Mr. Harley calls it), which hinders him from distinguishing between the guilty and the innocent, and makes him suffer the heir of his honour and fortunes to languish in indigence and obscurity.

You will readily allow that I was under the necessity of answering the letter, which I certainly should not have done had it contained only a declaration of love: but it was just to set him right with regard to the pecuniary obligation, as he considers it. Here then is what I wrote.

TO MR. HARLEY.

"SIR,

"IT was by my uncle's command that I enclosed to you the note which your grateful disposition seems to lay too great a stress upon. Both my uncle and myself were under the highest obligations to you, who hazarded your own life to prevent our suffering a slight inconvenience. It is but just that you should know this was the sense he had of your generous behaviour; and the accident that befell you, in consequence of it, being likely to produce some inconveniences to you, who was far from home, and unattended—this was the cause of the liberty he took in offering you some assistance. I am apprehensive, from the turn of your letter, that you will reject what you consider as an obligation, when you know it came from him. This is what I sincerely wish to prevent, for it will be a means of increasing and continuing that ill-will which has unhappily taken place between your families. As in the circumstances we both are, I can neither receive nor answer any more letters, without hazarding my uncle's displeasure. I take this opportunity to assure you that I am, with all the esteem that is due to you, Sir,

Your very humble servant,
MARIA HARLEY."

Tell me, my dear Euphemia, have I done right in answering his letter thus, or indeed in answering it at all? I shall not be easy till I have your approbation, which is so respected and revered by me, that I should prefer it to reason itself, if they were two things that could be separated, and one of them left to my choice. Adieu.

MARIA HARLEY.

Letter XIX.
MRS. NEVILLE TO MISS HARLEY.

I AM just returned from Lord S.'s seat, where I have spent a week. It was a farewell visit; and, like all other farewell visits, was begun in pleasure and ended in tears. The very day after my return, your Lady Jackson called upon me, introducing herself with a letter from you. I could not open it with any propriety, as I heard from her that you were in health, so I missed the advantage of knowing her character without the help of my own observations; but, to say the truth, there is no need of any great acuteness to make one's self mistress of the subject; for the features of her mind are as strongly marked as those of her face; and, like a book printed in a large letter, the weakest eyes may read her.

With a familiarity, which she borrowed from the notion of her superior rank, she invited herself to tea with me; and in less than half an hour professed, and claimed in return, an ardent and inviolable friendship. Having thus laid the foundations of an entire confidence, she entertained me with the history of her life, in which, like all other romances, love made the principal part—she is a perfect homicide. There was no end to the murders of her eyes; then, for conjugal affection, none ever equalled her. Those widows, whose tears antiquity hath hallowed, were but the shadows of her substantial grief. She left me at length, after a strict embrace, to the pleasure your letters always afford me. Your former large packet found me at Lord S.'s; it is full of adventure, my dear Maria. The unexpected meeting between your uncle and Mr. Harley has had consequences that will certainly produce some interesting events. The merit of the young man, and the natural good disposition of Sir John, prepare a scene, in which you will perhaps have a part. How greatly am I obliged to you for giving me, in your charming journal, so large a share of your conversation. The scene will soon change with me, and then my narratives may become interesting, for at present my days run on in one dull tenor, and afford nothing to engage your attention.

I have another letter from you this moment—things have fallen out just as I expected.—Mr. Harley is your conquest. Well, there is nothing surprising in that, *he has a heart, and you have conquering eyes.* You compliment too highly when you lay so great a stress upon my advice and approbation. You have no need of any precepts, nor indeed of any instruction; you cannot wander from the right if you go not astray from your own inclination, nor do amiss, if you borrow not a frailty which is none of your own. Your letter seems dictated by prudence itself. I wish, indeed, there had been no concealment in the case; but I see not how you could have shewn Mr. Harley's letter to your uncle: there is one severe expression in it, which would doubtless have given him great offence, and would, perhaps, have clouded for ever those dawnings of good-will, which broke out, in spite of himself, in consequence of his engaging behaviour.

We are to dine to-morrow on board the man of war[1] which is to carry the colonel and his family, of which we are considered as a part, to New York. I know the mention of this circumstance will raise some tumults in your breast; but you must accustom yourself, my dear Maria, to bear these preludes to our parting, that the parting itself may not fall so heavy upon you.

Mrs. Benson has settled all her affairs; and having no relations but such as are much richer than herself, she has sunk part of her little fortune in an annuity for her life, and the remainder she has bequeathed to me. Her good sense and obliging manners endear her to every one that knows her. I am most happy in this consideration, that having lost my mother, and upon the point of being separated from you, I have the comfort to enjoy such a companion—such a monitor and friend.

I am to spend this evening with Lady Jackson, in consequence of so pressing an invitation, that I know not how to refuse. It shall

---

1 A navy warship.

not be my fault if our intercourse of visits do not end here. She would be my friend, that is, according to her notion of the thing— a companion in my amusements—one who returns my visits most punctually, never fails to send daily enquiries after my health if I am the least indisposed, and a most strict observer of all the civil duties of life. But by a friend, I mean a witness of conscience, a physician of secret griefs, a moderator in prosperity, and a guide in adversity. How little are such as she qualified to act that part? But you tell me she styles herself an idolater of my character. A good opinion, it has been said, lays one under an obligation, let it come from whom it will; but it is only truly valuable when it proceeds from the wise, the candid, and the virtuous.

AT NIGHT.

I cannot close my letter without giving you an account of a most extravagantly kind proposal Lady Jackson made me.—I was obliged to stay till the rest of her company were gone, two of whom, she said, were her intimate friends, married ladies, whose husbands she gave me to understand were, to her great grief, so much in love with her, that she lived in continual apprehension, lest their unfortunate passions should be discovered by their wives, whose peace of mind such a discovery would entirely destroy.

As she seemed impatient for my opinion and advice upon this very hard case, I told her gravely, that I had no advice to offer her but to keep the secret carefully herself, in order to prevent, as far as lay in her power, the bad consequences she apprehended. She then suddenly changed the discourse, loaded me with a thousand professions of friendship, and called it a misfortune to have known me, since she was to lose me so soon; execrated my husband's uncle for driving him, by his unjust parsimony, to the necessity of going abroad.

"But I have thought of a way," said she, "to prevent that necessity, if you will do me the honour to accept my offer. I have some money unemployed; I will lay it out in the purchase of a small estate in any county in England that will be most agreeable to you. It shall be yours for ever, if you will; yours at least as long as you may want it. Tell me you will accept my offer—tell me so, and make me happy."

My first emotions on this speech were all gratitude and surprise at the uncommon generosity it displayed: but her looks and manners bore so little affinity with her words, that a moment afterwards I could scarce persuade myself she was in earnest: for, while she was pouring out these effusions of friendship and benevolence, she had her eyes often turned towards the glass, with a complacency that shewed how much her thoughts were taken up with the object it represented. And, in the midst of her earnest entreaties that I would accept her offer, her hands were often employed in setting the flounces of her petticoat, adjusting her tucker,[1] or pinning up a curl. These observations cooled the first warmth of my gratitude: I expressed my acknowledgments, however, for the generosity of her offer in civil terms, assuring her I should never forget it, but that I had some very powerful reasons for declining it. She would know my reasons.—I told her my husband was obliged in honour to fulfil his engagements; and that, however painful it might be to me to leave my friends and my country, I hoped I should always be able to sacrifice my inclination to his duty and reputation. That I had received from a dear and valuable friend, with whom I had been connected from my earliest youth, offers of the same generous nature with her's, and which, on the same account, I had been obliged to refuse.

She seemed satisfied with my excuse; but lamented, in very passionate terms, her misfortune in being hopeless to prevail upon me. We parted, with great cordiality on her side, and much civility on mine.

When I related what had passed in this visit to my husband and Mrs. Benson, they diverted themselves extremely with my credulity, which they thought much greater than it was; for I did not endeavour to undeceive them, being really in some doubt whether I should wrong her by suspecting her sincerity. I shall be able, when I write next, to tell when our voyage is determined upon. Adieu! My dear Maria.

Letter XX.
MRS. NEVILLE TO MISS HARLEY.

WELL, my dear friend, I have six weeks good yet. This news was like a reprieve to one under a painful sentence, for I reckoned upon no more than a fortnight at farthest. May I not hope then to have one week of your dear society granted by your uncle? Do, my Maria, make the request now, while Sir John is with his friend; your absence will be more easily supported by him. Tell

---

1 A flounce is a wide piece of ornamental material that is gathered and sewn by the upper edge, around a woman's skirt, so that the lower edge is full; a tucker is a bib or neckcloth.

him I entreat this favour, and I will number it among the many instances I have received of his goodness, which will live in my memory for ever.

Never having been on board a ship in my life, you will easily conceive, my dear Maria, how much I was affected with a sight so new and strange as that of the — man of war, where I dined yesterday, in company with Colonel Bellenden, his lady, and eldest daughter. It was a beautiful, but to me terrific, object, when I considered, that in such a frail building I was to traverse an immense ocean; every thing I saw produced astonishment, and excited my curiosity, so that I asked a thousand foolish questions, which were, however, answered with great civility by the gentlemen about us, by whom we were conducted round this little world, and shewn every thing worthy our observation.

The commander is a young man, very genteel in his person and dress; his manners are polite, soft, and insinuating; but in my opinion he has too much of the courtier, and too little of the chief. He suffered greatly in the comparison with Colonel Bellenden, who in his person and manners unites dignity with sweetness, the martial air of a soldier with the elegance of the gentleman, the noble frankness of his profession with the politeness of a man of quality.

The captain presented his principal officers to Colonel Bellenden and the ladies. Miss Bellenden had reason to be pleased with the effect of her charms; every eye was riveted upon her; every tongue seemed ready to pronounce her beautiful. I wish I could say she received this involuntary homage with greater propriety; she even seemed to claim more than was paid her; a conscious simper, an affected toss of her head, a careless air, and a wandering eye, that seemed searching for new victims to gratify her pride of conquest, proclaimed the temper of her mind.

The handsome, it has been said with great truth, can never be seen without respect, and their youth hath not more days than their beauty hath triumphs—they conquer as often as they appear; but the mischief of it is, that their triumphs are short, their youth is not lasting, and the handsome at last grow ugly. Queens and princesses, said your Mr. Neville once in my hearing, grow old; and there is no ancient beauty but that of the sun and the stars. What a pity it is then, that the generality of our sex neglect to acquire, in youth, those qualities which may preserve them from contempt when they are old, and secure esteem when they can no longer excite admiration.

I suspected that my husband and Mrs. Benson, by their whispering and significant smiles at each other whenever I mentioned

Lady Jackson, and her uncommonly generous offers, had some mischief in their heads; and to-day it came out. I had passed the whole morning in the city, making some purchases for our approaching voyage; during which Lady Jackson paid me a visit. Mrs. Benson received her in my absence, and listened for a whole hour to her extravagant professions of friendship for me, and repinings at my cruel reserve, which would not permit her to be of some use to me. Mrs. Benson excused me upon that delicacy which made persons born in affluence, and accustomed to bestow, not to receive favours, shy of laying themselves under great and unreturnable obligations. This called forth an ostentatious display of the most liberal sentiments from Lady Jackson, delivered with an impetuosity of voice and action peculiar to herself. Again she regretted her misfortune in not being permitted to shew the ardour of her affection for me by some substantial proofs.

Mrs. Benson seemed moved with the enthusiasm of her friendship; and after a little pause said—"It is a pity such generous warmth should fail of its purpose; I have thought of a way by which you may gratify your earnest desire of serving Mrs. Neville, without wounding her delicacy."

"Pray name it," said Lady Jackson, with a look and accent in which much of her former fervour was abated.

"Why, Madam," said Mrs. Benson, "you must certainly have heard of the fatal wreck of my friend's once shining fortunes; and that all those possessions, to which she was born the heiress, fell by her father's imprudence into the hands of his creditors. In a day or two she is likely to suffer a very sensible mortification by the sale of a very fine collection of pictures, which her father, in a tour through Italy, purchased at an immense expence. Some of these pictures were so highly valued by her mother, whose memory she almost adores, that I am persuaded you could not do her a more acceptable service than to prevent them from going into other hands, by purchasing them for her. If you please I will attend you to the auction-room, and point out to you those particular pictures which she so ardently wished to be possessed of; so that when the sale takes place you may have them."

"You are very obliging," said Lady Jackson, with a confused accent, and a freezing look—"I shall not fail to give you notice when I am more at leisure than at present, being really very particularly engaged." She then rose up, and took her leave, leaving kind compliments for me.

When I came home, I found Mr. Neville, and Mrs. Benson enjoying their triumph over my credulity; and Mr. Neville, after his usual manner, dictating to me upon the choice of my friends, and affirming, that he only was the proper judge of what persons I ought to admit into my friendship and confidence. I pleaded hard for an exemption with regard to my female acquaintance; but he insisted that we were no better judges of one another than we are of the men; and that a wife has nothing to do but to leave the choice to her husband's discernment. You may be sure I did not yield this point without a little contest; but in regard to Mr. Neville, I have often experienced the truth of that observation, that with some persons it is not safe to be reasonable. Whenever it happens that my arguments press home upon him, he has recourse to an expedient that never fails to silence me,—he falls into a passion—I say not a word more—happy if silence will shelter me; but that is seldom the case, for he pursues me even to this last retreat, and nothing will serve him but my confession that he has convinced me I am in the wrong. For the sake of peace I submit to this; and presently afterwards, in some new instance, this confession is turned against me, with "Why will you pretend to debate this matter with me? You know you are generally wrong—nay, you acknowledge it too. Why will you depend upon your own judgment, which you are so often obliged to own always misleads you?" However, as we both agree in our high opinion of you, my Maria, I may, without fear of rebuke, subscribe myself ever your faithful and affectionate

EUPHEMIA NEVILLE.

P.S. I have just learned that Lady Jackson is gone out of town for a week, by which time she knew the sale of the pictures would be over. Is not this a strange woman? I was vexed this trial was made: a very little reflection might have served to convince me, that she meant nothing by all those high-sounding professions and offers.—Truth is simple and modest; and when she cannot shew herself by real effects, will scorn to do it in words.

You will be pleased to hear that Lord S. has actually promised to purchase those pictures for me which my mother most valued. My husband and Mrs. Benson knew this, when they thought fit to make this trial of the lady's sincerity, otherwise I should have thought it an unpardonable meanness.

If I am to be indulged with a visit from you, give me speedy notice of it, that I may enjoy the blessing by anticipation.

E.N.

Letter XXI.
MISS HARLEY TO MRS. NEVILLE.

YES, my dear Euphemia, our wishes are granted; I am permitted to stay a week with you. My uncle did not wait to be requested; he kindly proposed this little excursion to me as soon as he knew that the time was fixed for your leaving England. Oh! that thought! but I will not distress you by my useless grief.

I have had an interview with Mr. Harley. You are surprised;— you blame me, perhaps; but hear how it happened, and you will acquit me I hope, of imprudence, since it was really out of my power to prevent it.

I had wandered into that delightful wood, where, since my abode at this seat, I have passed so many hours in sweet, yet painful recollection. I was employed in reading some of your letters, when the sound of steps at a distance made me turn to see who was coming. Guess my surprise when I saw it was Mr. Harley. I stopped, uncertain what to do, or how to take this unexpected intrusion. He advanced with a slow and timid pace, his hat under his arm, his eyes cast on the ground, as if he was fearful to meet my quick-enquiring glance. I remained immoveable; he approached me, bowing respectfully.

"Do not be surprised, Miss Harley," said he; "do not be offended, that being soon to absent myself from you, perhaps for ever, I have ventured to break in upon your solitude; I could not depart without the satisfaction of breathing at your feet those vows my heart made at the first moment I beheld you." And he actually, my dear, threw himself at my feet with the air of an Orondates.[1]

The place, his posture, his language, had all so romantic an air, that I could not help smiling as I desired him to rise. He did rise, but with a disconcerted look, while a deep blush overspread his cheeks.

I perceived the fault I had been guilty of, and was angry with myself for having wounded a sensibility so affecting. The alteration in my looks and manner relieved his confusion.

---

1 Also Oroondates or Oroondate. Hero of the ten-volume romance, *Cassandre* (1642-45, trans. 1652 as *Cassandra*) by Gautier de Costes La Calprènade, a French novelist and dramatist. Oroondate, Prince of Scythia, vied with Alexander the Great for the love of Statira, daughter of the defeated Persian king, Darius and eventually wins her.

"May I hope," said he, "that you will pardon my presumption in coming to find you here?"

"The presumption of this visit, Sir," said I, "may be easily pardoned; but the imprudence of it, I am afraid, all things considered, cannot be justified. Have you not called my uncle implacable? And indeed to you, perhaps, he appears so."

"And is he not so, Madam," replied he, "to my family? I am sorry to arraign the conduct of a person who has had judgment enough to do justice to your merit; but can his long continued enmity to my father, the friend and companion of his youth, his nearest kinsman, be excused?"

"Not unless he had received some great injury," replied I.

"From my father, Madam," interrupted he, "impossible! my father is not capable of injuring any one, much less his friend, his relation, and, as I have heard, his benefactor."

I cast down my eyes, and was silent; the noble warmth, the filial tenderness, that appeared in his words, his accent, and his looks affected me. I tried to dissipate a starting tear; it would not do, and I applied my handkerchief to my eyes—he looked eagerly at me—

"What can this mean?" said he. "You seem greatly moved, Madam; do you know the cause of this long continued hatred on the part of Sir John? For as for my father, he appears to have no resentment against him; he speaks of him with respect, nay kindness. What can he have done to offend him so highly?"

"Nothing," replied I, "unless you will allow it was an offence to supplant him in his love for a most amiable object."

"Nothing!" exclaimed he eagerly, "do you call that nothing which was to stab him to the heart?—It was worse,—it was to make him live wretched. But was it his fault that he was the successful lover? Yet that word *supplant*, implies some baseness in his conduct. Baseness! My father act basely! that cannot be. I conjure you, Madam, speak plainly. I perceive you are well acquainted with the particulars of this affair—I wish to know them; what has escaped you has given me great uneasiness: pray inform me further."

"If what I have said," replied I, "has given you uneasiness, why should I increase it by complying with your request? I must beg to be excused from saying any more."

"I see how it is," said he; "my father will suffer by this explanation—I must not expect it from your delicacy—every way I am unhappy."—He sighed deeply, and was silent for a moment,—then added:

"Well, Madam, every thing concurs to shew me the imprudence, the hopelessness of that passion I have dared to entertain.—I came to take my leave; but do not imagine that I expect my cure from absence—perhaps I do not wish it."

"Pray no more of this," said I confused, as you may well imagine at this conversation—"but tell me where you are going?"

"I am going to seek my fortune in the Indies," said he, "for I lie here a dead weight upon my father, who finds it difficult enough to bring up a large family of girls upon his slender income."

"To the Indies!" interrupted I; "pray in what capacity? Are you to be dignified with a commission, and the title of captain or colonel in the Company's troops; or are you to be a trader yourself?"—"I have no talents for either," said he smiling.—He was going on, when I heard my uncle's voice calling me at a distance.

"I would not have you seen here," said I, "on any account; pray retire. If you are resolved to go to the Indies, make Mr. Greville acquainted with your design; he is your friend, and will be glad of an opportunity of serving you."

I pointed out to him the path he was to take, in order to avoid meeting my uncle; and curtseying, turned from him. He followed me two or three steps, and taking my hand respectfully, raised it to his lips; I felt it wet with a falling tear. He darted like lightning from me, and in an instant was out of sight.

I met my uncle a moment afterwards; he said he had been looking for me; and pointing to Mr. Greville, who was following him—"Our host," said he, "is come to take leave of you; he has received news which obliges him to set out for the North immediately." Mr. Greville accordingly joined us, and we walked with him to the gate, where his post-chaise waited.

I was very much concerned at his departure, on Mr. Harley's account, to whom I know he wishes well. I was not without hope that his representations of the young gentleman's case might have made some impression upon my uncle, and induced him to prevent the heir of his title and fortune from seeking a subsistence in so distant a part of the globe, for my uncle is naturally good; but the best virtues have need of some standard to guide them.

We are to return to the Hall to-morrow, and the next day I am to set out for London. Oh! this meeting, what joy would it afford me, were it not so soon to be followed by a long, long absence! How can I support the thought? There is no friendship in the world of so much use to me as yours: it is my defence in all my contests—it is my consolation in all my distresses: but what is still more, it is my oracle in all my doubts. That which, before I have your advice, I propose to myself with diffidence, when once I have your approbation I make it a maxim. Adieu! my dearest friend. On Wednesday I shall have the happiness to embrace you.

MARIA HARLEY.

Letter XXII.
MISS HARLEY TO MRS. NEVILLE.

IT is done, I have taken a long, long leave of you, perhaps for ever, for my heart sinks within me, and tells me I shall not live to hail your return; do not chide me, my dear, my valuable friend, pardon the weakness of a vulgar mind, which feels no crosses lightly, and falls flat to the earth at the very first stroke of adverse fortune; perhaps in prosperity I should behave better, and I do not think that happiness would make me insolent, but in affliction I am less than nothing; and that which would not leave a scratch upon the skin of a stoick,[1] pierces me to the heart; if light evils wound me so deeply, what think you I must suffer from this great, this remediless calamity?—a separation from you. I have laid upon my wound all the balm that my small share of philosophy can administer; but methinks my grief is to me in the place of my friend. I possess it with a kind of sweetness, and I am so fond of it, that I should think it a second loss if I had it not to pass my time with.

My uncle, in his reception of me at my return, seemed to accommodate his looks and behaviour to mine; for my grief, I confess, made me silent, unsociable, and incapable of any conversation but with my own sad thoughts: however, when I reflected upon the respect and affection I owed my generous uncle, I resolved to put a constraint upon myself, and meet him at breakfast next morning with cheerfulness in my looks and language.

Alas! my dear Euphemia, I was mistaken in the cause of my uncle's reserve—he is offended with me; I have lost his esteem; doubtless he thinks me unworthy of the benefits he has bestowed upon me. How then can I enjoy them with any satisfaction? He has heard of my interview with Mr. Harley—he thinks me

---

1 I.e., stoic. The Stoic philosophy of Ancient Greece emphasized patient fortitude in the face of great distress.

ungrateful, designing, false—his cold looks, his altered behaviour, the hints he sometimes throws out, stab me to the very heart!—Oh! what needed this new affliction to one already overwhelmed with distress? Why did I not make him acquainted with all that has passed between Mr. Harley and me? I know you disapprove my conduct upon this occasion; but I had not you to advise with at the time. I remember, in speaking of this affair, you told me that concealment always implies something wrong: it is true, and appearances are against me; to be thought ungrateful, capable of taking advantage of that independence which his goodness bestowed on me, and contrary to his will—I cannot bear it; I will be justified in his opinion, and become once more dependant on his bounty.

But this dear, this affectionate, this more than father, shuns me; and having already condemned me in his thoughts, is unwilling to hear my defence; before the servants, and in company, his behaviour, though less tender, is still polite; but when we are left alone, he is silent, reserved, and even stern: and either retires to his own apartment, or orders the carriage to take an airing, without asking me to accompany him.

He is this moment returned from one of these little excursions; I will go to him; he is alone in his library; either he must acquit me of any design to offend him, which Heaven knows is the truth, or take back those gifts which, by making me independent of him, have exposed me to his suspicions. Oh! that you were here to advise, to direct me! I think I know how you would act on such an occasion; I will endeavour to imitate you; you are all openness, candour, and sincerity—so innocence should be; and I am sure I have no willful offence, with regard to my uncle, to charge myself with. Well, I will go, I will speak to him; I will act this humiliating part; for surely nothing can be more so than, conscious of innocence, to have a character to defend—but I will delay no longer—I go.

This dreaded interview is over. I found my uncle in his library; he was reading; he looked up on my entrance. I asked if he was busy; my countenance, and the tone of my voice, which partook, I suppose, of the perturbation of my heart, affected him I believe, for he answered with his usual sweetness; "not if you have any thing to say to me"; and rising, drew a chair for me opposite to his.

"Till I can remove the prejudices you have entertained against me, I am," said I, "unworthy to sit in your presence, and far, far, unworthy of that affluence your lavish gifts have raised me to;

resume those gifts, I beseech you, Sir; suffer me to return to my former dependence on your bounty, and let my behaviour be the measure of your future generosity to me."

"You are strangely moved," said my uncle, looking earnestly on me; "what do you complain of, Maria?" "I do not presume to complain, Sir," replied I, "but I lament the loss of your favour, which is but too apparent from your altered behaviour to me."

"Are you conscious," said he, "of having done any thing to give me cause of complaint against you?"

"I am, Sir," answered I!

"That is honest," said he, "well, since you have got so far in your confession, pray go on, and let me have the whole."

He spoke this with a half smile, which gave me courage to proceed.

"The fault I have to confess, Sir," said I, "is my having received a letter from Mr. Harley, and answering it, without communicating either his letter, or my answer to you. I have also seen him; and this circumstance, likewise, I have concealed from you."

"And was this right?" said my uncle, a little sternly.

"My intention was not wrong, Sir," replied I. "The principles of good actions," interrupted my uncle, "are good inclinations; if you meant well, how did it happen that you have acted ill?"

"You will be a judge, Sir," said I, "how far I have acted ill on this occasion, if you will condescend to read the papers I have in my hands; here is Mr. Harley's letter to me, and a copy of my answer to it."

"Give them to me," said my uncle, with some precipitation.

I did so; he walked to the window, and I could perceive that he read both the letters twice over with great attention. He did not return them to me, but threw them both upon the table, and resuming his seat—

"So the son of my greatest enemy," said he peevishly, "has made you a declaration of love? You whom I have considered as my daughter, and for whom I have the affection of a father."

"My dear uncle," said I, "my more than father, Heaven is my witness I would rather die than offend you!" I could not utter these words without tears. He looked at me, I thought, kindly. "You have read my answer to Mr. Harley's letter, Sir?" pursued I; "is there any thing in it which offends you?"

"Why, I cannot say," said he, "that your letter is much amiss, considering that you certainly were not displeased with his declaration."

"Does that appear, Sir?" said I. "I think it does," replied he.

Now, my dear Euphemia, this surprised me: you have read this letter, do you think it will bear that inference? I am sure I did not intend it should; I was vexed,—I was confused; I could not bear my uncle's looks, which were fixed upon me. I cast down my eyes, and was silent.

He seemed to wait for some reply; but finding I said nothing—

"Taking it for granted," said he, "what you have as good as confessed, that the addresses of my enemy's son are far from being unwelcome to you, and that your heart is very, very favourably disposed towards him—"

I rose up precipitately.

"Oh! Sir," said I, "I have not deserved this!" my tears flowed fast, I covered my face with my handkerchief, and curtseying without looking at him, I was hastening out of the room.

My uncle rose up also, and getting between me and the door, took my hand, and led me back to my chair; he removed my handkerchief from my eyes; and still holding my hand—

"Nay, you must hear what I have more to say," said he, and smiling, repeated, "taking it for granted that your heart is very favourably disposed towards this young man, who is the son of my mortal enemy, and who has himself offended me, by presuming to declare a passion for you, and endeavouring to engage you in a clandestine correspondence with him; you whom I love, whom I have considered as my daughter, and from whom I might expect some returns of affection, and even duty: have I not reason to complain of you, Maria, for encouraging pretensions which you knew I could never approve?"

I ventured to interrupt him here.

"Does it appear, Sir, by my answer to his letter, that I have encouraged his pretensions?" said I.

"It does not appear by your letter," said he, "that you have *discouraged* them.

'He comes too near who comes to be denied,'[1]

said a poet very skilful in these matters; and one denial, it seems, will not serve his turn, else why is he continually hovering about my house, in hopes of some opportunity of speaking to you?"

Now this circumstance, my dear Euphemia, I was till then quite ignorant of—I blushed—my uncle observed it. "I do not

---

1 "He comes too near that comes to be denied"—from "The Lady's Resolve," by Lady Mary Wortley Montagu (1713).

wish to distress you, Maria," said he, "I pretend not to control your inclinations—you are your own mistress; I suspected that you had acted disingenuously with me; and it was this notion which produced the coldness you complain of. I have been too hasty in my conclusions, I believe; I do not perceive that you are much to blame in this business; but I shall always think it a misfortune, that the person nearest and dearest to me in the world, should form connections with those I have most reason to hate."

At that moment Mr. Greville was announced—I rose up, and being unwilling to be seen in the disorder I then was, I hurried out of the room, saying only these few words to him—

"Depend upon it, Sir, you shall be satisfied with me; I would not displease you for the world."

I have often observed, my dear Euphemia, that most persons consider less the reasons of what is proposed to them contrary to their inclinations, than the motives which may have obliged the person who proposes them to make use of those reasons; had I attended only to my uncle's motives for the disapprobation he expressed of Mr. Harley's addresses to me, I might have thought them rather unjustifiable; but the reasons he brought to influence my conduct were unanswerable. As my parent, my friend, my benefactor, he had a right to my obedience; which, by having so nobly made me independent of his control, is an effect of my will, not of constraint: and I could not disoblige him, without being guilty of the highest ingratitude.

I hesitated not a moment in resolving to put an end to Mr. Harley's hopes, if he entertained any; and to forbid him absolutely from seeking opportunities to write or speak to me any more. My first intention was to write to him; but I found I could not please myself in the terms I was to use: these appeared too harsh, those not decisive enough. I tore my letter, and concluded that my best way was to engage Mr. Greville to acquaint him with my intentions, and to prevail upon him to desist from his pursuits.

This seemed so happy a thought, that I became composed enough to take my place at table, without shewing, in my countenance and behaviour, any traces of the disorder I had been in so lately.

I perceived that my uncle observed me heedfully, and seemed pleased. I found an opportunity to have a quarter of an hour's private conversation with Mr. Greville, to whom I related, not without some confusion, all that had passed in regard to Mr. Harley; and as I knew he often saw him, begged he would prevent my having any further disquiet upon his account.

Mr. Greville promised to execute my commission, for he acknowledged that I had no other part to act. The next news I shall hear perhaps is, that the poor youth is gone to the Indies. Well, what of that? You are going to America; can I think of that dreadful circumstance, and suffer any meaner regrets to mix with so just, so poignant an affliction? Adieu!

MARIA HARLEY.

Letter XXIII.
MISS HARLEY, IN CONTINUATION.

MR. Greville, it seems, soon met with an opportunity of delivering my message, which he charged himself with two days ago, and is this morning returned to give me an account of his commission; he appeared affected with the gentle sorrow, for so he phrased it, with which Mr. Harley received my absolute rejection of him; it never rose to complaint, said he, much less to murmurings against your commands; silent dejection, and some half-suppressed sighs, and a promise faintly pronounced—that he would obey you, were all his answer.

Mr. Greville really seemed moved himself, when he repeated this: so you see it is not so very difficult to make philosophy feel compassion sometimes. "I hope Sir John will now be satisfied with me," said I, without taking notice of his pathetic description.

"If you had a little more sensibility," replied he, "I should say you have shewn great heroism on this occasion; but as it is, I can only compliment you upon your prudence and good sense."

"I do not think I have done any more than my duty," said I, "which my uncle pointed out to me; and when once one is assured of the skill of one's guide, it is afterwards a pleasure to be led."

"I am not sure," replied Mr. Greville, gravely, "that my good friend is quite right in all this; the limits that part justice from wrong, are not so well marked out, but that we may pass them before we are aware. Mr. Harley is not answerable for his father's faults, and he has virtues that render him not unworthy even of you,—and that is saying a great deal."

I will dispatch this letter to the post immediately; my uncle keeps his chamber with a slight indisposition. I shall be employed in sending to him all day. My dear Euphemia, I expect a letter from you every moment, and would you think it, I tremble at the very thoughts of receiving one, lest it should fix the day of your departure. Oh! my friend, my fortitude grows less every day; I feel it does,—how shall I bear the loss of you? But I will not wound you with my vain regrets. Adieu!

Letter XXIV.
MRS. NEVILLE TO MISS HARLEY.

NO, my dear friend, this letter will not fix the day of my departure, which may perhaps be yet more distant than I imagined; for the Bellenden family do not seem to have finished half their preparations yet. They propose to set out in a very splendid style, suitable to the rank the colonel will hold in the province, and the taste the people of our colonies have, as I am informed, for expence. I think I can perceive the colonel is only passive in these affairs; that innate grandeur of soul which he possesses, neither seeks nor needs the aid of outward shew.

How shall I thank you, my dear Maria, for the unbounded generosity of your presents to me? Your jeweller was with me this morning, and in a few instants I was made so rich by your munificence, that Mr. Neville was struck with astonishment, and seemed to doubt whether he was not in a dream. Gratitude is the best virtue of the poor, and that Heaven knows my heart is full of; so full indeed, that no words seem adequate to its feelings; and were you present with me, I could only thank you with a silent tear.

I cannot express how much I admire you, for being able to maintain so noble a conduct under your present trials and difficulties—I repeat it, my friend, trials; for, although you have not been pleased to open your whole heart to me; yet that heart, incapable of disguise, displays itself even in the midst of all your delicate reserve. Would I could congratulate, as well as praise; for I had rather see the virtue of my friend employed in wisely using well-deserved prosperity, than in nobly bearing unmerited distresses. If Heaven hears my ardent prayers, I shall yet be able to leave you in a more tranquil situation than you are at present. Adieu!

EUPHEMIA NEVILLE.

Letter XXV.
MISS HARLEY TO MRS. NEVILLE.

MY DEAR EUPHEMIA,

YOU have a right to all occasions of doing good; I think it therefore incumbent upon me to offer you one. There is a young woman in my neighbourhood, for whom I have a great esteem, on account of her good sense and amiable qualities. Some disappointments she has lately met with, makes her very desirous to go abroad. She will think herself happy to be about your person, for she knows enough of your character to love and revere you with a kind of enthusiasm: her history is briefly this:

Her parents, who were persons of genteel birth and education, dying when she was very young, left her wholly unprovided for, to the charitable cares of an aunt, who was a widow, without children, and in tolerable circumstances. She bred up the little girl as her own, gave her a good education, and declared she would leave her all she was worth. The merit of the girl, and the dutiful and affectionate returns she made to her kindness, made this disposing of her property seem not more an act of affection than justice. The old gentlewoman being seized with a dangerous fit of sickness, sent for an attorney, in great practice here, to make her will: a man remarkable for his success in his profession, by which, being likewise very fortunate in the numerous legacies that have been bequeathed him, he has made a very considerable fortune in a few years.

The old lady died; and when the will was opened, Mr. D. the attorney, was, to the astonishment of every one, appointed her executor, and sole heir to her fortune, which was about two thousand pounds—her once-loved niece being cut off with a shilling!—This strange and unexpected reverse of fortune drew on a still more poignant affliction: A young man, who had courted her with the consent of his parents, and to whom she was soon to have been married, was ordered by them to see her no more. He loved her, and persisted in his resolution to marry her, though at the hazard of losing the greatest part of his fortune by disobliging his father.—Poor Fanny! though she loves him tenderly, has had the generosity to give him a positive denial, and to avoid his importunities; and doubtful, perhaps, of her own resolution, is anxiously desirous of leaving England. When I mentioned recommending her to you, she was in transports. If you approve of my proposal, I will send her to London in the stagecoach, under the care of our housekeeper, a good matronly woman, who has a great kindness for her, with whose absence I must dispense for a few days, that I may have the satisfaction of delivering her safe to your protection.

I am very uneasy about my uncle; I am afraid he is going to have a severe attack of his old distemper, the gout; at present it is but slight, yet he is more restless and impatient than usual. I read to him continually; but he does not seem to give much attention, and often interrupts me to tell me, that my voice is low and faint, and that my spirits seem greatly depressed. It may be so; and sure I have cause, so soon to be separated from the friend of my heart, the companion of my youth, my comfort in adversity, and my example for virtue.

Mr. Greville will have it that my uncle is not quite satisfied with his conduct towards young Mr. Harley, which, doubtless, said he, was harsh, if not unjust; and yet, if he was here (so he is gone you see, my Euphemia), it is probable he would not alter it. Now I cannot be of this opinion. I am sure, if my uncle thought he was wrong in this case, he would make haste to be right: bad men justify their faults, the good amend them.

I was obliged to lay down my pen, being summoned to Sir John, who was taken extremely ill. The physicians were afraid the gout was getting into his stomach. I have not been in bed these two nights: my dear, suffering uncle, seeing me continually by his bedside, expressed great uneasiness, lest my health might suffer by so constant an attendance upon him, and insisted upon my retiring to rest. It was not possible for me to obey him; so I kept out of his sight, yet without quitting his apartment.

This morning, when I approached his bed, as if just come down from my own chamber, he took notice that I looked very pale, and said, "He was afraid I had not slept well." He comforted me with an assurance that he was better; and pressing my hand affectionately, "You are a good girl," said he, "your whole conduct is of a piece. I never will forget the generous sacrifice you have made me on a late occasion."

I felt my face all in a glow; I was not able to make him any answer. The physicians coming in relieved my confusion; they pronounced him better: and now being in some measure free from my racking apprehensions, I really retired to my chamber, and threw myself upon my bed. Two hours sleep refreshed me so much, that when I entered my uncle's apartment again, he perceived the alteration in my looks.

I found the servants had informed him that I had not been in bed for three nights; he tenderly reproached me with the deceit I had practised upon him; but added, "that as he hoped for some rest himself to-night, the physicians having ordered something to compose him, he would never pardon me if I did not go to bed."

Mr. Greville is come to pass a day or two here. I left the two friends together, and retired to my own apartment, to have the pleasure of conversing with you, my dear friend; for when I am writing to you, and relating all the little occurrences that help to vary the dull scene of my life, I fancy you are present, and I am talking to you. Adieu! however, for a little time.

I have a strange and terrible circumstance to tell you, my Euphemia, which I shall never wholly lose the remembrance of, and which, as often as it is recollected, will probably occasion the same horrors that I feel now.

This evening, when I went into my uncle's chamber to take leave of him for the night, he told me he would take the draught that was ordered for him then, that he might have the pleasure of taking it from my hands. Accordingly, after having read the label, I poured the medicine into a cup, and gave it into his hand: in the very moment that he was raising it to his lips Martin came into the room, and perceiving what my uncle was doing, cried out, with eyes all wild and staring, and in a voice scarce articulate, from the violence of his agitation—"Hold, Sir! For Heaven's sake do not drink!"

"What is the matter with the man," said my uncle; "are you mad?"

"You have not drank any of it, have you, Sir," said he, eagerly taking the cup out of his master's hand, "are you sure you have not?"

"Well," replied my uncle, "I have not, and what then?"

"Heaven be praised!" said the good old man. "Why, Sir, if you had drank it, you would have been dead by this time; it is poison."

"How! Poison!" said my uncle astonished. As for me, I was near fainting, and should have fallen to the ground, if my dear uncle, weak as he was, had not raised himself up in his bed to support me: in the mean time Mr. Greville was examining the medicine.

"I believe it is laudanum,"[1] said he; "and sure enough you would, as Martin says, have been a dead man if you had taken this dose. But pray, my good friend," said he to Martin, "how did it happen that you knew this?"

"Sir," said Martin, "two moments since a man and horse came to the gate; he must have rode hard indeed, for the horse was all over in a foam. 'If your master has not yet drank the potion that was sent him by Mr. Allen, the apothecary,[2] this evening,' said he,

---

1 Originally prepared primarily with opium; later, a painkiller containing morphine and alcohol.

2 One who prepares drugs and other medicines for sale.

'haste—prevent him—it is poison. Allen will be here soon after me and explain,'—and he rode away instantly."

Mr. Greville now congratulated my uncle on his escape, who seemed touched with the sincerest gratitude to Heaven for his preservation, and said some very kind things to Martin, who had been, under Providence, the happy instrument of it.

It was some time before I could recover any degree of composure, so greatly had I been affected by my uncle's danger. He pressed me earnestly to go to bed; but all inclination to sleep was vanished, and I was resolved to sit up, and hear what the apothecary had to say.

I retired, however, for a few moments, to write you an account of this strange accident, which was likely to have been so fatal a one, both to him and me; for I think I never should have forgiven myself for having, though innocently, administered the deadly draught to him.

These ill-shaped letters and crooked lines are an effect of that agitation under which I still labour.

Sure the apothecary must be come by this time.—I am impatient to hear how this dreadful mistake happened. For the future I shall tremble to take their medicines; for how can one be sure of their exactness? Jenny tells me Mr. Allen is this moment arrived.

ONE IN THE MORNING.

Well, my dear friend, here I am, in my own chamber, without the least desire of going to bed to night. Joy is as great an enemy to sleep as grief; and I am overjoyed, I own it. You are surprised—you are impatient to know what happened to produce a sensation I am so little acquainted with—so long unfelt, and almost despaired of. Take then things in order, and share, largely share in the satisfaction of your friend.

Mr. Allen entered my uncle's apartment a moment after me; his countenance retained the traces of the great perturbation he had been in.

"Heaven be praised! Sir," said he to his patient, "that this mistake has had no other consequences than to make me, for some hours, the most wretched man in the world."—"I can easily conceive the fright you have been in," said Sir John; "but prithee, Allen, how did it happen that you sent me this fatal dose."

"Sir," replied the apothecary, "a patient of mine, a gentlewoman in years, is accustomed to take small doses of laudanum every night: she is miserable if it is not always at hand; so I generally send her two ounces at a time. I had prepared your draught, and wrote the labels for both the phials, when a servant of a dear friend of mine, who lived about a quarter of a mile distant, came to tell me that I must go instantly and bleed his master, who was in an apoplectic fit.[1]

"My journeyman,[2] who had always been remarkable diligent and careful in his business, was just ready to mount on horseback to take your medicine to the Hall. I gave him the label; and shewing him the phial, bid him tie it on, and set out with it immediately; and I hastened to relieve my friend. My man, who, during the five years that he has lived with me, never made any mistake of this kind before, took the phial which contained the laudanum, put the label on it designed for your draught, and rode away.

"When I came home, about an hour afterwards, I discovered the dreadful mistake; the draught designed for you being still on the counter. I concluded that the other was by this time delivered, and probably taken. I was almost distracted, having no horse but that my journeyman rode on, I determined to set out on foot for the Hall; but, however anxiety and terror might have quickened my pace, I must have come too late, when a gentleman alighting at my door, desired me to dress his hand, which by some accident he had cut dreadfully. I answered, that it was impossible; that Sir John Harley was in danger of being poisoned by a mistake of my man, who had carried him a large dose of laudanum instead of the prescription I had prepared for him. Saying this, I rushed by him, scarce knowing what I did.

"The gentleman instantly re-mounted his horse, and putting him in full gallop, cried out to me as he passed by me, that he would be at the Hall in less than ten minutes, and hoped to prevent the mischief. Then, and not before, I recollected who he was."—"And who is he?" said my uncle eagerly; "The reverend Dr. Harley's son," replied Mr. Allen, "I know him very well."

My uncle hearing this name, clasped his hands together with great emotion, and casting his eyes first upon Mr. Greville, then on me, with a look big with meaning, he turned himself about in his bed, and continued silent. His piercing glance at me filled me, I know not how, with confusion. I felt my face covered with blushes. I could not look at Mr. Greville, who exclaimed two or

---

1 A stroke.
2 Assistant.

three times, in a transported accent—"Generous, noble fellow! What think you of this, my friend," said he to Sir John, approaching his bed. My uncle made him no answer; but I thought I heard him sigh deeply.

Mr. Greville then observing that Mr. Allen must be greatly fatigued with so long a walk in such agitation of mind (and indeed the poor man looked like a ghost), desired him to walk into the next room, where he would find something to refresh him, and in the mean time he would give directions for a horse to be saddled, to carry him home.

Mr. Allen withdrew; and Martin appearing upon Mr. Greville's ringing the bell, my uncle interrupted the orders he was giving, to ask him eagerly if he knew the person who brought the message from the apothecary.

"Yes, Sir," said Martin, "it was Mr. Harley." "And why did you not tell us this circumstance?" said my uncle. Martin cast down his eyes.

"How did he look,—what did he say to you?" asked my uncle.

"He seemed to be in great agitation: Sir," replied Martin, "his horse was all in a foam, and himself seemed almost breathless."

"'Has your master,' said he, 'taken the medicine that Mr. Allen sent here this morning?' I replied, No. 'Fly, prevent him, it is poison,' said he; 'the apothecary is following me, he will explain the mistake.' The porter has since told me, that he rode away instantly, and that he thought he was wounded, for his handkerchief was bound round his left hand, and seemed covered with blood."

My uncle then bid Martin go and attend Mr. Allen; when Mr. Greville repeating,

"What think you of all this, my friend?"

"I think," replied Sir John, "that this young man is the noblest of all human beings. My life stood between him and an ample fortune; and, what is more, between him and a blessing which he sets perhaps a much higher value upon. Yet he has saved that life with the hazard of his own, and done as much for his enemy as he would have done for his father."—Then pausing a little—"And a father I will be to him now," added he; "from this moment I will consider him as my son. Why is he not here, that I may embrace and call him so?" My uncle spoke this in so affectionate a manner, as moved even the lively Mr. Greville.

"Where shall I find him," pursued he—"who will bring him to me? That wound in his hand alarms me. I feel already the anxiety of a father for him." Then looking at me with a tender smile,

"Maria," said he, "will not, I hope, be jealous of this new-sprung affection for a person so worthy." I was silent; for what indeed could I say? Mr. Harley's merits are too great for praise—for my praise. My uncle seemed to have a just sense of them; and for this I could not but rejoice.

Mr. Greville, who sat musing for some time, at last said, "The appearance of young Harley in these parts surprises me. I know he took leave of his family a week ago, in order to go on board the—Indiaman, which I thought had sailed by this time. Perhaps I may get some intelligence from Allen; I'll go to him." He did so, and returned again in a quarter of an hour; during which time my uncle and I had not spoke a word to each other.

"Allen tells me," said Mr. Greville, "that he met Mr. Harley when he had got about half way to the Hall. He called out to him in a joyful tone, and told him all was safe. He complained of the hurt in his hand, and said, he would stop at his house, and get his journeyman, if he was come home, to put some dressings upon it." Mr. Allen begged he would stay till he came back if he did not find his man at home. Mr. Harley replied, 'that he had not a moment to spare; that he was going to hire a post-chaise at the Rose-Inn, and intended to travel all night, being apprehensive that the ship would sail without him; his father's sudden illness having detained him longer than he expected.'

"So, then," interrupted my uncle, in a tone of deep distress, "he is gone!"

"No, no, I hope not," replied Mr. Greville; "I have dispatched Allen on horseback, with directions, if he finds the youth at his house, as I doubt not but he will, to tell him that he must not stir from thence till I have seen him, which shall be early in the morning. Allen can accommodate him with a bed."

"This will not do," cried my uncle vehemently, "this voyage must be prevented, or I shall never enjoy a quiet moment. Bid Martin get on horseback instantly; and if he does not find Harley at Allen's, let him go on with all speed to the Rose-Inn. Dear Greville hasten him; mean time I will write a line myself to Harley. Maria, give me pen, ink and paper."

My uncle's impetuosity put us all in motion. Mr. Greville hastened to give Martin his orders; I brought my uncle what he desired; he sat up in bed, and made shift to scrawl a few lines. Here is a copy of them:

TO MR. HARLEY.

"Worthy young man! you have saved my life; but if you would not embitter the remainder of it, think no more of your voyage to India; return with my messenger, and expect for the future to find a father, an affectionate father, in

JOHN HARLEY."

Mr. Greville inclosed this note in one from himself; and Martin, who seemed excessively pleased with his commission, assured us he would not return without the blessed young gentleman that had preserved his master.

Sir John seemed now quite exhausted with the different agitations his mind had suffered this evening; and a few minutes after Martin's departure, fell into a profound sleep. I wished Mr. Greville a good night, and retired to my chamber, where I have ever since been employed in writing to you.

Mr. Greville told me at parting, that he would sit up an hour or two longer, in expectation of Martin's return, who, if he is not here by that time, said he, we may conclude he did not meet Harley at Allen's, and is gone after him to the inn.

Well, we may now conclude that Martin has not succeeded, for he might have been here long ere this time. I hear Mr. Greville crossing the gallery, to go to his own chamber, so he has given up all hope. He calls to me as he passes by my door, seeing a light still in my chamber.—Sure he has heard some news.

This is what Mr. Greville told me through the door, for I would not open it, being all undressed.

Martin has sent a man home with the horse he rode out with; and in a note to Mr. Greville informs him, that Mr. Harley had called at Allen's, and got his hand dressed, which he had hurt by a fall from his horse, and immediately afterwards set out for the inn. Thither Martin followed; and hearing that Mr. Harley was gone away a quarter of an hour before in a post-chaise, he thought he could not do a more acceptable piece of service to his master than to follow him, and endeavour to overtake him: accordingly he ordered post-horses and a guide, and was just ready to set out when his messenger came away. Mr. Greville added, in a melancholy accent, that he feared all this would end at last in disappointment and regret. Indeed I fear so too, and am in pain for my uncle, who will be most sensibly afflicted: so now, my dear Euphemia, being not too happy to sleep, I wish you a good night, and retire to bed.

Letter XXVI.
MISS HARLEY, IN CONTINUATION.

I ROSE early this morning, and had the satisfaction to hear that my uncle had had a good night, and was still asleep. Mr. Greville being also up, and in my uncle's library, I joined him there. He was beginning to rally me on the subject of Mr. Harley; but presently altered his tone, being strongly apprehensive that the youth would be on board, and the ship sailed before Martin could overtake him.

"Poor fellow!" said he with a sigh, "he is too good to be a favourite with Fortune, who seldom bestows any thing upon the virtuous, because she knows she cannot bribe them with her gifts."

My uncle having sent to desire we would drink our chocolate by his bedside, we attended him immediately. He was very low spirited, having heard from his valet that Martin was not returned. Mr. Greville read his billet[1] to him, which was not calculated to remove his fears of the bad success of his expedition. He was full of uneasy reflections; he railed at fortune, he railed at himself, but still he was more inclined to find fault with his stars than himself.

Mr. Greville put him in mind of the great danger he had so lately escaped, by means so unlikely and unexpected.

"Yes," replied my uncle, "my life is preserved, but he who preserved it is out of the reach of my gratitude, which will be a continual source of vexation and regret to me. The favours I receive," pursued he in a peevish tone, "are so husbanded, that I cannot recover an eye but by losing a leg; my causes of complaint never cease, they only change their places."

We have had a melancholy day of it; I never saw my uncle so fretful and impatient: he recals every circumstance to his mind that is likely to increase his remorse for his unkindness to Mr. Harley. He reprobates his own churlish conduct at the inn, where he first saw him, and received so strong a proof of the generosity and sweetness of his disposition, which I repaid, said he, by a tyrannous exertion of the power I had to make him miserable. I must ever despise and hate myself for it.

"Come, come," said Mr. Greville, "we must not suffer you to be too severe a censurer of yourself; a man shews himself greater

___

1 Letter.

by being capable of owning a fault, than by being incapable of committing it."

"I would repair that fault," replied my uncle impatiently, "and fortune puts it out of my power—it is this that makes me wretched." His physician was surprised when he visited him to-day to find him so much worse. He said he had a considerable degree of fever; he seemed unwilling to take any medicines, telling him the danger he had escaped, which he could not do without sighing deeply several times.

Dr. Irwin told him he would carry his prescriptions himself to the apothecary, see them made up, and send them by one of his own servants; and this expedient has made us easy on that head. But as we have no tidings yet of Martin, and my uncle apparently suffers in his health from the inquietude of his mind, we are under great apprehensions on his account. Mr. Greville utterly condemns his too great sensibility on this occasion. The best virtues, he told him, when in excess, partake so much of vice, that even extreme right is no better than extreme wrong. My uncle answered peevishly, that his philosophy was very unseasonable; and turning himself in his bed, seemed as if he was desirous of taking some rest; but I really believe he sought only to indulge his melancholy reflections without interruption.

Mr. Greville walked into the garden, and I retired to my chamber, and wrote thus far. I am now going down to make him some tea.—No news of Martin yet.

AT NIGHT.

Mr. Greville being obliged to visit a friend in our neighbourhood to-day, I have been reading the whole evening to my uncle, in order to detach his thoughts from the subject of his uneasiness. His friend is now with him; he tells him that Martin's not return-ing is a good sign, for if he had not had hopes of overtaking Mr. Harley, he would have been back ere now. There is some proba-bility in this; but my uncle is so out of humour with himself, that he admits of nothing which may tend to relieve his disquiet.

What an enormous packet you will receive this time! but I am willing to keep it open while our suspense continues, that you may either rejoice or grieve with us for the event. I wish, yet dread, to have a letter from you—your next will probably fix the very moment of your departure. It is late; and with this sad expectation on my mind I will go to bed, I cannot say to rest.

Well, my dear Euphemia, Martin is returned. Has be brought

back Mr. Harley? you ask: he has, but not to us. This morning, as I was going into my uncle's chamber, I met Mr. Greville, who, beckoning to me to come to one of the gallery windows, which looked out into the court-yard, shewed me Martin just arrived alone, and looking melancholy. We were in doubt whether we should let him see my uncle immediately, till we had prepared him for the ill news he brought. But he, who had already been informed that he was come, rang his bell impetuously, upon which we both went into his chamber.

"So," said he, as soon as he saw us, "Martin is come, and alone it seems: it is as I expected. Did ever any thing happen according to my wish?"

Martin coming in, put a stop to these fretful complaints; but, as it should seem, he was afraid to ask him any questions, for he said not a word to him. Upon which Mr. Greville said, "I am sorry to see you are come alone, friend."

"I am sorry too, Sir," replied Martin; "and Mr. Harley hopes, Sir," addressing himself to his master, "when you know his reasons, you will have the goodness to excuse him."

"You have seen him then," cried my uncle impatiently, "and he has refused to come: well, I might have expected this. But did he receive my invitation with disdain—did he express any bitterness against me?"

"Oh, Sir," said Martin, "I wish you could have seen with what respect he received your Honour's letter. At the very first words he read of it, his face seemed all in a glow. He read it over, I believe, twenty times; and kissing it respectfully before he put it in his pocket, I observed his eyes full of tears. I ventured to say to him, 'May I hope, Sir, you will lay aside all thoughts of your intended voyage, and return with me to the Hall?'

"'Can you doubt it, my good friend?' said he, 'if you were not so much fatigued as I see you are, I would this moment set out with you, for I shall think every moment an age till I can throw myself at the feet of your noble master, to thank him for the unmerited goodness he expresses for me in this letter.' He then took it out of his pocket again, and read it over half a dozen times, I believe."

"But why is he not here?" interrupted my uncle with his usual impatience; "where is he—when shall I see him?"

"Sir," replied Martin, "he is gone to his father's."

"How!" interrupted my uncle, "gone to his father's!"

"Oh, Sir!" resumed Martin, "the poor young gentleman heard the most melancholy piece of news when he came to the Rose-

Inn last night, where we only stopped till fresh horses were put to the chaise. I walked out with him into the inn-yard, to hasten them, when a country fellow espying him, came running up to him, crying 'Master Harley, I am glad to see you, faith! What, have you heard the sad news then.—But you must make haste, I can tell you that, or you will not see your father alive; he was just giving up the ghost when I came from —— and that is five or six hours ago.'

"Oh, Sir!" pursued Martin, wiping his eyes—"I shall never forget the sad condition poor young Harley was in; I had just time to catch him in my arms, where he lay, without sense or motion, for several minutes. As soon as he recovered, he begged me, with his eyes all drowned in tears, to tell you the sad circumstances he was in; and then eagerly throwing himself into the chaise, which was now ready, he bid the post-boy drive with all the speed he could to ——. He just pronounced your Honour's name, and would have added something; but a violent burst of grief stopped his voice; he fell all along the seat, sighing as if his heart would break, and the chaise driving away furiously, he was presently out of sight. I was obliged to stay several hours after him, not being able to get any conveyance here till five o'clock this morning."

You will easily imagine, my dear Euphemia, that we were all greatly affected with this sad tale. I wept, I own it; my uncle discovered great emotion, and Mr. Greville walked to the window in a pensive mood.

My uncle, after a silence of some minutes, told Martin he would allow him this day to rest himself after his fatigue, and that to-morrow he must set out early for Dr. Harley's—. The post is just going out; I shall have only time to make up my packet. Adieu! then, my dear Euphemia.

MARIA HARLEY.

Letter XXVII.
MISS HARLEY TO MRS. NEVILLE.

SIR John is so well recovered, that he took an airing this morning in his chariot.[1] Mr. Greville has left us, and Martin is dispatched to Dr. Harley's, with a kind message to the afflicted family, and his pocket-book stuffed with bank bills for Mr. Harley; and a short billet, in which my uncle earnestly requests him to come to

---

1 A light four-wheeled horse-drawn carriage.

the Hall as soon as he possibly can. His health seems to improve every moment. Joy is a great restorative. Yet he now and then breathes a half-suppressed sigh to the memory of his once-loved friend, whose offences towards him could only, it seems, be cancelled by death.

Martin is returned. Dr. Harley lived two hours after the arrival of his beloved son. He was perfectly sensible; and Mr. Harley had the comfort to remove his anxiety for the future fortunes of the young family he left behind him, by acquainting him with the happy change in Sir John's disposition towards him.

The family are in great affliction. Mr. Harley wrote a few lines to my uncle, which seem to please him greatly. He did not read them to me, but this was his observation upon them: "This young man," said he, "receives a benefit with the same grace with which he confers one. His gratitude loses nothing of its force by the dignity of his expression." Why have I not a letter from you? Yet when it comes I shall fear to break the seal, lest it should tell me what I dread to know. Adieu!

MARIA HARLEY.

Letter XXVIII.
MRS. NEVILLE TO MISS HARLEY.

I RETURNED last night from another visit to Lord L.'s. I could not resolve to leave England without visiting once more the place where the dear remains of my mother are deposited. As I was leaving the church I met Mr. Neville, who was just arrived at Lord L.'s seat, in order to conduct me home; and hearing to what place I was gone, came himself to fetch me. My mind, softened by the tender, melancholy ideas which the sight of my loved mother's tomb inspired, was so sensibly affected with the obliging solicitude of my husband, that I flew to meet him with a transport, which was instantly repressed by the austerity of his looks, and the harshness of his reproofs, for the indulgence of a grief which he treats almost as a crime. There is no doubt but he meant well; and this severity was an effect of his concern for me: but he has so little delicacy, is so ungracious, that he converts even the best intentions into offences, by his unfortunate manner of expressing them.

This meeting, therefore, as you may well imagine, did not contribute to calm my mind. I came home sufficiently mortified and dejected; but the society of my dear Mrs. Benson, her wise reasonings, and tender soothings, restored me to some degree of tranquillity.

You have made me a most acceptable present in the young person who has the honour to be recommended by you. Oppression has ever been, in my opinion, a sufficient ground for protection; but the testimony you give of her merit, and her own engaging appearance and manner, will secure her a large share of my kindness and esteem. Her situation with me shall, in every respect, be made as agreeable to her as you would wish. Mrs. Benson is much pleased with her; she is her bedfellow, and they are very seldom asunder.

I have got your second packet; my hopes, my wishes, my expectations, are answered—you will be the wife of Mr. Harley. Excellent young man! but he is, as you justly observe, above all praise. He is worthy of you, my friend, lovely as you are in person and mind.

Sir John Harley's character rises greatly upon me in your agreeable narrative—he has acted both a just and a generous part. You have painted him with great force; I see him in all the turns and changes of his temper, and in every view he is pleasing. Your gay philosopher, your lively, yet sententious Mr. Greville, was in my opinion much to blame, when he placed the most amiable virtue of the mind in the number of its maladies and infirmities. Sir John's sensibility is certainly very great; and if it be necessary, as some have said, that limits and bounds should be set in all cases, they cannot be unfit in acts of acknowledgment. If there is a fault opposite to ingratitude, he has fallen into it; and thus, by the excess, he has avoided the defect; but the defect is so horrid, and the excess so beautiful, that he must be a rigid moralist indeed who calls it an infirmity.

And now, my dear Maria, that I see you possessed of so much happiness at present, and so much greater in prospect, I shall with the less reluctance tell you, that our ship will absolutely sail within these ten days. All the fortitude I can boast would have been scarce sufficient to have supported my spirits under this separation, if I had left you in that uneasy state of mind which your delicacy but half unveiled, but which your candor and amiable simplicity made but too apparent to an observation interested like mine.

Yes, my dear friend, you have loved Mr. Harley all this time; and your gentle mind has had some severe conflicts to sustain between your inclination for him, and the obedience you owed Sir John, who, as your uncle and benefactor, had a double title to it. The virtues of Mr. Harley have made this sacrifice no longer necessary, and that which justifies your choice secures you the possession of its object.

I earnestly intreat you, my Maria, not to suffer the present sunshine of your fortune to be clouded with your apprehensions for me. Our separation is the only circumstance that ought to give you some concern, and that is common to us both. It is true, I have but little contentment but what I derive from reason and philosophy; that sort of philosophy I mean which teaches us submission to the will of Heaven. I see nothing terrible in this long voyage but my absence from you. I apprehend nothing worse than what has already happened to me; and I will never believe that ill fortune will follow me so far, or that it is possible for one to fall, who already stands so low. You may render absence tolerable to me by frequent letters. Continue your charming narratives; while I read your lively descriptions, I see, I converse with you—I partake your fears, I am elevated with your hopes, I sympathise with your sorrows, and enjoy your happiness.

As for me, it will be the chief comfort of my life to write to you, and make you acquainted with all the events of it. I propose to devote some part of every day to this dear *converse* I will call it, which will make you present with me; and, although I cannot hope to give you equal entertainment, yet I will be punctual if not liberal, and send you that which I promised, if I cannot send you what I would. Adieu!

EUPHEMIA NEVILLE.

Letter XXIX.
MISS HARLEY TO MRS. NEVILLE.

MR. Greville is just come from Dr. Harley's afflicted family, where he has been to pay a consolatory visit. He has brought a letter from Mr. Harley to my uncle, which he keeps to himself. I am extremely glad that the youth, in accepting my uncle's liberal present, discovers nothing of that pride of spirit which appeared in that letter of his to me upon a former occasion. I mentioned this circumstance to Mr. Greville, as what had given me some apprehensions.

"You are right," said he, "for nothing is more likely to create distrust in a new reconciliation than to shew a shyness to be obliged to those with whom we are reconciled. But Harley, you know, is now his son by adoption; and now I think of it," pursued he, with a sly leer, "you are too just not to have this worthy young man's interest extremely at heart; would it not be more for his advantage, think you, for Sir John to call him his nephew than his son?"

I blushed like a fool; but recollecting myself, I answered him gravely, "that he had acted like a father by me, who was only his niece; and that whichsoever of those characters he chose to consider Mr. Harley in, I did not doubt but he would shew himself equally affectionate."

I was afraid of the archness I saw rising in his looks; therefore, to prevent his mischievous raillery, I asked him a great many questions concerning Mrs. Harley and the young ladies; and he let me into a secret which surprised me greatly. Mrs. Harley was, it seems, bred up by her mother in the Roman Catholic religion; and although obliged, on account of her husband's profession, to conceal her principles while he lived, yet being a bigot to its tenets, she is determined to spend the remainder of her days in a convent in France,[1] where she proposes to complete the education of her daughters. I believe this scheme will meet with some opposition from Sir John, who, I know, intends to take care of them.

To-day at dinner my uncle told me, that he expected a visit from Mr. Harley in a day or two; and he desired me to give orders to the housekeeper to prepare that apartment for him which was formerly mine; for since Lady Harley's death I have, by his

---

1 Mrs. Harley's Catholicism is treated here with the usual eighteenth-century British negativity and it acts as a judgment against her. After the Protestant Reformation in England, lands belonging to the Catholic Church were sold, and monasteries and convents closed; while the state religion was Anglicanism, many citizens continued to practice their Catholic faith, albeit surreptitiously as such behavior was considered a threat to national wellbeing, especially during the late seventeenth century. The Glorious Revolution in 1688 seemed to assure Britain of Protestant rule, though this was challenged by the Jacobite Revolution in 1745 when Stuart sympathizers led by Charles Edward Stuart advanced from Scotland into the midlands of England. During the eighteenth century, Catholics in Britain and Ireland were penalized with a number of social, political, and educational restrictions. In general, adherents to the Catholic faith during this time were viewed with suspicion and belittled as superstitious and small-minded. France, on the other hand, was sympathetic to the Catholic religion and the country's many convents served as places of refuge for British women young and old, Catholic and Protestant—those who had been widowed, disappointed in love, or whose parents wanted a safe and isolated place for them.

express command, occupied her's. I answered hesitatingly, "Yes, Sir," for both the gentlemen threw me into such confusion by their fascinating looks, that I scarce knew what I said.

As soon as the cloth was removed[1] I retired to my own apartment; instead of giving the housekeeper orders myself, I bid my maid tell her, her master wanted her. She received his directions, and came to tell me, with great joy, that we were to have Mr. Harley for a guest.

"We are all debtors to this charming young gentleman," said she, "for the life of our good master."

Now, my dear Euphemia, no one has a higher sense of this obligation than I have; but my situation is a little awkward. Mr. Greville's raillery, and my uncle's fixed looks on me, which seem as if they were exploring the inmost recesses of my heart, often distress me greatly—I escape from them when I can.

I am summoned this moment to make tea. I wish Mr. Greville was gone—I never thought his company tiresome before. Do you not think it is indelicate in him, my Euphemia, to pursue me thus with his raillery?—So! A second summons—I must go.

Sir John and his friend imagined a fine scheme to divert themselves with my embarrassment. Who do you think I saw upon my returning to the room where I had left them together?—Even Mr. Harley, whom I had been taught not to expect these two days. But this mischievous design did not succeed entirely to their wish; for, although my surprise was indeed very great at this unexpected sight of him, yet I felt my confusion decrease, in proportion as the tender melancholy in his looks fixed my attention upon the recent cause.

A transient blush overspread his cheeks on my first appearance; but instantly gave place to that paleness which the death of a father, whom he had loved excessively, seemed to have planted there.

He approached me with an air of deep respect, but with a sedateness which he borrowed from his melancholy situation, and made me a short compliment; which I received, and answered, without other emotion than what arose from a partic-

---

1 Cloth removed: Removal of the table-cloth and all vestiges of the meal. This was a signal for the ladies to depart for the "withdrawing room" where they would visit together and wait for the arrival of the gentlemen, who stayed at table for postprandial drinks and to smoke. The gentlemen would eventually join the ladies for tea; note Euphemia is "summoned to make tea," below.

ipation in a grief so just and so affecting. He led me to my chair; and resuming his seat, which was next my uncle, he continued his discourse upon some indifferent matters, which my coming had interrupted.

Sir John and Mr. Greville were evidently disappointed, that this first interview had passed over without any of that discomposure which would have laid a foundation for some future raillery. I enjoyed their disappointment, I confess, and saw, with some little triumph, Mr. Greville's arch looks, and my uncle's significant glances, give place to a seriousness, which was better suited to the circumstances of our young guest.

The evening passed over very agreeably; my uncle seemed delighted with Mr. Harley's conversation; for although he was far from making an ostentatious display of his powers of pleasing, yet, through all his modesty, there appeared a fund of knowledge and an elegance of expression, which captivated the attention, and gave an advantageous idea of his understanding and improvements.

He took occasion once to mention his great obligations to my uncle; he employed but few words; for he seemed well aware of the justness of that observation, that the dignity of truth is wounded by much professing: but his look and accent were so affecting, that Sir John seemed touched to the soul, and grasping his hand with an eager pressure—

"Talk not to me of obligations," said he, "your worth outstrips all my power of rewarding."

Mr. Greville was cruel enough, at that moment, to cast a glance full of meaning, at me, to add to the confusion with which I was overwhelmed. I perceived, as soon as I was able to look up, that this mischievous look had not escaped Mr. Harley's observation: his face was covered by a deep blush. With a timid and disconcerted air he raised my uncle's hand, which still held his fast clasped to his lips, and told him, in a low but ardent accent, that it should be the business of his life to deserve his good opinion.

Our common persecutor now seemed to pity the embarrassment he had occasioned, and instantly began a conversation on indifferent matters.

I retired early to my own apartment, to be at liberty to continue my letter to you. It was late, and I was still engaged in this dear employment, when Mrs. Groves, who had carried the candle before Mr. Harley when he retired to his chamber, where she left him with Martin, who was ordered to attend him, came into my room, and begging pardon for her intrusion, broke into the most extravagant praises of the young gentleman.

This good woman loves to talk, and says every thing that comes into her head, without regarding time, or place, or persons; and she is indulged in this liberty on account of her long-tried rectitude and fidelity.

"Do you know, Madam," said she, "that I have found out that there is a great likeness between you and Mr. Harley. He has the very air of your countenance, your fine large eyes," said the flatterer, "and dimpled mouth; only his complexion is not like yours—his is a lovely brown, and yours, to be sure, is as fair as alabaster. I think he resembles you too in the air of his person—no disparagement to you neither, Madam, for I think he is one of the genteelest young men I ever saw.

"Well, but I must tell you something, Madam: You must know, that as we passed through that room which was formerly your dressing-room, your picture, that hangs over the chimney, took his eye in a minute; well, what did he do, but, with great eagerness, he takes one of the candles out of my hand, goes up close to it, and there he stood looking and looking, as if he could never be tired. So I made bold to say, 'Sir, that is my young lady's picture; it was drawn when she was about fourteen: do you think it is like her?'

"'It is like your young lady,' said he, 'but she is vastly improved since this was painted.'

"Well, Madam, he staid looking and looking at it so long, till I was down-right tired with standing; at last, he begged my pardon, and returned me the candle; and, as sure as you are alive, Madam, he fetched a deep sigh when he took his eyes off it."

"Well, Mrs. Groves," said I, smiling, "what is all this to the purpose?"

"Why, Madam," replied she, "what I *refer*[1] from all this is, that Mr. Harley has certainly a great kindness for you, and that you would make a charming couple."

Now, my dear Euphemia, I do not doubt but the wise assembly[2] of the housekeeper's room have settled already all the preliminaries of this match, and as good as concluded upon it. I was unwilling to hear any more upon the subject; so I called my maid to assist me in undressing, and bade the loquacious housekeeper good night.

---

1 Refer: i.e., infer.
2 Assembly: A gathering for social purposes.

And a thousand thousand times good night to you, my dear friend, whom I always see in my dreams, but with melancholy omens; for, alas! you are torn from me; the distance between us seems to increase, and sometimes I lose sight of you entirely. But sure we shall meet again; do you not think we shall? I must, I will indulge this hope, for without it I shall be miserable.

Letter XXX.
MISS HARLEY, IN CONTINUATION.

MR. Harley has left us, and I am just escaped from that unceasing teaser, Mr. Greville, to give my dear Euphemia an account of what has passed during this interesting day.

At breakfast, my uncle asked Mr. Harley if it would be inconvenient to him to stay another day. The youth replied, that a longer absence at this time would be severely felt by his afflicted family.

"Well, then, you shall go, my dear Edward," said my uncle, "my horses and groom shall attend you, unless you choose to have the post-chariot."[1] Mr. Harley thanked him, and said, as the day was fair he would rather ride.

"You will reach —," said my uncle, "before dark, though you do not set out these two hours; therefore," pursued he, rising, "as I wish to have a little discourse with you in private before you leave us, I will expect you in my library as soon as you have finished your breakfast."

Mr. Harley, who rose up when my uncle did, told him he was ready to attend him then; and accordingly followed him, after bowing to me with an air so timid and embarrassed, as threw me, I know not why, into confusion likewise.

I durst not raise my eyes to Mr. Greville, who, I supposed, was making his malicious observations; so both of us continued ridiculously silent for several minutes, when he thought fit to relieve me, by desiring me to give him another dish of tea. I did so; and he then asked me gravely, if I could guess what was likely to be the subject of Sir John's conversation with Mr. Harley?

I told him I really could not.

"And have you no curiosity about it?" said he.

"Not much," I answered.

---

1 A light four-wheeled carriage used for carrying mail and passengers, with a driver's seat in front.

"Not much!" repeated he; "this indifference is not very obliging to Mr. Harley."

"You are mistaken, Sir," replied I, "I am not indifferent to any thing that concerns Mr. Harley; his interests will always be of some consequence to me, esteeming his so justly as I do. But I have no anxiety on my mind on account of this private conference, and therefore little curiosity, because I have no doubt of the greatness and permanency of my uncle's affection for him, as it is founded upon his merit, and the grateful sense he has of his obligations to him."

The openness of my answer disconcerted Mr. Greville, who, I perceived, expected I should say something that would give him an opportunity of teazing me, as was his custom. He looked at me, I thought, with complacency; and that moment my uncle called out, *Greville.*

"Now," said he, rising to go to him, "I shall know all; and to punish you for your reserve, I will not tell you a word of what I know."

"Yes you will," replied I, laughing, "when I have curiosity enough to ask you."

He went to my uncle, and I took my usual walk upon the terrace, where, in about half an hour afterwards, I was joined by Mr. Greville and Mr. Harley. There was something in the countenance of the latter so full of meaning, that, I knew not why— but I could neither look at nor speak to him. He was silent too; and in this stupid way we followed Mr. Greville, who led us from one walk to another, pointing out to Mr. Harley somewhat or other to admire in the disposition of the grounds, which, you know, are laid out in the most beautiful taste imaginable.

All of a sudden he seemed to recollect something he had to say to Sir John; and telling us he would be with us again in a few minutes, left us together.

This silly contrivance of leaving me alone with Mr. Harley, was not calculated to lessen that unaccountable embarrassment into which his coming had thrown me. I was impatient to free myself from this awkward situation; and therefore, pretending to be apprehensive that it would rain, I mended my pace, in order to get as soon as possible into the house; but he respectfully retaining me, begged me not to have the cruelty to deprive him of the only opportunity he had yet had of speaking to me alone. I then walked slower, but still towards the house, though he fought to turn my steps to another path.

"The tide of favour here," said he, "flows so strongly for me, as might indeed carry my hopes very far, did not your coldness, Madam, or rather aversion, reduce me to despair."

"My aversion," said I, "Mr. Harley, how can you imagine that I have any aversion to you—you who have so just a right to my esteem?"

"And I am honoured with your esteem, Madam," replied he eagerly; "and may I presume to hope that the tender, the ardent passion, with which you inspired me the first moment I beheld you, is not displeasing to you? Speak, I conjure you, Madam," pursued he, "relieve me from this agony of doubt—suffer me not to depart uncertain of my fate."

Being still out of sight of the house, he threw himself at my feet, holding one of my hands, which he several times pressed to his lips, in spite of my endeavours to withdraw it.

This liberty was not altogether agreeable, any more than the parade of his posture, still kneeling. I moved a step back; and laughing, as I did once before on the same occasion, told him, that I supposed he had lately read Cassandra and the grand Cyrus,[1] for his language and manners had all the air of an Orondates.

I confess to you, my dear Euphemia, that I was willing to relieve the embarrassment this very passionate address had thrown me into, by a little raillery, which detached my reflexions upon the silly figure I must have made during this short scene; but I was much concerned when I perceived the effect my ill-judged gaiety had upon him.—He dropped my hand submissively, and rising, bowed low, asking me pardon for the liberty he had taken in declaring his sentiments so freely. He was now convinced, he said, that my indifference, or rather dislike of him, was not to be overcome; that he could have borne my anger with more fortitude than my scorn, by which his presumption was too severely punished to leave him an excuse for ever repeating his offence.

I heard him sigh—I saw his eyes full of tears; I was shocked, perplexed—I knew not what to say to him. I am sure my heart was far from being in that disposition towards him which he seemed to apprehend. Scorn! Good Heaven! Mr. Harley an object of scorn! how could a thought so injurious to his acknowl-

---

1 Madeleine de Scudéry (1607-91), French romance writer, used classical characters and themes for her multi-volume romances, which included *Artamenes, ou le Grand Cyrus* (1649-53), of which Cyrus is the hero.

edged merit rise in his mind? I wished to erase it; but nothing proper to be said recurred to my mind.

I continued silent; and, without attending to what I did, walked fast towards the house. Doubtless he understood this to be in consequence of my eagerness to get rid of him; for again I heard him sigh deeply; but he spoke not a word.

Mr. Greville, who was come out again, joined us before either of us perceived him. He seemed surprised and vexed at the disorder that appeared in Mr. Harley's countenance: it was indeed sufficiently apparent, for at that moment I ventured to cast my eyes upon him; but instantly removed them again, being, I own it, greatly affected by the tender distress expressed in every line of his face.

Mr. Greville, who heedfully observed us both, cast an upbraiding glance on me; and being now arrived at the house, he said to Mr. Harley, I intend to accompany you a few miles; the horses are at the gate—I believe we shall find Sir John there likewise.

Mr. Harley then made me a most respectful bow; but uttered not a word, nor raised his eyes to my face. I curtseyed also in silence, though I am sure I secretly wished him a good journey, and retired to my own apartment, where I have been ever since.

I have a most oppressive weight upon my spirits; I dread seeing Mr. Greville again—I hate his scrutinizing looks; but I must resolve to meet them; for my maid tells me that dinner is ready to be served, and that Mr. Greville is returned from his ride. Why did he return? I think he takes root here.—Well, I must go.

My uncle looked very grave upon me all dinner-time; Mr. Greville was serious and reserved.

When I drank my uncle's health, he took no other notice of me than by a bow lower than usual, without his wonted smile of complacency. Just as I was rising from table, my maid brought me a letter from you. I took it out of her hand with a visible emotion, I suppose, for the gentlemen smiled. I asked leave to retire to read it; and, without waiting for an answer, flew up stairs.

Oh! my Euphemia, what do you tell me? a few days more, and I shall be separated from you, perhaps, for ever. Have I so anxiously wished for this letter, which, when it came, was to pierce my heart with its fatal tidings? Do not chide me, my dear friend, this stroke, though long expected, falls heavy on me. I must lay down my pen, my tears blind me; when I am more composed I shall finish my letter.

I have passed a sleepless night:

Thought followed thought, and tear succeeded tear.[1]

But I am now, if not easy, yet resigned, since to remediless evils nothing but patience can be opposed. But be assured, neither time nor absence will be able to weaken my affection—Your idea will always be present with me. I shall dream continually of you, and find no image in my memory so pleasing as that which presents me the time of our being together. You shall have letters from me by every conveyance; and thus, though oceans roll between us, our minds may often meet and converse with each other.

Your picture travels continually from one room to another; wherever I am likely to spend most of my time, thither it is removed; but this is not sufficient, I would have you always near me. I conjure you then, my dear friend, sit immediately to —— for a miniature.[2] You will still have time enough, if you set about it instantly. When the painter has done his part, send it to my jeweler, he has some diamonds of mine unemployed; I will write to him, and give him directions. I dispatch this pacquet to the post, without staying to consider some things in your last letter, which have given my thoughts a good deal of employment. Adieu! my dear Euphemia.

MARIA HARLEY.

Letter XXXI.
MISS HARLEY TO MRS. NEVILLE.

I HAVE loved Mr. Harley all this time you say, my dear Euphemia; and this circumstance, which has hitherto been a secret to myself, you have, it seems, discovered, from my first mention of him. I will not call your penetration in question, nor will you, I am sure, doubt my candour when I declare, that the sentiments I entertained for Mr. Harley, and which I freely avowed to you, appeared to me to be such as every friend to virtue must feel for one so truly virtuous.

You call him an excellent young man; and so he certainly is. It was natural to wish well to the worth I esteemed—to feel for his situation, and to be anxious for his prosperity. I never thought it

---

1   A paraphrase from Book 8 of *The Odyssey*, translated by Alexander Pope (1725-26): "Fast fell the tears, and sighs succeeded sighs."
2   Miniature: A small-scaled portrait, usually in watercolor (*OED*).

necessary to question my own heart about the nature of sentiments which appeared to me so reasonable and so just.

I remember a saying that once fell from you—"A young woman has passed over the first bounds of reservedness, who allows herself to think she is in love." Nor would your delicacy have permitted you to speak so plainly to me on this subject, if you had not supposed, that from the great and just degree of favour Mr. Harley is now in with my uncle; his pretensions to me will be authorised by his consent; without it I am sure, however favourably I might think of him, he could never have hoped for success.

But although, according to you, my *inclinations* and duty are now reconciled, you are not likely to leave me so happy as you imagined; for my uncle is offended, Mr. Greville reproaches me, and Mr. Harley perhaps hates me; and all these misfortunes I have drawn upon myself with the most innocent intentions imaginable.

Some time ago I suffered in my uncle's opinion for being willing to do justice to the merits of this young man, when I thought he was harshly used; and I was suspected of favouring addresses from the son of his ancient enemy; and now he reproaches me with caprice, and a tyrannical use of my power over a person whom he loves and esteems, and to whom he has the highest obligations. In the former case I shewed a ready obedience to his will, by giving Mr. Harley an absolute rejection; in the latter, whatever my sentiments were with regard to him, I thought myself obliged to act with great reserve, till my uncle was pleased to declare his intentions to me. Mr. Greville calls my conduct, in this instance, a too scrupulous prudence, which does nothing for fear of doing ill. "Your uncle's prejudices," said he, "have all given way to the conviction of his better judgment; for sensible persons only taste of an error, of which the ignorant drink till they are intoxicated. You could not, my dear Miss Harley, be ignorant what designs Sir John entertained in favour of Mr. Harley. Why then treat him with a coldness that saddened all his delightful prospects?" And he was angry with me in good earnest, for sending his young friend, as he calls Mr. Harley, away in despair.

It is no unpleasant thing to see a philosopher in choler. I only smiled at his reproaches, though I could easily have justified myself. He was malicious enough to leave me alone with my uncle this afternoon, who he knew was resolved to chide me; and accordingly he began to rail at the caprice, the obstinacy and inconsistency of our sex, in very severe terms. I was determined not to make any particular application, and listened to him very patiently, which reduced him to the necessity of being more explicit.

"I hoped you had been, in a certain degree, free from those faults, Maria," said he; "but you have convinced me, by your behaviour to Mr. Harley, that you are a very woman; and that to give steadiness to your inclinations, it is necessary you should meet with opposition.

"Here, now," pursued he, (without waiting for my answer, and indeed I had none ready for him) "when, to my shame be it spoken, I viewed young Harley in no other light than as the son of an ungrateful man, who had deceived and betrayed me, you were very favourably disposed towards him, and some very tender letters passed between you."

"Oh, Sir," interrupted I with some emotion, "is this a candid representation of my conduct? You have copies of my letters to Mr. Harley; will they bear such a comment?"

"Well, well," resumed Sir John, "letting the letters pass, if Mr. Harley was indifferent to you, where was the merit of your rejecting him to comply with my unreasonable prejudices? That sacrifice, Maria, for so I considered it, redoubled my affection for you; great as it was before, it has been greater since; but you have spoiled all, by your unaccountable behaviour. Is this young man less amiable in your eyes, because mine are open to his virtues?

"Has he not deserved you by his noble disinterestedness? And can I do less for him who saved my life, at a time when it stood between him and happiness, than bestow on him a gift which he values, I am sure, more than my estate? Which must be his whether I will or not, since I have no other heir."

My dear uncle spoke all this so affectionately, that I was melted into tears. He mistook the cause of my emotion; and starting from his chair, began to pace about the room in great agitation.

I was confounded, not being able to guess at the cause of this transport; when suddenly coming up to me, and seizing my hand, he looked earnestly at me for a moment, then exclaimed—

"Is it possible! have you really any dislike to Mr. Harley? And must I be disappointed in the pleasing design I had formed of making my preserver happy?"

"Dislike to Mr. Harley, Sir," replied I, "No, on the contrary—" I stopped, for his eyes were fixed upon me.

"Go on," said he, "your contrary, come."—

"Every one must be a friend to Mr. Harley who knows him," said I.

Now, my dear Euphemia, the discovery you think you have made coming into my head that moment, I felt my face glow like fire.

"Very well," said my uncle, "that blush is honester than your words, and we are friends again, my Maria; so I will answer for you, 'since Mr. Harley is your choice, Sir, he shall be mine'; have I hit your meaning?"

"You may always depend upon my obedience, Sir," replied I; "for I am sure you will never command any thing that is not reasonable."

"Mighty well, mighty well," cried my uncle, in a joyful accent, "I am satisfied." Mr. Greville, coming in at that moment—"Greville," said Sir John, "write to Harley instantly, tell him, I say he is a fool."

I hastened out of the room, not being willing to hear more: though, it must be acknowledged, my uncle has not, on this occasion, been inattentive to the claims of female delicacy. Here is a prodigious change in my affairs: a happy one I know you will think it. But, alas! that happiness comes clogged with the painful idea of our separation.

Letter XXXII.
MISS HARLEY TO MRS. NEVILLE.

MY DEAR EUPHEMIA,

I DISPATCHED my last letter to the post, without waiting till I could give you an account of my interview with Mr. Harley, which I expected would soon take place; for a messenger was immediately dispatched to him, with a letter from my uncle, which it was probable would soon bring him to the Hall; and indeed he came so early the next morning, that Sir John was not risen.

By his order, however, he was introduced into his bed-chamber, where they had a conference of more than an hour. I had already finished my morning walk, when they came together into the garden to meet me, for you know I am an early riser.

While they were yet at some distance, I could perceive so much heartfelt satisfaction in my uncle's looks, in Mr. Harley's so much joy, which yet seemed checked by a certain timidity that encreased as he approached me, that it was easy to guess their conversation had been very interesting.

I summoned up all my courage, in order to conquer my confusion, and prevent my acting a silly part in the trying scene that was preparing for me; and accordingly I paid my compliments to my uncle, with an air very unembarrassed as I thought; but when

I curtseyed to Mr. Harley, my half raised eyes were encountered with so passionate a glance, at the same time that he bowed to me with the most profound respect, as quite disconcerted me; and I felt that I blushed, and blushed the more because I felt it.

My uncle did not give me time to recover myself.

"It is in vain to dissemble, Maria," said he, eagerly; "I have betrayed your secret to my young friend here. I have told him, that you have been kind enough to put it in my power to reward his nobleness of mind, and pay him back some part of the vast debt of gratitude I owe him, by a gift, which, knowing your merit so well as I do, I will call a precious one."

"Receive her hand from me, Harley," proceeded he; "I promise you it is not an unwilling one—Is it, niece?"

"If it were, Sir," said I, "I am sure you would not give it, nor would I." I could not bring out another word—I was half dead with confusion.

Mr. Harley, as if remembering my rebuke a day or two before, and fearful of incurring the same censure, received my hand half bending on one knee, but kept it glewed to his lips with so passionate an action, that my uncle, willing, as it should seem, to relieve me, called out laughing—

"What, have you nothing to say to her!"

"We receive the answers of oracles, Sir," replied he, rising, in awful silence; "true devotion is dumb; and all words," pursued he, taking my uncle's hand, which he kissed respectfully, "would be too weak to paint the excess of my transport and acknowledgment."

"You have done pretty well now, however," said my uncle, still smiling, and giving his hand a hearty shake—"and now we will go in to breakfast."

Just as we were preparing to enter the house we perceived Mr. Greville coming to meet us; he drew near, laughing,

"I have rare news for you, Sir John," said he; "who do you think is come to breakfast with you? Even the learned and scientific Lady Cornelia Classick, with the Diana of our fortress, the fearless huntress Miss Sandford, who, at the age of forty-five, declares her fixed resolution never to marry, though an Endymion[1] were to court her; and boasts of her wonderful art in keeping men at a distance."

---

1 In Greek myth, Endymion was the son of Zeus and Calyce. He was so beautiful that Artemis (Diana in Roman myth, goddess of the moon, and partron of hunting and chastity), fell in love with him.

"Alas! to what am I condemned for two hours at least?" said Sir John.

"Aye," replied Mr. Greville, "you must resolve to be patient; but as for you, Miss Harley," pursued he, "fall upon your knees, and thank me for sparing you the mortification of sharing this tremendous visit; for I have told her, that you are confined to your chamber with a sore throat, a disorder she is infinitely afraid of, so you may breakfast quietly in your dressing-chamber, either alone or with company," looking at Mr. Harley, who would not venture to understand this proposal otherwise than by speaking a look.

I thanked Mr. Greville very cordially for the good office he had done me at the expence of his veracity; and, without taking notice of his insinuation with regard to my having company to breakfast with me, I told him, I would employ the happy exemption he had afforded me in writing to you.

He charged me with a thousand thousand good wishes for you; and we parted.

Mr. Harley, notwithstanding a little cloud upon his brow, contrived, unseen, to kiss my hand with a mighty passionate air; and here have I been ever since in company with my dear Euphemia; but I must quit you soon, I suppose, for my maid tells me the ladies are going. I hear their carriage draw up to the gate—I must have one look at them.

There is my uncle leading Lady Cornelia with the most gallant air imaginable. By the motion of her hand and head it would seem that she is discussing some deep question in politics, theology, or the belles lettres;[1] and my uncle, by his assenting nods, is fully convinced I observe.

But here comes the virgin huntress, with Mr. Greville on one side of her, and Mr. Harley on the other. I protest she does not accompany Lady Cornelia in the carriage, but mounts her steed with most masculine agility, to escort her female friend. Her military riding-habit, the fierce cock of her hat, the intrepid air of her countenance, make her have the appearance of a very respectable guard. Ah! what a pity she has petticoats!—My uncle looks up to me as he passes, and beckons me. I come, my dear Sir—again! Pray do not be impatient. Adieu! then, my dear Euphemia, for a short time only, for I shall dispatch this letter to the post to-day.

---

1 Literary writings, especially essays, criticism, etc.

I found the gentlemen entertaining themselves very freely with the singularities of their female visitants. How absurd does it seem in our sex to step out of nature, in order to be more agreeable! And how mortified would these mistaken candidates for general admiration be, if they could, unseen, hear the censures and ridicule that are cast on them, instead of the praises they expect.

My uncle congratulated me on having escaped this disagreeable visit; however, said he, your part would only have been silence; for wherever Lady Cornelia is no one talks but herself.

"Lady Cornelia," said Mr. Greville, "does not mix in company to converse, but to make orations. She will stun her female visitants of sixteen with learned gibberish; gives rules for epic and dramatic poetry, and cannot endure a comedy that is not within the law of four-and-twenty hours."[1]

"Ah! if your charming friend," pursued Mr. Greville, looking at me (can you guess who he meant, my dear?), "had been here, what a contrast might we not have observed between true genius and an affectation of knowledge—elegant language, and pedantic stiffness, just sentiment and unintelligible conceit: when the other preached she would only speak; and, as some one justly observes, by making plain and simple answers to her riddles, and giving definition to her confusion, she would have done her at least the good office of expounding her to herself."

"A man makes a silly figure," said Mr. Harley, "in company with so learned a Lady, and her Amazonian friend.[2] Talents so masculine, and so ostentatiously displayed, place them above those attentions and assiduities to which the charming sex have so just a claim, and which we delight to pay. Women should always be women; the virtues of our sex are not the virtues of theirs. When Lady Cornelia declaims in Greek, and Miss Sanford vaults into her saddle like another Hotspur,[3] I forget I am in

---

1 In his *Poetics*, Aristotle suggests that the action of a tragedy should take place within a twenty-four hour period; this principle was important to the neo-classical writers and critics of the eighteenth century.

2 The Amazons were a mythical tribe of female warriors near Greece who, it was said, cut off their right breasts in order to use the bow more easily, and who saw men as adversaries. Hence the adjective in the eighteenth century would denote a masculine woman, one who is inappropriately confident and aggressive.

3 In Shakespeare's *I Henry IV*, the nickname of Sir Henry Percy, a hot-tempered opponent of Prince Hal.

company with women: the dogmatic critic awes me into silence, and the hardy rider makes my assistance unnecessary."

"You do well," said Mr. Greville, laughing, "to find an excuse for not flying to take up Miss Sandford's handkerchief when she dropped it, nor attending to a question put to you in Latin by Lady Cornelia."

"Oh! as for that," replied Mr. Harley, "Lady Cornelia answered herself, and Miss Sandford drew up her handkerchief with the end of her whip so dexterously, that I had no opportunity of serving her."

"I do not think hunting," said my uncle, "a proper sport for ladies; it spoils their complexion, gives them masculine manners, and hardens their tempers. A woman who, like Miss Sandford, leaps every five-bar gate,[1] is ready to join the huntsman's hollow,[2] and would grieve if she is not in at the death,[3] may make a jolly companion over a flask of wine, but must not expect to inspire a delicate passion. I would as soon marry the female pedant, her friend, as one of those Amazonian ladies."

"Ah, Sir," replied Mr. Harley, "if you have seen the young, the noble, the beautiful Louisa join the chace, under the conduct of a fond father, and affectionate brothers, you would confess, that female delicacy may be preserved even in that habit; and that exercise, by the elegance and propriety of her dress, she loses none of the tender graces of her sex and years; her charming face retains all its sweetness, her form all its delicacy, and her mind all its native softness. The happy innocent animal, whom she pursues but to save, as if conscious of her generous intention, takes shelter at her feet, and there is sure of protection."

"You have rescued one of our fair huntresses from Sir John's general censure," said Mr. Greville. "Do you think we could not find a lady eminently distinguished for her erudition, who yet is free from pedantry and ostentation?" "You, Sir, know such a one, I am sure," replied Mr. Harley. "The wise, the pious, the virtuous Eleonora, superior to most of our sex in learning, in gentleness equal to the most gentle of her own. The poets describe Modesty as blushing at her own motion. Eleonora engages in discourse with timidity and is surprised, confused, to find her superiority

---

1   Fence of five bars' height that horses jump during the hunt as they pursue the fox; only an accomplished horse and rider would be able to jump such a high fence successfully.

2   Halloo, or cry hunters use to alert other riders to the location of the fox.

3   I.e., the death of the fox.

acknowledged by those, whose higher attainments she considered with awe."

"Then this lady does not stun one with her Latin and Greek like Lady Cornelia," said my uncle.

"So far from it, Sir," replied Mr. Harley, "that unless her extraordinary acquirements are called forth by some apt and unavoidable occasion, one may converse with her for whole years as a sensible and amiable woman, without discovering her to be a great genius."

Mr. Harley, this moment, tapped at my door, and presented me a small box, which contained your dear picture, which he would suffer no one to bring up to me but himself. I could not help thanking him very cordially, for the satisfaction he shewed in doing me this kind office.

After we had spent some time in admiring those features, which so powerfully express the beauty of the soul that animates them, I ordered my woman to tie the ribbon, to which I had fastened it round my neck; this task, also, he would perform, and did very dexterously. And now, I would have had him leave me, that I might be at liberty to indulge, alone, the sad, yet pleasing ideas, with which this dear image filled my mind, when, with a look of sympathising tenderness and concern, he drew from his pocket your letter.

Oh! my Euphemia, my foreboding heart told me this would be the last I should receive from you in England. With trembling haste I broke the seal.—Your first lines confirmed the melancholy truth—I burst into tears; and vainly repeated to Mr. Harley, my earnest desire to be left alone. He threw himself at my feet, and while he held one of my hands, and prest it to his lips, I felt it wet with a sympathising tear.

"Yes," said I, "you would love her, as I do, if you knew her; and, like me, you would grieve at being separated from her—for ever." He soothed my sorrows, by a tender participation in them. He comforted me with hope; and, when he found me a little composed, he told me, that if I had any letters ready, the messenger who brought the picture would procure a safe and speedy conveyance for them, his brother being to set out immediately for London; but that I had not a moment to lose. Alas! I have a thousand thousand things to say to you, and not a moment to say them. Farewell then, my Euphemia! and to that Almighty Power, to whom such piety and virtue must be dear, I trust the preservation of my friend! Farewell! farewell!

MARIA HARLEY.

Letter XXXIII.
MRS. NEVILLE TO MISS HARLEY.

THIS will be the last letter you will receive from me in England, my dear Maria; and could I not, at the same time that I tell you this disagreeable news, congratulate you on your approaching union with the virtuous youth who has so well deserved you, my full heart would have found it very difficult to bid you farewell; but I leave you happy, happy as my fondest wishes for you could require. And once more, I earnestly intreat you, not to repine that my lot has not been cast so favourably as yours.

A well disposed mind will extract good out of evil; for, whatever happens to us, there is some virtue or other to be exercised; either patience or gratitude, moderation or humility, charity or resignation, and they are all equally productive of peace here, and happiness hereafter.

And do you count it a small matter that I enjoy such a friendship as yours? I tell you, my Maria, with such a friendship I can despise ill fortune; and it affords me comforts, which high fortune seldom enjoys.

My picture will accompany this letter; the person who carries it will bring me back what letters you have ready. I shall begin a kind of journal from the day I leave England, and continue it as long as I am able to hold a pen; and thus I shall have the pleasure of conversing with you every day.

The more splendid and active scenes of *your* life will hardly afford you equal leisure to gratify me with packets as large as those I shall send you; but I am persuaded you will neglect no opportunity of making me happy by your letters. Fanny writes to you by my messenger, who is this moment ready to set out. I must then, my Maria, I must bid you farewell—Most loved, most amiable of friends, farewell, farewell!

EUPHEMIA NEVILLE.

Letter XXXIV.
MRS. NEVILLE TO MISS HARLEY.

Portsmouth.

MY DEAR MARIA,

IT was a great comfort to me that I did not miss your last packet, which was delivered to me a few hours before I set out from

London. It brings me a confirmation of your happiness; and can I then, loving you as I do, be less than happy, when you are supremely so? Mrs. Bellenden insisted upon my performing my journey to this place in her coach, though I made a fifth in it; but the three young ladies accommodated themselves very easily on the back seat, and I was obliged to sit next their mother, whose polite attention to me, I am afraid, was not properly repaid by one, whose thoughts were so much engrossed by the absent.

The Colonel and Mr. Neville, with the men-servants, rode on horse-back, the maids were disposed of in the stage-coach,[1] and my worthy Mrs. Benson and Fanny were together in a post-chaise. We were hospitably entertained two nights, at the house of a friend of the Colonel's; and next morning Captain Wilmot sent the boat, full manned, to bring the Colonel and his train on board the ship.

After all the ceremonies of our reception were over, we retired to our several little apartments. The Colonel and his family are all lodged near each other very commodiously. One of the lieutenants, an old acquaintance of Mr. Neville's, having very obligingly resigned his cabin to me during the voyage, I found a small writing desk in it, which I shall make good use of. Mrs. Benson and Fanny continue to be bedfellows, and are to be very near me.

Captain Wilmot gave us an elegant dinner, and did the honours of his table very gracefully. The beautiful Miss Bellenden drew his particular attention, though her vivacity seemed a little clouded by her regret at leaving England, or rather, her beloved London, alone, the scene of all her triumphs.

I happened to be seated at table near a lady, who I found was a relation of the Captain's; she had the air and manner of a woman of fashion, but seemed sunk in so profound a melancholy, that, although she answered with great politeness to the usual civilities that pass between persons at the same table, yet she did not engage at all in the conversation, but seemed wholly taken up with her own sad thoughts.

I observed her eyes were continually turned upon a most beautiful and elegant boy, about twelve years of age, who sat opposite to her, and when she removed them, it was always with a sigh, that seemed to rend her heart.

The boy, whenever he met her eager glance, turned pale and red alternately, while his sweet eyes seemed full of tears, which he

---

1 A large closed horse-drawn coach that ran at regular intervals between two places, stopping at set places along the way.

strove to hid, by forcing a smile at an austere looking gentleman next him, who watched his looks attentively, and never failed to repel the rising softness by a dreadful frown.

While I was busied in observing their different emotions, which greatly affected me, the lady, whose stifled grief had almost risen to a suffocation, asked me, in a voice scarcely articulate, for a smelling-bottle, I immediately produced one, and proposed to her to leave the company for a few minutes, and go into fresher air.

She accepted my supporting arm; the ladies were now all in motion to assist her, as well as the gentlemen; but she begged to be permitted to withdraw for a few moments with me, on whom she still leaned.

"Aye, aye," said the stern gentleman, whom I found was her husband, "take a little air, my dear, this will go off." And nodding significantly at Captain Wilmot, "Women will be foolish," said he, "there is no help for it."

The sweet boy rose up eagerly, as if he would have gone with us, but was withheld by the frowning fire; he yielded submissively; but his eyes followed us to the door with such an expression of tender anxiety, as moved me greatly.

I led the lady to my little apartment, and seated her on the bed. She burst into a violent passion of tears, which seemed a little to relieve her labouring heart. I endeavoured to sooth her, and begged of her to tell me, if I could in any way be useful to her.

"Ah! Madam," said she, "I ought to ask your pardon, for being thus troublesome to you with my grief; but when you are a mother, you will be able to guess what my sufferings are this moment.

"I am upon the point of being separated, perhaps for ever, from the darling of my soul. That boy, that lovely boy! you saw at table, he is my son, he is my only child; the most dutiful, the most affectionate of children; he will be torn from me this day; his father will have it so; I cannot survive this parting—I wish not to survive it."

Another shower of tears now burst from her eyes: somebody tapping gently at the door, I opened it, and Captain Wilmot appeared, leading the boy; who seeing the disorder his mother was in, sprung into her arms; and leaning his head over her shoulder, while she pressed him to her sobbing bosom, he wept in silence, anxious, as it should seem, to hide his tears.

"It is you cousin," said the lady, casting an upbraiding glance at the captain, "it is to you that I am indebted for this severe affliction. Why would you encourage Mr. Mansel in this odious design of sending our son to sea? Is he not born to an easy fortune? was he not prosecuting his studies with the greatest application and success?"

"My dear cousin," interrupted the captain, "you accuse me unjustly; I found Captain Mansel determined to bring up his son to the sea-service, a service in which he himself has acquired reputation. I neither encouraged nor dissuaded him from his resolution, but desired to have him on board my own ship; and will it not be a greater satisfaction to you, that he should make his first voyage under my care and protection, than with a stranger?"

The poor little boy now interposed; and taking one of his mother's hands, which he kissed tenderly several times, said, in a soothing voice—"My dear mamma, make yourself easy, I shall be very happy under my cousin's protection, he will bring me back safe to you; and if upon this trial I should not like the sea, or be found unfit for it, my papa may be persuaded to alter his mind."

The weeping mother made no reply; but strained him again in her arms, as if determined never to let him go from thence. The captain and I employed every argument we could think of to console and satisfy her mind; without attending to what we said, she exclaimed—

"Ah, my child, this boisterous element may not agree with the delicacy of your constitution. Who now will watch over your health? Who will attend to your complaints?"

"I will, Madam," cried I, eagerly—"I will supply your place during this voyage; in my cares and assiduity Master Mansel shall find another parent."

"Oh! what comfort do you give me, Madam," said Mrs. Mansel; "if any thing can support me under this afflicting separation, it will be this kind promise of yours. Edmund," said she to her son, "this sweet lady will be your mother now; I need not bid you love and respect her, for you have a grateful heart." The boy answered only by a most expressive look, and a bow low as the ground.

Captain Mansel now burst in upon us.

"What! have you not done whimpering yet?" said he to his lady. "Come, come, every body has been enquiring for you."

He strutted before her, and Captain Wilmot giving her his hand to lead her to the company, I addressed some trifling conversation to Master Mansel, in order to begin our acquaintance, and lessen his reserve.

While Mrs. Mansel was apologizing to the company for her

absence, I took care to seat myself next to my young charge, as I now considered him. I talked to him familiarly, and lessened his diffidence insensibly. He served me with my tea and coffee with a grace and freedom, and at the same time with an assiduity, that shewed at once the elegance of his manners, and the particular pleasure he took in attending me.

My heart glowed with transport when I observed that the mother, who watched our behaviour, beheld the growing intimacy with a satisfaction which seemed to suspend her grief. She took an opportunity to approach me—and grasping my hand with an eager pressure—

"I see my son will be happy in your favours to him," said she; "this goodness of your's has preserved me from despair. You are all over angel," pursued she in a transported accent: "you look and act like one; and Heaven surely sent you to my relief on this trying occasion."

I stopped this rhapsody, by calling her attention to the little schemes we had formed for our amusement during the voyage. I promised to make him acquainted with the colonel's young daughters; and assured her he would pass his time very agreeably in such society.

The evening now approached: I expected she would be soon summoned to depart. I felt for her so sincerely, that I dreaded the fatal moment, and could not help trembling when I saw Captain Wilmot advancing towards us. He seemed disconcerted, and unwilling to tell her, that she must take leave of her son; but Captain Mansel spared him the disagreeable task.

"The boat is ready, my dear," said he, with an unfeeling abruptness. "Edmund, God bless you! Come, my dear, give him a kiss, we must be gone."

A paleness, like that of death, overspread her countenance. She stood motionless, uttering not a word, nor shedding a tear, whilst the boy, who on his knee had received his father's blessing, now prostrated himself at her feet; and struggling to suppress his sighs and tears, while he held her hand, which he eagerly kissed several times, uttered in broken accents—

"Will you not give me your blessing, my dear mamma? Pray look upon me—do not grieve, I shall soon return to you—indeed I shall."

Mrs. Mansel, whom I had supported all this time, after breathing a deep sigh, turned her eyes upon her son, who was still kneeling, and spreading her arms, he sprung into her embrace, weting her bosom with tears, which now flowed fast from her eyes also.

This scene affected even the men who were present. Mrs. Bellenden was greatly moved, and the young ladies were drowned in tears.

Captain Mansel's sterness put an end to it. He seized his wife's hand, and told her in a voice, not very tender, that she was to blame to work upon the boy's passions, by giving way to her extravagant grief.—"See how he blubbers," continued he—"what a milk-sop[1] you make of him! Come, I shall lose all patience if you go on thus."

The poor lady, who evidently was in great awe of him, suffered herself to be led upon the deck. I followed her with Master Mansel, giving her, as we passed on, the most tender assurances of my attention to him. She seemed struggling to repress her anguish, and assume some degree of fortitude; and being now ready to seat herself in the chair, by which she was to be let down into the boat, after saluting the ladies, and the rest of the company, she took a more cordial leave of me, whispering, "Remember what you have promised me." Then folding her son once more in her arms, she breathed an ardent blessing on him, and still preserved some composure, till she was got into the boat. I then saw her suddenly sink into her husband's arms, apparently in a fainting fit.

Her son, who had kept his eyes fixed upon her, cried out to me in a mournful voice, "Ah! Madam, my mother!" and hiding his face to conceal his tears. I endeavoured to comfort him, but in vain; till perceiving she was recovered, I bid him look up, and shewed him his tender mother, now standing waving her handkerchief to him—which he returned with repeated bows, till the boat was out of sight.

We are got under sail; all the ladies, except Mrs. Bellenden and myself, are sea-sick. My dear Mrs. Benson struggled with the same disorder for some hours, in order to keep me company; but she was at last forced to yield to it; and she, as well as Fanny, is confined to her bed.

I sat upon the quarter-deck, as it is called, more than two hours this morning, under an awning, which Lieutenant Crawford, my husband's friend, caused to be set up for me, with no other company than my young charge, who never leaves me but when he retires to his studies, under the direction of the captain; as for Mr. Neville, he always finds most amusement where I am

---

1 A child still being fed only milk, or a coddled young man.

not. My eyes follow the receding shores, while I revolve a thousand tender melancholy ideas, and many a heavy sigh I breathed, which was constantly echoed back by my little friend, who, observing me taken up with my own thoughts, did not offer to interrupt them by any conversation. At last I asked him, "Why he sighed so often?"—"Some of my sighs are for myself, Madam," replied he, "but the greater part are for you: when I see you melancholy, I think it is my mother that I see so—and can I choose but sigh then?"

Mr. Neville that moment came to us.

"So, so, young gentleman," said he, "what, always with the ladies! you will make a fine sailor at this rate; come, I heard the captain ask for you—I will bring you to him." Master Mansel, after making me a low bow, followed him.

We have now lost sight of land—all is sky and ocean; tremendous prospect! My mind feels its awful influence—my ideas are all solemn and sad. I have recourse to my books to dissipate them; for Mrs. Benson continues still too much indisposed to relieve me by her agreeable conversation. My sweet Edmund is sick likewise, but Fanny is better, and able now to assist me in my office of nurse to him and my friend.

To-day Mrs. Bellenden and I, accompanied by the colonel, took an airing upon deck. This lady has a charming flow of spirits, and so much natural as well as acquired politeness, that although her understanding is not one of the first-rate, yet her company is sometimes very desirable. When I left her, to retire to my own apartment, I was most agreeably surprised to find Mrs. Benson there, quite recovered, her sickness having left her as suddenly as it had come on; and she is, as it is common it seems in these cases, the better for having been ill. I embraced, and congratulated both her and myself for this change: but as the good things of this life are often mixed with the bad, I found Master Mansel worse, and even with some symptoms of a fever. I staid with him great part of the day; and in the afternoon Mrs. Benson and I went to visit our sick friends. Mrs. Bellenden we found busy in nursing her daughters; for all their female attendants were so sick, that she could have but little assistance from them. Miss Bellenden, wrapped in a white satin negligee, with a most becoming night-dress on her head,[1] lay reclined on some cushions, moaning grievously. Our young naval commander had, I found,

---

1 Nightcap.

been extremely assiduous about her, never failing to enquire a dozen times in a day concerning her health; and when his visits were permitted, expressed great solicitude for her. But this single adorer could not comfort her for the gay scenes she had abandoned; and the general admiration she supposed she had attracted, when in the midst of them, she suffered more from discontent than sickness—she is sullen, fretful, and impatient.

When I came into their apartment, I found her mother gently reproving her for her behaviour, which, she said, greatly affected her father, who is very fond of her.

"He thinks it strange, my dear," said Mrs. Bellenden, "that you should shew so much reluctance to follow him to any place where his duty calls him: this peevishness alters you so, that one would hardly know you."

"Alters me, Madam!" repeated Miss Bellenden, roused to attention by these interesting words.

"Yes, my dear," replied Mrs. Bellenden, "I appeal to Mrs. Neville for the justness of my observation."

"Pray be free, my dear Mrs. Neville," said Miss Bellenden, eagerly, "Tell me, am I really altered?"

"My dear Miss," said I, "I am sorry to be obliged to tell you so disagreeable a truth; but if you suffer this depression of spirits to gain upon you, it may produce the jaundice, a distemper which is often the effect of continued discontent."

"Oh Heavens!" cried Miss Bellenden, taking out her pocket-glass, and fixing her eyes upon it, "how you terrify me!"

Colonel Bellenden and Captain Wilmot that moment entered; the latter observing the young lady so intently gazing upon her own image that she did not perceive him, went close up to her, and whispered her to beware of the fate of Narcissus.[1]

"Had Narcissus the jaundice, then?" said she, turning to him.

"The jaundice!" repeated the captain, surprised.

"Aye," said Miss Bellenden; "here is Mrs. Neville and my mamma have been frightening me out of my wits; they tell me I am grown quite shocking with this sea-sickness; I shall hate the sea while I live; I wish we could have gone to this New-York by land."

---

1 In Greek mythology, the son of Cephisus and Liriope; his love for himself was so strong that he spurned other lovers. He was punished for this arrogance by Artemis who caused him to fall in love with his own reflection in a pool. When he began to pine away, he was changed into the flower that bears his name.

"I am glad that was not possible," said Captain Wilmot, half smiling, "for then I should not have had the pleasure of conducting you."

I heard no more of the sprightly dialogue that ensued, being engaged in discourse with the colonel and his lady, and in paying my compliments to the two youngest ladies, who are as ill as their sister, but not quite so impatient. Presently afterwards Mrs. Benson and I took leave of them.

When she left me to retire for the night, I had recourse to my pen. It is a great comfort to me to be this way with you, and that from time to time I can make you read, that your image is the dear companion of all my solitary hours.

When I visited Master Mansel this morning I was greatly alarmed to find his fever very high: Captain Wilmot ordered the surgeon to attend him immediately. This gentleman, who is a grave, sensible man, and, as far as I can judge, very skilful, thinks his distemper will be the small-pox. Mrs. Mansel, it seems, never had courage enough to have him inoculated:[1] unhappy, yet amiable weakness, in a mind so full of maternal tenderness!

I am now fixed by his bed-side: I give him all his medicines, he refuses nothing from my hand. At times he is delirious, and then he takes me for his mother. Giving me that tender appellation, which he accompanies with such affectionate expressions of duty and obedience, as go to my heart. My anxiety is inexpressible! I fear for him, I fear for his mother—I fear for myself, for I feel a mother's tenderness for him.

The surgeon tells me, the symptoms are all favourable. He approves my method of nursing him; but I have some contests to sustain with Mr. Neville, who is prejudiced in favour of all the old methods; he is indeed diseased with opinion, and infected by custom. He says I starve the youth; and, although the weather is

---

1 A viral disease characterized by fever and rash, then pustulates. The smallpox was a virulent and deadly disease during the eighteenth century; if it did not kill its victim, it often severely disfigured him or her if the eruption of the vesicles was severe. Lady Mary Wortley Montagu brought back the inoculation for smallpox from her travels in Turkey in the early 1720s, inoculating her own son so that she might show by example the efficacy of this method of fighting the disease. While many accepted and benefited from such medical progress, there were others, like Mr. Neville, who chose to rely on "old methods" of treating small-pox sufferers such as keeping the room in which the patient lay shuttered and the windows closed, using poultices, etc.

very warm, mutters sadly when I suffer the fresh air to enter the little cabin. He asks me, "How I will answer it to Mrs. Mansel if I kill her son by my improper management?" I generally get off by referring him to the surgeon, whose directions I tell him I am resolved to follow. He retires, shrugging up his shoulders; and I, in this case, persist in my own way.

I have passed some days under the most uneasy solicitude; but now, thank Heaven! all goes well: the eruption is so favourable, that the surgeon assures me we have nothing to fear. But the dear boy's sensibility is so great, that he even oppresses me with the excess of his gratitude. He employs the warmest acknowledgments, the most endearing expressions, to testify the sense he has of what he calls my kindness to him. I am obliged to leave him sometimes for half an hour together, to put a stop to these strong effusions of his grateful heart, lest they should act too powerfully upon his spirits.

I have the pleasure to tell you, my dear Maria, that notwithstanding all Mr. Neville's fatal prognostications, at which I own I have been weak enough to be sometimes alarmed, that my young friend is perfectly recovered, and will lose nothing of his beauty. The little redness that remains on his face will, the surgeon assures me, leave no marks. The Bellenden family, and Captain Wilmot in particular, have congratulated me upon this event in the most obliging terms.

Mr. Neville, however, persists in arraigning my skill as a nurse; calls Master Mansel's recovery a lucky hit, in which the odds were ten to one against him; and declares, when he is so happy as to be a father, he will treat this distemper, when his child has it, his own way.

"Heaven forbid you should have a daughter then," cried Miss Bellenden; "sure you do not intend to spoil her face! Why, what a cruel man are you?"

"Your mamma was more cruel," said Captain Wilmot to her, in a low voice, for he always contrives to sit next her, "when she prevented what you think such a misfortune; she may be called the first cause of all the murders you have committed."

Miss Bellenden smiled graciously at this gross flattery, which encouraged the gallant captain to add:

"Confess, now, have you the least remorse at being able to kill your thousand in a day?"

Clara, the lively Clara, that moment raising her eyes from a book which she had been reading, and casting them archly on her sister, repeated, *What! a whole day, and kill but one poor thousand!*

The powerful expression of her look and voice charmed me, and rivetted the captain's attention upon her for a minute, which Miss Bellenden observing, said peevishly,

"I suppose, Miss, you found that piece of wit in your book there."

"Indeed I did," said Clara; "here, you may read it if you please," and offered her the book, which Miss Bellenden rejecting with a contemptuous frown, the sweet girl gave it to me; "see, Mrs. Neville," said she, "how truly my sister has guessed; and guessing work it must always be with my sister," whispered she to me, "for she hates reading, and always joins with my mamma when she chides me for being fond of it."

Captain Wilmot now hastily stepped up to me; and looking over my shoulder, as I held the book open in my hand:

"Ah!" said he, "it is Dryden's tragedy of the Duke of Guise, and Marmontier—the charming Marmontier[1] speaks the sprightly line."

He begged me to give him the book; and resuming his seat near Miss Bellenden, read out the scene, which is full of extravagant passion, all which he applied to the fair coquet with too little ceremony I thought; but she seemed highly delighted, though he read so ill, that Clara could not hide her dissatisfaction, but murmured softly, "Poor Dryden, you have got into bad hands, I perceive."

When the Colonel joined us, the conversation took another turn; for Captain Wilmot is extremely reserved in his address to Miss Bellenden before her worthy father; however, as this gentleman's private fortune is very considerable, his present station respectable, and his interest great, he certainly would be no bad match for the young lady; but a coquet generally uses her advantages so ill, that these sudden attachments seldom produce any serious consequences.

The winds seem to favour the passion of our gallant commander; and, in order to keep the charming object near him, have lulled themselves into so perfect a calm, that we make, in the sailor's phrase, very little way, and our voyage is likely to last long: however, as our sick are now in a fair way of being well, we pass our time very agreeably. We have music often, cards sometimes, and feasting every day.

Colonel Bellenden and the captain keep splendid tables:[2] we

---

1 In John Dryden and Nathaniel Lee's *The Duke of Guise* (1679).
2 Put forth excellent food and drink.

have constant invitations to both; but I am never happier than when I am permitted to pass a day in private with my own family, in the pleasing vicissitude of conversation, reading, work, and writing to you.

Poor Miss Bellenden is in a state of mortification at present. Notwithstanding the gratification her vanity has met with in the sighs of the enamoured Captain Wilmot, she has always pined in secret after the fuller triumphs she enjoyed in the gay metropolis, where she was a general toast.[1] The uneasiness of her mind has brought on hysteric fits, to which it seems she is subject.

Hitherto she has been a very charming invalid; and both her languor and her deshabille have been alike becoming: and being well aware of this circumstance, her adorer has not been kept at a distance on account of her indisposition, which only rendered her charms more interesting: but it is quite another thing with an hysteric fit.[2]

Captain Wilmot happened to be present yesterday when she was suddenly seized with one, which proved to be very violent; her frantic screams, the distortions of her countenance, her struggles, in which she exerted such strength, that it was with difficulty her mother, assisted by two maids and myself, could hold her. Her lover stood motionless for some minutes with amazement; and strong marks of disgust, mixed with some transient gleams of pity, appeared in his countenance. He hastened to send the surgeon, and in the mean time the young lady recovered her senses. I left her after she had taken some drops, and meeting Captain Wilmot, as I was returning to my own apartment, he led me to the door of it, enquiring with more curiosity, as I thought, than concern after the sick lady; I told him she was in no danger; he smiled, but in a grave accent said, it was a terrible malady, he had never seen any thing like it.

We have, for this week past, had, what the sailors call, a brisk wind, and that so favourable, that the Captain tells us we may soon expect to reach our desired port. The weather is now very warm, and a few days ago it was so intensely cold, that we were scarce able to endure its rigour; this effect was produced, it seems, by our passing near an island of ice, which rose up in the

---

1 General toast: popular at London social events.
2 Hysteria was viewed as a woman's disease whose symptoms could include overly dramatic, volatile behaviour, even amnesia, along with tremor, and convulsions that seem to have no physiological cause.

midst of the ocean to a surprising height, exactly in the form of a sugar-loaf, which it resembled in colour as well as shape.

I went upon deck with the rest of the ladies to take a view of it, but was not able to stay more than a few moments; my limbs seemed all benumbed with cold, and my teeth, as the phrase is, chattered in my head. Happily this inconvenience did not last long; we soon lost sight of this beautiful, but uncomfortable object, and its freezing influence was no longer felt.

Providence has been pleased to grant us hitherto so favourable a navigation, that nothing has happened to act, even upon the fears of ignorance and inexperience like mine, except a few squalls, as the sailors call a sudden gust of wind. The hurry and bustle these would occasion among the mariners, seemed to me a certain indication that we were going to the bottom; but the danger, as well as the apprehension, was soon over.

The sailors are now emulously climbing up to the top-mast head, as they call it, looking out for land; from this fearful height they seem no bigger than crows. Happy will the man be who first discovers it; he will be presented with a handsome purse,[1] the joint offering of all the passengers. We are all full of pleasing anxious expectation.

In this interval of hope and suspense, I often amuse myself with observing what passes between the Captain and Miss Bellenden; the lover—lover now no more since the adventure of the hysteric fit, is become a much more agreeable companion, now that his attention is not wholly engaged by one object—the lady's malady has restored him to health; he converses freely, and, in general, his eyes are no longer rivetted upon one face; he is at leisure to attend to all the little complaisances and assiduities, which a polite man pays to every female in company, but which a lover confines to one.

He disguises his indifference, however, under a most profound respect; Miss Bellenden seems amazed, confounded; she calls forth all her attractions; she varies her posture twenty times in a minute in vain, his attention is wholly disengaged; she grows peevish, complains of the length of the voyage, enquires impatiently when it will be at an end? The Captain tells her, he hopes soon to have the pleasure of congratulating her upon the sight of land.—She stares—He enters into some indifferent discourse with Mrs. Bellenden or myself. She is now down-right angry, and

---

1 I.e., a monetary reward.

frowns; he does not perceive it; but, in the course of the conversation, addresses her with the same free unembarrassed air as any other person in the company, and when she sullenly neglects to answer any question he happens to ask her, he shews not the least surprise, but repeats it with all the apparent simplicity imaginable, till she think fit to answer him.

Her coquetry is now at a stand; smiles and frowns, peevishness and good humour, produce no alteration in his countenance and behaviour; he is always polite, always respectful, and always indifferent.

It is common with persons of deeper thinking than Miss Bellenden, to change their opinions of others by their kindness or unkindness to them. This young lady has now found out, that Captain Wilmot is a very silly fellow, rude, unpolished, in a word, a mere sailor, and is much mortified to find, none of us can be persuaded to think as she does. However, she condescended yesterday to throw out, what she thought, a lure for him; which produced an effect quite contrary from what she expected, and which, to some of us who knew the secret, was a very diverting one.

The young ladies and myself were together in the gallery, admiring the most beautiful landscape imaginable, formed by the setting sun, when Captain Wilmot joined us. He had scarce paid his compliments, when we were alarmed with a cry, that one of the sailors had fallen over board; though this bad news was immediately contradicted, yet it had such an effect upon the tender nerves of Miss Bellenden, that she sighed out, "Oh! I shall faint!" and would actually have fallen, if I had not supported her; for the Captain, who was still nearer her, being apprehensive that she was going to have another hysteric fit, instead of receiving her in his arms, ran away as fast as he could to send the Doctor; and we could hear him calling aloud for him long after the lady was recovered. Miss Bellenden looked mortified to the last degree, and retired, led by her two sisters.

I met the Captain some time afterwards, and rallied him a little upon his want of gallantry. He assured me, he had not fortitude enough to bear the sight of a lady in an hysteric fit, and he thought the best thing he could do, was to send the Doctor to her assistance.

If this young lady could be convinced, that these fits, to which she is so subject, prove a powerful antidote against the effects of her charms, she might possibly endeavour to restrain the violence of her temper, for it is to that, and not to the weakness of her constitution, that she owes this disgusting malady.

I was just risen this morning, when the sound of *land! land!* reached my ears, and which was soon afterwards repeated by a hundred voices at once. A good we ardently wish for, always appears uncertain till we are in possession of it. This may be an illusion, thought I, a mistake arising from too great eagerness for the promised reward; but I was scarce dressed, when the good news was confirmed to me by Master Mansel, who, with a countenance like an April day, half smiles, half tears, came to wish me joy that our voyage would soon be happily concluded.

"Methinks, my dear little friend," said I, "your satisfaction on this occasion, is not altogether unmixed with some chagrin; what is the reason?"

"Because, Madam," replied he, "I shall soon lose you; you will forget me I fear, and this parting will be almost as terrible to me as the separation from my mother; for have you not been a mother to me?" pursued he, respectfully kissing my hand, which I felt wet with his tears, "and can I help loving you like a son?"

I comforted him with assurances, that I would always love him tenderly, and that while Captain Wilmot remained on the coast, I would make frequent opportunities of seeing him.

I now went to pay my compliments to the Colonel and his family. Mr. Neville, who, it must be acknowledged, is very exact in his observance of all due respect to his commander, was already in his apartment, which was soon filled with several of the naval officers. When Captain Wilmot joined the company, Miss Bellenden affected the most extravagant joy, at the prospect of being soon delivered from her confinement on board an *odious* ship. The Captain, without taking notice of an expression, that insinuated so great a dislike to her present situation, appeared to enjoy the universal satisfaction. He gave us an elegant entertainment, at which the mortified fair sat sullen and silent. He assures us, we shall make the harbour in two days.

The wished-for port is now in sight; we are all busy in making preparations for our landing. Miss Bellenden and her maid have been in close consult for many hours. The article of dress, on this occasion, is an arduous affair with this young lady.

We are entering fast the harbour.—I have now a sight of this new world; my heart throbs with sensations unfelt before—I dread, I hope, I wish I know not what—my thoughts are all confused. I know not whether to rejoice or weep; but I feel a disposition to do both.

I am roused from this revery [sic] by the noise of the cannon from the fort. The city of New-York seems to rise from the waves, and, viewed from the sea, makes a fine appearance. The noise of the salutes, given and received from all the ships in the harbour, as well as the citadel, stuns me. We have now cast anchor. I must lay down my pen. Mr. Neville tells me the ladies expect me.— The barge is ordered. My next letter will be dated from the city now in my view.

★ ★ ★ ★ ★

New-York.

Till this moment, my dear Maria, I have not had leisure to resume my little narrative, though I have been already two days upon this island.

When I waited upon Mrs. Bellenden in the great cabin, I found the ladies all ready to embark in the ship's barge, which was full manned; the streamers flying, and every decoration, both for state and convenience, ordered by the Captain, to accommodate Colonel Bellenden and his family.

When Miss Bellenden came upon deck, in the full blaze of dress and beauty, I observed Captain Wilmot look at her attentively, not without some emotions of surprise and pleasure, as I thought; but they were soon checked by the silly consciousness she betrayed of her own charms, and the scornful, yet exulting glances, she cast upon him. And he now, having taken a polite leave of Mrs. Bellenden, addressed her with the most perfect indifference, associating myself and the young ladies, her sisters, in his parting compliments.

When we were all seated in the barge, with Mrs. Bellenden at our head, I observed to her smiling, that she had a numerous suite; and indeed her charming daughters, Mrs. Benson, myself, and Fanny, with the female servants, who were all well drest, formed a respectable train.

The Governor's[1] coaches waited our landing; the Colonel put

---

1 Euphemia refers to the governor's wife as "Mrs. Montague" four paragraphs below this mention of the governor, and later, in Volume III, "Mr. Mountague" clearly denotes the governor. However, there is no record of a Governor Montague or Mountague as governor of colonial New York. John Montgomerie served as governor from 1728-31; Robert Monckton in 1761; Henry Moore from 1765-69; and John Murray from 1770-71; perhaps Lennox means one of these. The governor in colonial New York was appointed by the king in Britain and was answerable to

me into the first coach with his lady and daughters; Mrs. Bellenden would have it so; he went in the next himself, with Mrs. Benson, Mr. Neville, and Fanny; who modestly declined the honour; but the colonel insisted upon taking her.

We were carried to a very large house, the principal tavern in the place, where a magnificent dinner was provided. Here we found a gentleman waiting our arrival, who complimented the Colonel from the Governor, and introduced some ladies, wives to some of the principal merchants, one of whom did the honours of the table very politely.

The Governor had caused Colonel Bellenden to be informed, that he would wait upon him in the evening; but the Colonel, ever strictly attentive to all the duties of his station, with great politeness prevented this visit, which was intended as a mark of high respect, and paid a visit himself to the Governor after dinner, taking Mr. Neville along with him. In the evening, we went to the several lodgings provided for us in the town, and had reason to be satisfied with their neatness and convenience.

This city is situated upon an island about fourteen miles long, but not more than two broad. This island is just in the mouth of the river Hudson, one of the noblest rivers in America, and is navigable for more than two hundred miles. Albany, the next principal city of the province, is situated on the same river, at about a hundred and fifty miles distant from New-York. There Colonel Bellenden, being second in military command to the Governor, will generally reside; half of the troops being constantly quartered there; and there also we must settle, my husband being one of the Colonel's lieutenants.

Mrs. Bellenden received a visit today from the Governor's lady; she brought with her three of her daughters, all handsome, their manners easy and engaging—so easy, that after the first ceremonies were over, they entered into the most familiar conversation with the Colonel's daughters; and before they parted, made them a thousand professions of friendship, with surprising cor-

---

him. He was given the title "Captain General and Governor in Chief." The colonial governor had the power to veto laws, adjourn the general Assembly, administer oaths, and establish judicial courts, among others, and, as the title implies, he was commander in chief of the military forces in the state. The powers of the governor became a major issue mid-century when the State Assembly challenged the governor's office for shared power; the Assembly ultimately backed down and reached a compromise position with the governor.

diality, which ceased to be surprising, when I found these suddenly formed attachments is the custom of the place. When Mrs. Bellenden presented me to the Governor's lady, she in a very graceful manner just mentioned my family, in order to procure me a more distinguished notice; and it must be acknowledged, that Mrs. Montague answered her intention perfectly well by the reception she gave me.

Yesterday we dined at the Governor's, and were most splendidly entertained. He resides in a very spacious house within the fort, where a lieutenant's guard mounts every day. It being Sunday, we heard divine service in the Governor's chapel. It is small but elegant; the Governor and his family sit in a little covered gallery, decorated with velvet hangings and cushions; they enter it by a door from one of their own apartments. The principal officers and their wives, who are considered as the nobility of the place, the Secretary of the Province,[1] and some other persons in civil employments, have pews in this chapel, and are always invited to the Governor's table, who is very hospitable, very polite, and, without descending from his dignity, extremely affable. He has the reputation of being a man of distinguished understanding.

A succession of visits, balls, and entertainments, for these ten days past, have fatigued me greatly, which, together with the heat of the climate, at this season of the year, brought on a little fever, for which Mrs. Montague prescribes change of air, and insists upon my passing a week at a little cottage of her's, as she calls it, about two miles from the city, where she promises to join me in a day or two; I shall set out accompanied only by Mrs. Benson and Fanny.

Mr. Neville is perpetually engaged; and pleads in excuse for his not attending me in this little excursion, the importunities of the numerous friends he has made since his arrival here, who will not suffer him to have an hour at his own disposal.

Mrs. Benson tells him, that it is a great misfortune to be so much beloved, for that one of whom so many others have need, can be of little use to himself. "For my own part," added she, "I

---

1   The Secretary of the Province or State of New York assisted the governor and maintained the authority of the king; he was sometimes a member of the governor's Advisory Council. In terms of rank within the government, he took precedence over members of the Commons, the House of Assembly, the Mayor and Aldermen, but was beneath the Attorney General, the Treasurer, and the Lt. Governor and Governor.

think it better to be less agreeable; and, as somebody says, never to sacrifice to the graces at all, than to become the victim of the sacrifice."

Mr. Neville looked a little grave at first, not knowing whether to take what she said as a compliment or banter; but self-love explained it to his own advantage, and the cloud that was gathering on his brow soon dispersed.

A ride of about half an hour brought me to Mrs. Montague's little villa; a cottage for its simplicity; but it is a palace for elegance and convenience.—The scene is sweetly romantic. I seem already to inhale health and spirits form the balmy breeze, impregnated with a thousand sweets from the flowers, which in vast profusion bloom around me. How sweet is solitude, to a mind capable of relishing its calm and rational pleasures! Yet it is true, that your absence is a perpetual drawback upon every thing that gives me joy; and possessing you but in idea, it requires a very strong imagination to make me desire nothing more.

Mr. Neville favoured me with a visit this morning, to tell me that a ship will sail to-morrow for England, and that I must make up my packet, which he will take care to put into proper hands, that it may be safely delivered. I have been so short a time here, that I can say but little of the place and its inhabitants. The city of New-York, as I observed before, makes a good appearance, viewed from the sea; but its streets are irregular.—The houses are of brick, and some of them built in the Dutch taste, who were the first settlers; and many of their descendants remain here. The town has a flourishing trade, which produces great profits. The merchants are wealthy; and the people in general, comfortably provided for, and that with very moderate labour. There seems to be great freedom of society among the better sort, who are rich and hospitable. The officers live in a stile suitable to the distinguished rank they hold here.—And the Governor, though easy of access, and very affable in his manners, keeps up a proper state and dignity.

The soil of this country, I am told, is extremely fruitful, abounding not only in its native grain, Indian corn, but in all such as have been naturalized here from Europe. Here is wheat, they say, in such abundance, and so excellent, that few parts of the world, for the part that is cultivated, exceed it in either of these qualities; nor in barley, oats, rye, and every sort of grain which you have. They have here a great number of horned cattle. Horses, sheep, hogs—all the European poultry, abound here. Game of all kinds is extremely plenty.—Wild turkies of a vast size, and equal goodness; and a beautiful species of pheasants, only found, they say, in this country. Every species of herbs, or roots, which you force in your gardens, grows here with great ease, as well as every kind of fruit; but some, such as peaches and melons, in far greater perfection than you have them.

From the account I have given you, my dear Maria, of the productions of this clime, you will readily agree, that an epicure may find sufficient gratifications here for his predominant passion.

Mr. Neville bids me haste and conclude. He is going back to town immediately, and only waits for my packet. I inclose a few lines for my Lord L. which I intrust to your care; he is the only person, among my relations, who, I believe, is anxious to hear from me.

This letter will, perhaps, reach your hands in three weeks, if the wind is favourable, and the ship not becalmed, as ours was; and, perhaps, one from you is upon its road to me.—Oh! that thought, how I enjoy it! I am charged with a thousand compliments to you from Mrs. Benson and Mr. Neville. Your Fanny is well and happy, and tells you so herself, in a letter which I inclose. Say every thing that is respectful and kind, in my name, to Sir John and Mr. Harley. And from your own heart, my dearest friend, judge of the unalterable affection of your

EUPHEMIA NEVILLE.

END OF THE SECOND VOLUME.

EUPHEMIA
VOL. III

LETTER XXXV.
MRS. NEVILLE TO MISS HARLEY.

MY DEAR MARIA,

I AM still in this delightful solitude; Mrs. Montague, on account of a slight indisposition of the governor, could make me but a short visit: but finding my health so much mended since I have been here, she very obligingly pressed me to continue a week longer; and left me the key of a closet which contains her books, among which she said I might possibly find some that would please me. They are indeed generally well chosen.

New-York.

Here I am, again, in the midst of balls, concerts, long dinners, late suppers, and a perpetual succession of visits. Miss Bellenden declares it is a charming place: she is universally admired, but has not made one conquest—a circumstance that often attends mere beauty.

In three days, however, we are to set out for Albany. Miss Bellenden hangs her fair head at this intelligence. That town is remarkable for nothing but the great trade it carries on with the Indians. The inhabitants are chiefly Dutch, and keep up the customs and manners of their ancestors—the ancient settlers. The officers and their families must furnish all the gay society she is likely to find there. It is true, her pride will be soothed. Her father is commandant there, and first commissioner likewise in civil affairs.[1] He will live in great state; but she will not be happy.

---

1 Col. Bellenden will command the military forces at the fort in Albany, and oversee interaction between fort personnel and townspeople. Patricia Bonomi suggests that the "intrusion" of military personnel in Albany society was an uncomfortable one: "Friction between soldiers and the civilian population was not unusual in the colonies, but at Albany it took on the added dimension of a clash between two cultures" (*AFP* 52), in that the British gentry at the forts found the Dutch civilian population ridiculous. This is clearly the view of the Bellenden girls towards the Dutch citizens they meet in Albany; given this, one wonders how effective a commissioner of civil affairs Col. Bellenden could have been.

However the Colonel, at his lady's request, has taken a house in this city, which he proposes to visit once a year; and Miss Bellenden is a little comforted by this arrangement.

We are to perform this long voyage, of a hundred and fifty miles, on Hudson's river, in one of those little yachts,[1] great numbers of which are continually sailing between New-York and Albany with the Indian trade. We went on board one of them this morning, in order to examine the accommodations we are likely to meet with; for calms, or contrary winds, sometimes lengthen this passage to a week or ten days. These vessels are made extremely convenient for passengers.—There are two cabins in each, destined for their use, one has six beds, three on each side; the space in the middle, contains a large table, chairs, and other conveniences; the furniture of the beds, chairs, and windows is of delicate figured calico.[2] Nothing can exceed the neatness which reigns in every part of these little vessels; the boards, even on the deck, are as nice as those of a lady's dressing-room.[3]

Although the Colonel has sent most of his servants already to Albany, yet our company is still large enough to require three of these yachts to convey us. It is settled, that Mrs. Bellenden, the three young ladies, myself, and Mrs. Bellenden's woman, are to go in one sloop; Mrs. Benson, with Fanny and some female servants, will occupy the cabin in another; the Colonel, with Mr. Neville, and some officers from New-York, who, out of respect, attend him to Albany, will lead the van. Tomorrow will be devoted to farewel visits; and the next day we shall embark.

Albany.

Not one line have I been able to write to my dear Maria for these ten days past. Our voyage lasted eight days, because we would have it so.—I will explain this circumstance to you in due time. And now being tolerably well settled, and having full leisure for the sweetest employment of my life, conversing (so I will call it) with you—I will go on with my usual prolixity.

After a tedious day spent in the ceremonial of leave-taking, we retired early to rest, hoping to go on board quietly in the

---

1 Originally, light, fast sailing ships, used to carry important people. Later, the term referred to small, light ships using wind or engine power.
2 The furniture is upholstered in a heavy, patterned white cotton cloth.
3 I.e., the floor aboard ship is as satisfactory as that in a lady's dressing room, so polished, smooth.

morning, without any further parade; but in this we were mistaken.—All the officers, and many of the principal gentlemen in the place, came to wait upon the Colonel, and attend him to the water side: some ladies also paid the same compliments to Mrs. Bellenden; in a word, we had a numerous train.

Captain Wilmot brought my sweet Edmund to take leave of me again. I thought I should never get loose from his arms; he hung about me in tears, even sobbing with the violence of his emotions; the Captain, at last, forced him away.

The cannon from the battery[1] saluted the Colonel's yacht as it passed; and the ladies of the fort family (for that is the phrase here), did us the honour to come out, and waved their handkerchiefs to us. We had little wind, but that favourable; and we sailed slowly along upon the most delightful river[2] imaginable, the shores on each side exhibiting a prospect, sometimes all beautifully wild and romantic, sometimes rich with flourishing plantations, and elegant mansions.

When the dinner-time approached, the skipper (for that is the title given to the Dutch commander of these little vessels) told us, that if we chose to dine on shore, he would come to an anchor near any spot we liked best; that the trees would afford us shade, and the mossy banks a table and seats. We all approved of this hint; Clara especially, who is a little romantic.

We pitched upon a very pastoral scene, and the boat carried us on shore; we sent it immediately to fetch Mrs. Benson; and soon afterwards the Colonel, who from his yacht had observed what was doing, joined us with his company. We had a very elegant cold collation; for our good friends at New-York had, unknown to us, sent a profusion of delicacies to increase our stores.

We did not part till the evening, when, a fresh breeze springing up, we hastened on board our separate vessels, and made a great deal of way in the night; but in the morning we were again becalmed, and as we moved slowly along the liquid plain, which was as smooth as glass, we were at leisure to admire the magnificent scene that presented itself to our eyes.—The river here being very narrow, running between a ridge of mountains on each side, whose tops, covered with groves of lofty trees, seemed to hide their heads in the clouds, while their sloping sides were adorned with the most beautiful verdure, and trees of many species unknown to us. The awful gloom from the surrounding

---

1   Group of artillery.
2   I.e., the Hudson River.

shades, the solemn stillness, inspired a soft and pleasing melancholy, which we enjoyed in silence, being, as the poet says, "rapt in pensive musing."[1]

Miss Bellenden, mean time, diverted herself with asking our skipper a thousand silly questions; and he, in the course of their conversation, informed her, that even among these wilds some inhabitants were to be found, who lived there secluded from all converse with their species, except, sometimes, a straggling Indian or two would stumble, by chance, upon their dwellings in the labyrinth of the woods. They subsisted, he said, upon the milk of their cows, some game, when they were able to catch it, and the spontaneous fruits of the earth.

Our curiosity was strongly excited by this account; we were impatient to see these persons, whose manners, we supposed, must be as savage as their way of life.

The skipper attended us on shore.—And Mrs. Bellenden, as lively and enterprising as the youngest of us, walked the wild, fearless and untired; but no human creature could we see; and, after traversing many a rugged path, and climbing up many a steep ascent, we were upon the point of giving over our fruitless search, when we heard the tinkling of a bell; we followed the sound, and presently discovered a cow, paceing slowly along a winding path in the woods, which, we supposed, led to some habitation.

We pursued her tract, and in a few moments came to a delightful spot, entirely cleared of under-wood, shaded with trees of a most beautiful foliage, with flowering shrubs between, and a luxurious growth of honeysuckles twining round their trunks. A spring of the clearest water ran meandering amongst their roots, and meeting with a hollow, which seemed to have been a little assisted by art, formed a bason that supplied the necessities of the family.

At a small distance stood an oven built of clay; a large platter, formed of the same materials, hardened in the sun, stood upon the top, full of wild pigeons, of which, in this season of the year, it seems there is a great plenty; they had been baked in the oven, which was preparing a second dish to furnish out the repast, consisting of peaches, which grow wild in such plenty, that they feed their hogs with them all over this country.

---

1 Alexander Pope's "Eloisa to Abelard" (1717): "In these deep solitudes and awful cells,/ Where heav'nly-pensive, contemplation dwells,/ And ever-musing melancholy reigns;/ What means this tumult in a Vestal's veins?" (lines 1-4).

We now ventured to enter the cottage; the sides of which were clay, supported on the out-side by thick branches of trees strongly fastened together, the roof thatched very firmly, and the chimney very well contrived, and formed of bricks, which seemed to have been the work of the same architect.

I took notice, that the fire-place was of an enormous size; the skipper said, not larger than was needful. The winters here are intensely cold, it seems; and the inhabitants of this cottage can, with very little labour, supply themselves with plenty of fuel.

In one corner was their bed, composed of dry leaves and bear skins. On some rudely fashioned shelves, we saw several large clay vessels full of milk, which had thrown up a very rich cream. We were very desirous of taking some away with us for our tea, but was at a loss what to put it in.—Miss Clara, searching about, found some cocoa-nut shells, which had been sawed in two, and were ranged like tea-cups on a shelf; we filled one of these with cream, which we skimmed with a wooden spoon we saw there; and having deposited some half-crowns and shillings, as payment for what we had taken, were preparing to depart, when the Dutchman, looking at us with a mixture of contempt and sur-prise in his countenance, exclaimed—"No, no, this must not be," and was sweeping all the money, except one shilling into his hat, when Mrs. Bellenden observing what he was about, ordered him, in a peremptory tone, to put it back; which he did, with a sor-rowful look, shrugging up his shoulders, and shaking his head at the same time.

We now heard a coarse voice, which, however, seemed to be that of a woman, calling aloud; at which we were a little fright-ened; but the skipper told us, it was the mistress of the cottage calling her cow by name; we went out to meet her; but the poor creature was in so much astonishment and terror at our appear-ance, that she seemed ready to fall to the ground.

A child about two years old, which she held in her arms, seeing us approach, almost stunned us with its screams; and even the cow, who, obedient to the call of its mistress, was hastening to her, no sooner saw us, than, as if struck with a panic likewise, it turned about, and trotted back to the woods.

It was impossible to help laughing at the general consternation our appearance had occasioned. We would fain have entered into some conversation with the good woman, but, besides that she did not understand a word of English, and we could not talk Dutch, when we offered to go near her, she would draw back a few paces in evident terror.

Our conductor having spoke to her a few minutes in Dutch, she seemed better reconciled to us, and paid her respects often, in somewhat between a bow and a curtsey. We shewed her the cream we had taken, and pointed to the money we had left in return for it; to which we added something more; and observing that the poor woman was wretchedly clothed, and that the infant was more than half naked, we collected our cambrick pocket-handkerchiefs together, and even added our aprons, and gave her.

She received our gifts with strong expressions of gratitude, and accompanied us part of our way to the boat, often calling on her husband, who, however, did not appear, and who was probably not within hearing.

The condition of these poor people seems to be bad; and I do not find that they receive much relief from the wealthy owners of the rich plantations, which are in the neighbourhood of these high lands. The many that need, and the many that deny pity, make up the bulk of mankind.

★ ★ ★ ★ ★

Albany.

Our navigation down this delightful river lasted eight days; it is true, we protracted it to this time, by the frequent excursions we made on shore.—Some of these I have given you an account of, which, I am afraid, will appear rather tedious; for it is no easy matter to entertain eyes that are not accustomed to fix upon vulgar objects, and to administer pleasure to a mind that is actuated only by lawful passions.

The Colonel was received here with much ceremony: the cannon from the fort was fired; the soldiers, headed by their officers, were drawn up on the beach; the mayor, with the principal citizens, attended his landing, and conducted him to the fort, where the commanding officer always resides.

This is a regular fortification, situated upon a steep hill, which overlooks the town, and has within it a large and elegant house for the commander, and convenient barracks for the soldiers, with a guard-room, and a handsome apartment for the lieutenant upon duty.

Mrs. Bellenden had reason to be satisfied with the care and diligence of her servants, who had been sent some weeks before with the baggage.—She found her apartments in very good order; and I left her and the young ladies in high spirits, delighted with the new and strange objects around them, and retired to a ready furnished house in the town, which Mr. Neville had taken care to have provided for me.

This town is worse built than New-York; few of the houses have an elegant appearance on the out-side, but an excessive neatness reigns within. The language, the manners, the dress, all Dutch.

During the whole time of my residence in New-York, I had never seen any of the savages; but they are often to be met with here. The Indian trade is very considerable, and has enriched many of the inhabitants of Albany; who at present, however, do not make the enormous profits they did formerly. The Indians, under such excellent masters of traffic as the Dutch, have acquired a knowledge of the successful artifices of trade, and are sometimes a match even for them in knavery.

They take great liberties with the town's people, entering their houses freely, if they find the doors open, and seating themselves wherever they like best, remain several hours together without being disturbed.

I had as yet seen an Indian only from my window. When going one day into my kitchen, to give some orders to my cook, I was extremely alarmed to see one of these savages seated by the fire, smoking his pipe very composedly.[1] His appearance had driven away all my servants, but a black woman,[2] employed in the

---

1 He most probably belongs to the Mohawk tribe, since Albany and its environs was "the Mohawks' country." One of the Six Nations that composed the Iroquois confederacy, the Mohawks were allies to the British, against the French. Indeed, it is this relationship, and the relationship the Mohawks had with the Dutch before the English arrived, that caused many of the tribes in the eastern portion of North America to fear them. Another reason was their involvement with the League of the Five Nations, to which they belonged along with the Onondaga, Cayuga, Oneida, and Seneca tribes, and in 1722 the Tuscarora tribe. By the mid-eighteenth century, the League's territory included the Ohio Valley to the west, and southeast of Lake Champlain.

2 Jacqueline Jones notes that while slavery was outlawed in New York in 1827, in the mid-1700s "all but a few thousand black women and men in the colonies were slaves" ("Race, Sex, and Self-Evident Truths: The Status of Slave Women during the Era of the American Revolution," in *Women in the Age of the American Revolution*, ed. Ronald Hoffman and Peter Albert [Charlottesville: UP of Virginia, 1989], 330). Thus it is likely that the woman Euphemia sees "employed in the drudgery of the

drudgery of the kitchen; and, indeed, that appearance was shocking enough to justify their fears.

He had a fierce and and menacing look; his copper-coloured face was painted in round spots of red, yellow, and black; his hair strewed up with some kind of powder of a deep red, which looked like blood streaming from different wounds in his head; his ears were stretched to an enormous length by the weight of the strange ornaments he wore in them, pieces of tin, glass, strings of shells, brass rings, and even slips of woolen cloth of several colours, which hung down to his shoulders.

His dress was a shirt made of Osnaburgh linen,[1] a short petticoat of the same, which reached to his knees, in the manner of the Scotch highlanders, and, over all, a mantle of coarse flannel, which, being a beau,[2] was adorned with several narrow borders of scarlet list.—He had a large knife hanging at a kind of girdle, unsheathed, ready for mischief, as I thought. This tremendous

---

kitchen" is a slave, though there were, according to Peter Kalm, a traveller from the Netherlands to America in the 1740s, some free Blacks living in New York State at that time, those who had been bought by Quaker masters and, after serving them for a time, were freed. He writes: "At present they seldom bring over any negroes to the English colonies [from Africa], for those which were formerly brought thither have multiplied rapidly" (*Travels in North America I*, 206). From Kalm's point of view, American Blacks were better treated than those in the West Indies since they were equal to other servants in all things except liberty. Gary Nash, in *Red, White and Black* (Englewood Cliffs, NJ: Prentice-Hall, 1974), notes that New York was the "largest importer of slaves north of Maryland. In the mid-eighteenth century, the areas of original settlement around New York and Albany remained slaveholding societies with about twenty percent of the population composed of slaves and thirty to forty percent white householders owning human property" (165). However, Selma Williams, in *Demeter's Daughters* (New York: Atheneum, 1976), writes that the total slave population in New England "never reached more than three percent in the eighteenth century" (67), though New York, "the northern colony with the greatest number of slaves" during the eighteenth century, had fourteen per cent of that total. Séjourné notes that of the total population of Albany in 1737, fifteen per cent was Black (8,941 Blacks to 51,496 Whites) (83, n. 152).

1 A coarse, inexpensive linen originally made in Osnabruck, Germany but subsequently manufactured in England and Scotland, this material was popular with colonists in the eighteenth century, and with the native populations with which they traded.

2 From the French word for handsome, a dandy, or one who is overly concerned with his dress and appearance.

object continued to smoke his pipe, without taking any notice of me, while I stood motionless with surprise and fear. When the black girl came up close to me, whispering in her gibberish, "You must be no fraid of Indian, my lady," said she, "if Indian see you fraid of him, he be quite mad."

This hint made me endeavour to recollect myself; and, all trembling as I was, I ventured to approach him, and very humbly dropt him a curtsey, which he returned with a nod, crying, "Hoh, hoh!" in a voice, however, less terrible than his looks.

I then ordered some cold meat and bread to be set before him, at which he seemed greatly pleased; and making him another curtsey, with trembling knees, for I was still dreadfully frightened, I went to find Mrs. Benson, and related my adventure; she, not at all dismayed, was eager to take a view of my savage guest; her courage emboldened Fanny and the cook. The Indian, without minding them, eat like a wolf, and when he was satisfied, fell fast asleep.

We knew not how to get him away; when, fortunately, Mr. Neville came in. We told him in what perplexity we were; and he immediately marched into the kitchen, making, on purpose, a great noise on his entrance, which roused the Indian, who, seeing him dressed in regimentals, for he was just come off guard, started up, shook hands with him very cordially, and went away.

They pay great respect to the military, and never presume to come uninvited into their houses; a circumstance I was extremely glad to hear; for such intrusion, if frequent, would have made me very miserable.

This city, as I have already observed, carries on a great trade with the Indians, who barter furrs for blankets, Osnaburgh shirts, guns, hatchets, knives, kettles, powder and shot, and many other articles. Here the treaties, and other transactions, between us and the Iroquois Indians are negociated. And every third year, the governor of New-York comes here to meet them, and renew the alliance.[1]

This nation, or rather combination of five nations, united by an ancient and inviolable league among themselves, are the

1 Conferences between the governor of New York and the Iroquois were actually held more frequently than Euphemia suggests: Séjourné notes that such a meeting occurred in 1733, 1735, 1737, 1740, 1742, and 1744. Harriot Stuart also states that the meetings took place every three years, a mistake Séjourné attributes to Lennox's probably having witnessed the 1740 meeting, the only one during the period when Lennox was probably in New York to take place after a gap of three years (126).

oldest, the most steady, and most effectual ally we have found among the Indians. By their unanimity, firmness, military skill, and policy, they have raised themselves to be the most formidable power in all America. They have reduced a great number of other nations under their dominion; and a territory twice as large as the kingdom of France.

The five nations of the Iroquois compose the most celebrated commonwealth of Indians in America.

The nations of America are at a great distance from each other, with a vast desert frontier, and hid in the bosom of hideous, and almost boundless forests. The Mohawks, a tribe of Iroquois, who dwell nearest our settlements, are converted to Christianity, and consequently, in some degree, civilized. The government pays a clergyman, who officiates in their chapel, which was built for them by Queen Anne,[1] who likewise presented them with a fine set of alter-plate, and other decorations for it.

There is a fort here, called by the name of a former governor,[2] in which there is a small garrison, commanded by a lieutenant, who may be relieved every year; but the present officer, Mr. Butler,[3] either because he is fond of command, or the emoluments arising from it, petitioned to be continued in it, and has actually lived there ten years. The Indians love him, and have presented him with lands to a considerable value.—They have been equally generous to their spiritual pastor, who is likewise a great favorite with them.

It is these Mohawks who come amongst us so frequently at Albany. Though converts to our faith, they preserve most of their ancient customs.—Religion seems to have but little influence upon their conduct and manners. Their virtues are their own; their vices often copied from their enlightened allies.

The Indians are tall, their limbs strait and well proportioned,

---

1 Anne (1665-1714), Queen of Great Britain and Ireland.

2 Originally named Queen Fort, it was renamed in 1719 after the then governor of New York Robert Hunter (1666-1734) who served in that office from 1710-19.

3 The lieutenant commanding Fort Hunter during the early 1740s was indeed Walter Butler. He had served at the fort since 1728, with intermittent duties at the fort at Oswego in the northern part of the state. Well liked by the aboriginal peoples, he conducted heavy trade with them and bought a great deal of land from them, which is perhaps one reason he was loathe to leave the area and return to England.

their bodies are strong, but of a species of strength, it is said, rather fitted for much hardship, than to continue long at any servile work, by which they are quickly consumed. Their heads are flattened by art, their features are regular, but their countenance fierce; they have long black lank hair, no beards, their skins a reddish brown, a colour admired among them, and improved by the constant use of bear's-grease and paint.

The whole fashion of their lives is of a piece, hardy, poor, and squalid; and their education, from their infancy, is solely directed to fit their bodies for this mode of life, and to form their minds to a capacity of enduring and inflicting the greatest evils.

Their only occupations are war and hunting; agriculture is left to the women; for merchandize they have the greatest contempt. When their hunting season is past, the fatigues of which they suffer with much patience, and in which they exert great ingenuity, they pass the rest of their time in an entire indolence—sleep half the day in their huts, and observe no bounds in eating. Drinking they were not addicted to, having no spirituous liquors among them; but since they have acquired this taste, it has given a spur to their industry, and enjoyment to their repose.

This is the principal end of all their treaties with us; and from this they suffer inexpressible calamities; for having once begun to drink, they observe no measure, but continue a succession of drunkenness as long as the means of procuring liquor lasts.— Even the Mohawk Christians are guilty of this excess; and, when intoxicated, are capable of committing the greatest cruelties.

They are grave even to sadness in their deportment, upon any serious occasion; observant of those in company, and respectful to the old. Their temper cool and deliberate; never in haste to speak before they have well considered the matter, and are sure the person who spoke before them has finished all he had to say. They express great contempt for the vivacity of the Europeans, who interrupt each other, and frequently speak all together. The tone of their voice is soft and agreeable; that of the women, I am told, is wonderfully sweet and harmonious.

All I have told you of the Indians, and much more that I have yet to tell you, you must not imagine is the result of my own observations, for which I have had but a few opportunities yet; but the substance of some conversations with a very sensible man, whom Mr. Neville met with at the Colonel's, and introduced to my acquaintance. He came to America merely to gratify a curiosity, which has carried him over half the world, I believe, and is but lately returned from Oswego, a factory[1] on the lake Ontario, which is at a great distance from hence. We have a fort there, by which most of the Indians pass in their way to Montreal.

In this wild region, inhabited only by savages, did Mr. Euston pass a whole year. The officer who commanded the detachment sent thither to relieve the small garrison being his friend, he accompanied him in this tedious march; and came back with him when he also was relieved in his turn.

It seemed to me surprising that a man, formed by nature, and enabled by fortune, to enjoy all the elegances of life, could voluntary waste so great a part of his time among a race of beings, in appearance truly wretched. He smiled at the compassion, mixed with horror, which I testified for their condition; and combated my notions in a manner so new and amusing, that I cannot forbear giving you a specimen of some of his arguments, which, he told me, were all drawn from the celebrated Abbé Reynal.[2] "It is in the nature of man, says the sensible and elegant writer," pursued he, "that we must look for his means of happiness. What does he want to be as happy as he can be?—Present subsistence; and if he thinks of futurity—the hopes, and certainty of enjoying that blessing. The savage who has not been driven into, nor confined within the frigid zones by civilized societies, is not in want of this first of necessaries; if he lays in no stores, it is because the earth and seas are reservoirs, always open to supply his wants—fish and game are to be had all the year, and will supply the want of fertility in the dead seasons.

"The savage indeed, says the elegant writer whose words I quote, has no house well secured from the access of external air, or commodious fireplaces; but his furs answer all the purposes of the roof, the garment, and the stove. He works but for his own occasions; sleeps when he is weary, and is a stranger to watchings and restless nights. War is a matter of choice to him; danger, like labour, is a condition of his nature, not a profession annexed to his birth—a national duty, not a domestic servitude.

"The savage is serious, but not melancholy; his countenance seldom bears the impression of those passions and disorders, that

---

1 A company's trading station.
2 Guillaume Thomas François Raynal (1713-96), French writer of the popular *Histoire philosophique et politique des établissements et du commerce des Européens dans les deux Indes*, published in 1770 and translated by J. Justamond in 1776 as *A Philosophical and Political History of the British Settlements and Trade in North America*. See Introduction and Appendix C.

leave such shocking and fatal traits on ours. He cannot feel the want of what he does not desire; nor can he desire what he is ignorant of. Most of the conveniences of life are remedies for evils he does not feel. He seldom experiences any of that weariness that arises from unsatisfied desires; or that emptiness and uneasiness of mind, that is the offspring of prejudice and vanity. In a word, the savage is subject to none but natural evils."

My philosopher, observing I listened to him with pleasure, went on with his quotations. "What greater happiness than this, says the Abbé, does the civilized man enjoy? His food is more wholesome and delicate than that of the savage; he has softer clothes, and a habitation better secured against the inclemencies of the weather. But should he live under a government, where tyranny must be endured under the name of authority—to what outrages is not the civilized man exposed! If he is possessed of any property, he know not how far he may call it his own; when he must divide the produce between the courtier, who may attack his estate; the lawyer, who must be paid for teaching him how to preserve it; the soldier, who may lay it waste; and the collector, who comes to levy unlimited taxes."

It must be confessed, this picture, though a little overcharged, is not ill drawn. Mr. Neville listens with great pleasure to this gentleman's account of the customs and manners of the American nations. He is so fond of change of scene, and of varying his modes of life, that I should not be surprised to find him envying Mr. Butler's situation, and soliciting to have his turn in that command, in order to enjoy the new and untried pleasures of an abode on the lake Ontario.

The ladies of the fort have had full employment, for some weeks past, in receiving the visits of all the Dutch families who have pretensions to the honour of being received there. Their manners, their dress, their conversation, are so strange, so uncouth, so rudely familiar, that I am not surprised at the disgust they create. Mrs. Bellenden, who is perfectly well bred, and who ranks politeness, I believe, amongst the cardinal virtues, conceals, with the utmost caution, her dislike of these strange visitants; and the less they seem intitled to her delicate attentions, she is the more assiduous in practising them, as if she hoped to civilize them by example.—Meantime they stare, and are confounded when she addresses them, and either do not answer at all, or in a manner so rude and strange, that she blushes, is confused, and silent.

Miss Bellenden seldom speaks, but her looks express a contempt of her company, which her mother often checks by a significant glance. As for Clara, she continues to be extremely busy with her knotting,[1] apparently to prevent the ludicrous ideas, that are excited in her mind, from appearing in her countenance; but the archness of her stolen glances do not escape the notice of her mamma, who seems extremely apprehensive, lest the young ladies should fail in any article of politeness to her unpolished guests.

Mrs. Benson understands the Dutch language sufficiently to enable her to keep up a little conversation with these ladies, which is a great relief to Mrs. Bellenden, and equal pleasure to them; who, although they can all speak English, yet are very shy in conversing in that language, so that they discoursed chiefly with each other.

My rank not giving me the privilige of being as slow in returning their visits[2] as Mrs. Bellenden, Mrs. Benson and I have already paid our respects to several of the chief families here. We were entertained in a very hospitable manner, which, it seems, is the custom of the place; for immediately after the tea equipage was removed, a large table was brought out, and covered with a dramatic table cloth, exquisitely white and fine; upon this table were placed several sorts of cakes, and tea-bread, with pats of the most delicate butter, plates of hung-beef and ham, shaved extremely fine, wet and dry sweetmeats,[3] every kind of fruit in season, pistachio and other nuts, all ready cracked with an instrument for that purpose; the liquors were cyder, mead,[4] and Madeira wine.—All these things were served in the finest china and glass; and if we did not eat heartily, it was not for want of example, for our good hosts shewed as keen an appetite for this, their third meal since the morning, as if they had not till then broke their fast.

Our thin European regale of a dish of tea, and a slice of cake, must have appeared very parsimonious to persons accustomed to

---

1 A piece of decorative work made by tying knots in yarn to form a pattern.
2 The higher up one was on the social scale the more leniency one received in paying visits. Euphemia, as the wife of a lieutenant, would be expected to return visits expeditiously, whereas Mrs. Bellenden, wife of a colonel, would receive the benefit of the doubt if tardy in returning a visit as it would be assumed she was kept from doing so by important affairs having to do with her husband's responsibilities and rank.
3 Confectionaries, candied fruits, sugared nuts, etc.
4 Fermented honey and water.

such plentiful afternoon collations; and I resolved, when I was visited next by my new friends, I would endeavour to treat them in their own way. But Mrs. Bellenden was totally against complying with this custom; not from an over-attention to œconomy, for she is hospitable in the highest degree, but because it seemed a great offence to delicacy, and against every rule of decorum, to turn a visit into a coarse substantial meal.

This lady is indeed not only hospitable, but has a taste for expence, which, in some measure, defeats the purpose for which the Colonel, her husband, left his native country, at an age somewhat advanced, to pass the remainder of his days in America, that he might save fortunes for his children.

The distinguished rank the Colonel holds in this province, obliges him to observe certain forms, which indeed include a considerable expence, but which is made much more considerable by the high notions Mrs. Bellenden entertains of what his station requires of him. On all public days,[1] it is usual for the mayor, the aldermen, and the principal inhabitants of the city, to appear at the fort in their best dress to compliment the commandant; on these occasions, not only cake and wine are, by Mrs. Bellenden's orders, handed about in great plenty, but there is always a ball at night, and an elegant supper for a select party. Besides this, her table is open to all strangers of any fashion, who visit Albany; and there is now a greater resort than ever, drawn by the beauty of the young ladies, and the hospitable and elegant manners of the commandant and his lady.

It is chiefly of such strangers that the assembly Mrs. Bellenden holds every fortnight, is composed; for except the officers and their wives, and two or three of the most polished persons in the place, none of the inhabitants are either qualified, or indeed desirous, to assist at these entertainments.

The Colonel, always keeping his laudable purpose in view, would willingly draw his expences within a narrower circle, that is, such as he thinks merely ostentatious; but whatever his rank really requires, he willingly assents to it; and to the calls of generosity and benevolence he attends with unrestrained liberality.

One instance I must give you, my dear Maria, of this worthy man's humanity and greatness of soul.

Soon after his arrival here, his first lieutenant, who held the command during his absence, presented him a list of men in his

---

1 I.e., When the fort is open to the townspeople.

own company, who being, on account of their age and infirmities, judged wholly unfit for the easiest duty, were ordered home to be received into Chelsea hospital.[1]

The Colonel, hearing that some of these soldiers were near an hundred years of age, desired to see them particularly; accordingly they were all presented to him in the great hall, where the ladies of the fort, myself, and some other company were assembled to view them.

Of this venerable group, the youngest was eighty-two years old, several were an hundred, and one was an hundred and ten. Here was a strong proof of the goodness of the climate; and it is said, and experience has proved it true, that the Europeans who come hither young generally live to a very great age.

These old men looked surprisingly healthy; but they seemed discontented, and even sad. The Colonel, after conversing with each of them a few moments, at length observed the melancholy air of their countenances, and asked them the cause.—One of the oldest then came forward, and making a low reverence,

"Sir," said he, "my companions and I are in great trouble, and if your Honour will be pleased to listen to our grievances, we shall be bound to pray for your honour."

"Listen to your grievances!" interrupted the Colonel, with an affectionate tone, "Aye, my good friends, and redress them too, if in my power."

"Oh, Sir," replied the old man, "we have all heard, before you came, that you are a noble gentleman.—God bless you for your kind speech. This, please your Honour, is our very hard case—

"I and my companions here, Sir, were young fellows when we left Old England; and yet we have seen some service too—and we have been upon hard service in our time here too, and fought with French and Indians, and spilt our blood for Old England and this here America, which is all one as our native land to us now. We married wives here, and have children and grand-children, and great-grand-children; and all we love is here, and we are used to the climate; so that it is a great hardship to be sent to die from our friends.

"Some years ago, please your Honour, seventeen of our comrades were sent over, very old men they were, and eleven of them died on board the ship, and never set foot on land; and the other six did not live many weeks after they came on shore. And it is

---

1 A hospital for old or disabled soldiers located in London.

likely it will be the same with us, for we are very old; and if we should be strong enough to bear the voyage, and the change of climate, we shall break our hearts at leaving our children and friends."

The poor old soldier ended his simple and affecting oration with another low reverence, and retired backward to his rank. We could perceive a tear or two drop on his silver beard. His companions discovered great emotion all the time he was speaking; and they all waited the Colonel's answer with apparent anxiety.

The Colonel, approaching them with an air of ineffable sweetness and benevolence, bid them not be uneasy; he would consider their case, and they should have no reason to complain.

They were beginning to express their joy and gratitude, in praises and blessings on their commander, when the lieutenant I mentioned before, whose name is Blood,[1] a name well suited to his nature I believe, went hastily up to the Colonel; the old men, observing this motion, became silent on a sudden, and beheld him with looks, in which fear and aversion were strongly marked.

"Sir," said Mr. Blood to the Colonel, "permit me the liberty of representing to you the consequence of these men's petition.— They have been on the superannuated list for several months, excused from duty, and are consigned to Chelsea-hospital. Their names are struck out of the muster-roll, and their places supplied by six effective men who have been enlisted in their stead, so that your company is complete; and if these men are not sent to England, their pay must, for the future, come out of your own pocket."

The Colonel with a smile, not wholly free from contempt, made no reply, but turned from him; and addressing himself to the anxious veterans—

---

1 Séjourné suggests that this character is modeled on Lieutenant Edmund Blood who "had come to America as early as 1710 ..., for the Canada Expedition; in 1723 his lieutenancy in one [of] the Independent Companies was confirmed ...; later on we find him repeatedly in Albany, Schenectady and Oswego" (103). Like Lennox's Blood, the historical Lt. Blood took over the command for his superiors when they had to leave the country for a time or when they retired and the fort was waiting for a successor. And, like Lennox's character, "Blood was by far the oldest lieutenant around 1740" when Charlotte Ramsay's father was serving in Albany; whether the historical Blood shared his fictional counterpart's jealous nature, dark anger, or mean-spiritedness is unclear. There is also no evidence that Edmund Blood was sent to Oswego for punishment as was Blood in *Euphemia*.

"My friends," said he, "this matter depends wholly upon me I find, therefore I am not willing to leave you a moment in suspence. None of you shall be sent to England; you shall stay here among your friends, and end your days in ease and quiet. Your pay shall run on as usual; and now you may withdraw, and drink the King's health."[1] Saying this, he ordered a servant to conduct them to the butler's pantry, and directed that they should have a plentiful repast, and a proper quantity of liquor.

The gratitude of these old men was now too great for words; but their emphatic silence, accompanied with tears, and eyes and hands lifted up to Heaven in mental prayer for their benefactor, affected us all extremely. Every eye was fixed on the Colonel, with an expression of admiration and delight; every tongue congratulated him upon the heartfelt satisfaction he had, by this noble act, both given and received. But Mr. Blood, sullenly silent, scowled scorn and anger from his black-beetle brows, and bowing more carelessly than became him, withdrew.

Mr. Neville tells me, this officer is universally hated by the soldiers, for his pride, rapaciousness, and severity. He has lived here many years, and being the oldest lieutenant in the service, when the commandant dies the command of the garrison, and all the forces here, devolves upon him, till another is appointed by the King, and arrives here.

He has had the good luck to survive four of his commanders, and, during each interval of another appointment, has enjoyed all the power and emoluments of their post. Hence he seems to claim a prescriptive right to possess this dignity, and has been heard to boast, that Colonel Bellenden, who does not seem built for duration, he says, will not long keep him out of it.

Heaven grant he may be mistaken! What a pity that the life of a man, who is an honour to human nature, should be short. Yet

---

1 George II (1683-1760) came to the throne of Great Britain and Ireland in 1727 and ruled until 1760 when his grandson George III (1738-1820) took the throne and ruled until 1820 (though during the last ten years of his reign, his son was regent due to the king's poor physical and mental health). Since the historical time period of the novel remains somewhat unclear, though much of the novel's atmosphere reads like Lennox's first novel, *Harriot Stuart*, which takes place roughly in the 1740s, and the parallels between characters and events in *Euphemia* and historical fact suggest this time period as well, it is difficult to say with certainty that the king referred to is George II, but he is the more likely choice here.

surely, he who may compute his existence, not by the number of his years, but his good actions, may be truly said to live long; for good actions are the seeds of immortality.

I am transported with joy, my dear Maria! I have a letter from you this moment; it was brought in the Colonel's packet. Oh! how generous, how kind, to be thus diligent in writing to me. I have locked myself up, and am visible to no eye, that I may enjoy uninterrupted the dear luxury of conversing with you.

Letter XXXVI.
MISS HARLEY TO MRS. NEVILLE.

MY DEAR EUPHEMIA,

IT is now five months since you left England: time has not lessened my regrets for our separation, nor weakened the ardor of my unavailing wishes for the blessing of your society. I remember all the arguments your good sense employed to comfort me; I approve them all, but I can apply none of them yet. My uncle rallies, reproaches, and even threatens me for the obstinacy of my grief for your loss. He tells me it will have a dangerous effect upon Mr. Harley, who has reason to be jealous of a friendship that leaves him but the second place in my affection. But, without settling the article of precedence in this case, I referred him to what Mr. Harley said a few days after your departure, as it was repeated to me by Mr. Greville.

"Miss Harley's sensibility on this occasion," said he, "is the foundation of all my hopes. From a heart so capable of a sincere attachment, the man who is so happy as to be her choice, may expect all the refinements of a delicate passion, with all the permanence of a generous friendship."

This young man has, by his amiable qualities, so endeared himself to my uncle, that he is uneasy when he is absent, even for a day; but to the claims of a mother, neither his gratitude nor his love can render him in the smallest degree inattentive. Sir John had obliged him to fix his residence at the Hall; but he never fails to visit Mrs. Harley three or four times a week, and often stays a night at her house.

I have been twice to wait on her, and was received with a profusion of kindness. She affected to call me daughter, and the young ladies caressed me like a sister. With their caresses indeed I was much pleased, and returned them very affectionately; but, whether I was prejudiced against Mrs. Harley's sincerity by the account I had received of the early part of her conduct, or that the professions she made me wanted the ingenuous and cordial air which carries them directly to the heart, I received them with fewer marks of gratitude than were due to them, if sincere; but I made up in respect what I wanted in tenderness, and my acknowledgments, such as they were, passed current with a heart which seemed too little interested in them to take the trouble of distinguishing between appearances and reality.

This lady, my dear Euphemia, has been very beautiful; she has one of those mischief-making faces which have produced much disorder in the world, and which, but too often, make an effectual apology for the faults of the head and heart. I took notice that she blushed when I delivered her a compliment from my uncle, which at that time I thought I could easily account for, but which I have since better understood.

When we returned from this visit, Sir John was very particular in his enquiries concerning the brothers and sisters of Mrs. Harley; but in what regarded Mr. Harley he appeared extremely cold and indifferent. She soon after, at my desire, received an invitation to spend some days at the Hall with her young family.

Mr. Harley set out in my uncle's coach to conduct her, and Mr. Greville drove me up in the phaeton[1] as far as —— to meet them. During our ride, he was very urgent with me to give him my opinion of Mrs. Harley; but in this case I kept within a reserve, which I thought due to the character in which I was shortly to regard this lady.

"Come, come," said he, "I know you have too much sincerity to deceive the world, and too much understanding to be deceived yourself. You will never be a favourite with your mother-in-law that is to be—it is impossible to be virtuous with the approbation of those who are not so themselves; but you may be very easy with her, provided you can be contented with appearances.

"All commerce with the world in general," pursued he, "is merely amusement, and tends to make one believe that people only meet together to impose upon each other: the reasonable few are friends, and see each other as they are; the rest are only acquaintances, and make up one great masquerade."

Mr. Greville having gone thus far, which was plainly with an intention to put me upon my guard against those natural impulses of affection and confidence, which young and innocent

---

1 A light, open, four-wheeled horse-drawn carriage with forward facing seats.

minds are apt too freely to indulge towards persons with whom they are newly connected, and which, when not returned with equal sincerity, produce discontent, complaints, and sometimes indecent quarrels and reproaches; changed the discourse to subjects more agreeable, till the coach, with our expected guests, appeared in view.

Mr. Harley, who rode on horseback, no sooner perceived the phaeton, than he galloped up to us with a speed and impetuosity, which made Mr. Greville look at me, and smile. The carriages met, and stopped: after a few compliments had passed, I desired Mrs. Harley to permit me to accompany her in the coach the rest of the way. She appeared to take this as I wished, an instance of respect; for which Mr. Harley, in gratitude, I suppose, thought fit to kiss my hand with a most lover-like ardour, as he helped me into the coach.

The children were rejoiced to see me; and Mrs. Harley said a great many obliging things, and was in high spirits. I was surprised at her deportment; the occasion indeed seemed to call for fortitude, which she doubtless possessed in an uncommon degree. She was soon to see a man whom she had deceived, injured, and forsaken, yet to whose generosity she must owe her future subsistence, and the establishment of her children. These circumstances did not appear to excite any uneasy reflexions, or produce the least perplexity in her behaviour.

I watched her looks when the coach drove up the avenue; they were perfectly serene. My uncle very politely, but not without some little discomposure, came to help her out of the coach. With an unaltered cheek, and an air perfectly easy, she gave him her hand; and as he led her up the stairs, addressed some indifferent conversation to him, which he answered with great gravity.

As soon as we entered the room, she presented her two daughters and her little boy to him. The girls are pretty and genteel. He gave them an obliging reception, and caressed the boy, who is extremely like his brother.

During this ceremony Mr. Greville remained silent, observing all that passed with a fixed attention. Mr. Harley had drawn me to a window, to listen to some tender trifles, which, I confess, interested me much less than the scene between Mrs. Harley and my uncle.

She had not neglected her dress, which, being second mourning, admitted some elegances very advantageous to her person; and she seemed still conscious of its attractions, and to think they had not yet lost all their force upon a heart which was once enslaved by them.

Sir John, taken up with the children, had not yet met her looks, which, armed with all their fascinating powers, were levelled full at him, as he now, for the first time, raised his eyes to her face, but he stood the shock with such unaffected composure and indifference, as seemed to mortify her a little; however, she soon recovered herself, and the conversation becoming general, my uncle mixed in it with his usual good humour and politeness.

At night, when I left her in her apartment, she embraced me with great tenderness, and seemed perfectly satisfied with the progress she had made that day in her design of pleasing; for vanity is easily led, and the many little engaging arts she practised, to draw my uncle's notice upon her, sometimes produced their effect, and gave to those attentions, which politeness demanded of him, a certain gallant air, which she explained as she pleased.

She had continued a fortnight at the Hall, without giving the least intimation when she meant to put an end to her visit. Her design upon my uncle's heart seemed apparent; Mr. Greville looked grave upon it.—And one day, after heedfully observing her manner, he drew me aside to a window.

"What can this woman mean," said he, "by the airs she gives herself? Harley had need to look about him; or he may have the singular good fortune to be cut out of his succession, by the selfish views of a mother."

This was carrying his suspicions very far. I combated them for the honour of my sex. But reflecting upon Mrs. Harley's ungenerous conduct in the early part of her life, the thing did not seem improbable.

Mr. Greville protracted his visit to an unconscionable length, as he himself observed, that he might not leave his friend exposed without succour to such a dangerous attack. I could perceive that his presence often checked Mrs. Harley in her career of coquetry, and that she wished his abscence most devoutly; for he watched her motions so assiduously, that she could never gain an opportunity of being with Sir John alone.

He was boasting of his dexterous management, on this occasion, one day as he was standing with me at one of the windows of my dressing-room, which overlooked the terrace, when I pointed out to him Mrs. Harley and my uncle walking together, engaged, as it seemed, in a very serious conversation.

"How could this happen?" said he, with some emotion. "I left Sir John in his library; and Mrs. Harley, you said, complained of some indisposition this morning. Well, I am resolved to interrupt them, however." He took his hat immediately, and crossing the terrace, as if he meant to go into one of the alleys, my uncle called to him, and he joined them, not greatly to the satisfaction of Mrs. Harley, as he told me afterwards, which appeared too plainly by her looks.

These tête-à-tête airings became, at length very frequent; and Mr. Harley, charmed with the good intelligence that subsisted between his mother and Sir John, implored me to consent to his making use of her growing interest with him, to press the conclusion of our marriage; a subject he could not take the liberty to enter upon himself. This, for obvious reasons, I would not consent to; so that there were some discontented faces among us. I could not approve of Mrs. Harley's behaviour; Mr. Greville was enraged at it; and her son seemed apprehensive of delays, without knowing why.

Things were in this state, when one day, after a long conversation with Mrs. Harley in private, my uncle sent for me into his library, and immediately afterwards, desired a servant to tell Mr. Greville he wanted to speak with him. Upon his entrance, my uncle shutting the door after him, took his hand, and leading him up to the window where I stood, wondering what this preparation was to end in.

"I wished to consult you both," said he, "upon a matter which presses my thoughts very much. I know not whether what I have resolved on will meet with your approbation; but I am sure I mean well; and the world—"

"Prithee, my good friend," said Mr. Greville, interrupting him impatiently, "tell us the matter without any further preface. If you have resolved, why let the world talk.—It is not the first time it has talked, you know."

"Of what?" replied my uncle, a little surprised. "The world knows nothing of my intentions in this case."

"Oh, no," said Mr. Greville, smiling, "but the world is very good at guessing sometimes."

"You are a part of this world," said my uncle, "tell me what have you guessed, that I may know whether I have answered, or fallen short of your expectations."

"I guess then," said Mr. Greville, "that in this business, you have followed your inclinations; and in that respect, I am sure, you have not fallen short of my expectations."

My uncle did not perceive that these words were spoken rather peevishly; he took them in a very favourable sense; and with a smile of complacency, replied—

"It would be a very sensible mortification to me to be condemned by a judgment, which it would lie heavy on my conscience not to subscribe to. My dear Edward, I am afraid, murmurs in secret, that I have delayed his happiness so long."

"It is a maxim with me," said Mr. Greville, "never to be long in doing that which can be done at once. But I can answer for your Edward, that, with all the impatience of a lover, he has all the submission and reverence of a son. However, I hope he will never be more than your nephew."

"How is that?" said my uncle, hastily, "I protest, I do not understand what you drive at, Greville. But if, as Edward's friend, you are chagrined at my delaying his marriage, hear my reasons.—I was willing, before this event took place, to set him entirely at ease with regard to the situation of his mother and his family; and by making them independent, to prevent any further claims upon him, which, perhaps, might not be regulated by reason on one side, nor prudence on the other.

"For this purpose, I have sought opportunities of engaging Mrs. Harley's attention on this subject; but it is hard to guess at this woman's meaning. An affair of such importance to her she treats with the most childish carelessness, and turns the discourse upon subjects which have not the least connexion with it, and trifles in so egregious a manner, that I was almost out of patience with her.

"This morning, however, I demanded her attention, in a decisive tone, to what I had to say to her, on subjects of importance to herself and her family. I began with telling her, my resolution to complete the marriage between my niece and her son (her worthy son I justly called him) in a few weeks.

"By the way, Maria," pursued my uncle, looking at me (which this last hint had, as you may imagine, thrown me into a little confusion), "I believe you are not so great a favourite with her as you might reasonably expect, for she received this plain declaration of my intentions, with a cold civility that surprised me."

I smiled, and was silent; but Mr. Greville said, "Aye, aye, this is natural enough; it is ourselves that we generally love in others; but where there is no resemblance, there is no foundation for partiality."

"I believe you are right," replied my uncle. "However, I passed over this circumstance, and proceeded to tell her, that I had resolved to settle two thousand pounds on each of her daughters, and, if she had no objection, would place them at the same boarding-school where my niece was brought up, and take the expence of their education upon myself. As for little Charles, who is really a promising boy, Greville, I told her, it was my intention to breed him up a scholar; that he should be educated in my own house, under the tuition of my chaplain, till he was fit for the university; and as I designed him, with her concurrence, for the church, I would keep the living of ——, which his father had possessed, vacant for him; and for future preferment, he would have all his brother's interest.[1]

"To all this," pursued my uncle, "Mrs. Harley made no other answer than to bow her head; which appeared a sacrifice to politeness, rather than an expression of approbation; so that being a little embarrassed by her behaviour, I entered rather abruptly into an explanation of my intentions with regard to herself.

"Your income, Madam," said I, "I propose to increase, by a settlement of two hundred pounds a year, which I hope you will think adequate to your occasions; and now, these necessary preliminaries being settled, we have nothing to do but to make preparations for the marriage of our children."

While my uncle was speaking, several self-accusing glances passed between Mr. Greville and me; although we had never explicitly declared to each other the suspicions these long and private conversations with Mrs. Harley had suggested; yet, conscious that we had really entertained such injurious thoughts of him, our hearts upbraided us with injustice; and my emotions impelled me to cast myself at his feet, to implore his pardon for my offence.

I checked this involuntary transport, however; but was delighted to see Mr. Greville give way to his sensibility; he embraced my uncle eagerly, crying, "You have acted like yourself, wisely, nobly, greatly!"

"Oh! mighty well," said my uncle, "I am glad you are pleased. But what think you was the lady's answer? Why truly, she paused a little, dropt me a formal curtsey, and said, she would consider of what I had been saying."

"Why truly," said Mr. Greville, "it required some time to deliberate, whether she would accept a genteel portion for her daughters; a plentiful income for herself; and a certain provision for her little son.—The matter was something difficult."

---

1 Charles Harley would have his older brother Edward's interest/influence to advance him in his future career.

"Well, I have done my part," interrupted my uncle. "And now, my dear Greville, find out Edward, and bring him to me; and as for you, niece, I shall leave it to your lover to prevail upon you to fix an early day for his, and, I hope, your happiness."—I curtsied in silence, and left the room.

Retiring to my own apartment, I saw Mr. Harley crossing the gallery to go into his mother's chamber. He did not see me, and I took no notice of him, being unwilling to interrupt a conversation that was likely to lead to a discovery of his mother's sentiments, which appeared to me to be very misterious. I sat alone till the hour of tea approached; when I went into the drawing-room, where I found Mr. Harley alone, leaning on the back of a chair, his arms folded and lost in thought. On my entrance, he started up, and running to me, took my hand, which he kissed with great emotion.

"Have you heard, my Maria," said he, "how your generous uncle, your noble uncle, means to provide for my mother and her family?" "I have," said I, "and I hope Mrs. Harley is quite satisfied with his plan." He cast his eyes down in some confusion, and was silent a moment; then dropping my hand with an air of despondency—

"How will it be possible for me," exclaimed he, "to bear the answer to Sir John!—Would you think it, my dear Maria, my mother, brought up in the principles of the Roman Catholic religion, is so bigoted to her mode of faith, that, rather than not carry her point, she will risk the displeasure of her benefactor, and the loss of her children's hopes; and is unkind enough to insist upon my acquainting Sir John with her intentions."

"And what are these intentions?" said I.

"To retire to France," replied he, "with my brother and sisters; and take upon herself the care of their education."

"And so she means to make your sisters nuns, and your brother a friar," said Mr. Greville, who had stolen upon us unobserved, and heard Mr. Harley's last words. "But come," pursued he, "I have been looking for you, Sir John expects you in the library; he has ordered coffee there, so we shall not attend your tea-table this afternoon, young lady," said he to me.

They went away together; and I sent to let Mrs. Harley know I waited tea for her; she excused herself on account of some indisposition; but her daughters, and her little son came to me.

The passages of the day gave my thoughts such full employment, that I was but a dull companion for my little visitors; so I went with them into the garden, and leaving them to stroll about as they pleased, retired to an alcove to indulge my meditations. I had not been here more than half an hour, when I saw Mr. Harley, joy sparkling in his eyes, advancing hastily towards me; I rose to meet him at the entrance of the alcove; but he prevented my going out; and taking my hand, which he pressed to his lips, with equal tenderness and respect, led me back to my seat, at the same instant throwing himself at my feet. I desired him to rise, with a smile, which he well understood.

"Oh! pardon the transports of a lover," said he, "who finding himself authorised to press you to conclude his happiness, can think of no posture too humble for such a request. Do not, my adored Maria, be less favourable to my ardent wishes than your uncle.—He bids me bring him your consent for an early day, to conclude our marriage. Can you, will you not answer his generous intentions?" "Methinks," said I, "Mrs. Harley ought to decide this matter—I will be directed by her." "Say rather by your uncle," interrupted he, "your more than father, my glorious friend and benefactor, say by him." "Well then," resumed I, "let my uncle determine for me."

This concession produced new transports; which I checked, by asking him, how Sir John had received Mrs. Harley's proposals?

"Mr. Greville," said he, "took upon him to acquaint Sir John with my mother's fatal infatuation."—"And how," said I eagerly, "how has he determined in consequence of it?"

"Like himself," replied he, "with equal dignity and justice.— He consents to my sisters going to France with my mother, since she will have it so; but insists upon her leaving my brother to my care, as my father with his last breath directed. I foresee," said he, sighing, "that this will produce some contest between my mother and me. Having always been used to pay her the utmost submission and respect, it will be a painful task to contradict her."

"But, surely," replied I, "the consideration of her own interest, and that of the child, will have some weight with her, besides the will of her late husband."

"Ah! against that," interrupted Mr. Harley, "she pleads the will of Heaven. Her church allows no salvation out of its own pale; and she thinks it would be a less misfortune to see her child poor and dependent, than a heretic."

"She is to be pitied," said I, "since her error is founded upon principle." He pressed my hand with ardour, upon my saying this.

"How excellently good are you," said he, "to view in so

favourable a light my mother's conduct on this occasion. I never was so happy as to enjoy an equal portion of her affection with any of her other children—but I love her most tenderly; and must regret a separation, which being her choice, proves her indifference towards me."

I was greatly moved with the affectionate manner in which he spoke these words, heightened by a look of extreme sensibility. This cloud, however, was soon dispersed by the sunshine, as he called it, of his present fortune; and, till we joined our little companions, he breathed nothing but the warmest effusions of gratitude, love, and joy.

Mr. Greville, in the mean time, had paid a visit to Mrs. Harley, in her own apartment; and had disposed her, by arguments which he well knew how to enforce, to an acquiescence with my uncle's intentions with regard to her little son; it was a sullen acquiescence, however; for she appeared at supper with looks so cold and reserved, as disconcerted us all.

Sir John, in a formal accent, and a look composed to great gravity, told her, that if she had no objection, he had fixed upon this day fortnight for the celebration of our marriage. Certainly, she said, she could have no objection; and turning to me, made me some common-place compliments, but delivered with surprising coolness.

My uncle added, that he intended the ceremony should pass with great privacy; and that all our parade should be reserved for our appearance in town, the ensuing winter,[1] whither he proposed to accompany us.

Dear generous man! My heart overflowed with gratitude; which was sufficiently apparent in my looks, I believe; for he several times smiled upon me with great complacency. Mr. Harley's acknowledgments were expressed with a fervor which seemed to move him much, and were answered by a most affectionate embrace.

---

1 While the London season was marked by the opening and closing of Parliament, beginning some time after Christmas and ending in early summer, the New York and other American social seasons were tied to weather conditions, so the New York season began in the fall, when the upper classes returned from their summer homes, and ended in the spring, when they left for the summer. At this time fashionable society congregated in these cities to partake of a round of assemblies, balls, musical evenings, and other entertainments. Young girls of marriageable age "came out" during the London or New York season, and were paraded at balls for eligible young men to see.

My uncle settles upon Mr. Harley twelve hundred pounds a year.—We are to live with him at the Hall; and it is in our own choice to spend the whole, or part of every winter in London; a permission I shall seldom make use of; because the air of that crowded city does not agree with his health; and it is equally my inclination, and my duty, to be absent from him as little as possible.

While all these arrangements were making, Mrs. Harley appeared to take very little interest in them, and kept a profound silence. Her son could with difficulty conceal his confusion at this behaviour; he often turned his expressive eyes upon her, full of respectful expostulation; which she did not, or would not, understand. When we separated for the night, she told Sir John, that as her son's marriage was to be celebrated *so soon*, it would be necessary for her to go home for a few days, in order to make some preparations for her own and her daughters appearance; and that she proposed to set out early in the morning. My uncle made no opposition to this design, so suddenly taken up, but gave orders for the coach to attend her at what hour she pleased, together with Martin and two of the footmen. She thanked him with a cold politeness; and when I waited on her to her chamber, told me, with a forced smile, that she hoped I would have no objection to her son's accompanying her, at least part of the way.

I blushed, and answered with some confusion, "Surely, Madam, I can have no objection to Mr. Harley's doing what his affection and his duty require of him."

"Oh! you are very obliging, my dear Miss," said she, and curtseying very ceremoniously, wished me a good night.

I desired to know, at what hour she intended to set out in the morning, that I might attend her at breakfast. She said, she would send to me as soon as she was risen; and we parted.

I rose earlier than usual the next morning, but still not time enough to see Mrs. Harley; for my maid informed me, she had been gone half an hour; for as soon as I had left her at night, she sent for her son, and desired him to give directions for the coach to be ready at five o'clock. He had acquainted my uncle with his intentions, of conducting his mother as far as ——, in her way home, and promised to return by dinner time. Mrs. Harley's behaviour had been so extraordinary, that I expected my uncle would have taken some notice of it to me; but, whatever his thoughts were, he kept them to himself.

Mr. Greville told me, that he was convinced, her sullenness was occasioned by the disappointment of her designs upon Sir

John. "Her confidence in her own charms," said he, "is prodigiously great; and the power they once had over the heart of my friend, persuaded her, that it would be no difficult matter to revive a passion, which the resentment he had preserved against her husband, for supplanting him, by continuing his whole life, proved that it had never been quite extinguished.

"Selfish and interested, to the last degree, a title had allurements sufficient to make her insensible to the injury she was preparing for the most amiable and most deserving of sons, by cutting him, perhaps, out of the succession; and, perhaps, the prospect, in case she had succeeded, of a long minority,[1] had its weight with her. I know," pursued he, "Sir John views her conduct in the same light that I do; but he has too much delicacy to explain himself."

It was painful to me to feel, for the mother of Mr. Harley, those emotions of contempt and dislike, which such a conduct naturally inspired. I could not conceal my astonishment at it.

"This woman," said he, "never had any sensibility. They who blush not at their faults, but add confidence to their guilt, have no motive left to restore them to the practice of virtue."

Mr. Harley did not return to dinner; at which we were not much surprised; as it was natural to suppose, that in conducting his mother on her way, he might exceed the limits he proposed to himself. But when night came, and he did not appear, my uncle became uneasy; and I, I own it, was greatly alarmed. I retired to my chamber, to conceal emotions it was not in my power to suppress. Either he neglects me, thought I, or some fatal accident has happened to him.

I passed a considerable time in this state of anxiety, when one of the footmen came back, and related, that Mr. Harley had been suddenly taken ill at an inn, where they stopped for some refreshment; and that his mother had thought proper to take him home to her own house.

As not a single line came from Mr. Harley on this occasion, we concluded he must certainly be in a very dangerous way. The

---

1 The period during which a person is under age. If Mrs. Harley had married Sir John Harley, and had a son by him, she would have effectively kept her eldest son from inheriting his uncle's estate since such a child would be a nearer relation to Sir John (a son rather than a nephew) and thus the new heir; and, if she had no children by Sir John, she'd still be able to keep Mr. Harley from his inheritance as Sir John's widow, who would have control of much of his estate as long as she lived.

servant either could not, or would not, give us any certain account, so that we all passed an uneasy night.

The next day, just as my uncle was going to send one of the grooms to Mrs. Harley's, we saw Martin arrive. My uncle and Mr. Greville had not patience to wait till he entered the house, but hastened to meet him. I remained in the room where they had left me in great anxiety, and trembling for the event.

Mr. Greville returned in a minute—"Do not be alarmed," said he, hastily, "our friend is in no danger; though he is indisposed—I flew to tell you this, which is all I have yet heard." He left me instantly, to go to my uncle; who had ordered Martin to follow him to his library, where he was giving him an account of what had happened.

The few words he had uttered, seemed to have removed a mountain from my breast. I began to breathe again; and for a few minutes enjoyed some little composure; but doubts and fears returned, and I was beginning to relapse into all my former inquietude, when Mr. Greville again entered; and drawing a chair close to me—"Now," said he, "you shall know all that has passed."

"Ah!" said I, with an emotion which I was not aware of, "you have deceived me—What is become of Mr. Harley? What fatal accident has happened?"—He smiled. The smile relieved my fears; but awakened me to a sense of shame, at the transport to which I had so indiscreetly given way.

"Nothing," said Mr. Greville, gravely, observing my confusion, "that we suffer, is so bad as what we fear. Mr. Harley is not well enough to be with us to-day, but we shall certainly see him to-morrow. Martin tells us, that his disorder was occasioned by a contest he was obliged to sustain with his mother, whose violent temper is well known. She obliged him, after they had travelled a few miles, to dismount, and come into the coach to her.—There an altercation ensued, so very lively, as to be heard distinctly by the servants, and particularly by Martin, who rode sometimes very near the coach. The subject was, Sir John's ungenerous use of the power her dependent situation gave him over her, in taking her youngest son out of her hands. She seemed disposed to contest this point with him: and upon Mr. Harley modestly, yet steadily, insisting upon his fulfilling the last injunctions of his father, with regard to this child, his mother set no bounds to her rage, but loaded him with the severest reproaches.

"Mr. Harley finding all his expostulations, intreaties, and submissions, were employed in vain to bring her to a better temper, reminded her of his promise to return to the Hall to dinner; and stopping the coach, ordered the servant, who led his horse, to come up.

"A very good inn being in sight, Mrs. Harley peremptorily insisted upon his dining with her on the road; which he complied with, in hopes, as it should seem, of leaving her more composed. But after dinner, the storm began with more violence than before. She ordered him, with an imperious air, to accompany her home. He pleaded his promise to Sir John; and assured her, if she would permit him to leave her then, he would return to her the next day. This medium[1] she refused; and continuing to rail, in the most indecent terms, against all he most loved and revered in the world, a thousand conflicting passions seemed to rend his heart; his tongue maintained a respectful silence, but his inward agitations were apparently very violent.

"Mrs. Harley now ordered the horses to be put to the coach, and with an imperious air bid her son, as he handed her into it, to come in likewise; he begged to be excused; and mounting his horse, rode on before, so swiftly that he was presently out of sight. A heavy shower of rain now fell, and continued so long and with such violence, that it was apprehended Mr. Harley would suffer greatly, unless he found shelter somewhere, which was not likely, as there was no inn upon the road, from thence to the parsonage house.[2]

"The coachman drove furiously, in order to overtake him; and accordingly they came up with him; but he had alighted, tied his horse to a tree, under which he stood himself drenched though with the rain. In this wet condition, he was prevailed upon to come into the coach; and after an hour's ride they reached the parsonage house. Mr. Harley, who had not uttered a single word all the time he was in the coach, desired a bed to be prepared for him; and bowing low to his mother, retired; apparently so ill, that she thought it necessary to send for the apothecary of the village, who, after visiting him, pronounced him to be feverish, and ordered him some medicines. Martin, however, rode to the next town to get a physician;[3] who thought his fever rather high, but did not apprehend any dangerous consequences from it. He had a tolerable night, it seems; and the next morning calling Martin

---

1 Compromise.
2 The house provided for the parson.
3 While the apothecary often came to a home to dispense drugs, and in so doing offer a diagnosis, the physician was legally able to practice medicine.

to his bed-side, directed him what account he was to give Sir John concerning the accident that detained him. Accordingly Sir John is but half-informed of the truth," added Mr. Greville, "and what I have told you, the honest and discreet old man imparted to me in private."

Mr. Greville accounts very naturally for this violent conduct in Mrs. Harley.—Her pride, mortified by the indifference of Sir John; her ambitious views disappointed, she proposed to herself a malicious pleasure, in interrupting that happiness which she could not participate.

I cannot help agreeing with Mr. Greville, that a woman so rash, so selfish, and imprudent, is not fit to have the guidance of any of her children. But she will never yield to persuasions. "It is superfluous to employ reason with those who have none," says he; "she must be forced to comply. Extremes are always dangerous; but they become wise means, when they are necessary. It is true, indeed, they never work by halves, but will decide the matter one way or other."

My uncle could not be satisfied with the favourable account Martin brought of Mr. Harley's present condition; he seemed determined to go and see him, and to carry his own physician with him; but Mr. Greville, apprehensive that Mrs. Harley might give him some disgust, prevailed upon him to lay aside all thoughts of this journey himself, and consent to his going with the doctor; who was immediately sent to; and they both went away early in the morning.

This was a melancholy interval. Fear is a great magnifier of evils.—My uncle reasoned so long upon the probable consequences of what had happened to Mr. Harley, that he almost reduced me to despair. The doctor's return restored us to some degree of tranquility; he assured us, that Mr. Harley was in no degree of danger, and that we might expect to see him the next day, Mr. Greville staying to accompany him. His arrival was impatiently expected by my uncle, who obliged me to walk with him several times down the avenue, in hopes of meeting the carriage.

Alas! it came not that day, nor the next; but the servants, who were dispatched each day to the parsonage-house, always brought us favourable accounts from Mr. Greville, which, however, contributed but little to the relief of our anxiety; and my uncle, now determined to set out himself, which I no longer opposed. While his post-chaise was getting ready, we took our usual melancholy walk, and, to our inexpressible joy, the carriage appeared in sight.—My uncle left me, and, forgetting his gout, actually ran towards it.

Mr. Harley got out, and threw himself into his arms. When I came up to them, I was amazed at the alteration I perceived in his countenance. Joy, at the sight of me, overspread his face with a faint blush, which instantly gave place to an ashy paleness.—His eyes had lost their sparkling vivacity; but they still retained that melting softness with which his partiality always beheld me.

The sight of him, thus altered, affected me so much, that I could have wept like an infant, had not shame restrained me. My uncle would needs support him as he walked to the house. Mr. Greville, as we followed them, took an opportunity to tell me, that Mrs. Harley was much altered in her behaviour; that she was perfectly complaisant, docile, and obliging; and ready to approve of every arrangement, in her own and her children's affairs, which Sir John should think fit to propose.

"Weak persons," he observed, "never yield at the time they ought to do. It was not possible for her to recover the ground she had lost by her former violence; but as her present conduct seemed to promise no farther opposition, we had reason to be contented."

Sir John took not the least notice of her behaviour to Mr. Harley, but employed all his attention in forwarding his recovery; and, indeed, he mends so fast, that we have reason to hope, his health will soon be perfectly re-established.

My dear Euphemia, good fortune, as well as evil accidents, seldom come alone. I have this moment your dear, your welcome packet. Sir John's agent in London[1] took care to forward it to me by one of his clerks, who is to take back what letters I have ready.

A ship for New-York, he tells me, being to sail immediately, I have but just time to run it over; and, to my inexpressible satisfaction, I find you have had an agreeable voyage, are well, and not unhappy. What a feast do you prepare for me, by writing thus to the moment,[2] and making me present to all the occur-

---

1 An agent is one who acts for another.

2 Maria refers to Euphemia's bringing her up to date on events in her life, but the phrase also recalls Samuel Richardson's *Pamela* (1741), the popular novel in which the titular character, a young girl, suffers the advances of her employer and writes a journal in which she documents his attempts on her virtue. Pamela's writings often took the form of entries which chronicled the events as if they were occurring in the present moment (hence, "writing to the moment"), a technique which some readers, including novelist Henry Fielding, found ridiculous.

rences of your life.—All, all are of consequence to me! Heaven grant, that you may never send me less pleasing news! You cannot complain, nor be unhappy, by yourself alone; I partake of all your good or evil fortune; and feel so lively a reflexion of any uneasiness you suffer, that there needs but one blow to give two wounds.

My uncle interrupts me, to tell me, the messenger waits for my packet.—He sends a thousand kind remembrances to you. You know what a favourite you are with Mr. Greville; he forgot, that it is not decent for a wise man to be transported with joy or grief, on any occasion whatever, but the news of your health, and safe arrival at your destined port, threw him so much off his guard, that he discovered little less sensibility than myself.

Mr. Harley would fain have me believe that he admires and loves you as much as I do; but that is impossible, because, he does not know you as well.—But he begs me to tell you, that he joins me, in every fond and tender wish for your health and happiness.—Adieu, my ever loved and valued friend—Adieu!

MARIA HARLEY.

P.S. You must make me acquainted with your kind and sensible friend, Mrs. Benson, whose affectionate attachment to you entitles her to my love and respect. Poor Fanny! she has written me a very pretty letter; remember me kindly to her. Her lover bewails her absence with unaffected sorrow, and, I am persuaded, will never forget her.—This circumstance you may either disclose, or conceal from her, as your prudence shall judge best.

Letter XXXVII.
MRS. NEVILLE TO MISS HARLEY.

MY DEAR MARIA,

WERE it possible for me to be less interested than I am in all your concerns, yet your agreeable narrative would have acted very powerfully upon my hopes and fears. When I reflect upon some passages you have related, I cannot help smiling at the blunders which distance produces. At the very moment when I had reason to fear that fortune was preparing some obstacles to your happiness, that happiness was already secured; and I hope and believe, that you were then the wife of that noble and generous youth who only could deserve you.

I shall be very glad to hear that Mrs. Harley pursues her intention of retiring to France; a mother-in-law of her complexion will be best conciliated at a distance. Ceremony between persons so nearly connected, but ill supplies the place of cordiality and friendship, and leaves a craving void in the heart, which will sometimes be filled with peevishness and discontent; and a formal civility is all that can subsist between characters so opposite as yours and hers.

In Mrs. Bellenden, this acquired quality of politeness is almost a virtue; and indeed it has the semblance of many—it makes her patient with absurdity, gentle with impertinence, forgiving with rudeness, and easy with all persons and on all occasions. You would admire her pleasing behaviour, and the grace with which she accommodates herself to the boorish manners of the men, and the awkward ignorance of the women of this place.[1] She has actually taken a great deal of pains to acquire as much knowledge of the Dutch language as to enable her to address some trifling uncouth visitants, with whom the young ladies are so much disgusted, that they have contrived to keep them out of the assembly Mrs. Bellenden holds every fortnight, which is now pretty numerous, from the resort of many strangers of fashion to this city.

Among these Mr. Euston holds a distinguished rank; elegant in his person, polite in his manners, and engaging in his address: he throws off the philosopher in the charming circle formed by the Colonel's daughters. Miss Bellenden has thought him worthy of her chains, and calls forth all her attractions to enslave him. The dignified Louisa looks as if his adorations might be *endured*; and Clara, without seeming to have the least design upon his heart, aims only at improving her understanding, by listening with the most respectful attention to all he says, when any opportunity offers to engage him in conversation.

Two nights ago Mrs. Bellenden gave a ball and supper, on occasion of the arrival of a young gentleman, son to the late governor of New-York, who is appointed third lieutenant to the Colonel. We had some music; all the young ladies sing and play, and Mrs. Bellenden does both excellently.

Mr. Neville and myself were among the performers; but nobody thought of asking the philosophic Mr. Euston to make

---

1 See Introduction for discussion regarding tensions between the Dutch and the British in eighteenth-century New York.

one. Mrs. Bellenden, however, heedfully observing him during the performance of Dryden's Ode on St. Cecilia's Day,[1] exclaimed—"I am sure Mr. Euston understands music!"—He smiled.

"Ah! I thought so," pursued she; "come, Sir, I insist upon your joining us." Miss Bellenden rose immediately from the harpsichord, and offered her place; and Mr. Neville presented his German flute.[2] Mr. Euston chose the harpsichord; and sitting down, sung that beautiful little song of Ben Johnson's in the Silent Woman, which you know I admire so much.

> Still to be fine, still to be drest,
> As you were going to a feast:
> Still to be powdered, still perfum'd,
> Lady, it is to be presum'd,
> Tho' art's hid causes are not found,
> All is not *genuine*, all not sound:
> Give me a look, give me a face
> That makes simplicity a grace;
> Robes loosely flowing, hair as free,
> Such sweet neglect more taketh me,
> Than all th' adulteries of art—
> They strike mine eyes, but not my heart.[3]

The company were so delighted with the song and the performance, that we encored it three times. This little incident unraveled a mystery which had hitherto puzzled us all. Mr. Euston's long stay at Albany, and his assiduous attendance at the Fort, created something more than a suspicion, that his heart had been surprised by the charms of one of the young ladies; but he was so much upon his guard, that it was not possible to guess which was the distinguished fair one.

He sung the last stanza with so much feeling, such pointed expression in his eyes, and such particular application to Clara, that his preference of her was no longer a secret. The elegant sim-

---

1 John Dryden "A Song for St. Cecilia's Day" (1687) or "Alexander's Feast; or The Power of Musique. An Ode, in Honour of St. Cecilia's Day" (1697). The reference is probably to "Alexander's Feast." The original music was by Jeremiah Clarke, but George Frederick Handel scored it in 1736.

2 Transverse flute, which displaced the recorder about 1750.

3 Ben Jonson's comedy, *Epicene, or The Silent Woman* (1609), 1.1.87-98.

plicity of her dress brought her exactly within the poet's description; a white lutestring robe, so fitted to her shape, as to disguise nothing of its admirable symmetry; the graceful folds, not distorted by the Gothic invention of a hoop,[1] swept the ground, but with no enormous train, like that of a tragedy queen. A girdle of black velvet, bordered with small pearls, circled her slender waist; her hair was loosely tied up behind with a knot of pale pink ribbon, and some strings of pearls, of the same size with those bound round her girdle, confined its shining ringlets from falling too low over her forehead and temples.

This dress, in which nothing seemed designed for ornament, but all for use, formed a striking contrast with that of Miss Bellenden's, where flowers, feathers, fringes, streamers, flounces, trimmings, formed an assemblage of gay colours and figures, on which, as Young observes,

"The dazzled eyes could find no rest."[2]

Miss Louisa was dressed with more propriety, but she was fine; and her deportment, like her dress, stately.

Mr. Euston's manner was too particular to escape notice—Miss Bellenden reddened—Clara seemed wholly unconcerned.

"What an odious old-fashioned song," said the mortified beauty, "was that the preaching gentleman gave us; and the music was as bad as the words." I defended both.—Clara was silent; but her eyes, which are great talkers, spoke sufficiently plain.

"I do not doubt but Clara thinks she has made a conquest," said Miss Bellenden, spitefully; "but I am sure nobody will envy her."

"Ah! why," repeated Clara, looking earnestly at her sister,

"'Will Beauty blunt on fops her fatal dart;
Nor claim the triumph of a letter'd heart?'"[3]

---

1 The hoop was a circle of flexible material (whalebone or steel) worn under a petticoat to expand a woman's skirt. Lennox views it as a "Gothic" or barbarous invention since it obfuscates a woman's natural shape for the sake of fashion.
2 Unidentified.
3 Samuel Johnson's "The Vanity of Human Wishes" (1749), lines 151-52: "Should Beauty blunt on Fops her fatal Dart,/ Nor claim the Triumph of a letter'd Heart."

"'A letter'd heart!'" exclaimed Miss Bellenden, laughing aloud. "For Heaven's sake! what is a letter'd heart? I protest I will ask Mr. Euston himself; he is so wise, he knows every thing—he shall tell me what a letter'd heart is."

Clara, anxious that her sister should not expose her ignorance, yet not daring to contradict her, gave me a beseeching look.

"No, no," said I, holding her, "he will laugh at us."

"Ah!" replied Miss Bellenden, "I thought it was nonsense. But pray, dear Clara, let us have no more of your rhimes; indeed they make you appear very silly; and you know my mamma cannot endure your reading those books so much."

It is true, that Clara is fond of quoting her beloved poets; but she does it so aptly, her voice is so harmonious, and her expression so just and beautiful, yet without the least affectation, or even consciousness of her powers of charming in this way, that every one, except her mother and sister, are delighted, when she either reads or repeats.

Mr. Euston, though not a declared lover, has the marks strongly on him.—He scarce ever loses sight of his young charmer.—The ladies are sure to meet him wherever they go; this happens by chance, to be sure, as he would have it appear.—And chance was very favourable to us on this occasion, which I am going to acquaint you with. For, since I must always be writing to you, and the simple tenor of my life affords no great and striking events to interest your curiosity, you must give me leave to entertain you, by selecting from those little occurrences, which every day produces such as are more worthy your attention.

You must know, then, that among the many contrivances we form, to vary our amusements in this place, Clara, who is a little romantic, proposed one, which met with general approbation:— This was, to make an excursion into the woods, which we beheld so beautiful in prospect, from the ramparts of the Fort, and to pass the afternoon amidst their shades.

Mrs. Bellenden not opposing our scheme, we set out early after dinner; the young ladies, Mrs. Benson, and myself, attended by Miss Bellenden's maid, and two men-servants, who carried a large basket, filled with every thing necessary for tea. Clara soon found out a proper place.—It was a little valley, surrounded with lofty trees. The servants filled the tea-kettle at a spring of delicate water, with which these woods abound; and lighted a fire at a convenient distance, while we seated ourselves, as well as we could, and began our different employments.

Miss Bellenden produced her netting, Louisa her flower-piece,

Mrs. Benson and I our plain-work,[1] and Clara her book. This was a novel, newly published in your world; and because it has uncommon merit, I suppose you have read it. Mr. Euston presented it to Clara; and told us, that Cecilia[2] is the performance of a young lady, whose elegant genius is generally admired.

Many of the incidents in this very sensible novel are extremely affecting, and made me weep like a child. I am not ashamed to own, that I have been much moved by such agreeable fictions; and that it was not for real evils I shed tears, but the ingenious fancies of another person, that excited these strong emotions. This has been called a tyrannical power, which the senses usurp over reason; and proves, that the neighbourhood of the imagination is extremely contagious to the intellectual part.

Clara was permitted by Miss Bellenden to read to us, while our tea was preparing.

In the midst of this pleasing entertainment, we were alarmed with a hideous noise, which, to our terrified imagination, seemed like the howling of wild beasts. Miss Bellenden screamed aloud, her sisters echoed her cries, and clung round Mrs. Benson and me, hiding their faces in our bosoms. We were half dead with fear ourselves, yet endeavoured to comfort the young ladies.

"These are Indians, Madam," said one of the men-servants to me; "and by their shouting I imagine they are drunk. They will be upon us, presently, I suppose. For Heaven's sake! do not discover any signs of fear; you will enrage them if you do."

I had been told this before; and therefore earnestly recommended it to our young friends, to appear as composed as possible.

They had just raised their heads, and dried their eyes, when three savages bolted out of the wood, and presented their hideous figures to our eyes. As soon as they perceived us, they set up a frightful yell, and stood still, gazing upon us with fixed attention.

Louisa and Clara, notwithstanding all their efforts to appear calm, even sobbed with the violence of their emotions. Miss Bellenden, though pale and trembling, adjusted her hair, and drew herself up, with an air that shewed her consciousness of her

---

1 Netting and flower piecing were ornamental work done by women for the home—especially by unmarried women as advertisements of womanly skill meant to impress suitors. Euphemia and Mrs. Benson do plain-work, simple, rather than decorative, work.

2 A reference to *Cecilia* (1782), by English novelist, playwright, and diarist Frances Burney (1752-1840).

charms. Such is the force of habit, that even in this moment of terror, her thoughts were not wholly diverted from their usual course, and the desire of charming was always uppermost.

The two men-servants took no notice of the savage intruders, but appeared to be very busy about their tea; and Mrs. Benson, very complaisantly, presented them with some cakes, which they accepted with a kind of surly satisfaction. She then offered them some tea; they tasted it, and returned the cups, shaking their heads; and made signs which we did not understand; but one of the footmen told us they wanted rum.[1]

I bid him make them comprehend, that we had not any; at which they looked displeased, and talked to each other. It appeared to us, that they supposed we had some of this darling liquor, and would not part with any to them; and this thought encreased our apprehensions; besides, we heard one of our servants say, in a whisper to his companion, "They are dreadfully drunk, I am afraid they will be mischievous."

We knew not what to do—to stay was dreadful—and if we offered to go, it was probable they would hinder us. However, Mrs. Benson, in order to sound their intentions, bid the servants put up the tea equipage in the basket.

The Indians looked angry at this motion; and one of them, moving from the place where they had both, till now, stood like statues, kicked the basket with his foot, and threw it down, seeming mightily pleased with the crash of the china.

The young ladies, no longer able to restrain their fears, screamed aloud. The Indians looked at them with a fierce and menacing air, and moved towards us.—We gave ourselves over

---

1 The British gave the aboriginal peoples rum, to which they were not accustomed, to make them drunk, and therefore more pliable and ineffective as traders. Edmund Burke, in *An Account of the European Settlements in America*, actually saw the addition of alcohol to the aboriginal peoples' lives as a positive thing, giving them "a spur to their industry, and enjoyment to their repose" (433), though he goes on to qualify this more positive judgment by noting that alcohol "is the principal end they pursue in their treaties with us; and from this they suffer inexpressible calamities; for, having once begun to drink, they can preserve no measure, but continue a succession of drunkenness as long as their means of procuring liquor lasts. In this condition they lie exposed on the earth to all the inclemency of the seasons, which wastes them by a train of the most fatal disorders ...; in short, excess in drinking ... is a public calamity" (433).

for lost.—When to our inexpressible joy, Mr. Euston appeared, brought thither by Miss Bellenden's maid, whom we had not missed; and who, upon the first appearance of the Indians, left us, and ran towards the Fort, in order to procure some assistance, if necessary.

Mr. Euston, whom the screams he had heard very much alarmed, approached us with great anxiety in his looks. He addressed his enquiries in general, but his eyes were almost always turned upon Clara. Finding, by our answers, that the savages had behaved peaceably enough, he entered into some conversation with them, in their own language; after which he informed us that these Indians were stragglers from a large party of their friends, a tribe of Iroquois Indians, who had come down the river to celebrate one of their festivals,[1] in the neighbourhood of Albany. He told us, we had nothing to fear, those nations being our good allies; that when they were intoxicated with liquor, they were apt to be troublesome; but if they had known who we were, they would have behaved with more civility.

We soon found, by their altered looks and manners, that Mr. Euston had given them some information concerning us. They gathered up the fragments of china they had broke, and gazed on them with wishing eyes; but did not offer to take any, till Mrs. Benson made signs to them, that they might have them; this present seemed very acceptable; and finding that we were preparing to go, they marched before us, officiously clearing our path from the underwood and broken boughs that obstructed our walk. They accompanied us to the gates of the Fort, and then took leave of us, with many tokens of reverence and respect.

We had now so effectually overcome our fears, that when Mr. Euston proposed our going the next day to visit the Indians' little camp, we eagerly accepted it. The Colonel, however, chose to be of the party; this drew in Mrs. Bellenden, and Mr. Neville, and all the officers that were not upon duty, attended us; which, with some servants, made up a large train.

---

1 The Iroquois, who inhabited central and western New York State, might have followed the Mohawk River southeast to where it joins the Hudson River, which runs north to south through the eastern part of the state from Albany to New York City. The Iroquois, in order to honor and to pacify the Great Spirit, held "seasonal festivals of thanksgiving. The more important were the Maple Festival in the spring, the Strawberry Festival in the summer, and the Green Corn Festival in the autumn" (*HNY* 14).

The Indians were assembled in a little plain; a great number of huts[1] might be seen among the trees. These huts consisted of three poles, covered on the top with the bark of trees, and lines with their branches, to keep out the sun. The women and children sat at the entrance of the huts.—Their husbands and fathers lay indolently along within, smoking or drinking.

The young men were differently employed; some in dancing, others in shooting at a mark with their arrows, and not a few busy in preparing the feast.

Several large kettles, full of venison, were suspended by a rope, fastened to two trees at a convenient distance, between which a large fire was kindled. As soon as our company appeared, they instantly quitted their sports and employments, and crouding together, formed a circle, and continued gazing on us in a profound silence.

Mr. Euston approached them, and pointing to Colonel Bellenden, told them who he was. The Indians, considering this visit from the great chief, as they called him, as a high honour, prepared, in token of respect, to entertain him with a dance. They kindled a large fire in the midst of the plain, threw their mantles over their shoulders, each holding up a large knife in one hand, they danced round the fire in a ring, their feet keeping time to a slow and barbarous strain, and their eyes fixed on the ground. This ceremony, which we thought very frightful, but with which we affected to appear extremely pleased, lasted half an hour.

As soon as the Indians had finished their dance, they resumed their former sports, and we mixed among the women, some of whom were tolerably handsome. We took notice of the children; and were delighted to hear the women speak, though we could not understand them, the tone of their voices was so exquisitely sweet and harmonious.

While we were ranging from hut to hut, Miss Bellenden observed two young Indians at a distance, leaning against a tree with a discontented air.—Their figures were pleasing, and their dress mighty smart; their heads were adorned with feathers; their ears loaded with strings of wampum,[2] and their mantles trimmed

---

1   The Iroquois lived in separate bark-covered houses around a larger long house in which ceremonies and meetings were held. A circle of pointed logs surrounded these and outside were the cornfields and then forest. The gathering Euphemia describes is a temporary village set up on the plain for the brief period of the governor's conference.

2   Wampum consisted of strings of beads made of polished shells worn as decoration or used as money.

with several rows of tinsel lace.[1] These young men had neither joined the dance, nor mixed in any of the sports. Curious to know the cause of their exclusion, we went up to them; and Mr. Euston asked them, why they continued apart from the rest?

Without changing their posture, and scarce raising their eyes to look on us, they told him, that not being of the party, they had no right to eat, and therefore had no inclination to dance.

We now searched our pockets for some trifles,[2] to present to these poor neglected young savages. One of us produced a small pen-knife, another a little snuff-box, Miss Bellenden made an offering of her pocket-glass, and Louisa gave a knot of ribbons; Clara blushed, because she could find nothing in her pocket but her Pastor Fido,[3] which, as she was now studying Italian with great application, she always carried about her; not willing, however, to appear less liberal than the rest of the company, she presented her cambric pocket handkerchief with a bashful air, which the Indian who received it immediately tore in two, tying a piece round each arm. We left them extremely delighted with our civility, and returned to the Fort. Adieu, my dear Maria, I must close my letter here—A sloop is this instant going off for New-York, and will take my packet.

EUPHEMIA NEVILLE.

---

1   The lace trim on the Iroquois' clothing glitters, or more derogatively, is showy.

2   The items given by Euphemia and her friends include everyday items: the snuff box was used to hold snuff, a powdered tobacco which one inhaled through the nose; the pocket-glass is a mirror; Louisa's knot of ribbons may be hair ribbons, or it may be an ornamental rosette, such as those used for cockades on soldier's hats; Clara's handkerchief is made of cambric, a white linen or cotton cloth, very simple and practical, not meant for decoration but for use.

3   *Il Pastor Fido* was an Italian pastoral play written by Battista Guarini in 1585. A tale of the trials and tribulations of two lovers, which ultimately ends happily, it was made into an opera by Handel, with a libretto by Rossi, and performed for the first time at the Queen's Theatre in London in 1712.

Letter XXXVIII.
MRS. BENSON TO MISS HARLEY.

MADAM,

IT shall never be laid to my charge that you speak of me favourably, and that I hear of it without gratitude; a good opinion lays one under an obligation from whomsoever it comes; but when judgment like yours commends, not to be vain would be to be above human frailty. He who said Socrates[1] was prouder of one word spoke by the oracle in his favour, than of all the praises the world bestowed upon him, speaks my sentiments. In return for your making me vain, Madam, which, the cause considered, I can scarce allow to be a fault, I will make you happy by informing you, that your valued and amiable friend is a mother, and has given us a lovely boy, who is called after a young gentleman, whom we hope has been for some time the happiest man in the world.

I write this by Mrs. Neville's bed side, who is, with some little alteration of the old phrase on this occasion, better than could be expected.

To explain this I must tell you, that when the affair was all over, the lady in bed, and in a sweet sleep, I retired to take some rest, having been up the whole night; but was soon waked by a loud and confused noise of many tongues speaking all at once. Among these I distinguished Mr. Neville's, who by the oaths he threw out in quick succession, I understood to be in a violent rage. Alarmed and confounded at a clamour so preposterous at such a time, I flew down stairs: at the entrance of Mrs. Neville's chamber I met Mr. Neville, who seizing my arm with a dreadful gripe, exclaimed—"Oh! Madam, come in, see what these Dutch devils have done,—they have killed my wife!"

I entered the room, trembling, and saw one part of it newly scoured, and streams of water running over the other, which issued from a large pail that had been overturned.

While Mr. Neville continued cursing and raving at the nurse, who, being entitled by her age and her wealth to wear a forehead cloth,[2] a distinction which the matrons here are extremely fond

---

1 See Xenophon, *Memorabilia*.
2 "Forehead cloth" was a term used during the sixteenth and seventeenth centuries for a band covering the front of a woman's head, often triangular. Among the Dutch, the wearing of the forehead cloth was a mark of respectability.

of, considered herself as highly affronted by his behaviour. I enquired of Fanny, who stood in great agitation, the meaning of the strange appearances I beheld.

She told me the nurse, as soon as I was retired, had called up the housemaid, and ordered the room to be scoured. "I remonstrated against it in vain," pursued Fanny, weeping, "and said it would kill my lady—that it was not the custom in our country. But finding that I could not prevail, I called my master, who was so shocked at their having wetted the room, which he said would kill his wife with cold, that he kicked down the pail in a rage, and set all afloat as you see."

I ordered a large fire to be made in the room; and, collecting all the carpets in the house, laid them one upon another on the floor. Mrs. Neville was anxious only for her child. I opposed very bad arguments to her reasonable fears, but it was absolutely necessary to quiet her mind; as for Mr. Neville, he continued to rail and swear.

"Did you ever hear of such a savage custom?" said he, "what! scour the chamber of a lying-in woman!"[1]

"The greatest mischief," I replied, "is likely to happen from the pail of water that was thrown down."

"Aye," said he, "that was unfortunate, to be sure; but it was very natural for me to be in a passion you know, when my wife's life was endangered by that old Dutch woman's absurdity."

To persuade Mr. Neville that he can ever be wrong is a task no human understanding is equal to. I suffered him therefore to march off in triumph, at having silenced me with so complete a defence, and took care to prevent any future blunders of the nurse, who only followed the custom of her country, to which we were strangers, and therefore could not guard against.

Mrs. Neville and the child are perfectly well. She makes an admirable nurse, and loses none of her delicacy by doing the duty of a mother.[2] This little stranger has been received with great joy

---

1 A woman who is in the process of giving birth. Among those wealthy enough to afford it, the term also referred to the month after parturition when it was expected that the woman would rest and receive few visitors.

2 Lennox here refers to the controversy waged during the eighteenth century over the merits of breastfeeding. At different times during the century the practice was viewed positively, to the point where even women of the upper classes would breastfeed their babies; at other times during the period, however, breastfeeding was viewed as uncouth, and infants were put out to nurse with wet nurses, women who had enough milk for their own children as well as those of others, and who were paid for their services, though usually only minimally.

by the father, who having now an heir to his uncle's estate, is not apprehensive of its going out of his line.

Mrs. Neville has given you an account, Madam, of our adventure in the woods with the two drunken savages; her situation made me tremble for the consequences of the fright she must necessarily have been in, which, however, she concealed so well, as to make me tolerably easy; but our little boy bears under his left breast the distinct mark of a bow and arrow,[1] the arms born by one of these savages. This power of imagination has been denied with such force of argument by some learned writers, that nothing but the evidence of my own eyes could force my assent to the possibility of it.

A troublesome affair has fallen out within these few days, which I have been fortunate enough to conceal from my friend, whose keenness of observation it is difficult to elude.

Mr. Neville and Lieutenant Blood had a dispute about some trifle, which was managed with such heat on both sides as to produce a quarrel; and a challenge[2] ensued on the part of Mr. Neville. The day, the hour, and the place of meeting were all settled, but happily the colonel was informed of the design time enough to prevent it, and put them both under arrest.

The only difficulty now was to reconcile them, that nothing of the kind might be apprehended for the future. The colonel undertook Mr. Blood, who on such occasions, being endowed with that docility with which the valiant reproach the wise, was prevailed

---

1 The use of the birthmark was popularized in the English novel with Henry Fielding's *Joseph Andrews* (1742) where Joseph's strawberry birthmark reveals his birthright, and indeed Edward's birthmark will serve to identify him later in the novel, but Lennox is also referring here to the notion that a baby can be "marked" by his mother's experiences before its birth. Expectant mothers were kept from potentially upsetting experiences so that their babies would not be marked physically. As the passage above suggests, this notion is beginning to lose currency in the period.

2 To a duel. Despite the fact that dueling was illegal in Britain and its colonies, it was a popular means of resolving conflict between men during the eighteenth century. As such, it was a great social concern, and many writers—including Richardson, Fielding, Addison, and Steele—decried its practice. Lennox registered her criticism of the practice in *Harriot Stuart* as well when she paints Harriot's brother and her lover, Belmein, as ridiculous figures for engaging in such an irresponsible act, while pointing to the potential for tragic outcomes of such behavior in Belmein's wounding of another adversary.

upon by his commander's arguments, enforced by his authority, to lay aside his wrath. I had more trouble with Mr. Neville, who is passionate and obstinate, but I carried my point at last, by reasons partly serious, partly jesting.

"If Heaven," said I, "had given you three or four lives, you might at any time venture one, and sometimes, in a fit of valour, let one go, knowing you have another in store; but to be prodigal in poverty, and to be careless of the only head you have, when no art can make you a new one, is unreasonable to the last degree." Mr. Neville at length agreed to let the Colonel settle the difference; and all was made up over a bottle of wine at the Fort.

I have now, Madam, acquainted you with every thing that has passed here worthy your notice; and have nothing to add, but I am with the greatest esteem and respect, your obedient servant,

C. BENSON.

Letter XXXIX.
MRS. NEVILLE TO MISS HARLEY.

I REMEMBER I once told you, my dear Maria, that I was resolved to turn philosopher, and so be revenged on Fortune for all her cruelties to me. I am now called to a new trial, which yet is not so severe as some I have already sustained; but you, who on all occasions feel for me, perhaps, more than I do for myself, will think it sufficiently mortifying.

I had just begun to taste something like happiness.—My dear little boy repays my care, with every advantage a fond mother can desire,—health, beauty, sweetness of temper, and early reason; a wise and faithful friend at home; some agreeable companions abroad; and a growing taste for the climate, and the wild yet not unpleasing scenes around me.

How truly has it been said, that the limits of our joy is but the absence of some degree of sorrow. Within these few days Mr. Neville has informed me, that he has obtained a promise of Colonel Bellenden, to be appointed to the command of a fort in Schonectady.[1]

---

1 As late as 1690, Schenectady was viewed as the northern frontier, and vulnerable to attack by the French, who burned the village in that year. Even during the eighteenth century, it was a small, somewhat isolated Dutch settlement, and the Dutch inhabitants actively discouraged any immigrants from settling in the town. In 1757, William Smith described

This is a little town, distant about thirty miles from Albany, inhabited by some Dutch traders. Seldom visited by any strangers, but Indians, who straggle hither, not only from the five nations of the Iroquois, our allies, but the savages of Canada, and other barbarous nations.

Whether impelled by that restlessness of temper, which makes every change, even for the worse, desirable; or the strange pride, of being greatest where all is little, I know not, but Mr. Neville is fixed in his resolution; and when he acquainted me with the approaching change in my situation, it was not to hear my opinion, to ask my advice, or to sooth me into a consent, but barely to signify his will to me; to which I offered no opposition, well knowing that it would produce no other effect, but ill humour, and unjust reproach.

When Mr. Neville left me, after this unwelcome communication, Mrs. Benson, alarmed at the sullenness of his aspect as he passed by her, came eagerly to my chamber, to enquire the cause of his apparent dissatisfaction; when I told her what had passed, she paused for a few moments, casting on me now and then a soft and sympathising look—then recollecting herself, she took my hand, which she tenderly prest—

"My dear child," said she, "of evils, the least is the best. Your days will pass less unhappily in this, I will suppose, wild solitude, than they can possibly do here; though here you have some agreeable society, and some elegant amusements. Mr. Neville's discontent would embitter all; nor would you be free from a little self-accusation, although you could carry your point, if it cannot be done without violating that obedience which you have solemnly vowed at the altar.

"All the evil in the world, my dear," pursued she, "consists, as I have somewhere read, in the disagreement between the object and the appetite; as when a person has what he desires not, or desires what he has not, or desires amiss. He that composes his spirit to the present accident, hath a variety of instances for his

---

it as being "sixteen or eighteen miles North-west from Albany ... on the banks of the Mohawks Branch, which falls into Hudson's River 12 miles to the North of Albany. The village is compact and regular, built principally of brick, on a rich flat of low land, surrounded by hills. It has a large Dutch church, with a steeple and town clock near the center. The windings of the river through the town, and the fields (which are often overflowed in the spring) form, about harvest, a most beautiful prospect" (*HPNY* I, 212).

virtue, but none to trouble him; because his desires are not at war with his present fortune. You have heard the philosopher," she went on, smiling, "now hear the friend.

"Doubt not but I will follow you to this savage solitude; and we shall be able to strike out amusements, which, as they will depend entirely upon ourselves, will always be within our reach.—We have books, we have music, and ideas I hope, to furnish out an agreeable and profitable conversation. Your little boy will soon be of an age to exercise you in higher cares than those of a tender and diligent nurse. Our judgment is formed by experience; the principles of truth unfold themselves by degrees with the natural progress of reason.—That progress, in this sweet plant, you will watch, direct, and improve; and having no temptations to divert your attention from so delightful, so laudable an employment, you will with the more ease perform the task which God and Nature have assigned you."

It was thus that this worthy woman reasoned with me, soothed me, and reconciled my will to a dispensation, which my heart murmured at before; so that when Mrs. Bellenden came to condole with me, upon a separation so unexpected, and offered, if I would consent to it, to manage matters so with the Colonel as to prevent this wild scheme, (as she called it), of my husband's, taking place, I earnestly intreated her to form no obstacle to his designs, declaring my voluntary acquiescence to them.

This lady is too good a wife to disapprove of my conduct on this occasion. She promised me to make my banishment as tolerable as possible, by a frequent intercourse of visits. I smiled, and pointing to the now dreary prospect around us, for winter, which in this country sets in with a sudden transition from extreme heat to intense cold, had already covered the ground with snow, at least three feet deep.—One pure expance of white meets the dazzled eye, as far as its sight can reach; the branches of the trees, loaded with snow, look like enormous plumes of feathers spangled with gems, formed by the frost. That beautiful river,[1] where we used to see innumerable elegant little sloops, sailing to and from New-York, is now become an icy plain; and bears on its frozen bosom deep loaded carriages, called sledges, drawn by horses, which seem to fly over the glassy surface.[2]

---

1 The Hudson.
2 From the Middle Dutch "sleedse," it is a low vehicle, on runners, often drawn by horses or dogs, and used to transport heavy loads or passengers over snow or ice.

"See, Madam," said I, "what a stern appearance Nature has put on; can friendship find a way through those pathless woods, to visit the poor exile at Schonectady?"

"Never doubt it, my dear Mrs. Neville," replied the good lady, "those pathless woods shall yet afford us a passage to you, when we need it, but happily that will not be till spring; for Lieutenant G— is not to be relieved till then." This was pleasing news to all, but Mr. Neville, who is impatient to enter upon his new command.

Alas! my dear Maria, you can have no conception of the rigor of a North American winter. We have had a fall of snow, which continued three days, which now lies upon the ground, to the depth of five feet, and is frozen so hard that it feels like the solid earth. We are, it seems, to expect no abatement of this extreme rigor these five months; but the constant serenity of a cloudless sky, and the enlivening rays of the sun, increase that cheerfulness which we owe to our now well-braced nerves; but it is cold, intensely cold; I can scarce keep myself tolerably warm, though I sit by a fire, where half the forest is blazing.

Mrs. Benson looks over my shoulder as I am writing, and tells me, laughing, that metaphor is carried very high.—But seriously, although my standish[1] is placed upon the steel hearth, it is with difficulty the ink is kept from freezing, and flakes of black ice frequently fall out of my pen upon the paper.—This will account for some of the many blots you meet with.

I was interrupted by a visit from Mr. Euston. He is much altered—Clara's attractions have proved too powerful for his philosophy. He reasons less, though he talks more than he used to do; but all his discourse bears some analogy to the present disposition of his heart; and, whatever be the subject, it leads him insensibly to the object that fills his thoughts. Hitherto he has declared himself no otherwise, than by assiduities, and the silent rhetoric of looks and sighs. But he has a rival, whom he must either supplant, or yield to; and this circumstance will decide the matter.

With this rival I would fain make you acquainted; if I knew how to describe a creature, to whom no distinction can belong for more than ten minutes together. He is every thing and nothing.—Mrs. Benson says, he is more fool than wise, and more a wag than fool. At the very moment, when he has been talking

---

1 A stand for writing materials.

so much to the purpose that you would pronounce him a sensible young fellow, he throws out something so wretchedly silly, as to deserve the appellation of a fool. One while the stupid solemnity of his countenance excites a laugh, at another, the archness of his look and satirical smiles, make one afraid of him.

He is son to the late Governor, and nephew to the Earl of H—, by whose interest he was appointed third lieutenant to Colonel Bellenden; and came from England to take possession of his new post. He has a fine face, and a figure remarkably elegant; his manners are often polite, and often clownish; his address sometimes courtly, and sometimes awkward; in a word, he is a perfect contradiction. But you will be better able to form an idea of him, from a few traits, which my memory furnishes me with for your information.

A few days after his arrival, being at the Fort, where a large company was assembled, and where the beauty of his person, the elegance of his dress, and the politeness of his behaviour, engaged every one's attention, Miss Bellenden happened to drop her glove; he took it up, and presented it to her with a grace that was infinitely pleasing, entreating her at the same time to permit him the honour of drawing it on; she smiled and held out her arm, on which, white as it is, a few freckles appeared.

Mr. C.— looked earnestly on it for a minute, then exclaimed—

"Heavens! why you are spotted like a toad." She blushed, and frowned. Those persons who were near enough to hear what he said, expressed in their looks the utmost astonishment.

Clara, who sat next him, laughed; upon which Mr. C.—, finding Miss Bellenden sat sullen and silent, and would not even look at him, turned to her sister, and with the easiest and most gallant air imaginable, entered into a conversation with her full of sprightliness, and of turns, which, if they could not be called witty, were at least very like wit. Clara took occasion to rally him upon the coarse speech he had made to her sister, but he defended himself with such an arch simplicity, as quite confounded her.

Colonel Bellenden knows not how to treat him; respectable on account of his birth and connexions, he has a certain air of grandeur diffused over his whole person, that keeps contempt at a distance, in spite of all his absurdities.

On the day that he was to be presented to the troops, who were drawn up upon the parade, headed by their officers, with colours flying, drums beating, and all the *pomp and circumstance* of military ceremonial, he appeared, instead of regimentals, in white and silver, and a plume of feathers in his hat without a cockade.[1] The Colonel perceived him before he came to the gates, and hastily ran to prevent his entering, and exposing himself to the derision of the soldiers.

"What is the meaning of your appearing in this dress, Sir," said he, with an indignant frown; "Do you not know what is to be done to-day?"

"We are to have a ball, Sir; are we not?" replied Mr. C.—, with an air highly respectful, but not in the least disconcerted. The Colonel was absolutely taken in by the steady composure of his looks, and the seeming simplicity of his answer.

"What strange misapprehension," said he, "is this! Go, Sir, put on your regimentals, and appear in your proper character." He then desired Mr. Neville to accompany him, and inform him what was to be done.

Mr. C.— retired, making a low obeisance; and in a short time afterwards returned, dressed *en militaire*.[2]

Nothing could exceed the elegance and dignity of his figure in this dress—there was something so noble in his air, so interesting in his countenance, that every eye beheld him with pleasure.

The deep respect with which he received his pike[3] from the Colonel was accompanied with equal dignity; and the grace that appeared in his motions and attitude, when he took his post, drew a kind look of approbation from his benevolent commander. But what was his confusion and disappointment when this young man, forgetting his duty and his station, faint with heat, and fatigued as it should seem with holding his pike, gave it into the hand of a serjeant, who stood nearest him, and quitting his rank, ran towards the ladies, snatched a fan out of Miss Bellenden's hand, and began to fan himself with the utmost composure, amidst the general astonishment his extravagant action occasioned.

At first all eyes were fixed on him with silent wonder; then an ill suppressed laugh ran through the ranks; the officers caught the

---

1 A parade is a place where troops assemble for parade; the colours refer to the regimental flag; regimentals are military uniforms, and the white and silver would denote a dress uniform; the cockade is a ribbon worn in the hat to denote rank.
2 French for "in the military manner."
3 A long wooden shaft with a pointed iron or steel head used as a weapon by infantry forces.

contagion, but quickly recovered themselves, attentive to the motions of the colonel, who for a moment stood gazing on the strange youth with a severe and steady eye; then advancing towards him—

"Boy," whispered he to him, "a fool's cap and bells would better become you than this respectable dress and manly profession." Then calling Mr. Neville, he spoke to him in a low voice; and turning again to Mr. C.—, who by this time had given Miss Bellenden her fan with his usual graceful manner—

"Go, Sir," said he, "follow this officer, and learn how ill the behaviour of a buffoon fits upon a gentleman and a soldier."

Mr. C.— either was, or affected an extreme surprise in his looks at this reprimand; but, silent and submissive, he bowed profoundly low to the colonel, then to the ladies, and went off the parade with Mr. Neville.

The business of the day, concluding thus ridiculously, afforded us sufficient matter for discourse. Mr. Neville placed a centinel at the door of Mr. C.—'s lodgings, and informed him he was put under an arrest. After some ridiculous enquiries concerning the nature of his offence, and the duration of his confinement, he sent his respectful compliments to the commandant; and ordering his servant to bring his flute, Mr. Neville left him entertaining himself very agreeably.

Colonel Bellenden sent for him the next day, and they had a private conference, that lasted near two hours. I suppose he softened the colonel by his submission; for he appeared to be received into some degree of favour. The soldiers, to a man, are loud in his praise, for he ordered a noble largess[1] to be distributed among them; and they can see no faults in an officer who is so liberal.

He met with some mortifications, however, in Mrs. Bellenden's circle that evening. She looked grave upon him; Miss Bellenden treated him with contempt—Louisa shunned him—Clara, moved by the natural sweetness of her disposition, took pity on him, and suffered him to engross her conversation the whole night. This kindness completed the conquest of his heart; he is become seriously in love with her, and much less extravagant in his behaviour than usual. I can perceive that Mr. Euston is uneasy, notwithstanding his endeavours to conceal it.

---

1   A generous gift, often of money, given on a notable occasion by a
    person in a high position.

"Our new Cymon," said he to me one day with a forced laugh, "improves daily."—"Not so much," replied I, "as to give him hopes of obtaining his Iphigenia."[1]

"Why not," said he, "the miracle would not be new, though he were to become a wise man. Love, which has sometimes made a philosopher a fool, may make a fool a philosopher."

The people of this country have begun their winter amusements. Nothing is to be seen on the river but sledges full of happy parties:—these are the only carriages in use in this severe season.

There is an odd custom among the younger and meaner sort, which it is impossible to reconcile with good order and decency.

A company of a dozen young Dutchmen, and as many girls, agree to go out upon a *froolick*[2] as they call it. These are distributed into six sledges, two couples in a sledge: as they go at a prodigious rate, they sometimes travel forty and fifty miles in a day, to the different farm-houses they propose to visit.

As soon as they appear, all hands are set to work, to provide an entertainment for them; and great is the slaughter among the poultry and pigs to furnish out the feast. They sit long at table, and conclude the evening with dancing, for they always carry a fidler along with them.

When they are disposed to go to rest, the largest room in the house is prepared for their reception. They spread before an enormous fire a quantity of mats and carpets, over which they lay feather beds and coverlets. The company lie down in their clothes, and sleep as well as they can, till morning, when a plentiful breakfast of tea, cream, hot cakes, and hung beef, is provided for them; after which they drive away to their next stage, which is generally at a great distance, where they meet with the same welcome and equal hospitality.

In this manner they traverse the country, spending sometimes a week, sometimes a fortnight, in these excursions; the farmers, wherever they chuse to stop, being, by an ancient custom, obliged to receive them, and treat them well.

I went out yesterday for the first time in our new winter carriage. Mrs. Benson, Miss Clara, and Mr. Euston, made up my

---

1 This is a reference to a story told in Boccaccio's *Decameron* and later used by John Dryden in his poem "Cymon and Iphigenia." In it, an ignorant rustic falls in love with the sleeping Iphigenia and, because of that love, is inspired to become a polished and elegant courtier (the poem is found in Dryden's *Fables, Ancient and Modern* (1700).

2 I.e., frolic.

party, for Mr. Neville was upon guard. We were well wrapped up in furrs, and our feet defended from the piercing cold by several bear-skins, that were laid at the bottom of the sledge. Happy was it for us that Mr. Euston was with us, for an accident happened that might have had the most dangerous consequences.

Our road lay through the woods: as we flew along, (for so the motion of these vehicles over the frozen snow may be called) suddenly I perceived the two fore paws of an animal upon the lower part of the sledge, on that side where I sat. The driver that instant lashing his horses, the creature by this increased velocity lost his hold: Mr. Euston, at the same moment, seized a loaded horse-pistol, which was carried by the servant who sat behind the carriage, and jumped out. We then perceived our danger. The furious bear, for a bear it was, had followed the sledge, and was come almost near enough to spring upon us, when our gallant friend, opposing himself to its assault, levelled his piece, and took so sure an aim, as laid the fierce creature weltering in its blood at his feet.

The explosion of the gun, repeated by a thousand echoes, the hideous howling of the dying animal, mixed with our screams, filled the wild solitude around us with sounds more dreadful than imagination can conceive. We were by this time at a considerable distance; for our driver did not slacken his pace; and had not the sledge been overturned, passing over the body of a large tree, that lay across the road, which in his terror he did not observe, we should have been out of sight.

None of us received the least hurt by this accident; for the overturning of a sledge is seldom attended with any danger, being open on each side, and having no top.

Mr. Euston now came up to us, and anxiously enquired if we were safe. We congratulated him upon his victory; and with the most heart-felt gratitude thanked him for our preservation. Clara said little; but that little was accompanied with a look so expressive, as seemed to have a powerful effect upon her lover's heart, for he gazed on her for a moment with extreme tenderness, and heard not one word that Mrs. Benson and I said to him about his combat.

At length he helped us into our carriage; and, as he was stepping into it himself, Clara grasped my hand eagerly and whispered—"Ah! Madam, he bleeds."

"He does indeed," said I, greatly alarmed, perceiving then, for the first time, that one of his legs was covered with blood.—"You are hurt, Sir," said I.

"I have got a scratch," replied he, smiling; "the creature made an attack upon my leg, but my fire had the good fortune to take place before I received much damage."[1]

"You must give us leave, however," said Mrs. Benson, "to bind up your wound with what linen we can collect." We all contributed; Clara, who till then had looked pale as death, now blushed excessively as she offered her help. Mr. Euston suffered us to do as we pleased—his whole attention was fixed upon my amiable young friend. We ordered the driver to make what haste he could back to the Fort, where his wound was dressed by the surgeon of the garrison, who eased us of our fears by declaring that it was not in the least dangerous.

The colonel and his lady were full of acknowledgments to this gentleman for his gallant defence of us; and indeed we had all reason to be grateful; for had he not by springing out of the sledge exposed himself singly to the assault of the ferocious animal, it is uncertain which of us might have been seized upon.

Such accidents as this, however, are very rare so near any of the settlements, and in the day too. But love, Mrs. Benson says, laughing, was determined to favour so respectable a votary, by affording him an opportunity of shewing how well he deserved the preference which Clara, notwithstanding all her bashfulness and reserve, seems disposed to give him over his young rival. But this rival is countenanced by Mrs. Bellenden, who, seduced by the splendour of his family, and the large fortune he is likely to inherit, is willing to overlook all his extravagancies. The colonel, I believe, if left to his own judgment, would favour Mr. Euston, and prefer an easy independence for his daughter, with a man of his character, to the superior advantages of birth and fortune, clogged with the absurdities of Mr. C.—.

I heard him speak highly in his praise one day to Mrs. Bellenden, who does not seem to relish his conversation.

"What was formerly said of a great man," said he, "to whom I had the honour to be known, may be very well applied to Mr. Euston. As nature has given him the good qualities that cannot be acquired by study, so his own study hath procured him all the good qualities that are not the gifts of nature."—This was a fine eulogium, my dear Maria; and I took care the worthy man should not be ignorant of it.

I have a very pretty letter from young Mansel, with one enclosed from his mother, full of the most affectionate acknowl-

---

1 He managed to fire his gun before the bear could do too much damage to him.

edgments for my kindness to her son. She has sent me some very valuable presents, which prove how much her grateful disposition has over-rated the little services I was able to do the amiable youth she is so justly fond of.

Colonel Bellenden sends for my letter to enclose in his packet, which is this moment setting out for New York. Some ships are expected to sail from thence in a few days. Adieu, then, my dear Maria; my ever loved, my ever valued friend, Adieu!

EUPHEMIA NEVILLE.

Letter XL.
MRS. NEVILLE TO MRS. HARLEY.

I WAS almost reduced to despair, my dear Maria, when I heard that several ships were come from England; and after waiting three weeks, in anxious expectation, no letter from you appeared. But one* has now come to comfort me; and that I got it at length, after so long a delay, I owe to the remorse of a man unknown, who being but half wicked, contented himself with only opening it, but would not by any means that I should lose it.

How do I rejoice, that all your little difficulties are over, and that you have been for some months the happy wife of the worthiest and most amiable young man in the world.

I love you dearly, for the matronly style in which you make your enquiries after my little boy; and I do not think I need offer you any apology for entertaining you with nursery tales—of the perilous adventures we have atchieved against the small-pox, measles, cutting of teeth, and other rocks and quicksands, to which the poor little bark¹ of infancy is exposed. And I have no doubt but you will believe me, when I tell you, that my Edward is very handsome, surprisingly witty, and is the most agreeable companion in the world. I pass the greatest part of my time with him, and never think the time so passed is tedious.

But all is hurry and bustle now in Albany; the town is full of strangers of fashion; nothing but balls and entertainments at the fort. The Governor is soon expected here, in order to meet in congress our good allies, the Iroquois, and pay them the usual

---

* This Letter does not appear.

---

1 Bark: Ship.

subsidies, in blankets, hatchets, iron-kettles, glass jewels, and the like; a ceremony which is renewed every third year.

Great numbers of these Indians are already arrived. Already we behold a large town rising in a plain, behind the fort, consisting of houses made of branches of trees, interwoven with each other and fastened to a number of stakes. These people subsist upon the produce of hunting, fishing, and some spontaneous[1] fruits. We sometimes visit the women and children in their huts, and make them little presents; but we never go but in large companies, and well attended; for most of the men have a savage fierceness in their looks, that is very terrible, though no real danger is to be apprehended.

Mrs. Benson and I are in great affliction—Mr. Euston has left Albany, and will soon leave the whole province, as he proposes to return to England this summer. It is no difficult matter to perceive, that he has left his heart behind him; and although he pleaded pressing affairs, which demanded his presence at home, yet it is certain, that the ill success of his passion for Clara, is the true cause of his sudden departure.

I learn from my young friend, that he had, in the most respectful manner imaginable, solicited Mrs. Bellenden to favour his suit, and procure the Colonel's consent; giving such an account of his family, his fortune, and character, which, as they knew to be true, by the testimony of the first persons in the province, they could form no reasonable objection to.

Mrs. Bellenden, however, received his proposals with great coldness, though with her usual politeness; and being pressed for a decisive answer, frankly owned, she had other views for Miss Clara, and begged he would desist from all future pretensions to her. He bowed, was silent, and from that moment avoided all occasions of entertaining the young lady particularly.

The evening before he left Albany he spent with me; and notwithstanding an apparent depression of spirits, his conversation was so agreeable and instructive, as to fill me with the deepest regret for the loss of it.

I was at the fort the next morning, when he came to take leave of the family. Miss Bellenden, when she saw him enter the room, whispered me exultingly—

"Thank Heaven! the Preacher, (so she always calls him) is going to leave us."

---

1 Uncultivated.

The Colonel pressed his hand affectionately, and expressed much concern at his leaving Albany; Mrs. Bellenden said the civilist things in the world upon the occasion. He addressed himself to Miss Bellenden and Louisa, with an easy polite air; but his compliment to Clara was confused, inarticulate, and accompanied with evident emotion.

She curtsied low, with an air of deep respect, without once raising her eyes, or uttering a word. As soon as he was gone, she withdrew, and was followed by a sarcastic laugh from her eldest sister; who is very angry that her triumphs are lessened, by the conquests made by this little girl, who possesses the power of pleasing in a higher degree than any one I ever saw.

Mr. C.— is more pert than ever since the departure of Mr. Euston, in whose company he had sensibility enough to appear awed and abashed. Mrs. Bellenden is continually giving him lessons of decorum, and he promises to practice them all, in hopes of pleasing Miss Clara, whose coldness and reserve to him are increased since the absence of his rival. He has made a formal application to the Colonel for his consent to address his youngest daughter; and was told, that he must first procure the approbation of his friends. This he immediately set about, by writing to the Governor, under whose direction he is placed, intreating him to propose the affair to his mother, and the Earl of H—, his uncle.

The Governor has taken no other notice of his request, than to send orders for his leaving Albany immediately, and returning to New-York.

In his Excellency's letter to the Colonel, upon this occasion, he hints at the reason of his sudden order. The Colonel answered with that noble frankness which marks his character; and gave him an account of the young man's application, and the answer he had thought proper to give him; treating the matter, however, in so careless a manner, as gave him to understand, that he had scarce considered it as meriting any serious attention.

Mrs. Bellenden charges the Governor with unpoliteness on this occasion, and want of due respect to her husband; whose birth, she hints, is equal if not superior to that of the Governor; although he holds but the second rank in the province.

It is certain, that the immediate order he sent for the young man's leaving Albany, seemed suggested by a very unnecessary caution, if we consider the noble principles which influence all the actions of Colonel Bellenden. His generous character could not be unknown to the Governor; and Mrs. Bellenden is, possibly, not much in the wrong, when she insinuates, that his extreme caution was the result of a thorough acquaintance with his own heart, which would not suffer him to be scrupulous, if an advantageous offer for one of *his* daughters was made him.

When Mr. C.— received the Governor's letter, he flew to the Fort, and entered Mrs. Bellenden's apartment with it open in his hand. She was beginning to condole with the disappointed lover, when he interrupted her by exclaiming, "Was there ever any thing so mortifying, Madam? here am I commanded to return to New-York; and so I shall lose the fine sight you will have here soon. This meeting with the Indians must needs be very entertaining, and would have afforded me something to talk of, when I returned to England. I never will forgive the Governor for playing me this trick."

Mrs. Bellenden, amazed and confounded at this new absurdity, looked at him for a moment with great contempt.

"I know not," said she, at last, "whether you will have any thing to talk of when you return to England, but I am sure, whoever has seen and conversed with you, will have something to talk of as long as they live."

He bowed with the most satisfied air imaginable; then begged permission to wait upon Miss Clara.

"Why, what have you to say to her, Sir?" said Mrs. Bellenden.

"Say to her, Madam!" replied he, "why she has heard, I suppose, that I am ordered back to New-York."

"And what then?" said Mrs. Bellenden.

"What then, Madam!" repeated he, staring at her with signs of surprise.—

"This order does not affect her," resumed the lady, "*she* will not lose the fine sight."—She smiled.—The youth looked a little disconcerted.

"To be plain with you, Mr. C.—," pursued she, "Clara has received orders from her father, to see you no more. When your relations think proper to make any proposals to Mr. Bellenden, it will then be time enough to consider, whether we will accept them or not."

Some company coming in, prevented any further discourse upon the subject. Mr. C.— being to set out that afternoon, Mrs. Bellenden invited him to dinner; and as I was taking leave of her, she followed me to the door of her apartment, and, in a whisper, desired me to take Clara home with me, and to tell her, she was permitted to pass the day at my house. This offer was highly acceptable, both to the young lady and myself. The ridiculous character of her lover afforded us great diversion; and I could perceive she was in transports at being thus freed from his addresses.

Mrs. Bellenden has since told me, that Mr. C.— had not the least appearance of a despairing lover all dinner time, where he eat very heartily, and talked a great deal of nothing, as usual.

This young man's volubility is really surprising. The reason Hudibras[1] gives, why those who talk on trifles speak with the greatest fluency, is, that the tongue is like a race-horse, which runs the faster the less weight it carries; and Mr. C.— never fails to distance all his opponents.

But scarce was the cloth removed, and the servants retired, when suddenly starting up, he, with a melancholy earnestness in his looks, begged the Colonel to give him an audience for a few moments in his closet—the Colonel complied. As soon as they were entered, he shut the door, and falling down upon his knees, with his hands clasped, and tears in his eyes, he implored the Colonel to give his consent, that the chaplain might marry him to Miss Clara, before he went away. The Colonel endeavoured to raise him, and smiling, said, he asked a thing which his honour would not permit him to grant. But to get rid of his importunities, told him, that if my Lord H— would write to him, and give his free consent to his marriage with his daughter, he should have liberty to see her; but as *her* free consent was no less necessary, he must next endeavour to gain that.

The young man, as if all difficulties were now removed, rose up in a transport, kissed his hand, and returning to the room where he had left Mrs. Bellenden and her two daughters, took leave of them very politely; the Colonel accompanying him to the water-side, where he staid till he saw him embark, on board the sloop that waited for him.

Yesterday the arrival of the Governor was announced, by the firing of the cannon of the Fort. The river was covered with the sloops that carried his train, which was increased by a crowd of persons, whom curiosity induced to join them. Mrs. Bellenden took me in her coach to the water-side, to see the manner of his reception. His Excellency had reason to be pleased with Colonel Bellenden's attention on this occasion; he had never been wel-

---

1 A character in Samuel Butler's (1612-80) prose satire, *Hudibras* (in three parts—1663, 1664, 1678), which satirized Cromwell and the Puritans. Hudibras was a member of Cromwell's roundheads and his adventures are treated mock-heroically.

comed, it was said, with equal distinction. I was struck with this circumstance, so much to the honour of the commandant. Mrs. Bellenden and her daughters were in raptures, when the Colonel, at the head of the troops, saluted the Governor as he passed. This ceremony, which is in itself very graceful, was performed by the Colonel with peculiar elegance, to which the dignity of his person and air greatly contributed.

The Governor was attended by an immense crowd, to the house that had been provided for him; for he absolutely refused to accept an apartment in the Fort, for fear of incommoding the family. He took notice to those about him, of the particularly honourable reception, Colonel Bellenden had given him. And that he might not be outdone in generosity, took the very extraordinary resolution of paying him a visit that same evening; accordingly, he slipped away from the obsequious crowd, and attended by only five or six gentlemen of his train, took his way on foot to the Fort.

I was walking with the ladies upon the ramparts, and the Colonel had just joined us, when the centinels at the gate, sent to inform him, that the Governor was coming up the Fort-hill.

The Colonel immediately ordered the guard to turn out to receive him; but Mr. Blood, the lieutenant who mounted guard that day, was not to be found.

Colonel Bellenden, who without considering his rank, thought only of paying the Governor the accustomed honours, performed the duty of a lieutenant upon guard, headed the men himself, and saluted the Governor as he entered the gates.

Mr. Mountague, surprised, ran up to him with some precipitation; and laying hold of his pike, which he himself gave into the hands of a soldier, embraced him with the warmest expression of kindness and respect, and arm in arm they walked together into the house; where the Colonel introduced him to his wife and family.

The Governor, who is a very well bred man, soon dispersed, by the politeness of his compliments, the cloud upon Mrs. Bellenden's brow, who retained some resentment in her heart against him, for the supposed slight they had received on Mr. C—'s account. His Excellency looked earnestly at Clara, and singling her out, entered into some conversation with her. He afterwards said, to a gentleman in his company, who repeated it to Mr. Neville, that he was surprised C—, who was a blockhead, had taste enough to fall in love with her.

He was willing, as it should seem, to prove that he did not

condemn his taste; for when Mr. Blood, by the Colonel's orders, went to receive the watch-word[1] from the Governor, the gallant old gentleman gave this young lady's name for the word; and, by his directions, the lieutenant repeated it aloud to the Colonel, before all the company, saying—

"Sir, the word is—*Clara*."

This piece of gallantry produced different effects on the company; Mrs. Bellenden looked pleased, Miss Bellenden bit her lips almost through with spite, Clara blushed, all were surprised, but Mr. Blood thought proper to assume a disapproving sneer.

"Your Excellency," said the Colonel, "has paid a dangerous compliment to the ladies; remember, it was a woman that betrayed the capitol."

"Aye," replied Mr. Mountague, with a side glance at Mr. Blood, whose impertinent looks had not escaped his notice, "but it was a goose that saved it[2]—You may depend upon your lieutenant, I suppose, Colonel?"

Mr. Blood left the room, with fury in his countenance; and afterwards declared to Mr. Neville, that if Mr. Montague had not been commander in chief, he would have challenged him, for calling him, by implication, a goose. He continues violently out of humour, blusters, and talks big.

Mrs. Benson diverts herself, and every one else, with the singularities of this doughty lieutenant. "The whole man," says she, "as a wit once observed of such another Drawcansir,[3] consists only of a pair of black menacing brows, and two fierce mustachios; and, therefore, utterly to defeat him, there needs only three or four clips of a pair of scissors. It is not possible to be afraid of him in earnest, for all his big looks." She thinks he hath choler enough, but does not believe he has any heart. She reckons him in the number of beasts that are skittish and rusty, but not furious and dangerous. The Colonel told her, he had been often in the field. "I believe it," she replied, "but then it had been rather to feed than to fight."

★ ★ ★ ★ ★

---

1 Password.
2 Tarpeia betrayed Rome to the Sabines, but ancient Roman tradition has it that geese cackling saved Rome from the Gauls' invasion of the capitol.
3 A loud-mouthed braggart in Villier's *The Rehearsal* (1672) who enters a battle and kills both friend and enemy alike.

I was present to-day at the first meeting between the Governor and the chiefs of the Indian tribes. The assembly was held in a large hall.—The Governor sat in state, attended by all the officers and gentlemen of his train; our commandant sat on his right hand; the mayor, and the other magistrates, on his left. The Indian chiefs, who were placed opposite to him, were venerable old men; they spoke in turn by their interpreter, and delivered themselves gracefully enough. I regretted that I did not understand their language; I am told it is highly figurative.[1] Their tone of voice is soft and agreeable; and their passions, as it should seem, very obedient; for although many matters were discussed, which included complaints, reproaches, and even threats, yet all was uttered with great gravity and composure.

The next day, the Governor gave them his answer. All was amicably settled; and on the third day, the government's presents, to the amount of five hundred pounds, were distributed among the tribes. The ceremony concluded with one of their war dances, at which none of us women chose to be present.

They are now preparing to return home; a circumstance which no one regrets. The rum, which was given them in large quantities, I think, very injudiciously, produces a great many disorders among them, and made them very disagreeable neighbours.

★ ★ ★ ★ ★

Albany is now quite deserted.—The Governor is gone, and has carried away with him all our gaiety. We have lived for these ten days past, in a continual succession of balls, entertainments, and parties of pleasure; but they are over, and have left a melancholy void, which cannot be filled up with our usual simple amusements. Miss Bellenden is fretful, Louisa solemn, and Clara silent and pensive.

My departure from this place, is fixed for next month.—A new source of disquiet among our little society, in which the absence of Mrs. Benson and myself, will be very sensibly felt, because

---

1 The languages of North American aboriginals resemble Chinese in their idiomatic construction. Raynal writes in *A Philosophical and Political History of the British Settlements and Trade in North America* "of the three original languages ... spoken in Canada; the Algonquin, the Sioux, and the Huron.... painted ... natural objects in strong colouring, and their discourses were quite picturesque, [with] ... figurative expression [and] ... gesture" (VI, 16). The language was highly metaphorical and poetic.

there are none to fill our places. However, Miss Bellenden will be easily comforted, for she has obtained leave of the Colonel and her mother, to spend three months at New-York: Miss Louisa goes with her. They are to be under the care of the wife of one of the principal merchants there, who is very deserving of such a trust.

Clara thinks herself happy, in being indulged in her request of remaining at home; she has lost much of her usual sprightliness; a soft and gentle melancholy appears in her looks, and runs through all her conversations. It is the opinion of her family, and her friends, that her heart has received a deep impression in favour of Mr. Euston; but this circumstance, which her modesty and reserve have concealed from herself, no one would be indelicate enough to hint to her. His acknowledged merit, and the respectful passion he expressed for her, might well produce this effect. I believe Mrs. Bellenden now thinks, she was rather too precipitate in rejecting his proposals, since her favourite scheme has not taken place.

Mr. Euston is actually gone to England; Clara was present when the Colonel mentioned it, as a piece of news he had just heard; every one carefully avoided looking at her. As I sat close to her, I could hear her hem away a sigh; she left the room on some pretense soon afterwards, and when she returned, no other alteration appeared in her countenance, than that her seriousness was a little encreased.

Mrs. Bellenden, with a view to divert her daughter, as well as to oblige me, has given her leave to be of my party to Schonectady. Mr. Neville proposed this little excursion, in order to take a view of the fort he is to command there, and to acquire some knowledge of the place, and the inhabitants among whom we are soon to reside.

From thence we are to go to Fort-Hunter; where we shall have an opportunity of becoming acquainted with the Mohawks, a tribe of Iroquois, who are converted to Christianity, and have their village, or castle, as they call it, in the neighbourhood of that fort. We reckon upon being absent a week upon this excursion.

Mrs. Bellenden insists upon having my little boy with her, till my return; he will be attended by Fanny, of whom he is extremely fond, and whose care and tenderness I can depend upon; so that I have nothing to make me uneasy, but a separation, which, however, will be but for a short time. I shall now close this packet, and leave it with the Colonel, that if any opportunity offers, while

I am away, of sending it to New-York, it may not be lost. I ever am, my dear Maria, your's most affectionately,

EUPHEMIA NEVILLE.

Letter XLI.

MRS. NEVILLE TO MRS. HARLEY.

Schonectady.

MY DEAR MARIA,

I NEVER go far from home without carrying with me materials for writing, that I may seize every opportunity of conversing with you in idea, at least; an employment which constitutes one of the greatest pleasures of my life.

We arrived here, after a very pleasant journey, early in the evening. Lieutenant Granger came out to meet us, and conducted us to his little fortress, which we found a very simple structure. The town, or rather village, (for so it is in appearance) consists of a small number of houses built in the Dutch taste,[1] and inhabited only by persons who carry on a trade with our Indian allies.—No language but Dutch is spoke here. There are some plantations pleasantly situated, and the country about is romantic and picturesque.

Mrs. Granger is a Dutch woman, a little more polished than her neighbours; an advantage which she owes to the conversation and instructions of her husband, who is a civil well bred man. She talks English tolerably well, and gave me all the information I could expect concerning the place, the people, and the manner of living here.

Observing that I sighed two or three times during her discourse, she told me, that to be sure, it was not so *fine* a place as Albany, and the people were not so rich, nor lived so grand, but that my husband might save a great deal of money here, and that you know, said she, is the chief thing to be considered in this world.

---

1 Dutch homes at this time were often steep-roofed, thick-walled and built of local stone, except for flat yellow bricks brought from Holland to outline the windows and door. These homes often had gambrel roofs and towers, were structured with a hall running between two rooms and openings in the wall for defense by muskets against aboriginal attacks.

I could not help smiling at this remark, which she took for a sign that I understood the force of her argument perfectly well.

I do not find that I shall be tempted to make any acquaintance here, unless it is with an old lady, of whom she gave me this account; that she is an English woman, the widow of an officer who once commanded here, and whom she has survived near twenty years.

"When her husband died," said Mrs. Granger, "she resolved never to leave the place, but to die here herself, that she might be buried with him; so she built herself a pretty little house near the skirts[1] of the town, and lives upon her pension and the profits of her negroes' work: she has four of them, and they love her so well, that they think they can never work hard enough for her. But she is a strange sort of a woman, for she will take but half of their earnings; the other half she lodges in safe hands, that it may be a provision for them when she dies, when she intends they shall be free.

"She has other odd fancies too; for when she stands god-mother to a child, as soon as it is three years old, she takes it, whether boy or girl, and breeds it up till it is ten years old, teaching it English and French, and writing and accompts,[2] for she is very learned. She is never without one of these god-children in the house with her. My husband thinks it a great favour when she will allow him to visit her, which is but seldom, for she does not love company, and is never without a book in her hand; and every year she has a cargo of them comes from New-York."

To meet with a person of such a description in this solitary place, is surely a fortunate circumstance. I hope I shall not find her difficult of access, for most eagerly shall I solicit her acquaintance.

Mrs. Benson and Mr. Neville are very busy in projecting alterations and improvements in the house and garden. The security one derives from living in a fortress in this wild country, and among these savage inhabitants, contribute not a little to reconcile me to my situation; and, all things considered, my condition will not by the wise be thought bad.

We have been here two days. Our hospitable host is very unwilling to part with us, and pressed us much to visit the Falls

---

1 Outskirts.
2 Accounts, "counting, reckoning, calculation" (*OED*).

of Cohas[1] in his company. Accordingly, we set out the next morning in a kind of covered waggon, in which our whole party was very well accommodated. We had clear sunshine, not a cloud appearing above the horizon, and very little wind at all. However, when we came near the Fall, there was a continual drizzling rain, occasioned by the vapours which rose from the water during its fall, and was carried about by the wind, so that our clothes were wetted as if there had been a shower of rain. This cataract,[2] which is in the river Mohawk before it falls into Hudson's river, is said to be very remarkable. Both above and below are solid rocks; the rock there, Mr. Granger told us, is three hundred yards broad. At the fall there is a rock crossways in the river, running every where equally high, and crossing in a straight line with that side that forms the fall: it represents, as it were, a wall towards the other side, which is not quite perpendicular. The heighth of this rock over which the water rolls, appears to be about four and twenty yards. We carried a cold collation with us, and dined very comfortably in a hut, built for the accommodation of travellers,[3]

---

1 Cahoes Falls, near Schenectady. Peter Kalm in his *Travels in North America* (1770 English trans.) describes "the waterfall near Cohoes, in the Mohawk River, before it empties into the Hudson River.... Above and below the falls both sides and the bottom are of rock, and there is a cliff at the fall itself, running everywhere equally high, and crossing the river in a straight line with the side which forms the fall" (I, 351). He suggests the height of the fall is 20 or 24 yards, and then cites the authoritative measurement given by an engineer of Philadelphia that the falls were 900 English feet broad and 75 feet high. When he saw the falls there was not much water cascading over the side, though close to the falls "vapors ... rose from the water during its fall" (352). See also Timothy Dwight's *Travels in New-England and New-York*, in Appendix D, for a description of "the celebrated cataract of the Mohawk."

2 Waterfall.

3 By the mid-eighteenth century, when the novel is set, and certainly by the end of the century, when *Euphemia* was published, the American landscape had attracted the attention of painters and travellers who sought out particular sights for their aesthetic qualities. The hut meant for travellers alluded to here is a recognition of the existence of American tourism, which was not as well established as the Grand Tour, for instance, but suggests that people viewed America as providing entertainment and instruction enough to justify the discomfort and danger of travel there. The hut would provide a marker to indicate the falls worthy of touristic consideration; protection from the elements; separation of the viewer from the object viewed—the sublimnity of the falls requiring such distance for full appreciation. See Introduction and Appendix C.

whose curiosity induces them to visit this place; and got home early in the evening, sufficiently fatigued with our journey.

★ ★ ★ ★ ★

Fort Hunter.

We reached this place early in the afternoon. The river, which is navigable for several miles beyond it, afforded us a most delightful passage, though in a canoe which was rowed with paddles by four careful Dutchmen, who observed a profound silence all the time. We were often willing to interrupt it, by asking several questions which curiosity suggested, but to no purpose, for they were not disposed to be in the least communicative.

This frail and simple vessel, which was nothing more than a large tree hollowed, at the bottom of which we sat upon mats and bear skins, carried us swiftly up the stream, while on each side our eyes wandered over the wild but charming scenes of the romantic shores, detached woods, adding beauty to the tops of the verdant mountains, cast a sweet yet dreadful gloom on either hand; and, assisted by the gentle dashing of the little oars, disposed the mind to no unpleasing melancholy.

Clara, lost in thought, was only roused from her reverie by the shouts of a number of Indians, who were ranged along the shore near the place where we were to land. Several of them jumped officiously into the river, and drew the canoe on shore. Mr. Butler, who loves parade it seems, received the daughter of the commandant with great ceremony. The flag was displayed on the bastion;[1] and the guard drawn up; a great crowd of Indians followed us to the gates, and some of the chiefs were permitted to enter, one of whom, in a set speech of several minutes, addressed to Clara, invited us, as we were told by Mr. Butler, to their castle.

To-day, being Sunday, we heard divine service in the Mohawk chapel, which is a pretty neat building. A great deal of finery is displayed on the pulpit and the alter, and there is some fine wrought plate for the communion table.

The chaplain preached in Dutch. Every sentence of the sermon was repeated to the Mohawks in their own language by an interpreter. The common-prayer and Psalms are translated

---

1 A five-sided fortification jutting from the main artillery fort for defense from many sides.

into the Mohawk tongue, and I observed that many of the Indians had their books in their hands.[1]

I never heard the Psalms sung more delightfully. The voices of the men are strong and clear; those of the women exquisitely melodious. We walk often on the ramparts, from whence we have a fine view of the country and the Indian plantations, where all the work is done by the women, the sole employment of the men being hunting and fishing; and when they have brought in game sufficient to supply their families, they spend the rest of their time in drinking and smoaking in their huts, relating their past exploits in war, and planning new expeditions.

These poor females work in the fields with one or more infants at their backs; and thus encumbered, bring home heavy burdens, their husbands being too lazy and too insolent to partake their labours.

We went to visit the Indian town to-day, well accompanied; for Captain Butler ordered some of the soldiers to attend us, in appearance to do us honour, but in reality to quiet our weak apprehensions, which he had in vain endeavoured to convince us was very ill founded. But it was not possible to persuade us we were safe without a guard, among such a great number of savages, whose appearance we thought very frightful.

We were obliged, in order to avoid giving offence by an appearance of preference, to enter the houses or *wigwams*, as the Indians call them, of all who invited us. Most of these *wigwams* were large enough to accommodate several families, each of which occupied no more than a square of eight or ten feet, that contained their bed, and a few other necessaries. The fire-place, which is in the middle of the hut, and is common to all, had a large opening in the roof to let out the smoke, of which however sufficient remained to blind us.

The *squaus*, so the Indian women are called, were extremely pleased with the notice we took of their children; and, in return for the presents we made them, gave us garters composed of

---

1   When St. Paul's Chapel was built in 1712 in the Mohawk Valley, it was the first and only royal chapel outside of Britain. Queen Anne presented it with a Bible, silver communion service and prayer books. Chief Joseph Brant (1742-1807) translated these prayer books into the Mohawk language. This would be rather late for the mid-century setting of *Euphemia*, but other anachronisms exist in the novel as well, and this may be one of those; or, the Mohawks' command of English may have been sufficient to the task of reading the prayer books.

wampum, strung in figures, and dyed of the most beautiful colours imaginable.

The principal chief of this nation has a house built and furnished in the European taste, for he is fond of imitating our manners; and here we actually drank tea; the *squau*, his lady, being ambitious to entertain us.

The Indian chief thought proper to confer the honour of adoption[1] upon Miss Clara, as his brother did upon me. This is considered as a high mark of respect among them, which conferred upon us all the rights and claims of a Mohawk by birth. We each of us received an Indian name upon this occasion. Their names always bear a relation to some real or imputed quality of body or mind. Clara's signified the morning star, and mine an ear of Indian wheat, denoting fruitfulness, for my present situation[2] was not unnoticed by them.

The ceremony concluded with one of their terrific dances, which we beheld from the ramparts of the Fort. Mr. Neville procured a quantity of their darling liquor rum, which he sent to them for their feast: it made them very quarrelsome, as usual; but we, safe behind our walls, suffered no inconvenience from them.

★ ★ ★ ★ ★

Albany.

We returned here yesterday evening, and I had the pleasure to resign my fair charge to her mother, in good health, and tolerable spirits, receiving in return her hostage, as she called my little boy, who was so delighted to see me again, that he almost smothered me with kisses, and lisped out a thousand prettinesses to engage me always to stay with him, for it seems he took my absence very heavily.

We have received here an alarming account of an intended insurrection of the Negroes at New-York:[3] the plot was happily

---

1 It was a custom to adopt across friendly tribes, as in this instance (considering, as the Mohawk would, the British as constituting a tribe).

2 Euphemia is pregnant with her second child.

3 The Negro Plot of 1741, which began in New York City, where several buildings in the fort and in the city were burned before the slaves could be brought under control, was one among many such unrests during this period, if the most substantial. Euphemia's fears that the insurrection would extend to Albany are strong enough that she and Mr. Neville dismiss their black servant and flee to the safety of the fort.

discovered before it was ripe for execution. We hear of nothing but informations, prosecutions, tortures, and death. Should the infection spread, the danger here would be very great, where the Negroes are still more numerous than at New-York. I had but one black servant in my house, a woman, and her I have sent away. There is no safety, I think, any where but in the Fort; and Mrs. Bellenden has been so good as to accommodate me with an apartment in it, where I shall remain till we remove to Schonectady, and there I shall be within walls and ramparts again. The Colonel's daughters left New York but three days before the conspiracy was discovered.

I am now settled at Schonectady. My dear Mrs. Benson came here some days before me; and I found my house fitted up with an elegant neatness, which left me nothing to wish for on that article.

Mr. Neville had been at as great an expence in improvements, as if he was to settle here for the remainder of his days. It is our opinion of things that is the measure of their value: like Cæsar, he had rather be the first man in a village than the second in Rome; nor is he happy only in the gratification of his ambition, he contrives to amuse himself in a way that suits his taste:—He likes field sports, his bottle, and the pleasures of the table. He makes frequent excursions to Albany and Fort Hunter; and spends much of his time at the neighbouring plantations, where, if he does not meet with polite manners, and sensible conversation, he is sure of finding good cheer, excellent wine, and unrestrained mirth.

Meantime I enjoy, in its highest perfection, what my favourite poet[1] emphatically calls

The feast of reason and the flow of soul,

In the society of my dear Mrs. Benson, that wise and affectionate friend. With the widow lady I mentioned to you we are become very intimate; for she is extremely amiable in her manners, and

---

1 Alexander Pope (1688-1744). Pope was one of the preeminent poets and critics of the first half of the eighteenth century in England. He struggled throughout his life with debilitating illness, but his poetry sets human life within a cosmic setting and emphasizes a rational, if sociable, approach to living a meaningful life. The quotation is from Pope's *Imitations of Horace* 2.1 (1744) in which the poet praises the company of his friend Henry St. John, Viscount Bolingbroke.

possesses a large share of good sense, improved by reading and reflection.

With such companions, with your dear animated letters, which make you present with me; with that never-failing, that extatic source of delight, my lovely boy, now rising to my fondest hopes—this wild, this savage region blooms a paradise.

With this account of my present situation, which I know will be welcome to you, I will close my letter; for a servant is just arrived from Albany, sent by the Colonel, to let me know that he is to send off some dispatches to-morrow to New-York, and will enclose any letters I have ready, that may be sent by the first ship that sails for England. Adieu, then, my dear Maria. Need I tell you that I am and ever will be yours most affectionately,

EUPHEMIA NEVILLE.

Letter XLII.
MRS. BENSON TO MRS. HARLEY.

DEAR MADAM,

YOUR reproaches for our long silence would be just, had any thing but the severest of calamities, produced this seeming neglect. Your amiable, and now unhappy friend, Madam, concluded her last letter to you in a strain, not only of content, but joy.—Her will wholly resigned to her present fortune, her heart glowing with the most delightful hopes of the future, she was eager to communicate, to her beloved friend, part of the transports that filled her breast. Ah! what a reverse, in the space of a few months, did she experience! But take the melancholy tale in order, since I have now acquired composure enough to give you all the circumstances of it.

A friend of Mr. Neville's, whom some private affairs had brought to New-York, accepted his invitation to stay a few days with us at Schonectady. Mr. Neville carried him to every place worthy his notice; the Falls of Cohas he had not yet seen, and a day was fixed upon for this little excursion. Mrs. Neville would willingly have avoided being of the party, the little Maria not being yet weaned;[1] but Mr. Neville having resolved to take his son with him, the tender anxious mother would not stay behind.

---

1 Maria is still nursing at her mother's breast.

All our party were in high spirits, except Mrs. Neville; her heart seemed to labour with some unknown oppression, her speech was often interrupted with sighs, an air of melancholy overspread her face. I asked her several times, if she was well: she assured me she felt no other disorder, but a strange tremor on her spirits, for which she could not account.

Observing Mr. Neville to appear dissatisfied, at her being less chearful than usual, she endeavoured to dispel the gloom that hung upon her, and met his contracted brow with her wonted smile of complacency.

I marked the painful effort—I saw the starting tears that glistened in those eyes, which she turned upon him with an assumed chearfulness. Uneasy and apprehensive, I whispered, "My dear Euphemia, you are not well." "I am well, indeed I am," she replied; "but my spirits are uncommonly low today, that is all."

Our guest having sufficiently satisfied his curiosity with the view of the cataract, our servants spread a cloth upon the rustic table, in the hut where we had dined before; and a cold collation being provided, we all sat down to it. But the keenness of that appetite, which I had borrowed from the air, and unusual exercise, was instantly checked, when I perceived that Mrs. Neville could not eat, but trifled with her knife and fork, in order to escape observation.

The gentlemen drank their wine pretty freely; meantime, my dear Euphemia, heavy from fatigue, and yet more with the unusual weight that oppressed her mind, gave the smiling infant, that hung upon her breast, into Fanny's arms, who sat next to her; and reclining her head upon a mossy pillow, fell into a profound sleep.

Mr. Neville now rose up, and proposed to his friend to walk into the woods, till the servants had dined, and the carriages were ready for our departure. They took little Edward with them, that his innocent prattle might not interrupt his mother's repose; and, attended only by Mr. Neville's own servant, they set out upon their walk.

Mrs. Neville slept sound and easy; I was happy in the hope, that this salutary rest would restore her strength and spirits. When Fanny said, softly, "Are you not surprised, Madam, that Mr. Neville stays so long?" I had never thought of this circumstance; I looked at my watch, and was astonished to find it so late.

That instant Mr. Neville entered the hut; with wild impatience in his look and accent, he enquired if Edward was with us.

"With us!" said I, trembling, "did he not go with you?"

"Oh! Sutton," said Mr. Neville to his friend, who had followed him, "my boy is not here!"

This exclamation was uttered so loud, that it awoke Mrs. Neville; her husband seeing her open her eyes, rushed out of the hut, and was followed by his friend. Fanny and I remained motionless; fear and amazement strongly pictured in her face, and, I suppose, in mine; for Mrs. Neville, surprised at her husband's abrupt departure, turned towards us to ask the reason; but at the first glance, she uttered a piercing shriek.

"Ah! I understand those looks," said she, turning her eyes alternately upon Fanny and me; "some dreadful accident has happened—My dear boy! my Edward! Is he dead? Oh! tell me, I conjure you," pursued she, clasping her hands together, "tell me the truth—is my child dead?" Her supplicating look and action, pierced my heart. "Heaven forbid!" was all I could say. "Then he is not dead," said she; "Heaven be praised! I breathe again; from what agonizing pangs am I relieved! Oh! if you knew what I felt in that dreadful moment of suspense, which realized all the strange forebodings that have tortured my imagination this day."

Mr. Neville's servant that moment appeared at the door, and rolling his eager enquiring eyes about the place, exclaimed—

"Oh! he is not here! he is lost! I shall go mad!"

Mrs. Neville starting up, cried, "who is lost?—My child! tell me—"

"Oh! detain me not, Madam," said he, for she held him by the arm; "let me go in search of him, I will find him, or never return." He broke from her loosened hold; she rushed out after him, with a distracted pace. Unable to follow her, I received the sleeping infant out of Fanny's arms, who flew after her miserable mistress, and both were in an instant concealed from my sight by the impervious woods.

Thus desolate, alone, my heart torn with anguish, expecting every moment to hear of some new calamity, no creature of whom I could make any inquiries, for all our people had dispersed themselves about the forest in search of the dear lost boy; trembling lest the baby should awake, and prest by wants I had no means of supplying, rent my afflicted heart with its tender wailings, I abandoned myself, I own it, I abandoned myself, for a few moments, to despair.

Reflection at length returned, and brought with it sober councils.

"Is this," said I to myself, "the part of a Christian, to shrink thus meanly in the hour of trial? where is that confidence in the goodness, that resignation to the will of God, which, till I was called upon to exert, I thought I possessed? Alas! in health and happy days, it is easy to talk of putting our trust in God; we readily trust him for life when we have health, for necessaries when we have competence, and for deliverance when we have escaped from any danger; but when dangers assault, when calamities oppress us, we forget that he is powerful to save, and compassionate to relieve."

I pursued this train of thought; and every moment, as a pious resignation gained upon my soul, I blessed, I adored the sacred power of religion, that could thus produce good out of evil, and make my present affliction the means of attaining eternal happiness.

The calm uninterrupted sleep of the infant, afforded in my altered mind, matter for gratitude and praise; for how could I have stilled its cries, or procure proper food for it in this desert, unused, as it had hitherto been, to any nourishment but its fond mother's milk.—It slept, while I wept over it with tenderness, and prayed with fervor.

At length I heard the sound of steps, I turned my eager eyes, my beloved Euphemia appeared, Mr. Sutton and her faithful Fanny supporting her. Now quick, now slow, was her faultering pace; her countenance pale as death; her eyes, one instant raised to Heaven with supplicating tears, the next in wild despondence fixed on the ground; her closed hands wringing each other as if she would burst their sinews.

She threw herself on the bank beside me, without uttering a word; one tender glance she cast upon her sleeping infant in my arms, then burst into a flood of tears.

Mr. Sutton begged her to compose herself if possible, saying, he would go again into the woods, and never give over his search, till he could bring her some news of her son. He went away instantly; and I took occasion from his last words, to draw some motives of consolation for her.

"Oh! do not amuse me with false hopes," said she; "I shall never more see my child. He is, doubt it not, he is a prey to savage beasts, or savage men, still worse than beasts. Oh! thou delight of my heart and eyes, was this the fate to which thou wert born?— Mangled—torn—devoured—"

At this sad thought she shrieked aloud, and sunk lifeless into Fanny's arms. With difficulty we recovered her; but it was but for a moment; successive fainting fits made us tremble for her life.

Still I indulged some gleams of hope, that the sweet boy might yet be found. But when Mr. Neville returned, his frantic looks proclaimed the irremidable calamity.

"He is lost!" groaned he out, "he is gone!—for ever gone!"

"Ah!" cried I, "see here," pointing to his wife, who lay pale and motionless on Fanny's knees.—He gazed on her for a moment—"What is to be done?" said he; "tell me, advise me."

"By all means," said Mr. Sutton, "let Mrs. Neville be carried home; place her in the carriage, thus insensible as she is; believe it, when she recovers sense and thought, it will be difficult to get her from hence."

This, in the sad extremity to which we were reduced, was the best thing that could be done. Fanny got into the coach, and received her, still fainting, in her arms; I placed myself opposite to them with the child, whose sleep seemed, by Providence, to be prolonged for our comfort.

Mr. Neville declared he would not leave the place, but continue his search till he found his son dead or alive. His friend staid with him, and the unhappy servant to whose care the child had been entrusted.

This man, in his looks and behaviour, expressed the most poignant remorse and agonizing grief; accusing himself, with floods of tears, as being the cause of what had happened. Its seems the little boy, tired with walking, desired to sit down under a tree, till his father and Mr. Sutton, who chose to go further, returned; William sat down with him. Overcome with the heat, and lulled by the dashing sound of the cataract, which may be heard at a great distance, they fell asleep.

The man awakening, missed the child; and not yet much alarmed, supposing he had only strayed a few paces from him, called him several times aloud, and ran about in search of him. Not finding him, his fears increased; he wandered through the woods, still calling him in vain: then fondly hoping, that he should meet him, perhaps, in the place where he had so unfortunately fallen asleep, he returned thither; but instead of the child, saw Mr. Sutton and his master, who were looking for them.

Mr. Neville seeing him alone, exclaimed, with an eager look and tone, "Where is Edward?" The man, confounded, terrified, amazed, answered not a word. Mr. Neville, in a transport of fear and rage, seized him by the collar, and giving him a violent shake, "Rascal," said he, "have you lost my son?"

Mr. Neville, now worked up almost to a delirium of fury, drew his sword, and had not Mr. Sutton held his arm, the poor fellow had fallen a victim to the tempest that raged within his soul.

"Let us go in search of your child," said his friend to him; "let us take different ways."

"What, hope of finding him safe in these wild woods!" said the sighing father: "Ere this he is become a prey to some furious animal, or some human savage.—My fears distract me."

With a furious pace he rushed into the thickest of the woods, calling his son. Mr. Sutton took a different path; as did the servant. Alas! all were unsuccessful.

The motion of the carriage, aided by some drops that Fanny applied, at length brought Mrs. Neville out of her fainting fit. With her senses, recollection—dreadful recollection! returned. She appeared not to consider where she was, or whither she was going, but groaned as if in the agonies of death. I begged her not to banish hope; that there was at least a possibility the child might be safe; that Mr. Neville and his friend were still in search of him; that enquiries would be made at every farm-house for many miles around, and that so many persons would be employed in seeking him; that we were sure of having some intelligence.

"Could you think it possible," said she, "that I should ever be so transcendently miserable as to wish I may hear my boy is dead by a fall, by a sudden fit, or that he is drowned; but, oh! to have him torn to pieces by wild beasts, or mangled by those savage hunters of men, who, when hunger presses, devour their species.[1]—Can I think that this is his fate, and not be mad? Talk not to me of hope.—Oh! when I think what my child has suffered, and is, perhaps, suffering now!"—Again her spirits, her sense forsook her. Scarce did it seem charity to use any efforts to recover her from this state of insensibility.

In these temporary deaths, from which our cares rescued her only to fall into them again, was this melancholy journey passed. At length we reached the Fort; we carried her up to her chamber, we put her to bed; a violent fever seized her; her ravings shewed the horrid images that filled her imagination.

Sometimes she fancied she saw her son in the paws of a wild beast; sometimes sprawling upon the lance of some ferocious Indian, writhing in the agonies of death. Her cries, her heart-rending complaints, filled all who heard her with the deepest anguish. Mrs. Lawson shared in all my sorrows and all my fatigue on this sad event.

---

1   The Algonquin root of "Mohawk" is "man-eater," or "cannibal." The tribe was named for the vicious and ruthless fighting style of its men.

From the Bellenden family we experienced every effort of tender sympathizing friendship. A very skilful physician was, by their means, brought from New-York. He gave us little hope, and her death was hourly expected.

Mr. Neville returned, after an absence of eight days, which he had spent in incessant wanderings, with beating heart. We crouded round him as soon as he appeared:—"'Tis all over," said he; "there is no more room for hope or fear—my boy is dead."

"The manner," cried I, almost breathless with terror—"tell us the manner of his death."

"Heaven be praised!" said he, "that was not so horrid as I feared—he was drowned—he had strayed too near the river, he fell in. A countryman, (for William has not been heard of since) saw the listless corse of the dear innocent carried away by the stream."—A burst of grief here stopped his speech for a moment; then recovering—"Tell me *your* tale of horror now," said he; "my wife, where is she?"

Mrs. Lawson with some caution informed him of her condition, and would have prevented him from going into her chamber, but the physician was of opinion that the sight of him might have an effect very contrary to what we feared. She had known none of us for several days, and still continued to rave, and paint those horrid scenes that filled her tortured imagination

Mr. Neville just shewed himself. She started—she screamed—he retired. She rose up in her bed, and eagerly drew back the curtain.

"Where is he?" said she, "did I not see him?"

"Who, my dear Euphemia," said I, "who did you see?"

"My husband," she replied; "where is he gone? why will you not let him come to me?"

Transported at this instance of her returning to reason, I called to him to approach. She seized his hand with an eager pressure—

"Have you found his mangled limbs?" said she: "have you buried him? Was he, Oh! tell me, was he not devoured?"

Mr. Neville was silent, not knowing what to say to her, when the physician interposed—

"Tell her the truth," said he; "the truth will be less dreadful than the horrid ideas that possess her fancy."

"My dear Euphemia," said Mr. Neville, "be patient, be

resigned—our child was drowned."—she paused a moment; then looking earnestly at him—

"You say he was drowned," said she; "are you sure of it?" The physician whispered—"Say you saw him dead."

"Alas!" said he, "I am too sure of it."

"Now then may I weep," said she, after a pause of a moment—"now I may grieve; it is *sorrow* now, before it was distraction. Oh! my dear boy, you are dead, I shall never see you more; but you was not devoured." She threw her arms about my neck as I was leaning over her; and hiding her face in my bosom, burst into tears.

Oh! how I blest the salutary shower; and, although I felt that the strong agony of sorrow shook her whole frame as I held her in my arms; yet, while her tears bedewed my bosom, I was cheered with the hope of a favourable change in her distemper.

Fatigued at length, and almost fainting, her head sunk upon her pillow, she closed her eyes, and but for the frequent sighs that forced their way, we should have thought her dead.

The physician, who had caused a composing medicine to be prepared for her, now gave it her himself. She swallowed it without uttering a word or opening her eyes, and soon afterwards fell into a profound sleep, that lasted several hours.

This first symptom of her amendment was followed by others that confirmed our hopes. When she awoke she knew us all; desired to see the little Maria, who had been consigned to Fanny's care, and was perfectly well. She kissed and blessed her; spoke with great tenderness to her husband, and thanked Mrs. Lawson for her friendly attention. To me she spoke not, but held my hand fast clasped in hers, and sometimes pressed it to her lips. She often sighed, and I could observe tears steal down her cheeks continually.

In this calm silent sorrow she remained several days; meantime her fever abated fast; the physician pronounced her out of danger; and all we had now to do, he said, was to endeavour to recruit her strength and spirits. Mrs. Bellenden came herself to fetch her to Albany; and it seemed to be the chief business of the whole family to soothe, to comfort, and amuse her.

Patient now as suffering infancy, and full of devout resignation, her grief is calm, sedate, and silent; but still she grieves. She has lost her usual chearfulness, but the sensibility of her heart is increased; always tender and compassionate, she is now more so than ever, and feels the woes of others as if she had none of her own to lament.

I love, I admire her if possible more than ever. Well has it been said, that adversity is the shining time of the wise and good. None are more miserable than those who never experienced calamity; how can it be known whether they be good or bad? Such virtues as are only faculties and dispositions, deserve little praise; but every *act* of virtue has in itself the principles of its own reward.

Such arguments as these I pressed upon my dear Euphemia, when I apprehended her grief for the loss of her son would exceed the bounds her good sense and piety seemed to prescribe for it. I put her in mind of the noble stand she made against immoderate sorrow, when she lost her excellent mother; a loss that was followed by many cruel disappointments and mortifications.

"Alas!" she replied, "it is but an accidental fortitude we can boast, when we bear misfortunes so unequally. I know—I feel my weakness, but I am not able to overcome it." The sighs and tears that accompanied this confession, proved its truth.

"No affliction, my child," said I, "is greater than despair; it turns a natural evil into an intolerable one, and constitutes the punishment to which the wicked are condemned."

When I found a calm and steady resignation take the place of that poignant anguish which had so long filled her heart: When I saw her return to her usual employments, if not with equal vivacity, yet with an air serene and composed: When I saw her cares for the little Maria give full employment for her maternal tenderness, without any of those sad retrospective thoughts which used to cast a damp upon the pleasure she received from the innocent caresses of this lovely child: then my hopes of her returning peace were confirmed. I congratulated her upon a change, so ardently desired by her friends, so salutary for herself. Never shall I forget her look and accent when she thus answered me:—

"My dear Mrs. Benson; those who will not suffer their portion of misery here, deserve to be something less than human, but nothing better."

Thus, Madam, have I fulfilled the sad task my situation imposed upon me, of giving you this sad narrative. You will weep—you will mourn for the sufferings of your amiable friend; but when you have paid that tender tribute to her misfortunes, remember, that she is no longer in the first paroxysms of her grief; that while your imagination represents her sinking beneath their weight, reason and religion have produced that resignation, which philosophy teaches, but which true piety alone can reach.

That heaven may preserve you from such severe trials, is my first and ardent wish; that your fortitude and patience may be equal to her's, my next. I am, with great truth, Madam, your faithful humble servant,

BENSON.

END OF THE THIRD VOLUME.

EUPHEMIA
VOL. IV

Letter XLIII.
MRS. NEVILLE TO MRS. HARLEY.

MY DEAR MARIA,

IT is not surprising that we should be so long in receiving each other's letters, considering how many hazards they must run through in these days of legal piracy,[1] before they reach, if they reach at all, their destined port. Your last wandered about by sea and land for near eight months before it came to my hands; but when it came I forgot the anxiety of long expectation, for it brought me comfort in the dear assurance that you were well and happy.

Depend upon it I never miss any opportunity of writing to you; such a neglect would be unpardonable to you, who have so many claims upon my gratitude, my love, my *veneration*. Quarrel not with that great word; it is strictly just when applied from me to you; but I will not say more, lest I should pain that modesty, which makes you shun the praises which you are never weary of deserving.

My letters cannot merit the value you set upon them on any account, but that they convey the sentiments of a heart devoutly yours.

You give me encomiums which I could not expect from your judgment, but that you have corrupted it by your too great partiality to me. You think too favourably of a spirit that is more than

---

1 Refers to practice in which armed merchant ships—privateering vessels—carrying a commission or letter of marque from the admiralty of a country were entitled to search out merchant ships of enemy countries and commandeer their contents. Lennox writes in *Harriot Stuart* (1750) of her heroine's being taken on board a Spanish privateer during the War of Jenkins' Ear (which ended in 1748). English privateers were outfitted in New York and encouraged to enter the war by the British government who reduced their taxes on prizes captured. These vessels acted as protection for English merchantmen, but also harassed French and Spanish traders. France and Spain retaliated with their own fleet of privateering vessels. Maria and Euphemia's letters are a casualty of such warring.

half extinguished; and consider not, that melancholy, which is indeed, as some have observed, ingenious and fruitful when it is a natural temperament of the mind; but stupid and sterile, when it proceeds from the continual outrages of adverse fortune.

In the state I was long, too long in, there is none but yourself that could have made me write; and, although several years have elapsed since the fatal blow was struck, which bleeding memory still presents fresh to my imagination, I recollect with shame that I never did a greater work in my life than when I dictated my pen to the few lines I first wrote to you after it.

But, alas! to what purpose should I grieve for a blessing that is out of my reach, and anxiously hunt after all the defects of my situation? This tedious banishment from my country, this worse than banishment, that includes my absence from you!

Mr. Neville seems resolved never to return to England, till his uncle's death puts him in possession of a fortune that will enable him to live in a style to which he has annexed ideas of respect—consideration—happiness; ideas unworthy of a man of sense, who possesses advantages which money cannot bestow. A lottery ticket may put a groom[1] upon a footing with a peer in point of affluence, make him a senator, introduce him at court; but can it make him a gentleman? can it supply the defects of low habits and a mean education? can it inform his mind with knowledge, fashion his person to elegance, or tincture his behaviour with politeness?

A clown in his gilt chariot will be still a clown; and a gentleman, even in poverty, will still preserve that distinction, if he unites dignity of sentiment and manners with the advantages of birth and education.

I sometimes venture to throw out hints like these, when Mr. Neville is repining at his situation: but this he considers as advice, a liberty not to be endured in a woman and a wife.

---

1   The earliest reference to a lottery in the *OED* is dated 1567, and novelist Henry Fielding writes in 1731 of the lottery as a means of making a young man's fortune. In 1726 the Netherlands formed what is now the oldest lottery still in operation, and in 1775 a lottery was authorized in order to raise funds for the colonial army. Through the winning of a lottery prize, some of which were in the tens of thousands of pounds in the eighteenth century, a young man—even a groom, a male servant of low position or birth, who often looked after horses—could make his fortune, though this would not make him a peer, a person of high rank in society.

He is careful, however, to provide amusements for himself, that may soften the rigour of his fate. He has obtained leave to be absent from his command, at different times, for a month together, which he has spent in excursions to Philadelphia, Boston, and other places whither curiosity or a desire of changing the scene has led him.

Meantime I have passed my days in the enjoyment of domestic happiness, as much as my heart is capable of, since the fatal —. But oh! I would not cast a glance that way. At home I have the society of my dear Mrs. Benson, whose excellent understanding affords me a perpetual feast; whose virtue and piety are at once my example and my guide. My daughter, whose unfolding sweets of person and of mind give me a foretaste of future as well as the possession of present delight.—Her education employs the greatest part of my time; under the direction of Mrs. Benson, whose deputy I am, I teach her French, Italian, and music; her father, when he is at home, teaches her writing and accompts; and, as she has a taste for drawing, he has taken some pains in instructing her, so that she has made a tolerable proficiency in that agreeable art. The meaner, but not less useful arts of the needle, are Fanny's province; and the œconomy of a family makes part of mine. My daughter, whether her lot is cast for riches or poverty, will not come unqualified to act her part decently in either condition.

Her father, being solicitous to prevent any rusticity from the retirement we live in, among a rude and unpolished people, insists upon my taking her to New-York every summer, where we spend three months very agreeably with the Bellenden family, who have an elegant house there. Here we see some good company; and Maria, under the care of a very skilful and diligent dancing master, has acquired a grace and elegance in her air and manner, which give a polish to all her other endowments.

In one of these excursions I became acquainted with a lady, who, because there is something singular in her character, and because that acquaintance was productive of an adventure which might have had very fatal consequences, I shall be particular in my description of her.

Mrs. Mountfort is the widow of a gentleman who was secretary to this province; her family is genteel, and her fortune considerable. Although bred up in all the fashionable amusements of London, and engaged in all its politer circles, having married the man of her choice, she had no reluctance to follow him to America, and pass her days in this distant province of the empire.

Mrs. Mountfort is in her forty-fifth year; she has been a complete beauty, and still retains as many charms as are consistent with that age. Her conversation is sensible and engaging; and there is an air of sprightliness in her look, her motion, and her manner, which it is plain is the effect of habit, not of affectation; and, as such, creates no disgust, though it is not altogether suitable to her years.

This lady, having courted my intimacy very assiduously, and being indeed extremely obliging to me on many occasions, I passed much of my time with her, and we conversed together with the freedom of old acquaintance.

In one of our tête-à-têtes, which happened very frequently, I heard her sigh several times; and expressing my concern, as well as surprise, at this appearance of uneasiness in a temper so uniformly chearful, as her's had always appeared to be,—

"And only in appearance," interrupted she; "for, strange as you will think it, I am, my dear Mrs. Neville, one of the most unhappy persons in the world."

"Unhappy!" repeated I, with some emotion.

"Yes," said she, "unhappy; and from causes so vain, so frivolous, so absurd, that I deserve no pity, and almost despise myself."

"You astonish me," replied I; "but I hope you are not serious. Surely this is one of your lively sallies, to amuse me."

"Ah! those lively sallies," interrupted she, casting down her eyes, "how ill do they become my faded person and declining years."

I smiled at this remark, delivered in so solemn an accent.

"Chearfulness," replied I, "is becoming in every age; and your's—"

"I know what you would say," resumed she, hastily. "But I am not merely chearful; I am gay, my dear Mrs. Neville; and that gaiety is not the effect of my temper, but of affectation; it springs from an inordinate desire of pleasing, which at my age is ridiculous."

"All I understand of this discourse," said I, "is, that you are a very severe censurer of yourself; and that, if you have any foibles, you are disposed to magnify them; a disposition, for which I can by no means account, in a person of your good sense and candour on other occasions."

"Well," replied she, "hear what I have to say of myself, and then judge if I do not deserve to be, what I really am, unhappy.

"I have been young and handsome; I forget that I am no longer so; I have lost the power of pleasing, but the inordinate desire of it remains. I am surprised to find myself practicing those coquet airs, which are excusable in youth and beauty, but which are ridiculous in one of my age; I blush at my folly one minute, and the next, dragged on by habit, I fall into it again. Among the young and gay, I find I am overlooked, and I am ready to die with vexation.

"When I look in my glass, I perceive the ravages time has made in my face, and I am ready to laugh at myself for my silly expectation, that such a face should raise any emotions but dislike, or at least, be beheld with any thing more than indifference; but when I am dressed, and mix in company, I forget the faithful monitor.—Habit is a thing which we often fall into by flying it, just as a person swears that he will not swear. I call forth attractions, which no longer exist; I expect the effect, when the cause has ceased; and the disappointment, that necessarily follows, loads me with chagrin.

"Since I cannot be younger, I wish to be older; at fifty I should cease to desire; what at forty I am absurd enough to endeavour to obtain. Confess now, my dear Mrs. Neville, is not this a terrible malady of the mind, and the more terrible, as it is absolutely incurable?"

"Oh! do not say so," replied I; "you who can so candidly acknowledge the disease, who can reason so justly upon its effects and consequences, could not fail of finding a cure, if you would but heartily endeavour it."

"Can you suggest one?" said she.

"Return to your family and friends," replied I, "whom you left to follow a husband you loved, and to whom, report says, you made an excellent wife. I shall be a loser by your yielding to this advice, but it is the best I can give. In the caresses of your affectionate relations, you will find employment for your sensibility; friendship will afford you rational and durable pleasures. One friend to your virtues, is worth a hundred admirers of your person."

"I have heard your Socratina" (so she calls Mrs. Benson) "say," interrupted she, "that the two greatest enemies in the world, are passion and reason. My vanity will not suffer me to take your advice, which yet I allow to be good. I left England in the bloom of youth and beauty; how can I bear the thoughts of returning thither, thus altered, that none of my former friends would know me.—They would seek for Harriet Mountfort, in Harriet Mountfort herself; and their astonishment at the sight of me, would be a mortal stab to my pride.

"Were I a Roman Catholic, I would bury myself in the gloom of a cloister; where the dreams of superstition would succeed to the illusions of vanity, and the spiritual pride of the devoted swallow up the regrets of the mortified beauty. However, I am resolved to become a recluse, and leave the world, since the world has left me.

"I will betake myself to some retirement, where I can have no opportunity of indulging ideas, which ought long since to have been banished from my mind. I will endeavour to forget every thing in which I formerly delighted; and above all, I will endeavour to forget myself; and like the antiquated coquet I have read of, cry out—

'Venus, take my votive glass,
Since I am not what I was;
What from henceforth I shall be;
Venus let me never see.'"[1]

"While you can rally thus," said I, "upon your imputed frailty, you are not far from the kingdom of sober reason. But pray tell me, what spot you have fixed upon for your hermitage?"

"I have proceeded further in this design than you imagine," replied she. "I have actually bought a plantation, which was lately the property of an Irish gentleman, who is returned to his own country, to take possession of an estate that has been bequeathed to him. My agent, who has transacted this business, tells me, that Mr. Casney has laid out his ground with some taste; and that the situation is, even in this romantic country, particularly romantic. But what gives it its greatest value with me, is its neighbourhood to Schonectady; being but ten miles distant from the fortress where you reside. I have not yet seen my purchase, but I intend to visit it before the winter sets in, and give what directions may be necessary for my removal thither next summer."

I endeavoured to prevail with her to leave New-York when I did; it being settled, that I should return to Schonectady in the course of a fortnight, the season now being far advanced; but she has business, she said, which would detain her a week or two after me.

---

1 Matthew Prior (1664-1721), English poet, prose satirist, and secret agent during Queen Anne's reign. This verse is from his "The Lady Who Offers Her Looking-Glass to Venus" (1718).

When I took leave of her, she assured me, I might depend upon seeing her soon at Schonectady. She came indeed, but so long after the time prefixed, that many threatening appearances warned us winter was at hand. Mr. Neville told her, she had chosen an unfavourable season to take the first view of her rural retirement. "Oh!" she replied, "to judge of true beauty, we must see it in an undress. If my new purchase pleases me in the state it now is, I shall be charmed with it, when it puts on all the ornaments of the spring and summer."

As soon as our guest had recovered from the fatigue of her journey from New-York, we set out to visit Casney, now Mountfort-Place: Mrs. Mountfort, Mrs. Benson, my little girl, and myself, with Fanny, in the coach, and Mr. Neville, with one servant, on horseback. We carried provisions for two days with us, not expecting to find very good entertainment in a place where the live stock had been all disposed of, and where there were no other inhabitants, but the husbandman and his wife, and one negro.

We had not proceeded more than three miles on our journey, when it began to snow. Alarmed at this appearance of winter, which, in this country, is extremely rapid in its approaches, having before-hand engaged Mrs. Mountfort's acquiesence with my intention, I begged Mr. Neville to let us return; he would not hear of it, alledging, that this little fall of snow would be of no consequence, and that we might still expect fine weather.

We pursued our route: the snow continued to fall so thick and fast, that Mr. Neville, almost petrified with cold, begged we would take him into the coach; we did so, and then Mrs. Mountfort and Mrs. Benson joined me in entreating him, to order the horses heads to be turned towards home, lest the road should become impassable, as would certainly be the case, if it continued much longer to snow with such violence.

Mr. Neville was immoveable in his opinion, that this severity of weather, being premature, would not hold long; that the snow would be melted before the next morning, when we should have no other difficulty to encounter in our return home, but wet roads.

His servant now rode up to the coach, and begged leave to assure him, that the road would be impassable for coach-wheels by to-morrow.

The poor fellow's interposition drew upon him a severe rebuke. We were obliged to submit; and at length reached Mountfort-Place.—Wet, cold, spiritless, we entered the house, which was yet but half finished. The husbandman and his wife heaped the parlour fire with nut-wood, which blazing up instantly, refreshed us with its comfortable warmth.

We sat down to dinner with keen appetites; and Mr. Neville being in high good humour, past hardships were forgot; but the dread of the future hung upon my mind, for the honest rustic told me, that the snow, which still continued falling very fast, was at that time very deep.

Mrs. Mountfort, however, seemed perfectly satisfied with the place; and although her eyes encountered nothing from the windows but a dreary waste, for all distinction of objects were lost in one uniform face of snow,—yet she amused herself with projecting improvements to make her farm a delightful retreat:— green vallies, shady groves, cool grottos, and meandering streams, were to diversify the scene, and a new Arcadia[1] was to rise amidst the wilds of America.

Mr. Neville drank his wine, and bowed assent to all these operations of her fancy; meantime Fanny visited the bed-chambers, and caused large fires to be made in each. We soon retired to rest, being heartily fatigued with our uncomfortable journey. As it had ceased to snow for some time before we went to bed, Mr. Neville foretold that we should have pleasant weather for our return, and applauded himself for not yielding to my silly apprehensions, which would have prevented Mrs. Mountfort from gratifying her curiosity with the view of her new purchase. But he was greatly mortified next morning at his rising, when going to the window, he found a prodigious quantity of snow had fallen in the night. I guessed what had happened by the gloominess of his looks, but I would not venture to ask him any questions, lest he should, as was very likely, construe my anxiety into a reproach for his obstinacy in not going back while it was yet in our power.

He left the room in a sullen silence; and Mrs. Benson and my little girl came in immediately afterwards. Maria threw herself upon my neck, all in tears; "Ah, mamma," said she, "we shall die to be sure in this frightful place—we shall never get from hence." I looked at Mrs. Benson, and was greatly alarmed at the consternation that appeared in her countenance; but before I could speak to her, Mr. Neville returned.

"We are in a fine way here," said he; "these foolish people have neglected to lay in their winter provision before the bad weather

---

1   In Virgil's *Eclogues*, Arcadia was the ideal pastoral world.

set in; we are in danger of being starved, for they tell me there is not three days subsistence in the house, and there is no getting hence without a thaw comes on, which is not to be hoped for, as the frost is already very severe. No relief is to be expected from without; for there is not any inhabitants within reach of us, and winter has now provided barricadoes for us, which no human strength or skill can break through."

I was thrown so much off my guard by this melancholy picture of our condition, that I exclaimed—"Oh! what imprudence to venture on, when the first fall of snow warned us of what we had to expect."

"And who hindered you?" retorted Mr. Neville, with a severe look, "from going back?"

Apparently he had had forgot that it was himself who had opposed it, and so vehemently, that no one had courage to press a measure which yet every one knew to be absolutely necessary; but Mr. Neville, who cannot bear the least touch of blame, whenever the event shews that he has determined wrong, either totally forgets that it was he who had determined so, or defends the measure itself in spite of conviction. This is one of his peculiarities, which I am now so used to, that I never, on such occasions, contradict him. Mrs. Benson, for the sake of peace, is silent likewise, and hears him with indifference.

As soon as I was dressed I went into the parlour, where I found Mrs. Mountfort waiting breakfast for us. She appeared greatly concerned at our melancholy situation, and took all the blame upon herself as being the cause of it, which Mr. Neville was too polite to contradict. So great a quantity of snow had fallen, that it was not possible to take a step without sinking in it almost up to the middle. The Indians indeed have snow shoes, which enable them to travel over the frozen snow without any inconvenience; but we had no resource.

All we could now hope for was, that the winter, being not yet far enough advanced to make a thaw improbable, that happy circumstance might intervene to save us from destruction.

On the fourth day of our captivity, we began a minute examination into the state of our provisions. Those we had brought from Schonectady, though sparingly used, were all exhausted. The house could produce nothing but a small cask of flour, some pieces of smoked beef, part of a stitch of bacon, and a few potted pigeons: the cow had been dry for two days, and was not expected to calve for some time. From this slender stock a family of nine persons were to draw their subsistence.

We gazed on each other with a melancholy despondence. Mr. Neville fretted and stormed; my little girl wept, not for herself, but for me, her father, and her friends. Mrs. Benson endeavoured to comfort us, and to calm the transports of Mrs. Mountfort, who was continually upbraiding herself as being the cause of this misfortune.

One evening, when we were taking our last regale of tea, we were surprised to hear the voice of an Indian shouting in their barbarous way, at a little distance from the house. The Negro was immediately dispatched to conduct him in; and every heart now glowed with expectation of some relief, from this unexpected incident.

The negro returned in a few minutes, with an Indian about forty years of age. He told us in Dutch that he came from the Mohawk Castle, and was journeying to Albany, but had lost his way; and appeared half starved, having met with no game to subsist on.

Mr. Neville ordered some food to be set before him, gave him a large glass of rum, of which there was indeed a good quantity in the house, and promised him a reward if he would carry a letter to the person who commanded the fort at Schonectady in his absence.

The Indian agreed willingly to the proposal; and as soon as his hunger was satisfied, he fell fast asleep upon some bear skins that were provided for him before the kitchen fire, intending to set out the next morning as soon as it was light.

Meantime Mr. Neville wrote to his officer, directing him to send the sledge, with a file of soldiers to break the road, and also a supply of fresh provisions.

In the morning our friendly savage, having breakfasted plentifully upon our slender store, received the letter and all necessary instructions, promising our people should be with us the following day. He insisted upon taking a large bottle, which held two quarts of rum, with him, which we durst not refuse; and he set out, leaving us full of hope, and gratitude to that Providence, which had thus interposed for our preservation.

Towards noon the next day, every eye was employed in looking out for the expected relief; every heart beat with anxious expectation—the hours wore away—our convoy did not appear.—That they did not appear, when the evening came on, must have been owing to the savage having deceived us; for the number of men Mr. Neville ordered for this service of breaking the road, might easily have performed it within that time.

With the departing light our hope abandoned us; and now all was despondence and vain reasoning upon the cause of our disappointment. It was late, and no one thought of going to bed; for rest, in our situation, it was impossible to expect. We retired however, at length, to our several chambers, and passed the night tortured with a thousand gloomy apprehensions.

In the morning, Mr. Neville, who had risen early, returned hastily into my room to tell me a piece of news that entirely banished what little hope remained; for at intervals we were willing to flatter ourselves, that our deliverance, though delayed, would still be effected by means of the Indian we had employed. Alas! Mr. Neville told me, this poor savage was found dead about a quarter mile from the house, by the Negro who had been sent out to bring in the wood.

The bottle, which he had taken with him filled with rum, was empty, and it was supposed, that having drank the greatest part of it before he had proceeded half his journey, he had returned to demand more; and being quite intoxicated before he could reach the house, had fallen a victim to his insatiate appetite for that fatal liquor.

Mr. Neville, when he had given me this account, left me abruptly; and, while I was relating this sad accident to Mrs. Benson, who came in as he went away, Fanny entered the room, and told me, that she had made a fortunate mistake, and put up a small canister of tea instead of one of snuff, which Mrs. Benson had directed her to bring with us.

This little incident gave us as much pleasure as we were capable of receiving in our distressed circumstances; but Mr. Neville not coming to breakfast, and the old husbandman who went to seek him returning without him, and declaring he was no where to be found, filled me with the most dreadful apprehensions. My friends endeavoured to calm my fears, and persuaded me to wait patiently for the return of the Negro, who had been dispatched to several places in search of him. But I was now grown incapable of listening to him, and was running out of the house to seek him myself; for when fear has risen to a certain pitch, it produces the same effects as temerity; when the servant, whom we brought with us to this disastrous place, threw himself in my way, and respectfully stopping me, begged me to return, and he would inform me what was become of his master.

Although his looks and the tone of his voice announced nothing unfortunate, yet my mind was so possessed by the apprehension of some fatal accident, that I expected nothing but a confirmation of it.

"Do not be alarmed, Madam," said he, "I doubt not but my master will return in safety—it was impossible to hinder him from going."

"From going whither?" said Mrs. Benson; for surprise and terror rendered me incapable of uttering a word.

"Why, Madam," replied he, "the case was this: my master going to look at the poor dead Indian, a thought struck him that his snow shoes might serve him for the same purpose for which he had been employed; so he ordered me to take them off and put them on his feet. I did so; and it was surprising to see with what ease and security he walked upon the surface of the snow, without sinking an inch. He then told me, that he was resolved to set out for Schonectady without delay. I begged him to permit me to go; but he said, he would trust this business to none but himself: so ordering me to tie up a small quantity of bread in a handkerchief, and a pint bottle of rum, lowered[1] with water, he wrapped himself up warm as he could, and set out, directing his course by the sun. I sent a thousand good wishes and prayers after him; and as soon as I had dug a hole in the snow, and laid the body of the Indian in it, as he ordered me, I came to tell you, Madam, what had happened."

Mrs. Mountfort and Mrs. Benson, although anxious for the safety of Mr. Neville, yet could not but be cheared with this prospect of deliverance from our melancholy confinement; but it was quite different with my poor little girl and me. The danger the father and the husband was exposed to, hung heavy upon our spirits, and rendered us insensible to the hope which animated our friends.

We passed an anxious day and restless night: we had reason to expect, if no misfortune had befallen him, that he would be with us early the next evening. The evening came, he did not appear; it was no longer anxiety, it was terror and despair. We gazed over the wide expanse of snow as long as one ray of light remained, and retired at length to give ourselves up to tears and complaints.

While we were thus absorbed in grief, and our friends at a loss what to say to comfort us, we heard a kind of noise at a distance, but could not distinguish whether it was the sound of human voices or the howling of wild beasts. The servants ran out of the

---

1 Diluted.

house to listen. They returned in transports, and assured us our deliverance was at hand, for they were certain they heard the voices of men.

"Perhaps it is a party of savages," said I, trembling, between hope and fear. We now plainly heard several shouts; and Robert, who had staid after the others to listen, came in and assured us he could plainly distinguish his master's voice.

We were not long in suspense: Mr. Neville actually presented himself at the door. He had left his pioneers, he said, and the sledge at a small distance, and, impatient to relieve our anxiety, trusted to his snow shoes for a quicker conveyance to us; for the sledge could not move but as the soldiers, who marched before, cleared a passage for it.

We crowded round him, eager to hear the particulars of his hazardous journey; but he declared he would not satisfy our curiosity till he could treat us with something better than news, for he was sure we were half famished; and indeed he was pretty near the truth, there being scarce any thing left in the house fit to eat.

The sledge arrived about half an hour after him; it was loaded with provisions of every kind: we sat down in high spirits, to a table spread, as it appeared to us, with the most exquisite delicacies. The soldiers were regaled in the kitchen with plenty of food and liquor; and, what was still more comfortable to them, an enormous fire.

Mr. Neville's heroism, in atchieving this perilous adventure, was the subject of extravagant praises from us all. He listened to us for some time, smiling, as if mightily flattered with the sounding epithets we gave to this action; at length he told us, that the whole merit of it was in the attempt, for he had encountered no dangers, overcome no difficulties, nor suffered any hardships.

"I had travelled," pursued he, "about four or five miles, when, by some observations I made, I perceived I was out of my way; and being thus uncertain to what point to turn, I was overtaken by two Dutchmen, who were returning to their own village from Oswago, whither they had been to trade. They not only directed me the right course I was to pursue, but offered to accompany me to Schonectady; for which, when we parted, I gave them a handsome gratuity.

"I arrived at the Fort, time enough to make all the necessary preparations for my return hither the next day. My pioneers set out some hours before me, in order to clear a passage for the sledge, which carried me and the good things I have brought you;

but I soon overtook them, for the work was tedious and heavy, which was the cause that I came here so late."

We were so impatient to leave a place where we had suffered so much distress, and were so apprehensive of future accidents, that we would not allow Mr. Neville more than one night to rest from his fatigue. The next morning, as soon as we had breakfasted, we set out in the sledge, well defended against the cold with bear-skins and stoves.

Mrs. Mountfort's people, who were left in the house, were plentifully supplied with provisions, for a longer time than was sufficient to provide their winter stores; and this care she took upon herself.

When our adventure was known, we were loaded with congratulations from our friends all over the province. The kind Mrs. Lawson welcomed us with tears of joy. Colonel Bellenden did us the honour to come and pass two days with us, and brought his lady and daughters with him. My house was large enough to accommodate this respectable company; and Mrs. Mountfort was so pleased with her situation, that she was easily persuaded, the winter being now set in with all its rigour, not to think of returning to New-York till the next summer, part of which she proposes to spend at her plantation. The Bellenden family have planned so many agreeable parties, and schemes of amusement, that she will not, I believe, think her stay tedious. She seems to have made a great progress in the cure of that vanity, of which she accused herself; and either her reason has overcome the disease, or the disease, by preying upon itself for want of other food, is entirely consumed, for she now appears quite easy in her own mind, and is more agreeable than ever.

★ ★ ★ ★ ★

Schonectady.

Your last letters, my dear Maria, found me at Fort Albany, as happy in the society of the dear and respectable friends I have there, as the misfortunes of my life will admit. To know that you are well, that all you love are so likewise, is one of my greatest comforts in distress; and in less disastrous circumstances, would give me a higher relish of the good I enjoy.

Mrs. Mountfort proved a very agreeable companion to me the whole winter. She left me as soon as the frost broke up, to return to New-York; but she promises I shall see her and the butterflies together. She proposes to spend the summer at her plantation, to direct the improvements to be made in it; and when her plans are executed, it will be a delightful retreat.

I am to set out in a few days for Philadelphia, with Colonel Bellenden and the ladies, who obliged Mr. Neville to consent that my little girl and myself should be of their party. I shall then be able to give you some account of that celebrated city; whose founder, in my opinion, is not much inferior to Solon,[1] or any of the wise lawgivers of antiquity. When I date my next, it will probably be from thence.

Fort Albany.

My life is so full of melancholy events, that I have neither festival nor day of rest; and when my own ill fortune ceases, for a short time, to persecute me, I suffer by the distresses of my friends.

A few days past, all was serene and happy in this family of love.[2] Our intended excursion to Philadelphia afforded us a pleasing prospect of amusement, and the day was fixed for our setting out on our journey; when the very evening before, as the Colonel, Mrs. Bellenden, and myself, were engaged in a party at quadrille,[3] the Colonel suddenly fell back in his chair in a fainting fit.

---

1 Solon, born into a well-to-do family in Athens c. 600 BCE, was a lawmaker there and contributed to the growth of democracy and the written constitution. In his *Travels in North America*, Peter Kalm describes Philadelphia in 1748 as "the capital of Pennsylvania, a province which forms part of what formerly was called New Sweden, ... one of the principal towns in North America and next to Boston the greatest. It is situated almost in the center of the English colonies.... [It] was built in the year 1683 ... by the well-known Quaker William Penn, who got this whole province by a grant from Charles the Second, king of England, after Sweden had given up its claims to it." The streets, he notes, are broad, regular, and "pretty"; the houses make a good appearance; there are a multitude of churches, including English, Swedish, German Lutheran, Presbyterian, Quaker, Catholic, etc.; the Town Hall is an impressive building, as is the Library, begun in 1742 by Benjamin Franklin; and despite Quaker opposition, the town is fortified (I, 18).

2 A phrase which recalls the conclusions of Henry Fielding's popular novels, including *Tom Jones* and *Joseph Andrews*, published mid-century. In these, the lovers and their families retire to an idyllic country setting, away from urban crime and corruption, to become a "family of love."

3 A fashionable card game.

Mrs. Bellenden uttered a piercing shriek; and springing to him, clasped him in her arms, wetting his pale face with a shower of tears.—The young ladies, distracted with their fears, ran about calling of help. I alone preserved some composure in this scene of affliction.—I administered some drops. He was just beginning to open his eyes, when the surgeon to the garrison attended; he bled him, and directed that he should be put to bed immediately. Some cordials[1] were given him; and he soon afterwards fell into a quiet sleep. Hope dawned in the face of his wife and daughters; but upon pressing the surgeon with their anxious enquiries, his answers, I could perceive, were vague and illusive.

I sought, and found an opportunity of speaking to him in private, when he owned to me, with tears starting to his eyes, that it was a paralytic stroke, and that the Colonel was in great danger. I took upon myself to dispatch a messenger immediately to New-York, for a physician of eminence, not being willing to alarm Mrs. Bellenden, whom the least idea of her husband's danger, would have thrown into a state of distraction.

I was by the Colonel's bedside when he awoke.—He asked for some drink, but with a voice scarce intelligible; and I could perceive, that it was with great difficulty he uttered those few words.

He continued in this state several days; sometimes raising our hopes by an appearance of amendment, sometimes depressing them by unfavourable symptoms.

When the physician arrived, he disapproved of the bleeding; but ordered some medicines, which produced a surprising effect.

To-day the Colonel was able to leave his bed, and leaning on Clara's arm, walked about his chamber for several minutes together. While she was thus employed, I could observe her often smile tenderly upon her mother, who sat with trembling anxiety, watching every step, and gazing with inexpressible tenderness upon that countenance, which, though pale and languid, had lost nothing of its benignity.

The servants, transported with joy at these first symptoms of their beloved master's recovery, communicated their hopes to the troops in the garrison, among whom one universal face of sorrow had prevailed, during the whole time that he was in the greatest danger.

Three of the old soldiers, still survived; these grateful veterans could not be persuaded to quit the hall for a moment, during his

---

1 A stimulating drink.

illness. They sat silent and sad, never stirring from their seats, or uttering a word; but when any of the servants appeared, then they would all eagerly rise, and ask, with trembling emotion, if he was better. Scarce could they be persuaded to return to their quarters at night; and as soon as the morning dawned, they came again to their melancholy post.

All the officers, except Lieutenant Blood, expressed in their looks and behaviour, the sincerest sorrow. And so powerfully does the innate goodness of this worthy man operate upon all hearts, that even the phlegmatic Dutchmen, appear with eyes wet with the dew of pity, and pray for his recovery.

The soldiers to a man execrate the First Lieutenant, whose brutal joy at the prospect of the Colonel's death, which will give him once more the temporary command, he neither can, nor seems to wish he could conceal.

One brutal act of his was within a little of raising a mutiny among them.

While the Colonel was judged to be in the greatest danger, the guard was relieved without beat of drum, and the sound of this noisy warlike instrument was, on other occasions, flattened as much as possible. When it came to Mr. Blood's turn to mount guard, he not only ordered every thing to be performed in the usual way, but upon some pretence or other, made the reveille[1] be beat upon the bastion nearest the Colonel's apartment.

The noise awaked him from a gentle slumber, which he had fallen into after a restless night. I was by his bedside, and almost choaked with grief and rage at this barbarous interruption of his sleep.—I approached him, lamenting the accident.

He asked me who commanded the guard? and when I told him it was that worst of men, Captain Blood, he answered, with a melancholy smile, "Weak man! he longs for my death, that he may wear the poor pageant of authority again."

The other officers have had some lively altercations with the First Lieutenant, on account of his indecent behaviour; and it was not their fault that they were not followed by some fatal consequences; but Mr. Blood, on some occasions, shews that he is possessed of a surprising command of temper.

This is the fourteenth day of the Colonel's illness; he mends, I think, but slowly; yet his family cherish the most flattering hopes—and who can have the cruelty to undeceive them? He

---

1 The signal to awaken, usually given by bugle or drum.

appears perfectly calm; asks his physician no questions, and takes whatever is prescribed for him, with an indifference that seems to have its source in a certain conviction, upon his own mind, that they will be ineffectual; so my foreboding heart interprets it. He passes much of his time in his closet; and I doubt not, has settled both his spiritual and temporal affairs. The life of a good man is a continual prayer: and Colonel Bellenden is indeed a good man.

To-day the Colonel proposed to dine with his family, in the usual dining parlour; for since his illness, dinner has been served in Mrs. Bellenden's dressing-room, for the conveniency of being near him. This proposal was received with joy by his wife and daughters, who considered it as a token of his amendment, and a happy omen of his perfect recovery.

He joined us with a chearful air, being led in by his eldest daughter, whose hand he politely kissed for rendering him this piece of service, which in doing, I thought, she looked more beautiful than ever.

At table I observed him heedfully.—He fixed his eyes often on his wife, with a tender and melancholy air, then on each of his daughters; a suppressed sigh, and a starting tear, accompanied the fond regards he cast upon them. Once, when he thought no one observed him, after gazing attentively upon them, he raised his eyes to heaven, as it should seem, in fervent ejaculation, for his lips moved. Most ardently did I join in mental prayer, the petition he was, doubtless, that moment offering up for his afflicted family.

When dinner was ended, he called for a glass of wine and water, and after drinking his wine, drank to each of his daughters severally, and even to me, with a cordiality that went to my heart.

About an hour afterwards he declared he was sleepy: we all attended him to his chamber.

"I think I will go to bed for the night," said he; and he was accordingly put to bed. Before he lay down he embraced Mrs. Bellenden affectionately, afterwards each of his daughters; then turned upon his side, and lay still and composed.

My soul was full of melancholy forebodings: I persuaded the ladies to retire that we might not disturb his repose. They complied; silent, and wrapped in dismal musings, with cautious tread they left the room. I followed them, but could with difficulty prevent them from returning every minute to enquire if he still slept: at length I told them, I would go myself, and bring them word.

When I entered the Colonel's room, I saw the physician sitting by the bedside, feeling his pulse.—I approached him, trembling with my fears; he whispered, "All is over! he has but a few minutes to live.—For Heaven's sake! keep the afflicted family out of the chamber."

His words shot a ball of ice through my throbbing heart. "One look! one last look!" I cried.—I saw him.—His hands were clasped, as in prayer; his eyes devoutly lifted up. Spite of my efforts, sighs forced their way, and tears drowned my eyes. He gently moved his head; he looked at me—oh! my Maria, he smiled upon me!—This was too much; I could not bear it—I sunk down. No one attended to me: for a moment afterwards, I heard the last agonizing groan; and the physician, in a melancholy accent, say, "He is dead!"

I sprung from the ground; I took one of his now lifeless hands, and pressing it to my lips, I eased my loaded heart by a shower of tears.

Death, in that amiable countenance, seemed divested of all its horror; it still preserved its wonted grace and benignity, and the sweet smile that sat upon every feature, seemed to tell us, he was happy.

The physician, after respectfully kissing his hand, drew me reluctant from the bedside.

"Suppress this useless grief, Madam," said he, "and employ all your cares in comforting the unhappy family; this will be the most acceptable service you can now render your departed friend."

The duty he pointed out to me, I prepared to perform; and drying my eyes, I went to Mrs. Bellenden's apartment, uncertain in what manner I should disclose the melancholy tidings. Alas! they had already too sure a presage of them; the loud laments of the servants had reached their ears.

I met Mrs. Bellenden wildly rushing out of her room; on seeing me she stopped, and gazing eagerly upon me, she clasped her arms about me, and sunk upon the floor. While I leaned over her, supporting her, she cried out, "Tell me if—Yet do not, oh! do not tell me, that I have lost him."

I could answer her no otherwise than by my tears; they spoke too plainly—she fainted in my arms; and while her maid and I were busy in laying her on a bed, the young ladies flew to their father's chamber, in a state almost of distraction; but instantly returned, led by the physician, and Mr. Neville, who was just arrived; for the chamber was crowded with the officers, and the chief men of the city.

Mr. Neville afterwards told me, it was a most affecting scene.

The officers, as they kissed the hand of their deceased commander, bathed it with their tears, enumerating his virtues, and lamenting his loss.

The citizens bore a willing testimony to the truth of their eulogiums, and regretted his death. But some of them, like true traders, ever attentive to the prospect of gain, was making interest with the house-keeper, who sat weeping at the head of the bed, to be employed in furnishing mourning[1] for the family.

Meantime Captain Blood, whose stature, as well as fierceness, seemed to be increased by this event, after having dispatched an express to New-York, with an account of it to the Governor, was blustering among the grieved soldiers, treating their sensibility as a crime, and doubling the duty of those who appeared most afflicted. He sneeringly told the old veterans, as they retired, oppressed with sorrow, to their quarters, that there was nothing now to hinder them from visiting again their native country.

One of them, upon this indirect menace, shook his head, expressing a mixture of contempt and anger in his looks; which so provoked his brutal officer, that he was not ashamed to give the old man, already sinking with the weight of years and sorrow, a blow, which staggered his weak frame, and he would have fallen to the ground, had he not been supported by one of the soldiers nearest him.

A murmur of pity and indignation now ran through the ranks. Captain Blood looked fiercely round him, and singling out one soldier, he seized him with a tremendous gripe, and gave him in custody to a serjeant, ordering him to be put in the black-hole,[2] and to remain there till he was taken out to receive his punishment, which he swore should not be less than a hundred lashes.

* * * * *

How justly has it been observed, that misfortunes seldom come alone.—"They love a train," says the melancholy Young.[3] My

---

1 Making/providing mourning clothes.

2 The punishment cell of a barracks.

3 From *The Complaint, or Night Thoughts on Life, Death, and Immortality* (1742-45), by Edward Young (1683-1765), English writer who wrote tragedies early in his career, satires, and poetry later in life, contributing to the Graveyard school of poetry in which melancholy perspectives on life and death were represented. "Woes cluster; rare are solitary woes;/ They love a train, they tread each other's heel" (III. 63-64).

heart bleeds for the distresses of this family, now increased by an unthought of, least expected accident.

The agent in whose hands Colonel Bellenden placed the greater part of his savings, during all the years that he had enjoyed his lucrative post here, is become a bankrupt, and all is lost. Such are the accounts brought by the last ships from England.

It was necessary that Mrs. Bellenden should be informed of this last stroke of fortune.—The sad task fell to me. After long struggles, I went to her apartment; I attempted to speak, but the words died upon my tongue; and when I looked upon her, and reflected that I was going to add a new weight of affliction, to the almost insupportable load she already laboured under, my tears were ready to gush out; and it would have been difficult to have concealed my disorder from her, if her own sad thoughts had not entirely engrossed her attention.

Clara's penetration, however, was not to be deceived; she looked earnestly to me, and giving me a sign to follow her, went out of the room.

"Speak out, Madam," said she to me; "you have some disagreeable news to tell us. Alas! what can happen now, worse than we have already suffered?"

I gave her the Governor's letter to Mr. Neville; whom he directed to acquaint Mrs. Bellenden, in the most cautious manner possible, with all the circumstances of this new misfortune.

Clara ran it over; and returned it to me with dry eyes, and a composed countenance.

"Since this fatal stroke was to fall on us," said she, "how much reason have we to thank Heaven, that my father was ignorant of it; and that his last moments were not disturbed, with anxious solicitude about the future subsistence of his family."

In this thought, all her regrets for the unhappy change of her circumstances, seemed to be absorbed. Mrs. Bellenden received the news with a kind of apathy, which she borrowed from an affliction too great to admit of an increase.

Meantime, Captain Blood offered every insult in his power to the memory of his late worthy commander. He was continually making new arrangements in the garrison, displacing persons whom the Colonel had distinguished by his favours, and promoting others, of whom, it was known, he had no favourable opinion. He encouraged, and even suggested, pecuniary demands upon the widow, which amounted to considerable sums; and the facility with which they were paid by the poor afflicted lady, who would have thought it a sacrilege to dispute any claim upon her husband, invited many unprincipled persons to practise upon her generosity.

Mr. Neville, who knew how greatly the Governor interested himself in the affairs of the distrest family, took the liberty to write to him an exact account of all these proceedings. He also informed him, that Captain Blood was for hurrying on the Colonel's funeral; having intimated his intention of removing, with his wife and family, to the Fort; and had marked out the Colonel's late apartments for his own residence.

The Governor, animated with a generous indignation at this brutal conduct of the First Lieutenant wrote to him himself, and reproved him in very severe terms for it. He ordered him not to think of taking up his residence in the Fort, which could not be done without some inconvenience to the Colonel's family, which he would not permit. He forbad him to interfere in the matter of the late commandant's funeral; the time and ordering of which, he took upon himself to determine; and strictly charged him, to trouble Mrs. Bellenden no more about pecuniary claims; all which he would settle himself when he came to Albany, the time for meeting the Indians now drawing near.

This letter was brought by an officer, deputed by the Governor to see his intentions executed, and who, with several others, came from New-York to attend the Colonel's funeral.

It was performed with all due military honours, suitable to his rank; and being, by his post, first commissioner likewise in civil affairs, the magistracy of the city[1] attended it in their formalities. But the highest honours that were paid him, were the tears of all good men, to whom his memory will ever be dear. He lies interred in the chapel belonging to the Fort.

This was a melancholy day for the family.—I shut myself up with them, in the most retired part of the house; by these means, great part of the hurry and bustle escaped their notice: but the noise of the firing threw them into agonies, which it was difficult to calm.—Mrs. Benson assisted me in this sad office; and my dear little girl, by the tender sympathy she shewed, sometimes attracted their grateful attention.

* * * * *

---

1   A civil officer of the law. Magistracy refers to "magistrates collectively; the whole body of magistrates."

To-day several large boxes were brought from New-York, which contained every article of dress for the family mourning, all of the most elegant kind. The millinery in the genteelest taste imaginable; accompanied with a letter from the Governor's daughters, filled with tender sympathy, and professions of friendship, apologizing for their officiousness in taking this business upon themselves; being sensible, they said, that nothing proper could be procured at Albany.

Persons in affliction, set a double value upon every instance of kindness, and it is just they should; for it has been well observed, that a pretended affection is not easily discernable from a real one, unless in seasons of distress; for adversity is to friendship, what fire is to gold, the only infallible test to discover the genuine from the counterfeit, as in all other circumstances they both bear the same common signature.

Mrs. Bellenden was extremely moved with this polite and generous attention to her situation; and Clara wrote an answer to the ladies, which, without departing from that dignity of sentiment suitable to her birth, expressed all the warmth of a grateful heart, impressed with the strongest sense of obligation.

As some allay to the satisfaction this incident afforded them, they met with a new mortification from Mr. Blood, who, although restrained by the measures the Governor had taken to prevent the effects of his insolence, yet gladly seized every opportunity of shewing his ill will.

The poor soldier, who had laboured all this time under the dread of that unjust sentence he had passed upon him, being informed that in two days his punishment was to take place, got a petition presented to Mrs. Bellenden, imploring her to procure his pardon from the First Lieutenant.

"I have no interest," said she, with a melancholy smile, "with the present powers.—But the nature of this poor man's offence, give me great concern for him."

She could not resolve to ask a favour of Mr. Blood herself; but she directed Miss Bellenden to send a card to him, requesting, if a pardon could not be granted, at least a mitigation of the soldier's punishment.

Mr. Blood had the insolence to return an answer to this effect:—

That the influence of fair ladies in the garrison, had for some years past, occasioned a great relaxation of discipline; but that while *he* had the honour to hold the command, he would endeavour to restore it to its former vigour.

The soldier was accordingly brought out to receive his punishment.—He was tied up to the halbards,[1] surrounded by the guard on duty. Mr. Neville told us, that his apprehensions at first seemed very strong, and spread a paleness over his countenance; but he was quickly encouraged, by the significant smiles and nods of his companions, and even of the two drummers, who were to execute the sentence.

Mr. Blood saw all this, but affected not to see it; for the defection was so general, that he was afraid to take notice of it. The man received his hundred lashes; but they were laid on so lightly, that a school-boy would have been ashamed to complain of the smart.

Mr. Blood seemed almost choaked with vexation. This was observed by a young fellow, who had lately enlisted in a fit of despair, occasioned by a disappointment in love, whose friends had in vain solicited Mr. Blood for his discharge: having had the advantage of a tolerable education, he passed for a wit among his companions.

This youth approached Mr. Blood with deep respect; and with great solemnity of countenance, as if he had something of wonderful importance to communicate, begged he would give him a private audience for a moment: the lieutenant went aside with him.

"I have read, Sir," said he, "that under governments like your's, where a wholesome severity prevails, informers were not only countenanced, but rewarded; I hope, therefore, I shall be entitled to your favour, for the intelligence I bring you."

Mr. Blood perceived something in this prelude to stir his spleen, but his curiosity predominated, so that in a loud voice he bid the fellow go on.

"Sir," said he, "you have been pleased to punish my comrade yonder with a hundred lashes, for making a sorrowful face for the death of his late commander; but there is one amongst us, whom, if you please, I can point out to you, who no longer ago than yesterday, was caught in the fact of weeping at his grave, and lamenting his loss."

Mr. Blood now almost mad with rage, gave the poor wit so many heavy blows, with a thick oaken stick he had in his hand,

---

1 Soldiers of the infantry, when flogged, were tied to three halberds (a combination battle axe and spear) set up in a triangle, with a fourth across them.

that he laid him sprawling at his feet; while several of the soldiers cried out, "Strike on, strike on, noble Lieutenant! you know he dare not strike again."

The behaviour of the garrison, carried such a face of mutiny, as made it necessary for the officers to shew their disapprobation of it; yet in private, they remonstrated against the severity exercised upon the feigned informer; but, notwithstanding all they could say, he was by Mr. Blood's order confined in the black-hole, which was all the salve he had for his bruises.

★ ★ ★ ★ ★

The Indians have been assembled in the plain behind the Fort this week past, in expectation of the Governor's arrival. They expressed great concern for the death of the late commandant; the Mohawk tribe in particular, many of whom had seen him. The request they made, to be permitted to pay their compliments of condolance to the widow and daughters of the Great Chief, as they stile him, shew, that these untutored savages, have in their minds those natural principles of humanity, which is the foundation of true politeness.

They deputed five of the most respectable men of their nation, to wait upon Mrs. Bellenden.—As soon as they entered her apartment, they seemed sensibly affected with the melancholy air of every thing they saw.

The sable dress of the family, the grief in the countenance of Mrs. Bellenden, the languid looks of the young ladies, who, pale and motionless, scarce raised their eyes to look upon their strange visitors, drew from them a murmur of sympathising feeling, which was strongly expressed in their looks.

The oldest of these Indians approached Mrs. Bellenden with a respectful air, and spoke two or three words to her in the Indian language, which none of us understood; she bowed her head, and they immediately withdrew, retiring backwards to the door by which they came in.

I was struck with this piece of politeness; but more with the tears, which I actually saw standing in the eyes of him who had addressed her.

This brought to my recollection, what I once heard Mr. Euston say, concerning the manners of these Indians.—"Let us never believe," said he, "that gentleness and humanity are qualities of the earth and air; they are, says a learned friend of mine, neither goods of the East, nor captive virtues of the Greeks; they are wandering and pasant.—All climates receive them in their turn; and it is not the Cymbrick Chersonesus any longer, it is Athens and Achaia[1] that are at this day barbarous."

* * * * *

Yesterday the Governor landed at Albany. The usual honours were paid him; but it was observed, that in his countenance and behaviour, there was a seriousness that approached to melancholy, which the numerous friends of Colonel Bellenden were charmed with.

His Excellency would not enter the lodgings prepared for him, till he had visited Mrs. Bellenden. He came up to the Fort with only a few gentlemen in his train, most of whom were officers, who wore a black scarf tied round their right arm, as did the Governor, who was drest in regimentals likewise.

Mr. Blood had not thought fit to pay this respect to the memory of the deceased Colonel Bellenden; a singularity which the Governor did not fail to take notice of.

Mrs. Bellenden, who had not yet left her chamber, received the Governor there. He drew a chair close to her's, and conversed with her, in a low voice, for near half an hour. I had joined the young ladies, who, accompanied by Mrs. Benson, were receiving the compliments of the gentlemen, who had attended the Governor in this visit.

Guess my surprise, my dear Maria, when I perceived Mr. Euston among them. Apparently Miss Clara had not yet seen him, for he had given place to the officers, who came up first to pay their respects, and stood at a little distance gazing on her with fixed attention, while she was answering the officers civilities with silent courtesies; her eyes, because they were full of tears, bending their looks upon the ground.

Mr. Euston now approached, unnoticed by her; but when he spoke, the sound of a voice so little expected, made her start; she raised her eyes, which encountering an ardent glance from his, a faint blush overspread her cheeks.—The sight of a person, whom she had lost all hopes of ever seeing again, and for whom her father had a particular respect, seemed to awaken a thousand tender remembrances; her eyes overflowed, sobs rose to oppress

---

1 I.e., just as the Thracians (of the Chersonese peninsula) were deemed the most barbarous people, until that honor went to the Athenians and Achaeans, so the old order will give way to the new.

her; she withdrew to a window, and for a moment hid her face with her handkerchief.

I saw Mr. Euston was greatly affected; I made haste to relieve him, by welcoming him again to America, and particularly to Albany.

Our conversation, as you may well imagine, turned upon our late dear and honoured friend. Mr. Euston spoke of him with an enthusiasm, which did honour to the goodness of his heart. He enquired, in a tender accent, how Clara bore her irreparable loss; but I had no opportunity of answering him, for the Governor, having taken leave of Mrs. Bellenden, came forward to speak to the young ladies and me, while Mr. Euston, with the other gentlemen, paid their compliments to Mrs. Bellenden, who expressed great satisfaction at the unexpected return of this gentleman.

When the Governor retired, Mr. Blood, at the head of the guard, saluted him; his Excellency just moved his hat; and when this officer waited upon him in the evening for the watch-word, he told him, he hoped he was prepared to answer to the several complaints that had been made against him.

The Lieutenant replied, he had always done his duty.

"I wish it may be found so, Sir," said the Governor, and turned from him. This reception of the First Lieutenant, occasions a thousand conjectures.—He is universally disliked, and no one will be sorry for any mortification he meets with.

* * * * *

Mr. Euston is again a constant visitor at the Fort. Mrs. Bellenden always receives him in the most obliging manner imaginable. It is not to be doubted, but he is still passionately in love with Clara; his eyes eagerly follow all her motions; if she leaves the room but for a moment, he falls into a languor, that makes him silent and inattentive to every thing about him; but when she appears again, joy lights up every feature, and he becomes agreeable, lively, and entertaining. An absence of two years seems to have made no alteration in his sentiments; and proves the truth of that observation, that distance from the beloved object, lessens small passions, and increases great ones; as the wind extinguishes tapers,[1] and makes fires burn more fiercely.

---

1 Wax candles.

These changes are obvious to us all, and are a plain indication of his sentiments, with regard to my young friend; but as he has not yet declared himself, although he must know Mr. C——'s disappointment, Mrs. Bellenden is apprehensive that he resents her former refusal of him; and in her present circumstances, the loss of such an establishment for her daughter is a real misfortune.

Since this poor lady's mind is become a little more composed, and she can now dispense with the absence of Clara, who used to be constantly employed in reading to her, she indulges herself in her beloved retirement with her books; so that Mr. Euston has few opportunities of seeing and conversing with her. But he always singles me out, and withdraws to a window, where she never fails to be the subject of our discourse. He was anxious to know how she bore the shock of her father's death, and the change of her fortune.

"The change of her fortune," I replied, "seemed to give her no concern; and it was only in those moments, when her attendance upon her afflicted mother could be spared, that she poured her tribute of tears for the loss of a father, whom she almost adored; while Miss Bellenden, frantic with her grief, gave employment to the whole house with her fits; and Louisa vented her sorrow, in groans and complaints, Clara represt her tears, smothered her sighs, and exerted all her persuasive powers to moderate her mother's affliction; reading whole hours to her the Scriptures, and other books of devotion, calculated to compose her mind to resignation and peace.

"While she was thus employed, I have often observed her breast labour with painfully supprest emotions, and the silent tear fall on the blotted page; but instantly checking herself, her voice would recover its melodious tones, and her looks their mild resignation; till having got through her task, she was at liberty to retire to her own chamber, there unobserved, to indulge her sorrow."

"And yet, I think, I never saw her look more lovely, than she does now," interrupted Mr. Euston; "from the obedient passions of her mind, there rises neither wind nor cloud, to stain the pureness of her complexion, which is like certain temperate climates, where the roses bloom all the year round."

Mr. Euston seemed disposed to have lengthened out this conversation; and, perhaps, it might have led to a free discovery of his motives for this unexpected visit to Albany; but Miss Bellenden joining us, put an end to it. However, I am persuaded, it is neither a visit of ceremony to the afflicted widow, nor merely an effect of his politeness to swell the train of the Governor; it is love that has brought him back, and love will, I hope, finish his work, and make my young friend happy in a husband, who knows how to value her merit.

The Governor surprised Mr. Neville to-day very agreeably; he told him, that so many complaints of Mr. Blood's exactions, tyranny, and insolence, had been laid before him, and fully proved, that he was resolved to deprive him of the command; a measure which, he was sure, would be approved by the new commandant of Albany, whenever he arrived.—"And you, Sir," added he, to my husband, "by your rank as Second Lieutenant, as well as your good conduct since you have been in the province, are entitled to succeed him in this post; which, I doubt not, you will fill to your own honour, and the satisfaction of the garrison and city."

Mr. Blood, it seems, has reason to think himself happy that he gets off so easily; so many odious accusations were preferred against him, that if he had been subjected to a court-martial, the censure might have been much more severe. The Governor spared him on account of his age.

The garrison, the officers, the citizens, are all highly pleased with this event. The first dawn of pleasure that has appeared on the countenance of Mrs. Bellenden, since the death of the Colonel, broke forth, when the Governor informed her himself of this new regulation; she thanked him for it, as for a favour conferred upon herself. He told her, he hoped she would now have no reluctance to continue her residence in the Fort, as long as her affairs required, or her inclination made it agreeable to her.

Mr. Neville, out of respect, ordered the house we formerly lived in, in Albany, to be got ready for us; but Mrs. Bellenden insisted, not only upon his coming to live in the Fort, but upon his occupying Colonel Bellenden's late apartment, all the elegant furniture of which is left standing for our use.

★ ★ ★ ★ ★

His Excellency having finished the affairs that brought him to Albany, paid a farewell visit to Mrs. Bellenden to-day. He behaved with great cordiality to her, and begged she would at all times command his best services.—He took a very particular notice of Clara; who, I observed, changed colour when she saw Mr. Euston among the gentlemen that attended him in this visit.

My anxiety was still more apparent than her's; and being less able, and less obliged to hide it than she was, I broke through the crowd rather impatiently to get to him.

"Sure you are not going to leave us so soon, Mr. Euston?" said I.

"That look and that accent, are very obliging to me, Madam," replied he; "and I could almost flatter myself that you wish my longer stay."

"Indeed I do," resumed I; "and I am certain, that in this, I speak the sense of the whole family."

"The *whole* family!" repeated he, sighing.—"Well, Madam, this family has an absolute power over me, and may command either my absence or my stay, if by staying I can be of the least use to them."

The Governor having taken leave of Mrs. Bellenden, he went up to her immediately; she looked disconcerted and uneasy, supposing he was going to bid her farewel.

Clara, who was standing close by her, turned pale, and cast down her eyes, as if fearful that her emotions would be observed.—Her lover *did* observe it, and interpreting her sweet confusion in his favour, answered to Mrs. Bellenden's abrupt enquiry, if *he* was going also.

"No, Madam, I *cannot* go." He spoke this in an eager accent, without taking his eyes off Clara's face, who now blushed excessively. Mrs. Bellenden smiling, rose, and giving Mr. Euston her hand, led him a little aside.

"I see how it is," said she, as he afterwards told me; "you have not forgot your former friendship for us."

"I never can forget it, Madam," said he, "nor never can have less."

"But I hope you will forget how little I once deserved it," replied she; "and may you depend upon it, you shall be satisfied with me for the future."

This discourse led to an explanation, which left Mr. Euston at liberty to prosecute his addresses to Clara. The lover is all joy and gratitude, and the young lady all obedience.

I take so tender an interest in every thing that concerns this family, with whom I have, for so many years, lived in constant intercourse of kind offices, that they scarce feel more satisfaction than I do, at an event which settles the youngest, and, by me, best loved daughter of it, so advantageously; for Mr. Euston is one of the most agreeable, as well as the most worthy of men; has a very considerable fortune, and very genteel connexions.

Mrs. Bellenden has had an opportunity of convincing Mr. Euston of the sincerity of her regard for him, by the preference she now gives him over his rival, Mr. C.—, who lately arrived in New-York from England. I send you a copy of his extraordinary letter to her; which she did not shew Mr. Euston till she had dispatched an answer to it, containing an absolute rejection of his offers. This letter she inclosed in one to the Governor, leaving it to him to prevent the young gentlemen's journey to Albany.

"Dear Madam,

"I hope soon to be entitled to address you, by the style of *honoured* Madam, as will become a dutiful son, and to give you that appellation many years; though at your time of life, you may think that an unreasonable expectation. I have, I thank Heaven, been of age[1] a long time; master of myself and fortune, which, together with a title in reversion,[2] I lay at the feet of my *divine* Clara. Pray, my dear Madam, do not take offence at that word; because, you are very devout, and may think it, perhaps, misapplied to a frail human creature; but I am a lover, and Clara is a *divinity* to me, therefore, I may with more propriety call myself her *adorer*.

The Governor's concurrence in this affair, is now no longer necessary; I am no longer under his controul, except in a military way; he is my commanding officer, it is true; he may, if the war[3] should come here, send me to storm a fort, to force my way through the *imminent deadly breach*,[4] or expose me to the danger of being scalped, by some of our copper-coloured foes; but all the cannon in Fort St. George,[5] where he holds his haughty sway, can

---

1 21 years of age in English law.
2 A title he will receive once the present holder dies.
3 Between 1689 and 1783 England and France fought several wars over trade and territory. The war to which Lennox refers here is probably King George's War (1744-48), which corresponded to the War of the Austrian Succession in Europe. It most definitely does not refer to the American Revolutionary War, though the novel was published after the Revolution's end.
4 *From Shakespeare's Othello* 1.3.134, in Othello's description to Desdemona of his past exploits: "... spake of most disasterous chances,/ Of moving accidents by flood, and field,/ Of hair-breadth 'scapes: the imminent deadly breach."
5 May refer to Fort George at Niagara-on-the-Lake, Ontario, Canada, where several battles took place during the War of 1812, though this fort was not built until after the 1783 Treaty of Paris.

never dislodge my heart, which your daughter keeps in sweet captivity. I do not expect any answer, though you should be inclined to honour me with one, for it is probable I shall be with you before my courier who brings this; he will be only carried by the tide and winds to you, but I shall be borne on the wings of love! I would not renew your grief, by offering you compliments of condolance, on the death of my late worthy commandant; he was not favourable to my wishes—but no matter for that—I paid due respect to his memory, by wearing mourning a whole week; though I do not become black, and the court was in gala for the grand victory[1] we have obtained over the French.—I am sorry we are at war with them, faith, for both their wine and their fashions are delightful. Dear Madam, writing to you I forget all time; my courier waits.—He will soon be followed by

Your very obedient servant,
C.C.—."

Mr. C.— followed his messenger so closely, that he was in Albany several days before Mrs. Bellenden's letter could reach the Governor. As soon as he came up to the Fort, he was introduced immediately to Mrs. Bellenden, who chose to receive his first visit alone, that she might, by acquainting him with his disappointment in the gentlest terms, prepare him to see the rest of the family without much emotion.

She told me that he seemed so confident of success, and so happy in that belief, that it gave her some pain to undeceive him. He appeared disposed at first to contest his claim with Mr. Euston; but when she assured him, that her daughter's affections had been long engaged to that gentleman, he expressed the utmost astonishment; obliged her to repeat her assurances of this truth several times, and when he was convinced, laughed heartily, hummed an opera tune, and then began to entertain Mrs. Bellenden with all the London news he could recollect, till he had tired her and himself sufficiently.

At parting, he told her, he hoped he might be permitted to pay his respects to the ladies in the afternoon, which being granted,

---

1 Possibly refers to the British capture of Louisbourg, Canada from the French in 1745 during King George's War, or it may be a reference to the 1758 battle at Louisbourg in which the British took the fort from the French once again during the French and Indian War, or the 1759 battle at Quebec in which the British took the city from France.

he went away; and she came to tell us, how much she was surprised at his behaviour; which, however, appeared strange to none but herself.

He brought the same good humour with him in the evening; addressed Clara with the most unembarrassed air imaginable; and when Mr. Euston came in, accosted him with the cordiality of a friend, who sincerely shared in his happiness, and seemed so perfectly at ease, that for three hours he kept all the discourse to himself, and on some subjects was not unentertaining.

Our young loquacious guest was impertinent enough to rally Mr. Euston upon his taciturnity; upon which he replied, smiling in his face, "I had rather be silent, than not say something that is better than silence." This stroke was not felt; and, perhaps, it was not intended that it should; for who indeed, as Pope expresses it—

"Would break a butter fly upon a wheel?"[1]

My dear Maria, I have this moment delivered into my hands a large packet from you. I cannot chuse a better time to conclude this long letter, than when I am in possession of so much happiness, as these dear papers will afford me. I do not take leave of you,— I go to enjoy your conversation, and by the force of imagination, to have you present with me.

EUPHEMIA NEVILLE.

Letter XLIV.
MRS. HARLEY TO MRS. NEVILLE.

MY DEAR EUPHEMIA,

YESTERDAY Mr. Harley came into my dressing-room, with a newspaper in his hand, and in a transported accent exclaimed—

"Joy! joy! to my dear Maria:—You will soon see your charming friend; the period of her banishment is arrived." He then read an article in the paper, to this effect—"'Yesterday died of an apoplectic fit, at the age of eighty-one, Robert Neville, Esq.'"

Good Heavens! what were my emotions at that moment! Joy operated upon my agitated mind like grief; and had not tears

---

1 Alexander Pope's "Epistle to Dr. Arbuthnot" (1735), lines 307-08.

relieved me, my strong sensations would have thrown me into a fainting fit.

My husband, alarmed, supported me in his arms, and whispered the kindest, softest soothings, mixed with congratulations, upon the happiness I should soon enjoy in your society.

As soon as I was a little recovered, I would read this interesting article myself; and, I believe, I read it over a dozen times, never thinking I could be too secure that there was no mistake; and now I resigned myself freely to the transporting expectation of meeting soon my beloved friend, never never more to part.

My uncle, and Mr. Greville, who is often with us, shared my joy; and never did a happier party sit down to table, than your four friends.

Ah! my dear Euphemia, how soon was this joy clouded by disappointment? A servant announced Mr. Granby, who was just arrived from London. From this gentleman, who was well acquainted with your husband's uncle, we expected a confirmation of this important news; and scarce were the first civilities over, when Mr. Harley impatiently asked him, if it was true that old Mr. Neville was dead?

"Dead!—No," replied he. "He was well and hearty last night."

"Why, here is an account of his death," said my uncle, "in this paper." Mr. Granby read it, and smiled.

"These mistakes will happen," said he; "but I assure you, he was perfectly well last night." There was something indecent, I thought, in the mortified air of our countenances upon this intelligence. I retired to my own apartment, and was soon followed by Mr. Harley, who appeared smiling, and in high spirits.

"For once," said I, a little peevishly, "there is no sympathy in our minds; you are gay, and I am sorrowful."

"I am gay," replied he, kissing my hand, "because I bring you pleasing news.—You will not be disappointed; you will soon see your friend."

"Then Mr. Granby has deceived us," said I.

"Not so either," replied my husband. "He is a wag,[1] and, like Bays,[2] loves to elevate and surprise.—He was mortified to find our credulity had been beforehand with him, and rendered the tidings he brought less important."

---

1 Joker, wit.
2 Bays: A reference to the character of Bayes (a satirical poke at John Dryden) in George Villiers, second Duke of Buckingham's *The Rehearsal* (1672).

"Pray, explain," interrupted I, impatiently.

"I dare not," said he, laughing; "Granby will fight me if I do; but come, hear from himself what he has to tell you."

He led me down stairs. I found Mr. Granby laughing with my uncle; he advanced to meet me.

"You are very cruel," said I to him, "to divert yourself with my anxiety."

"Hear me, Madam," said he, leading me to a chair, and standing before me with an air of assumed importance. "I had rode post to bring you intelligence, that I know would rejoice you; and expected I should have heard you, in a transported accent, exclaim, 'Blessed are the feet of those that bringeth good tidings!'"

"No more of this," interrupted I, gravely; "but let me know your tidings."

"When, behold," pursued he, "I lost all my importance with you, because, upon the credit of a newspaper, you had anticipated my errand, and my news was cold."

"Well then," said I, "the old gentleman *is* dead."

"No, upon my honour," replied he.—I looked at Mr. Harley, who checked the smile that sat upon his features, and insisted upon Mr. Granby's teazing me no longer; so drawing a chair close by me, he went on.—

"You must know, Madam, my old friend Neville has had a dangerous fit of sickness; his physicians gave him over, and, as is usual now in the practice, pronounced his sentence."

"The poor man was surprised, shocked, and terrified.—The *buggabo* Death, which, being but fourscore and odd, he had fancied at an immense distance, put serious thoughts into his head. His conscience took the alarm, and told him plainly, that he was very wicked, to keep his nephew and heir in a tedious banishment from his country and friends, for want of a little of the pelf, of which he had ten times more than he could use.—Hereupon, he made a kind of saving bargain with Heaven, and devoutly promised and vowed, that if he recovered his health, he would settle one half of his estate immediately upon his nephew, and furnish him with a sufficient sum to purchase a commission in the Guards, that he might not be out of the military line, of which he knows he is fond.

"Contrary to all expectation, he recovered his health; and, what is still a greater miracle, he is firmly resolved to fulfil his vow; and has commissioned me to acquaint Mr. Neville with his resolution, which he has confirmed under his own hand, earnestly inviting him to hasten to England with his family, that they may yet, he modestly says, spend some years together with cordiality."

So now, my dear Euphemia, my wishes, my prayers are answered, and I shall once more be happy in the society of my beloved friend. Mr. Granby tells me, the packet sails in three days. He returns to town early to-morrow morning, and will take my letter with him. You will soon have an account of this happy, this unexpected event.

All here is joy and festivity.—They murmur at me for retiring to write long letters, and spending any part of this day of jubilee in my closet; and it is scarce civil, my uncle sends me up word, to withdraw myself from congratulations, which are at once a tribute to your merit, and a compliment to my just sense of it.

There is something in this gentle rebuke, which can be only answered by obedience; therefore, I will lay down my pen.

The house is full of men visitors.—I am retired to my closet, and the whole evening being at my own disposal, it is yours and mine, my dear Euphemia. I have a most affecting history to relate to you, of the sweet companion of our early youth, the beautiful, the accomplished Miss Damer, of whom we were both equally fond. We were mere girls when she left the boarding-school to be married to Mr. Freeman, yet we had sense enough to rejoice, that her merit had obtained her so advantageous a settlement, merit being her only fortune; a sort of riches, which pass current with those few only, who are capable of transferring to virtue and talents, the respect usurped by insolent unfeeling wealth.

Miss Damer had all the reason in the world to love her husband; he had a fine person, a well-cultivated understanding, and he adored her. Those persons who envied her good fortune, affected to blame her for setting out in so high a style of living, which was by no means suitable to her circumstances; for his income, though very large, arose from a place under the government, and must necessarily cease at his death. She would have been thought more prudent, to have drawn her expences within a narrower circle, in order to provide for a family which was every year increasing.

But you and I, who know her well, and saw her perform all the offices of a nurse to the little cherubs she produced, knew that domestic employments were not more her duty than her taste; and she would have preferred a much less showy appearance, if it had been equally agreeable to Mr. Freeman, to whose inclinations she paid a most implicit obedience.

It has been observed, that the world, ungenerous as it is, is oftener ready to reward false merit, than to do justice to true; and the reason, I think, is plain:—real worth extorts applause; affected virtue solicits it. To seem generous is more soothing to vanity, than to be merely just. The proud are better pleased to bestow a gift than pay a debt. Amongst the discerning few, Mrs. Freeman found friends, whose candour made her amends for the envy which the uncommon loveliness of her person excited in the ill-judging, malignant part of our sex.

You left her happy, my dear Euphemia, and she continued so long enough to confide in the stability of her good fortune; and, perhaps, she never was less apprehensive of a reverse, than at the very moment when the fatal storm broke out, in which her peace, her honour, and her life, were all at once wrecked and lost.

In one of those changes among the great, Mr. Freeman was deprived of his employment.—One minute saw him in possession of all the elegant enjoyments of life; the next, plunged in all the horrors of indigence.

Mrs. Freeman, with an infant at her breast, and four children besides, three of whom were daughters, of which the eldest was but fifteen years of age, bore this stroke with amazing fortitude; and without regretting the past, or seeming to dread the future, applied herself assiduously to all the duties of her present situation.

Their magnificent house, in one of the most elegant squares in London, was now exchanged for small inconvenient lodgings, in a remote part of the town; and of all their servants, one only was permitted to attend her in this retreat.

Her beautiful little girls immediately became notable housewifes, and filled up their little departments in the household affairs, with a sweet officiousness, that spoke the pleasure they took in being employed.

Mrs. Freeman superintended all, mixed in all, and was the soul that animated them. Her husband sat down to his frugal table with equal order and neatness, if not with equal splendor as formerly. Sure of meeting nothing but smiles of complacency in the charming face of his wife, who, when he would express his admiration of the equanimity of her temper, under such severe trials, used to tell him, that she was too busy to be unhappy.

Meantime Mr. Freeman left no means untried, that prudence and good sense suggested, to recover his former situation. He visited all his former friends and patrons, who in the days of his prosperity, were lavish of their professions of kindness and promises of service: of some of these he found the doors irrevocably barred against him; others received him with countenances that froze him; some made him compliments of condolance, in a tone that expressed the most stabbing indifference; and others, whose high rank set them above the necessity of dissimulation, carried the dagger directly to his heart, by talking to him of the beauty of his wife, and the blooming graces of his eldest daughter, as if they meant to point out to him the only road to success in his applications.

Mr. Freeman retired from these fruitless attempts with indignation; and wisely resolving to seek in his own industry alone, for those resources which he vainly hoped to have found in the patronage of the great, he bent all his endeavours to procure some employment, which, though humble if compared with his former situation, might enable him to procure a subsistence for his family.

"To avoid the temptations of poverty," said he to his lovely wife, "it concerns us not to over-rate the conveniences of our station, and in estimating the proportion fit for us, to fix it rather too low than too high; for our desires will be proportioned to our wants, real or imaginary, and our temptations to our desires.

"I am aware," pursued he, recollecting himself, "that these reflexions ought to have been made before; but a sickly fortune produces wholesome councils; and we reap this fruit from adversity, that it brings us at last to wisdom."

It was this just way of thinking, that made them readily approve the advice of a sensible female friend, who proposed to them, the placing Miss Freeman as an attendant upon the person of some lady of quality, who would have the goodness to accept her, though not qualified to fill up at present all the duties of such a situation, but which a little time and experience would enable her to perform.

Miss Freeman, happy in the thoughts of lessening, by her removal, the expence which her tender anxious parents were little able to support, was impatient till such a settlement could be procured for her; and an opportunity soon offered of gratifying her wishes.

The sister of the young Earl of N— wanted a woman; Miss Freeman immediately offered her service, and was by the housekeeper, to whom her friend had applied, introduced to Lady Louisa.

That young lady, who was very amiable both in her person and manners, was extremely struck with the appearance of Miss Freeman; her extreme youth, her beauty, an air of dignity diffused over her whole person, which even her amiable modesty, and the humiliating circumstance she now appeared in, could not lessen, inspired at once tenderness and consideration.

Lady Louisa rose from her seat, and approaching her with the softest complacency in her looks, desired to know her name and family.

Miss Freeman, with a deep blush, and a sigh half supprest, told her name.

"Freeman!" repeated the lady.—"What, the daughter of Mr. Freeman of the —?" Miss Freeman courtsied.

"Alas! my dear Miss," said Lady Louisa, taking her hand, and leading her to a chair, which she drew quite close to her own, "I am grieved for the cause of this application; but most happy in the power of offering you a situation not wholly unworthy of you.—You shall live with me, my dear, as my companion and friend. Tell me, do you think you shall like my company? Will such a settlement be agreeable to you?"

The poor girl, unable to speak, could only kiss the kind hand which held her's within it gently prest; and when she raised her timid eyes upon her fair benefactress, shewed them all suffused with tears.

Lady Louisa said the kindest things imaginable to her; and when she saw her quite composed, told her, if it was agreeable to her, she would go herself to her mama, and make the proposal to her.

Miss Freeman assented with a transport, which the simplicity of her age and manners suffered to appear in all its force.

Lady Louisa immediately ordered her chariot, and taking her young friend with her, drove to Mrs. Freeman's lodgings.

All was soon settled in the most obliging manner imaginable on Lady Louisa's side, and the most grateful sensibility on the part of Mrs. Freeman; with whose person and manner the young lady was so absolutely charmed, that she could talk of nothing else to her brother when she returned.

The Earl approved of his sister's intention, to make Miss Freeman a yearly present of a sum sufficient to enable her to make a proper appearance as her companion; and would fain have doubled it, but this the lady's delicacy would not permit.

The first sight, however, of this beautiful girl fixed her destiny, by inspiring him with a passion as honourable as it was ardent; at the same moment that he declared his sentiments to her, he offered her his hand, and implored her permission to apply to her father for his consent.

Miss Freeman confused, astonished, trembling, and unable to speak, quitted him hastily, without daring to look at him. As she was hastening to her own chamber, Lady Louisa met her, and surprised at the agitation she appeared to be in, led her into her dressing-room; and after dismissing her woman, eagerly enquired into the cause of her disorder.

The poor innocent burst into tears.—"Oh! Madam," cried she, "you will be angry with me; my Lady Countess will be angry with me.—I shall lose your favour for ever."

"Angry with you!" repeated the young lady—"lose my favour for ever! Impossible, my dear! What do you mean? explain yourself."

"Oh! Madam," exclaimed she again,—"my Lord"—she stopped; her face was in an instant covered with blushes. She was not able to meet the penetrating glance of Lady Louisa; but bending her fixed looks upon the ground, she continued silent and motionless before her.

"You parted just now from my brother," said Lady Louisa; "what was he saying to you? I hope he did not affront you?"

"Affront me! Madam," exclaimed Miss Freeman eagerly; "my Lord is too polite, too generous, too good, to affront a young person under your protection. And yet, if he was in earnest in what he said, I am sure I shall have reason to think myself very unhappy; for you will think me in fault, perhaps, and will never forgive me."—This thought brought tears into her eyes.

Lady Louisa embraced her tenderly, "Compose yourself, my dear Emma," said she; "my brother loves you; he has told you so.—There is nothing surprising in that; though there is in the noble frankness of your mind, which has made you thus explicit. Make yourself easy; whatever turn this affair may take, you may depend upon my unalterable friendship for you."

Upon the entrance of the Countess, Miss Freeman retired; her little heart fluttering with a thousand different emotions, in which fear, notwithstanding the encouraging kindness of Lady Louisa, was still predominant.

At table she appeared bashful, apprehensive, and confused; yet she met with nothing but kind looks and obliging language from the ladies; and from Lord N——, an unrestrained attention, equally tender and polite.

All these circumstances which I have already related, my dear Euphemia, as well as those extraordinary ones which follow, I had from Lady Louisa herself, so that you may depend upon their authenticity.

The little girl had reason to be surprised at the behaviour of the ladies, after what she had communicated. But it will be easily accounted for, when it is considered, that Lord N—'s relations had nothing so much at heart as his marriage, he being the last of an illustrious line, and his immense estates, if he died without issue, being entailed upon a family whom they detested.

The young nobleman had hitherto discovered an insurmountable aversion to the married state; neither the youth, beauty, high birth, and splendid fortunes, of any of the young ladies who had been proposed to him, were capable of shaking his resolution. His friends began to be apprehensive of the extinction of his noble name, with the additional misfortune of their enemies' triumph over their ruined hopes. When on a sudden, that heart, deemed so impenetrable, became subjected at a time when they least expected it.

No objection could be made to his choice of Miss Freeman, but her want of fortune, which, his great wealth considered, could have no weight. Her birth was genteel, her person eminently lovely, her innocent and virtuous manners, rendered her worthy of the rank to which he resolved to raise her, and her accomplishments of adorning it. His whole family was pleased with his choice: and in less than two months after her first introduction to Lady Louisa, Miss Freeman became Countess of N—.

Her good fortune included that of her father, who was reinstated in his post. Grown wise by experience, he no longer affected to make a splendid appearance as formerly, but substituted an elegant economy, in the place of an ostentatious display of affluence; and by laying up a future provision for his children, at the expence of sacrificing some of his predominant tastes and inclinations, he endeavoured to atone for his former indiscretion.

Mrs. Freeman, whose health was very delicate, and who loved the country, passed the greatest part of her time at her son-in-law's magnificent seat, where she was treated with all imaginable respect and deference.

This splendid solitude was sometimes enlivened by visits from the young Earl and his bride, who were now launched upon the stream of fashionable pleasures, and were not often willing to interrupt their course; and sometimes endeared by the affectionate converse of her tender and amiable husband, who always flew to her, whenever the duties of his employment would afford him so much time.

But these visits were neither frequent or long enough, to prevent a certain languor and satiety of her present lonely situation, from increasing fast upon her.

"I am no longer a wood-nymph, a dryad, as you used to call me," said she, in one of her letters to me from this place; "I am not always disposed to ramble alone amidst the groves and vales, to listen to the song of the nightingale, and be lulled to sleep by the gentle dashing of a neighbouring stream. Solitude, to be sure, is a charming thing, as Voltaire says; but well does he add, in his lively way, One is always willing to have somebody to whom one may say, *solitude is a charming thing*:[1] And at this moment, what would I not give to have you seated by me, that I might tell you how I am charmed with this beautiful prospect of variegated nature, which now meets my eyes."

The fashionable season for visiting the country being come, Lord N— and his young bride, to keep up the rules of decorum, repaired to their seat, where they were soon joined by the dowager Countess, and Lady Louisa. The hurry and bustle of their arrival, occasioned great resort of company; and the continual succession of balls and entertainments, proved more fatigueing than delightful to Mrs. Freeman, who sometimes sighed for the calm pleasures of solitude again. But her daughter was now pregnant, and this circumstance dilated every heart, and gave up every day to new scenes of festivity.

In the midst of this general joy, Lord N—, on a sudden, became pensive, and even melancholy; he avoided company, he seldom mixed in conversation, and when he did, it was with a distraction of thought, and incoherence of expression, that shewed his mind was wholly employed on something within itself, which left it free to no other impression.

Lady N— wept in secret, at the too obvious abatement of his tenderness for her; yet his behaviour to her was polite, obliging, and even some times attentive; but his attentions did not seem to flow from the heart, they were the effects of recollection, that decency required of them.

"Novelty is to love," says the discerning Rochfrecault, "what the bloom is to fruit; it gives it a luster which is easily effaced, and never returns."[2] The Countess perceived this charm so pow-

1 Voltaire, pseud. of Francois-Marie Arouet (1694-1778), French satirist. "The happiest of all lives is a busy solitude" (*Philosophical Dictionary*, 1764).
2 From *Reflexions ou Sentences et Maximes Morales* (1665) by Duc de François de Marsillac La Rochefoucauld (1613-80), French essayist.

erful while it lasts, was broke; it was what she feared, it was what she expected from the impetuosity of his youth, and the suddenness of his attachment; and before she left the Earl's seat to retire to her own, earnestly recommended it to him to watch assiduously over the health of his wife, and preserve her peace of mind in her present condition, in which his whole family was so much interested.

The Earl started and blushed at this remonstrance; was a moment silent, and then answered in a sigh, that he was not conscious of having failed in any instance of affection to her.

After the departure of his mother and sister, his gaiety seemed in some degree to return. He was now seen constantly in his wife's dressing-room, to which her frequent indispositions confined her. Mrs. Freeman was almost always there; her wit and vivacity had charms to dispel his chagrin; and, except a deep drawn sigh now and then, he appeared easy and even chearful; yet still he shunned company, and every amusement the country afforded.

The servants were the first who made malicious remarks upon his conduct: they took notice that he was never seen with his lady, but when his mother-in-law was with her; that it was in her presence only, that a dawn of chearfulness ever appeared upon his countenance; that his eyes were constantly fixed upon her in the most passionate manner imaginable; that he watched all her motions, and never failed to follow her in her evening excursions, in the noble park that belonged to the house, where it was his custom to direct her steps to the most sequestered parts of it, and had often been heard, by some *undesigned* listener no doubt, entertaining her with discourse fitter for a lover, than the husband of her daughter.

These insinuations spread by degrees among the tenants, and from them to the neighbouring gentry, whose unwelcome visits became more frequent, impelled by curiosity to discover what truth there might be in them.

Their keenness of observation, produced remarks still less favourable to the reputation of Mrs. Freeman; whose vanity, they did not scruple to say, was so much soothed by the attentions of this young nobleman, which approached even to adoration, that she seemed to forget he was her son-in-law.

The consummate loveliness of her person, seemed to justify the conclusions they drew from his uncommon attachment to her. Although a mother of five children, she had but just reached her thirty-second year; her form had all the delicacy, her charming features all the softness, and her complexion all the bloom of early youth. To this attractive person was joined, a wit always lively and entertaining, the sweetest sensibility was diffused over her countenance, in her least actions an unaffected dignity and grace.

Lord N—, these whisperers observed, had no eyes for any other object while she was present: his half suppressed sighs while he gazed on her, the trembling awe with which he approached her, the languor and listlissness that took possession of him when she was absent, the sudden transport that lighted up every feature in his face the moment she appeared again; every look, word and action, bore the marks of a violent passion; of which none but the object of it appeared to be ignorant, except the person most concerned, his young and innocent wife; who perceived that he loved her no longer; but not even guessing the motive of his change, perplexed her tender mind with fears, that she had by some means or other offended him, and wept in secret, for fear of offending him more by complaints.

Lord N—'s unwarrantable passion, and the unhappy situation of his wife, were now generally talked of, though in dark hints, sly insinuations, and oblique, but severe, censures: not one tongue, my Euphemia, was found candid enough to defend our too lovely and amiable friend, from the imputed guilt of encouraging, by her coquetry, this shocking infatuation.—So true it is, that our bad actions do not expose us to so much persecution and hatred, as our good qualities, and that a certain degree of merit is fatal to the possessor.—Calumny is a public thief, which robs the community of all that benefit, which it might justly claim, from the worth and virtue of particular persons, by rendering their virtues utterly insignificant.

Mrs. Freeman's meritorious behaviour under her late misfortunes, was forgot; the calm resignation with which she filled up all the duties of the humble condition, into which she had fallen; her uncorrupted virtue amidst the snares that were laid for her, were sunk in the torrent of that scandal, which now poured in upon her.

She received by the post some anonymous verses, in which this affair was treated with so much witty malice, as not only to alarm her modesty, but to excite the most dreadful apprehensions, of the loss of her character, and her husband's affections. She balanced not a moment concerning the step she ought to take; and although her daughter's condition required the presence and soothing of a mother, whose tenderness for her children was carried to almost a faulty extreme, yet the horror she conceived, at the base suspicions that were entertained of her, and conscious, perhaps, of the fatal effect of her charms, she resolved to leave Lord N—'s seat immediately; and pretending some urgent affairs that called her to London, she acquainted Lady N—, with all possible precaution, with her intention to set out the next day.

The poor young lady burst into tears, hung upon her, and earnestly entreated her not to leave her. Mrs. Freeman clasped her in her arms, mixed her tears with her's, and to comfort her, promised to return when her presence was necessary.

All this time Lord N— sat pale and motionless in his chair, with his eyes fixed on the ground. The young lady turning to him, said, sobbing—

"Why, my Lord, don't you join with me, to persuade my mamma not to leave me? Try what you can do; you see I cannot prevail."

Lord N—, rising from his chair, approached the ladies, as if intending to say something; but fearful, as it should seem, that his emotions might betray him, he rushed out of the room, having first cast a glance at Mrs. Freeman, which shewed her his eyes swimming in tears; a deep blush overspread her face, which she endeavoured to conceal from the observation of her own maid, who was present, by bending over her daughter, as she leaned her head upon her bosom, and was weeping bitterly.

It was from this servant that I learned these particulars.—She added, that Mrs. Freeman, at last, succeeded in reconciling Lady N— to her departure, by a promise to send her two sisters to keep her company, and a solemn assurance, that she would return herself, as soon as she had finished the business that called her to London.

They passed a melancholy evening together; Lord N—, under pretense of indisposition, not appearing at supper. Lady N—, who for several nights past, had slept in a separate chamber, within her lord's, anxiously enquiring how he did, as she passed by his bed, found him really feverish, which, adding to the uneasy state of her mind, she ordered her woman to stay with her all night, being apprehensive of fainting fits, to which she was subject.

About midnight, she complained she was not well, and ordered this attendant to go into her mother's chamber, and bring her a bottle of hartshorn, which she recollected to have seen in the evening upon her toilet.

The woman was hastening to obey her, when Lady N—, fearing she would awake her mother, whose tenderness she knew would take the alarm, on seeing her at such an hour, said she would rise and go herself.—Accordingly she slipped on a loose night-gown, and with great precaution, passed through her lord's chamber into her mother's dressing-room, and from thence into her bed-chamber; where the first object that met her eyes, was Lord N— kneeling at her bedside.

She shrieked aloud: the wax-taper which she held in her hand, fell out of it; and she herself sunk down in a fainting fit upon a sofa, that happened fortunately to be near her.

Her woman, in great terror, flying to her assistance, Lord N—, with looks all wild and furious, rushed by her as she entered the room, and went directly to the apartment of his valet, where he knew a pair of loaded pistols always hung over the chimney; he seized one.—The servant, who had been awakened by the noise his lord made in opening his door, perceived by the light of the moon, that shone strongly on the window, what he was about, and leaping out of bed, seized his hand, just as he had raised the fatal instrument of death to his temple; he threw that, and the other likewise, out of the window, and then, with trembling emotion, approached his lord, who had thrown himself upon the bed, where he lay groveling in all the agonies of despair.

His old and faithful servant falling on his knees before him, with tears, begged to know what had happened?

"Oh! Wilson," cried Lord N—, violently grasping his hand, and staring wildly on him, "my rash, my frantic folly, has ruined the best and loveliest of women! I have undone her, Wilson! Innocent, as she is, her reputation is ruined for ever!"

This thought seemed to sting him even to madness. With a furious motion he sprung from the bed, and seizing the poor fellow by the throat, "Rascal," cried he, "how didst thou dare to prevent my purpose? I cannot, I will not live under this load of misery!"

The man, who could comprehend nothing of the truth from these exclamations, disengaged himself from his hold, and replaced him on the bed, watching his motions, and attentive to his preservation, he durst not leave him a moment to call for assistance, but remained kneeling and weeping by him.

Meantime all was horror and confusion in Mrs. Freeman's apartment; the report of the pistols, which went off in their fall, filled her mind with the dreadful idea, that a murder had been committed by Lord N—, either upon himself or some other person.—She fell into successive faintings.—Her daughter, still insensible, was carried into her own chamber, and laid in bed.

The female servants, who had crowded into Mrs. Freeman's room upon the noise and bustle they heard there, were informed by Lady N—'s woman, of the occasion, who falsely and maliciously added, that she had seen Lord N— throw himself out of Mrs. Freeman's bed; and when he rushed by her to get out of the room, he was quite undressed.

Mrs. Freeman's maid, who saw him as he passed, for she slept in a little room adjoining to her lady's, and had risen in a fright upon hearing the young Countess scream, declared Lord N— was in his morning dress. Her testimony had no weight, as she was supposed to be attached to her mistress, and perhaps in the secret; though it was afterwards confirmed by another witness, who saw him immediately afterwards.

Lady N— was now under the care of her nurse, a sensible prudent woman, who had been some time in the house, attending the time of her lying-in. This person perceived that the young lady, when she recovered her senses, had not the least notion that her Lord's being in her mother's chamber, at that hour, involved any suspicion of guilt; but upon seeing him had concluded, that she was taken dangerously ill, or perhaps dying; and it was this fear that, operating violently upon her spirits, occasioned her screams, and the faintings that followed.

The nurse, therefore, peremptorily insisted upon her woman's not being permitted to enter her apartment, lest she should communicate her odious slanders to the unsuspecting innocent. And to account for Mrs. Freeman's not visiting her herself, she was told, that she was really ill, but not dangerously, her disorder being a little fever from a cold, which was likely to be soon removed.

Can you conceive, my dear Euphemia, a distress more poignant than that of our poor friend? Under circumstances so suspicious to be exposed to the insolence of a rabble of servants, who she knew, from the notices she had received, had before made free with her character; and now, under pretence of zeal for their lady, muttered reproaches in her ears—circumstances which would be thought decisive by the malignant and prejudiced, and doubtful even by the most candid.

When her senses returned, all the horrors of her situation appeared in its full force. She was set right as to the accident of the pistols, but plunged in the deepest despair; she neither raised her eyes, nor uttered a word, but to inquire after her daughter's health.

Her maid took care to tell her the only circumstance that could alleviate her sorrows; that it was Lady N——'s anxious concern for her, which alone, she said, had occasioned her terror, upon seeing her lord by her bedside. Mrs. Freeman discovered some sensibility of this hint, by just lifting up her eyes to heaven; but after that she continued motionless, silent, and regardless of every thing that passed.

The messenger who was sent to town the next day to acquaint the Countess and Mr. Freeman with what had happened, omitted no circumstance of the distressful scene. Mr. Freeman, in a transport of rage and grief, threw himself into a post-chaise, and set out immediately for the Earl's seat.

On his arrival he learned, that his daughter was just brought-to-bed of a son, which, though born some weeks before full time, was strong, and likely to live, and the young Countess herself in a fair way; but that Lord N—— was confined to his bed with a violent fever, which had already deprived him of his senses.

"And where," said the unhappy husband, "where is ——." He hesitated—he stopped—he could not name his wife. Her maid, who saw him alight, ran to meet him with tears in her eyes. He followed her to Mrs. Freeman's apartment. As he was about to enter, with an emotion that terrified her, the poor girl threw herself upon her knees.

"Believe me, Sir," cried she, "my mistress is slandered—all here are her enemies; every thing has been vilely misrepresented." Perceiving him stepping forwards—"Only permit me, Sir, to tell her you are here; she is so weak—so ill—the sight of you, unprepared, will kill her." He sighed deeply, and hindered her not from entering the chamber first, but followed her so close, that she had but just some time to say, "Madam, my master is here."

The poor unfortunate was lying on a sofa. On his appearance she rose, and endeavoured to stand; but her trembling knees, unable to support her, she sunk down again. He started from the chair into which he had thrown himself—he approached her eagerly; but finding her not in a fit, as he apprehended, drew back as hastily, resumed his seat, and, after gazing on her pale face, and scarce animated form, a few minutes, with mingled grief and indignation, he sighed out—"Art thou not, say—art thou not most vile? Oh, Emma! Cruel, ungrateful, most abandoned Emma!" groaned he out at intervals. Mrs. Freeman the while lay on the sofa like one dead; her face hid with the cushions; and, only by the convulsive heavings of her agitated bosom, could it be perceived that she was alive. Her maid interrupted this sad scene, to tell Mr. Freeman Lady N—'s nurse begged to speak with him. From her he learned, that the young lady was wholly ignorant of the malicious conclusions that had been drawn from her Lord's being in her mother's chamber at that late hour. She also assured him, that several circumstances of that affair, so as to give it a criminal appearance, had been greatly exaggerated. Mr. Freeman gave her a patient hearing, but made no answer. At her entreaties he consented to visit his daughter, and to conceal his emotions from her as much as possible. It was agreed that he should tell her, Mrs. Freeman's illness, though not dangerous, obliged her to keep her bed, which prevented her from coming into her chamber.

He found Lady N— in a mixed state—between joy and grief: to be the mother of an heir to an illustrious family, by whom such an event was so ardently wished for, elated her young mind; but her mother's illness, and the accident which they had told her had happened to her Lord, of violently straining his ancle so as to be obliged to keep his bed, filled her with uneasy apprehensions.

Mr. Freeman kissed and blessed her; but the mention of those two fatal names threw him into an agitation which, though unobserved by Lady N—, affected the nurse so much, that it was with difficulty, she said, she could restrain from tears. Still the young lady continued to talk of her mamma and husband, pressing him to tell her truly if the illness of either of them was dangerous; till no longer able to suppress his emotions, he was obliged to withdraw, telling her that being fatigued with his journey, he would go take a little rest.

Fresh horses being put to the chaise, he sent to tell Mrs. Freeman he was ready to conduct her home. She rose immediately from the sofa, where she had lain all this time without answering a single word to all her maid's tender inquiries and earnest solicitations, that she would take some refreshment, and suffer her to make some little alteration in her dress.

With faultering steps, a dying paleness in her face, and eyes fastened on the ground, she was led by her into the hall, where she found Mr. Freeman, who helped her into the chaise, and took his place by her; her maid having orders to follow in another with her trunks, which had been all packed up two days before.

During this journey, which lasted till late at night, Mrs. Freeman kept a dismal silence, lost as it should seem in agonizing thought, while her unhappy husband, whose breast was torn with conflicting passions, mixed tender expostulations with reproaches, tears with invectives, and fond complaints with threats of vengeance. That she answered nothing to all these bursts of passion, might have been construed into sullenness or insensibility, had not her heart-felt groans, the frequent wringing of her hands, the tears that flowed continually from her eyes, been sure proofs how deeply she suffered.

When the carriage stopped at their own house, she was obliged to be lifted out like an infant, so totally was she bereft of strength and spirits, and her husband himself carried her up the stairs in his arms into her bed-chamber, where she sunk almost lifeless on a chair. He ordered some wine to be warmed; he gave her a glass himself; she took it trembling from his hand, drank it, but raised not her eyes. He continued walking about the room in great agitation till her maid arrived, whom he ordered to have another chamber prepared for him to sleep in. A sudden crimson at this order, took, for a moment, the place of that ashy pale with which her lovely face had been overspread. Her husband observed her emotion; he fixed his eyes on her for a moment; then striking his forehead vehemently with both his hands, he rushed out of the room.

Mrs. Freeman permitted her maid to undress her and put her to bed, and in a few moments she appeared to be in a profound sleep. Some time afterwards Mr. Freeman entered; he took hold of her hand, and felt her pulse: "She is feverish," said he to her maid; "you must not leave her apartment." The girl said she would only lie down in her clothes upon the sofa in her mistress's dressing-closet, where she should be certain to hear her if she stirred or called: with which he was satisfied, and went to his own chamber.

The girl, fatigued both in body and mind, was soon fast asleep.

Alas! my dear Euphemia, how I relate the sad scene that followed? About an hour afterwards Mrs. Freeman, who doubtless had only dissembled sleep, perceiving all still and quiet in the house, rose softly; and, wrapping herself in a loose gown, took the wax taper that was burning in her chamber, and went into the adjoining room, where she remembered as she passed through it to have seen her husband's sword lying on a table. She drew it instantly; and setting the pummel on the ground, and directing the point to her side threw herself with all her remaining strength upon it.

The noise she made in falling was heard distinctly by Mr. Freeman, who lay in a chamber over that room, and who had been kept waking by his tormenting thoughts; he ran down stairs, he entered the room with precipitation. Think, my friend, what must be his amazement—his grief—his horror, when he beheld his wife whom at once he adored and hated, lamented and execrated, stretched upon the floor, weltering in her blood, with the fatal instrument of her death lying at her feet.

For a moment he stood fixed like a statue, gazing on her with distracted looks, till roused by her maid, who cried out—"Oh! Sir, what shall we do?" He with her assistance, raised her from the ground, and carried her to the bed. This motion recalled her senses; she half-opened her eyes, and uttered a deep sigh. Mr. Freeman, transported at this sign of life, flew out of the house himself to get assistance, and returned in a few moments with Mr. B—d, who had thrown himself out of bed at the affecting summons, and had scarcely given himself time to put on his clothes. This gentleman, whose skill in his profession can only be equaled by his humanity and benevolence, dressed the wound, and endeavoured to comfort the afflicted husband, who, supporting the lovely victim in his arms during the operation, shed a torrent of tears.

Mrs. Freeman had recovered her senses perfectly; and although the surgeon afterwards declared, that the pain she suffered must have been to the last degree excruciating, she never uttered a groan, nor discovered the least sign of impatience.

The surgeon had not yet given a decisive opinion in her case. Mr. Freeman apprehending the worst, could not be prevailed on to quit her for a moment, but passed the anxious hours kneeling at her bedside, bedewing her hand, which he held clasped in his, with tears. She often stole a look at him, full of the softest tenderness, but spoke not a word. Every time her wound was probed, the strong agony she felt could only be guessed at by her countenance, for not the least complaint escaped her.

On the fourth day, Mr. B—d being no longer doubtful of the event, was obliged to be explicit with Mr. Freeman. Had the sentence of his own death been pronounced, it could not have shook his soul with more violent emotions. As soon as he had recovered some degree of calmness, he returned to his wife's chamber. He found her sitting half-raised in bed, her maid silently weeping as she supported her in her arms. Mrs. Freeman, who had not spoke one word to her husband since the time of their fatal meeting at Lord N—'s seat, and always with deep sighs averted her eyes when they met his mournful glance, now seemed to regard his entrance with pleasure, and with a beseeching look made a motion to him to be seated near her.

With streaming eyes he took the place of her maid; and while he tenderly supported her in his arms, often cried—"Oh! Emma, unkind, rash Emma! what have you done?"

"My dear husband," replied she, pressing his hand, "now I may dare to call you so, since I am sure I have not many hours to live. The ease I enjoy convinces me a mortification is begun—I feel my death approaching. In these last awful moments hear me protest my innocence, and restore me to your good opinion. Oh! tell me, tell me," cried she, earnestly fixing her beautiful though dying eyes upon him, "do you now believe me guiltless?"

"Alas!" cried he, straining her to his tortured bosom, "you have given a fatal, a cruel proof that you are innocent; yes, Emma, a cruel one to me and to your children."

She then repeated these two lines, which I have somewhere read, though I do not remember where:

> "'The fatal scene was so severely wrought,
> Except I died I must be guilty thought.'"[1]

A faint blush, he said, overspread her face at a recollection, even then painful to her quick sense of virtue.

Mr. Freeman, who is never weary of talking of this last affecting scene, represented her as filled with remorse, for having dared, by her own hands, to abridge her days; yet owning she could not endure life, with the loss of reputation and his affection.

"But, Oh! at what a price," said she, "have I perhaps purchased this exemption from evils that appeared more terrible to me than a thousand deaths."

After repeatedly recommending her children to his care, she begged to be at liberty to spend the short remainder of her time with the worthy clergyman, who had regularly visited her during her illness, whose pious exhortations she had always listened to with the most submissive attention, interrupted only by her sighs and tears, and whose prayers she had joined with strong indications of the most fervent devotion.

Mr. Freeman, when he embraced her for the last time, fainted in the arms of Mr. B—d, who, with the assistance of his servant, carried him out of the room. Her streaming eyes pursued him while in sight; then raising them ardently to heaven, she seemed to implore that mercy for him which she trembled to ask for herself.

---

1 Unidentified.

The clergyman passed the greatest part of the night with her in prayer. About four in the morning she expired without any struggles, and almost without a groan.

Such was the end of our lovely, our unfortunate friend, my dear Euphemia, who, had she not been a Christian, might have been ranked among the noblest heroines of antiquity; though a Christian poet makes it a doubt whether it is

"A crime in heaven to act a Roman part."[1]

It has been observed by the great Lord Verulum,[2] that there is no passion in the human mind so weak, but it equals and even conquers the fear of death. Love, says he, despises it, honour aspires to it, and grief flies to it. Poor Emma felt all three in their extremest force: she doated on her husband, whose esteem she had lost. She had the highest value for reputation; and her's was sunk in a charge of infamy, which, from a fatal concurrence of circumstances, she had no means of refuting. The manner of her death redeemed her fame; but Oh! as she herself observed, it is dreadful to think what price she paid for it.

That her sufferings by the fatal wound were exquisite, and her patient endurance of them unexampled, her surgeon and physician witnessed by their tears; and to her deep repentance of the fatal deed, the learned and pious clergyman who constantly attended her in her illness, and during her last moments, bears ample testimony. Let us then with humble hope look up to the mercies of a righteous God, and the all-atoning merits of a divine Saviour and mediator, for comfort under our doubts and fears for her future sentence.

The Dowager Countess and Lady Louisa, who had never for a moment doubted the innocence of Mrs. Freeman, heard with astonishment, from the mouth of Lord N— himself, in his lucid intervals, an acknowledgment of his passion for his too lovely mother-in-law. But he protested that he had no other design in going that fatal night to her chamber, than to prevail upon her, by his tears and entreaties, not to quit his house, which he found her immoveably determined to do.

When the news of her tragic death arrived, these two ladies, shuddering with horror, and drowned in tears, lamented her; one

---

1 From *Cato* (1713) iv.i, by Joseph Addison.
2 Francis Bacon, Baron Verulam. The quotation is from Bacon's *Essay*, "Of Death."

with the tenderness of a mother, the other with the affection of a sister. In the first violence of their grief they almost hated, almost execrated the guilty cause of such a dreadful event: but nature resuming its rights in the hearts of a parent and a sister, awakened their fears for the unhappy youth. They took all possible care to prevent his being informed of it; but their cares were fruitless: an indiscreet domestic dropped some words in his hearing, which he compelled him, by frantic threats, to explain. His fever that instant returned with redoubled violence; he grew delirious, and expired two days afterwards, raving on Mrs. Freeman, whom he fancied he saw continually before his eyes.

The persons about young Lady N— were more attentive and more successful; and she is to this day ignorant of her mother's fate. When Mrs. Freeman's absence could no longer be excused, they told her, that having fallen into a swift decline, her physicians hurried her to Bristol; and thus prepared, she was, with proper precautions, informed she was dead.

A hard task still remained. Lady Louisa took this upon herself; she attempted not to comfort her, but mixed her tears with her's, till each compassionating the other's sorrows, they mutually endeavoured to give that consolation which for a long time neither were capable of receiving. They are all now at the German Spa,[1] and with them the little boy, born under the most disastrous circumstances; but the hope, the delight of the noble family, which but for his birth had been extinct; a circumstance that endears the young widow to her noble relations, as well as her gentle manners and irreproachable conduct.

Mr. Freeman is gone to pass some months in France, overwhelmed with melancholy. The family have done every thing in their power to alleviate his misfortunes. His income is enlarged by another very lucrative and honourable employment; and his daughters educated at the expence and under the inspection of the Countess Dowager of N—.

My dear Euphemia, this history, which I was willing to give you in all its circumstances, and which kept me up half the night to write, leaves me scarce a moment to bid you adieu. Mr. Granby waits impatiently for my letter. I see him from my window; he is actually got on horseback—he dispatches Mr. Harley to hasten me.—Well, then, adieu! my dearest friend, adieu! for a short time only, for I may soon expect to see you. Oh!

---

1 Possibly Baden Baden.

that thought, what joy it gives me! All here are yours; but most your ever faithful and affectionate

MARIA HARLEY.

Letter XLV.
MRS. NEVILLE TO MRS. HARLEY.
IN CONTINUATION.

Albany.

MRS. Bellenden and her family will leave Albany very soon; the preparations I continually see making for their departure, draw some heart-felt sighs from me. Their society has enlivened many a languid hour; their tender sympathy softened many a grief; and by their friendly exertions, many of the difficulties of my situation have been lessened. But I console myself with the reflection, that they will be the happier for what is a source of regret to me. They are leaving a place, where every object reminds them of the good they have lost, and renews their sorrows.

I have the satisfaction also to know, that their circumstances, which a little time ago had so unfavourable an aspect, are altered greatly for the better. Mrs. Bellenden has received assurances from her friends in England, that in consideration of her late husband's birth and long services, a pension[1] will be granted her, sufficient to support her genteely; and in Mr. Euston, she has now a most affectionate son-in-law, and a firm and unalterable friend.

Clara's marriage was celebrated last week, without any external shew, or noisy festivity; but under the happiest auspices, if we consider the great worthiness of *her* choice, the sweet and amiable qualities of *his*. Miss Bellenden does not appear at all mortified, that her youngest sister is so advantageously settled, while she continues still unsought for. The New World is not civilized enough to have a taste for charms like her's; and she expects upon her return to England, to have all her triumphs renewed. Her glass, however, might instruct her, that Time has not spared her; and that beauty is not a treasure that can be long

---

1 Séjourné notes that officers' widows were granted pensions on a case by case basis, and not automatically. Charlotte Ramsay Lennox's mother, Catherine, received such a pension, but not until 1752, ten years after her husband's death.

possessed; and, if it be generally true, what somebody observes, that as great riches often lead to great indigence, so great beauty in decay produces frightful ugliness, she has some reason for uneasy apprehension.

Miss Louisa has not been without admirers, but none whose rank and fortune seemed to entitle them to her notice. She has lost no part of the stateliness of her manners, by the depression of her fortune; but as she possesses a great share of her mother's politeness, she never gives offence, and her reserve is oftener ascribed to seriousness than pride.

Mr. C.— has of late appeared very much attached to her; he dresses at her,[1] sings, dances, and is witty, only for her. His singularities sometimes force a smile from her; but it cannot be perceived that she is disposed to give him any encouragement, either because she is too haughty to listen to a rejected lover of her sister, or that she is doubtful of his sincerity; but as she is ambitious enough to set a proper value upon so splendid an offer, it is to be presumed, that it is the latter reason that weighs most with her. He seems resolved to consider her indifference merely as a mask; and an incident happened the other day, which, by a mixture of humour and absurdity, he improved in such a manner, as to afford him an opportunity of persuading others to have the same opinion.

Louisa and I were walking in the fields below the Fort; Mr. C.— returning from his evening's ride, spied us at a distance, and immediately put his horse in a gallop to come up to us: by some accident the horse threw him, within a few paces of us; we both screamed; and Louisa running up to him, as he lay stretched on the ground, cried out, "Oh! Mrs. Neville, he is dead! he is certainly dead!"

The strange creature, who was not hurt, starting up instantly, clasped her in his arms, as she was stooping over him, and exclaimed in a theatrical tone,

"'See Marcia, see! the happy Juba lives!
He lives to catch that dear embrace,
And to return it too with mutual warmth!'"[2]

Louisa, blushing, fretting, and ready to weep, struggled in vain to free herself from his arms; he held her fast, blessing Heaven for

---

1 He dresses for her, to impress her.
2 From *Cato* (1713), 4.3 by Joseph Addison.

the happy accident, that had forced her to disclose her sentiments! thanking her, with the utmost warmth of gratitude! and vowing eternal love and constancy in return.

I could not help laughing at this scene; when Louisa, highly provoked at these insinuations, burst into tears; and having, with my assistance, disengaged herself from his hold, ran home with such speed, that it would have been difficult for him to have overtaken her, as he would have attempted, if I had not kept him back with all the strength I could exert.

He drank tea with us the next day, but Miss Louisa, still full of resentment, did not appear. He wrote a most passionate billet to her, which he would fain have persuaded one of us to be the bearer of; and in particular, solicited Mr. Euston's good offices with his charming sister, which he promised, with a great deal of good nature.

"You see," said he, "my desires to not wander out of the family; and I verily believe, if Miss Louisa should continue cruel, which Heaven forbid! I should even offer myself to Miss Bellenden here," bowing to her profoundly low, as if he expected what he said should be taken as a great compliment. This ridiculous speech brought a smile into every face, but Miss Bellenden's, who bridling, replied—

"And you would be rejected, Sir, as you have been twice already." He stared at her, smiled, and made her another low bow; then turning to Mr. Euston, with an air half serious, half gay—

"You carried off my first love from me," said he; "but I acknowledge you deserved her better than me. You are now the happiest of men; but the happier you are, the greater must have been my disappointment: you ought to consider this, and since I am once more passionately in love, afford me your friendship, and if you have any influence over Louisa, employ it in my favour."

"And so I will," answered Mr. Euston, taking his hand, and shaking it very cordially. Mr. C.—, thus encouraged, drew him apart from the company to a bow-window; where he talked to him for half an hour, with great eagerness, and many significant gestures.

This young man is so much in earnest, and he is really so advantageous an offer for Miss Louisa, that Mr. Euston is of opinion, he ought not to be rejected. Mrs. Bellenden favours him of course; but her obligations to the Governor weigh so much with her, that she is resolved to give him no encouragement, till she has consulted his Excellency upon the affair. However,

Louisa is directed to treat him civilly, and she obeys with so little reluctance, as to draw upon herself a great deal of coarse raillery from her elder sister, who is now in the unfortunate circumstance of being considered as an old maid, and her peevishness, a natural appendage to that state, is increased.

★ ★ ★ ★ ★

We are just now informed, that our new commandant is arrived in New-York. He is a young Scotch nobleman, very sensible and polite, with whom Mr. Euston was intimately acquainted in England; so that we may hope—But why do I talk of hope on this side of the Atlantic? My hopes, my wishes, my comforts, all spring from the happy land where my beloved friend resides. I have your welcome letters this moment; always welcome, but doubly so, now that they recall me to you, to my native country, to the ashes of my ever honoured mother, with which mine, I may now expect, will be mixed.

I flew to congratulate Mr. Neville upon this happy, this unexpected change of his fortune. I found him reading Mr. Granby's letter; which, when he had finished, he gave into my hand, with a countenance so grave, or rather austere, that I was alarmed, and expected to meet with some fatal reverse.—But I was pleasingly surprised to find, by a very solid proof, that my husband's uncle is indeed in earnest in his proposals; for Mr. Granby, by his orders, has inclosed bills for five hundred pounds upon some of the principal merchants in New-York, to pay off any incumbrances we may have here, and to defray the expences of our voyage to England. Such a circumstance, added to all his other liberal offers, might, one would think, have lightened Mr. Neville's countenance into smiles; but it is certain, that he is never less disposed to be chearful, than when he has most reason to be so; and any unexpected favours from Fortune, produce what Mrs. Benson stiles superciliousness, but I cannot consent to give it so harsh a name,—a seriousness then let me call it, which freezes one, and closes up the before expanded heart, which sought at once to receive, and to communicate delight.

★ ★ ★ ★ ★

Yesterday Lord R— landed at Albany; and he was received with the usual honours, and came up immediately to the Fort, to pay his compliments to the widow and family of his predecessor.

Although our stay here is likely to be very short, we have left the Fort, and have taken up our residence in the house we formerly lived in. Lord R— pressed us very politely not to remove, and would have contented himself with lodgings while we continued in Albany, but this we could not consent to.

Mrs. Bellenden and her family go to New-York in a few days, to prepare for their embarkation: meantime Lord R— is settled in the late commandant's apartments; and being in the same house with Miss Bellenden, who plays off all the artillery of her eyes upon him, she plumes herself already upon her imaginary conquest; but—

"Vain is the art that would itself deceive!"[1]

Lord R—'s heart is impenetrable. "I have often heard," said he to Mr. Euston, "of this celebrated beauty, but I can perceive nothing touching in it; she has no mind in her face." He complimented his friend upon his choice of Clara.—"She will be charming," said he, "when she is no longer young—'A lively wit, and a cultivated understanding,' says Rochfrecault,[2] 'never grow old.'"

The First Lieutenant pays most assiduous court to his new commandant: He attends all his motions, watches every glance of his eye: to all his affirmatives he says, yes; to all his negatives, no. The forbidding stateliness of Lord R—'s manners, inspires him with more awe than the mild dignity of Colonel Bellenden. Mr. Blood is more than obsequious, he is servile.—A mean understanding cannot distinguish between pride and true greatness of mind. Lord R—'s stiffness of behaviour, which Mr. Euston compares to a verse, where every syllable is measured, keeps him[3] at a slavish distance; which he never breaks through, but to pour in some coarse flattery, that disgusts every one but the person to whom it is addressed; who hears it, however, with a chilling indifference.

Mr. Euston diverts himself, with observing the indefatigable pains this worthless old man takes to recommend himself to his commander, by his despicable adulation. "An ordinary flatterer, as I have somewhere read," said Mr. Euston, "will have always at hand, certain common attributes, which may serve every man. A

---

1 Unidentified.
2 From *Reflexions ou Sentences et Maximes Morales* (1665) by La Rochefoucauld.
3 Pronoun refers to Lt. Blood.

cunning flatterer will follow the arch-flatterer, which is a man's self, and whatever great or amiable quality he is pleased to dignify himself with, will swear him into the possession of; but the impudent flatterer, will observe well in what a man is conscious to himself that he is defective, and is most ashamed of being charged with, and he will entitle him to the contrary virtue by main force."

"He was acting this last part," replied Clara, smiling, "three days ago, when he complimented Lord R— upon his noble liberality to the troops, when he took the command of them."

"Ah! I understand this arch hint," replied Mr. Euston, snatching her hand, and kissing it passionately. Lord R— is not generous, he has been charged with the contrary extreme; his *largesse* to the soldiers was beneath his rank, and even his fortune, though that is not high. But the old Lieutenant's arts will not succeed: Lord R—, whether prejudiced against him by the Governor, or really engaged by promise, to mortify him for his past conduct, has appointed him to the command at Oswago; where he may wear out the remnant of his days, among the most savage of all the Indian tribes in our alliance.[1] This news was far from being unpleasing to any of us; the family, however, whom it most concerned, in having deeply suffered by the brutal insolence of this man, were decently silent upon this occasion.

Mr. Neville is gone to New-York to obtain leave of the Governor for his voyage to England, to settle his affairs. His request will be readily granted, as it is known that he intends to dispose of his lieutenancy, which Mr. Montague wishes to purchase for a nephew of his, who is upon the spot. Mrs. Bellenden will also leave this place in a few days; and I shall not be long behind her. When Mr. Neville has settled his affairs with the Governor, he will return to fetch me, and we shall all embark together.

With this agreeable prospect before me, how shall I account for an oppression of heart, which forces many an involuntary sigh from me, and sometimes draws tears from my eyes. You will call me weak, if I tell you that I have been greatly affected by a dream, which I had two nights ago; not that I can possibly draw either a good or bad presage from it, were I superstitiously disposed, which indeed is not the case; and I have often been surprised to find persons of good sense, lay so much stress on dreams, as to be uneasy or joyful according as they interpreted them. The true

---

1 Oswego. The Mohawks had the reputation for being savage warriors.

reason, perhaps, why any credit is given them, is, because people mark when they hit, but never when they miss: my dream affected me because it called up some sad ideas, which to suppress has been a task to which all the fortitude I can boast has scarcely been equal.

Methought I was passing to the water-side, where a boat lay ready to carry me to the ship in which I was to embark for England. I had taken leave of my surrounding friends, and was preparing to step into the boat, when a youth crossed my path, and in an accent that harrowed up my soul exclaimed—"Ah, will you leave me! if you leave me now, you will never see me more."

I looked up; it was my child, my dear drowned boy, that stood before me;—his very air and features, with no other difference than what nine years growth might be supposed to make in his appearance. I screamed aloud—I clasped him in my arms; the strong emotion waked me; and I found I had my daughter, who slept with me, pressed close to my bosom, and her face all wet with tears.

Oh! my Maria, what melancholy scenes did this dream recal to my mind! I passed the night in tears and wailings:—but no more on this sad theme: I will not suffer these bitter remembrances to cloud the happier prospects which our meeting again, after this long separation, affords me.

It is possible I may be the bearer of this letter myself; for we shall certainly embark in the first ship that sails. Mr. Neville writes me word, that he has settled every thing with the Governor, and that I will do well to set out with Mrs. Bellenden for New-York, without giving him the unnecessary trouble of coming to fetch me. I think so too; and am making all the necessary preparations to obey him.

Although flattered with the dear hope of seeing you soon, I cannot give up the pleasure of conversing with you by my pen as usual; and I retire as regularly every day to my closet to tell you every little incident relating to my friends here and myself, as if the date of my banishment was still undetermined.

Miss Louisa has surprised us all with an exploit, which seemed to require a more enterprizing temper, and sentiments more free than from her apparent reserve, and stateliness of manners, could be expected. She has been upon a visit for several days past to Mrs. Mountfort, at her charming little villa, where she now generally resides; the carriage and servants were sent to bring her home, and we expected her yesterday, but she did not appear. Mrs. Bellenden was not pleased with this delay; and Mr. Euston was preparing to take horse this morning to conduct her home, when Mrs. Mountfort suddenly entered Mrs. Bellenden's apartment, laughing as if for a wager. Mrs. Bellenden inquired for her daughter in vain,—Mrs. Mountfort could not answer her for laughing. I was a little disconcerted for my friend, who, I perceived, was got into one of her flighty whims, and made signs to her to recollect herself, but was not regarded; meantime Mrs. Bellenden, crossing her arms in a very composed manner, looked earnestly on her, without speaking a word.

Mrs. Mountfort, attempted two or three times to speak, but interrupted herself as often with a laugh, which, as it should seem, she was not able to suppress. This scene was growing very tiresome, when Mr. C.— entered the room; his features bore the same air of pleasantry.—"I am glad you are come," said Mrs. Mountfort to him, "pray tell your own story if you please." The young gentleman drew near Mrs. Bellenden, and bending one knee, took her hand, which he kissed with a very respectful air.

"What do you mean by this foolery?" said Mrs. Bellenden, in a peevish accent.

"I mean to inform you, Madam," said he, "that I have the happiness and honour to be your son-in-law; and crave your blessing, as the custom is."

"My son-in-law!" repeated Mrs. Bellenden, greatly surprised, as indeed we all were, though a little doubtful whether he was in earnest or jest.

"My son-in-law!" cried Mrs. Bellenden again.

"Yes, upon my soul am I," said the strange creature, starting up; "Louisa, the charming Louisa is mine. Winds, catch the sound,[1] *and so forth*." Then dropping his theatric tone—

"This manœuvre was not mine, Madam," said he, "though my whole soul was in it—it was planned by my charming friend here," taking Mrs. Mountfort's hand, which he kissed half-a-dozen times: "and charming you will be, in spite of time, let me tell you that for your comfort," said he, in a loud whisper. "Yes, Madam," pursued he, turning to Mrs. Bellenden, "it is to this

---

1 The ending of Nahum Tate's *King Lear* in which Cordelia lives, and will take the throne: Lear says:

Cordelia then shall be a Queen, mark that:
Cordelia shall be Queen; Winds catch the Soung
And bear it on your rosie Wings to Heav'n.
Cordelia is a Queen.

lady you are obliged for the most dutiful and affectionate son-in-law in the world."

Mrs. Bellenden not knowing how to take this matter, looked earnestly at Mrs. Mountfort, who, recovering from a little confusion which Mr. C.—'s absurd compliment, that touched a tender string with her, occasioned—said smiling—

"Come, Madam, you must not be angry with me for having spared your punctilio, and completed an honourable match for your daughter, without embroiling you with the Governor, for whom you have so much regard and deference."

"Mrs. Mountfort has reason," said Mr. Euston, willing to assist Mrs. Bellenden on the difficult task before her, (for she knew not whether to seem angry or pleased, the one being contrary to her sentiments as the other to her nice notions of decorum).—"We are obliged to Mrs. Mountfort for assisting these lovers to get over the difficulties my mother's delicacy threw in their way."

"But tell me," interrupted Mrs. Bellenden, addressing herself to Mrs. Mountfort, with a very serious air—"how has this matter been carried; where was the ceremony performed?"

"In a Protestant chapel, my dear mother," said Mr. C.—eagerly; "by the Reverend Mr. Salter, chaplain to the regiment, whom you have so often entertained at your table; and in return for your good cheer, seemed very glad to do my Louisa this good office. The licence[1] I procured myself in my last trip to New-York; present Mrs. Mountfort, her woman, the clerk, and my valet. Every thing passed in due form, I assure you; and I have been a grave married man these six hours."

Mrs. Bellenden, half smiling, shrugged up her shoulders, and again submitted her hand to the happy bridegroom, breathing out a pious prayer for his and her daughters happiness; to which, with great emphasis, he said "Amen."

"The dear girl," said he, "durst not present herself before you till the matter was first broke to you; so as soon as she entered the house she flew up to her own room, and locked herself in; but now that her pardon is sealed, I will bring her to receive your blessing."

Away he went, followed by Mrs. Euston; and Louisa appeared soon afterwards, led in by her sister and her husband, and all

---

1 For the marriage to be legally binding, a marriage license needed to be obtained from the governor in New York City if banns could not be published three consecutive Sundays in a parish church.

covered with blushes. She threw herself at her mother's feet, who, pitying her confusion, embraced and blessed her, without even hinting her displeasure.

"And now, my dear mother," said Mr. C.—, "I hope you will give us a dinner and a dance."—"By all means," said Lord R—, who entered the room that moment, and walking up to the bride, saluted and wished her joy.

"Sure, my Lord, you were not in the secret," said Mrs. Bellenden.

"Indeed I was not, Madam," said he, "but it is no secret now; for the servants by this time have sufficiently blazed the news; neither the garrison nor the town will be long ignorant of it in a few moments."

His Lordship was in the right; the bells were set a-ringing. The soldiers gathered round the house, and were loud in their wishes and prayers for the happiness of their young lieutenant and his charming bride. Mr. C.— gratified them with a noble present; and they retired to shew their gratitude and joy, by drinking largely to their healths. We had an elegant repast, and a dance in the evening. Every face was dressed in smiles, but Miss Bellenden's: her silence and reserve were sufficiently remarkable, without the absurd yet humourous endeavours of her new brother-in-law to raise her spirits; however, she cleared up towards the evening. Lord R—, whose partner she was, soothed her into chearfulness by two or three well-turned compliments, and a polite attention, with which she seemed quite elated.

Mrs. Bellenden has had a letter from the Governor, in answer to one from her, apologizing for the manner in which this affair was carried. His Excellency treats the matter with a kind of laughing indifference, and concludes with very heartily wishing the young people all manner of happiness: so this rub is well got over. But as all the good things of this life is mixed with the bad, this lady will have a severe shock to sustain in parting with Louisa, who is her favourite daughter. She looks very melancholy, and sighs often; and it is easy to perceive that Louisa is sometimes in tears; the gay prospects before her cannot lessen her regret at being separated from her family.

To-morrow I shall bid adieu, an eternal adieu to this city. The sloop that is to convey us to New-York is at anchor in our view; our baggage is all on board. The ship in which our passage is taken for England will sail, Mr. Neville writes me word, in a few days. Every fleeting moment brings me nearer the happy time when I shall once more embrace my dearest friend, and see my native country: my heart bounds within my bosom at the thought—I am all pleasing expectation. Methinks I see my beloved Maria; I hear her joyful exclamations; I am folded in her affectionate arms!—I anticipate all the charming circumstances of this happy meeting.

* * * * *

No, my Maria, no; you will not see your unhappy friend so soon as you expect—alas! perhaps I am destined never to enjoy happiness. Born to perpetual disappointments, I am only mocked with shows of blessings which are never, never to be realized. My condition is more truly pitiable now than ever. I am here in this wild country, without friends, without society, without comfort; for my frequent cruel disappointments have even banished hope, the last resource of the afflicted.

The evening before we were to go on board the sloop, my dear Mrs. Benson was seized with a violent fever: this disorder had been coming on her for some time, but she carefully concealed it, fearful of damping my joy, and deranging my measures. She lay in a delirium while my dear friends and companions took leave of me, drowned in tears, and bitterly regretting her misfortune, mine and their own disappointment. The deprivation of her charming intellects, prevented those contests which I must have sustained from her generous regard to *me*: for no consideration for herself would have made her submit to my stay.

I have the best medical advice I can procure. I nurse her, (alas! is it not my duty to do so?) with more than the tenderness of a daughter, with the solicitude of a grateful friend, whom her goodness has laid under the highest obligations.

The worthy Mrs. Lawson, whom I mentioned to you in one of my letters, has quitted her retreat, to come and comfort me in this my forlorn condition; for I was left quite alone, my dear Maria. Mr. C— and his lady went to New York with Mrs. Bellenden; and Mrs. Mountfort, to her great regret, was called thither likewise, by some pressing affairs. My dear Mrs. Benson's fever being pronounced infectious, I durst not keep your goddaughter with me; she is gone under the care of my faithful Fanny to the country-house of one of our officers. My dear child, clinging round my neck, and almost suffocated with her tears, was obliged to be torn out of my arms. Her cries, her tender entreaties to be permitted to stay with me, still sound in my ears, and press upon my thoughts. Fanny, struggling with her own strong emotions, that she might be able to supply my place to her, at length bore her from my sight; my heart sunk within me; all was a melancholy void; a still and dreadful silence! only interrupted by the faint groans of my friend, my second mother, my pious monitress, my virtuous guide.

Thus desolate, and ready to sink under the present calamity, Mrs. Lawson, like my good angel, broke upon my dismal solitude, and shed a ray of comfort round me. At sight of her, the weight upon my sad heart grew lighter. I lifted up my eyes in grateful acknowledgments to the Almighty goodness that sent me this relief, and ran into her embrace, mingling tears with the welcome I gave her.

When these first emotions subsided, I recollected the danger to which she exposed her health, and would have hurried her out of the chamber, where the air she drew might be fatal to her; but she prevented me with the smile of a pitying angel.

"Can you imagine," said she, "that these poor dregs of life, which now remain in me, are of such high estimation, that to preserve them I should neglect to fulfil the duty of a Christian, the obligations of humanity, and the sympathy of friendship, for two objects so worthy as you and Mrs. Benson? No, my dear Mrs. Neville, I come to share your fatigues, to weep with you if we must lose this estimable woman; but I rather hope to rejoice with you on her recovery."

A friend has been called the medicine of life. Oh! how powerfully did this salutary medicine act upon my sick mind! It gave me hope, to invigorate my necessary attendance upon my dear patient, strength to go through the fatigues of it, fatigues which the good Mrs. Lawson shared with me, for we never leave her night nor day.

A feigned affection, says Cicero, is not easily discernable from a real one, unless in seasons of distress;[1] for adversity is to friendship what the fire is to gold, the only infallible test to discover the genuine from the counterfeit; in all other circumstances they both bear the same signatures. That I can boast the possession of such an invaluable blessing in you, my Maria, in Mrs. Lawson, and the dear woman who now presses a sick-bed, is sufficient to compensate for all the misfortunes of my life. She still continues in

---

1 Letters of Cicero, XXIII, to L. Papirius Paetus (at Naples), Tusculum, July 46 BC. Marcus Tullius Cicero (106-43 BCE), Roman philosopher and politican.

the same condition; but not to grow worse is a foundation for expecting an amendment.

I have a letter from Mr. Neville, in which he at once condemns and approves my resolution not to abandon my friend in this situation; and produces so many good reasons for not delaying his own voyage upon this account, that I cannot reasonably blame him for leaving me. He tells me, that a king's ship is expected to touch at New-York in the course of a few weeks, in which the Governor will procure me a passage to England: he seems in high spirits, and bids me farewell with great fortitude. I have letters from the Bellenden family, filled with tender regret for my situation, and their own disappointment in not having me the companion of their voyage. Mr. C——, not being able to bear the tears of his bride, has taken a resolution to go to England: this step is irregular; but his lieutenancy is of little consequence to him, who has an ample fortune in possession, and such great reversionary expectations.[1]

My dear Mrs. Benson has had a tolerable night, the physician is just come from her; he tells me her fever is abated, that a favourable crisis may be expected; in a word, he has hopes, my dear Maria.—Mr. Neville's messenger waits for my packet, which he proposes to deliver to you himself. I will not add another word to the news I have communicated, which opens to me the prospect of seeing you soon; but that I am, and ever must be, your faithful and affectionate

EUPHEMIA NEVILLE.

Letter XLVI.
MRS. BENSON TO MRS. HARLEY.

MADAM,

MY dear Euphemia puts the pen into my hand, that upon the first opening of this packet, the certainty of my recovery may be an earnest of her speedy return to you. I no longer regret that I was the cause of a delay which cost you so much uneasiness, and your sweet friend so much fatigue and distress, since that delay was graciously ordered by Providence to produce an effect so surprising, so unhoped for, so happy.—But my Euphemia com-

---

1 Mr. C— is the heir to a large fortune.

mands me to give you an account of it in all its preparatory circumstances. I could have wished she had been willing to take this task upon herself, and have given it you in her own agreeable manner, which I cannot hope to imitate: so truly has it been observed, that the art of narration, which so many practice, and so few understand, is however easier to be understood than put in practice.

My recovery, Madam, was as rapid as the progress of my disease had been; and my Euphemia's pious cares were rewarded with the re-establishment of my health in three weeks after Mr. Neville's departure.

Her friends at New-York now earnestly solicited her to take up her residence in that gay city, till an opportunity offered for her return to England; but she chose to pass her time at Mrs. Mountfort's villa, preferring the society of that agreeable woman, that of the sensible and pious Mrs. Lawson, and even mine, to the amusements she might have expected there, for which indeed she had little taste. "Conversation," said she, "has been properly stiled the air of the soul; they who value the health and ease of the mind, ought to chuse an element pure and serene for it to breathe in."

I had nothing remaining of my former disorder but a little weakness, which lessened every day, and which did not prevent me from taking my early morning's walk as usual. In one of these excursions Mrs. Mountfort accompanied me: the weather being very warm I sat down under a tree, and took out my netting,[1] while she went to visit some other part of the plantation. While I was thus employed, I heard the sound of steps behind me. I rose up; and turning my eyes that way, perceived an Indian advancing towards me. Having now a full view of me, he stood still, expressing, by some very significant gestures, surprise and joy; at meeting me (Mrs. Mountfort was out of sight); I was a little uneasy at this encounter, and immediately took the same path she had done, with some precipitation.

The Indian perceiving that I was under apprehensions, stopped, and called out in English, "Madam, Mrs. Benson! pray do not be afraid; don't you know me, Madam?"

Struck with the sound of his voice, which I thought was not wholly unknown to me, I stopped in great agitation: he came up to me; and bowing low, said, "I am William, Madam, Mr.

---

1 Netting: Decorative mesh-work.

Neville's servant, have you quite forgotten me?" Speechless with astonishment, I gazed eagerly on him; and notwithstanding the dark hue his skin had acquired, his habit, and the alteration that years had made in his countenance, I perceived all the features of William.

The fatal accident which his carelessness had been the cause of, now rushed upon my memory, and I burst in to tears.

"Ah, what brings you here in this disguise?" said I, as soon as I was able to speak. "Take care, and do not appear before your afflicted mistress; your sight will renew her sorrows. If you want my assistance, I am ready to afford it you; but never let my dear Euphemia see you."

He answered with a smile,—"My mistress should not see me if I could not bring her comfort. Look there, Madam," added he, pointing to a young Indian, who that moment shewed himself between the trees, and upon this man's beckoning him came forward slowly, with his eyes bent on the ground.

Amazement seized me!—In the countenance of this Indian boy I perceived a strong resemblance to my Euphemia. While I stood trembling, unable to speak, and my eyes fixed upon his face, William, throwing aside his mantle, bared his bosom, and shewed me the mark of the bow and arrow with which he was born.

Convinced of what till that moment I dared not to hope, astonishment and joy deprived me of all caution; I screamed aloud; and, throwing my arms about the dear boy, held him close embraced, without being able to utter a word. Mrs. Mountfort, who was not far distant, heard my cry, and came running in great terror to my assistance. The persons she saw me with, the attitude she found me in, filled her with astonishment.

"What is the meaning of all this?" said she, after a silence of some moments. "What is this Indian boy to you, that you embrace him so fondly? Is this man the father? Good Heaven!" pursued she, looking earnestly in the face of the dear creature I still held in my arms, "how handsome he is! Here is some mystery: speak to me, my dear Mrs. Benson; tell me what all this means!"

"He is found," cried I, almost breathless with my emotions; "my Euphemia's son is found! he whom we thought drowned— he is alive, this is he; see the indelible mark he was born with. But where is my Euphemia? Let us fly to her."—Mrs. Mountfort checked my transports.

"Take care how you communicate this news to Mrs. Neville,"

said she; "the surprise, the joy of such a discovery, will operate too powerfully on her spirits, unless it is managed with great caution."

"You are right," replied I; "but how, how shall we break it to her? how long shall we keep her ignorant of her happiness?"

That moment William exclaimed—"Sure, that is my mistress yonder—she is coming this way." "It is her—it is your mother, Sir," said he in French to the dear boy; who instantly withdrawing his hand from mine, sprung eagerly forwards a few paces, as if he intended to go and meet her, but was prevented by Mrs. Mountfort, who led him back. He yielded submissively, but still turned his eyes towards her, while on his expressive countenance all the various emotions that agitated his young breast were strongly painted.

Our two feigned Indians struck into the wood behind us; and Mrs. Mountfort and I hastened to meet Mrs. Neville. As soon as we came up to her she chid me gently for taking a walk so long for one so newly recovered from a dangerous illness: when looking earnestly upon me—

"My dear Mrs. Benson," said she, "you are pale—you tremble. Alas! you are ill; let me lead you to the house."

"No, no, my dear child," replied I; "I am not ill, my spirits have been hurried a little, that is all."

"Has any thing happened to alarm you?" said she eagerly.

Mrs. Mountfort now looked uneasy, and apprehensive that I should be indiscreet; but I went on.

"We met an Indian in our walk, who had so strong a resemblance to William, Mr. Neville's unfortunate servant, that—"

"William!" interrupted Mrs.Neville, sighing deeply; "did he resemble William, do you say?"

"So much," replied I, "that for some moments I could scarce persuade myself that is was not really him I saw."

Mrs. Neville now appeared greatly agitated: she looked earnestly upon me for a moment—"My dear Madam," said she, "you would not have said so much if you had not more to say—you have really seen this man. Is it not so?"

"You have guessed right," I replied; "your penetration seldom deceives you. I *have* seen William." She now leaned her head upon Mrs. Mountfort's shoulder, who tenderly supported her, and shed some tears.

"I cannot see him," said she; "the sight of him will open a wound that neither time nor reason have yet entirely healed; if he has need of my assistance he shall have it; but I cannot see him."

"Indeed you will do well to see him," I replied; "he brings you some news that will be very acceptable to you."

"News!" repeated she; "what news? of whom?"

"Of your son," said I; "he will have it that he was not drowned; nay, more, he thinks he has reason to believe that he is alive."

Mrs. Mountfort shook her head at me, fearing I had gone too far; for my Euphemia trembled so much, that it was with great difficulty she could support her.

William, who heard all that past, taking my last words as a signal for him to shew himself, now appeared in view, leading our dear Edward. At that moment, Euphemia raising her eyes, encountered those of her son, which were fixed upon her, and all bathed in tears.

"Oh! Heavens!" cried she, "the very form I saw in my dream."

Mrs. Mountfort called for help, for she sunk from her enclosing arms upon the ground in a deep swoon.

It was so long before she recovered, that the sweet boy, who had thrown himself on the ground beside her, thought she was dead, and filled the air with his lamentations. He was the first object that met her eyes when she opened them, for he was leaning over her, watering her face with his tears. She gazed a little wildly upon him; then turning to me—

"Tell me," said she, "do I dream still—can this be real? Is it indeed my child that I see—and does he live—is it really he?" Mrs. Mountfort pointed to the mark on his breast: she saw it: she strained him eagerly in her arms, her eyes at the same time raised to heaven, while she uttered with the most affecting earnestness, an ardent ejaculation of gratitude and praise to the Almighty giver, for the blessing she had thus unexpectedly recovered. For a long time all was wonder and tumultuous joy; no one thought of returning home; and the whole day had probably been wasted in this place in tears of joy and tenderness, in fond embraces, and strains of rapturous gratitude to Providence for the unhoped for blessing, had not the little Maria, attended by Fanny, come running to fetch her mamma home.

"See your sister," said Euphemia to her son, in French; for by this time she had learned from William that he did not understand English. Smiles of joy and tenderness lighted up his face at sight of the little blooming girl; but finding that when he approached her she clung to Fanny, he modestly drew back.

Mrs. Neville told her, he was her brother, and that she must love him.

"I shall never love him," said she, bursting into tears, "for all he is so handsome; he is an Indian: I shall always be afraid of him."

"He is no Indian," said Mrs. Mountfort, "he is only dressed like one; you will love him when you see him in his proper clothes." She made no answer, but continued gazing upon him; while Fanny, who had learned from me some particulars of this wonderful event, held him in her arms, mixing tears of joy with her embraces.

We now returned home. The footman accommodated William with linen; but our dear Edward was obliged to keep on his Indian dress, till a taylor, who was immediately sent for from Albany, could provide him with another.

I shall be able to acquaint you with all the particulars of his wonderful preservation, as we have learned them from William and himself; for the ship by which we send this packet does not sail for some days: we should have taken our passage in it, but, besides that it is too small to afford us proper accommodations, the Governor, who very kindly interests himself in every thing that regards Mrs. Neville's security and convenience, insists upon her going in the man of war which is expected soon at New-York, and will sail for England soon afterwards.

Your now happy friend, Madam, employs all the moments she can spare from the company of conversation of her son, in writing to Mr. Neville. I must bring you acquainted with the person and character of this sweet youth, when I take up my pen again; at present I can only add, that I am, with great truth, your faithful and obedient servant,

C. BENSON.

Letter XLVII.
MRS. BENSON TO MRS. HARLEY.

MRS. Neville is busy in teaching her son English, who, to great quickness of apprehension, and a most retentive memory, joins an application that must soon conquer all difficulties. He is now dressed in a European habit, in which his easy and graceful air would have surprised us, if we had not known his history. Although he is but twelve years of age, he is as tall as some boys at fifteen. Nothing can be more elegant than his form; and, when I tell you he is very like his mother, I need not add that he is very handsome.

There is something so sweet and innocent in the tones of his voice, so interesting in his countenance, so gentle, yet manly in his manners, as disposes every heart to love him with the affection of a parent. If this charming countenance, so full of sensibility, spirit and sweetness, had none but ordinary qualities to treat us with, it had been a trick put upon us by nature to deceive us, by hanging out a false sign; but his mind corresponds with the loveliness of his outward form. His mother, every moment more sensible of the value of the blessing she has recovered, never looks on him but feels her heart expanded with awful gratitude to that beneficent Power who has restored him to her.

You will be surprized to hear, that our handsome Indian is, considering his youth, a good classical scholar; that he has had a polite as well as a learned education. This appears strange to you, almost incredible; but your wonder will cease when you are acquainted with all the particulars of his history, which I am now going to give you.

You may remember, Madam, when I sent you the melancholy relation of his loss, that I mentioned William's disappearing, having declared that he would find him or never return. He informs us, that, traversing the wood in search of him, in great agitation of mind, he thought he heard the feeble cry of a child. He flew to the place from whence the sound proceeded; he saw, with inconceivable transport, his dear little charge lying at the foot of a tree. The child perceived him, and with a joyful scream made a motion to rise, but was evidently too weak, being almost spent with his wanderings in the pathless forest.

William took him in his arms; and while he prest him to his bosom, his transport breaking out in tears, the little creature stroked his cheeks, and gave him a hundred kisses, in token of his joy and gratitude.

Uncertain which way he should direct his steps, in order to carry him soonest back to the place where he had left his master, he stood a few moments looking round him, when suddenly a party of about twenty Indians came pouring from an eminence behind him, two of them seized him, and a third took the child out of his arms.

William in agonies, lest they should hurt the child, implored their mercy with tears and supplicating gestures, which they took no notice of. But the screams of the child seemed to give the Indian offence; for he shook him with a menacing air, which had such an effect upon him, that he became instantly silent, and held up his little hands for pardon.

This action was observed by an Indian woman in their company, on whom the beauty of little Edward had seemed to make some impression. She approached the Indian who held him, and spoke some words to him, upon which he delivered the child to her, who, feeling itself encouraged by those signs of compassion that were strongly marked in her countenance, held out its arms to her; which seemed to please her so much, that she put him tenderly to her bosom, and covered him with her mantle, where, tired with his wanderings, he soon fell asleep.

These Indians, who belonged to a Huron village in the dependance of Canada, and who had come down to the English settlements to dispose of their furs, now prepared to return to their canoes, which they had drawn ashore at the distance of five miles. They bound William's hands behind his back, and led him along with a cord they had tied round his waist, regardless of his tears and entreaties. They told him in French, (of which the Canadian Indian tribes, who have missionaries settled amongst them, all understand a little), that having lost one of their companions in this expedition, by an accident, they were carrying him to the mother of the deceased, in order, that by adopting him, she might replace her dead son.

William understood enough of the language to be able to comprehend all the horror of his destiny, which was greatly aggravated by his reflections on the distress he had brought upon his master and mistress, in the loss of their child; whose fate he lamented, he said, more than his own.

The Indian women are extremely fond of their children, and take the utmost care of them while they are young. She who had adopted little Edward, shewed an affection for him equal to that she had felt for her own son, who died a few days before she accompanied her friends in this expedition.

These Indians belonged to a tribe called *Hurons*, who were settled about three leagues from Montreal.—They are Christians, and have a missionary who always resides amongst them, and for whom they have the highest respect and reverence. During their journey to their own village, which was very tedious, and sometimes performed in canoes, sometimes by land, the Huron woman was very attentive to the preservation of the child, feeding it plentifully with a preparation of maice, which they call *sagamity*.[1]—They boil it in the ear while it is yet tender, after-

---

1 Maize is the corn indigeneous to North America, and sagamite is a corn porridge.

wards roast it a little, then separate it from the ear, and leave it to dry in the sun: in this state it will keep a long time. They commonly make their provision of it for long journies, and complete the dressing of it, when they want it, by boiling it in water, and it has then an excellent flavour.

William, who often travelled in the same canoo with this Huron woman and his young master, saw with pleasure that the child began to relish this food; but was pierced to the heart, he said, when he would innocently ask, when he should see his mamma? and when she would come to him?

At length they reached their village: the Huron woman carried Edward to her cabin. The family, who had lost a relation in this expedition, willingly received William in his place. Some days afterwards a feast was made, during the course of which, he received, in solemn manner, the name of him whom he replaced; and from thence forth, not only succeeded to all his rights, but likewise became liable to all his obligations.

The missionary, who was of the order of the Jesuits, finding William was bred a Protestant, immediately set about converting him to the Catholic Faith, as he termed it. William listened to his documents with great attention, and shewed a docility which pleased the father greatly; who expressed a friendship for him, that gave him hopes, he might be able one day, by his means, to recover his liberty, and restore Edward again to his parents. But it was necessary to observe great caution in this design; for if the Indians had received the least intimation of it, they would have put him to death, nor could the father have protected him; who, when he was informed by him, that Edward was the son of an English officer of family and fortune, expressed some compassion for his fate, and the grief his parents must feel for his loss; but his zeal, flattered with the expectation of making him a good Catholic as he grew up, and his fear of endangering the success of his mission, if he gave any offence to the Indians by endeavouring to effect his deliverance, prevented him from forming any scheme in his favour.

William had been now four months in the Huron village, when he was obliged to join a hunting party composed of several young Indians, to whom, by the right of adoption, he was now related. He told us, that when he went to take leave of little Edward, his emotions, which he considered as a sad presage that he should see him no more, were so violent, as exposed him to the ridicule of his companions, and obliged him to affect a more than ordinary degree of alacrity afterwards, in order to wear off the unfavourable impression.

His apprehensions were realized.—Being obliged to go to a great distance from their own village, in quest of game, they were encountered by a more numerous party of the Algonguins, a tribe of Indians, with whom the Hurons were always at enmity; a battle ensued; several of the Hurons were killed, and two of the Algonguins; William was wounded and taken prisoner. He had the good fortune to be again adopted; the mother of an Algonguin, who was killed, consented to replace her son by this captive, whose figure pleased her.

His condition here was much worse than it had been with the Hurons; he was not only separated from the dear child, who was his only comfort, and whose deliverance he always hoped to accomplish, but he was now adopted into an idolatrous nation, whose savage customs and manners, filled him with horror and dismay.

Here, my dear Madam, we must leave the unfortunate William, and return to our dear little boy, who in a few weeks after his departure, lost his affectionate nurse, who was seized with a fever, which proved mortal.

When the missionary attended her to receive her confession, and prepare her for death, she surprised him with a declaration, that she could not die in peace, unless he promised to use his utmost endeavours to restore her adopted child to his natural parents.

The Huron Indians of this village are, it seems, very sincere Christians; they respected this woman's pleas of conscience, and readily consented that the father should take what measures he thought fit to fulfil her request. She died contented, after embracing the child with the strongest marks of affection.

The missionary immediately took him to his own cabin, where he treated him with great tenderness. He wrote to the Father Rector of the Jesuits College in Montreal,[1] gave him an account of the whole affair, and desired his advice in what manner he should proceed.

The Rector sent for the child. His beauty and sprightliness pleased him.—In a short time, the amiableness of his manners, and his insinuating sweetness and gentleness of disposition,

---

1 College of Our Lady of the Angels, an elementary school for boys, founded in 1635. Lessons were conducted in Huron, Montagnais, and French. It was closed after the British conquest of Quebec in 1760.

engaged his affections so powerfully, that not being able to bear the thoughts of parting with him, he was less active than he ought to have been, in his endeavours to restore him to his parents.

It is true, that the missionary could give him but little intelligence.—All he had learned from William, with whom he never chose to converse upon the subject, was, that he was the son of an English officer of family and fortune, but his name he knew not, nor where he was stationed. The place indeed where the Indians found him, might naturally have led him to conclude, that his father belonged to the troops of New-York; and the singular mark upon the child's breast could not fail of making him be acknowledged.—But still there were many difficulties to be got over, before this could be done; and the Father Rector made the most of them.

Meantime, finding in him an astonishing capacity, he cultivated his natural abilities with the utmost care. Being a man of genius, and an excellent scholar, the little Edward, under his tuition, advanced so fast in his learning, that he was considered as a prodigy. He was not only a favourite in the college, but all the persons of any fashion in Montreal, were fond of the handsome little Huron; for a good grace is to the body, what a good sense is to the mind, it creates respect and conciliates kindness. He learned to dance, to fence, to ride, with the principal youth of the city. He was admired and beloved—but he was not happy: as his years increased, he sighed in secret for that sweet intercourse of parental affection, and filial duty and tenderness; impressions which he had received from nature, which he felt in early childhood, and were strengthened with the growth of his reason.

His preceptor had taken care to sow the seeds of piety in his mind; but these seeds, being to spring up and flourish in a religion loaded with inextricable difficulties, defaced by absurdities, errors, and contradictions, which his natural sagacity, aided by reflexion uncommon at his age, enabled him to discover: no wonder that their growth was checked, and that he was involved in a labyrinth of doubts and perplexities, which was likely to have the fatal tendency, of making him indifferent to religion itself.

One of Mrs. Neville's first cares, was to prevent this misfortune, by giving him right notions of the Christian religion, as taught by the divine founder of it. He grows more enlightened every day, and improves in the study of the Scriptures; and when he has English enough, the excellent sermons of Doctor

Clarke,[1] the best expounder of them, will make, I hope, a good Protestant of a very indifferent Roman Catholic.

The people at Montreal had a suspicion, that the Father Rector, from the high opinion he entertained of our Edward's natural abilities, had formed the design of making a Jesuit of him, conceiving that he would, in time, become an ornament to their order; and hence might arise the indifference he expressed about restoring him to his parents and his country; a design universally disapproved. But if this *was* his design, Providence defeated it, by enabling William, at length, to escape from the Algonguins, and to arrive at Montreal, after having surmounted dangers, and suffered hardships, to which human nature seemed wholly unequal.

His intention was to proceed to Quebeck, and to petition the Governor in behalf of Edward; hoping to interest his justice and compassion, for the son of an officer, who was heir to a considerable name and fortune.

In order to know if the dear boy was still alive, he went to the Jesuit College, where the Huron missionary was sometimes to be met with. He presented himself at the gate, at the very moment when the Father Rector, accompanied by the principal gentlemen of Montreal, were coming out, among whom was Edward. The squalid appearance of this Indian, as William was supposed to be; his body almost sinking with fatigue, and emaciated with famine, drew every eye upon him, while his were eagerly fixed upon our dear boy, whom he instantly knew. He threw himself upon his knees, thanking Heaven for so happy a meeting! then suddenly clasping him in his arms, wet his face with a shower of tears. The company thought he was intoxicated, as the Indians are too apt to be, and pushed him away: but Edward, who now perfectly recollected him, cried out, with great emotion—

"Oh! do not drive him away—it is William!"

"And who is William, child?" said the Father Rector.

"I am his father's servant, Sir," said William. "Captain Neville is his father, and my master; a gentleman of high fortune. A party of Hurons carried the child and me off, about eight years ago. I

---

1 Samuel Clarke (1675-1729), English philosopher and Chaplain to Queen Anne from 1706. In 1709 he became rector of St. James's, Westminster. His work on the *Trinity* (1712) and his *Demonstration of the Being and Attributes of God* (1704-05), which he delivered as Boyle lecturer, are his best known contributions to theological debate and exemplify his arguments for Protestantism over Catholicism, to which Lennox here alludes.

became a prisoner to the Algonguins, and was adopted by them: but fortunately, after a long captivity, have made my escape from them: and now, if I can carry my master's son back to him, and his afflicted lady, I shall be contented."

The Father Rector stood silent a few moments; during which time, William was kissing the hands of Edward, and bathing them with his tears.

"Your master's son," said the Rector, "had a singular mark upon his breast; do you know what it is?" "Yes, Sir," replied William; "it is a bow and arrow."

"There needed not this confirmation," said a gentleman, who had always been particularly solicitous that Edward should be restored to his parents: "The young gentleman immediately recollected this man, notwithstanding he was so young when they were separated, and the alteration that years and misery have made in his person.—It is just that he should be immediately sent back to his parents; the Governor will, doubtless, be of the same opinion."

"There is no necessity for any application to the Governor," said the Father Rector, who thought fit to yield with a good grace; "I have no reason to be ashamed of the improvements my young pupil has made under my tuition; I will complete the good work, and take upon myself the care of providing for his return to the English colonies."

He was as good as his word. William's strength was restored by proper nourishment, and decent clothing was provided for him.

Edward's time was sufficiently employed till their departure, in paying farewell visits to his numerous friends and admirers at Montreal, and in attending to the departing documents of the Father Rector; among which religion held the first place.

When the moment of parting came, the good father mixed so many tears with his embraces, that Edward, quite overcome with gratitude, tenderness, and grief, almost fainted in his arms. They were obliged to carry him away by force; and it was many hours before his mind was free enough from those impressions to entertain those natural emotions of joy which the expectation of seeing his parents excited.

This joy, however, was not without alloy: it was possible one or both his parents might be dead; and he might be again an orphan, without having the good fortune to meet with such a protector as he had found in the good Jesuit. His mind was thus fluctuating between hope and fear, when they arrived at Oswego;

and here William assured him they should get certain intelligence of all they so much desired to know.

When they presented themselves at the gate of the Fort, William desired to be immediately introduced to the commanding officer. It is the detestable Lieutenant Blood who now holds that place, Madam, and whom fortune now furnished with an opportunity of gratifying the hatred that boiled in his breast against Mr. Neville, ever since the Governor had removed him from the command at Albany to give it to him.

As soon as William came into his presence, after making many a low bow, the fierce and haughty air of this petty commander, seeming to exact such homage, he begged to be informed if Captain Neville and his lady were living, and still in the province?

"And what business have you, fellow, with Captain Neville?" said the Lieutenant in a surly tone. William told him, he was that gentleman's unfortunate servant, who nine years ago had been carried off by a party of the Hurons, together with his master's son, then a child of three years old, and had ever since been a prisoner among the Indians. He proceeded to give him an account of all that had happened to them from that period; to which the Lieutenant listened with an air or incredulity and contempt. When he had finished—

"And so, fellow," said he with a dreadful frown, "you expect I should believe this fine tale, do you?"

William, in great surprize, asked him if he did not recollect that Captain Neville lost his only son at the Fall of Cohas, who was supposed to be drowned?

"I remember nothing of the matter," replied he.

The man, now more astonished, leading up Edward to him, and shewing him the mark on his breast, "This is my master's son," said he; "this mark, with which he was born, will make him be acknowledged."

"You are both imposters," said the Lieutenant in a rage.

Edward, whose indignation at this reception, he was no longer able to suppress, (for William explained to him what he said), came up to him with a countenance and air so full of spirit, that he astonished the old man, and said in a haughty tone—

"We came not here to ask any assistance of you; we are very well provided for the remainder of our journey; we came to inquire whether my parents are still living, and in the province: questions which any person in this garrison, I suppose, can answer, as well as you, Sir; we will trouble you therefore no further."

The Lieutenant, who did not understand French, asked the surgeon who stood near him what the boy said; "for by his haughty air," said he, "he seems to threaten us."

The surgeon, who gazed on him while he was speaking, with admiration and delight, repeated his words in English; which so provoked the Lieutenant, that rising from his seat, he seized him with one hand, while with the other he endeavoured to reach a stick, with which he threatened to correct him severely.

Our sweet boy, whose stature and strength greatly exceeds his age, disengaged himself from his hold with a force that made the feeble old man stagger; and was leaving the room, beckoning William to follow him, when the Lieutenant, foaming with rage, called to a sarjeant—"Take that fellow into custody," said he, pointing to William. "I am convinced he is a spy, employed by the French for some bad purposes; lodge him safe in the barracks, together with this audacious boy, whom I shall know how to deal with."

William, pale and trembling, attempted to speak; but Edward, pushing back the sarjeant, proclaimed aloud in French that he was Captain Neville's son, and that the officer had no right to detain him in his garrison.

The surgeon now took the Lieutenant aside; and after talking to him a few minutes in a low voice, Mr. Blood came forwards, and said aloud—

"Well, I consent to it: do you take charge of them till to-morrow, meantime I will consider what course to take with them."—The surgeon then courteously invited Edward to go with him, who no longer made any resistance: William was ordered to follow them.

Mr. Parker, for that was his name, carried them to his quarters: he left them there for a few minutes, to order a dinner to be prepared; and, returning, tenderly embraced our little hero.

"Your father, Sir," said he in French, "honoured me with his friendship; he recommended me to Colonel Bellenden, who appointed me surgeon to this garrison."

"Oh! say," interrupted Edward, "is he alive? Is he in the province? Does my mother live?"

"I am informed," replied Mr. Parker, "that Captain Neville sailed for England about two months ago, to take possession of a considerable fortune; your mother was prevented from going with him by some accident, but she is well,—she is in the province, and you will see her. Be not alarmed at what has passed here; I know Lieutenant Blood has an inveterate hatred to your father—he has some ill designs against you, but I shall take care to prevent his carrying them into effect."

Edward, transported with joy and gratitude, threw himself on Mr. Parker's neck, and embraced him fondly. The worthy young man repaid his tenderness with interest: he had the complaisance to answer all his numerous enquiries concerning his parent, as circumstantially as his insatiable curiosity required. In the evening he left him to go to the Lieutenant, in order to gain a full intelligence of his designs.

This interval was passed by Edward in a delightful anticipation of the happiness he was soon to enjoy in the embraces of a mother, whose character, faintly drawn by William, and more fully displayed by the eloquence of the young surgeon, added to the force of natural affection, all the admiration, respect, and reverence, so justly her due.

Mr. Parker returned to his quarters in the evening, with so much concern and perplexity in his countenance, that Edward, dismayed, cried out—

"Ah, you have some bad news to tell us; speak, is it not so?"

"This old man's malignity," said Mr. Parker, "is astonishing; it has suggested to him a design worthy of a fiend."

"Why, what does he intend to do?" replied our dear boy, in a tone, William said, that expressed at once indignation and grief.

"He is resolved," said Mr. Parker, "notwithstanding all my arguments, to consider you as two criminals, who have fled from justice at Canada, and to send you, under a guard of soldiers, back to Montreal."

"There," replied Edward briskly, "we shall be certain of being cleared:" but, after a little pause, he burst into tears. "My mother, my dear mother!" cried he, "I shall not see you then—I shall be torn from you again—perhaps we shall never meet." This thought affected him so much, that the surgeon could with difficulty pacify him, though he gave him repeated assurances that he would contrive some method to get him out of the Lieutenant's power.

Finding him a little composed, he left him, in order, he said, to execute a plan he had formed, which he did not doubt would succeed. He staid long; and this interval was passed in cruel agitation by the two prisoners. At length the surgeon returned; and now, with such marks of satisfaction in his looks, as revived all their hopes.

"Make yourself easy, my sweet young friend," said he to

Edward; "you shall be at liberty this night. Hear how I have settled the matter:

"There is now in the Fort two of the Mohawk Indians, who have been here some time, trading for furs. They have finished their business, and propose to return to their village to-morrow. They are both sensible honest fellows, of some consequence in their tribe; they know your father, and are highly provoked at the cruelty and injustice of the Lieutenant: I have engaged them to take you and William under their conduct. See here," pursued he, shewing them a bundle which he had brought in under his cloak; "here is a complete Indian dress for each of you. We have nothing to do but to pare off some of the length of this mantle, and you will be well fitted," said he to Edward. "The Indians have agreed to set out to-night, which is dark enough to favour your escape. The sentinel at the gate, supposing you to be all Mohawk Indians, who go in and out of the garrison freely, will ask no questions.—But, come, (added he), we have no time to lose; put on your disguises, the Indians will be here immediately."

William soon appeared a perfect Indian, his hair being already cut[1] in their frightful fashion. But Edward, unwilling to part with his fine curling locks, was in some perplexity.

"You have nothing to do," said Mr. Parker, "but to wrap part of your mantle about your head; the Mohawk Indians often wear theirs in that manner."

While Edward was dressing, he expressed his concern for the difficulties this friendly action would draw upon Mr. Parker.

"You may be quite easy upon that score," said the worthy young man; "I have provided against the effects of the Lieutenant's rage: all I have to expect is to be put under an arrest, but my confinement will not last long. One of the Indians, for a reward, has undertaken to proceed to New-York with a letter from me to the Governor, in which I shall give him an account of Mr. Blood's tyranny and injustice. As soon as you are out of danger of a pursuit, which however I think he will hardly attempt, I will tell him that circumstance, which I know will operate so strongly upon his fears, that he will not dare to treat me with any severity."

Mr. Parker sat down to write his letter, which was but just sealed when the Indians arrived. He furnished the travellers with

---

1 The Mohawks cut their hair so that the sides were shorn, leaving a long strip from forehead to back of neck where the hair grew long.

what refreshments he could procure; and, after tenderly embracing Edward, recommended him to Providence, and dismissed them, following them at some distance till he saw them safely out of the gate. They soon reached their canoes, in which they embarked immediately.

I will not trouble you now, Madam, with an account of all the difficulties and distresses they met with in this expedition; concerning which William was very circumstantial, as well as in that from Canada. You will hear the whole some other time: when you are all happily met, these adventures will furnish matter for many interesting conversations.

The Indian who was to proceed to New-York, having been lately at Albany, was able to give Edward some intelligence of his mother, which threw him into transports of joy. He told William, who understood the Mohawk language, that he saw her at Mrs. Mountfort's villa, whither he went with a Dutchman, who had some business with that lady. Edward, therefore, all eager impatience to see her, would not stop at the Mohawk village to refresh himself, after the incredible fatigue he had endured, where Mr. Butler, who commanded the Fort there, would have given him a cordial reception, but insisted upon proceeding.

The Indians faithfully performed their engagement, for which they were well paid. They landed their fellow travellers at a creek, within three miles of the place where Mrs. Mountfort resided. Here he who was the courier to New-York, took leave of them, and pursued his rout to Albany; from whence, if he did not find a sloop ready to sail for New-York, he was to continue his journey by land. And the other, having conducted them within sight of the house, went back to his canoe, and returned to his own village.

You know the rest, Madam. Your amiable friend, after so many severe trials of her patience and fortitude, is now happy—happy beyond her most sanguine hopes, beyond her fondest wishes.— For what hopes, what wishes, could reach an event, that seemed, not only out of the bounds of probability, but almost impossible?

Mr. Neville, by his eagerness to gratify his own inclinations, to which he sacrificed even the appearance of tenderness for the most deserving of women, will be sometime longer before he partakes the happiness she now enjoys. A selfish person, our great Bacon[1] compares to the earth, which stands fast only on its own

---

1 Francis Bacon's *Essays (Civil and Moral)* (1597), "Of Wisdom for a Man's Self."

centre; whereas, all things that have affinity with the heavens, move upon the centre of another, which they benefit.—Such is the difference between their two minds.

We have congratulations from all parts, on the surprising restoration of our dear boy. The Governor, in his letter on this subject to Mrs. Neville, tells her, that the King's ship that was expected in the port, is arrived; and that she will soon see a friend, with whom he expects she will set out for New-York. The curiosity to see the handsome young Huron, is universal there.

We have a letter from Mr. Parker, brought by an Indian courier, in which he informed us, that Lieutenant Blood was so much intimidated by the steps he had taken to inform the Governor of his base treatment of Captain Neville's son, and the wicked scheme he had formed for his ruin, that he not only forbore to take any revenge upon him, but his apprehensions increasing, the more he reflected upon the consequences of what he had done, he was seized with a fever, and that there was no probability of his recovery.

Mrs. Neville has sent this worthy young man, a diamond ring of great value, with other considerable presents. She designs a noble donation to the Father Rector, for his college, which is but indigent; and has no doubt but Mr. Neville will readily adopt her views: meantime she is obliged to content herself with expressing her gratitude only in words. Her letter, enclosed in one from Edward, which breathes the most affecting strains of love, reverence and gratitude, is sent to Mr. Parker, to be transmitted to him by some of those Indians who trade between Montreal and Oswago.

The friend, mentioned by the Governor in his letter to Mrs. Neville, was no other than young Mansel, who is, it seems, Third Lieutenant of the man of war in which we are to embark for England. He arrived here this morning; Mrs. Mountford introduced him, smiling, for the remembered kindness there was between him and my Euphemia.

"Here," said she, "I bring you another son, to share your affections with the handsome Huron."

Edward, surprised, rose from his seat, retiring to a little distance, to make way for the young officer, who, with an impetuosity that shewed how much he was affected with the sight of Mrs. Neville, threw himself at her feet, kissing each of her hands alternately. Mrs. Neville raised him, and tenderly embracing him, expressed great joy at this unexpected meeting.

Meantime, Edward, still keeping at a respectful distance,

looked sometimes at his mother, sometimes at Mr. Mansel, with an air of perplexity: at last—

"Have I a brother?" said he to me, in a low voice, which, however, was heard by Mr. Mansel.

"Yes," said he, turning to him with a look of surprise and pleasure, at the beauty of his face and figure, "you have a brother; the son of that dear lady, will always be considered as a brother by me." Edward received his affectionate embrace with a grateful sensibility in his looks, and seemed to admire the free open air of his new friend, and the tenderness and benevolence of his aspect, which character is at once his profession and his heart.

It is settled that we shall set out for New-York in two days. Mrs. Mountfort will accompany us; but we must leave Mrs. Lawson behind us. This separation sits heavy upon my dear Euphemia; the good woman observes the tear starting to her eyes, when she looks upon her; and guessing her thoughts—

"Why," said she to her to-day, "will you, by these tender regrets, cloud the satisfaction I take in a separation that will restore you to your country, your friends, and an ample fortune? You are going to take a journey, which, I hope, will lead you to all the happiness you so well deserve: and I am entering upon a much longer one, for which, I trust, I am not wholly unprepared."

No certainly, not unprepared; for her whole life has been one uniform preparation for it. The placid air of her countenance, the perpetual chearfulness of her temper, and uncommon share of health, for a person of her age, prove the powerful influence of a good conscience upon every stage of our existence here. The religious pleasures of a well disposed mind, says a writer, with whose works I am sure, you are well acquainted, move gently, and therefore constantly; they do not affect with rapture and extasy, but are like the pleasures of health, still and sober.[1]

New-York.

Yesterday we arrived safe here, under the conduct of Mr. Mansel; and were received on our landing by a croud of friends, whose curiosity to see the handsome Huron, would not permit them to wait for us at our abode, which, during our stay here, will be at

---

1 From *The Tatler* No. 211 (1710) "Uses of Sunday—on Devotion," by Richard Steele (1672-1729).

Mrs. Mountfort's house. Visitants are announced every moment of the day; I withdraw unobserved, for they all press young Edward, gazing, and asking him a thousand questions. His French education has given him an air and manner, so unembarrassed, so polite, and even gallant, which, joined with a true English solidity of understanding, makes him pass for a prodigy. If he stays here much longer, he will certainly make some conquest among the rising generation of beauties; for, notwithstanding his youth, his stature is so advantageous, that no one considers him as a boy. He is now gone to wait on the Governor, who sent his coach for him, and carried him off from a little world of his admirers.

Mrs. Neville is so taken up with entertaining these people, that she has not a moment to spare for writing, which she regrets the less, she obligingly says, as she can command my pen. The expectation of seeing you, so contracts the distance between you, that it seems as if a few days would bring you together.

Our sweet boy is returned decorated with a most flattering mark of the Governor's esteem for him; and what is still more soothing, of the favour of the young lady, his Excellency's youngest daughter. When he was preparing to depart, the Governor produced a sword, that had been made for his son when he was about Edward's age, and had an ensign's commission in the Guards bestowed on him.—The hilt, silver; most richly enchased;[1] and the belt, the most elegant thing, of the kind, I ever saw. The Governor, giving it into his daughter's hands, ordered her, with a smile, to gird on the belt round the waist of his young friend: she took it from his hands, courtesying low; and with a deep blush, yet evident marks of satisfaction, prepared to obey him.

A youth of less presence of mind than Edward, would have been a little disconcerted at this ceremony; which the Governor, who is full of wit and spirit, had contrived before-hand; but he, with admirable quickness of thought, bending one knee to the ground before her, kissed the sword; and adopting the language of ancient chivalry, begged leave to vow himself her knight, and to dedicate that sword to her service and protection.

Miss Mountague, blushing more than before, made haste to fasten a sword-knot of white and silver ribbon, which her own fair hands had made up; and retiring a step or two backwards, to give

---

1 Engraved.

the new knight an opportunity of rising, made a profound courtesy to his bow, which was low and almost to prostration; and
then joined her mother, who, with her sisters and some other
ladies, were in another part of the room, delighted with all that
had passed.

I must make up my packet immediately. Euphemia has but
just time to write* a few lines to you which you will find enclosed.
She pleases herself with the happiness her letters will communicate to her husband. The vessel that carries them, sails but a few
days before that in which we are to embark; so that before you
have done wondering at the event they inform you of, you will
find yourself in her arms. I am, with great respect, dear Madam,
your faithful humble servant.

E. BENSON.

Letter XLVIII.

London.

MY DEAR MARIA,

AFTER a tedious, though not unpleasant voyage, during which
we were treated with the greatest kindness and respect by the
commander of the ship, and had every accommodation that the
unremitting attention of Mr. Mansel could procure us, we arrive
safe in the Downs last Thursday. Mr. Neville's impatience to see
his son brought him there two days before. He came off in a boat
to the ship, and the moment he got upon the deck the dear boy
was at his feet. Mr. Neville, with an eager curiosity, gazed at him
a few moments; at last recollecting himself, he raised and
embraced him with a most edifying philosophic calmness, as
Mrs. Benson observed. Your little god-daughter meantime hung
on his arm, and, with a speaking look, put in her claim to his
notice also. After all due compliments were paid to our kind pro-
tectors, we landed, and got in to a coach and four, which Mr.
Neville had provided, and arrived safely, though much fatigued,
at his uncle's house, where it seems we are to take up our abode
for the present.

We found the old gentleman very much indisposed; he seemed

---

* This Letter does not appear.

glad to see me, and takes great notice of our handsome Huron, observing, (for he has heard as much of his history as Mr. Neville would be at the trouble to communicate) that he had not an *outlandish* look; and piously hoped he never worshipped the devil when he was among the cannibals.

"But you have been used to idol worship, Ned?" said Mr. Neville; "your friends the Jesuits would not dispense with that?"

"It is a great misfortune, Sir," replied our dear boy, "to be in a situation where one must do things contrary to one's reason."

"Upon my word," replied his father, "your reason was very early matured, if you entertained such scruples at that time." He spoke this in a tone of voice that disconcerted his son, and brought a blush into his cheeks; but presently recollecting himself—

"My mamma, Sir," said he, "has taken a great deal of pains to set me right in many things respecting religion; and I hope her instructions on that head, as well as on many others, will not be thrown away."

He spoke this in French, which Mr. Neville understands very well. He made no answer, but rose from his chair, and whistling a tune as he walked about the room, with a vacant air; which his son observed with marks of surprise and confusion in his countenance.

Alas! my dear Maria, the contempt which Mr. Neville has always affected to treat my notions with, will, if it operates as perhaps he intends it should upon his son, render me much less useful to him than I hoped to be.

* * * * *

Here is your dear, your amiable Mr. Harley, come with a coach and six[1] to carry me to the Hall. You are dying with impatience to see me, he says; and although you have lain in but a fortnight, he is in doubt whether you will not set out for London next week, unless he can bring me and my children to you. How shall I be able to tell you that I must deny myself a happiness which I have so long sighed for, and which I vainly thought was within my reach. Old Mr. Neville is dangerously ill; he has taken a great liking to me. My attentions and assiduity about him are so

---

1   A coach is a large, horse-drawn carriage, and in this case, there are six horses pulling the carriage.

acceptable, that they seem to soften his pains. He complains bitterly of my husband's unkindness, who, he say, has neglected him cruelly since he came to England; seldom vouchsafing him (that was his expression) a quarter of an hour of his company, although he has acted so generously by him.

Our tenderness is said to encrease for those persons on whom we have conferred benefits, in the same manner as we hate those with violence whom we have injured. The old gentleman has more than fulfilled the liberal promises he made his nephew; and the unkind returns he thinks he has made him, seems to affect him with more grief than resentment.

I excuse my husband as well as I can, and redouble my own attentions to him. His condition requires all my cares, which my dear Edward would gladly share with me, but his father engrosses him all, carrying him to every scene of pleasure and amusement, in such quick succession, that he has no time to prosecute his studies, and can afford his uncle and me but a small share of his conversation. He is in less danger, however, of acquiring a taste for dissipation, which his natural love of knowledge, and early habits of study and retirement, render him rather averse to, than of being reduced by false shews of kindness and regard, into connexions with persons of dangerous principles, which it is impossible his unsuspecting youth, his open and candid temper, should enable him to discover, till it is too late. Nothing seems more easy to young persons than to gain affection; and they reckon their own friendship a sure price of another persons: but I tell him, that when an experience shall have shewn him the hardness of most hearts, and the deceitfulness of others, he will find that a friend is the gift of God, and that He only who made hearts can unite them.

Mr. Harley calls upon me this moment for my letter; he tells me, with half a smile, that he is afraid to appear before you without me in his hand; but I am sure that his appearance after even this short absence will leave your heart free to no other emotions but joy, for some time at least; after which friendship may put in its claim, to some regret, that our meeting is still delayed—*delayed* only, my dear, mark that; and but for a short time: be this thought your consolation, as it is mine. Mr. Harley would fain take my Edward with him to the Hall; he is charmed, he says, with his mind, his person, his manners: how soothing is the praise of such a man as him to the heart of a fond mother! He says your god-daughter is like you; and the little girl holds up her head upon it more than before. I ask him a thousand questions about his son; his answer is only Come and see. And so I will, my Maria, doubt it not, the moment I am at liberty. Till then adieu, my dearest friend!

EUPHEMIA NEVILLE.

P.S. I am excessively obliged by the kind remembrances of Sir John and Mr. Greville; and hope soon, if Mr. Neville grows better, to make them my acknowledgments in person.

Letter XLIX.
MRS. BENSON TO MRS. HARLEY.

DEAR MADAM,

YOU must accept of a letter from me instead of one from your amiable friend, who is constantly employed about our sick gentleman, who seems uneasy if she is a moment out of his sight. It is not surprising that he, who has known none of the comforts of domestic life, and in sickness has been used to the awkward attendance of servants, their blunders, and unfeeling assistance, should be so sensible of the mighty difference between their services and those of his charming niece, as he always calls her. She is indeed, with all her delicacy of figure and constitution, the most active and most useful nurse in the world: that forethought, that provides against all contingencies; that quickness of apprehension, which seizes instantly every possible means of assistance; that tender sympathy, which seems to partake the pain she is endeavouring to alleviate; and that generous disregard of her own ease and health, while she is performing the duties of the office she has undertaken, excite the admiration of all who are witnesses of her behaviour. But I should not say *all*: there is one who can neither feel nor do justice to her excellence—so hard, nay even impossible, it is to be virtuous with the approbation of those who are not so.

"A man," says the immortal Bacon, "who has no virtue in himself, is sure to decry virtue in others; for men's minds will either feed upon their own good, or upon others' evil; and he who wants the one, will prey upon the other."[1]

My dear Euphemia, fearful of my endangering my ill confirmed health, will not permit me to partake of her fatigue; the

---

1 Francis Bacon, *Essays (Civil and Moral)* (1597), "Of Envy."

task of answering letters, and receiving the visits of her numerous friends, falls to me. Among these every branch of the Bellenden family are most assiduous; even that ghost of beauty, Miss Bellenden, glides here sometimes, in her way to those scenes of splendour and gaiety which she still haunts, and where she is received with an effect that might well mortify her, if it were possible for vanity ever to be extinct in the heart of a toast.

★ ★ ★ ★ ★

Mr. Neville's recovery is despaired of; he seems sensible that his end is approaching, and prepares for it with decent fortitude. He has had several private conferences with Mr. Granby, who yesterday introduced a lawyer to him. This circumstance has given a solemnity to his nephew's countenance, very proper on this melancholy occasion.

★ ★ ★ ★ ★

The old gentleman is no more. Mr. Neville, with all decent haste, has opened his will, which was confided to Mr. Granby's care. He there found, to his great surprise, that his uncle had bequeathed fifteen thousand pounds, the produce of his savings for many years past, to Mrs. Neville, for her sole use and benefit, not subject to the controul of her husband, and entirely at her own disposal; that she may have it in her power, as the testator expresses it, to reward her children, according to the measure of duty and affection she receives from them. The precautions taken to secure this legacy in its full extent and design to Mrs. Neville, is an indirect reflexion upon Mr. Neville, who makes great use of the circumstance to veil his disgust at so marked a preference. Mr. Neville comes into the possession of a very good estate, which by certain restrictions, that sets bounds to his thoughtless extravagance, must descend to his heir, free from all incumbrances.

Mrs. Neville undertakes to be at all the expence of completing her son's education—an offer her husband accepts as what he had a right to demand. This will throw power enough in her hands, to enable her to follow the light of her own excellent understanding, in an affair of too much consequence to be left to the guidance of a man, who is always counselled by his passions, appetites, and caprice. Since her return from America, she has taken every opportunity to remind him of the great obligations they lie under to the Father Rector, who, under Providence, was the means of preserving their son to them, and added to that benefit, the inestimable advantage of an early virtuous and learned education; and has earnestly entreated him to make a suitable return for it, but was not able to prevail. And often lamented with me, her want of power to pay the mighty debt of gratitude she owed him.

"Heaven knows," she says, "that my intentions are good, and with Heaven they are accepted; but with regard to men, good intentions are little better than dreams, unless they are put in act." She may now indulge her generous disposition. She destines five hundred pounds for a donation to his college. Mr. Euston, who has some connexions in Canada, has undertaken to get this money properly transmitted to the Rector; to which she has added some valuable presents for himself in particular.

Fanny's lover is just arrived from the country.—The meeting between those two, was full of transport on his side, of grateful sensibility and modest joy on her's. There is now no obstacle to their union; his parents have left him in easy circumstances, and their mutual constancy, under so long a separation, promises them a solid and durable happiness.

My Euphemia desires me to leave room for her to add a line in her own hand.—Adieu then, dear Madam! and believe me, with great respect, your most obedient servant,

M. BENSON.

My presence being no longer necessary here, my dear Maria may expect me at the Hall in two days. I shall bring your god-daughter with me; but our dear Huron stays till the funeral ceremony is over; his father will then conduct him to me. You will see him, my dear Maria—you will see this son, so long lamented as dead, so wonderfully preserved, so unexpectedly recovered: you will see again your friend, so long banished from you to a new and savage world, and you will see her happy.—This is the work of Heaven:—Whether unfortunate or happy, may I ever adore its decrees!—

"Thus blessings ever wait on virtuous deeds;
And tho' a late, a sure reward succeeds."[1]

---

1 William Congreve's *The Mourning Bride* (1697), 5.12.

Mrs. Benson forced the pen out of my hand to add the foregoing quotation, which her partial fondness applies to me. I tell her, in the words of a very good judge of human nature,[1] That our enemies come nearer the truth, in their judgments of us, than our friends.—She admits this, but with exceptions. The post is going out. Adieu, my dear *Maria*; for a short—a very short time, adieu!

EUPHEMIA NEVILLE.

FINIS.

---

1 From La Rochefoucauld's *Reflexions ou Sentences et Maximes Morales* (1665).

Appendix A: Reviews of Euphemia

1. *Critical Review*, LXX (July 1790): 81-83

If we enlarge our account of this pleasing work, it is chiefly because we think it uncommon in its construction, and interesting from some of its descriptions; accounts of a country which, though long in our possession, has scarcely ever been described in a picturesque narrative. Euphemia does not appear, at first, the most striking personage of the history. We begin where novels usually end, by her marriage; a marriage dictated by duty and convenience rather than affection. The character of Mr. Neville, her husband, is drawn only in the little incidents of Euphemia's correspondence; and it seems to be copied from nature, where similar inconsistencies are sometimes found. Haughty, positive, feeling a rational well grounded affection, which his lordly pride will not always permit him to acknowledge, eager to be distinguished as well as to command, his failings are the source of Euphemia's distress, and afford her not only an opportunity of establishing her own character, but of giving a striking example to wives in similar situations: yet the conclusion does not leave the mind wholly at rest: the trials of our heroine are not at an end; and, though in possession of many sources of happiness, the whole may be tainted by the inconsiderate, hasty conduct of such a husband. But Mrs. Neville's story affords no instance of sudden attachments, of improper connections, or romantic adventure. If historic truth (for we see many reasons to lead us to think this story a copy from real life), had not prevented, we could have wished Mr. Neville had been sent to sleep with his fathers; and a more suitable companion provided for the gentle, the benevolent, the affectionate Euphemia. The loss of her son, her again recovering him, and the incidents which happened during the separation, are told with great feeling, and are highly interesting. The description of the Bellenden family, of Mr. C. and of lieutenant Blood, are well drawn sketches, seemingly from real life; and the history of Mrs. Freeman, in many respects, truly interesting and pathetic. If we could have separated any part of this story from the rest with propriety and effect, we should have added it as a specimen. The account too of the family being confined in a distant house by a sudden fall of snow, in consequence of the premature commencement of winter, and in danger of famishing, with the circumstance of their relief, is not less attractive; but we cannot convey its effect by a partial extract, and we are unwilling to tell it in any but Mrs. Lennox's words. We shall therefore transcribe a specimen of the descriptive powers of our author from the voyage up Hudson's River: it must be remembered that the æra of these events is previous to the late unfortunate war in America.

[The reviewer includes the section from the novel which describes the cottage in the woods belonging to the Dutch woman and her child and the meeting between them and the travellers, pp. 220-22]

... The history of Euphemia's friend, Miss Harley, approaches more nearly to the general style of novels, but it exceeds the greater number, though it does not reach the first of the first rank. The characters, however, though drawn without any splendid traits, are sufficiently distinct, and very ably supported: indeed, in every part of these volumes, we see characters delineated with so much apparent fidelity, and preserved with such strict consistency, that we almost forget we are reading a novel. This last work of Mrs. Charlotte Lennox, if it should prove her last, will not sully her fame. If she does not shine with meridian splendor, she sets with a mild radiance, more pleasing and more attractive.

2. *The European Magazine and London Review* (August 1790): 121-22

The epistolary form of writing, when applied to the subject of Fictitious History, renders, in general, the narrative extremely languid, by delaying that quick succession of events in which the charm of romance is made at present principally to consist. In the work now before us, however, this defect is judiciously avoided by confining the correspondence between two persons only, each of whom are made to disclose a different story in such a manner as to form a kind of double plot, intricated with great art, and unravelled with an ingenuity that produces a very pleasing effect. The scenes are very correct representations of *real life*; and to those who feel domestic comfort, an important ingredient in the cup of human bliss, the incidents will be peculiarly interesting. Mr. Neville, the husband of Euphemia, is a character, the resemblance of which we have frequently seen in *the World*, but never before to our recollection in *a Novel*, and furnishes a useful lesson to the numerous progeny of novel-writers, that a discriminating attention to the variety of the species is the true School of Genius and Originality. The character of Euphemia is a model of female excellence: not that she is arrayed in that abundant perfection which distinguishes and adorns the heroines of modern romance; but, possessing a moderate portion of reason and good sense, she exercises them in the discharge of her duty, to the disappointment of adversity, the enjoyment of virtue, and the attainment of happiness. Among the traits which distinguish the character of old Harley, we now and then perceive a glimmering resemblance of Mr. Western in Tom Jones;[1] particularly in the unconquerable partiality he feels for his lovely niece; and his sudden transitions from the transports of rage and resentment to the feelings of tenderness and reconciliation.—The picturesque beauties of the province of New York, the manners and customs of its inhabitants, together with the vagrant life of the savages, are described, in the course of this correspondence, with great beauty and effect. As to the general merits of the work, we may truly say, that if it be, as it most certainly is, the duty of a Novelist "to convey instruction, to paint human life and manners, to expose the errors into which we are betrayed by our passions, to render virtue amiable, and vice odious," Mrs. Lenox has performed the important task with no inconsiderable degree of success; and although it may perhaps appear less brilliant than the former productions of her sensible and entertaining pen, to us the mild radiance of a setting sun is more agreeable than the intense heat of its meridian beams.

3. *Monthly Review*, Series 2, Volume III (September 1790): 89

We have been better pleased with Mrs. Lennox's Novel, than with many others of the same class, which have lately passed under our review; though indeed there is no prodigality of commendation in this sentence, as most of them have excited our displeasure. The language of *Euphemia* is easy, though not always accurate; the sentiments are, generally, just, though they may not entirely possess the recommendation of novelty; the incidents are

---

1 Mr. Western in *Tom Jones*: Squire Western appears in Henry Fielding's novel *The History of Tom Jones* (1749) as the loving if rather irascible father of Sophia.

frequently natural, though in some instances they are carried beyond the bounds of probability; and the characters are well preserved, though they are not drawn with any appearance of bold design or nice discrimination.—Of the personages to whom we are introduced, Euphemia deserves the chief praise, as her manners approach nearest to what is seen in common life, and her conduct is marked by fortitude and judgement. If we could admit of any agreement between the terms, *utility* and a *Novel*, it should be admitted where such characters as Euphemia are described. Indeed, the chief merit of Mrs. Lennox's book is, that it will amuse those who read it, without depressing their minds with unnecessary apprehensions, and rendering them unable to perform with cheerfulness their duties in life. To this testimony of its merit, there may, however, be found exceptions; particularly in the story of Mrs. Freeman, in which our feelings are preposterously harrassed with accumulated and improbable distress.

Whatever may be deemed imperfections in this work, it must, on the whole, be allowed a considerable degree of merit.—We always imagined, with respect to the literary abilities of this Lady, (whose productions are nearly coeval with the existence of our Review), that it was impossible for a writer endowed with so much genius, to offer any performance to the public, that would prove unworthy the perusal of readers who have any pretensions to the praise of discernment and taste;—and we are still of the same opinion.

4. *The General Magazine and Impartial Review*, IV (1790): 313-15

We heartily congratulate all who have any relish for works of imagination on the publication of a novel, which we can freely recommend, without any apprehension of injury to innocence. But, apart from the easy, familiar, and lively style in which it is written, we must apprise our readers, that there is nothing in the commencement or outset of the story either attractive or prepossessing; and such as are incapable of relishing the charms of honest simplicity, good sense, and elegant expression, may find it a difficult task to support their attention to the end of the first volume. Here, however, the business becomes sufficiently explicit to give the dullest reader a very sensible interest in the sequel.

The plan, as might have been expected from such a writer, is by no means crouded with bustle, incident, or romance. The whole is a genuine draught of nature in private life, taken, as it should seem, either by a party concerned in what is going forward, or a witness at least, and on the spot, while the facts are recent, and the impression they make strong and vivid; the writer, consequently, never deals in heroics, or has any recourse for materials to those common-place expedients, which well may be called the *stale trick of Romance*. She possesses, in a very high degree, powers which can never be at a loss, and writes from a fund of real genius, enriched by a good education, and matured by long experience and observation.

The story is indeed without any formal plot, and contains nothing more than a detail of the fortunes of two amiable young ladies, who, on the reader's first acquaintance with them, appear rather aukwardly situated. One of these, *Maria Harley*, is dependent on *Sir John Harley*, a rich uncle, who, although a worthy man, is apparently duped by a young, designing wife, to whom the niece is a kind of eye-sore, and who she endeavours to supplant and ruin in her uncle's estimation. The other, *Euphemia Lumley*, has the misfortune to lose her father while her education is yet hardly finished. What renders this calamity the greater in her case is, that he dies insolvent, while in general thought very rich. From the distress to which her mother is reduced by this sudden reverse of fortune, she is impelled, from a painful sense of duty, to marry Mr. Neville, a man neither agreeable nor affluent. The work consists of letters between these ladies, who mutually communicate whatever they deem material in their history and adventures to each other. Mrs. Neville goes with her husband, who is an officer in the army, to America; and, notwithstanding an eligible settlement offered to her in England by her amiable friend and correspondent, she has the virtue to prefer her duty in this instance also to her inclinations. Miss Harley too, by her prudent, delicate, and becoming behaviour, regains her uncle's confidence, nothwithstanding the secret machinations of an invidious aunt, who dies of the spleen, in consequence of Sir John's detecting her treacherous practices both against himself and Miss Harley.

It is by uniformly acting right under every contingency of difficulty or embarrassment, that these virtuous young ladies survive all their enemies and troubles, and are ultimately as happy as affluence, human connections, peace of mind, and a modest confidence in Providence can make them. In this placid and agreeable termination the morality of the whole consists. Every character, every action, every speech, and every occurrence in an intercourse peculiarly varied, and under circumstances often enough abundantly perplexing, have all this tendency; and whoever reads these volumes with due consideration, and is blessed with a heart susceptible of the highest instruction, will derive no trifling advantage from the perusal. There is not a word, or an incident, in any part of the performance to strengthen one bad habit, prompt one loose passion, or relax one good principle. The only lesson inculcated from the beginning to the end is expressed in no very elegant verse, as quoted at the conclusion:

Thus blessings ever wait on virtuous deeds;
And though a late, a sure reward succeeds.

The characters in this work are not numerous, but all happily drawn, and uniformly well supported. It abounds in maxims peculiarly beautiful, and the result of an intimate acquaintance with human nature, a perfect knowledge of the world, a polished taste, and an understanding happily expanded and enriched by all the stores of ancient and modern philosophy. These are more truly useful than whole circulating libraries of vapid novels. We select a few only as a specimen of the rest:

"Men of wit and ridicule have a very relaxed moral on certain occasions.
"Truth is simple and modest; and when she cannot shew herself by real effects, scorns to do it in words.
"The dignity of truth is wounded by much profession.
"The many that need, and the many that deny pity, make the bulk of mankind.
"It is ourselves we generally love in others; but where there is no resemblance, there is no foundation for partiality.
"They who blush not at their foibles, but add confidence to guilt, have no motive left to restore them to virtue.
"One friend to your virtues, is worth a hundred admirers of your person.
"The life of a good man is a continual prayer."

Most of the interesting scenes lie in America, and that romantic country is always prolific of adventure. The writer knows it well; and her information has this advantage, that it is authentic. Her language is very elegant and precise; and no author knows better how to interest, to command, to please, and to improve the human heart.

Appendix B: Marriage Tracts

1. From Mary Astell, *Some Reflections upon Marriage, Occasion'd by the Duke & Duchess of Mazarine's Case; Which is also consider'd*. London: John Nutt, 1700

[The early feminist Mary Astell (1666-1731) likens the relationship between wife and husband to that of the subject and his king, but suggests that while sometimes men rule "with an iron fist," marriages must be built upon mutual trust, respect and love. While a woman has a duty to her husband, and puts herself in a man's power, he has the duty to treat her well in return.]

... It is the hardest thing in the World for a Woman to know that a Man is not Mercenary, that he does not Act on base and ungenerous Principles, even when he is her Equal, because being absolute Master, she and all the Grants he makes her are in his Power, and there have been but too many instances of Husbands that by wheedling or threatening their Wives, by seeming Kindness or cruel Usage, have perswaded or forc'd them out of what has been settled on them.[1] So that the Woman has in truth no security but the Man's Honour and Good-nature, a security that in this present Age no Wise Person would venture much upon. A Man enters into Articles very readily before Marriage, and so he may, for he performs no more of them afterwards than he thinks fit. A Wife must never dispute with her Husband, his Reasons are now no doubt on't better than hers, whatever they were before; he is sure to perswade her out of her Agreement, and bring her, it must be suppos'd, *Willingly*, to give up what she did vainly hope to obtain, and what she thought had been made sure to her. And if she shew any Refractoriness, there are ways enough to humble her; so that by right or wrong the Husband gains his will. For Covenants between Husband and Wife, like Laws in an Arbitrary Government, are of little Force, the Will of the Sovereign is all in all....

---

1 Marriage settlements; entering into Articles: Before a woman married, her family and her prospective husband's family legally settled property upon her, and perhaps on the children of the marriage. Her prospective husband "entered into Articles" when he accepted these terms.

... [I]t is not enough to enter wisely into this State;[1] care must be taken of our Conduct afterwards. A Woman will not want being admonish'd of her Duty, the custom of the World, Oeconomy, every thing almost reminds her of it. Governors do not often suffer their Subjeccts to forget Obedience through their want of demanding it, perhaps Husbands are but too forward on this occasion, and claim their Right oftner and more Imperiously than either Discretion or good Manners will justifie, and might have both a more cheerful and constant Obedience paid them if they were not so rigorous in Reacting[2] it. For there is a mutual Stipulation, and Love, Honor and Worship, by which certainly Civility and Respect at least are meant, is as much the Woman's due, as Love, Honour and Obedience is the Man's, and being the Woman is said to be the weaker Vessel, the Man should be more careful not to grieve or offend her. Since her Reason is suppos'd to be less, and her Passions stronger than his, he should not give occasion to call that supposition into Question by his pettish outrage and needless Provocations. Since it is the *Men,* by which very Word Custom wou'd have us understand not only strength of Body, but even greatest firmness and force of Mind, he shou'd not play the *little Master* so much as to expect to be cocker'd, nor run over to that side which the Woman us'd to be rankd in; for according to the Wisdom of the *Italian, Volete? Si dice a gli ummalati: Will you? Is spoken to sick Folks.*

Indeed Subjection, according to the common Notion of it, is not over easie, none of us whether Men or Women but have so good an Opinion of our own Conduct as to believe we are fit, if not to direct others, at least to govern our selves. Nothing but a sound Understanding, and Grace the best improver of natural Reason, can correct this Opinion, truly humble us, and heartily reconcile us to Obedience. This bitter Cup therefore ought to be sweetened as much as may be, for Authority may be preserv'd and Government kept inviolable, without that nauseous Ostentation of Power which serves to no end or purpose, but to blow up the Pride and Vanity of those who have it, and to exasperate the Spirits of such as must truckle under it.

Insolence 'tis true is never the effect of Power but in weak and cowardly Spirits, who wanting true *Merit* and Judgment to support themselves in that advantage ground on which they

---

1 I.e., the married state.
2 I.e., repulsing or resisting.

stand, are ever appealing to their Authority, and making a shew of it to maintain their Vanity and Pride. A truly great Mind and such as is fit to Govern, tho' it may stand on its Right with its Equals, and modestly expect what is due to it even from its Superiors, yet it never contends with its Inferiors, nor makes use of its Superiority but to do them Good. So that considering the just Dignity of Man, his great Wisdom so conspicuous on all occasions, the goodness of his Temper and Reasonableness of all his Commands, which makes it a Woman's Interest as well as Duty to be observant and Obedient in all things, that his Prerogative is settled by an undoubted Right and the Prescription of many Ages, it cannot be suppos'd that he should make frequent and insolent Claims of an Authority so well establish'd and us'd with such moderation, nor give an impartial By-stander (cou'd such an one be found) any occasion from thence to suspect that he is inwardly conscious of the Badness of his Title; Usurpers being always most desirous of Recognitions and busie in imposing Oaths, whereas a Lawful Prince contents himself with the usual Methods and Securities.

And since Power does naturally puff up and he who finds himself exalted, seldom fails to think he *ought* to be so, it is more suitable to a Man's Wisdom and Generosity to be mindful of his great Obligations than to insist on his Rights and Prerogatives. Sweetness of Temper and an obliging Carriage are so justly due to a Wife, that a Husband who must not be thought to want either Understanding to know what is fit, nor Goodness to perform it, can't be suppos'd not to shew them. For setting aside the hazards of her Person to keep up his Name and Family, with all the Pains and Trouble that attend it, which may well be thought great enough to deserve all the respect and kindness that may be, setting this aside, tho' 'tis very considerable, a Woman has so much the disadvantage in *most*, I was about to say in *all* things, that she makes a Man the greatest Complement in the World when she condescends to take him *for Better for Worse*. She puts her self intirely in his Power, leaves all that is dear to her, her Friends and Family, to espouse his Interests and follow his Fortune, and makes it her Business and Duty to please him! What acknowledgements, what returns can he make? What Gratitude can be sufficient for such Obligations? She shews her good Opinion of him by the great Trust she reposes in him, and what a Brute must he be who betrays that Trust, or acts any way unworthy of it? Ingratitude is one of the basest Vices, and if a Man's Soul is sunk so low as to be guilty of it towards her who has so generously oblig'd him, and who so intirely depends on him, if he can treat her Disrespectfully, who has so fully justify'd her Esteem of him, she must have a stock of Vertue which he shou'd blush to discern, if she can pay him that Obedience of which he is so unworthy.

... She then who Marrys ought to lay it down for an indisputable Maxim, that her Husband must govern absolutely and intirely, and that she has nothing else to do but to Please and Obey. She must not attempt to divide his Authority, or so much as dispute it, to struggle with her Yoke will only make it gall the more, but must believe him Wise and Good and in all respects the best, at least he must be so to her. She who can't do this is in no way fit to be a Wife, she may set up for that peculiar Coronet the ancient Fathers talk'd of, but is not qualify'd to receive that great reward, which attends the eminent exercise of Humility and Self-Denial, Patience and Resignation the Duties that a Wife is call'd to.

But some refractory Woman perhaps will say how can this be? Is it possible for her to believe him Wise and Good who by a thousand Demonstrations convinces her and all the World of the contrary? Did the bare Name of Husband confer Sense on a Man, and the mere being in Authority infallibly qualifie him for Government, much might be done. But since a wise Man and a Husband are not Terms convertible, and how loath soever one is to own it, Matter of Fact won't allow us to deny that the Head many times stands in need of the Inferior's Brains to manage it, she must beg leave to be excus'd from such high thoughts of her Sovereign, and if she submits to his Power, it is not so much Reason as Necessity that compels her.

2. From William Fleetwood, *The Relative Duties of Parents and Children, Husbands and Wives, Masters and Servants*. London: Charles Harper, 1705

[While he believed that women were meant to be governed, William Fleetwood (1656-1723) does suggest in this selection that marriage is a two-way street: "good Husbands make good Wives, and good Wives good Husbands," and that in return for her "obedience and submission," a wife deserves her husband's affection and respect.]

... And thus it is too frequently with many Husbands, who are full of Dominion, morosely Imperious, and sometimes Cruel and

Tyrannical, ever remembring the Submission, Duty, Honour and Obedience, that their Wives are tied by Reason and God's Command to pay them; but seldom or never thinking of what they owe themselves to those their Wives, by the same Reason and God's Commands. St. *Paul* here makes no difference, but having said, in Verse 18. *Wives submit your selves to your own Husbands, as it is fit in the Lord*; he adds immediately in Ver. 19. in the words of the Text, *Husbands love your Wives, and be not bitter against them*. Leaving it as much a Duty on the Husbands *to love their Wives*, as on the Wives to *submit themselves to their own Husbands*;[1] and indeed it is so well and wisely ordered by God Almighty, that whosoever obeys his Commands, in discharging the Duty of his Relation, does thereby make the surest and the readiest way, to the receiving what is due to him from his Correlative. A good Prince is the most likely to find good and obedient Subjects: and so the good and careful Parents and Masters are the most likely to make or find the most obedient, diligent, and faithful Children and Servants. And dutiful obedient Children, are the most likely to secure the care and affection of Parents to them; and the most diligent and honest Servants, are the most likely to find their Masters kindest and most careful of them; so that by discharging every one his Duty, the World in general would be happy, and each particular be easie in their Station and Relation. And this is also the bottom of that common Saying, which is also true and reasonable, that good Husbands make good Wives, and good Wives good Husbands; *i.e.*, there is nothing so likely to engage one partner to perform *his* Duty, as the other's performing *his*. There is no readier way for Husbands to have good Wives, affectionate, obedient, careful and faithful, than by following the Dictates of Reason, as well as the Commands of God, *to love them, and not be bitter against them*....

Now because it is impossible where there are two Persons and two Wills, but there will be dispute, in matters of debate and doubt, which shall be uppermost and superiour, God hath decided it, as well by natural Indications, as by positive Commands, that Man shall reign and govern, and therefore Women are to be obedient and submissive. But in return for this Submission and Obedience, Man is to love his Wife, and to affect *her*, above all the World. This he is commanded by God to do; and because it is not in Man's power, to love and like, whom and

---

1   The Epistle of Paul to the Colossians, 3.18-19.

wherever he will, he is in reason oblig'd to marry no where, but
where he can love, he cannot otherwise comply with God's Commands; the reasonableness and necessity of this, I have been
trying to shew, from many great inconveniencies and grievous
mischiefs that are likely, and do usually arise from marrying otherwise, upon mere Worldly Considerations. Not, that many other
things besides affection to the Person, are not to be well considered and sought after, for they are undoubtedly, and Men
without them never will or can be happy, especially Religious
education, virtuous and discreet Behaviour, and other good
Qualities, as well as Birth, and Fortune; but that all other Considerations are of little use to make a Marriage happy, where
affection to the Person is found wanting, all advantages imaginable will not make a Woman easie, where the affection of the Heart
is wanting; and since the Wife is to be made as happy as she can
by Marriage, a Husband cannot answer it to God, nor her, nor to
himself, that marries with aversion and dislike.

And it is yet more reasonable, that when the Men *are* Married,
they should still continue on their love; and in order to that,
should take all courses to confirm and strengthen their Affection,
and avoid all manner of occasions that may weaken and decay it.
Because without this personal love, they will be in great danger
of not continuing true and faithful to their Vows; and of not
making such Provision for them as is fit and reasonable, which
are the other particulars in which the love of Husbands is requir'd
to shew it self....

3. **From George Booth, Earl of Warrington,** *Considera-*
   tions upon the Institution of Marriage. **London: John**
   Whiston, 1739

[Warrington felt that marriages, as promises made before men,
not to God, and between equals should be dissolvable when necessary—if not by divorce, then by separation.]

... "For there is no Relation in the World, but there is a reciprocal Duty obliging each Party: there is no such thing as one
Person's requiring Love, Respect, Honour, Service or Obedience
from another, without being at the same Time obliged to do him
some good Turn for it, or for having done it already. No one can
require any thing from another as a Duty, to whom he does not
also *owe* something by way of Duty; for in all Relations, whether
natural or civil, each Party is mutually, tho' differently bound to

each other; and all the several Duties of Relations of all Sorts (none in the World excepted, no not that between the *Great Creator* and his *Creature*) do mutually infer each other, and are therefore due, and paid for the Sake of each other."[1]

... Now, among such relative Duties as must be paid by *one* Party, to render the *other* Party bound to those on his Part, we apprehend are the Duties mutually owing between *Husband* and *Wife*. And although it may perhaps be urged, that by Marriage we are laid under a *Sacred Vow*, from which *God* only can release us, and that it may be startling and surprizing to hear any Thing contradictory to so generally received an Acceptation; yet needs it not be much scrupled to enquire a little, whether the *Marriage Contract* be, strictly speaking, properly a *Vow* or not, when back'd by so great an Authority as Bishop *Sanderson*,[2] who [suggests] ... that Marriage can be a *Promise* or Obligation to *Man only*, and not to *God*. For how Solemnly soever God may be called into it, and the Parties so mutually engaging to each other, do set themselves in the Presence of God, yet he is called in only as a *Witness*, nor can with any Propriety of Speech, be said to be a *Party* in such Contract; and consequently, how sacred soever such Contract ought to be, it is still but a *Promise* only, and not a *Vow* in the strict Sense of that Word, and therefore releaseable by the *Parties* to such Promise.

... So, we may believe, that our Blessed Lord, in congruity with the Manner of giving *that* Law, did, in the giving of *his own* Laws, leave a great deal unsaid, which from the purport of what he had spoken, our own Reason would naturally supply. And therefore, though we should admit, that *only* Adultery and Desertion are *expressly* declared to be a Dissolution of the Bond of Marriage, or a lawful Cause for Separation; yet we may reasonably believe, that *every* Thing which totally frustrates *any* of the ends of Marriage, is likewise a just Cause for Separation; because it is to be presumed, that the Reason why our Saviour intended those *two Crimes* should dissolve the Contract, was, because *some* of the Ends of Marriage were by them frustrated....

---

1 Warrington is quoting William Fleetwood, *Relative Duties* (1705).
2 Bishop Robert Sanderson, seventeenth-century bishop of Lincoln, England who published *Some Short Tracts or Cases of Conscience* (1678).

4. From Philogamus, *The Present State of Matrimony: Or, The Real Causes of Conjugal Infidelity and Unhappy Marriages*. London: John Hawkins, 1739

[This pseudonymous essayist wisely suggests that people should be good friends before they marry, and that, once married, husbands should not tyrannize their wives. The essay's message is ultimately a conservative one in that it suggests that women's liberty should be curtailed if they are to remain virtuous: indeed, according to the author, virtuous women will concur with their husbands in reducing their liberty as they will recognize this is best for their marriages and therefore the well-being of the nation.]

... But to return to the more immediate Causes of unhappy Marriages, and conjugal Infidelities, so frequent of late Years: one of the Principal is that preposterous, unequal, and sometimes unnatural Way of matching our young People, very often without taking the least Care in examining and comparing the different Ages, Tempers, and Constitutions, of the Parties. Money and sordid Views are generally the prime Movers, unless some mad and foolish Passion intervenes, which when over, either turns to Hatred or Repentance, or both. However, Money is the prevailing Charm in both Sexes: neither difference of Birth, Years, Persuasion, Education, Tempers, or Constitutions, will have any Weight, if once the Balance is over-poised with Gold....

But to put our modern marriages in a more obvious Contrast, according to what is commonly the Case; particularly among People above the middle Rank; for the middling people are certainly more happy in the married State, than Persons of a more elevated Dignity; Suppose the Parents and Parties are equally considerable, if Portions and Jointures[1] will but tally together, what else is required? Perhaps a sweet good-natured Creature is tied to a Brute, scarce a Degree above a Savage; a gay, sprightly Temper, to a dark, gloomy, sulky Mortal, who shall take every innocent Freedom for a Step towards Cuckoldom; a Person of fine Sense, and distinguishing Taste, to a flat, lumpish Piece, that has nothing but Gold and Varnish to set it off; a fresh, hale, blooming Creature, capable of producing Heroes, to a poor,

---

1 I.e., if a woman's dowry (that which she brings to a marriage) is equal to the jointure or estate she will be left at her husband's death.

puling, worn-out Wretch, who, if by the Imputation of Insufficiency, thinks he is qualified for the Title of a Husband. In short, we see Beauty coupled to Deformity, Youth to Age, Innocency to Debauchery, Health to Diseases and Rottenness; that we may as well join Fire and Water, War and Peace, and all the Contraries in Nature, and expect a reasonable Result from them, as expect any solid Happiness in innumerable modern Marriages; tho' there should be a sort of Equality, as to Birth, Rank, Fortune, &c. without some Equality in their Years, Tempers, Constitutions, and the like. But suppose the young Couple, on a proper Acquaintance with each other's Temper, might be joined together without a perfect Equality in all Circumstances, where a prudent Person of either Side, for valuable Considerations, might render that State tolerable: but what do we do to settle them in such an Acquaintance? Or to establish a Liking of one another, before they put on the Yoke?[1] Why, if the Parents and Friends are agreed about the Fortune, the Parties, almost unknown to one another, are made to join their Hands; supposing that Love, or at least a prudent Dissimulation of it, will come after; a Supposition so directly against Reason and Experience, that, for one Time it happens, it has a thousand Times the contrary Effect. It is a much more probable Supposition, marry them without Love, and you are almost sure a Dislike, or perhaps Hatred, will follow: this is a more natural Supposition, than marry them first, and Love will come after.

It cannot be denied but, with all our Care, Marriage is a sort of a Lottery; nor can all the Precautions in the World insure its certain Happiness. Vast Difficulties occur in every Supposition; even Equality of Years, Humours, &c. will not always do. If they are both young and giddy, they will play together like Children, and fall out like Children; very often such Childrens' Quarrels are improved, with their Age, to a more steady Hatred: in that Case, what is not to be feared on either Side? The surest Way of all, is to have their Hearts engaged first, not by a foolish Passion, but by prudent Trials, if possible; particularly, let the Woman have the greatest Balance in the Choice. A Man may be a prudent, kind Husband, without the Fondness of Passion; but the Woman can hardly dissemble Love, unless for other Ends. If she takes a Dislike to him in her Heart, it must be an heroical Virtue, that will keep her within Bounds, which our modern Education gives

---

1 I.e., of marriage.

us very little Reason to expect; at least, real Happiness is not to be hoped for in such Matches; but at the best, Patience and Suffering, nay sometimes a living Martyrdom, which must be vastly agreeable to Parents, to think that they have made a Martyr of their Daughter....

Another of these Causes,[1] is the wrong Way of setting out; and the imprudent Conduct of the Parties themselves, on the Entrance of a State for Life, where they are tied, past Redemption, till Death, or something, almost worse, parts them. This very Thought, if they are capable of any, ought to give them the utmost Caution, how they begin; not to create the least Uneasiness in one another, at a Juncture where they are to lay the Foundation of a lasting Peace, instead of beginning an endless War. In which I shall be so impartial, as to impute the first Cause of Uneasiness to the Man's Fault, more than the Woman's; bating some extraordinary Cases, and Exorbitances, which could not be foreseen; or, if foreseen, might have been avoided, before he put Matters to the Risk. We will suppose the young Couple to be joined with such prudent Care, of the Parents, or themselves, or both, as to have escaped most of the former Inconveniences; they had been well and virtuously educated; of Equality of Years, Birth, Fortune, Humour, Inclination, &c. seemingly happy in one another, and easy in every Respect, as far as Infirmities of human Life will permit; yet, in a few Years, you see nothing but Jars, Dislikes, and at last mutual Hatred instead of mutual Love; with more dismal Consequences, which I leave to the Reader's Imagination. Without doubt, if we consider these Misfortunes, in their first Original, we shall see Faults on both Sides; such as want of sufficient Instruction in the reciprocal Duties incumbent on both, and proper Endeavours to comply with them; want of Reflection, too common with the unthinking giddiness of Youth; a false, or at least too great an Idea of Happiness, without Allay, which can never be found in this mortal State; want of complying with each other's Humours, which, it is impossible should be alike in any two Persons in the World, and will always require a great many mutual Forbearances and Allowances in Persons of the best Temper. To which may be added, too great an Opinion of their Love for each other; which will make them take Things amiss, as if unkindly done by so dear a Friend, which they would not mind from an indifferent Person. These Faults, or Imperfec-

---

1 I.e., of bad marriages.

tions, will, I fear, be found in most Marriages, and belong to both Sides, rendering each Side blameable, that does not timely guard against them; the best Way, in some of these Cases, is to take no Notice of them; or at least it must be done in earnest. There are other Causes of Dislike, which are more particular; nor can well be specified, or perhaps seen, but by the Parties themselves. However, on the whole, they require a great deal of Prudence, to prevent, moderate, or overlook, them. But, still I am inclined to think, that the first real Cause of Rupture proceeds from the Man, excepting some exotick and extravagant Tempers, as nothing can manage.

The first Cause of Dislike given to the Woman from the Man (supposing Essentials) is his putting on the Husband too soon; and exerting his Authority over a young Creature, who was made to believe, she was to be Mistress of his Heart, and should always be treated with the most endearing Tenderness. It is a hard Thing for human Nature to pass from one Extreme to another, all at once; from a State of Empire and Adoration to a State of Obedience and Subjection. All Women, before they are married, are accustomed to be flattered from their Infancy; are courted, attended, treated, caressed, and almost adored, by their Lovers, especially here in *England*; where we pay the greatest Deference to the Ladies of any Place in the World before Marriage, and the least after, of any People, who allow Women to be born free, as well as Men. Yesterday she was assured by her Lover, that his Life depended on her's; what she said or did, was a Law; one kind Look filled him with Raptures; an unkind one threw him into Despair: But as soon as the Parson has pronounced the fatal Words, he puts on the Lord and Master, and in a short Time lets her see, that she must obey. The Bird is lured into the Cage, where it may beat itself against the Sides, till it is forced to live in Thrall, or knock its Brains out. This must be extremely shocking, if we allow Women capable of any Reflexion; and will infallibly lessen all interior Love for her Tyrant, if not intirely sour her Temper; which cannot fail to have very ill Consequences; at the best great Uneasinesses must follow, when the most endearing Love is changed into Awe and Fear. This is so far from being an Exaggeration, that I am sure I have known some of the finest Women in the World reduced to a worse Condition, than scarce having an easy Moment, not very long after the Marriage Ceremonies were intirely over; and have seen the Husband put on the Tyrant, before the Wedding Night-Cap has been worn out. Women are justly called the tender Sex; their Nature, generally speaking, leads them that way, and requires to be treated with Tenderness. Nor is it possible to preserve their Friendship without it. When she sees the Reverse of so many Vows and Protestations, she will believe her ardent Lover was a false Dissembler; and he will come well off, if she only dissembles with him in Requital. However, the Husband's Tenderness ought still to be so contrived, as to retain a just Decorum of Superiority, that they may not think they can command, and subvert the Order of Obedience. They are made to be governed, not to govern: but you will never bring them to a just Sense of this Duty, by a rough, rude, and shocking Behaviour ... A Husband therefore, who puts on a morose domineering Temper over his Rib, and does not maintain his Prerogative by the softest Degrees imaginable, must not wonder, if she contrives to be even with him in her Turn, some Way or other; at first perhaps covertly; but at last openly in the Face of the World. It is then the Business of every Husband, who would seek domestick Content, and Happiness, (and who would marry without that View?) to take some Pains to preserve Love, as well as obtain it: which, as was said, he will never do by a rude and shocking Behaviour....

5. From Sarah Pennington, *An Unfortunate Mother's Advice to Her Absent Daughters: in a Letter to Miss Pennington*. London: S. Chandler, 1761

[Lady Pennington wrote this treatise on how to choose a husband in the form of a letter to her eldest daughter as she entered adulthood and the marriage market. Having been accused by her husband of being morally unfit to parent, and separated from her children, her only way of communicating with her children was through this public forum. In her practical comments on marriage, she speaks from bitter experience.]

... Be slow in contracting Friendship, and invariably constant in maintaining it: expect not many Friends, but think yourself happy, if, through Life, you meet with one or Two who deserve that Name, and have all the Requisites for the valuable Relation. This may justly be deemed the highest Blessing of Mortality; uninterrupted Health has the general Voice; but, in my Opinion, such a Friend as much deserves the Preference, as the mental Pleasures, both in Nature and Degree, exceed the Corporeal: the Weaknesses, the Pains of the Body may be inexpressibly alleviated by the Conversation of a Person, by Affection endeared, by

Reason approved; whose tender Sympathy partakes your Afflictions, and shares your Enjoyments; who is steady in the Correction, but mild in the Reproof of your Faults; like a guardian Angel, ever watchful to warn you of unforseen Danger, and by timely Admonitions prevent the Mistakes incident to human Frailty, and Self-partiality. This is the true Office of Friendship; with such a Friend, no state of Life can be absolutely unhappy; but destitute of some such Connection, Heaven has so formed our Natures for this intimate Society, that, amidst the Affluence of Fortune, and the Flow of uninterrupted Health, there will be an aking void in the solitary Breast, that can never know a Plentitude of Happiness. Should the Supreme Disposer of all Events bestow on you this superlative Gift, to such a Friend let your Heart be ever unreservedly open; conceal no secret Thought, disguise no latent Weakness, but bare your Bosom to the faithful Probe of honest Friendship, and shrink not, if it smart beneath the Touch; nor with tenacious Pride dislike the Person that freely dares condemn some favorite Foible; but, ever open to Conviction, hear with Attention, and receive with Gratitude the kind Reproof that flows from Tenderness; when sensible of a Fault, be ingenuous in the Confession, sincere and steady in the Correction of it.

Happy is her Lot, who in an Husband finds this invaluable Friend! yet so great is the Hazard, so disproportioned the Chances, that I could almost wish the dangerous Die was never to be thrown for any of you! ...

... The chief Point to be regarded in the Choice of a Companion for Life, is a real virtuous Principle, an unaffected, Goodness of Heart; without this you will be continually shocked by Indecency, and pained by Impiety. So numerous have been the unhappy Victims to the ridiculous Opinion, that a reformed Libertine makes the best Husband that, did not Experience daily evince the contrary, one would believe it impossible for a Girl, who has a tolerable Degree of common Understanding, to be made the Dupe of so erroneous a position, that has not the least Shadow of Reason for its Foundation, and which a small Share of Observation will prove to be false in Fact. A Man who has been long conversant with the worst Sort of Women, is very apt to contract a bad Opinion of, and a Contempt for the Sex in general; incapable of esteeming any, he is suspicious of all; jealous without Cause, angry without Provocation, and his own disturbed Imagination is a continual Source of ill Humour; to this is frequently joined a bad Habit of Body, the natural Consequence of an irregular Life, which gives an additional Sourness to the Temper. What rational Prospect of Happiness can there be with such a Companion? ...

... Be it your Care to find that Virtue in a Lover, which you must never hope to form in an Husband. Good Sense and good Nature are almost equally requisite; if the former is wanting, it will be next to impossible for you to esteem the Person of whose Behaviour you may have Cause to be ashamed; (and mutual Esteem is as necessary to Happiness in the married State, as mutual Affection); without the latter, every Day will bring with it some fresh Cause of Vexation; 'till repeated Quarrels produce a Coldness, that will settle into an irreconcilable Aversion, and you not only become each other's Torment, but the Object of Contempt to your Family and Acquaintance.

... Never be prevailed with, my Dear, to give your Hand to a Person defective in these material Points; secure of Virtue, good Nature, and Understanding, in an husband, you may be secure of Happiness; without the two former it is unattainable, without the latter, in a tolerable Degree, it must be very imperfect....

... Here should this Subject end, were it not more than possible for you, after all that has been urged, to be led by some inferior Motive, to the Neglect of the primary Caution; and either from an Opinion too hastily entertained, an unaccountable Partiality, or the powerful Prevalence of Perswasion, be unfortunately induced to give your Hand, where a bad Heart, and a morose Temper, concealed by a well practiced Dissimulation, may render every flattering Hope of Happiness abortive.... Most sincerely do I pray this may never be your Lot! And hope your prudent Circumspection will be sufficient to guard you from the Danger: but the bare Possibility of such an Event, makes it not unnecessary to lay down a few Rules, for the maintaining some Degree of Ease, under the Deprivation of Happiness. This is by far the most difficult Part of my present Undertaking; it is hard to advise here, and still harder to practice the Advice: the Subject also is too extensive to be minutely treated within the Compass of a Letter, which must confine me to the most material Points only; in these, shall give you the best Directions in my Power, ardently wishing you may never have Occasion to make use of them.

... Should the painful Task of dealing with a morose tyrannical Temper be assigned you, there is little more to be recommended than a patient Submission to an Evil which admits not of a Remedy. Ill Nature is increased, Obstinacy confirmed by Opposition; the less such a Temper is contradicted, the more supportable will it be to those who are under its baneful Influence. When all Endeavours to please are ineffectual, and a Man seems determined to find Fault with every Thing, as if his chief Pleasure consisted in tormenting those about him, it requires a more than common Degree of Patience, and Resolution, to forbear uttering those Reproaches which such a Behaviour may be justly allowed to deserve; yet it is absolutely necessary to the maintaining any tolerable Degree of Ease, not only to refrain all Expressions of Resentment, but even those disdainful Looks which are apt to accompany a contemptuous silence, both equally tending to encrease the Malady. This diabolical Delight in giving Pain, is most unwearied in the Search of Matter for its Gratifications, and can either find, or unaccountably form it in almost all the Occurrences of Life; but, when suffered unobstructed unregarded to run its malicious Course, will quickly vent its blunted Arrows, and die of Disappointment; whilst all Endeavours to appease, all Complaints of Unkindness, sharpens against yourself the Weapon's Edge, and by proving your Sensibility of the Wound, gives the wished Satisfaction to him who inflicts it. Prudence here directs more than ordinary Circumspection; that every Part of your Behaviour may be as blameless as possible, even to the abstaining from the least Appearance of Evil; and after having, to the utmost of your Power, strove to merit Approbation, expect not to meet with it; by this Means you will escape the Mortification of being disappointed, which, often repeated, is apt to give a gloomy Sourness to the Temper incompatible with any Degree of Contentment: you must also learn to be satisfied with the Consciousness of acting Right, according to your best Ability, and look with an unconcerned Indifference on the Reception every successless Attempt to please may meet with.

This, it must be owned, is a hard Lesson of Philosophy; it requires no less than an absolute Command over the Passions; but let it be remembered, that such a Command, will itself more amply recompence every Difficulty, every Pain the obtaining it may cost; besides, 'tis, I believe, the only Way to preserve any Tranquility of Mind under so disagreeable a Connection.

6. From Priscilla Wakefield, *Reflections on the Present Condition of the Female Sex*. London: J. Johnson and Darton and Harvey, 1798

[Priscilla Wakefield (1751-1832) laments that modern educational practices were not designed to produce a woman who was prepared to be her husband's helpmate and inspiration; but she credits wives with great power over their husbands', because in their virtuous behavior lies their husbands' happiness, and their own.]

... A happy marriage may be estimated among the rarest felicities of human life; but it may be doubted, whether the means used to accomplish it are adequate to the purpose.... It is not then sufficient, that a girl be qualified to excite admiration; her own happiness, and that of the man to whom she devotes the remainder of her days, depend upon her possession of those virtues, which alone can preserve lasting esteem and confidence.

The offices of a wife are very different from those of the mere pageant of a ball-room; and as their nature is more exalted, the talents they require are of a more noble kind: something far beyond the elegant trifler is wanted in a companion for life. A young woman is very ill-adapted to enter into the most solemn of social contracts, who is not prepared, by her education, to become the participator of her husband's cares, the consoler of his sorrow, his stimulator to every praise-worthy undertaking, his partner in the labours and vicissitudes of life, the faithful and oeconomical manager of his affairs, the judicious superintendent of his family, the wise and affectionate mother of his children, the preserver of his honour, his chief counsellor, and, to sum up all, the chosen friend of his bosom. If a modern female education be not calculated to produce these effects, as few surely will judge it to be, who reflect upon its tendency, it is incompetent to that very purpose, which is confessedly its main object, and must therefore be deemed imperfect, and require reformation....

Appendix C: Travel Narratives, Histories of North America, and the Picturesque

1. From Sarah Knight, *The Private Journal of a Journey from Boston to New York, in the Year 1704.* Albany: Frank Little, 1865

[Sarah Kemble Knight (1666-1727) was born in Boston and lived much of her married life in that city. In 1704 she took a business trip to New York on horseback, unaccompanied except for a guide (when she could find one), and in her diary recorded the progress of that journey. In the selection below she reveals she is a savvy traveler, handling herself well with the men and women whom she meets along the way. She is also observant of the variety of people whom she encounters, their customs, their economic situations as compared to her own, her cultural distance from them—this is especially true of the aboriginal peoples she encounters. Knight's journal was edited by Theodore Dwight and published in 1825.]

Tuesday, October ye third, about 8 in the morning. [1704]

... From hence we proceeded (about ten forenoon) through the Naragansett country, pretty Leisurely; and about one afternoon come to Paukataug River, wch was about two hundred paces over, and now very high, and no way over to to'ther side but this. I darid not venture to Ride thro, my courage at best in such cases but small, And now at the Lowest Ebb, by reason of my weary, very weary, hungry and uneasy Circumstances. So takeing leave of my company, tho' with no little Reluctance, that I could not proceed wth them on my Jorny, Stop at a little cottage Just by the River, to wait the Waters falling, wch the old man that lived there said would be in a little time, and he would conduct me safe over. This little Hutt was one of the wretchedest I ever saw a habitation for human creatures. It was suported with shores enclosed with Clapbords, laid on Lengthways, and so much asunder, that the Light come throu' every where; the doore tyed on wth a cord in ye place of hinges; The floor the bear earth; no windows but such as the thin covering afforded, nor any furniture but a Bedd wth a glass Bottle hanging at ye head on't; an earthan cupp, a small pewter Bason, A Bord wth sticks to stand on, instead of a table, and a block or two in ye corner instead of chairs. The family were the old man, his wife and two Children; all and every part being the picture of poverty. Notwithstanding both the Hutt and its Inhabitance were very clean and tydee: to the crossing the Old Proverb, that bare walls make giddy hows-wifes.

I Blest myselfe that I was not one of this misserable crew; and the Impressions their wretchedness formed in me caused mee on ye very Spott to say:

> Tho' Ill at ease, A stranger and alone,
> All my fatigu's shall not extort a grone.
> These Indigents have hunger with their ease;
> Their best is wors behalfe than my disease.
> Their Misirable hutt wch Heat and Cold
> Alternately without Repulse do hold;
> Their Lodgings thyn and hard, their Indian fare,
> Their mean Apparel which the wretches wear,
> And their ten thousand ills wch can't be told,
> Makes nature er'e 'tis midle age'd look old.
> When I reflect, my late fatigues do seem
> Only a notion or forgotten Dreem.

I had scarce done thinking, when an Indian-like Animal come to the door, on a creature very much like himselfe, in mien and feature, as well as Ragged cloathing; and having 'litt, makes an Awkerd Scratch wth his Indian shoo, and a Nodd, sitts on ye block, fumbles out his black Junk, dipps it in ye Ashes, and presents it piping hott to his muscheeto's, and fell to sucking like a calf, without speaking, for near a quarter of an hower. At length the old man said how do's Sarah do? who I understood was the wretches wife and Daughter to ye old man: he Replyed—as well as can be expected, &c. So I remembred the old say, and suposed I knew Sarah's case. Butt hee being, as I understood, going over the River, as ugly as hee was, I was glad to ask him to show me ye way to Saxtons, at Stoningtown; wch he promising, I ventur'd over wth the old man's assistance; who having rewarded to content, with my Tattertailed guide, I Ridd on very slowly thro' Stoningtown, where the Rode was very Stony and uneven.[1]

---

1 After leaving Pawcatuck river, Madam Knight evidently took the old country road, leading over the hills through the central part of Stonington to the head of Mystic river.—Letter of Miss Caulkins, June 1865 [Editor's note].

I asked the fellow, as we went, divers questions of the place and way, &c. I being arrived at my country Saxtons,[1] at Stonington, was very well accommodated both as to victuals and Lodging, the only Good of both I had found since my setting out....

About two a clock afternoon we arrived at New Haven, where I was received with all Posible Respects and civility.... There are every where in the Town as I passed, a Number of Indians the Natives of the Country, and are the most salvage of all the salvages of that kind that I had ever Seen: little or no care taken (as I heard upon enquiry) to make them otherwise. They have in some places Landes of theire owne, and Govern'd by Law's of their own making;—they marry many wives and at pleasure put them away, and on the ye least dislike or fickle humor, on either side, saying *stand away* to one another is a sufficient Divorce. And indeed those uncomely *Stand aways* are too much in Vougue among the English in this (Indulgent Colony) as their Records plentifully prove, and that on very trivial matters, of which some have been told me, but are not proper to be Related by a Female pen, tho some of that foolish sex have had too large a share in the story.[2]

If the natives committ any crime on their own precints among themselves, ye English takes no Cognezens of. But if on the English ground, they are punishable by our Laws. They mourn for their Dead by blacking their faces, and cutting their hair, after an Awkerd and frightfull manner; But can't bear You should mention the names of their dead Relations to them: they trade most for Rum, for wch they^d hazzard their very lives; and the English fit them Generally as well, by seasoning it plentifully with water....

The Cittie of New York is a pleasant well compacted place, situated on a Commodius River wch is a fine harbour for shipping. The Buildings Brick Generaly, very stately and high, though not altogether like ours in Boston. The Bricks in some of the Houses are of divers Coullers and laid in Checkers, being glazed look very agreeable. The inside of them are neat to admiration, the

---

1 Capt. Joseph Saxton, who died in 1715, lived some two or three miles east of Mystic. He is described in one document as formerly of Boston. "My Country" undoubtedly means "my countryman" and may indicate that they were both from Boston.—*Ibid.* [Editor's note].

2 This facility for obtaining divorce may have arisen from the degradation of marriage to a mere civil contract entered into before a magistrate. It was certainly in striking contrast with the strictness which could lead a grand jury to present a young man and woman "for sitting together on the Lord's day under an apple tree...." [Editor's note].

wooden work, for only the walls are plasterd, and the Sumers and Gist[1] are plained and kept very white scowr'd as so is all the partitions if made of Bords. The fire places have no Jambs (as ours have). But the Backs run flush with the walls, and the Hearth is of Tyles and is as farr out into the Room at the ends as before the fire, wch is Generally Five foot in the Low'r rooms, and the piece over where the mantle tree should be is made as ours with Joyners work, and as I supose is fasten'd to iron rodds inside. The House where the Vendue was, had Chimney Corners like ours, and they and the hearths were laid wth the finest tile that I ever see, and the stair cases laid all with white tile which is ever clean,[2] and so are the walls of the Kitchen wch had a Brick floor. They were making Great preparations to Receive their Govenor, Lord Cornbury from the Jerseys, and for that End raised the militia to Gard him on shore to the fort.[3]

They are Generaly of the Church of England and have a New England Gentleman[4] for their minister, and a very fine church set out with all Customary requsites. There are also a Dutch[5] and Divers Conventicles as they call them, viz. Baptist,[6] Quakers,[7]

---

1 Summers and joist. The summer, a word not now in very common use, was a central beam supporting the joist; such as is now sometimes called the *bearing-beam* [Editor's note].

2 The tiles were set into the wall; forming, as it were, a continuous border, or row, of the width of one tile (or perhaps sometimes of more), close to the upper line of the staircase. The Coeymans house, standing on the bank of the Hudson, just north of the village of Coeymans, still shows most of these peculiarities of buildings mentioned by Madam Knight:—the staircase laid with tiles; no plaster except on the walls; and heavy floor-timbers, strengthened at the ends by solid knees, planed and "kept very white scoured" [Editor's note].

3 On the block between Bowling Green, Whitehall, Bridge and State streets.—Valentine's *History of New York*, 28 [Editor's note].

4 William Vesey, previously "a dissenting preacher on Long Island. He had received his education in Harvard under that rigid Independent, Increase Mather, and was sent from thence by him to confirm the minds of those who had removed for their convenience from New England to this Province" [Editor's note].

5 The Reformed Dutch Church built in 1693 in what is now Exchange Place.—Greenleaf's *History of N.Y. Churches*, II [Editor's note].

6 Greenleaf however gives 1799 as the first Baptist preaching; that of Wickenden—*Documentary History of New York*, III, 480 [Editor's note].

7 The first Friends' Meeting House, a small frame building, standing on Little Green Street, is said to have been erected in 1696 or 1703.— *Greenleaf*, 116 [Editor's note].

&c. They are not strict in keeping the Sabbath as in Boston and other places where I had bin, But seem to deal with great exactness as farr as I see or Deall with. They are sociable to one another and Curteos and Civill to strangers and fare well in their houses. The English go very fasheonable in their dress. But the Dutch, especially the middling sort, differ from our women, in their habitt go loose, wear French muches wch are like a Capp and a head band in one, leaving their ears bare, which are sett out wth Jewells of a large size and many in number. And their fingers hoop't with Rings, some with large stones in them of many Coullers as were their pendants in their ears, which You should see very old women wear as well as Young.

They have Vendues very frequently and make their Earnings very well by them, for they treat with good Liquor Liberally, and the Customers Drink as Liberally and Generally pay for't as well, by paying for that which they Bidd up Briskly for, after the sack has gone plentifully about, tho' sometimes good penny worths are got there. Their Diversions in the Winter is Riding Sleys about three or four Miles out of Town, where they have Houses of entertainment at a place called the Bowery,[1] and some go to friends' Houses who handsomely treat them. Mr. Burroughs carry'd his spouse and Daughter and myself out to one Madame Dowes, a Gentlewoman that lived at a farm House, who gave us a handsome Entertainment of five or six Dishes and choice Beer and metheglin, Cyder, &c. all which she said was the produce of her farm. I believe we mett 50 or 60 slays that day—they fly with great swiftness and some are so furious that they'le turn out of the path for none except a Loaden Cart. Nor do they spare for any diversion the place affords, and sociable to a degree, they'r Tables being as free to their Naybours as to themselves.

2. **From Priscilla Wakefield, *Excursions in North America, Described in Letters from a Gentleman and His Young Companion, to Their Friends in England*. 2nd ed. London: Darton, Harvey, and Darton, 1810**

[Priscilla Wakefield (1751-1832) was born in England to a Quaker family. She wrote widely on educational issues, as well as

---

1   "A small tavern stood on the banks of the Harlem river. This tavern was the occasional point of excursion for riding parties from the City and was known as the 'Wedding place.' One or two small taverns were on the road between the town and the Bowery."—Valentine's *History of New York*, 69 [Editor's note].

writing several travel narratives, of which this epistolary novel is one. In the selection below, she presents a sympathetic view of the American aboriginal peoples through the peace that came after the Revolutionary War; she paints a picture of a people who remained firm in their desire to build confederacies with other people, despite the betrayals they had experienced. This work was first published in 1806 by Darton and Harvey.]

Letter XXIX.
Arthur Middleton to Edwin.

Albany.

My Dear Boy,

...The rest of the road to Albany lies in the midst of a mountainous district, but lately brought under the plough. We took up our quarters in this city for a week or ten days: it is full of Dutchmen and their descendants, and the appearance of the buildings so much like those in Holland; that I could have fancied myself in a Dutch town. It is distant from New York one hundred and sixty miles; has an extensive trade, and a good harbour. In the old part of the town the streets are narrow, and the houses ugly; being built with the gable end towards the street, the pyramidal part rising in steps, and terminating with large iron weather-cocks, in the form of men or animals: but the modern buildings are handsome, and the street broad. It is also well paved and lighted. Here are several places for worship, belonging to different sects; the most remarkable is the Dutch Lutheran church, a Gothic structure of singular appearance. I was much entertained with the manufactures of glass for windows and bottles, near the town; as well as with a set of mills for preparing tobacco, mustard, starch, and cocoa, worked by curious water machinery. A few years ago the chief of the inhabitants were of Dutch origin, but the advantages for commerce are so great, that strangers from all quarters have settled here. The trade is principally carried on with the produce of the Mohawk country, and reaches eastward as far as agriculture and cultivated lands extend. The exports mostly consist in timber and lumber of every sort, pot and pearl ashes, grain, and manufactured goods; which are brought hither in winter on sledges, and sent by the merchants to New York, whence they are frequently exported to Europe. Getting money is the grand object at Albany, and business the delight of most of the people; yet a few of the Dutch Dons have found leisure to entertain us with great civility. Their hospitality, and our acquaintance with an Indian Chief, have detained us here some time...

Letter XXX.
Mr. Henry Franklin to his Brother.

Albany.

Dear Brother,

This place is much resorted to by the Indians; and as I am particularly desirous of making acquaintance with them, wherever they cross my path, that I may gain a thorough knowledge of their character, I have lengthened my stay, and have been well recompensed by an introduction to Kayashota, a chief of the Mohawks, who has had an European education, and to great natural talents adds the most amiable manners. He has been with me every day, and has given me some curious particulars concerning the Six Nations, which inhabit the neighbourhood of the Great Lakes. He feels a patriotic warmth for the welfare of the Indians in general, and his own nation in particular; and sometimes speaks rather indignantly of the encroachments and arts, too often used by the European settlers, to diminish the territories of these, the native possessors of the soil. He loves to maintain the glory of the warlike achievements of the Indian heroes; and has communicated to me some interesting details of the war between these people and the Americans, which, though it will form a little volume, I shall transcribe for your amusement, believing it will be acceptable to you, from its novelty, and authenticity of facts very little known, related in the true Indian style, though in an English dress.

As I do not desire to increase the bulk of this packet, I shall introduce you immediately to my Indian friend, who, with his pipe in his hand, addressed me nearly as follows.

★ ★ ★ ★ ★

"The Six Nations form a confederacy, or federal union, without either having any superiority over the others. This league consists of the Mohawks, the Oneidas, the Onodagas, the Cayugas, the Senecas, and the Tuscaroras. Each of these nations is again divided into three tribes, or families, who are distinguished by different arms, or ensigns. The Tortoise, the Bear, and the Wolf, are the tokens put to all treaties by our chiefs, who maintain their authority by honour or shame, having no other restraint over the people."

... To my enquiry, What effects their intercourse with Europeans had had on their manners, he gravely replied: "The circumstances in which the American war placed the Indian confederacy, has injured their simplicity, and frequently so much changed their mode of life, as to oblige them to depend on the British forts for a supply of provision; their corn fields having been destroyed, and game being there too scarce to depend wholly on the chace. They were detained in the neighbourhood of Niagara, to assist us in its defence, and often employed in incursions on the American frontier. The intervals were too frequently spent in licentious dancing and drinking; vices to which in similar circumstances, the most polished nations are prone. The men neglected their hunting, and were fed and clothed as a reward for their warlike achievements; but there being no regular system in bestowing these donations, it often happened that the boldest fared the best, and that the gifts which were intended to be the recompence of bravery and merit, served only to stifle virtue and encourage vice. Nor did the decorum and industry of the female sex suffer less."

"Since that unhappy period, these irregularities are greatly vanished. The men have resumed the chace; and many of them are employed in the labours of the corn field. They practice the arts of building and fencing. Their cattle and horses have greatly increased, and numbers use the plough as well as the hoe, in the cultivation of the land."

... "Previously to the American war, the yellow fever had made great havock amongst the Mohawks and other tribes; so that, at its commencement, but few of the old warriors remained."

"The Mohawks, in the dispute between the mother country and the colonies, although in the midst of an American settlement, decidedly joined the king's interest, and went to Niagara, and prevailed with some of the other tribes to unite in the same cause."

"A great number of the Oneidas having been converted, by a missionary from New England, to the doctrines of the Presbyterians, and feeling a jealousy of the Mohawks, continued on the side of the Americans."

"The elders of the other tribes did not unanimously agree to enter into the war for a considerable time, because they considered the English and Americans as the same people, though they had quarreled; and that, when a reconciliation should take place between them, whatever side they had taken, they should gain the ill-will of both. Whilst these reasons restrained the chiefs from coming to a decision, a number of the warriors, inclined to war, took an active part. The surprise of some of their villages by parties of American soldiers, coinciding with other circumstances, drew them at last generally into hostilities...."

"In former times, when the Six Nations were united, and far more numerous than at present, with intrepid independent chiefs to conduct them, they were highly venerated in this part of the world; and though deprived of several of these advantages, their name is still respected by the neighbouring tribes. In their treaties they always hold the language of an independent people...."

... This, my dear brother, is the substance of my Mohawk's narrative; which, in many places, you must admire, for the simplicity and expression of the figures, whilst it describes the manners of these untutored nations, both in time of war and in council. I have nothing further to say, but, with Indian simplicity, to bid you farewell.

H. FRANKLIN.

Letter XXXI
Arthur Middleton to his Brother Edwin.

St. John's, on Lake Champlain.

Dear Edwin,

A Promise, my dear Edwin, should always be observed: I hasten to fulfill mine, and give you the particulars of our journey from Albany to Lake Champlain.

Cohoz is a small village, which is distinguished by the neighbourhood of a remarkable fall in the Mohawk river. Though a cataract is no great novelty for me, I was charmed with the sublimity of this, which differs in many respects from most I had before seen. The breadth of the river is three hundred yards; a ledge of rocks extends quite across it, and from the top of them, the water falls about fifty feet perpendicularly. The appearance of this grand spectacle varies according to the quantity of water: after heavy rains, it descends in an unbroken sheet, from one bank to the other; whilst, at other times, the greater part of the dark-coloured rocks are visible....

3. From Timothy Dwight, *Travels; in New-England and New-York*. 4 vols. New-Haven: Timothy Dwight, 1821

[Timothy Dwight (1752-1817), President of Yale College, offers descriptions of Albany, Schenectady and the Cahoes Falls, as well as historical information on the cities. He was interested in the way people build a society out of the wilderness, and he recognized that citizens need good models if they are to be good themselves. He located virtue not in the poor or the rich, but in the ways in which people responded to their environments.]

Vol. II
Letter XVI.

Dear Sir,

...The next morning we left Stillwater and rode to Schenectady: thirty-one miles; of which we lost four by our ignorance of the country. The first ten lay along the Hudson in the townships of Stillwater, and Half Moon. Then, turning Westward, we ascended the hills; or rather the brow of the elevated country, which borders the valley of this river. Between this ascent, and Schenectady, the country is chiefly composed of plains, and very gradual swells. The plains are covered with yellow pine; the swells principally with white pine, oak, and hickory. The plains are barren: the swells in favourable seasons yield good crops of wheat, peas, and grass. The three last miles, our journey was on the intervals of the Mohawk; and was very pleasant.

We arrived at Schenectady about seven. On Saturday a heavy rain commenced with a North-East wind; and continued three days. We were, therefore, prevented from pursuing our journey until the following Tuesday; but had no reason to regret our delay.

Schenectady is situated on the South side of the Mohawk fifteen miles North-West of Albany; and about the same distance from the confluence of the Mohawk with the Hudson. It is built on an interval anciently overflowed by the river, and now very little elevated above its highest freshets. On three sides it is nearly enclosed by the brow of a lofty pine plain; always an unsightly disagreeable object. The surface, as you would suppose, is level; and the soil rich. The streets cross each other often, and, in many instances, at right-angles; yet, from the difference of the distances between some, and the obliquity of other, streets, the eye receives no impression of regularity. The houses are chiefly ancient structures of brick, in the Dutch style: the roofs sharp; the ends toward the street; and the architecture uncouth. A great number of them have but one story. There are three churches here: a Dutch, a Presbyterian, and an Episcopal: all of them ordinary buildings. The town is compact; and one or two of the streets are paved. The number of inhabitants in this township was, in 1790, 4,228; and, in 1800, 5,289.

The people of Schenectady are descendants of the Dutch planters, mixed with emigrants from Scotland, Ireland, England, and New-England.

The government of this city is vested in a Mayor, Aldermen, and Common Council.

Schenectady formerly became wealthy by engrossing most of the trade, in furs and peltry, carried on with the Indians. In consequence of the Revolutionary war, and the settlement of the interiour country, this trade has for many years ceased; and with it, that accumulation of property, of which it was the source. Within a few years past the inhabitants have begun to throw off the burden of discouragement, under which they had long laboured, and to apply themselves to other business with considerable success. Since I passed through this place in 1792, a number of the old houses have been pulled down, and a great number of new ones built in the English style. Should this spirit increase; their wealth, which is still considerable, may become an active capital, and restore to Schenectady a part of its former prosperity.

The morals of the inhabitants, particularly of the inferiour classes, are, extensively, upon a low scale. Among other causes, this is one: the merchandise, which passes into the Western country, is usually embarked here, on the Mohawk. Of course, the numerous boatmen, employed in transporting it, make this their place of rendezvous: and few collections of men are more dissolute. The corruption, which they contribute to spread among the ordinary inhabitants, is a greater evil than a stranger can easily imagine....

... In the year 1690, Schenectady was destroyed by a party of Canadian French, and Indians: most of them Mohawks, whom the French had seduced from their attachment to the English. This party consisted of three hundred men; and was one of three, sent by the Count de Frontenac to distress the British Colonies. The other two proceeded against New-Hampshire, and the Province of Maine, where one of them, under Hertel de Rouville, destroyed Dover in the manner already related. The body, which attacked Schenectady, was commanded, according to Colden, by Monsieur De Ourville; according to Dr. Trumbull (for which he quotes the letters of Colonel Schuyler, and Captain Bull),[1] by D'Aillebout, De Mantel, and Le Moyn. The Mohawks were, or had lately been inhabitants, of Caghnawaga: a village up the river, about twenty-five miles from Schenectady. Of course they had been familiarly acquainted with the town, and often entertained by its citizens. The French were chiefly what are called Indian traders. They arrived in the neighbourhood on the 8th of February, when the season was so cold, and the snow so deep, that it was thought to be impossible for an enemy to approach. The French commander sent some of the Indians, as spies, to discover the state of the town. These men were seen lurking in the neighbourhood; and this fact was publickly announced; but the people were so satisfied of their safety, that they paid no regard to the information. Not even a sentinel was employed to watch the advent of the supposed enemy. This negligence was fatal to them. The French afterwards confessed, that they were so reduced by cold, hunger, and fatigue, as to have formed the resolution to surrender themselves as prisoners, if they found the least preparation for resistance. But, learning from the spies, that the town was perfectly defenceless and secure, they marched into its centre the following evening; raised the war-whoop; and, having divided themselves into little parties, broke open the houses, set them on fire, and butchered every man, woman, and child, on whom they could lay hands. "No tongue," says Colonel Schuyler, "can express the cruelties, which they committed." Some of the inhabitants sought for safety in flight; and ran naked through the snow into the fields, and forests. Others endeavoured to hide themselves within the town from the fury of their murderers; but were forced from their retreats by the flames, and either killed or carried into captivity. Sixty-three were butchered in this inhuman manner. Twenty-seven more were made prisoners. Of those who escaped, twenty-five lost their limbs by the severity of the cold.

The cruelties, perpetrated here, were only the customary consequences of a Canadian irruption. The French stimulated the Savages to every inhuman act; and, when charged with these fiend-like violations of every law, and every principle, apologized for themselves by declaring, that they were unable to restrain their barbarity....

---

1 Captain Bull was on the spot [Dwight's note].

Letter XVII.

Tuesday, October 4, we left Schenectady in the morning; and rode to Albany: sixteen miles. The road passes over a pitch-pine plain, nearly a perfect flat, chiefly covered with a forest; the soil miserably lean; the houses few, and poor; and the scenery remarkably dull, and discouraging. The road also is encumbered with sand; and, unless immediately after a rain, covered with an atmosphere of dust.

Albany is the second town in this State. From New-York it is distant one hundred and sixty miles; from Boston one hundred and sixty-five; from new-Haven one hundred and seven; and from Quebec South by West, three hundred and forty.

It was first settled about the year 1612; and the spot, where it was afterwards built, was visited by the celebrated English navigator, Henry Hudson, in 1609. It was first called Beverwyck; then Fort Orange; then Williamstadt. The name of Albany it received in 1664.

Albany was a Dutch Colony; and, until within a few years, the inhabitants have been, almost without exception, descendants from the original settlers. From this fact it has derived its whole aspect, and character. The houses are almost all built in the Dutch manner; standing endwise upon the street; with high, sharp roofs, small windows, and low ceilings. The appearance of these houses is ordinary, dull, and disagreeable. The house, first erected in this town, is now standing; and was built of bricks, brought from Holland. If I were to finish this picture according to the custom of poets and painters, and in obedience to the rules of criticism, by grouping with it animated beings; I should subjoin, that the master of the house, and often one or two of his neighbours, are regularly seen, sitting[1] in a most phlegmatic composure in the porch, and smoking with great deliberation from morning until night.[2]

---

1 1798 [Dwight's note].

2 That this custom is not new, may be seen in the following passage from the travels of Professor Kalm, June 1749. Speaking of Albany, he says, "The street doors are generally in the middle of the houses, and on both sides are seats, in which, during fair weather, the people sit and spend almost the whole day, especially on those which are in the shadow of their houses. In the evening these seats are covered with people of both sexes; but this is rather troublesome, as those who pass by are obliged to greet every body, unless they will shock the politeness of the inhabitants of this town." Kalm, Vol. 2, p. 92, 2nd edition, Lond. [Dwight's note].

The site of Albany is an interval on the Western side of the Hudson, and the brow of an elevated pine plain, rising rapidly at a small distance from the river. The soil of the elevation is clay. Both grounds easily imbibe, and retain, water. The streets therefore, few of which have been paved until very lately, have been usually incumbered with mud, so as at times to render traveling scarcely practicable. When I was in this city, in the year 1792, a waggon, passing through the heart of it, was fairly mired in one of the principal streets.

Since that period, an essential change has taken place in Albany. A considerable number of the opulent inhabitants, whose minds were enlarged by the influence of the Revolutionary war, and the extensive intercourse which it produced among them and their countrymen, and still more by education, and traveling, have resolutely broken through a set of traditionary customs, venerable by age, and strong by universal attachment. These gentlemen have built many handsome houses in the modern English style; and in their furniture, manners, and mode of living, have adopted the English custom. To this important change the strangers, who within a few years have become a numerous body of the inhabitants, have extensively contributed. All these, from whatever country derived, have chosen to build, and live, in the English manner.

The preference given to the customs of the English, must descend with increasing influence to their children. In the English language all accompts, instruments of conveyance, records and papers employed in legal processes must be written. The attainment of this language has, therefore, now become indispensable to the safety, as well as to the prosperity, of every individual. Urged by this necessity, and influenced by the example of their superiours, the humblest classes of the Dutch must, within a short period, adopt the English language, and manners. Within two generations there will probably be no distinction between the descendants of the different nations. Intermarriages are also becoming more frequent; and will hasten this event.

... The trade of Albany is extensive. It consists in the exchange of foreign commodities for the produce of a large, fertile, country; and must, I think, continue to increase through a long period. Heretofore the inhabitants pursued a profitable commerce with the Indians, and were for many years still more profitably employed in the lucrative business of supplying successive armies with almost every thing which armies consume. Many of the inhabitants have of course become rich. This has been the fact particularly since the formation of the present American government.

I know not that Albany has ever suffered any serious evils from the savages....

Vol. III.

Letter VI.

...Wednesday, Oct. 9th, we rode to Stillwater; twenty-eight miles. On our way we stopped to see the Cohoes; the celebrated cataract of the Mohawk, about one and a half miles from its confluence with the Hudson. The river is here about three hundred yards wide; and descends over the brow of a vast stratum of slate, spreading through this region to a great, but undefined extent. The brow of this stratum crosses the river in a direction somewhat oblique. Its face also is oblique in a small degree, and at the same time more regular than any distinguished object of this kind within my knowledge. Of course, it wants those wild and masculine features, which give so magnificent an appearance to several other cataracts in this country. The eye is disappointed of this grandeur, which it instinctively demands; and sees a tame and unanimated aspect, which ill supplies the place of that violence and splendour, imparted by rough and ragged precipices to descending water. Yet the height of the fall, which is not less than sixty feet, the breadth of the river, and the quantity of the water, when it is full, give this cataract no small degree of majesty.

The river was now low, and presented a collection of handsome cascades rather than a magnificent cataract. I had before seen it when the water was high.

The slate through which the Mohawk has worn its bed in this place, is exactly the same with that, mentioned in the description of Canajoharie creek; of the same dark colour; divided into thin laminae; equally friable; and equally dissoluble by water, and weather. Its banks, below the Cohoes, are not less than one hundred feet in height, black and precipitous. The fall has been evidently worn backward, during the lapse of ages, almost a mile by the united agency of the stream, and the atmosphere....

4. From Edmund Burke, *An Account of the European Settlements in America*. 2 Vols. Second edition. London: R. and J. Dodsley, 1758

[Like the Abbé Guillaume Raynal, Edmund Burke (1729-97) viewed North America in terms of its potential for trade. But, unlike Raynal, Burke's comments on the aboriginal peoples of

North America are ambiguous: while he has positive things to say about them, he does so in language that emphasizes their bestiality and savagery. This work, which Burke co-authored with his brother, William, was first published in 1757.]

The Aborigines of America, throughout the whole extent of the two vast continents which they inhabit, and amongst the infinite number of nations and tribes into which they are divided, differ very little from each other in their manners and customs; and they all form a very striking picture of the most distant antiquity. Whoever considers the Americans of this day, not only studies the manners of a remote present nation, but he studies, in some measure, the antiquities of all nations; from which no mean lights may be thrown upon many parts of the ancient authors, both sacred and profane. The learned Lafitau[1] has laboured this point with great success, in a work which deserves to be read amongst us much more than I find it is.

The people of America are tall, and strait in their limbs beyond the proportion of most nations: their bodies are strong; but of a species of strength rather fitted to endure much hardship, than to continue long at any servile work, by which they are quickly consumed; it is the strength of a beast of prey, rather than that of a beast of burthen. Their bodies and heads are fattish, the effect of art; their features are regular, but their countenances fierce; their hair long, black, lank, and as strong as that of a horse. No beards. The colour of their skin a reddish brown, admired amongst them, and improved by the constant use of bear's fat and paint.

When the Europeans first came into America, they found the people quite naked, except those parts which it is common for the most uncultivated people to conceal. Since that time they have generally a coarse blanket to cover them, which they buy from us. The whole fashion of their lives is of a piece; hardy, poor, and squalid; and their education from their infancy is solely directed to fit their bodies for this mode of life, and to form their minds to inflict and endure the greatest evils. Their only occupations are hunting and war. Agriculture is left to the women. Merchandize they contemn. When their hunting season is past, which

---

1   Joseph-François Lafitau (1681-1746), French, eighteenth-century Jesuit missionary to Canada. He tried to show that the aboriginal peoples of Canada were descended from the ancient Greeks in his two-volume *Mœures des Sauvages américains* (1724).

they go through with much patience, and in which they exert great ingenuity, they pass the rest of their time in an entire indolence. They sleep half the day in their huts, they loiter and jest among their friends, and they observe no bounds or decency in their eating and drinking. Before we discovered them they wanted spirituous liquors; but now, the acquirement of these is what gives a spur to their industry, and enjoyment to their repose. This is the principal end they pursue in their treaties with us; and from this they suffer inexpressible calamities; for, having once begun to drink, they can preserve no measure, but continue a succession of drunkenness as long as their means of procuring liquor lasts. In this condition they lie exposed on the earth to all the inclemency of the seasons, which wastes them by a train of the most fatal disorders; they perish in rivers and marshes; they tumble into the fire; they quarrel and very frequently murder each other; and in short, excess in drinking, which with us is rather immoral than very destructive, amongst this uncivilized people, who have not art enough to guard against the consequence of their vices, is a public calamity. The few amongst them who live free from this evil, enjoy the reward of their temperance in a robust and healthy old age. The disorders which a complicated luxury has introduced, and supports in Europe, are strangers here.

The character of the Indians is striking. They are grave even to sadness in their deportment upon any serious occasion; observant of those in company; respectful to the old; of a temper cool and deliberate; by which they are never in haste to speak before they have thought well upon the matter, and are sure the person who spoke before them has finished all he had to say. They have therefore the greatest contempt for the vivacity of the Europeans, who interrupt each other, and frequently speak all together. Nothing is more edifying than their behavior in their public councils and assemblies. Every man there is heard in his turn, according as his years, his wisdom, or his services to his country have ranked him. Not a word, not a whisper, not a murmur is heard from the rest while he speaks. No indecent condemnation, no ill-timed applause. The younger sort attend for their instruction. Here they learn the history of their nation; here they are inflamed with the songs of those who celebrate the warlike actions of their ancestors; and here they are taught what are the interests of their country, and how to pursue them.

There is no people amongst whom the laws of hospitality are more sacred, or executed with more generosity and good-will.

Their houses, their provision, even their young women are not enough to oblige a guest. To those of their own nation they are likewise very humane and beneficent. Has any one of them succeeded ill in his hunting? Has his harvest failed? Or is his house burned? He feels no other effect of his misfortune, than that it gives him an opportunity to experience the benevolence and regard of his fellow-citizens, who for that purpose have all things almost in common. But to the enemies of his country, or to those who have privately offended, the American is implacable. He conceals his sentiments, he appears reconciled, until by some treachery or surprise he has an opportunity of executing an horrible revenge. No length of time is sufficient to allay his resentment; no distance of place great enough to protect the object; he crosses the steepest mountains, he pierces the most impracticable forests, and traverses the most hideous bogs and desarts for several hundreds of miles, bearing the inclemency of the seasons, the fatigue of the expedition, the extremes of hunger and thirst with patience and chearfulness, in hopes of surprising his enemy, on whom he exercises the most shocking barbarities, even to the eating of his flesh. To such extremes do the Indians push their friendship or their enmity; and such indeed in general is the character of all strong and uncultivated minds.

Notwithstanding his ferocity, no people have their anger, or at least the shew of their anger, more under their command. From their infancy they are formed with care to endure scoffs, taunts, blows, and every sort of insult patiently, or at least with a composed countenance. This is one of the principal objects of their education. They esteem nothing so unworthy a man of sense and constancy, as a peevish temper, and a proneness to a sudden and rash anger. And this so far has an effect, that quarrels happen as rarely amongst them when they are not intoxicated with liquor, as does the chief cause of all quarrels, hot and abusive language. But human nature is such, that as virtues may with proper management be engrafted upon almost all sort of vicious passions, so vices naturally grow out of the best dispositions, and are the consequence of those regulations that produce and strengthen them. This is the reason that when the passions of the Americans are roused, being shut up, as it were, and converging into a narrow point, they become more furious; they are dark, sullen, treacherous and unappeasable.

★ ★ ★ ★ ★

The province of New York has two cities; the first is called by the name of the province itself. It was denominated New Amsterdam when the Dutch possessed it, but it has changed its name along with its masters. This city is most commodiously situated for trade, upon an excellent harbour, in an island called Manahatton, about fourteen miles long, though not above one or two broad. This island lies just in the mouth of the river Hudson, which discharges itself here after a long course. This is one of the noblest rivers in America. It is navigable upwards of two hundred miles. The tide flows one hundred and fifty.

The city of New York contains upwards of two thousand houses, and above twelve thousand inhabitants, the descendants of Dutch and English. It is well and commodiously built, extending a mile in length, and about half that in breadth, and has a very good aspect from the sea; but it is by no means properly fortified. The houses are built of brick in the Dutch taste; the streets not regular, but clean and well paved. There is one large church built for the church of England worship; and three others, a Dutch, a French, and a Lutheran. The town has a very flourishing trade, and in which great profits are made. The merchants are wealthy, and the people in general most comfortably provided for, and with a moderate labour. From the year 1749 to 1750 two hundred and thirty-two vessels have been entered in this port, and two hundred and eighty-six cleared outwards. In these vessels were shipped six thousand seven hundred and thirty-one tons of grain; of which I have no particular account. In the year 1755 the export of flax seed to Ireland amounted to 12,528 hogsheads. The inhabitants are between eighty and an hundred thousand; the lower class easy; the better rich, and hospitable; great freedom of society; and the entry to foreigners made easy by a general toleration of all religious persuasions. In a word, this province yields to no part of America in the healthfulness of its air, and the fertility of its soil. It is much superior in the great convenience of water carriage, which speedily and at the slightest expence carries the product of the remotest farms to a certain and profitable market.

Upon the river Hudson, about one hundred and fifty miles from New York, is Albany; a town of not so much note for its number of houses or inhabitants, as for the great trade which is carried on with the Indians, and indeed by connivance with the French for the use of the same people. This trade takes off a great quantity of coarse woolen goods, such as strouds and duffils;[1] note and with these, guns, hatchets, knives, hoes, kettles, powder and shot; besides shirts and cloaths ready made, and several other articles. Here it is that the treaties and other transactions between us and the Iroquois Indians are negotiated.

This nation, or combination of Five nations, united by an ancient and inviolable league amongst themselves, were the oldest, the most steady, and most effectual ally we have found amongst the Indians. This people, by their unanimity, firmness, military skill, and policy, have raised themselves to be the greatest and most formidable power in all America; they have reduced a vast number of nations, and brought under their power a territory twice as large as the kingdom of France; but they have not increased their subjects in proportion. As their manner of warring is implacable and barbarous, they reign the lords of a prodigious desert, inhabited only by a few scattered insignificant tribes, whom they have permitted to live out of a contempt of their power, and who are all in the lowest state of subjection. And yet this once mighty and victorious nation, though it has always used the policy of incorporating with itself a great many of the prisoners they make in war, is in a very declining condition. About sixty years ago it was computed, that they had ten thousand fighting men; at this day they cannot raise upwards of fifteen hundred. So much have wars, epidemical diseases, and the unnatural union of the vices of civilized nations with the manner of savages, reduced this once numerous people. But they are not only much lessened at this day in their numbers, but in their disposition to employ what numbers they have left in our service. Amongst other neglects, which I have no pleasure in mentioning, and no hopes of seeing amended, this of inattention, or worse treatment of the Indians, is one, and a capital one. The Iroquois have lately had three other nations added to their confederacy, so that they ought now to be considered as eight; and the whole confederacy seems much more inclined to the French interest than ours.

---

1 Coarse woolen goods, such as strouds and duffels: Strouds and Duffils (or duffels) were coarse woolen blankets made for sale to the aboriginal peoples of North America.

5. From Abbé Guillaume Thomas François Raynal, *A Philosophical and Political History of the British Settlements and Trade in North America*. Trans. J. Justamond. Edinburgh: C. Denovan, 1779

[In this work, which sold over 25,000 copies in seventeen editions between 1772, when it was first published in France, and 1780, Abbé Raynal (1713-96) is chiefly interested in trade in North America but despite this pragmatic concern, he also sheds significant light on the continent's aboriginal inhabitants—their plight as a result of the incursion of Europeans onto their land, and into their culture. While impressed by certain aspects of British America, he suggests that until the British "form one people" with others living in North America, they will not realize success as colonists.]

The first Europeans who went over to settle English colonies, found immense forests. The vast trees, that grew up to the clouds, were so encumbered with creeping plants, that they could not be got at. The wild beasts made the woods still more inaccessible. They met only with a few savages, clothed with the skins of those monsters. The human race, thinly scattered, fled from each other, or pursued only with intent to destroy. The earth seemed useless to man; and its powers were not exerted so much for his support, as in the breeding of animals, more obedient to the laws of nature. The earth produced every thing at pleasure without assistance, and without direction; it yielded all its bounties with uncontrolled profusion for the benefit of all, not for the pleasure or conveniences of one species of beings. The rivers now glided freely thro' the forest; now spread themselves quietly in a wide morass; from hence issuing in various streams, they formed a multitude of islands, encompassed with their channels. The spring was restored from the spoils of autumn. The leaves dried and rotted at the foot of the trees, supplied them with fresh sap to enable them to shoot out new blossoms. The hollow trunks of trees afforded a retreat to prodigious flights of birds. The sea, dashing against the coasts, and indenting the gulphs, threw up shoals of amphibious monsters, enormous whales, crabs, and turtles, that sported uncontrolled on the desert shores. There nature exerted her plastic power, incessantly producing the gigantic inhabitants of the ocean, and asserting the freedom of the earth and the sea.

But man appeared, and immediately changed the face of

North America. He introduced symmetry by the assistance of all the instruments of art. The impenetrable woods were instantly cleared, and made room for commodious habitations. The wild beasts were driven away, and flocks of domestic animals supplied their place; whilst thorns and briars made way for rich harvests. The waters forsook part of their domain, and were drained off into the interior parts of the land, or into the sea, by deep canals. The coasts were covered with towns, and the bays with ships; and thus the new world, like the old, became subject to man....

★ ★ ★ ★ ★

...The Dutch, who were the first founders of the colony, planted in it that spirit of order and oeconomy which is the characteristic of their nation; and as they always made up the bulk of the people, even after these had changed masters, the example of their decent manners was imitated by all the new colonists brought amongst them by the conquest. The Germans, compelled to take refuge in America by the persecution which drove them out of the Palatinate,[1] or from other provinces of the empire, were naturally inclined to this simple and modest way of life; and the English and French, who were not accustomed to so much frugality, soon conformed, either from motives of wisdom or emulation, to a mode of living less expensive and more familiar than that which is regulated by fashion and parade.

★ ★ ★ ★ ★

... It may easily be imagined that such nations[2] could not be so gentle nor so weak as those of South America. They shewed that they had that activity and energy which are always found in the northern nations, unless, like the Laplanders, they are of a different species from ourselves. They had but just attained to that degree of knowledge and civilization, to which instinct alone may lead men in the space of a few years; and it is among such people that a philosopher may study man in his natural state.

They were divided into several small nations, whose form of

---

1 At the end of the seventeenth century, Elector Charles Philip began a campaign of persecution against the Mennonites. Seeking religious freedom, many came to North America, especially to Pennsylvania.
2 The aboriginal peoples of North America.

government was nearly similar. Some had hereditary chiefs; others elected them; the greater part were only directed by their old men. They were mere associations, formed by chance, and always free; united, indeed, but bound by no tie. The will of individuals was not even over-ruled by the general one. All decisions were considered only as matter of advice, which was not binding, or enforced by any penalty. If, in one of these singular republics, a man was condemned to death, it was rather a kind of war against a common enemy, than of coercive power; good manners, example, education, a respect for old men, and parental affection, maintained peace in those societies, that had neither laws nor property. Reason, which had not been misled by prejudice or corrupted by passion, as it is with us, served them instead of moral precepts and regulations of police. Harmony and security were maintained with the interposition of government. Authority never incroached upon that powerful instinct of nature, the love of independence, which enlighted by reason produces in us the love of equality.

Hence arises that regard which the savages have for each other. They lavish their expressions of esteem, and expect the same in return. They are obliging, but reserved; they weigh their words, and listen with great attention. Their gravity, which looks like a kind of melancholy, is particularly observable in their national assemblies. Every one speaks in his turn, according to his age, his experience, and his services. No one is ever interrupted, either by indecent reflections, or ill-timed applause.[1] Their public affairs are managed with such disinterestedness as is unknown in our governments, where the welfare of the state is hardly ever promoted but from selfish views, or party spirit. It is no uncommon thing to hear one of these savage orators, when his speech has met with universal applause, telling those who agreed to his opinion, that another man is more deserving of their confidence.

This mutual respect amongst the inhabitants of the same place prevails between the several nations, when they are not in actual war. The deputies are received and treated with that friendship which is due to men who come to treat of peace and alliance. Wandering nations, who have not the least notion of a domain,

---

1 Burke uses similar language to describe the aboriginal peoples' behavior at their assemblies in his *Account of the European Settlements in America* (1758).

never negotiate for a project of conquest, or for any interests relative to dominion. Even those who have a settled home, never quarrel with others for coming to live in their district, provided they do not molest them. The earth, say they, is made for all men; no one must possess the share of two. All the politics, therefore, of the savages consist in forming leagues against an enemy who is too numerous or too strong, and in suspending hostilities that become too destructive....

As the savages possess no riches, they are of a benevolent turn. A striking instance of this appears in the care they take of their orphans, widows, and infirm people. They liberally share their scanty provisions with those whose crops have failed, or who have been unsuccessful in hunting or fishing. Their tables and their huts are open night and day to strangers and travellers. This generous hospitality, which makes the advantages of a private man a public blessing, is chiefly conspicuous in their entertainments. A savage claims respect, not so much from what he possesses as from what he gives away. Accordingly the whole provision of a six months chase is often expended in one day, and he who treats enjoys more pleasure than his guests.

None of the writers who have described the manners of the savages have reckoned benevolence amongst their virtues. But this may be owing to prejudice, which has made them confound antipathy and resentment with natural temper. These people neither love nor esteem the Europeans, nor are they very kind to them. The inequality of conditions, which we think so necessary for the well-being of society, is in their opinion the greatest folly. They are shocked to see, that, amongst us, one man has more property than several others put together; and that this first injustice is productive of a second, which is, that the man who has most riches is on that account the most respected. But what appears to them a meanness below that of the brute creation is, that men who are equal by nature should stoop to depend upon the will or the caprice of another. The respect we show to titles, dignities, and especially to hereditary nobility, they call an insult, an injury to human nature. Whoever knows how to guide a canoe, to beat an enemy, to build a hut, to live upon little, to go a hundred leagues in the woods, with no other guide than the wind and sun, or any provision but a bow and arrow; he is a man, and what more can be expected of him? That restless disposition which prompts us to cross so many seas, to seek a fortune that flies before us, appears to them rather the effect of poverty than of industry. They laugh at our arts, our manners, and all those customs which inspire us with vanity in proportion as they remove us from the state of nature. Their frankness and honesty is roused to indignation at the tricks and cunning which have been practiced in our dealings with them. A multitude of other motives, some founded on prejudice, but most on reason, have rendered the Europeans odious to the Indians. They have used reprisals, and are become harsh and cruel in their dealings with us. That aversion and contempt they have conceived for our morals, has always made them shun our society. We have never been able to reconcile any of them to the indulgences of our way of life; whereas we have seen some Europeans forego all the conveniences of civil life, go into the forests, and take up the bow and the club of the savage....

Many of these nations allow a plurality of wives; and even those that do not practice polygamy, admit of divorce. The very idea of an indissoluble tie never once entered the thoughts of these people who are free till death. When those who are married disagree, they part by consent, and divide their children between them. Nothing appears to them more repugnant to nature and reason than the contrary system which prevails among Christians. *The great spirit*, say they, *hath created us all to be happy: and we should offend him, were we to live in a perpetual state of constraint and uneasiness....*

The savages shew a degree of penetration and sagacity, which astonishes every one who has not observed how much our arts and methods of life contribute to render our minds slow and inactive; because we are seldom put to the trouble of thinking, and have only to learn what is already discovered. If they have brought nothing to perfection any more than the most sagacious animals, it is, probably, because these people, having no ideas but such as relate to the present wants, the equality that subsists between them lays every individual under a necessity of thinking for himself, and of spending his whole life in acquiring this occasional learning: hence it may be reasonably inferred, that the sum total of ideas in a society of savages is no more than the sum of ideas of each individual.

Instead of abstruse meditations, the savages delight in songs. They are said to have no variety in their singing; but we are uncertain whether those that have heard them had an ear properly adapted to their music. When we first hear a foreign language, the words seem all the same, we think it is all pronounced with the same tone, without any modulation or prosody. It is only by continued habit that we learn to distinguish the words and syllables, and to perceive that some are dull and others sharp, some long and others short. The same may be equally true with regard to the melody of a people, whose song must bear some analogy to their speech.

... When we consider the hatred which the hordes of these savages bear to each other; the hardships they undergo; the scarcity they are often exposed to; the frequency of their wars; the scantiness of their population; the numberless snares we lay for them; we cannot but foresee, that, in less than three centuries, the whole race will be extinct. What will posterity then think of this species of men, who will exist no more but in the accounts of travellers? Will not the times of savages appear to them in the same light as the fabulous times of antiquity do to us? They will speak of them, as we do of the Centaurs and Lapithae.[1] How many contradictions shall we not discover in their customs and manners? Will not such of our writings as may then have escaped the destructive hands of time, pass for romantic inventions, like those which Plato has left us concerning the ancient Atlantica?[2]

★ ★ ★ ★ ★

The first persons who landed in this desert and savage region were Englishmen who had been persecuted at home for their civil and religious opinions.

It was not to be expected that this first emigration would be attended with important consequences. The inhabitants of Great Britain are so strongly attached to their native soil, that nothing less than civil wars or revolutions can induce those among them who have any property, character, or industry, to a change of climate and country; for which reason the re-establishment of public tranquillity in Europe was likely to put an unsurmountable bar to the progress of American civilization.

Add to this, that the English, though naturally active, ambitious, and enterprising, were ill-adapted to the business of clearing the grounds. Accustomed to a quiet life, ease, and many conveniences, nothing but the enthusiasm of religion or politics

---

1 Centaurs and Lapithae: The epic battle between the mythical races of Lapithae of Thessaly in Greece and the Centaurs (half man, half horse) was depicted on the Parthenon, on vases, and by the artist Raphael.
2 Ancient Atlantica: Plato wrote of the legendary island of Atlantica, or Atlantis, in two dialogues, *Timaeus* and *Critias*.

could support them under the labours, miseries, wants, and calamities, inseparable from new plantations.

It is further to be observed, that though England might have been able to overcome these difficulties, it was not a desirable object for her. Without doubt, the founding of colonies, rendering them flourishing, and enriching herself with their productions, was an advantageous prospect to her; but those advantages would be dearly purchased at the expence of her own population.

Happily for her, the intolerant and despotic spirit, that swayed most countries of Europe, forced numberless victims to take refuge in an uncultivated tract, which, in its state of desolation, seemed to implore that assistance for itself which it offered to the unfortunate. These men, who had escaped from the rod of tyranny, in crossing the seas, abandoned all hopes of return, and attached themselves for ever to a country which at the same time afforded them an asylum and an easy quiet subsistence. Their good fortune could not forever remain unknown. Multitudes flocked from different parts to partake of it. Nor has this eagerness abated, particularly in Germany, where nature produces men for the purposes either of conquering or cultivating the earth. It will even increase. The advantage granted to emigrants throughout the British dominions of being naturalized by a residence of seven years in the colonies, sufficiently warrants this prediction.

... Let the British clear the ground, purify the air, alter the climate, improve nature, and a new universe will arise out of their hands for the glory and happiness of humanity. But it is necessary that they should take steps conformable to this noble design, and aim by just and laudable means to form a population fit for the creation of a new world. This is what they have not yet done.

★ ★ ★ ★ ★

... If any thing be wanting in British America, it is its not forming precisely one people. Families are there found sometimes re-united, sometimes dispersed, originating from all the different countries of Europe. These colonists, in what ever spot chance or discernment may have placed them, all preserve, with a prejudice not to be worn out, their mother-tongue, the partialities and the customs of their own country. Separate schools and churches hinder them from mixing with the hospitable people, who hold out to them a place of refuge. Still estranged from this people by worship, by manners, and probably by their feelings, they harbour seeds of dissention that may one day prove the ruin and total overthrow of the colonies. The only preservative against this disaster depends entirely on the management of the ruling powers.

6. From Dr. Benjamin Franklin, *Remarks Concerning the Savages of North America*. London: John Stockdale, 1784

[This tract treats aboriginal peoples with respect in order to represent America in positive terms. Benjamin Franklin (1706-90) suggests that perspective is relative: Americans and Europeans may view the aboriginal peoples as savage, but the aboriginal peoples see them similarly. Their spokesperson is the articulate and respected Iroquois chief, Canassetego, who offers an indictment against those who treat his people unethically.]

Savages we call them, because their manners differ from ours, which we think the perfection of civility; they think the same of theirs.

Perhaps if we could examine the manners of different nations with impartiality, we should find no people so rude as to be without any rules of politeness; nor any so polite as not to have some remains of rudeness.

... Having frequent occasions to hold public Councils, they have acquired great order and decency in conducting them. The Old Men sit in the foremost ranks, the Warriors in the next, and the Women and Children in the hindmost. The business of the Women is to take exact notice of what passes, imprint it in their memories, for they have no writing, and communicate it to their Children. They are the Records of the Council, and they preserve tradition of the stipulations in Treaties a hundred years back; which, when we compare with our writings, we always find exact. He that would speak, rises. The rest observe a profound silence. When he has finished, and sits down, they leave him five or six minutes to recollect, that if he has omitted any thing he intended to say, or has any thing to add, he may rise again, and deliver it. To interrupt another, even in common conversation, is reckoned highly indecent. How different this is from the conduct of a polite British House of Commons, where scarce a day passes without some confusion, that makes the Speaker hoarse in calling *to order*; and how different from the mode of conversation in many polite companies of Europe, where, if you do not deliver your sentence with great rapidity, you are cut off in the middle of it by the impatient loquacity of those you converse with, and never suffered to finish it.

The politeness of these Savages in conversation, is, indeed, carried to excess; since it does not permit them to contradict, or deny the truth of what is asserted in their presence. By this means they indeed avoid disputes; but then it becomes difficult to know their minds, or what impression you make upon them. The Missionaries who have attempted to convert them to Christianity, all complain of this as one of the great difficulties of their Mission. The Indians hear with patience the Truth of the Gospel explained to them, and give their usual tokens of assent and approbation: you would think they were convinced. No such matter. It is mere civility.

... When any of them come into our towns, our people are apt to croud round them, gaze upon them, and incommode them where they desire to be private; this they esteem great rudeness, and the effect of the want of instruction in the rules of civility and good manners. "We have," say they, "as much curiosity as you, and when you come into our town, we wish for opportunities of looking at you; but for this purpose we hide ourselves behind bushes where you are to pass, and never intrude ourselves into your company."

Their manner of entring one anothers' villages has likewise its rules. It is reckoned uncivil in travelling strangers to enter a village abruptly, without giving notice of their approach. Therefore, as soon as they arrive within hearing, they stop and hollow, remaining there till invited to enter. Two old men usually come out to them, and lead them in. There is in every village a vacant dwelling, called the strangers' house. Here they are placed, while the old men go round from hut to hut, acquainting the inhabitants that strangers are arrived, who are probably hungry and weary; and every one sends them what he can spare of victuals and skins to repose on. When the strangers are refreshed, pipes and tobacco are brought; and then, but not before, conversation begins, with enquiries who they are, whither bound, what news, &c. and it usually ends with offers of service; if the strangers have occasion of guides, or any necessaries for continuing their journey; and nothing is exacted for the entertainment.

The same hospitality, esteemed among them as a principal virtue, is practiced by private persons; of which *Conrad Weiser*, our Interpreter, gave me the following instance. He had been naturalized among the Six Nations, and spoke well the Mohock language. In going through the Indian Country, to carry a message from our governor to the Council at *Onondaga*, he called at the habitation of *Canassetego*,[1] an old acquaintance, who embraced him, spread furs for him to sit on, placed before him some boiled beans and venison, and mixed some rum and water for his drink. When he was well refreshed, and had lit his pipe, Canassetego began to converse with him: asked how he had fared the many years since they had seen each other, whence he then came, what occasioned the journey, &c.

Conrad answered all his questions; and when the discourse began to flag, the Indian, to continue it, said, "Conrad, you have lived long among the White People, and know something of their customs; I have been sometimes at Albany, and have observed, that once in seven days they shut up their shops, and assemble all in the great house; tell me, what is it for? What do they do there?"

"They meet there," says Conrad, "to hear and learn *good things*."

"I do not doubt," says the Indian, "that they tell you so; they have told me the same. But I doubt the truth of what they say, and I will tell you my reasons. I went lately to Albany to sell my skins, and buy blankets, knives, powder, rum, &c. You know I used to generally deal with Hans Hanson; but I was a little inclined this time to try some other Merchants. However, I called first upon Hans, and asked him what he would give for beaver. He said he could not give more than four shillings a pound. But, says he, I cannot talk on business now; this is the day when we meet together to learn *good things*, and I am going to the meeting. So I thought to myself, since I cannot do any business to-day, I may as well go to the meeting too, and I went with him. There stood up a man in black, and began to talk to the people very angrily. I did not understand what he said; but perceiving that he looked much at me, and at Hanson, I imagined he was angry at seeing me there; so I went out, sat down near the house, struck fire, and lit my pipe, waiting till the meeting should break up. I thought too, that the man had mentioned something of Beaver, and I suspected it might be the subject of their meeting. So when they came out, I accosted my Merchant."

"'Well, Hans,' says I, 'I hope you have agreed to give more than four shillings a pound.'"

"'No,' says he, 'I cannot give so much. I cannot give more than three shillings and sixpence.'"

---

1 Chief of the Onondagas.

"I then spoke to several other dealers, but they all sung the same song, three and sixpence, three and sixpence. This made it clear to me that my suspicion was right; and that whatever they pretended of meeting to learn *good things*, the real purpose was to consult how to cheat Indians in the price of Beaver. Consider but a little, Conrad, and you must be of my opinion. If they met so often to learn *good things*, they would certainly have learned some before this time. But they are still ignorant. You know our practice. If a white man in travelling through our country, enters one of our cabins, we all treat him as I treat you; we dry him if he is wet, we warm him if he is cold, and give him meat and drink, that he may allay his thirst and hunger; and we spread soft furs for him to rest and sleep on. We demand nothing in return.[1] But if I go into a white man's house at Albany, and ask for victuals and drink, they say, where is your money; and if I have none, they say, get out, you Indian Dog. You see they have not yet learned those little *good things*, that we need no meetings to be instructed in because our mothers taught them to us when we were children; and therefore it is impossible their meetings should be, as they say, for any such purpose, or have any such effect; they are only to contrive *the cheating of Indians in the price of Beaver.*"

7. From William Gilpin, *Remarks on Forest Scenery.* 3 vols. London: R. Blamire, 1791

[William Gilpin (1724-1804), a clergyman, fueled the interest in the picturesque in England with his writings on the landscapes of his country. He defined the picturesque against its companions the sublime and the beautiful as an aesthetic that partook of both but was different because marked by a dependence on variation in Nature: ruins, movement between the smooth and the irregular, the grandeur of a scene coming upon one unawares. These are transformed by the picturesque eye. This work contains some of his more controversial statements about the picturesque: the affin-

---

1 It is remarkable, that in all ages and countries, hospitality has been allowed as the virtue of those, whom the Civilized were pleased to call Barbarians; the Greeks celebrated the Scythians for it. The Saracens possessed it eminently, and it is to this day the reigning virtue of the wild Arabs. St. Paul too, in the relation of his voyage and shipwreck, on the Island of Melita, says, "The barbarous people shewed us no little kindness; for they kindled a fire, and received us every one, because of the present rain, and because of the cold" [Franklin's note].

ity for the general rather than the specific, the appreciation of distance which "hides many defects," the denial of the utilitarian.]

... We have already observed, that the wild and rough parts of nature produce the strongest effects on the imagination; and we may add, they are the only objects in landscape, which please the picturesque eye. Every thing trim, and smooth, and neat, affects it coolly. Propriety brings us to acquiesce in the elegant, and well-adapted embellishments of art: but the painter, who should introduce them on canvas, would be characterized as a man void of taste; and utterly unacquainted with the objects of picturesque selection.—Such are the great materials, which we expect to find in the skirts, and internal parts of the forest—trees of every kind, but particularly the oldest, and roughest of each.—We examine next the *mode* of scenery which results from their combinations.

In speaking of the glen, we observed that the principal beauty of it arose from those little openings, or glades, with which it commonly abounds. It is thus in the forest-woods. The great beauty of these *close scenes* arise from the openings and recesses, which we find among them.

By these I do not mean the *lawns*, and *pasturage*, which I mentioned as one of the great divisions of forest-scenery; but merely those little openings among the trees, which are produced by various circumstances. A sandy bank, or a piece of rocky ground may prevent the contiguity of trees, and so make an opening; or a tree or two may have been blasted, or have been cut down; or, what is the happiest of all circumstances, a winding road may run along the wood.—The simple idea, which is varied through all these little recesses, is the exhibition of a few trees, just seen behind others. The varieties of this mode of scenery, simple as it is, are infinite. Nature is wonderfully fertile. The invention of the painter may form a *composition* more agreeable to the rules of his art, than nature commonly produces: but no invention can reach the varieties of *particular objects*.

... Nor is the cottage, which is often found in the woody scenes of the forest, a circumstance without its effect. In *nature* at least it pleases: not only as the embellishment of a scene; but as it shews us a dwelling, where happiness may reside, unsupported by wealth—as it shews us a resource, where we may still continue to enjoy peace, tho we should be deprived of all the favours of fortune.

... The following remark I found in a work of Dr. Johnson's; which I transcribe, not only because it is judicious, and may be introduced here in place; but because it affords a new argument to shew the resemblance between poetry and painting. Johnson was a critic in the former; but I never heard, that he was a judge of the latter. His opinion therefore in a point of this kind, was unbiased.—"The business of a poet, says he, is, to examine—not the individual, but the species—to remark general, and large appearances. He does not number the streaks of the tulip, nor describe the different shades in the verdure of the forest. He is to exhibit in his portraits of nature such prominent, and striking features, as recall the original to every mind: and must neglect the minuter discriminations (which one may have remarked, and another have neglected) for those characteristics, which are alike obvious to attention and carelessness."[1]

★ ★ ★ ★ ★

... Such objects we often meet with in the wild scenes of the forest, spires, towers, lodges, bridges, cattle-sheds, cottages, winding pales, and other things of the same kind; which have often as beautiful an effect, when seen at a *distance*, as we have just observed they have, when sparingly met with in the internal parts of a forest. Only the nearer the object is, we expect its form must be the more picturesque. Distance, no doubt, hides many defects; and many an object may appear well in a remove, which brought nearer, would disgust the eye.

★ ★ ★ ★ ★

...The picturesque eye, in the mean-time, is greatly hurt with the destruction of all these sylvan scenes. Not that it delights in a continued forest; nor wishes to have a whole country covered with wood. It delights in the intermixture of wood, and plain; in which beauty consists. It is not its business to consider matters of utility. It has nothing to do with the affairs of the plough, and the spade; but merely examines the face of nature as a beautiful object....

---

1 Pr. Of Abyssin. p. 68 [Gilpin's note]. In *Rasselas, Prince of Abyssinia* (1759) by Samuel Johnson (1709-84).

Appendix D: Captivity Narratives

1. From Charlotte Lennox, *The Life of Harriot Stuart, Written by Herself*. London: J. Payne and J. Bouquet, 1750

[This selection from Charlotte Lennox's first novel, set partially in colonial New York describes Harriot's captivity at the hands of her disappointed lover, Belmein, disguised as a Mohawk and accompanied by members of the Mohawk tribe. It is set against the backdrop of one of the triennial meetings between the Governor of New York and the Iroquois Confederacy. It is an interesting use of the genre of the captivity narrative, as it transfers the expected violence and cruelty of the aboriginal peoples of North America to the European male, suggesting that the savage is really within the "civilized" breast.]

... The five Indian nations, with whom we were in alliance, were accustomed to come every third year to A—, and were met by the governour of N— to renew a treaty of peace with them, which was confirmed by presents to the extent of several hundred pounds, allowed by the government of Britain for that purpose. These savage people were assembled in great numbers, on the large plain behind the fort: they had brought with them their wives and children, and none but the aged and infirm were left behind. We saw, with astonishment, a new sort of city raised in the compass of a few hours: for these people, when they travel, carry with them the materials for building their houses, which consist of the bark of trees, and two or three wooden poles, with some bear skins to lye on: thus a square of ten feet will serve to contain a very large family; and it being now the middle of summer, their hutts were decorated with the boughs of trees on the outside, to keep out the sun, which (on account of their different verdure) formed a very new and beautiful prospect. I constantly spent some hours every evening in the garden, which was at a small distance from the fort, where I took great pleasure in viewing the Indians at a distance; for I was too much terrified at them, to walk out among their hutts, as several gentlemen and ladies who were come from N— did. The governour's intended interview with the Indians, drew great numbers of people from all parts of the country: my father was preparing to receive him with the usual formalities; but resolving to have me married before his arrival, he told me, in two days he would bestow me on Maynard, and omitted no arguments that could prevail upon me to obey him, without reluctance. I answered only with sighs and tears; and when my father left me, I retired into the garden alone, meditating on the difficult and dangerous part I had to act. My thoughts were so much employ'd, that I staid later than usual; night stole upon me unawares, and just as I was preparing to return, three or four Indians rushed into the garden; the gate, thro' the carelessness of the gardner, being left unfastened, they seized me immediately. The terror I was in facilitated their design of carrying me away: I fell into a swoon the moment I perceived them, and, when I recovered my senses, I found myself in a boat, rowing (with the utmost expedition) up the river. I gave a loud shriek the moment I opened my eyes, when one of the company, who supported me in his arms, begged me to compose myself; but, O heavens! what was my surprize, when the first word I heard informed me, it was the well-known voice of Belmein. "May I believe my senses," cried I (trembling with astonishment and joy) "is it Captain Belmein that I hear and see? am I not then abandoned entirely to the mercy of these savages?" My first emotions were all joy, but recollecting the violence that had been used to me, I hastily drew away my hand, which Belmein had all this time kept glewed to his lips. "But is it possible," resum'd I, "that Belmein (forgetting the respect he owed me) has acted the part of a brutal ravisher, and snatched me, with violence, from my family." "Ah! too cruel Harriot," interrupted he, "I have indeed taken you away without your consent; but have I not snatched you from a man whom you detested, and whom, notwithstanding, you were upon the point of marrying? Do I merit reproaches for having delivered you from so great a misfortune, at the hazard of my life; and must the excess of my love be imputed to me as a crime?" "If you hazarded your life," replied I, "by this action, you have also hazarded my reputation, which ought to be infinitely dearer to me than either your life or my own. Alas!" continued I (melting into tears) "what affliction is the family involved in upon my account! I am either lamented as unhappily lost, or reproach'd and detested for my criminal flight." ... The Indians who rowed us had all this time observed a profound silence, gazing upon us with a fix'd attention. The moon was now risen, and discovered to me the whole person of Belmein, so altered by his Indian dress, that it was impossible to know him: he wore the same kind of sandals, an Osnabrig's vest which reached to his knees, and a mantle of blue cloth trim'd with several rows of worsted lace; his face was painted, and his hair, which he had been obliged to cut short, was combed into their frightful fashion, and sprinkled, in the divisions, with a kind of fine red sand which looks like blood, and which the Indians affect, in order to give them a more tremendous appearance. You may imagine, dear Amanda, that a lover thus disfigured, was no very agreeable object in the eyes of his mistress: however, the fine shape and regular features of Belmein, shone thro' the savageness of his disguise; and tho' it would have been difficult to have believed him any other than an Indian, yet it must be confess'd he was a very handsome one. Having express'd some apprehensions of the Indians who rowed us, he informed me they were young men of quality in their own nation, the Mohocks, who were all converted to Christianity, and whom he had bound to his interests by large gifts and promises of future reward. These people being most religious observers of their oaths, he had exacted one from each of them, which made him quite secure of their secrecy. When they observed Belmein and I to be upon better terms than we were at first, they made me some complements in the Dutch language, which most of the Mohock Indians can speak fluently. Capt. Belmein explained what they said to me, and I should have fancied it was him who gave their expressions that gallant turn, had I not heard this nation frequently celebrated for its politeness. The whole night the Indians continued to row with all their strength; and Captain Belmein had so well fenced me against the air by several bearskins, which he had disposed advantageously about me, that I was in no danger of taking cold. The summer nights in this country are more pleasant and refreshing than can be well express'd; there is just coolness enough in the air to be agreeable, after the excessive heats of the day. The river we were upon[1] is one of the finest in the world; and the shore, on each side, presented nothing but thick woods to our view; yet there was such a beautiful variety of greens, and so romantic a wildness in the whole prospect, as forcibly attracted my observation, notwithstanding the confusion and distress of my mind. It was soon day, and the Indians still continuing their hasty progress up the river, I ask'd Belmein, in a tone that express'd the utmost resentment, where he intended to carry me. "You know," continued I, "my resolution is fix'd, I will never be yours without my father's consent: amidst all the persecutions I

---

1 The Mohawk River.

suffered, upon Maynard's account, I still reserved my heart for you; but this unjustifiable action has so entirely effaced that tenderness I once felt for you, that you are now both equally the objects of my aversion."

2. From Robert Eastburn, *A Faithful Narrative, of the Many Dangers and Sufferings, as well as Wonderful Deliverances of Robert Eastburn*. Philadelphia: William Dunlap, 1758

[Captured on his way to Oswego, New York, by a group of French soldiers and their aboriginal allies in 1756, Robert Eastburn, a blacksmith, later escaped. His captivity narrative is striking for its portrayal of the physical hardships endured on his journey with his captors to Montreal. Eastburn's adoption by an aboriginal tribe in Canada does not take because, as a deacon in the First Presbyterian Church of Philadelphia, he was unwilling to convert to Catholicism.]

When we came near Shore, a stout Indian took hold of me, and hauled me into the Water, which was Knee-deep, and very cold. As soon as I got a-shore, the Indians gathered round me, and ordered me to dance and sing, now when I was stiff with Cold and Wet, and lying long in the Cannoe; here I only stamped to prepare for my Race,[1] and was incompassed with about 500 Indians, who danced and sung, and at last gave a Shout, and opened the Circle; about 150 young Lads made ready to Pelt me with Dirt and gravel Stones, and on my setting off gave me a stout Volley, without my suffering great Hurt; but an Indian seeing me run, met me, and held me fast, till the Boys had stored themselves again with Dirt and small Stones, and let me run; but then I fared much worse than before, for a small Stone among the Mud hit my Right-Eye, and my Head and Face were so covered with Dirt, that I could scarce see my Way; but discovering a Door of an Indian House standing open, I run in. From this Retreat I was soon hauled, in order to be pelted more; but the Indian Women being more merciful interposed, took me into a House, brought me Water to wash, and gave me boiled Corn and Beans

---

1 Eastburn must run the gauntlet, a rite most captives endured at the hands of their captors. Those who survived the run were generally adopted by the tribe.

to eat. The next Day, I was brought to the Center of the Town, and cried according to the Indian Custom, in order to be sent to a Family of Indians, 200 Miles up Stream, at Oswegotchy, and there to be adopted, and abused no more. To this End, I was delivered to three young Men, who said I was their Brother, and set forward on our Way to the aforesaid Town, with about 20 more Indians, but by reason of bad Weather, we were obliged to encamp on a cold, stony Shore, three Days, and then proceeded on....

Set off on our Journey for Oswegotchy, against a rapid Stream, and being long in it, and our Provision growing short, the Indians put to Shore a little before Night; my Lot was to get Wood, others were ordered to get Fires, and some to Hunt; our Kettle was put over the Fire with some pounded Indian Corn, and after it had boiled about two Hours, my oldest Indian Brother, returned with a She Beaver, big with Young, which he soon cut to Pieces, and threw into the Kettle, together with the Guts, and took the four young Beavers, whole as they came out from the Dam, and put them likewise into the Kettle, and when all was well boiled, gave each one of us a large Dishfull of the Broth, of which we eat freely, and then Part of the old Beaver, the Tail of which was divided equally among us, there being Eight at our Fire; the four young Beavers were cut in the Middle, and each of us got half of a Beaver; I watched an Opportunity to hide my Share (having satisfied myself before that tender Dish came to Hand) which if they had seen, would have much displeased them. The other Indians catched young Musk-Rats, run a Stick through their Bodies, and roasted, without being skinned or gutted, and so eat them. Next Morning hastened on our Journey, which continued several Days, till we came near Oswegotchy, where we landed about three Miles from the Town, on the contrary Side of the River; here I was to be adopted, my *Father* and *Mother* that I had never seen before were waiting, and ordered me into an Indian House, where we were directed to sit down silent for a considerable Time. The Indians appeared very sad, and my Mother began to cry, and continued crying aloud for some Time, and then dried up her Tears, and received me for her Son, and took me over the River to the Indian Town; the next Day I was ordered to go to Mass with them, but I refused once and again, yet they continued their Importunity several Days, saying it was good to go to Mass, but I still refused; and feeling they could not prevail with me, they seemed much displeased with their new Son. I was then sent over the River, to be employed in hard Labour, as a Punishment for not going to Mass, and not allowed a Sight of, or any Conversation with my fellow Prisoners.

3. From Gilbert Imlay, *The Emigrants*. Dublin: Brown, 1794

[Whether Gilbert Imlay wrote this epistolary novel, originally published in 1793 and set in western Pennsylvania, with feminist Mary Wollstonecraft, his lover, or simply with the benefit of her influence, one of its thrusts is toward the support of divorce as a means of dealing with an unhappy marriage. In addition, like Lennox's two American novels, it uses the captivity narrative to counter the usual notions of the aboriginal peoples of North America as savages. Imlay (1754?-1828?), an expatriate American writer, also wrote about the geography of the wilderness areas of America as an aid for those wishing to move west, to further economic development in those areas.]

Letter LVII.

Mr. Il—ray to P. P—, Esq.

St. Vincent's, August.

MY DEAR SIR,

I received by the bearer within two days after date, the sad accounts of the capture of your lovely niece by the natives....

Unfortunate Caroline! How will her sensible[1] heart palpitate in the agonizing dereliction? How will her tender limbs support the fatigue of being hurried through briary thickets? How will her lovely frame be able to rest, without other covering than the cloud deformed canopy of the heavens? What will be the sensations of Arl—ton[2] when he hears of the fate of Caroline....

We must live in hope—after the effervescence of our passions, our cooler judgment searches for more stable ground to act upon; and it is from the loss we all have sustained, we are bound to demand that Caroline shall be given up; otherwise the whole race of savages, must expiate with their lives the robbery they have committed.

---

1 I.e., sensitive, feeling.
2 Caroline's lover.

Letter LIX.
Capt. Arl—ton, to Mr. Il—ray.

Kaskaskia, Sept.

MY DEAR FRIEND,

... It was early in the morning of the 30th. ult. that one of my hunters, who had been absent the whole of the preceding day, returned to camp in great haste, and informed me, that morning, immediately after the break of day, as he was watching for Buffalos, at a crossing about ten miles above where we lay, he saw a party of Indians put off from the shore, upon a raft, who appeared to have charge of prisoners; and the moment that he had seen them land upon the opposite bank, he had posted back to the party.

... How to rescue the prisoner, without endangering her life, was a difficulty I could not contrive to surmount—at length, I thought the only chance would be to wait until night, and in case they kept no guard, for they were now far removed from an enemy's country, and when they should be sleeping we might retake her, before they would have time to hear, or perceive us.— However that scheme was frustrated by their vigilance; when I devised the following stratagem:—

At the dawn of day I dispatched four of my men, keeping only the mountaineer with me, with orders to advance about one quarter of a mile in front of the Indians, there to discharge their pieces irregularly twice, as quick as possible, and then to make a small circuit and return with the greatest expedition. The plan succeeded....

We had travelled in the course of the preceding day upwards of forty miles beyond the Illinois, so that it was nearly 3 P.M. before we regained the bank of the river.

My active guide and mountaineer had embarked the baggage the moment of our arrival, when I first had an opportunity of recognizing our captive.

Ah! Il—ray how did my swelling heart beat for joy, which was instantly succeeded by sorrow, when I first caught a glance from the brilliant eyes of the most divine woman upon earth, torn into shatters by the bushes and briars, with scarcely covering left to hide the transcendency of her beauty, which to be seen by common eyes is a profanation, and it was only by the effulgence of her ætherial looks, that I could have known her?

Caroline has fallen into my hands!—She is at this moment decorating the gardens of this place while I am writing to you, and seems to give enchantment to the whispering breezes that are wafted to my window, and which in their direction as they pass her, collect from her sweets the fragrance of ambrosia, and the exhilarating charms of love itself.

She was sitting upon the bank of the river half harassed to death when I arrived, which from the horrors of a wilderness was converted into Elysium; when I, regardless of every appearance, fell at her feet, and then embracing her, I felt all the transports that the circumstances of our meeting and the divinity of feminine charms can inspire.

... Indeed I wondered that she was alive—but she was not only alive, my friend! but she looked more lovely than ever—the luster of her eyes was like the torch of love—her smiles like the genial hours of May when nature blooms in all its eradiated charms; and though her beauteous face had been lacerated with brambles, still the little loves seemed to vie with each other, as if to prove, which of her features were the most fascinating....

What a change has happened in the fortune of your friend?—Every thing conspires to make me the happiest man living—I have been almost three days alone, as it were, with Caroline.—She is the most charming woman alive, and as ingenuous as she is lovely....

Caroline has this moment entered with a humming bird that a little French lad caught and gave to her;—"behold," said she, as she came into the room where I was writing, "and look at the little captive, how sad it looks, because it has lost its mate."—"And was you sad, my Caroline," said I, taking hold of her hand and tenderly pressing it, "when you was hurried a prisoner from your friends?"—Her cheek was resting upon my breast—Ah! Il—ray, her murmuring accents, for she could not articulate, expressed the most unutterable things—"Go thou little innocent thing," said she to the bird, putting her hand out of the window at the same time to facilitate its escape, "you shall not be a moment longer confined, for perhaps, already I have robbed thee of joys, which the exertions of my whole life could not repay."—"Ah! Caroline," said I, "and who is to restore to us the rapturous pleasures of which we have been robbed?—or shall we find, my charming girl, a compensation for such a sequestration in our future endearments?" ...

Adieu!

J. Arl—ton.

Mr. Il—ray to P. P—, Esq.

St. Vincent's, October.

MY DEAR SIR,

I was so overjoyed at the reception of my friend's letter, announcing his having retaken your niece, the charming Caroline, that I was scarcely able to write a line, and which I hope will appear a sufficient excuse for my having written you so crude a letter upon the event....

Two things in Caroline's account of her captivity are very extraordinary; they are, that she never felt in the least harassed, or alarmed for her safety, as she had, from the moment she was captured, a *presentiment* that Arl—ton would retake her; and, that the Indians treated her the whole time with the most distant respect, and scrupulous delicacy.

The first appears to be natural, when we consider the enthusiasm of the human mind when it is in love; and the latter is corroborated, by the testimony of all decent looking women, who have been so unfortunate as to fall into their hands. Indeed, I have been told of instances, where women have been treated with such tenderness and attention by them, that they have from gratitude become their wives.

4. From James Seaver, *A Narrative of the Life of Mary Jemison*. 7th ed. New York: G.P. Putnam, 1910

[The events of this narrative began in 1755 when Mary Jemison was thirteen. She was captured, along with her family, by French soldiers and their aboriginal allies, and suffered at the hands of her captors emotionally as well as physically, as her family was killed and their scalps carried before her. She was adopted by the Seneca tribe, married, and bore children within the tribe. In 1784, the treaty of peace between America and the aboriginal peoples occurred at Fort Stanwix, near Rome, NY, one year after the treaty that ended the American Revolution; at that time, Mary Jemison was "freed" to return to white society, but not knowing if her kin were alive, and having made a life for herself with the Senecas, she decided to stay and chronicle the lives of the people with whom she had lived most of her adult life. This is the story she told James Seaver, and which was published in 1824.]

My former Indian masters and the two squaws were soon ready to leave the fort, and accordingly embarked—the Indians in a large canoe, and the two squaws and myself in a small one—and went down the Ohio. When we set off, an Indian in the forward canoe took the scalps of my former friends, strung them on a pole that he placed upon his shoulder, and in that manner carried them, standing in the stern of the canoe directly before us, as we sailed down the river, to the town where the two squaws resided.

On the way we passed a Shawnee town, where I saw a number of heads, arms, legs, and other fragments of the bodies of some white people who had just been burned. The parts that remained were hanging on a pole, which was supported at each end by a crotch stuck in the ground, and were roasted or burnt black as coal. The fire was yet burning; and the whole appearance afforded a spectacle so shocking that even to this day the blood almost curdles in my veins when I think of them.

At night we arrived at a small Seneca Indian town, at the mouth of a small river that was called by the Indians, in the Seneca language, She-nan-jee, about eighty miles by water from the fort, where the two squaws to whom I belonged resided. There we landed, and the Indians went on; which was the last I ever saw of them.

Having made fast to the shore, the squaws left me in the canoe while they went to their wigwam or house in the town, and returned with a suit of Indian clothing, all new, and very clean and nice. My clothes, though whole and good when I was taken, were now torn in pieces, so that I was almost naked. They first undressed me, and threw my rags into the river; then washed me clean and dressed me in the new suit they had just brought, in complete Indian style; and then led me home and seated me in the center of their wigwam.

I had been in that situation but a few minutes before all the squaws in the town came in to see me. I was soon surrounded by them, and they immediately set up a most dismal howling, crying bitterly, and wringing their hands in all the agonies of grief for a deceased relative.

Their tears flowed freely, and they exhibited all the signs of real mourning. At the commencement of this scene, one of their number began, in a voice somewhat between speaking and singing, to recite some words to the following purport, and continued the recitation till the ceremony was ended; the company at the same time varying the appearance of their countenances, gestures, and tone of voice, so as to correspond with the sentiments expressed by their leader.

"Oh, our brother! alas! he is dead—he has gone; he will never return! Friendless, he died on the field of the slain, where his bones are yet lying unburied! Oh! who will not mourn his sad fate? No tears dropped around him: oh, no! No tears of his sisters were there! He fell in his prime, when his arm was most needed to keep us from danger! Alas! he has gone, and left us in sorrow, his loss to bewail! Oh, where is his spirit? His spirit went naked, and hungry it wanders, and thirsty and wounded, it groans to return! Oh, helpless and wretched, our brother has gone! No blanket nor food to nourish and warm him; nor candles to light him, nor weapons of war! Oh, none of those comforts had he! But well we remember his deeds! The deer he could take on the chase! The panther shrunk back at the sight of his strength! His enemies fell at his feet! He was brave and courageous in war! As the fawn, he was harmless; his friendship was ardent; his temper was gentle; his pity was great! Oh! our friend, our companion, is dead! Our brother, our brother! alas, he is gone! But why do we grieve for his loss? In the strength of a warrior, undaunted he left us, to fight by the side of the chiefs! His warwhoop was shrill! His rifle well aimed laid his enemies low: his tomahawk drank of their blood: and his knife flayed their scalps while yet covered with gore! And why do we mourn? Though he fell on the field of the slain, with glory he fell; and his spirit went up to the land of his fathers in war! Then why do we mourn? With transports of joy, they received him, and fed him, and clothed him, and welcomed him there! Oh, friends, he is happy; then dry up your tears! His spirit has seen our distress, and sent us a helper whom with pleasure we greet. Deh-he-wä-mis has come: then let us receive her with joy!—she is handsome and pleasant! Oh! she is our sister, and gladly we welcome her here. In the place of our brother she stands in our tribe. With care we will guard her from trouble; and may she be happy till her spirit shall leave us."

In the course of that ceremony, from mourning they became serene,—joy sparkled in their countenances, and they seemed to rejoice over me as over a long-lost child. I was made welcome among them as a sister to the two squaws before mentioned, and was called Deh-he-wä-mis; which, being interpreted, signifies a pretty girl, a handsome girl, or a pleasant, good thing. That is the name by which I have ever since been called by the Indians.

I afterward learned that the ceremony I at that time passed through was that of adoption. The two squaws had lost a brother in Washington's war,[1] sometime in the year before, and in consequence of his death went up to Fort Du Quesne[2] on the day on which I arrived there, in order to receive a prisoner, or an enemy's scalp, to supply their loss. It is a custom of the Indians, when one of their number is slain or taken prisoner in battle, to give to the nearest relative of the dead or absent a prisoner, if they have chanced to take one; and if not, to give him the scalp of an enemy. On the return of the Indians from the conquest, which is always announced by peculiar shoutings, demonstrations of joy, and the exhibition of some trophy of victory, the mourners come forward and make their claims. If they receive a prisoner, it is at their option either to satiate their vengeance by taking his life in the most cruel manner they can conceive of, or to receive and adopt him into the family, in the place of him whom they have lost. All the prisoners that are taken in battle and carried to the encampment or town by the Indians are given to the bereaved families, till their number is good. And unless the mourners have but just received the news of their bereavement, and are under the operation of a paroxysm of grief, anger, or revenge; or, unless the prisoner is very old, sickly, or homely, they generally save them, and treat them kindly. But if their mental wound is fresh, their loss so great that they deem it irreparable, or if their prisoner or prisoners do not meet their approbation, no torture, let it be ever so cruel, seems sufficient to make them satisfaction. It is family and not national sacrifices among the Indians, that has given them an indelible stamp as barbarians, and identified their character with the idea which is generally formed of unfeeling ferocity and the most barbarous cruelty.

It was my happy lot to be accepted for adoption. At the time of the ceremony I was received by the two squaws to supply the place of their brother in the family; and I was ever considered and treated by them as a real sister, the same as though I had been born of their mother.

During the ceremony of my adoption, I sat motionless, nearly terrified to death at the appearance and actions of the company, expecting every moment to feel their vengeance, and suffer death on the spot. I was, however, happily disappointed; when at the

---

1   The French and Indian War, 1754-63. George Washington fought for the British, with aboriginal allies, against the French and their allies to gain control of the French forts in the west.

2   In Pittsburgh, taken in 1758 by the British from the French, during the French and Indian War, and renamed Fort Pitt.

close of the ceremony the company retired, and my sisters commenced employing every means for my consolation and comfort.[1]

Being now settled and provided with a home, I was employed in nursing the children, and doing light work about the house. Occasionally, I was sent out with the Indian hunters, when they went but a short distance, to help them carry their game. My situation was easy; I had no particular hardships to endure. But still, the recollection of my parents, my brothers and sisters, my home, and my own captivity, destroyed my happiness, and made me constantly solitary, lonesome, and gloomy.

My sisters would not allow me to speak English in their hearing; but remembering the charge that my dear mother gave me at the time I left her, whenever I chanced to be alone I made a business of repeating my prayer, catechism, or something I had learned, in order that I might not forget my own language. By practicing in that way, I retained it till I came to Genesee flats,[2] where I soon became acquainted with English people, with whom I have been almost daily in the habit of conversing.

My sisters were very diligent in teaching me their language; and to their great satisfaction, I soon learned so that I could understand it readily, and speak it fluently. I was very fortunate in falling into their hands; for they were kind, good-natured women; peaceable and mild in their dispositions; temperate and decent in their habits, and very tender and gentle towards me. I have great reason to respect them, though they have been dead a great number of years....

---

1 Seaver notes that "The Iroquois never exchanged prisoners with Indian Nations, nor ever sought to reclaim their own people from captivity among them. Adoption or the torture [by running the gauntlet] were the alternative chances of the captive" (61).

2 In New York State.

Works Cited and Recommended Reading

Altman, Janet Gurkin. *Epistolarity: Approaches to a Form*. Columbus: Ohio State UP, 1982.

Andrews, Malcolm. *The Search for the Picturesque: Landscape Aesthetics and Tourism in Britain, 1760-1800*. Stanford, CA: Stanford UP, 1989.

Axtell, James. *The Invasion Within: The Contest of Cultures in Colonial North America*. New York: Oxford UP, 1985.

Bailyn, Bernard. *The Peopling of British North America*. New York: Knopf, 1986.

Bannet, Eve Tavor. "The Theater of Politeness in Charlotte Lennox's British-American Novels." *Novel* 33.1 (Fall 1999): 73-92.

Beebee, Thomas. *Epistolary Fiction in Europe 1500-1850*. Cambridge: Cambridge UP, 1999.

Berg, Temma. "Getting the Mother's Story Right: Charlotte Lennox and the New World." *Papers on Language and Literature* 32 (Fall 1996): 369-98.

Bermingham, Ann. *Landscape and Ideology*. Berkeley, CA: U of California P, 1986.

Bissell, Benjamin. *The American Indian in English Literature of the Eighteenth Century*. New Haven: Yale UP, 1925.

Black, Frank Gees. *The Epistolary Novel in the Late Eighteenth Century*. Folcroft, PA: Folcroft Press, 1940.

Black, Nancy and Bette Weidman, eds. *White on Red: Images of the American Indian*. Port Washington, NY: Kennikat Press, 1976.

Blunt, Alison. *Travel, Gender and Imperialism*. New York: Guilford Press, 1994.

Bohls, Elizabeth. *Women and Travel Writers and the Language of Aesthetics, 1716-1818*. Cambridge: Cambridge UP, 1995.

Bolt, Christine. *The Women's Movements in the United States and Britain from the 1790s to the 1920s*. Amherst: U of Massachusetts P, 1993.

Brewer, John. *The Pleasures of the Imagination*. New York: Farrar, Straus, Giroux, 1997.

Burke, Edmund. *An Account of the European Settlements in America*. 2 vols. Second edition. London: R. and J. Dodsley, 1758.

Burnham, Michelle. *Captivity and Sentiment: Cultural Exchange in American Literature 1682-1821*. Hanover, NH: UP of New England, 1997.

Buzard, James. *The Beaten Track: European Tourism, Literature, and the Ways to "Culture," 1800-1918*. New York: Oxford UP, 1993.

Chard, Chloe. *Pleasure and Guilt on the Grand Tour*. Manchester: Manchester UP, 1999.

Copley, Stephen. "Gilpin on the Wye." *Prospects for the Nation*. Ed. M. Rosenthal et al. New Haven: Yale UP, 1997. 133-55.

Cott, Nancy. "Divorce and the Changing Status of Women in Eighteenth-Century America." *The American Family in Social-Historical Perspective*. Ed. Michael Gordon. New York: St. Martin's, 1978.

Davidson, Cathy. *Revolution and the Word: The Rise of the Novel in America*. New York: Oxford UP, 1986.

Ellison, Julie. "There and Back: Transatlantic Novels and Anglo-American Careers." *The Past as Prologue*. Eds. Carla Hay and Syndy Conger. New York: AMS, 1995. 303-24.

Ezell, Margaret. *The Patriarch's Wife*. Chapel Hill: U of North Carolina P, 1987.

Fairchild, H.N. *The Noble Savage*. New York: Columbia UP, 1928.

Ferguson, Moira. *Subject to Others: British Women Writers and Colonial Slavery, 1670-1834*. London: Routledge, 1992.

Flanders, W. Austin. *Structures of Experience*. U of South Carolina P, 1984.

Fliegelman, Jay. *Prodigals and Pilgrims: The American Revolution against Patriarchal Authority, 1750-1800*. London: Cambridge UP, 1989.

Garside, Peter. "Introduction." *Euphemia*. Charlotte Lennox. London: Thoemmes, 1992. v-xvi.

Geiter, Mary K. and W.A. Speck. *Colonial America: From Jamestown to Yorktown*. New York: Palgrave Macmillan, 2000.

Gottlieb, Beatrice. *The Family in the Western World*. London: Oxford UP, 1994.

Grant, Anne MacVicar. *Memoirs of an American Lady*. London: Longman et al., 1809.

Greenberg, Janelle. "The Legal Status of the English Woman in Early Eighteenth-Century Common Law and Equity." *Studies in Eighteenth-Century Culture* 4 (1975): 171-81.

Grinde, Donald and Bruce Johansen. "Exemplar of Liberty:

Native Americans and the Evolution of Democracy."
<www.ratical.com/many_worlds/6Nations/EoL/ch11.htm>.

Harold, Frederic. *Stories of New York*. Ed. Thomas O'Donnell. Syracuse: Syracuse UP, 1966.

Hay, Douglas and Nicholas Rogers. *Eighteenth-Century English Society*. London: Oxford UP, 1997.

Heilman, Robert. *America in English Fiction 1760-1800*. Baton Rouge, LA: Louisiana State UP, 1937.

Helsinger, Elizabeth. "Land and National Representation in Britain." *Prospects for the Nation*. Ed. M. Rosenthal et al. New Haven: Yale UP, 1997. 13-35.

Hill, Bridget. *Women, Work, and Sexual Politics in Eighteenth-Century England*. Oxford: Basil Blackwell, 1989.

Houlbrooke, Ralph. *The English Family 1450-1700*. London: Longman, 1984.

Howard, Susan Kubica. "Seeing Colonial America and Writing Home About It: Charlotte Lennox's *Euphemia*, Epistolarity, and the Feminine Picturesque." *Studies in the Novel* 37.3 (Fall 2005): 273-91.

Isles, Duncan. "The Lennox Collection." *The Harvard Bulletin* 19.4 (Oct. 1971): 416-35.

Jones, Jacqueline. "Race, Sex, and Self-Evident Truths: the Status of Slave Women During the Era of the American Revolution." *Women in the Age of the American Revolution*. Ed. Ronald Hoffman and Peter Albert. Charlottesville: University of Virginia Press, 1992. 293-337.

Kalm, Peter. *Travels in North America*. 2 vols. Trans. Adoph Benson. 1937. Reprint, New York: Dover, 1964.

Kawashima, Yasuhide. "Adoption in Early America." *Journal of Family Law* 20 (1982): 677-96.

Kolodny, Annette. *The Land Before Her*. Chapel Hill: U of North Carolina P, 1984.

——. *The Lay of the Land*. Chapel Hill: U of North Carolina, 1975.

Labbe, Jacqueline. *Romantic Visualities*. London: Macmillan, 1998.

Lawrence, Karen. *Penelope Voyages: Women and Travel in the British Literary Tradition*. Ithaca: Cornell UP, 1994.

Lennox, Charlotte. *The Life of Harriot Stuart, Written by Herself*. Ed. Susan Kubica Howard. Fairleigh Dickinson UP, 1995.

MacArthur, Elizabeth. *Extravagant Narratives*. Princeton: Princeton UP, 1990.

MacFarlane, Alan. *Marriage and Love in England*. London: Basil Blackwell, 1986.

Marshal, P.J. and Glyndwr Williams. *The Great Map of Mankind: British Perceptions of the World in the Age of Enlightenment.* Cambridge, MA: Harvard UP, 1982.

Marshall, David. "The Problem with the Picturesque." *Eighteenth-Century Studies* 35.3 (Spring 2002): 413-37.

Maynadier, Gustavus. *The First American Novelist?* Cambridge, MA: Harvard UP, 1940.

McNeil, David. "Charlotte Lennox's Fictionalization of New York: Gender, Curiosity and Colonial Venture." *Transatlantic Crossings: Eighteenth-Century Explorations.* Ed. Donald Nichol et al. St. John's: Memorial University of Newfoundland Press, 1995. 39-48.

Mills, Sara. *Discourses of Difference: An Analysis of Women's Travel Writing and Colonialism.* New York: Routledge, 1991.

Modell, Judith. *Kinship with Strangers: Adoption and Interpretations of Kinship in American Culture.* U of California P, 1994.

Narrett, David. "Men's Wills and Women's Property Rights in Colonial New York." *Women in the Age of the American Revolution.* Ed. Ronald Hoffman and Peter Albert. Charlottesville: U of Virginia P, 1992. 91-133.

O'Donnell, Thomas, ed. *Stories of York State.* Syracuse, New York: Syracuse UP, 1966.

Pearce, Roy Harvey. *The Savages of America.* Baltimore: Johns Hopkins UP, 1965.

Plumb, J.H. *The First Four Georges.* London: Beresford, 1972.

Preston, Thomas. "Smollett among the Indians." *Philological Quarterly* 61 (1982): 231-41.

Raynal, Abbé Guillaume Thomas François. *A Philosophical and Political History of the British Settlements and Trade in North America.* Trans. J. Justamond. Edinburgh: C. Denovan, 1779.

Regis, Pamela. *Describing Early America.* DeKalb: Northern Illinois UP, 1992.

Ross, Alexander. *The Imprint of the Picturesque on Nineteenth-Century British Fiction.* Waterloo, Ontario: Wilfrid Laurier UP, 1986.

Saar, Doreen A. "The Heritage of American Ethnicity in Crevecoeur's *Letters from an American Farmer.*" *A Mixed Race: Ethnicity in Early America.* Ed. Frank Shuffelton. New York: Oxford UP, 1993. 241-56.

Sears, John. *Sacred Places: American Tourist Attractions in the Nineteenth Century.* Amherst: University of Massachusetts Press, 1998.

Seelye, John. *Beautiful Machine: Rivers and the Republican Plan 1755-1825*. New York: Oxford UP, 1991.

Séjourné, Philippe. *The Mystery of Charlotte Lennox, First Novelist of Colonial America*. Aix-en-Provence: Publications des Annales de la Faculté des Lettres, 1967.

Sheridan, Frances. *Memoirs of Miss Sidney Bidulph*. London: R. and J. Dodsley, 1761; London: Pandora, 1987.

Slotkin, Richard. *Regeneration through Violence*. Middletown, CT: Wesleyan UP, 1973.

Small, Miriam Rossiter. *Charlotte Ramsay Lennox: An Eighteenth-Century Lady of Letters*. Yale UP, 1935; rpt. Archon Books, 1969.

Spender, Dale. *Mothers of the Novel*. London: Pandora, 1986.

Spurr, David. *The Rhetoric of Empire*. Durham, NC: Duke UP, 1993.

Staves, Susan. *Married Women's Separate Property in England 1660-1833*. Cambridge: Harvard UP, 1990.

Stone, Lawrence. *Family, Sex, and Marriage in England 1500-1800*. New York: Harper and Row, 1977.

——. *The Road to Divorce*. Oxford: Oxford UP, 1995.

Suleri, Sara. *The Rhetoric of English India*. U of Chicago P, 1992.

Todd, Janet. *The Sign of Angellica*. London: Virago, 1989.

Todorev, Tzvetan. *The Conquest of America: The Question of the Other*. Trans. Richard Howard. New York: Harper and Row, 1984.

Turner, Katherine. *British Travel Writers in Europe 1750-1800: Authorship, Gender, and National Identity*. Aldershot, England: Ashgate, 2001.

VanDerBeets, Richard, ed. *Held Captive by Indians: Selected Narratives 1642-1836*. Knoxville: U of Tennessee P, 1973.

Whitney, Lois. *Primitivism and the Idea of Progress in the English Popular Literature of the Eighteenth Century*. Baltimore: Johns Hopkins Press, 1934.

Wilson, Adrian. "The Ceremony of Childbirth and Its Interpretation." *Women as Mothers in Industrial England*. Ed. Valerie Fildes. London: Routledge, 1990. 68-107.

Wilson, Kathleen. "Empire of Virtue: The Imperial Project and Hanoverian Culture c. 1720-1785." *An Imperial State at War: Britain from 1689 to 1815*. Ed. Lawrence Stone. New York: Routledge, 1994. 128-64.

Wroth, Lawrence. *An American Bookshelf 1755*. Philadelphia: U of Pennsylvania P, 1934.

Zuckerman, Michael. "Identity in British America: Unease in Eden." *Colonial Identity in the Atlantic World, 1500-1800*. Eds. Nicholas Canny and Anthony Pagden. Princeton: Princeton UP, 1987. 115-57.